The New Testament

New International Version

*An Ecumenical
Bible Study Edition*

*Mr & Mrs William R Campbell
91 Bay Avenue
Atlantic Highlands, NJ 07716*

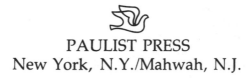
PAULIST PRESS
New York, N.Y./Mahwah, N.J.

Library of Congress
Catalog Card Number: 85-61004

ISBN: 0-8091-2733-4

Published by Paulist Press
997 Macarthur Boulevard
Mahwah, New Jersey 07430

Printed and bound in the United States of America

Contents

Preface

THE NEW INTERNATIONAL VERSION is a completely new translation of the Holy Bible made by over a hundred scholars working directly from the best available Hebrew, Aramaic and Greek texts. It had its beginning in 1965 when, after several years of exploratory study by committees from the Christian Reformed Church and the National Association of Evangelicals, a group of scholars met at Palos Heights, Illinois, and concurred in the need for a new translation of the Bible in contemporary English. This group, though not made up of official church representatives, was transdenominational. Its conclusion was endorsed by a large number of leaders from many denominations who met in Chicago in 1966.

Responsibility for the new version was delegated by the Palos Heights group to a self-governing body of fifteen, the Committee on Bible Translation, composed for the most part of biblical scholars from colleges, universities and seminaries. In 1967 the New York Bible Society (now the International Bible Society) generously undertook the financial sponsorship of the project—a sponsorship that made it possible to enlist the help of many distinguished scholars. The fact that participants from the United States, Great Britain, Canada, Australia and New Zealand worked together gave the project its international scope. That they were from many denominations—including Anglican, Assemblies of God, Baptist, Brethren, Christian Reformed, Church of Christ, Evangelical Free, Lutheran, Mennonite, Methodist, Nazarene, Presbyterian, Wesleyan and other churches—helped to safeguard the translation from sectarian bias.

How it was made helps to give the New International Version its distinctiveness. The translation of each book was assigned to a team of scholars. Next, one of the Intermediate Editorial Committees revised the initial translation, with constant reference to the Hebrew, Aramaic or Greek. Their work then went to one of the General Editorial Committees, which checked it in detail and made another thorough revision. This revision in turn was carefully reviewed by the Committee on Bible Translation, which made further changes and then released the final version for publication. In this way the entire Bible underwent three revisions, during each of

1

which the translation was examined for its faithfulness to the original languages and for its English style.

All this involved many thousands of hours of research and discussion regarding the meaning of the texts and the precise way of putting them into English. It may well be that no other translation has been made by a more thorough process of review and revision from committee to committee than this one.

From the beginning of the project, the Committee on Bible Translation held to certain goals for the New International Version: that it would be an accurate translation and one that would have clarity and literary quality and so prove suitable for public and private reading, teaching, preaching, memorizing and liturgical use. The Committee also sought to preserve some measure of continuity with the long tradition of translating the Scriptures into English.

In working toward these goals, the translators were united in their commitment to the authority and infallibility of the Bible as God's Word in written form. They believe that it contains the divine answer to the deepest needs of humanity, that it sheds unique light on our path in a dark world, and that it sets forth the way to our eternal well-being.

The first concern of the translators has been the accuracy of the translation and its fidelity to the thought of the biblical writers. They have weighed the significance of the lexical and grammatical details of the Hebrew, Aramaic and Greek texts. At the same time, they have striven for more than a word-for-word translation. Because thought patterns and syntax differ from language to language, faithful communication of the meaning of the writers of the Bible demands frequent modifications in sentence structure and constant regard for the contextual meanings of words.

A sensitive feeling for style does not always accompany scholarship. Accordingly the Committee on Bible Translation submitted the developing version to a number of stylistic consultants. Two of them read every book of both Old and New Testaments twice—once before and once after the last major revision—and made invaluable suggestions. Samples of the translation were tested for clarity and ease of reading by various kinds of people— young and old, highly educated and less well educated, ministers and laymen.

Concern for clear and natural English—that the New International Version should be idiomatic but not idiosyncratic, contemporary but not dated—motivated the translators and consultants. At the same time, they tried to reflect the differing styles of the biblical writers. In view of the international use of English, the translators sought to avoid obvious Americanisms on the one hand and obvious Anglicisms on the other. A British edition reflects the comparatively few differences of significant idiom and of spelling.

As for the traditional pronouns "thou," "thee" and "thine" in reference to the Deity, the translators judged that to use these archaisms (along with the old verb forms such as "doest," "wouldest" and "hadst") would violate accuracy in translation. Neither Hebrew, Aramaic nor Greek uses special pronouns for the persons of the Godhead. A present-day translation is not enhanced by forms that in the time of the King James Version were used in everyday speech, whether referring to God or man.

For the Old Testament the standard Hebrew text, the Masoretic Text as published in the latest editions of *Biblia Hebraica,* was used throughout. The Dead Sea Scrolls contain material bearing on an earlier stage of the Hebrew text. They were consulted, as were the Samaritan Pentateuch and the ancient scribal traditions relating to textual changes. Sometimes a variant Hebrew reading in the margin of the Masoretic Text was followed instead of the text itself. Such instances, being variants within the Masoretic tradition, are not specified by footnotes. In rare cases, words in the consonantal text were divided differently from the way they appear in the Masoretic Text. Footnotes indicate this. The translators also consulted the more important early versions—the Septuagint; Aquila, Symmachus and Theodotion; the Vulgate; the Syriac Peshitta; the Targums; and for the Psalms the *Juxta Hebraica* of Jerome. Readings from these versions were occasionally followed where the Masoretic Text seemed doubtful and where accepted principles of textual criticism showed that one or more of these textual witnesses appeared to provide the correct reading. Such instances are footnoted. Sometimes vowel letters and vowel signs did not, in the judgment of the translators, represent the correct vowels for the original consonantal text. Accordingly some words were read with a different set of vowels. These instances are usually not indicated by footnotes.

The Greek text used in translating the New Testament was an eclectic one. No other piece of ancient literature has such an abundance of manuscript witnesses as does the New Testament. Where existing manuscripts differ, the translators made their choice of readings according to accepted principles of New Testament textual criticism. Footnotes call attention to places where there was uncertainty about what the original text was. The best current printed texts of the Greek New Testament were used.

There is a sense in which the work of translation is never wholly finished. This applies to all great literature and uniquely so to the Bible. In 1973 the New Testament in the New International Version was published. Since then, suggestions for corrections and revisions have been received from various sources. The Committee on Bible Translation carefully considered the suggestions and adopted a number of them. These were incorporated in the first printing of the entire Bible in 1978. Additional revisions were made by the Committee on Bible Translation in 1983 and appear in printings after that date.

As in other ancient documents, the precise meaning of the biblical texts is sometimes uncertain. This is more often the case with the Hebrew and Aramaic texts than with the Greek text. Although archaeological and linguistic discoveries in this century aid in understanding difficult passages, some uncertainties remain. The more significant of these have been called to the reader's attention in the footnotes.

In regard to the divine name *YHWH*, commonly referred to as the *Tetragrammaton*, the translators adopted the device used in most English versions of rendering that name as "LORD" in capital letters to distinguish it from *Adonai*, another Hebrew word rendered "Lord," for which small letters are used. Wherever the two names stand together in the Old Testament as a compound name of God, they are rendered "Sovereign LORD."

Because for most readers today the phrases "the LORD of hosts" and "God of hosts" have little meaning, this version renders them "the LORD Almighty" and "God Almighty." These renderings convey the sense of the Hebrew, namely, "he who is sovereign over all the 'hosts' (powers) in heaven and on earth, especially over the 'hosts' (armies) of Israel." For readers unacquainted with Hebrew this does not make clear the distinction between *Sabaoth* ("hosts" or "Almighty") and *Shaddai* (which can also be translated "Almighty"), but the latter occurs infrequently and is always footnoted. When *Adonai* and *YHWH Sabaoth* occur together, they are rendered "the Lord, the LORD Almighty."

As for other proper nouns, the familiar spellings of the King James Version are generally retained. Names traditionally spelled with "ch," except where it is final, are usually spelled in this translation with "k" or "c," since the biblical languages do not have the sound that "ch" frequently indicates in English—for example, in *chant*. For well-known names such as Zechariah, however, the traditional spelling has been retained. Variation in the spelling of names in the original languages has usually not been indicated. Where a person or place has two or more different names in the Hebrew, Aramaic or Greek texts, the more familiar one has generally been used, with footnotes where needed.

To achieve clarity the translators sometimes supplied words not in the original texts but required by the context. If there was uncertainty about such material, it is enclosed in brackets. Also for the sake of clarity or style, nouns, including some proper nouns, are sometimes substituted for pronouns, and vice versa. And though the Hebrew writers often shifted back and forth between first, second and third personal pronouns without change of antecedent, this translation often makes them uniform, in accordance with English style and without the use of footnotes.

Poetical passages are printed as poetry, that is, with indentation of lines and with separate stanzas. These are generally designed to reflect the structure of Hebrew poetry. This poetry is normally characterized by parallelism in balanced lines. Most of the poetry in the Bible is in the Old Testament, and scholars differ regarding the scansion of Hebrew lines. The translators determined the stanza divisions for the most part by analysis of the subject matter. The stanzas therefore serve as poetic paragraphs.

As an aid to the reader, italicized sectional headings are inserted in most of the books. They are not to be regarded as part of the NIV text, are not for oral reading, and are not intended to dictate the interpretation of the sections they head.

The footnotes in this version are of several kinds, most of which need no explanation. Those giving alternative translations begin with "Or" and generally introduce the alternative with the last word preceding it in the text, except when it is a single-word alternative; in poetry quoted in a footnote a slant mark indicates a line division. Footnotes introduced by "Or" do not have uniform significance. In some cases two possible translations were considered to have about equal validity. In other cases, though the translators were convinced that the translation in the text was correct, they judged that another interpretation was possible and of sufficient importance to be represented in a footnote.

In the New Testament, footnotes that refer to uncertainty regarding the original text are introduced by "Some manuscripts" or similar expressions. In the Old Testament, evidence for the reading chosen is given first and evidence for the alternative is added after a semicolon (for example: Septuagint; Hebrew *father*). In such notes the term "Hebrew" refers to the Masoretic Text.

It should be noted that minerals, flora and fauna, architectural details, articles of clothing and jewelry, musical instruments and other articles cannot always be identified with precision. Also measures of capacity in the biblical period are particularly uncertain (see the table of weights and measures following the text).

Like all translations of the Bible, made as they are by imperfect man, this one undoubtedly falls short of its goals. Yet we are grateful to God for the extent to which he has enabled us to realize these goals and for the strength he has given us and our colleagues to complete our task. We offer this version of the Bible to him in whose name and for whose glory it has been made. We pray that it will lead many into a better understanding of the Holy Scriptures and a fuller knowledge of Jesus Christ the incarnate Word, of whom the Scriptures so faithfully testify.

The Committee on Bible Translation

June 1978
(Revised August 1983)

Names of the translators and editors may be secured
from the International Bible Society
144 Tices Lane, East Brunswick, New Jersey 08816.

The New Testament

Matthew

INTRODUCTION

The Gospel of Matthew was written in Greek, probably in Syria by a Jewish Christian trained as a scribe, during the decade 75–85 A.D., for an ethnically-mixed community of Jews and Gentiles. Although at first circulated anonymously, authorship was later attributed to the apostle Matthew to give special credence to what the early Church considered the most important of the Gospels, calling it the Church book. However, neither the Gospel itself nor modern scholarship confirms apostolic authorship.

As sources for the writing of his Gospel, the author (whom we shall designate as Matthew) uses oral tradition, the Gospel of Mark, and a hypothetical document called Q (from the German word Quelle, meaning source). Matthew combined the deeds of Jesus taken from Mark, and the teachings of Jesus taken from Q, with the oral tradition to which he fell heir, and injected into this literary composite his own purpose and theology to show how Jesus made the kingdom of God present in the lives of people.

Convinced that Jesus was the culmination of Jewish messianic expectations, Matthew presents him as directing his ministry initially to Israel. However, his own people reject Jesus and finally participate in his execution. Following his resurrection, Jesus commissions his apostles to create among the Gentiles a new Israel, the Church. Matthew saw the time between the resurrection and the delayed second coming of Jesus as a sacred time, the time of the Church, a time for the teaching of Jesus and for obedience to his new law of love, and a time when he would continue to be with his people to the end of the age.

An awareness of his topical and structural arrangement is helpful to the readers of the Gospel of Matthew. Following an introduction of Jesus as the long-awaited Messiah who has fulfilled Old Testament prophecies, five collections or units of the teaching material of Jesus are presented. Each collection, consisting of narrative and discourse, is concluded with a formula such as, "When Jesus had finished saying these things . . ."

The Sermon on the Mount (5:1—7:29), often thought of as a parallel to the Mosaic law revealed on Mount Sinai, constitutes Matthew's first teaching unit. As a "greater Moses" Jesus introduces a new law of love for Christians that both completes and transcends the earlier Mosaic teaching because he is the lawgiver of the end time and the supreme interpreter of God's will.

The second unit (9:35—11:1) details the characteristics and the ministry of a true disciple. Absolute loyalty to the master and a profound faith that can move mountains are prerequisite to preaching the imminent coming of the kingdom, healing the sick, casting out demons, and raising the dead.

The kingdom, presented through parables, is the subject of the third teaching unit (13:1–53). Entrance into the kingdom is possible for the believer through Jesus, but full sharing in the kingdom of the Father will be realized only with the second coming of Jesus.

The fourth collection (18:1—19:2) reflects the life of the Christian community two or three generations after the death of Jesus. Matthew weaves his understanding of the post-resurrectional era into his account of Jesus' public ministry.

A searing denunciation of the scribes and the Pharisees, professional transmitters and interpreters of the law, is found in Matthew's fifth collection of the teachings of Jesus (19:3—23:39). The harshest anti-Jewish diatribe in the New Testament, it may reflect the antipathy that existed between Christians and Jews in Matthew's day.

The commissioning of his apostles by the risen Jesus (28:16–20) climaxes the Gospel and reveals the dominant themes of Matthew: (1) God's new and final revelation of himself is Jesus, understood through his teaching; (2) believers can relate to God through obedience to the teaching of Jesus as interpreted by the Church; (3) the Church is guided and the believer sustained through the continuing presence of the risen Lord.

Matthew's community and future readers, as well, are disciples, heirs to the new revelation and to the task of accepting, obeying, and transmitting it. No one need feel alone in this charge; the risen Lord is and will be present always, to the close of the age, as the source of power and authority.

SYLVIA MAURER, C.S.C.

Points for Reflection

1. Do the qualities and characteristics demanded by Jesus for his disciples have relevance for a Christian in the modern world?
2. Two primary prescriptions of Matthew's Church were forgiveness without limit and acceptance of authority. Are these prescriptions likewise a challenge to present Church, civic, and social communities?
3. Matthew's concept of the *one* Church extended to all nations. Does a divided, multi-denominational Church have New Testament approbation?
4. Reflectively consider Matthew, chapter 18, as a challenge to any presently-existing denominational Church.
5. Formulate a commissioning statement which would be meaningful today to any religious community.

The Genealogy of Jesus

1 A record of the genealogy of Jesus Christ the son of David, the son of Abraham:

²Abraham was the father of Isaac,
Isaac the father of Jacob,
Jacob the father of Judah and his brothers,
³Judah the father of Perez and Zerah, whose mother was Tamar,
Perez the father of Hezron,
Hezron the father of Ram,
⁴Ram the father of Amminadab,
Amminadab the father of Nahshon,
Nahshon the father of Salmon,
⁵Salmon the father of Boaz, whose mother was Rahab,
Boaz the father of Obed, whose mother was Ruth,
Obed the father of Jesse,
⁶and Jesse the father of King David.

David was the father of Solomon, whose mother had been Uriah's wife,
⁷Solomon the father of Rehoboam,
Rehoboam the father of Abijah,
Abijah the father of Asa,
⁸Asa the father of Jehoshaphat,
Jehoshaphat the father of Jehoram,
Jehoram the father of Uzziah,
⁹Uzziah the father of Jotham,
Jotham the father of Ahaz,
Ahaz the father of Hezekiah,
¹⁰Hezekiah the father of Manasseh,
Manasseh the father of Amon,
Amon the father of Josiah,
¹¹and Josiah the father of Jeconiah[a] and his brothers at the time of the exile to Babylon.

¹²After the exile to Babylon:
Jeconiah was the father of Shealtiel,
Shealtiel the father of Zerubbabel,
¹³Zerubbabel the father of Abiud,
Abiud the father of Eliakim,
Eliakim the father of Azor,
¹⁴Azor the father of Zadok,
Zadok the father of Akim,
Akim the father of Eliud,
¹⁵Eliud the father of Eleazar,
Eleazar the father of Matthan,
Matthan the father of Jacob,

[a]11 That is, Jehoiachin; also in verse 12

¹⁶and Jacob the father of Joseph, the husband of Mary, of whom was born Jesus, who is called Christ.

¹⁷Thus there were fourteen generations in all from Abraham to David, fourteen from David to the exile to Babylon, and fourteen from the exile to the Christ. ᵃ

The Birth of Jesus Christ

¹⁸This is how the birth of Jesus Christ came about: His mother Mary was pledged to be married to Joseph, but before they came together, she was found to be with child through the Holy Spirit. ¹⁹Because Joseph her husband was a righteous man and did not want to expose her to public disgrace, he had in mind to divorce her quietly.

²⁰But after he had considered this, an angel of the Lord appeared to him in a dream and said, "Joseph son of David, do not be afraid to take Mary home as your wife, because what is conceived in her is from the Holy Spirit. ²¹She will give birth to a son, and you are to give him the name Jesus, ᵇ because he will save his people from their sins."

²²All this took place to fulfill what the Lord had said through the prophet: ²³"The virgin will be with child and will give birth to a son, and they will call him Immanuel"ᶜ—which means, "God with us."

²⁴When Joseph woke up, he did what the angel of the Lord had commanded him and took Mary home as his wife. ²⁵But he had no union with her until she gave birth to a son. And he gave him the name Jesus.

The Visit of the Magi

2 After Jesus was born in Bethlehem in Judea, during the time of King Herod, Magiᵈ from the east came to Jerusalem ²and asked, "Where is the one who has been born king of the Jews? We saw his star in the eastᵉ and have come to worship him."

³When King Herod heard this he was disturbed, and all Jerusalem with him. ⁴When he had called together all the people's chief priests and teachers of the law, he asked them where the Christᶠ was to be born. ⁵"In Bethlehem in Judea," they replied, "for this is what the prophet has written:

⁶" 'But you, Bethlehem, in the land of Judah,
    are by no means least among the rulers of Judah;
 for out of you will come a ruler
    who will be the shepherd of my people Israel.'ᵍ"

⁷Then Herod called the Magi secretly and found out from them the exact time the star had appeared. ⁸He sent them to Bethlehem and said, "Go and make a careful search for the child. As soon as you find him, report to me, so that I too may go and worship him."

ᵃ17 Or Messiah. "The Christ" (Greek) and "the Messiah" (Hebrew) both mean "the Anointed One."
ᵇ21 Jesus is the Greek form of Joshua, which means the Lᴏʀᴅ saves.   ᶜ23 Isaiah 7:14
ᵈ1 Traditionally Wise Men   ᵉ2 Or star when it rose   ᶠ4 Or Messiah   ᵍ6 Micah 5:2

[9]After they had heard the king, they went on their way, and the star they had seen in the east[a] went ahead of them until it stopped over the place where the child was. [10]When they saw the star, they were overjoyed. [11]On coming to the house, they saw the child with his mother Mary, and they bowed down and worshiped him. Then they opened their treasures and presented him with gifts of gold and of incense and of myrrh. [12]And having been warned in a dream not to go back to Herod, they returned to their country by another route.

The Escape to Egypt

[13]When they had gone, an angel of the Lord appeared to Joseph in a dream. "Get up," he said, "take the child and his mother and escape to Egypt. Stay there until I tell you, for Herod is going to search for the child to kill him."

[14]So he got up, took the child and his mother during the night and left for Egypt, [15]where he stayed until the death of Herod. And so was fulfilled what the Lord had said through the prophet: "Out of Egypt I called my son."[b]

[16]When Herod realized that he had been outwitted by the Magi, he was furious, and he gave orders to kill all the boys in Bethlehem and its vicinity who were two years old and under, in accordance with the time he had learned from the Magi. [17]Then what was said through the prophet Jeremiah was fulfilled:

> [18]"A voice is heard in Ramah,
>   weeping and great mourning,
> Rachel weeping for her children
>   and refusing to be comforted,
> because they are no more."[c]

The Return to Nazareth

[19]After Herod died, an angel of the Lord appeared in a dream to Joseph in Egypt [20]and said, "Get up, take the child and his mother and go to the land of Israel, for those who were trying to take the child's life are dead."

[21]So he got up, took the child and his mother and went to the land of Israel. [22]But when he heard that Archelaus was reigning in Judea in place of his father Herod, he was afraid to go there. Having been warned in a dream, he withdrew to the district of Galilee, [23]and he went and lived in a town called Nazareth. So was fulfilled what was said through the prophets: "He will be called a Nazarene."

John the Baptist Prepares the Way

3 In those days John the Baptist came, preaching in the Desert of Judea [2]and saying, "Repent, for the kingdom of heaven is near." [3]This is he who was spoken of through the prophet Isaiah:

---

[a]9 Or *seen when it rose*   [b]15 Hosea 11:1   [c]18 Jer. 31:15

"A voice of one calling in the desert,
'Prepare the way for the Lord,
    make straight paths for him.' "^a

⁴John's clothes were made of camel's hair, and he had a leather belt around his waist. His food was locusts and wild honey. ⁵People went out to him from Jerusalem and all Judea and the whole region of the Jordan. ⁶Confessing their sins, they were baptized by him in the Jordan River.

⁷But when he saw many of the Pharisees and Sadducees coming to where he was baptizing, he said to them: "You brood of vipers! Who warned you to flee from the coming wrath? ⁸Produce fruit in keeping with repentance. ⁹And do not think you can say to yourselves, 'We have Abraham as our father.' I tell you that out of these stones God can raise up children for Abraham. ¹⁰The ax is already at the root of the trees, and every tree that does not produce good fruit will be cut down and thrown into the fire.

¹¹"I baptize you with^b water for repentance. But after me will come one who is more powerful than I, whose sandals I am not fit to carry. He will baptize you with the Holy Spirit and with fire. ¹²His winnowing fork is in his hand, and he will clear his threshing floor, gathering his wheat into the barn and burning up the chaff with unquenchable fire."

The Baptism of Jesus

¹³Then Jesus came from Galilee to the Jordan to be baptized by John. ¹⁴But John tried to deter him, saying, "I need to be baptized by you, and do you come to me?"

¹⁵Jesus replied, "Let it be so now; it is proper for us to do this to fulfill all righteousness." Then John consented.

¹⁶As soon as Jesus was baptized, he went up out of the water. At that moment heaven was opened, and he saw the Spirit of God descending like a dove and lighting on him. ¹⁷And a voice from heaven said, "This is my Son, whom I love; with him I am well pleased."

The Temptation of Jesus

4 Then Jesus was led by the Spirit into the desert to be tempted by the devil. ²After fasting forty days and forty nights, he was hungry. ³The tempter came to him and said, "If you are the Son of God, tell these stones to become bread."

⁴Jesus answered, "It is written: 'Man does not live on bread alone, but on every word that comes from the mouth of God.'^c"

⁵Then the devil took him to the holy city and had him stand on the highest point of the temple. ⁶"If you are the Son of God," he said, "throw yourself down. For it is written:

" 'He will command his angels concerning you,
    and they will lift you up in their hands,

---

^a3 Isaiah 40:3   ^b11 Or *in*   ^c4 Deut. 8:3

so that you will not strike your foot against a stone.'[a]"

[7]Jesus answered him, "It is also written: 'Do not put the Lord your God to the test.'[b]"

[8]Again, the devil took him to a very high mountain and showed him all the kingdoms of the world and their splendor. [9]"All this I will give you," he said, "if you will bow down and worship me."

[10]Jesus said to him, "Away from me, Satan! For it is written: 'Worship the Lord your God, and serve him only.'[c]"

[11]Then the devil left him, and angels came and attended him.

Jesus Begins to Preach

[12]When Jesus heard that John had been put in prison, he returned to Galilee. [13]Leaving Nazareth, he went and lived in Capernaum, which was by the lake in the area of Zebulun and Naphtali— [14]to fulfill what was said through the prophet Isaiah:

> [15]"Land of Zebulun and land of Naphtali,
>   the way to the sea, along the Jordan,
>   Galilee of the Gentiles—
> [16]the people living in darkness
>   have seen a great light;
>   on those living in the land of the shadow of death
>   a light has dawned."[d]

[17]From that time on Jesus began to preach, "Repent, for the kingdom of heaven is near."

The Calling of the First Disciples

[18]As Jesus was walking beside the Sea of Galilee, he saw two brothers, Simon called Peter and his brother Andrew. They were casting a net into the lake, for they were fishermen. [19]"Come, follow me," Jesus said, "and I will make you fishers of men." [20]At once they left their nets and followed him.

[21]Going on from there, he saw two other brothers, James son of Zebedee and his brother John. They were in a boat with their father Zebedee, preparing their nets. Jesus called them, [22]and immediately they left the boat and their father and followed him.

Jesus Heals the Sick

[23]Jesus went throughout Galilee, teaching in their synagogues, preaching the good news of the kingdom, and healing every disease and sickness among the people. [24]News about him spread all over Syria, and people brought to him all who were ill with various diseases, those suffering severe pain, the demon-possessed, those having seizures, and the paralyzed, and

[a]6 Psalm 91:11,12   [b]7 Deut. 6:16   [c]10 Deut. 6:13   [d]16 Isaiah 9:1,2

he healed them. ²⁵Large crowds from Galilee, the Decapolis,^a Jerusalem, Judea and the region across the Jordan followed him.

The Beatitudes

5 Now when he saw the crowds, he went up on a mountainside and sat down. His disciples came to him, ²and he began to teach them, saying:

> ³"Blessed are the poor in spirit,
>   for theirs is the kingdom of heaven.
> ⁴Blessed are those who mourn,
>   for they will be comforted.
> ⁵Blessed are the meek,
>   for they will inherit the earth.
> ⁶Blessed are those who hunger and thirst for righteousness,
>   for they will be filled.
> ⁷Blessed are the merciful,
>   for they will be shown mercy.
> ⁸Blessed are the pure in heart,
>   for they will see God.
> ⁹Blessed are the peacemakers,
>   for they will be called sons of God.
> ¹⁰Blessed are those who are persecuted because of
>   righteousness,
>   for theirs is the kingdom of heaven.

¹¹"Blessed are you when people insult you, persecute you and falsely say all kinds of evil against you because of me. ¹²Rejoice and be glad, because great is your reward in heaven, for in the same way they persecuted the prophets who were before you.

Salt and Light

¹³"You are the salt of the earth. But if the salt loses its saltiness, how can it be made salty again? It is no longer good for anything, except to be thrown out and trampled by men.

¹⁴"You are the light of the world. A city on a hill cannot be hidden. ¹⁵Neither do people light a lamp and put it under a bowl. Instead they put it on its stand, and it gives light to everyone in the house. ¹⁶In the same way, let your light shine before men, that they may see your good deeds and praise your Father in heaven.

The Fulfillment of the Law

¹⁷"Do not think that I have come to abolish the Law or the Prophets; I have not come to abolish them but to fulfill them. ¹⁸I tell you the truth, until heaven and earth disappear, not the smallest letter, not the least stroke of a pen, will by any means disappear from the Law until everything is accomplished. ¹⁹Anyone who breaks one of the least of these command-

^a25 That is, the Ten Cities

ments and teaches others to do the same will be called least in the kingdom of heaven, but whoever practices and teaches these commands will be called great in the kingdom of heaven. [20]For I tell you that unless your righteousness surpasses that of the Pharisees and the teachers of the law, you will certainly not enter the kingdom of heaven.

Murder

[21]"You have heard that it was said to the people long ago, 'Do not murder,[a] and anyone who murders will be subject to judgment.' [22]But I tell you that anyone who is angry with his brother[b] will be subject to judgment. Again, anyone who says to his brother, 'Raca,'[c] is answerable to the Sanhedrin. But anyone who says, 'You fool!' will be in danger of the fire of hell.

[23]"Therefore, if you are offering your gift at the altar and there remember that your brother has something against you, [24]leave your gift there in front of the altar. First go and be reconciled to your brother; then come and offer your gift.

[25]"Settle matters quickly with your adversary who is taking you to court. Do it while you are still with him on the way, or he may hand you over to the judge, and the judge may hand you over to the officer, and you may be thrown into prison. [26]I tell you the truth, you will not get out until you have paid the last penny.[d]

Adultery

[27]"You have heard that it was said, 'Do not commit adultery.'[e] [28]But I tell you that anyone who looks at a woman lustfully has already committed adultery with her in his heart. [29]If your right eye causes you to sin, gouge it out and throw it away. It is better for you to lose one part of your body than for your whole body to be thrown into hell. [30]And if your right hand causes you to sin, cut it off and throw it away. It is better for you to lose one part of your body than for your whole body to go into hell.

Divorce

[31]"It has been said, 'Anyone who divorces his wife must give her a certificate of divorce.'[f] [32]But I tell you that anyone who divorces his wife, except for marital unfaithfulness, causes her to become an adulteress, and anyone who marries the divorced woman commits adultery.

Oaths

[33]"Again, you have heard that it was said to the people long ago, 'Do not break your oath, but keep the oaths you have made to the Lord.' [34]But I tell you, Do not swear at all: either by heaven, for it is God's throne; [35]or by the earth, for it is his footstool; or by Jerusalem, for it is the city of the Great King. [36]And do not swear by your head, for you cannot make even

[a]21 Exodus 20:13   [b]22 Some manuscripts *brother without cause*   [c]22 An Aramaic term of contempt   [d]26 Greek *kodrantes*   [e]27 Exodus 20:14   [f]31 Deut. 24:1

one hair white or black. ³⁷Simply let your 'Yes' be 'Yes,' and your 'No,' 'No'; anything beyond this comes from the evil one.

An Eye for an Eye

³⁸"You have heard that it was said, 'Eye for eye, and tooth for tooth.'ᵃ ³⁹But I tell you, Do not resist an evil person. If someone strikes you on the right cheek, turn to him the other also. ⁴⁰And if someone wants to sue you and take your tunic, let him have your cloak as well. ⁴¹If someone forces you to go one mile, go with him two miles. ⁴²Give to the one who asks you, and do not turn away from the one who wants to borrow from you.

Love for Enemies

⁴³"You have heard that it was said, 'Love your neighborᵇ and hate your enemy.' ⁴⁴But I tell you: Love your enemiesᶜ and pray for those who persecute you, ⁴⁵that you may be sons of your Father in heaven. He causes his sun to rise on the evil and the good, and sends rain on the righteous and the unrighteous. ⁴⁶If you love those who love you, what reward will you get? Are not even the tax collectors doing that? ⁴⁷And if you greet only your brothers, what are you doing more than others? Do not even pagans do that? ⁴⁸Be perfect, therefore, as your heavenly Father is perfect.

Giving to the Needy

6 "Be careful not to do your 'acts of righteousness' before men, to be seen by them. If you do, you will have no reward from your Father in heaven.

²"So when you give to the needy, do not announce it with trumpets, as the hypocrites do in the synagogues and on the streets, to be honored by men. I tell you the truth, they have received their reward in full. ³But when you give to the needy, do not let your left hand know what your right hand is doing, ⁴so that your giving may be in secret. Then your Father, who sees what is done in secret, will reward you.

Prayer

⁵"And when you pray, do not be like the hypocrites, for they love to pray standing in the synagogues and on the street corners to be seen by men. I tell you the truth, they have received their reward in full. ⁶But when you pray, go into your room, close the door and pray to your Father, who is unseen. Then your Father, who sees what is done in secret, will reward you. ⁷And when you pray, do not keep on babbling like pagans, for they think they will be heard because of their many words. ⁸Do not be like them, for your Father knows what you need before you ask him.

⁹"This, then, is how you should pray:

" 'Our Father in heaven,

ᵃ38 Exodus 21:24; Lev. 24:20; Deut. 19:21   ᵇ43 Lev. 19:18   ᶜ44 Some late manuscripts *enemies, bless those who curse you, do good to those who hate you*

hallowed be your name,
¹⁰your kingdom come,
your will be done
on earth as it is in heaven.
¹¹Give us today our daily bread.
¹²Forgive us our debts,
as we also have forgiven our debtors.
¹³And lead us not into temptation,
but deliver us from the evil one. ^{a'}

¹⁴For if you forgive men when they sin against you, your heavenly Father will also forgive you. ¹⁵But if you do not forgive men their sins, your Father will not forgive your sins.

Fasting

¹⁶"When you fast, do not look somber as the hypocrites do, for they disfigure their faces to show men they are fasting. I tell you the truth, they have received their reward in full. ¹⁷But when you fast, put oil on your head and wash your face, ¹⁸so that it will not be obvious to men that you are fasting, but only to your Father, who is unseen; and your Father, who sees what is done in secret, will reward you.

Treasures in Heaven

¹⁹"Do not store up for yourselves treasures on earth, where moth and rust destroy, and where thieves break in and steal. ²⁰But store up for yourselves treasures in heaven, where moth and rust do not destroy, and where thieves do not break in and steal. ²¹For where your treasure is, there your heart will be also.

²²"The eye is the lamp of the body. If your eyes are good, your whole body will be full of light. ²³But if your eyes are bad, your whole body will be full of darkness. If then the light within you is darkness, how great is that darkness!

²⁴"No one can serve two masters. Either he will hate the one and love the other, or he will be devoted to the one and despise the other. You cannot serve both God and Money.

Do Not Worry

²⁵"Therefore I tell you, do not worry about your life, what you will eat or drink; or about your body, what you will wear. Is not life more important than food, and the body more important than clothes? ²⁶Look at the birds of the air; they do not sow or reap or store away in barns, and yet your heavenly Father feeds them. Are you not much more valuable than they? ²⁷Who of you by worrying can add a single hour to his life^b?

²⁸"And why do you worry about clothes? See how the lilies of the field

^a13 Or *from evil*; some late manuscripts *one,* / *for yours is the kingdom and the power and the glory forever. Amen.*   ^b27 Or *single cubit to his height*

grow. They do not labor or spin. ²⁹Yet I tell you that not even Solomon in all his splendor was dressed like one of these. ³⁰If that is how God clothes the grass of the field, which is here today and tomorrow is thrown into the fire, will he not much more clothe you, O you of little faith? ³¹So do not worry, saying, 'What shall we eat?' or 'What shall we drink?' or 'What shall we wear?' ³²For the pagans run after all these things, and your heavenly Father knows that you need them. ³³But seek first his kingdom and his righteousness, and all these things will be given to you as well. ³⁴Therefore do not worry about tomorrow, for tomorrow will worry about itself. Each day has enough trouble of its own.

Judging Others

7 "Do not judge, or you too will be judged. ²For in the same way you judge others, you will be judged, and with the measure you use, it will be measured to you.

³"Why do you look at the speck of sawdust in your brother's eye and pay no attention to the plank in your own eye? ⁴How can you say to your brother, 'Let me take the speck out of your eye,' when all the time there is a plank in your own eye? ⁵You hypocrite, first take the plank out of your own eye, and then you will see clearly to remove the speck from your brother's eye.

⁶"Do not give dogs what is sacred; do not throw your pearls to pigs. If you do, they may trample them under their feet, and then turn and tear you to pieces.

Ask, Seek, Knock

⁷"Ask and it will be given to you; seek and you will find; knock and the door will be opened to you. ⁸For everyone who asks receives; he who seeks finds; and to him who knocks, the door will be opened.

⁹"Which of you, if his son asks for bread, will give him a stone? ¹⁰Or if he asks for a fish, will give him a snake? ¹¹If you, then, though you are evil, know how to give good gifts to your children, how much more will your Father in heaven give good gifts to those who ask him! ¹²So in everything, do to others what you would have them do to you, for this sums up the Law and the Prophets.

The Narrow and Wide Gates

¹³"Enter through the narrow gate. For wide is the gate and broad is the road that leads to destruction, and many enter through it. ¹⁴But small is the gate and narrow the road that leads to life, and only a few find it.

A Tree and Its Fruit

¹⁵"Watch out for false prophets. They come to you in sheep's clothing, but inwardly they are ferocious wolves. ¹⁶By their fruit you will recognize them. Do people pick grapes from thornbushes, or figs from thistles? ¹⁷Likewise every good tree bears good fruit, but a bad tree bears bad fruit. ¹⁸A

good tree cannot bear bad fruit, and a bad tree cannot bear good fruit. ¹⁹Every tree that does not bear good fruit is cut down and thrown into the fire. ²⁰Thus, by their fruit you will recognize them.

²¹"Not everyone who says to me, 'Lord, Lord,' will enter the kingdom of heaven, but only he who does the will of my Father who is in heaven. ²²Many will say to me on that day, 'Lord, Lord, did we not prophesy in your name, and in your name drive out demons and perform many miracles?' ²³Then I will tell them plainly, 'I never knew you. Away from me, you evildoers!'

The Wise and Foolish Builders

²⁴"Therefore everyone who hears these words of mine and puts them into practice is like a wise man who built his house on the rock. ²⁵The rain came down, the streams rose, and the winds blew and beat against that house; yet it did not fall, because it had its foundation on the rock. ²⁶But everyone who hears these words of mine and does not put them into practice is like a foolish man who built his house on sand. ²⁷The rain came down, the streams rose, and the winds blew and beat against that house, and it fell with a great crash."

²⁸When Jesus had finished saying these things, the crowds were amazed at his teaching, ²⁹because he taught as one who had authority, and not as their teachers of the law.

The Man With Leprosy

8 When he came down from the mountainside, large crowds followed him. ²A man with leprosy^a came and knelt before him and said, "Lord, if you are willing, you can make me clean."

³Jesus reached out his hand and touched the man. "I am willing," he said. "Be clean!" Immediately he was cured^b of his leprosy. ⁴Then Jesus said to him, "See that you don't tell anyone. But go, show yourself to the priest and offer the gift Moses commanded, as a testimony to them."

The Faith of the Centurion

⁵When Jesus had entered Capernaum, a centurion came to him, asking for help. ⁶"Lord," he said, "my servant lies at home paralyzed and in terrible suffering."

⁷Jesus said to him, "I will go and heal him."

⁸The centurion replied, "Lord, I do not deserve to have you come under my roof. But just say the word, and my servant will be healed. ⁹For I myself am a man under authority, with soldiers under me. I tell this one, 'Go,' and he goes; and that one, 'Come,' and he comes. I say to my servant, 'Do this,' and he does it."

¹⁰When Jesus heard this, he was astonished and said to those following

^a2 The Greek word was used for various diseases affecting the skin—not necessarily leprosy.
^b3 Greek *made clean*

him, "I tell you the truth, I have not found anyone in Israel with such great faith. ¹¹I say to you that many will come from the east and the west, and will take their places at the feast with Abraham, Isaac and Jacob in the kingdom of heaven. ¹²But the subjects of the kingdom will be thrown outside, into the darkness, where there will be weeping and gnashing of teeth."

¹³Then Jesus said to the centurion, "Go! It will be done just as you believed it would." And his servant was healed at that very hour.

Jesus Heals Many

¹⁴When Jesus came into Peter's house, he saw Peter's mother-in-law lying in bed with a fever. ¹⁵He touched her hand and the fever left her, and she got up and began to wait on him.

¹⁶When evening came, many who were demon-possessed were brought to him, and he drove out the spirits with a word and healed all the sick. ¹⁷This was to fulfill what was spoken through the prophet Isaiah:

> "He took up our infirmities
> and carried our diseases."[a]

The Cost of Following Jesus

¹⁸When Jesus saw the crowd around him, he gave orders to cross to the other side of the lake. ¹⁹Then a teacher of the law came to him and said, "Teacher, I will follow you wherever you go."

²⁰Jesus replied, "Foxes have holes and birds of the air have nests, but the Son of Man has no place to lay his head."

²¹Another disciple said to him, "Lord, first let me go and bury my father."

²²But Jesus told him, "Follow me, and let the dead bury their own dead."

Jesus Calms the Storm

²³Then he got into the boat and his disciples followed him. ²⁴Without warning, a furious storm came up on the lake, so that the waves swept over the boat. But Jesus was sleeping. ²⁵The disciples went and woke him, saying, "Lord, save us! We're going to drown!"

²⁶He replied, "You of little faith, why are you so afraid?" Then he got up and rebuked the winds and the waves, and it was completely calm.

²⁷The men were amazed and asked, "What kind of man is this? Even the winds and the waves obey him!"

The Healing of Two Demon-possessed Men

²⁸When he arrived at the other side in the region of the Gadarenes,[b] two demon-possessed men coming from the tombs met him. They were so violent that no one could pass that way. ²⁹"What do you want with us, Son

---

[a]17 Isaiah 53:4   [b]28 Some manuscripts Gergesenes; others Gerasenes

of God?" they shouted. "Have you come here to torture us before the appointed time?"

³⁰Some distance from them a large herd of pigs was feeding. ³¹The demons begged Jesus, "If you drive us out, send us into the herd of pigs."

³²He said to them, "Go!" So they came out and went into the pigs, and the whole herd rushed down the steep bank into the lake and died in the water. ³³Those tending the pigs ran off, went into the town and reported all this, including what had happened to the demon-possessed men. ³⁴Then the whole town went out to meet Jesus. And when they saw him, they pleaded with him to leave their region.

Jesus Heals a Paralytic

9 Jesus stepped into a boat, crossed over and came to his own town. ²Some men brought to him a paralytic, lying on a mat. When Jesus saw their faith, he said to the paralytic, "Take heart, son; your sins are forgiven."

³At this, some of the teachers of the law said to themselves, "This fellow is blaspheming!"

⁴Knowing their thoughts, Jesus said, "Why do you entertain evil thoughts in your hearts? ⁵Which is easier: to say, 'Your sins are forgiven,' or to say, 'Get up and walk'? ⁶But so that you may know that the Son of Man has authority on earth to forgive sins. . . ." Then he said to the paralytic, "Get up, take your mat and go home." ⁷And the man got up and went home. ⁸When the crowd saw this, they were filled with awe; and they praised God, who had given such authority to men.

The Calling of Matthew

⁹As Jesus went on from there, he saw a man named Matthew sitting at the tax collector's booth. "Follow me," he told him, and Matthew got up and followed him.

¹⁰While Jesus was having dinner at Matthew's house, many tax collectors and "sinners" came and ate with him and his disciples. ¹¹When the Pharisees saw this, they asked his disciples, "Why does your teacher eat with tax collectors and 'sinners'?"

¹²On hearing this, Jesus said, "It is not the healthy who need a doctor, but the sick. ¹³But go and learn what this means: 'I desire mercy, not sacrifice.'ᵃ For I have not come to call the righteous, but sinners."

Jesus Questioned About Fasting

¹⁴Then John's disciples came and asked him, "How is it that we and the Pharisees fast, but your disciples do not fast?"

¹⁵Jesus answered, "How can the guests of the bridegroom mourn while he is with them? The time will come when the bridegroom will be taken from them; then they will fast.

¹⁶"No one sews a patch of unshrunk cloth on an old garment, for the

ᵃ13 Hosea 6:6

patch will pull away from the garment, making the tear worse. [17]Neither do men pour new wine into old wineskins. If they do, the skins will burst, the wine will run out and the wineskins will be ruined. No, they pour new wine into new wineskins, and both are preserved."

A Dead Girl and a Sick Woman

[18]While he was saying this, a ruler came and knelt before him and said, "My daughter has just died. But come and put your hand on her, and she will live." [19]Jesus got up and went with him, and so did his disciples.

[20]Just then a woman who had been subject to bleeding for twelve years came up behind him and touched the edge of his cloak. [21]She said to herself, "If I only touch his cloak, I will be healed."

[22]Jesus turned and saw her. "Take heart, daughter," he said, "your faith has healed you." And the woman was healed from that moment.

[23]When Jesus entered the ruler's house and saw the flute players and the noisy crowd, [24]he said, "Go away. The girl is not dead but asleep." But they laughed at him. [25]After the crowd had been put outside, he went in and took the girl by the hand, and she got up. [26]News of this spread through all that region.

Jesus Heals the Blind and Mute

[27]As Jesus went on from there, two blind men followed him, calling out, "Have mercy on us, Son of David!"

[28]When he had gone indoors, the blind men came to him, and he asked them, "Do you believe that I am able to do this?"

"Yes, Lord," they replied.

[29]Then he touched their eyes and said, "According to your faith will it be done to you"; [30]and their sight was restored. Jesus warned them sternly, "See that no one knows about this." [31]But they went out and spread the news about him all over that region.

[32]While they were going out, a man who was demon-possessed and could not talk was brought to Jesus. [33]And when the demon was driven out, the man who had been mute spoke. The crowd was amazed and said, "Nothing like this has ever been seen in Israel."

[34]But the Pharisees said, "It is by the prince of demons that he drives out demons."

The Workers Are Few

[35]Jesus went through all the towns and villages, teaching in their synagogues, preaching the good news of the kingdom and healing every disease and sickness. [36]When he saw the crowds, he had compassion on them, because they were harassed and helpless, like sheep without a shepherd. [37]Then he said to his disciples, "The harvest is plentiful but the workers are few. [38]Ask the Lord of the harvest, therefore, to send out workers into his harvest field."

Jesus Sends Out the Twelve

10 He called his twelve disciples to him and gave them authority to drive out evil[a] spirits and to heal every disease and sickness.

[2]These are the names of the twelve apostles: first, Simon (who is called Peter) and his brother Andrew; James son of Zebedee, and his brother John; [3]Philip and Bartholomew; Thomas and Matthew the tax collector; James son of Alphaeus, and Thaddaeus; [4]Simon the Zealot and Judas Iscariot, who betrayed him.

[5]These twelve Jesus sent out with the following instructions: "Do not go among the Gentiles or enter any town of the Samaritans. [6]Go rather to the lost sheep of Israel. [7]As you go, preach this message: 'The kingdom of heaven is near.' [8]Heal the sick, raise the dead, cleanse those who have leprosy,[b] drive out demons. Freely you have received, freely give. [9]Do not take along any gold or silver or copper in your belts; [10]take no bag for the journey, or extra tunic, or sandals or a staff; for the worker is worth his keep.

[11]"Whatever town or village you enter, search for some worthy person there and stay at his house until you leave. [12]As you enter the home, give it your greeting. [13]If the home is deserving, let your peace rest on it; if it is not, let your peace return to you. [14]If anyone will not welcome you or listen to your words, shake the dust off your feet when you leave that home or town. [15]I tell you the truth, it will be more bearable for Sodom and Gomorrah on the day of judgment than for that town. [16]I am sending you out like sheep among wolves. Therefore be as shrewd as snakes and as innocent as doves.

[17]"Be on your guard against men; they will hand you over to the local councils and flog you in their synagogues. [18]On my account you will be brought before governors and kings as witnesses to them and to the Gentiles. [19]But when they arrest you, do not worry about what to say or how to say it. At that time you will be given what to say, [20]for it will not be you speaking, but the Spirit of your Father speaking through you.

[21]"Brother will betray brother to death, and a father his child; children will rebel against their parents and have them put to death. [22]All men will hate you because of me, but he who stands firm to the end will be saved. [23]When you are persecuted in one place, flee to another. I tell you the truth, you will not finish going through the cities of Israel before the Son of Man comes.

[24]"A student is not above his teacher, nor a servant above his master. [25]It is enough for the student to be like his teacher, and the servant like his master. If the head of the house has been called Beelzebub,[c] how much more the members of his household!

[26]"So do not be afraid of them. There is nothing concealed that will not be disclosed, or hidden that will not be made known. [27]What I tell you in

---

[a]1 Greek *unclean* [b]8 The Greek word was used for various diseases affecting the skin—not necessarily leprosy. [c]25 Greek *Beezeboul* or *Beelzeboul*

the dark, speak in the daylight; what is whispered in your ear, proclaim from the roofs. ²⁸Do not be afraid of those who kill the body but cannot kill the soul. Rather, be afraid of the One who can destroy both soul and body in hell. ²⁹Are not two sparrows sold for a penny^a? Yet not one of them will fall to the ground apart from the will of your Father. ³⁰And even the very hairs of your head are all numbered. ³¹So don't be afraid; you are worth more than many sparrows.

³²"Whoever acknowledges me before men, I will also acknowledge him before my Father in heaven. ³³But whoever disowns me before men, I will disown him before my Father in heaven.

³⁴"Do not suppose that I have come to bring peace to the earth. I did not come to bring peace, but a sword. ³⁵For I have come to turn

> " 'a man against his father,
>   a daughter against her mother,
>   a daughter-in-law against her mother-in-law—
> ³⁶   a man's enemies will be the members of his own
>   household.'^b

³⁷"Anyone who loves his father or mother more than me is not worthy of me; anyone who loves his son or daughter more than me is not worthy of me; ³⁸and anyone who does not take his cross and follow me is not worthy of me. ³⁹Whoever finds his life will lose it, and whoever loses his life for my sake will find it.

⁴⁰"He who receives you receives me, and he who receives me receives the one who sent me. ⁴¹Anyone who receives a prophet because he is a prophet will receive a prophet's reward, and anyone who receives a righteous man because he is a righteous man will receive a righteous man's reward. ⁴²And if anyone gives even a cup of cold water to one of these little ones because he is my disciple, I tell you the truth, he will certainly not lose his reward."

Jesus and John the Baptist

11 After Jesus had finished instructing his twelve disciples, he went on from there to teach and preach in the towns of Galilee.^c

²When John heard in prison what Christ was doing, he sent his disciples ³to ask him, "Are you the one who was to come, or should we expect someone else?"

⁴Jesus replied, "Go back and report to John what you hear and see: ⁵The blind receive sight, the lame walk, those who have leprosy^d are cured, the deaf hear, the dead are raised, and the good news is preached to the poor. ⁶Blessed is the man who does not fall away on account of me."

⁷As John's disciples were leaving, Jesus began to speak to the crowd about John: "What did you go out into the desert to see? A reed swayed by the wind? ⁸If not, what did you go out to see? A man dressed in fine

---

^a29 Greek *an assarion*   ^b36 Micah 7:6   ^c1 Greek *in their towns*   ^d5 The Greek word was used for various diseases affecting the skin—not necessarily leprosy.

clothes? No, those who wear fine clothes are in kings' palaces. ⁹Then what did you go out to see? A prophet? Yes, I tell you, and more than a prophet. ¹⁰This is the one about whom it is written:

> " 'I will send my messenger ahead of you,
> who will prepare your way before you.'ᵃ

¹¹I tell you the truth: Among those born of women there has not risen anyone greater than John the Baptist; yet he who is least in the kingdom of heaven is greater than he. ¹²From the days of John the Baptist until now, the kingdom of heaven has been forcefully advancing, and forceful men lay hold of it. ¹³For all the Prophets and the Law prophesied until John. ¹⁴And if you are willing to accept it, he is the Elijah who was to come. ¹⁵He who has ears, let him hear.

¹⁶"To what can I compare this generation? They are like children sitting in the marketplaces and calling out to others:

> ¹⁷" 'We played the flute for you,
> and you did not dance;
> we sang a dirge,
> and you did not mourn.'

¹⁸For John came neither eating nor drinking, and they say, 'He has a demon.' ¹⁹The Son of Man came eating and drinking, and they say, 'Here is a glutton and a drunkard, a friend of tax collectors and "sinners." ' But wisdom is proved right by her actions."

Woe on Unrepentant Cities

²⁰Then Jesus began to denounce the cities in which most of his miracles had been performed, because they did not repent. ²¹"Woe to you, Korazin! Woe to you, Bethsaida! If the miracles that were performed in you had been performed in Tyre and Sidon, they would have repented long ago in sackcloth and ashes. ²²But I tell you, it will be more bearable for Tyre and Sidon on the day of judgment than for you. ²³And you, Capernaum, will you be lifted up to the skies? No, you will go down to the depths.ᵇ If the miracles that were performed in you had been performed in Sodom, it would have remained to this day. ²⁴But I tell you that it will be more bearable for Sodom on the day of judgment than for you."

Rest for the Weary

²⁵At that time Jesus said, "I praise you, Father, Lord of heaven and earth, because you have hidden these things from the wise and learned, and revealed them to little children. ²⁶Yes, Father, for this was your good pleasure.

²⁷"All things have been committed to me by my Father. No one knows the Son except the Father, and no one knows the Father except the Son and those to whom the Son chooses to reveal him.

ᵃ10 Mal. 3:1   ᵇ23 Greek *Hades*

[28]"Come to me, all you who are weary and burdened, and I will give you rest. [29]Take my yoke upon you and learn from me, for I am gentle and humble in heart, and you will find rest for your souls. [30]For my yoke is easy and my burden is light."

Lord of the Sabbath

12 At that time Jesus went through the grainfields on the Sabbath. His disciples were hungry and began to pick some heads of grain and eat them. [2]When the Pharisees saw this, they said to him, "Look! Your disciples are doing what is unlawful on the Sabbath."

[3]He answered, "Haven't you read what David did when he and his companions were hungry? [4]He entered the house of God, and he and his companions ate the consecrated bread—which was not lawful for them to do, but only for the priests. [5]Or haven't you read in the Law that on the Sabbath the priests in the temple desecrate the day and yet are innocent? [6]I tell you that one[a] greater than the temple is here. [7]If you had known what these words mean, 'I desire mercy, not sacrifice,'[b] you would not have condemned the innocent. [8]For the Son of Man is Lord of the Sabbath."

[9]Going on from that place, he went into their synagogue, [10]and a man with a shriveled hand was there. Looking for a reason to accuse Jesus, they asked him, "Is it lawful to heal on the Sabbath?"

[11]He said to them, "If any of you has a sheep and it falls into a pit on the Sabbath, will you not take hold of it and lift it out? [12]How much more valuable is a man than a sheep! Therefore it is lawful to do good on the Sabbath."

[13]Then he said to the man, "Stretch out your hand." So he stretched it out and it was completely restored, just as sound as the other. [14]But the Pharisees went out and plotted how they might kill Jesus.

God's Chosen Servant

[15]Aware of this, Jesus withdrew from that place. Many followed him, and he healed all their sick, [16]warning them not to tell who he was. [17]This was to fulfill what was spoken through the prophet Isaiah:

> [18]"Here is my servant whom I have chosen,
>   the one I love, in whom I delight;
> I will put my Spirit on him,
>   and he will proclaim justice to the nations.
> [19]He will not quarrel or cry out;
>   no one will hear his voice in the streets.
> [20]A bruised reed he will not break,
>   and a smoldering wick he will not snuff out,
> till he leads justice to victory.
> [21] In his name the nations will put their hope."[c]

a6 Or something; also in verses 41 and 42   *b7 Hosea 6:6*   *c21 Isaiah 42:1-4*

Jesus and Beelzebub

²²Then they brought him a demon-possessed man who was blind and mute, and Jesus healed him, so that he could both talk and see. ²³All the people were astonished and said, "Could this be the Son of David?"

²⁴But when the Pharisees heard this, they said, "It is only by Beelzebub,ᵃ the prince of demons, that this fellow drives out demons."

²⁵Jesus knew their thoughts and said to them, "Every kingdom divided against itself will be ruined, and every city or household divided against itself will not stand. ²⁶If Satan drives out Satan, he is divided against himself. How then can his kingdom stand? ²⁷And if I drive out demons by Beelzebub, by whom do your people drive them out? So then, they will be your judges. ²⁸But if I drive out demons by the Spirit of God, then the kingdom of God has come upon you.

²⁹"Or again, how can anyone enter a strong man's house and carry off his possessions unless he first ties up the strong man? Then he can rob his house.

³⁰"He who is not with me is against me, and he who does not gather with me scatters. ³¹And so I tell you, every sin and blasphemy will be forgiven men, but the blasphemy against the Spirit will not be forgiven. ³²Anyone who speaks a word against the Son of Man will be forgiven, but anyone who speaks against the Holy Spirit will not be forgiven, either in this age or in the age to come.

³³"Make a tree good and its fruit will be good, or make a tree bad and its fruit will be bad, for a tree is recognized by its fruit. ³⁴You brood of vipers, how can you who are evil say anything good? For out of the overflow of the heart the mouth speaks. ³⁵The good man brings good things out of the good stored up in him, and the evil man brings evil things out of the evil stored up in him. ³⁶But I tell you that men will have to give account on the day of judgment for every careless word they have spoken. ³⁷For by your words you will be acquitted, and by your words you will be condemned."

The Sign of Jonah

³⁸Then some of the Pharisees and teachers of the law said to him, "Teacher, we want to see a miraculous sign from you."

³⁹He answered, "A wicked and adulterous generation asks for a miraculous sign! But none will be given it except the sign of the prophet Jonah. ⁴⁰For as Jonah was three days and three nights in the belly of a huge fish, so the Son of Man will be three days and three nights in the heart of the earth. ⁴¹The men of Nineveh will stand up at the judgment with this generation and condemn it; for they repented at the preaching of Jonah, and now oneᵇ greater than Jonah is here. ⁴²The Queen of the South will rise at the judgment with this generation and condemn it; for she came from the ends of the earth to listen to Solomon's wisdom, and now one greater than Solomon is here.

ᵃ24 Greek *Beezeboul* or *Beelzeboul*; also in verse 27   ᵇ41 Or *something*; also in verse 42

[43]"When an evil[a] spirit comes out of a man, it goes through arid places seeking rest and does not find it. [44]Then it says, 'I will return to the house I left.' When it arrives, it finds the house unoccupied, swept clean and put in order. [45]Then it goes and takes with it seven other spirits more wicked than itself, and they go in and live there. And the final condition of that man is worse than the first. That is how it will be with this wicked generation."

Jesus' Mother and Brothers

[46]While Jesus was still talking to the crowd, his mother and brothers stood outside, wanting to speak to him. [47]Someone told him, "Your mother and brothers are standing outside, wanting to speak to you."[b]

[48]He replied to him, "Who is my mother, and who are my brothers?" [49]Pointing to his disciples, he said, "Here are my mother and my brothers. [50]For whoever does the will of my Father in heaven is my brother and sister and mother."

The Parable of the Sower

13 That same day Jesus went out of the house and sat by the lake. [2]Such large crowds gathered around him that he got into a boat and sat in it, while all the people stood on the shore. [3]Then he told them many things in parables, saying: "A farmer went out to sow his seed. [4]As he was scattering the seed, some fell along the path, and the birds came and ate it up. [5]Some fell on rocky places, where it did not have much soil. It sprang up quickly, because the soil was shallow. [6]But when the sun came up, the plants were scorched, and they withered because they had no root. [7]Other seed fell among thorns, which grew up and choked the plants. [8]Still other seed fell on good soil, where it produced a crop—a hundred, sixty or thirty times what was sown. [9]He who has ears, let him hear."

[10]The disciples came to him and asked, "Why do you speak to the people in parables?"

[11]He replied, "The knowledge of the secrets of the kingdom of heaven has been given to you, but not to them. [12]Whoever has will be given more, and he will have an abundance. Whoever does not have, even what he has will be taken from him. [13]This is why I speak to them in parables:

"Though seeing, they do not see;
though hearing, they do not hear or understand.

[14]In them is fulfilled the prophecy of Isaiah:

" 'You will be ever hearing but never understanding;
you will be ever seeing but never perceiving.
[15]For this people's heart has become calloused;
they hardly hear with their ears,
and they have closed their eyes.
Otherwise they might see with their eyes,

---

[a]43 Greek *unclean*   [b]47 Some manuscripts do not have verse 47.

> hear with their ears,
> understand with their hearts
> and turn, and I would heal them.'[a]

[16]But blessed are your eyes because they see, and your ears because they hear. [17]For I tell you the truth, many prophets and righteous men longed to see what you see but did not see it, and to hear what you hear but did not hear it.

[18]"Listen then to what the parable of the sower means: [19]When anyone hears the message about the kingdom and does not understand it, the evil one comes and snatches away what was sown in his heart. This is the seed sown along the path. [20]The one who received the seed that fell on rocky places is the man who hears the word and at once receives it with joy. [21]But since he has no root, he lasts only a short time. When trouble or persecution comes because of the word, he quickly falls away. [22]The one who received the seed that fell among the thorns is the man who hears the word, but the worries of this life and the deceitfulness of wealth choke it, making it unfruitful. [23]But the one who received the seed that fell on good soil is the man who hears the word and understands it. He produces a crop, yielding a hundred, sixty or thirty times what was sown."

The Parable of the Weeds

[24]Jesus told them another parable: "The kingdom of heaven is like a man who sowed good seed in his field. [25]But while everyone was sleeping, his enemy came and sowed weeds among the wheat, and went away. [26]When the wheat sprouted and formed heads, then the weeds also appeared.

[27]"The owner's servants came to him and said, 'Sir, didn't you sow good seed in your field? Where then did the weeds come from?'

[28]" 'An enemy did this,' he replied.

"The servants asked him, 'Do you want us to go and pull them up?'

[29]" 'No,' he answered, 'because while you are pulling the weeds, you may root up the wheat with them. [30]Let both grow together until the harvest. At that time I will tell the harvesters: First collect the weeds and tie them in bundles to be burned; then gather the wheat and bring it into my barn.' "

The Parables of the Mustard Seed and the Yeast

[31]He told them another parable: "The kingdom of heaven is like a mustard seed, which a man took and planted in his field. [32]Though it is the smallest of all your seeds, yet when it grows, it is the largest of garden plants and becomes a tree, so that the birds of the air come and perch in its branches."

[33]He told them still another parable: "The kingdom of heaven is like

[a]15 Isaiah 6:9,10

yeast that a woman took and mixed into a large amount[a] of flour until it worked all through the dough."

[34]Jesus spoke all these things to the crowd in parables; he did not say anything to them without using a parable. [35]So was fulfilled what was spoken through the prophet:

> "I will open my mouth in parables,
> I will utter things hidden since the creation of the world."[b]

The Parable of the Weeds Explained

[36]Then he left the crowd and went into the house. His disciples came to him and said, "Explain to us the parable of the weeds in the field."

[37]He answered, "The one who sowed the good seed is the Son of Man. [38]The field is the world, and the good seed stands for the sons of the kingdom. The weeds are the sons of the evil one, [39]and the enemy who sows them is the devil. The harvest is the end of the age, and the harvesters are angels.

[40]"As the weeds are pulled up and burned in the fire, so it will be at the end of the age. [41]The Son of Man will send out his angels, and they will weed out of his kingdom everything that causes sin and all who do evil. [42]They will throw them into the fiery furnace, where there will be weeping and gnashing of teeth. [43]Then the righteous will shine like the sun in the kingdom of their Father. He who has ears, let him hear.

The Parables of the Hidden Treasure and the Pearl

[44]"The kingdom of heaven is like treasure hidden in a field. When a man found it, he hid it again, and then in his joy went and sold all he had and bought that field.

[45]"Again, the kingdom of heaven is like a merchant looking for fine pearls. [46]When he found one of great value, he went away and sold everything he had and bought it.

The Parable of the Net

[47]"Once again, the kingdom of heaven is like a net that was let down into the lake and caught all kinds of fish. [48]When it was full, the fishermen pulled it up on the shore. Then they sat down and collected the good fish in baskets, but threw the bad away. [49]This is how it will be at the end of the age. The angels will come and separate the wicked from the righteous [50]and throw them into the fiery furnace, where there will be weeping and gnashing of teeth.

[51]"Have you understood all these things?" Jesus asked.

"Yes," they replied.

[52]He said to them, "Therefore every teacher of the law who has been instructed about the kingdom of heaven is like the owner of a house who brings out of his storeroom new treasures as well as old."

[a]33 Greek *three satas* (probably about 1/2 bushel or 22 liters)   [b]35 Psalm 78:2

A Prophet Without Honor

⁵³When Jesus had finished these parables, he moved on from there. ⁵⁴Coming to his hometown, he began teaching the people in their synagogue, and they were amazed. "Where did this man get this wisdom and these miraculous powers?" they asked. ⁵⁵"Isn't this the carpenter's son? Isn't his mother's name Mary, and aren't his brothers James, Joseph, Simon and Judas? ⁵⁶Aren't all his sisters with us? Where then did this man get all these things?" ⁵⁷And they took offense at him.

But Jesus said to them, "Only in his hometown and in his own house is a prophet without honor."

⁵⁸And he did not do many miracles there because of their lack of faith.

John the Baptist Beheaded

14 At that time Herod the tetrarch heard the reports about Jesus, ²and he said to his attendants, "This is John the Baptist; he has risen from the dead! That is why miraculous powers are at work in him."

³Now Herod had arrested John and bound him and put him in prison because of Herodias, his brother Philip's wife, ⁴for John had been saying to him: "It is not lawful for you to have her." ⁵Herod wanted to kill John, but he was afraid of the people, because they considered him a prophet.

⁶On Herod's birthday the daughter of Herodias danced for them and pleased Herod so much ⁷that he promised with an oath to give her whatever she asked. ⁸Prompted by her mother, she said, "Give me here on a platter the head of John the Baptist." ⁹The king was distressed, but because of his oaths and his dinner guests, he ordered that her request be granted ¹⁰and had John beheaded in the prison. ¹¹His head was brought in on a platter and given to the girl, who carried it to her mother. ¹²John's disciples came and took his body and buried it. Then they went and told Jesus.

Jesus Feeds the Five Thousand

¹³When Jesus heard what had happened, he withdrew by boat privately to a solitary place. Hearing of this, the crowds followed him on foot from the towns. ¹⁴When Jesus landed and saw a large crowd, he had compassion on them and healed their sick.

¹⁵As evening approached, the disciples came to him and said, "This is a remote place, and it's already getting late. Send the crowds away, so they can go to the villages and buy themselves some food."

¹⁶Jesus replied, "They do not need to go away. You give them something to eat."

¹⁷"We have here only five loaves of bread and two fish," they answered.

¹⁸"Bring them here to me," he said. ¹⁹And he directed the people to sit down on the grass. Taking the five loaves and the two fish and looking up to heaven, he gave thanks and broke the loaves.Then he gave them to the disciples, and the disciples gave them to the people. ²⁰They all ate and were satisfied, and the disciples picked up twelve basketfuls of broken pieces that

were left over. ²¹The number of those who ate was about five thousand men, besides women and children.

Jesus Walks on the Water

²²Immediately Jesus made the disciples get into the boat and go on ahead of him to the other side, while he dismissed the crowd. ²³After he had dismissed them, he went up on a mountainside by himself to pray. When evening came, he was there alone, ²⁴but the boat was already a considerable distance *a* from land, buffeted by the waves because the wind was against it.

²⁵During the fourth watch of the night Jesus went out to them, walking on the lake. ²⁶When the disciples saw him walking on the lake, they were terrified. "It's a ghost," they said, and cried out in fear.

²⁷But Jesus immediately said to them: "Take courage! It is I. Don't be afraid."

²⁸"Lord, if it's you," Peter replied, "tell me to come to you on the water."

²⁹"Come," he said.

Then Peter got down out of the boat, walked on the water and came toward Jesus. ³⁰But when he saw the wind, he was afraid and, beginning to sink, cried out, "Lord, save me!"

³¹Immediately Jesus reached out his hand and caught him. "You of little faith," he said, "why did you doubt?"

³²And when they climbed into the boat, the wind died down. ³³Then those who were in the boat worshiped him, saying, "Truly you are the Son of God."

³⁴When they had crossed over, they landed at Gennesaret. ³⁵And when the men of that place recognized Jesus, they sent word to all the surrounding country. People brought all their sick to him ³⁶and begged him to let the sick just touch the edge of his cloak, and all who touched him were healed.

Clean and Unclean

15 Then some Pharisees and teachers of the law came to Jesus from Jerusalem and asked, ²"Why do your disciples break the tradition of the elders? They don't wash their hands before they eat!"

³Jesus replied, "And why do you break the command of God for the sake of your tradition? ⁴For God said, 'Honor your father and mother' *b* and 'Anyone who curses his father or mother must be put to death.' *c* ⁵But you say that if a man says to his father or mother, 'Whatever help you might otherwise have received from me is a gift devoted to God,' ⁶he is not to 'honor his father *d*' with it. Thus you nullify the word of God for the sake of your tradition. ⁷You hypocrites! Isaiah was right when he prophesied about you:

*a*24 Greek *many stadia*   *b*4 Exodus 20:12; Deut. 5:16   *c*4 Exodus 21:17; Lev. 20:9   *d*6 Some manuscripts *father or his mother*

^{8}" 'These people honor me with their lips,
  but their hearts are far from me.
^{9}They worship me in vain;
  their teachings are but rules taught by men.'^{a}"

^{10}Jesus called the crowd to him and said, "Listen and understand. ^{11}What goes into a man's mouth does not make him 'unclean,' but what comes out of his mouth, that is what makes him 'unclean.' "

^{12}Then the disciples came to him and asked, "Do you know that the Pharisees were offended when they heard this?"

^{13}He replied, "Every plant that my heavenly Father has not planted will be pulled up by the roots. ^{14}Leave them; they are blind guides.^{b} If a blind man leads a blind man, both will fall into a pit."

^{15}Peter said, "Explain the parable to us."

^{16}"Are you still so dull?" Jesus asked them. ^{17}"Don't you see that whatever enters the mouth goes into the stomach and then out of the body? ^{18}But the things that come out of the mouth come from the heart, and these make a man 'unclean.' ^{19}For out of the heart come evil thoughts, murder, adultery, sexual immorality, theft, false testimony, slander. ^{20}These are what make a man 'unclean'; but eating with unwashed hands does not make him 'unclean.' "

The Faith of the Canaanite Woman

^{21}Leaving that place, Jesus withdrew to the region of Tyre and Sidon. ^{22}A Canaanite woman from that vicinity came to him, crying out, "Lord, Son of David, have mercy on me! My daughter is suffering terribly from demon-possession."

^{23}Jesus did not answer a word. So his disciples came to him and urged him, "Send her away, for she keeps crying out after us."

^{24}He answered, "I was sent only to the lost sheep of Israel."

^{25}The woman came and knelt before him. "Lord, help me!" she said.

^{26}He replied, "It is not right to take the children's bread and toss it to their dogs."

^{27}"Yes, Lord," she said, "but even the dogs eat the crumbs that fall from their masters' table."

^{28}Then Jesus answered, "Woman, you have great faith! Your request is granted." And her daughter was healed from that very hour.

Jesus Feeds the Four Thousand

^{29}Jesus left there and went along the Sea of Galilee. Then he went up on a mountainside and sat down. ^{30}Great crowds came to him, bringing the lame, the blind, the crippled, the mute and many others, and laid them at his feet; and he healed them. ^{31}The people were amazed when they saw the mute speaking, the crippled made well, the lame walking and the blind seeing. And they praised the God of Israel.

^{a}9 Isaiah 29:13 ^{b}14 Some manuscripts *guides of the blind*

³²Jesus called his disciples to him and said, "I have compassion for these people; they have already been with me three days and have nothing to eat. I do not want to send them away hungry, or they may collapse on the way."

³³His disciples answered, "Where could we get enough bread in this remote place to feed such a crowd?"

³⁴"How many loaves do you have?" Jesus asked.

"Seven," they replied, "and a few small fish."

³⁵He told the crowd to sit down on the ground. ³⁶Then he took the seven loaves and the fish, and when he had given thanks, he broke them and gave them to the disciples, and they in turn to the people. ³⁷They all ate and were satisfied. Afterward the disciples picked up seven basketfuls of broken pieces that were left over. ³⁸The number of those who ate was four thousand, besides women and children. ³⁹After Jesus had sent the crowd away, he got into the boat and went to the vicinity of Magadan.

The Demand for a Sign

16 The Pharisees and Sadducees came to Jesus and tested him by asking him to show them a sign from heaven.

²He replied,ᵃ "When evening comes, you say, 'It will be fair weather, for the sky is red,' ³and in the morning, 'Today it will be stormy, for the sky is red and overcast.' You know how to interpret the appearance of the sky, but you cannot interpret the signs of the times. ⁴A wicked and adulterous generation looks for a miraculous sign, but none will be given it except the sign of Jonah." Jesus then left them and went away.

The Yeast of the Pharisees and Sadducees

⁵When they went across the lake, the disciples forgot to take bread. ⁶"Be careful," Jesus said to them. "Be on your guard against the yeast of the Pharisees and Sadducees."

⁷They discussed this among themselves and said, "It is because we didn't bring any bread."

⁸Aware of their discussion, Jesus asked, "You of little faith, why are you talking among yourselves about having no bread? ⁹Do you still not understand? Don't you remember the five loaves for the five thousand, and how many basketfuls you gathered? ¹⁰Or the seven loaves for the four thousand, and how many basketfuls you gathered? ¹¹How is it you don't understand that I was not talking to you about bread? But be on your guard against the yeast of the Pharisees and Sadducees." ¹²Then they understood that he was not telling them to guard against the yeast used in bread, but against the teaching of the Pharisees and Sadducees.

Peter's Confession of Christ

¹³When Jesus came to the region of Caesarea Philippi, he asked his disciples, "Who do people say the Son of Man is?"

ᵃ2 Some early manuscripts do not have the rest of verse 2 and all of verse 3.

¹⁴They replied, "Some say John the Baptist; others say Elijah; and still others, Jeremiah or one of the prophets."

¹⁵"But what about you?" he asked. "Who do you say I am?"

¹⁶Simon Peter answered, "You are the Christ,ᵃ the Son of the living God."

¹⁷Jesus replied, "Blessed are you, Simon son of Jonah, for this was not revealed to you by man, but by my Father in heaven. ¹⁸And I tell you that you are Peter,ᵇ and on this rock I will build my church, and the gates of Hadesᶜ will not overcome it.ᵈ ¹⁹I will give you the keys of the kingdom of heaven; whatever you bind on earth will beᵉ bound in heaven, and whatever you loose on earth will beᵉ loosed in heaven." ²⁰Then he warned his disciples not to tell anyone that he was the Christ.

Jesus Predicts His Death

²¹From that time on Jesus began to explain to his disciples that he must go to Jerusalem and suffer many things at the hands of the elders, chief priests and teachers of the law, and that he must be killed and on the third day be raised to life.

²²Peter took him aside and began to rebuke him. "Never, Lord!" he said. "This shall never happen to you!"

²³Jesus turned and said to Peter, "Get behind me, Satan! You are a stumbling block to me; you do not have in mind the things of God, but the things of men."

²⁴Then Jesus said to his disciples, "If anyone would come after me, he must deny himself and take up his cross and follow me. ²⁵For whoever wants to save his lifeᶠ will lose it, but whoever loses his life for me will find it. ²⁶What good will it be for a man if he gains the whole world, yet forfeits his soul? Or what can a man give in exchange for his soul? ²⁷For the Son of Man is going to come in his Father's glory with his angels, and then he will reward each person according to what he has done. ²⁸I tell you the truth, some who are standing here will not taste death before they see the Son of Man coming in his kingdom."

The Transfiguration

17 After six days Jesus took with him Peter, James and John the brother of James, and led them up a high mountain by themselves. ²There he was transfigured before them. His face shone like the sun, and his clothes became as white as the light. ³Just then there appeared before them Moses and Elijah, talking with Jesus.

⁴Peter said to Jesus, "Lord, it is good for us to be here. If you wish, I will put up three shelters—one for you, one for Moses and one for Elijah."

⁵While he was still speaking, a bright cloud enveloped them, and a voice from the cloud said, "This is my Son, whom I love; with him I am well pleased. Listen to him!"

ᵃ16 Or *Messiah*; also in verse 20   ᵇ18 *Peter* means *rock*.   ᶜ18 Or *hell*   ᵈ18 Or *not prove stronger than it*   ᵉ19 Or *have been*   ᶠ25 The Greek word means either *life* or *soul*; also in verse 26.

⁶When the disciples heard this, they fell facedown to the ground, terrified. ⁷But Jesus came and touched them. "Get up," he said. "Don't be afraid." ⁸When they looked up, they saw no one except Jesus.

⁹As they were coming down the mountain, Jesus instructed them, "Don't tell anyone what you have seen, until the Son of Man has been raised from the dead."

¹⁰The disciples asked him, "Why then do the teachers of the law say that Elijah must come first?"

¹¹Jesus replied, "To be sure, Elijah comes and will restore all things. ¹²But I tell you, Elijah has already come, and they did not recognize him, but have done to him everything they wished. In the same way the Son of Man is going to suffer at their hands." ¹³Then the disciples understood that he was talking to them about John the Baptist.

The Healing of a Boy With a Demon

¹⁴When they came to the crowd, a man approached Jesus and knelt before him. ¹⁵"Lord, have mercy on my son," he said. "He has seizures and is suffering greatly. He often falls into the fire or into the water. ¹⁶I brought him to your disciples, but they could not heal him."

¹⁷"O unbelieving and perverse generation," Jesus replied, "how long shall I stay with you? How long shall I put up with you? Bring the boy here to me." ¹⁸Jesus rebuked the demon, and it came out of the boy, and he was healed from that moment.

¹⁹Then the disciples came to Jesus in private and asked, "Why couldn't we drive it out?"

²⁰He replied, "Because you have so little faith. I tell you the truth, if you have faith as small as a mustard seed, you can say to this mountain, 'Move from here to there' and it will move. Nothing will be impossible for you.ᵃ"

²²When they came together in Galilee, he said to them, "The Son of Man is going to be betrayed into the hands of men. ²³They will kill him, and on the third day he will be raised to life." And the disciples were filled with grief.

The Temple Tax

²⁴After Jesus and his disciples arrived in Capernaum, the collectors of the two-drachma tax came to Peter and asked, "Doesn't your teacher pay the temple taxᵇ?"

²⁵"Yes, he does," he replied.

When Peter came into the house, Jesus was the first to speak. "What do you think, Simon?" he asked. "From whom do the kings of the earth collect duty and taxes—from their own sons or from others?"

²⁶"From others," Peter answered.

"Then the sons are exempt," Jesus said to him. ²⁷"But so that we may not offend them, go to the lake and throw out your line. Take the first fish

---

ᵃ20 Some manuscripts you. ²¹But this kind does not go out except by prayer and fasting.   ᵇ24 Greek the two drachmas you catch; open its mouth and you will find a four-drachma coin. Take it and give it to them for my tax and yours."

The Greatest in the Kingdom of Heaven

18 At that time the disciples came to Jesus and asked, "Who is the greatest in the kingdom of heaven?"

[2]He called a little child and had him stand among them. [3]And he said: "I tell you the truth, unless you change and become like little children, you will never enter the kingdom of heaven. [4]Therefore, whoever humbles himself like this child is the greatest in the kingdom of heaven.

[5]"And whoever welcomes a little child like this in my name welcomes me. [6]But if anyone causes one of these little ones who believe in me to sin, it would be better for him to have a large millstone hung around his neck and to be drowned in the depths of the sea.

[7]"Woe to the world because of the things that cause people to sin! Such things must come, but woe to the man through whom they come! [8]If your hand or your foot causes you to sin, cut it off and throw it away. It is better for you to enter life maimed or crippled than to have two hands or two feet and be thrown into eternal fire. [9]And if your eye causes you to sin, gouge it out and throw it away. It is better for you to enter life with one eye than to have two eyes and be thrown into the fire of hell.

The Parable of the Lost Sheep

[10]"See that you do not look down on one of these little ones. For I tell you that their angels in heaven always see the face of my Father in heaven. [a]

[12]"What do you think? If a man owns a hundred sheep, and one of them wanders away, will he not leave the ninety-nine on the hills and go to look for the one that wandered off? [13]And if he finds it, I tell you the truth, he is happier about that one sheep than about the ninety-nine that did not wander off. [14]In the same way your Father in heaven is not willing that any of these little ones should be lost.

A Brother Who Sins Against You

[15]"If your brother sins against you,[b] go and show him his fault, just between the two of you. If he listens to you, you have won your brother over. [16]But if he will not listen, take one or two others along, so that 'every matter may be established by the testimony of two or three witnesses.'[c] [17]If he refuses to listen to them, tell it to the church; and if he refuses to listen even to the church, treat him as you would a pagan or a tax collector.

[18]"I tell you the truth, whatever you bind on earth will be[d] bound in heaven, and whatever you loose on earth will be[d] loosed in heaven.

[19]"Again, I tell you that if two of you on earth agree about anything you ask for, it will be done for you by my Father in heaven. [20]For where two or three come together in my name, there am I with them."

---

[a]10 Some manuscripts *heaven.* [11]*The Son of Man came to save what was lost.*   [b]15 Some manuscripts do not have *against you.*   [c]16 Deut. 19:15   [d]18 Or *have been*

The Parable of the Unmerciful Servant

²¹Then Peter came to Jesus and asked, "Lord, how many times shall I forgive my brother when he sins against me? Up to seven times?"

²²Jesus answered, "I tell you, not seven times, but seventy-seven times.ᵃ

²³"Therefore, the kingdom of heaven is like a king who wanted to settle accounts with his servants. ²⁴As he began the settlement, a man who owed him ten thousand talentsᵇ was brought to him. ²⁵Since he was not able to pay, the master ordered that he and his wife and his children and all that he had be sold to repay the debt.

²⁶"The servant fell on his knees before him. 'Be patient with me,' he begged, 'and I will pay back everything.' ²⁷The servant's master took pity on him, canceled the debt and let him go.

²⁸"But when that servant went out, he found one of his fellow servants who owed him a hundred denarii.ᶜ He grabbed him and began to choke him. 'Pay back what you owe me!' he demanded.

²⁹"His fellow servant fell to his knees and begged him, 'Be patient with me, and I will pay you back.'

³⁰"But he refused. Instead, he went off and had the man thrown into prison until he could pay the debt. ³¹When the other servants saw what had happened, they were greatly distressed and went and told their master everything that had happened.

³²"Then the master called the servant in. 'You wicked servant,' he said, 'I canceled all that debt of yours because you begged me to. ³³Shouldn't you have had mercy on your fellow servant just as I had on you?' ³⁴In anger his master turned him over to the jailers to be tortured, until he should pay back all he owed.

³⁵"This is how my heavenly Father will treat each of you unless you forgive your brother from your heart."

Divorce

19 When Jesus had finished saying these things, he left Galilee and went into the region of Judea to the other side of the Jordan. ²Large crowds followed him, and he healed them there.

³Some Pharisees came to him to test him. They asked, "Is it lawful for a man to divorce his wife for any and every reason?"

⁴"Haven't you read," he replied, "that at the beginning the Creator 'made them male and female,'ᵈ ⁵and said, 'For this reason a man will leave his father and mother and be united to his wife, and the two will become one flesh'ᵉ? ⁶So they are no longer two, but one. Therefore what God has joined together, let man not separate."

⁷"Why then," they asked, "did Moses command that a man give his wife a certificate of divorce and send her away?"

ᵃ22 Or *seventy times seven*   ᵇ24 That is, millions of dollars   ᶜ28 That is, a few dollars
ᵈ4 Gen. 1:27   ᵉ5 Gen. 2:24

⁸Jesus replied, "Moses permitted you to divorce your wives because your hearts were hard. But it was not this way from the beginning. ⁹I tell you that anyone who divorces his wife, except for marital unfaithfulness, and marries another woman commits adultery."

¹⁰The disciples said to him, "If this is the situation between a husband and wife, it is better not to marry."

¹¹Jesus replied, "Not everyone can accept this word, but only those to whom it has been given. ¹²For some are eunuchs because they were born that way; others were made that way by men; and others have renounced marriage[a] because of the kingdom of heaven. The one who can accept this should accept it."

The Little Children and Jesus

¹³Then little children were brought to Jesus for him to place his hands on them and pray for them. But the disciples rebuked those who brought them.

¹⁴Jesus said, "Let the little children come to me, and do not hinder them, for the kingdom of heaven belongs to such as these." ¹⁵When he had placed his hands on them, he went on from there.

The Rich Young Man

¹⁶Now a man came up to Jesus and asked, "Teacher, what good thing must I do to get eternal life?"

¹⁷"Why do you ask me about what is good?" Jesus replied. "There is only One who is good. If you want to enter life, obey the commandments."

¹⁸"Which ones?" the man inquired.

Jesus replied, " 'Do not murder, do not commit adultery, do not steal, do not give false testimony, ¹⁹honor your father and mother,'[b] and 'love your neighbor as yourself.'[c]"

²⁰"All these I have kept," the young man said. "What do I still lack?"

²¹Jesus answered, "If you want to be perfect, go, sell your possessions and give to the poor, and you will have treasure in heaven. Then come, follow me."

²²When the young man heard this, he went away sad, because he had great wealth.

²³Then Jesus said to his disciples, "I tell you the truth, it is hard for a rich man to enter the kingdom of heaven. ²⁴Again I tell you, it is easier for a camel to go through the eye of a needle than for a rich man to enter the kingdom of God."

²⁵When the disciples heard this, they were greatly astonished and asked, "Who then can be saved?"

²⁶Jesus looked at them and said, "With man this is impossible, but with God all things are possible."

²⁷Peter answered him, "We have left everything to follow you! What then will there be for us?"

---

[a]12 Or *have made themselves eunuchs*   [b]19 Exodus 20:12-16; Deut. 5:16-20   [c]19 Lev. 19:18

²⁸Jesus said to them, "I tell you the truth, at the renewal of all things, when the Son of Man sits on his glorious throne, you who have followed me will also sit on twelve thrones, judging the twelve tribes of Israel. ²⁹And everyone who has left houses or brothers or sisters or father or mother*a* or children or fields for my sake will receive a hundred times as much and will inherit eternal life. ³⁰But many who are first will be last, and many who are last will be first.

The Parable of the Workers in the Vineyard

20 "For the kingdom of heaven is like a landowner who went out early in the morning to hire men to work in his vineyard. ²He agreed to pay them a denarius for the day and sent them into his vineyard.

³"About the third hour he went out and saw others standing in the marketplace doing nothing. ⁴He told them, 'You also go and work in my vineyard, and I will pay you whatever is right.' ⁵So they went.

"He went out again about the sixth hour and the ninth hour and did the same thing. ⁶About the eleventh hour he went out and found still others standing around. He asked them, 'Why have you been standing here all day long doing nothing?'

⁷"'Because no one has hired us,' they answered.

"He said to them, 'You also go and work in my vineyard.'

⁸"When evening came, the owner of the vineyard said to his foreman, 'Call the workers and pay them their wages, beginning with the last ones hired and going on to the first.'

⁹"The workers who were hired about the eleventh hour came and each received a denarius. ¹⁰So when those came who were hired first, they expected to receive more. But each one of them also received a denarius. ¹¹When they received it, they began to grumble against the landowner. ¹²'These men who were hired last worked only one hour,' they said, 'and you have made them equal to us who have borne the burden of the work and the heat of the day.'

¹³"But he answered one of them, 'Friend, I am not being unfair to you. Didn't you agree to work for a denarius? ¹⁴Take your pay and go. I want to give the man who was hired last the same as I gave you. ¹⁵Don't I have the right to do what I want with my own money? Or are you envious because I am generous?'

¹⁶"So the last will be first, and the first will be last."

Jesus Again Predicts His Death

¹⁷Now as Jesus was going up to Jerusalem, he took the twelve disciples aside and said to them, ¹⁸"We are going up to Jerusalem, and the Son of Man will be betrayed to the chief priests and the teachers of the law. They will condemn him to death ¹⁹and will turn him over to the Gentiles to be mocked and flogged and crucified. On the third day he will be raised to life!"

---

*a*29 Some manuscripts *mother or wife*

A Mother's Request

²⁰Then the mother of Zebedee's sons came to Jesus with her sons and, kneeling down, asked a favor of him.

[20]Then the mother of Zebedee's sons came to Jesus with her sons and, kneeling down, asked a favor of him.

[21]"What is it you want?" he asked.

She said, "Grant that one of these two sons of mine may sit at your right and the other at your left in your kingdom."

[22]"You don't know what you are asking," Jesus said to them. "Can you drink the cup I am going to drink?"

"We can," they answered.

[23]Jesus said to them, "You will indeed drink from my cup, but to sit at my right or left is not for me to grant. These places belong to those for whom they have been prepared by my Father."

[24]When the ten heard about this, they were indignant with the two brothers. [25]Jesus called them together and said, "You know that the rulers of the Gentiles lord it over them, and their high officials exercise authority over them. [26]Not so with you. Instead, whoever wants to become great among you must be your servant, [27]and whoever wants to be first must be your slave— [28]just as the Son of Man did not come to be served, but to serve, and to give his life as a ransom for many."

Two Blind Men Receive Sight

[29]As Jesus and his disciples were leaving Jericho, a large crowd followed him. [30]Two blind men were sitting by the roadside, and when they heard that Jesus was going by, they shouted, "Lord, Son of David, have mercy on us!"

[31]The crowd rebuked them and told them to be quiet, but they shouted all the louder, "Lord, Son of David, have mercy on us!"

[32]Jesus stopped and called them. "What do you want me to do for you?" he asked.

[33]"Lord," they answered, "we want our sight."

[34]Jesus had compassion on them and touched their eyes. Immediately they received their sight and followed him.

The Triumphal Entry

21 As they approached Jerusalem and came to Bethphage on the Mount of Olives, Jesus sent two disciples, [2]saying to them, "Go to the village ahead of you, and at once you will find a donkey tied there, with her colt by her. Untie them and bring them to me. [3]If anyone says anything to you, tell him that the Lord needs them, and he will send them right away."

[4]This took place to fulfill what was spoken through the prophet:

> [5]"Say to the Daughter of Zion,
> 'See, your king comes to you,
> gentle and riding on a donkey,
> on a colt, the foal of a donkey.' "[a]

[a]5 Zech. 9:9

⁶The disciples went and did as Jesus had instructed them. ⁷They brought the donkey and the colt, placed their cloaks on them, and Jesus sat on them. ⁸A very large crowd spread their cloaks on the road, while others cut branches from the trees and spread them on the road. ⁹The crowds that went ahead of him and those that followed shouted,

"Hosanna*ᵃ* to the Son of David!"

"Blessed is he who comes in the name of the Lord!"*ᵇ*

"Hosanna*ᵃ* in the highest!"

¹⁰When Jesus entered Jerusalem, the whole city was stirred and asked, "Who is this?"

¹¹The crowds answered, "This is Jesus, the prophet from Nazareth in Galilee."

Jesus at the Temple

¹²Jesus entered the temple area and drove out all who were buying and selling there. He overturned the tables of the money changers and the benches of those selling doves. ¹³"It is written," he said to them, " 'My house will be called a house of prayer,'*ᶜ* but you are making it a 'den of robbers.' *ᵈ*"

¹⁴The blind and the lame came to him at the temple, and he healed them. ¹⁵But when the chief priests and the teachers of the law saw the wonderful things he did and the children shouting in the temple area, "Hosanna to the Son of David," they were indignant.

¹⁶"Do you hear what these children are saying?" they asked him.

"Yes," replied Jesus, "have you never read,

" 'From the lips of children and infants
you have ordained praise'*ᵉ*?"

¹⁷And he left them and went out of the city to Bethany, where he spent the night.

The Fig Tree Withers

¹⁸Early in the morning, as he was on his way back to the city, he was hungry. ¹⁹Seeing a fig tree by the road, he went up to it but found nothing on it except leaves. Then he said to it, "May you never bear fruit again!" Immediately the tree withered.

²⁰When the disciples saw this, they were amazed. "How did the fig tree wither so quickly?" they asked.

²¹Jesus replied, "I tell you the truth, if you have faith and do not doubt, not only can you do what was done to the fig tree, but also you can say to this mountain, 'Go, throw yourself into the sea,' and it will be done. ²²If you believe, you will receive whatever you ask for in prayer."

ᵃ9 A Hebrew expression meaning "Save!" which became an exclamation of praise; also in verse 15
ᵇ9 Psalm 118:26   ᶜ13 Isaiah 56:7   ᵈ13 Jer. 7:11   ᵉ16 Psalm 8:2

The Authority of Jesus Questioned

²³Jesus entered the temple courts, and, while he was teaching, the chief priests and the elders of the people came to him. "By what authority are you doing these things?" they asked. "And who gave you this authority?"

²⁴Jesus replied, "I will also ask you one question. If you answer me, I will tell you by what authority I am doing these things. ²⁵John's baptism— where did it come from? Was it from heaven, or from men?"

They discussed it among themselves and said, "If we say, 'From heaven,' he will ask, 'Then why didn't you believe him?' ²⁶But if we say, 'From men'—we are afraid of the people, for they all hold that John was a prophet."

²⁷So they answered Jesus, "We don't know."

Then he said, "Neither will I tell you by what authority I am doing these things.

The Parable of the Two Sons

²⁸"What do you think? There was a man who had two sons. He went to the first and said, 'Son, go and work today in the vineyard.'

²⁹" 'I will not,' he answered, but later he changed his mind and went.

³⁰"Then the father went to the other son and said the same thing. He answered, 'I will, sir,' but he did not go.

³¹"Which of the two did what his father wanted?"

"The first," they answered.

Jesus said to them, "I tell you the truth, the tax collectors and the prostitutes are entering the kingdom of God ahead of you. ³²For John came to you to show you the way of righteousness, and you did not believe him, but the tax collectors and the prostitutes did. And even after you saw this, you did not repent and believe him.

The Parable of the Tenants

³³"Listen to another parable: There was a landowner who planted a vineyard. He put a wall around it, dug a winepress in it and built a watchtower. Then he rented the vineyard to some farmers and went away on a journey. ³⁴When the harvest time approached, he sent his servants to the tenants to collect his fruit.

³⁵"The tenants seized his servants; they beat one, killed another, and stoned a third. ³⁶Then he sent other servants to them, more than the first time, and the tenants treated them the same way. ³⁷Last of all, he sent his son to them. 'They will respect my son,' he said.

³⁸"But when the tenants saw the son, they said to each other, 'This is the heir. Come, let's kill him and take his inheritance.' ³⁹So they took him and threw him out of the vineyard and killed him.

⁴⁰"Therefore, when the owner of the vineyard comes, what will he do to those tenants?"

⁴¹"He will bring those wretches to a wretched end," they replied, "and

he will rent the vineyard to other tenants, who will give him his share of the crop at harvest time."

⁴²Jesus said to them, "Have you never read in the Scriptures:

" 'The stone the builders rejected
   has become the capstone*a*;
the Lord has done this,
   and it is marvelous in our eyes'*b*?

⁴³"Therefore I tell you that the kingdom of God will be taken away from you and given to a people who will produce its fruit. ⁴⁴He who falls on this stone will be broken to pieces, but he on whom it falls will be crushed."*c*

⁴⁵When the chief priests and the Pharisees heard Jesus' parables, they knew he was talking about them. ⁴⁶They looked for a way to arrest him, but they were afraid of the crowd because the people held that he was a prophet.

The Parable of the Wedding Banquet

22 Jesus spoke to them again in parables, saying: ²"The kingdom of heaven is like a king who prepared a wedding banquet for his son. ³He sent his servants to those who had been invited to the banquet to tell them to come, but they refused to come.

⁴"Then he sent some more servants and said, 'Tell those who have been invited that I have prepared my dinner: My oxen and fattened cattle have been butchered, and everything is ready. Come to the wedding banquet.'

⁵"But they paid no attention and went off—one to his field, another to his business. ⁶The rest seized his servants, mistreated them and killed them. ⁷The king was enraged. He sent his army and destroyed those murderers and burned their city.

⁸"Then he said to his servants, 'The wedding banquet is ready, but those I invited did not deserve to come. ⁹Go to the street corners and invite to the banquet anyone you find.' ¹⁰So the servants went out into the streets and gathered all the people they could find, both good and bad, and the wedding hall was filled with guests.

¹¹"But when the king came in to see the guests, he noticed a man there who was not wearing wedding clothes. ¹²'Friend,' he asked, 'how did you get in here without wedding clothes?' The man was speechless.

¹³"Then the king told the attendants, 'Tie him hand and foot, and throw him outside, into the darkness, where there will be weeping and gnashing of teeth.'

¹⁴"For many are invited, but few are chosen."

Paying Taxes to Caesar

¹⁵Then the Pharisees went out and laid plans to trap him in his words. ¹⁶They sent their disciples to him along with the Herodians. "Teacher," they said, "we know you are a man of integrity and that you teach the way of

---

*a*42 Or *cornerstone*   *b*42 Psalm 118:22,23   *c*44 Some manuscripts do not have verse 44.

God in accordance with the truth. You aren't swayed by men, because you pay no attention to who they are. [17]Tell us then, what is your opinion? Is it right to pay taxes to Caesar or not?"

[18]But Jesus, knowing their evil intent, said, "You hypocrites, why are you trying to trap me? [19]Show me the coin used for paying the tax." They brought him a denarius, [20]and he asked them, "Whose portrait is this? And whose inscription?"

[21]"Caesar's," they replied.

Then he said to them, "Give to Caesar what is Caesar's, and to God what is God's."

[22]When they heard this, they were amazed. So they left him and went away.

Marriage at the Resurrection

[23]That same day the Sadducees, who say there is no resurrection, came to him with a question. [24]"Teacher," they said, "Moses told us that if a man dies without having children, his brother must marry the widow and have children for him. [25]Now there were seven brothers among us. The first one married and died, and since he had no children, he left his wife to his brother. [26]The same thing happened to the second and third brother, right on down to the seventh. [27]Finally, the woman died. [28]Now then, at the resurrection, whose wife will she be of the seven, since all of them were married to her?"

[29]Jesus replied, "You are in error because you do not know the Scriptures or the power of God. [30]At the resurrection people will neither marry nor be given in marriage; they will be like the angels in heaven. [31]But about the resurrection of the dead—have you not read what God said to you, [32]'I am the God of Abraham, the God of Isaac, and the God of Jacob'[a]? He is not the God of the dead but of the living."

[33]When the crowds heard this, they were astonished at his teaching.

The Greatest Commandment

[34]Hearing that Jesus had silenced the Sadducees, the Pharisees got together. [35]One of them, an expert in the law, tested him with this question: [36]"Teacher, which is the greatest commandment in the Law?"

[37]Jesus replied: " 'Love the Lord your God with all your heart and with all your soul and with all your mind.'[b] [38]This is the first and greatest commandment. [39]And the second is like it: 'Love your neighbor as yourself.'[c] [40]All the Law and the Prophets hang on these two commandments."

Whose Son Is the Christ?

[41]While the Pharisees were gathered together, Jesus asked them, [42]"What do you think about the Christ[d]? Whose son is he?"

"The son of David," they replied.

[a]32 Exodus 3:6   [b]37 Deut. 6:5   [c]39 Lev. 19:18   [d]42 Or *Messiah*

⁴³He said to them, "How is it then that David, speaking by the Spirit, calls him 'Lord'? For he says,

> ⁴⁴" 'The Lord said to my Lord:
> "Sit at my right hand
> until I put your enemies
> under your feet." ' ᵃ

⁴⁵If then David calls him 'Lord,' how can he be his son?" ⁴⁶No one could say a word in reply, and from that day on no one dared to ask him any more questions.

Seven Woes

23 Then Jesus said to the crowds and to his disciples: ²"The teachers of the law and the Pharisees sit in Moses' seat. ³So you must obey them and do everything they tell you. But do not do what they do, for they do not practice what they preach. ⁴They tie up heavy loads and put them on men's shoulders, but they themselves are not willing to lift a finger to move them.

⁵"Everything they do is done for men to see: They make their phylacteriesᵇ wide and the tassels on their garments long; ⁶they love the place of honor at banquets and the most important seats in the synagogues; ⁷they love to be greeted in the marketplaces and to have men call them 'Rabbi.'

⁸"But you are not to be called 'Rabbi,' for you have only one Master and you are all brothers. ⁹And do not call anyone on earth 'father,' for you have one Father, and he is in heaven. ¹⁰Nor are you to be called 'teacher,' for you have one Teacher, the Christ.ᶜ ¹¹The greatest among you will be your servant. ¹²For whoever exalts himself will be humbled, and whoever humbles himself will be exalted.

¹³"Woe to you, teachers of the law and Pharisees, you hypocrites! You shut the kingdom of heaven in men's faces. You yourselves do not enter, nor will you let those enter who are trying to.ᵈ

¹⁵"Woe to you, teachers of the law and Pharisees, you hypocrites! You travel over land and sea to win a single convert, and when he becomes one, you make him twice as much a son of hell as you are.

¹⁶"Woe to you, blind guides! You say, 'If anyone swears by the temple, it means nothing; but if anyone swears by the gold of the temple, he is bound by his oath.' ¹⁷You blind fools! Which is greater: the gold, or the temple that makes the gold sacred? ¹⁸You also say, 'If anyone swears by the altar, it means nothing; but if anyone swears by the gift on it, he is bound by his oath.' ¹⁹You blind men! Which is greater: the gift, or the altar that makes the gift sacred? ²⁰Therefore, he who swears by the altar swears by it and by everything on it. ²¹And he who swears by the temple swears by

ᵃ44 Psalm 110:1   ᵇ5 That is, boxes containing Scripture verses, worn on forehead and arm
ᶜ10 Or *Messiah*   ᵈ13 Some manuscripts *to. ¹⁴Woe to you, teachers of the law and Pharisees, you hypocrites! You devour widows' houses and for a show make lengthy prayers. Therefore you will be punished more severely.*

it and by the one who dwells in it. ²²And he who swears by heaven swears by God's throne and by the one who sits on it.

²³"Woe to you, teachers of the law and Pharisees, you hypocrites! You give a tenth of your spices—mint, dill and cummin. But you have neglected the more important matters of the law—justice, mercy and faithfulness. You should have practiced the latter, without neglecting the former. ²⁴You blind guides! You strain out a gnat but swallow a camel.

²⁵"Woe to you, teachers of the law and Pharisees, you hypocrites! You clean the outside of the cup and dish, but inside they are full of greed and self-indulgence. ²⁶Blind Pharisee! First clean the inside of the cup and dish, and then the outside also will be clean.

²⁷"Woe to you, teachers of the law and Pharisees, you hypocrites! You are like whitewashed tombs, which look beautiful on the outside but on the inside are full of dead men's bones and everything unclean. ²⁸In the same way, on the outside you appear to people as righteous but on the inside you are full of hypocrisy and wickedness.

²⁹"Woe to you, teachers of the law and Pharisees, you hypocrites! You build tombs for the prophets and decorate the graves of the righteous. ³⁰And you say, 'If we had lived in the days of our forefathers, we would not have taken part with them in shedding the blood of the prophets.' ³¹So you testify against yourselves that you are the descendants of those who murdered the prophets. ³²Fill up, then, the measure of the sin of your forefathers!

³³"You snakes! You brood of vipers! How will you escape being condemned to hell? ³⁴Therefore I am sending you prophets and wise men and teachers. Some of them you will kill and crucify; others you will flog in your synagogues and pursue from town to town. ³⁵And so upon you will come all the righteous blood that has been shed on earth, from the blood of righteous Abel to the blood of Zechariah son of Berekiah, whom you murdered between the temple and the altar. ³⁶I tell you the truth, all this will come upon this generation.

³⁷"O Jerusalem, Jerusalem, you who kill the prophets and stone those sent to you, how often I have longed to gather your children together, as a hen gathers her chicks under her wings, but you were not willing. ³⁸Look, your house is left to you desolate. ³⁹For I tell you, you will not see me again until you say, 'Blessed is he who comes in the name of the Lord.'*ᵃ*"

Signs of the End of the Age

24 Jesus left the temple and was walking away when his disciples came up to him to call his attention to its buildings. ²"Do you see all these things?" he asked. "I tell you the truth, not one stone here will be left on another; every one will be thrown down."

³As Jesus was sitting on the Mount of Olives, the disciples came to him privately. "Tell us," they said, "when will this happen, and what will be the sign of your coming and of the end of the age?"

⁴Jesus answered: "Watch out that no one deceives you. ⁵For many will

ᵃ39 Psalm 118:26

come in my name, claiming, 'I am the Christ,*' and will deceive many. ⁶You will hear of wars and rumors of wars, but see to it that you are not alarmed. Such things must happen, but the end is still to come. ⁷Nation will rise against nation, and kingdom against kingdom. There will be famines and earthquakes in various places. ⁸All these are the beginning of birth pains.

⁹"Then you will be handed over to be persecuted and put to death, and you will be hated by all nations because of me. ¹⁰At that time many will turn away from the faith and will betray and hate each other, ¹¹and many false prophets will appear and deceive many people. ¹²Because of the increase of wickedness, the love of most will grow cold, ¹³but he who stands firm to the end will be saved. ¹⁴And this gospel of the kingdom will be preached in the whole world as a testimony to all nations, and then the end will come.

¹⁵"So when you see standing in the holy place 'the abomination that causes desolation,'ᵇ spoken of through the prophet Daniel—let the reader understand— ¹⁶then let those who are in Judea flee to the mountains. ¹⁷Let no one on the roof of his house go down to take anything out of the house. ¹⁸Let no one in the field go back to get his cloak. ¹⁹How dreadful it will be in those days for pregnant women and nursing mothers! ²⁰Pray that your flight will not take place in winter or on the Sabbath. ²¹For then there will be great distress, unequaled from the beginning of the world until now— and never to be equaled again. ²²If those days had not been cut short, no one would survive, but for the sake of the elect those days will be shortened. ²³At that time if anyone says to you, 'Look, here is the Christ!' or, 'There he is!' do not believe it. ²⁴For false Christs and false prophets will appear and perform great signs and miracles to deceive even the elect—if that were possible. ²⁵See, I have told you ahead of time.

²⁶"So if anyone tells you, 'There he is, out in the desert,' do not go out; or, 'Here he is, in the inner rooms,' do not believe it. ²⁷For as lightning that comes from the east is visible even in the west, so will be the coming of the Son of Man. ²⁸Wherever there is a carcass, there the vultures will gather.

²⁹"Immediately after the distress of those days

" 'the sun will be darkened,
    and the moon will not give its light;
the stars will fall from the sky,
    and the heavenly bodies will be shaken.'ᶜ

³⁰"At that time the sign of the Son of Man will appear in the sky, and all the nations of the earth will mourn. They will see the Son of Man coming on the clouds of the sky, with power and great glory ³¹And he will send his angels with a loud trumpet call, and they will gather his elect from the four winds, from one end of the heavens to the other.

³²"Now learn this lesson from the fig tree: As soon as its twigs get tender and its leaves come out, you know that summer is near. ³³Even so, when you see all these things, you know that itᵈ is near, right at the door.

ᵃ5 Or *Messiah*; also in verse 23   ᵇ15 Daniel 9:27; 11:31; 12:11   ᶜ29 Isaiah 13:10; 34:4   ᵈ33 Or *he*

[34]I tell you the truth, this generation[a] will certainly not pass away until all these things have happened. [35]Heaven and earth will pass away, but my words will never pass away.

The Day and Hour Unknown

[36]"No one knows about that day or hour, not even the angels in heaven, nor the Son,[b] but only the Father. [37]As it was in the days of Noah, so it will be at the coming of the Son of Man. [38]For in the days before the flood, people were eating and drinking, marrying and giving in marriage, up to the day Noah entered the ark; [39]and they knew nothing about what would happen until the flood came and took them all away. That is how it will be at the coming of the Son of Man. [40]Two men will be in the field; one will be taken and the other left. [41]Two women will be grinding with a hand mill; one will be taken and the other left.

[42]"Therefore keep watch, because you do not know on what day your Lord will come. [43]But understand this: If the owner of the house had known at what time of night the thief was coming, he would have kept watch and would not have let his house be broken into. [44]So you also must be ready, because the Son of Man will come at an hour when you do not expect him.

[45]"Who then is the faithful and wise servant, whom the master has put in charge of the servants in his household to give them their food at the proper time? [46]It will be good for that servant whose master finds him doing so when he returns. [47]I tell you the truth, he will put him in charge of all his possessions. [48]But suppose that servant is wicked and says to himself, 'My master is staying away a long time,' [49]and he then begins to beat his fellow servants and to eat and drink with drunkards. [50]The master of that servant will come on a day when he does not expect him and at an hour he is not aware of. [51]He will cut him to pieces and assign him a place with the hypocrites, where there will be weeping and gnashing of teeth.

The Parable of the Ten Virgins

25 "At that time the kingdom of heaven will be like ten virgins who took their lamps and went out to meet the bridegroom. [2]Five of them were foolish and five were wise. [3]The foolish ones took their lamps but did not take any oil with them. [4]The wise, however, took oil in jars along with their lamps. [5]The bridegroom was a long time in coming, and they all became drowsy and fell asleep.

[6]"At midnight the cry rang out: 'Here's the bridegroom! Come out to meet him!'

[7]"Then all the virgins woke up and trimmed their lamps. [8]The foolish ones said to the wise, 'Give us some of your oil; our lamps are going out.'

[9]" 'No,' they replied, 'there may not be enough for both us and you. Instead, go to those who sell oil and buy some for yourselves.'

[10]"But while they were on their way to buy the oil, the bridegroom

[a]34 Or *race*   [b]36 Some manuscripts do not have *nor the Son.*

arrived. The virgins who were ready went in with him to the wedding banquet. And the door was shut.

¹¹"Later the others also came. 'Sir! Sir!' they said. 'Open the door for us!'

¹²"But he replied, 'I tell you the truth, I don't know you.'

¹³"Therefore keep watch, because you do not know the day or the hour.

The Parable of the Talents

¹⁴"Again, it will be like a man going on a journey, who called his servants and entrusted his property to them. ¹⁵To one he gave five talents[a] of money, to another two talents, and to another one talent, each according to his ability. Then he went on his journey. ¹⁶The man who had received the five talents went at once and put his money to work and gained five more. ¹⁷So also, the one with the two talents gained two more. ¹⁸But the man who had received the one talent went off, dug a hole in the ground and hid his master's money.

¹⁹"After a long time the master of those servants returned and settled accounts with them. ²⁰The man who had received the five talents brought the other five. 'Master,' he said, 'you entrusted me with five talents. See, I have gained five more.'

²¹"His master replied, 'Well done, good and faithful servant! You have been faithful with a few things; I will put you in charge of many things. Come and share your master's happiness!'

²²"The man with the two talents also came. 'Master,' he said, 'you entrusted me with two talents; see, I have gained two more.'

²³"His master replied, 'Well done, good and faithful servant! You have been faithful with a few things; I will put you in charge of many things. Come and share your master's happiness!'

²⁴"Then the man who had received the one talent came. 'Master,' he said, 'I knew that you are a hard man, harvesting where you have not sown and gathering where you have not scattered seed. ²⁵So I was afraid and went out and hid your talent in the ground. See, here is what belongs to you.'

²⁶"His master replied, 'You wicked, lazy servant! So you knew that I harvest where I have not sown and gather where I have not scattered seed? ²⁷Well then, you should have put my money on deposit with the bankers, so that when I returned I would have received it back with interest.

²⁸" 'Take the talent from him and give it to the one who has the ten talents. ²⁹For everyone who has will be given more, and he will have an abundance. Whoever does not have, even what he has will be taken from him. ³⁰And throw that worthless servant outside, into the darkness, where there will be weeping and gnashing of teeth.'

The Sheep and the Goats

³¹"When the Son of Man comes in his glory, and all the angels with him, he will sit on his throne in heavenly glory. ³²All the nations will be gathered

[a]15 A talent was worth more than a thousand dollars.

before him, and he will separate the people one from another as a shepherd separates the sheep from the goats. ³³He will put the sheep on his right and the goats on his left.

³⁴"Then the King will say to those on his right, 'Come, you who are blessed by my Father; take your inheritance, the kingdom prepared for you since the creation of the world. ³⁵For I was hungry and you gave me something to eat, I was thirsty and you gave me something to drink, I was a stranger and you invited me in, ³⁶I needed clothes and you clothed me, I was sick and you looked after me, I was in prison and you came to visit me.'

³⁷"Then the righteous will answer him, 'Lord, when did we see you hungry and feed you, or thirsty and give you something to drink? ³⁸When did we see you a stranger and invite you in, or needing clothes and clothe you? ³⁹When did we see you sick or in prison and go to visit you?'

⁴⁰"The King will reply, 'I tell you the truth, whatever you did for one of the least of these brothers of mine, you did for me.'

⁴¹"Then he will say to those on his left, 'Depart from me, you who are cursed, into the eternal fire prepared for the devil and his angels. ⁴²For I was hungry and you gave me nothing to eat, I was thirsty and you gave me nothing to drink, ⁴³I was a stranger and you did not invite me in, I needed clothes and you did not clothe me, I was sick and in prison and you did not look after me.'

⁴⁴"They also will answer, 'Lord, when did we see you hungry or thirsty or a stranger or needing clothes or sick or in prison, and did not help you?'

⁴⁵"He will reply, 'I tell you the truth, whatever you did not do for one of the least of these, you did not do for me.'

⁴⁶"Then they will go away to eternal punishment, but the righteous to eternal life."

The Plot Against Jesus

26 When Jesus had finished saying all these things, he said to his disciples, ²"As you know, the Passover is two days away—and the Son of Man will be handed over to be crucified."

³Then the chief priests and the elders of the people assembled in the palace of the high priest, whose name was Caiaphas, ⁴and they plotted to arrest Jesus in some sly way and kill him. ⁵"But not during the Feast," they said, "or there may be a riot among the people."

Jesus Anointed at Bethany

⁶While Jesus was in Bethany in the home of a man known as Simon the Leper, ⁷a woman came to him with an alabaster jar of very expensive perfume, which she poured on his head as he was reclining at the table.

⁸When the disciples saw this, they were indignant. "Why this waste?" they asked. ⁹"This perfume could have been sold at a high price and the money given to the poor."

¹⁰Aware of this, Jesus said to them, "Why are you bothering this

woman? She has done a beautiful thing to me. ¹¹The poor you will always have with you, but you will not always have me. ¹²When she poured this perfume on my body, she did it to prepare me for burial. ¹³I tell you the truth, wherever this gospel is preached throughout the world, what she has done will also be told, in memory of her."

Judas Agrees to Betray Jesus

¹⁴Then one of the Twelve—the one called Judas Iscariot—went to the chief priests ¹⁵and asked, "What are you willing to give me if I hand him over to you?" So they counted out for him thirty silver coins. ¹⁶From then on Judas watched for an opportunity to hand him over.

The Lord's Supper

¹⁷On the first day of the Feast of Unleavened Bread, the disciples came to Jesus and asked, "Where do you want us to make preparations for you to eat the Passover?"

¹⁸He replied, "Go into the city to a certain man and tell him, 'The Teacher says: My appointed time is near. I am going to celebrate the Passover with my disciples at your house.' " ¹⁹So the disciples did as Jesus had directed them and prepared the Passover.

²⁰When evening came, Jesus was reclining at the table with the Twelve. ²¹And while they were eating, he said, "I tell you the truth, one of you will betray me."

²²They were very sad and began to say to him one after the other, "Surely not I, Lord?"

²³Jesus replied, "The one who has dipped his hand into the bowl with me will betray me. ²⁴The Son of Man will go just as it is written about him. But woe to that man who betrays the Son of Man! It would be better for him if he had not been born."

²⁵Then Judas, the one who would betray him, said, "Surely not I, Rabbi?"

Jesus answered, "Yes, it is you."ᵃ

²⁶While they were eating, Jesus took bread, gave thanks and broke it, and gave it to his disciples, saying, "Take and eat; this is my body."

²⁷Then he took the cup, gave thanks and offered it to them, saying, "Drink from it, all of you. ²⁸This is my blood of theᵇ covenant, which is poured out for many for the forgiveness of sins. ²⁹I tell you, I will not drink of this fruit of the vine from now on until that day when I drink it anew with you in my Father's kingdom."

³⁰When they had sung a hymn, they went out to the Mount of Olives.

Jesus Predicts Peter's Denial

³¹Then Jesus told them, "This very night you will all fall away on account of me, for it is written:

ᵃ25 Or "You yourself have said it"   ᵇ28 Some manuscripts the new

" 'I will strike the shepherd,
   and the sheep of the flock will be scattered.'[a]

[32]But after I have risen, I will go ahead of you into Galilee."

[33]Peter replied, "Even if all fall away on account of you, I never will."

[34]"I tell you the truth," Jesus answered, "this very night, before the rooster crows, you will disown me three times."

[35]But Peter declared, "Even if I have to die with you, I will never disown you." And all the other disciples said the same.

Gethsemane

[36]Then Jesus went with his disciples to a place called Gethsemane, and he said to them, "Sit here while I go over there and pray." [37]He took Peter and the two sons of Zebedee along with him, and he began to be sorrowful and troubled. [38]Then he said to them, "My soul is overwhelmed with sorrow to the point of death. Stay here and keep watch with me."

[39]Going a little farther, he fell with his face to the ground and prayed, "My Father, if it is possible, may this cup be taken from me. Yet not as I will, but as you will."

[40]Then he returned to his disciples and found them sleeping. "Could you men not keep watch with me for one hour?" he asked Peter. [41]"Watch and pray so that you will not fall into temptation. The spirit is willing, but the body is weak."

[42]He went away a second time and prayed, "My Father, if it is not possible for this cup to be taken away unless I drink it, may your will be done."

[43]When he came back, he again found them sleeping, because their eyes were heavy. [44]So he left them and went away once more and prayed the third time, saying the same thing.

[45]Then he returned to the disciples and said to them, "Are you still sleeping and resting? Look, the hour is near, and the Son of Man is betrayed into the hands of sinners. [46]Rise, let us go! Here comes my betrayer!"

Jesus Arrested

[47]While he was still speaking, Judas, one of the Twelve, arrived. With him was a large crowd armed with swords and clubs, sent from the chief priests and the elders of the people. [48]Now the betrayer had arranged a signal with them: "The one I kiss is the man; arrest him." [49]Going at once to Jesus, Judas said, "Greetings, Rabbi!" and kissed him.

[50]Jesus replied, "Friend, do what you came for."[b]

Then the men stepped forward, seized Jesus and arrested him. [51]With that, one of Jesus' companions reached for his sword, drew it out and struck the servant of the high priest, cutting off his ear.

[52]"Put your sword back in its place," Jesus said to him, "for all who draw the sword will die by the sword. [53]Do you think I cannot call on my

[a]31 Zech. 13:7   [b]50 Or "Friend, why have you come?"

55

Father, and he will at once put at my disposal more than twelve legions of angels? ⁵⁴But how then would the Scriptures be fulfilled that say it must happen in this way?"

⁵⁵At that time Jesus said to the crowd, "Am I leading a rebellion, that you have come out with swords and clubs to capture me? Every day I sat in the temple courts teaching, and you did not arrest me. ⁵⁶But this has all taken place that the writings of the prophets might be fulfilled." Then all the disciples deserted him and fled.

Before the Sanhedrin

⁵⁷Those who had arrested Jesus took him to Caiaphas, the high priest, where the teachers of the law and the elders had assembled. ⁵⁸But Peter followed him at a distance, right up to the courtyard of the high priest. He entered and sat down with the guards to see the outcome.

⁵⁹The chief priests and the whole Sanhedrin were looking for false evidence against Jesus so that they could put him to death. ⁶⁰But they did not find any, though many false witnesses came forward.

Finally two came forward ⁶¹and declared, "This fellow said, 'I am able to destroy the temple of God and rebuild it in three days.' "

⁶²Then the high priest stood up and said to Jesus, "Are you not going to answer? What is this testimony that these men are bringing against you?" ⁶³But Jesus remained silent.

The high priest said to him, "I charge you under oath by the living God: Tell us if you are the Christ,ᵃ the Son of God."

⁶⁴"Yes, it is as you say," Jesus replied. "But I say to all of you: In the future you will see the Son of Man sitting at the right hand of the Mighty One and coming on the clouds of heaven."

⁶⁵Then the high priest tore his clothes and said, "He has spoken blasphemy! Why do we need any more witnesses? Look, now you have heard the blasphemy. ⁶⁶What do you think?"

"He is worthy of death," they answered.

⁶⁷Then they spit in his face and struck him with their fists. Others slapped him ⁶⁸and said, "Prophesy to us, Christ. Who hit you?"

Peter Disowns Jesus

⁶⁹Now Peter was sitting out in the courtyard, and a servant girl came to him. "You also were with Jesus of Galilee," she said.

⁷⁰But he denied it before them all. "I don't know what you're talking about," he said.

⁷¹Then he went out to the gateway, where another girl saw him and said to the people there, "This fellow was with Jesus of Nazareth."

⁷²He denied it again, with an oath: "I don't know the man!"

⁷³After a little while, those standing there went up to Peter and said, "Surely you are one of them, for your accent gives you away."

ᵃ63 Or Messiah; also in verse 68

[74]Then he began to call down curses on himself and he swore to them, "I don't know the man!"

Immediately a rooster crowed. [75]Then Peter remembered the word Jesus had spoken: "Before the rooster crows, you will disown me three times." And he went outside and wept bitterly.

Judas Hangs Himself

27 Early in the morning, all the chief priests and the elders of the people came to the decision to put Jesus to death. [2]They bound him, led him away and handed him over to Pilate, the governor.

[3]When Judas, who had betrayed him, saw that Jesus was condemned, he was seized with remorse and returned the thirty silver coins to the chief priests and the elders. [4]"I have sinned," he said, "for I have betrayed innocent blood."

"What is that to us?" they replied. "That's your responsibility."

[5]So Judas threw the money into the temple and left. Then he went away and hanged himself.

[6]The chief priests picked up the coins and said, "It is against the law to put this into the treasury, since it is blood money." [7]So they decided to use the money to buy the potter's field as a burial place for foreigners. [8]That is why it has been called the Field of Blood to this day. [9]Then what was spoken by Jeremiah the prophet was fulfilled: "They took the thirty silver coins, the price set on him by the people of Israel, [10]and they used them to buy the potter's field, as the Lord commanded me."[a]

Jesus Before Pilate

[11]Meanwhile Jesus stood before the governor, and the governor asked him, "Are you the king of the Jews?"

"Yes, it is as you say," Jesus replied.

[12]When he was accused by the chief priests and the elders, he gave no answer. [13]Then Pilate asked him, "Don't you hear the testimony they are bringing against you?" [14]But Jesus made no reply, not even to a single charge—to the great amazement of the governor.

[15]Now it was the governor's custom at the Feast to release a prisoner chosen by the crowd. [16]At that time they had a notorious prisoner, called Barabbas. [17]So when the crowd had gathered, Pilate asked them, "Which one do you want me to release to you: Barabbas, or Jesus who is called Christ?" [18]For he knew it was out of envy that they had handed Jesus over to him.

[19]While Pilate was sitting on the judge's seat, his wife sent him this message: "Don't have anything to do with that innocent man, for I have suffered a great deal today in a dream because of him."

[20]But the chief priests and the elders persuaded the crowd to ask for Barabbas and to have Jesus executed.

[a]10 See Zech. 11:12,13; Jer. 19:1-13; 32:6-9.

[21]"Which of the two do you want me to release to you?" asked the governor.

"Barabbas," they answered.

[22]"What shall I do, then, with Jesus who is called Christ?" Pilate asked. They all answered, "Crucify him!"

[23]"Why? What crime has he committed?" asked Pilate.

But they shouted all the louder, "Crucify him!"

[24]When Pilate saw that he was getting nowhere, but that instead an uproar was starting, he took water and washed his hands in front of the crowd. "I am innocent of this man's blood," he said. "It is your responsibility!"

[25]All the people answered, "Let his blood be on us and on our children!"

[26]Then he released Barabbas to them. But he had Jesus flogged, and handed him over to be crucified.

The Soldiers Mock Jesus

[27]Then the governor's soldiers took Jesus into the Praetorium and gathered the whole company of soldiers around him. [28]They stripped him and put a scarlet robe on him, [29]and then twisted together a crown of thorns and set it on his head. They put a staff in his right hand and knelt in front of him and mocked him. "Hail, king of the Jews!" they said. [30]They spit on him, and took the staff and struck him on the head again and again. [31]After they had mocked him, they took off the robe and put his own clothes on him. Then they led him away to crucify him.

The Crucifixion

[32]As they were going out, they met a man from Cyrene, named Simon, and they forced him to carry the cross. [33]They came to a place called Golgotha (which means The Place of the Skull). [34]There they offered Jesus wine to drink, mixed with gall; but after tasting it, he refused to drink it. [35]When they had crucified him, they divided up his clothes by casting lots. [a] [36]And sitting down, they kept watch over him there. [37]Above his head they placed the written charge against him: THIS IS JESUS, THE KING OF THE JEWS. [38]Two robbers were crucified with him, one on his right and one on his left. [39]Those who passed by hurled insults at him, shaking their heads [40]and saying, "You who are going to destroy the temple and build it in three days, save yourself! Come down from the cross, if you are the Son of God!"

[41]In the same way the chief priests, the teachers of the law and the elders mocked him. [42]"He saved others," they said, "but he can't save himself! He's the King of Israel! Let him come down now from the cross, and we will believe in him. [43]He trusts in God. Let God rescue him now if he wants him, for he said, 'I am the Son of God.' " [44]In the same way the robbers who were crucified with him also heaped insults on him.

a35 A few late manuscripts lots that the word spoken by the prophet might be fulfilled: "They divided my garments among themselves and cast lots for my clothing" _(Psalm 22:18)_

The Death of Jesus

⁴⁵From the sixth hour until the ninth hour darkness came over all the land. ⁴⁶About the ninth hour Jesus cried out in a loud voice, *"Eloi, Eloi,ᵃ lama sabachthani?"*—which means, "My God, my God, why have you forsaken me?"ᵇ

⁴⁷When some of those standing there heard this, they said, "He's calling Elijah."

⁴⁸Immediately one of them ran and got a sponge. He filled it with wine vinegar, put it on a stick, and offered it to Jesus to drink. ⁴⁹The rest said, "Now leave him alone. Let's see if Elijah comes to save him."

⁵⁰And when Jesus had cried out again in a loud voice, he gave up his spirit.

⁵¹At that moment the curtain of the temple was torn in two from top to bottom. The earth shook and the rocks split. ⁵²The tombs broke open and the bodies of many holy people who had died were raised to life. ⁵³They came out of the tombs, and after Jesus' resurrection they went into the holy city and appeared to many people.

⁵⁴When the centurion and those with him who were guarding Jesus saw the earthquake and all that had happened, they were terrified, and exclaimed, "Surely he was the Sonᶜ of God!"

⁵⁵Many women were there, watching from a distance. They had followed Jesus from Galilee to care for his needs. ⁵⁶Among them were Mary Magdalene, Mary the mother of James and Joses, and the mother of Zebedee's sons.

The Burial of Jesus

⁵⁷As evening approached, there came a rich man from Arimathea, named Joseph, who had himself become a disciple of Jesus. ⁵⁸Going to Pilate, he asked for Jesus' body, and Pilate ordered that it be given to him. ⁵⁹Joseph took the body, wrapped it in a clean linen cloth, ⁶⁰and placed it in his own new tomb that he had cut out of the rock. He rolled a big stone in front of the entrance to the tomb and went away. ⁶¹Mary Magdalene and the other Mary were sitting there opposite the tomb.

The Guard at the Tomb

⁶²The next day, the one after Preparation Day, the chief priests and the Pharisees went to Pilate. ⁶³"Sir," they said, "we remember that while he was still alive that deceiver said, 'After three days I will rise again.' ⁶⁴So give the order for the tomb to be made secure until the third day. Otherwise, his disciples may come and steal the body and tell the people that he has been raised from the dead. This last deception will be worse than the first."

⁶⁵"Take a guard," Pilate answered. "Go, make the tomb as secure as you know how." ⁶⁶So they went and made the tomb secure by putting a seal on the stone and posting the guard.

ᵃ46 Some manuscripts *Eli, Eli*   ᵇ46 Psalm 22:1   ᶜ54 Or *a son*

The Resurrection

28 After the Sabbath, at dawn on the first day of the week, Mary Magdalene and the other Mary went to look at the tomb.

²There was a violent earthquake, for an angel of the Lord came down from heaven and, going to the tomb, rolled back the stone and sat on it. ³His appearance was like lightning, and his clothes were white as snow. ⁴The guards were so afraid of him that they shook and became like dead men.

⁵The angel said to the women, "Do not be afraid, for I know that you are looking for Jesus, who was crucified. ⁶He is not here; he has risen, just as he said. Come and see the place where he lay. ⁷Then go quickly and tell his disciples: 'He has risen from the dead and is going ahead of you into Galilee. There you will see him.' Now I have told you."

⁸So the women hurried away from the tomb, afraid yet filled with joy, and ran to tell his disciples. ⁹Suddenly Jesus met them. "Greetings," he said. They came to him, clasped his feet and worshiped him. ¹⁰Then Jesus said to them, "Do not be afraid. Go and tell my brothers to go to Galilee; there they will see me."

The Guards' Report

¹¹While the women were on their way, some of the guards went into the city and reported to the chief priests everything that had happened. ¹²When the chief priests had met with the elders and devised a plan, they gave the soldiers a large sum of money, ¹³telling them, "You are to say, 'His disciples came during the night and stole him away while we were asleep.' ¹⁴If this report gets to the governor, we will satisfy him and keep you out of trouble." ¹⁵So the soldiers took the money and did as they were instructed. And this story has been widely circulated among the Jews to this very day.

The Great Commission

¹⁶Then the eleven disciples went to Galilee, to the mountain where Jesus had told them to go. ¹⁷When they saw him, they worshiped him; but some doubted. ¹⁸Then Jesus came to them and said, "All authority in heaven and on earth has been given to me. ¹⁹Therefore go and make disciples of all nations, baptizing them in[a] the name of the Father and of the Son and of the Holy Spirit, ²⁰and teaching them to obey everything I have commanded you. And surely I am with you always, to the very end of the age."

[a]19 Or *into*; see Acts 8:16; 19:5; Romans 6:3; 1 Cor. 1:13; 10:2 and Gal. 3:27.

Mark

INTRODUCTION

Mark's Gospel was composed at a time when the society to which Christians had become accustomed was crumbling and the future loomed as a frightening uncertainty. The main focus of the crisis was the demise of Jerusalem as the secure center of Christianity, the base of apostolic activity, the home of the pillars of the Church (Gal 2:9). What precipitated this crisis was a series of events which culminated in the Roman armies of Titus crushing the Jewish revolt and destroying the temple in 70 A.D. In the course of these events, Christians, unwilling to participate in the revolt, had fled Jerusalem leaving Christianity without a center and leaving Christians everywhere perplexed and confused. Almost like a therapist who helps patients cope with the present by having them retrace and understand their past, Mark tells the story of Jesus in such a way as to enable Christians to understand the real meaning of their present existence.

Mark is concerned with a correct understanding of discipleship but the disciples in Mark's story do not serve as models for the reader. The reader is rather invited by Mark's story to identify with Jesus in much the same way as one identifies with the hero in a Greek tragedy. By reliving, through story, the tragic consequences of Jesus' utter fidelity to his nature and mission the reader arrives at a deeper appreciation of the saying, "If anyone would come after me, he must deny himself and take up his cross and follow me" (8:34).

The above quotation is taken from the scene at Caesarea Philippi (8:27—9:1), a scene which is crucial for appreciating the overall structure and flow of the narrative. Prior to this scene Jesus is presented as preaching the arrival of God's kingdom through his powerful words and deeds. The initial chapters (1–3) show Jesus working within the context of the Judaism of his day but insisting on a radical break: "No one pours new wine into old wineskins" (2:22f). The next chapters (4–5) show Jesus attempting to make the true meaning of his mission clear to his disciples, recognizing that "those on the outside" (4:11) will misunderstand. In the succeeding chapters it becomes increasingly clear that the disciples themselves misunderstand (6–8), and when Jesus, at Caesarea

Philippi, asks "Who do you say I am?" the response given by Peter "You are the Christ" (8:29), while correct, is also defective. It is easy to recognize a powerful leader on whom one can attach one's hopes for triumph over present evils. It is much more difficult to recognize the full dimensions of what Jesus is all about and make that recognition the basis of one's new existence in God's kingdom.

From the scene at Caesarea Philippi onward Jesus is presented as moving relentlessly to his passion and death. Three times he predicts his passion (8:31; 9:31; 10:33f), and each time has to correct his disciples' misunderstanding. Eventually he arrives in Jerusalem amid much cheering (11:1–11), but in the temple his actions and teaching arouse the enmity of the chief priests (11:15—12:44). His final discourse (ch. 13) is rich in symbols that could be understood in terms of the crisis facing the Church at the time of the composition of Mark's Gospel or in any age. The next two chapters (14–15) detail the final three days of Jesus' life. The stories of the anointing at Bethany and the Last Supper are told in a way that sheds light on the meaning of Jesus' eventual death and burial but the disciples fail to grasp their real meaning. When Jesus is arrested and led off to be crucified he is totally abandoned, an abandonment he had begun to feel and agonize over in Gethsemane. As Jesus meets his tragic end the reader is challenged by Mark's story to respond. The nature of the response is elicited by the story in its entirety but two scenes at the end are suggestive: the centurion at the cross becoming the first human in Mark's Gospel to confess that Jesus was "the Son of God" (15:39), and the women at the empty tomb saying "nothing to anyone, because they were afraid" (16:8).

TERENCE J. KEEGAN, O.P.

Points for Reflection

1. When we reach the end of Mark's Gospel we can ask ourselves how we would respond to the empty tomb. How strong is our faith when faced with crisis and uncertainty?
2. We, as readers, were told in the first verse of the Gospel that Jesus was the Son of God, but what do these words mean to us? Can we confess our faith with the depth of meaning involved in the centurion's confession?
3. Do we recognize that real triumph over evil comes with suffering, not in attempts to seize and exercise power? If we have become so caught up in the problems of the present day that our Christianity has consisted in confusing adjustments to contemporary culture, then Mark's Gospel can bring us back to our origins and allow us to experience anew the real meaning of the good news.

John the Baptist Prepares the Way

1 The beginning of the gospel about Jesus Christ, the Son of God. ª

²It is written in Isaiah the prophet:

> "I will send my messenger ahead of you,
>   who will prepare your way"ᵇ—
> ³"a voice of one calling in the desert,
> 'Prepare the way for the Lord,
>   make straight paths for him.' "ᶜ

⁴And so John came, baptizing in the desert region and preaching a baptism of repentance for the forgiveness of sins. ⁵The whole Judean countryside and all the people of Jerusalem went out to him. Confessing their sins, they were baptized by him in the Jordan River. ⁶John wore clothing made of camel's hair, with a leather belt around his waist, and he ate locusts and wild honey. ⁷And this was his message: "After me will come one more powerful than I, the thongs of whose sandals I am not worthy to stoop down and untie. ⁸I baptize you withᵈ water, but he will baptize you with the Holy Spirit."

The Baptism and Temptation of Jesus

⁹At that time Jesus came from Nazareth in Galilee and was baptized by John in the Jordan. ¹⁰As Jesus was coming up out of the water, he saw heaven being torn open and the Spirit descending on him like a dove. ¹¹And a voice came from heaven: "You are my Son, whom I love; with you I am well pleased."

¹²At once the Spirit sent him out into the desert, ¹³and he was in the desert forty days, being tempted by Satan. He was with the wild animals, and angels attended him.

The Calling of the First Disciples

¹⁴After John was put in prison, Jesus went into Galilee, proclaiming the good news of God. ¹⁵"The time has come," he said. "The kingdom of God is near. Repent and believe the good news!"

¹⁶As Jesus walked beside the Sea of Galilee, he saw Simon and his brother Andrew casting a net into the lake, for they were fishermen. ¹⁷"Come, follow me," Jesus said, "and I will make you fishers of men." ¹⁸At once they left their nets and followed him.

¹⁹When he had gone a little farther, he saw James son of Zebedee and his brother John in a boat, preparing their nets. ²⁰Without delay he called them, and they left their father Zebedee in the boat with the hired men and followed him.

ª1 Some manuscripts do not have *the Son of God*.   ᵇ2 Mal. 3:1   ᶜ3 Isaiah 40:3   ᵈ8 Or *in*

Jesus Drives Out an Evil Spirit

²¹They went to Capernaum, and when the Sabbath came, Jesus went into the synagogue and began to teach. ²²The people were amazed at his teaching, because he taught them as one who had authority, not as the teachers of the law. ²³Just then a man in their synagogue who was possessed by an evil^a spirit cried out, ²⁴"What do you want with us, Jesus of Nazareth? Have you come to destroy us? I know who you are—the Holy One of God!"

²⁵"Be quiet!" said Jesus sternly. "Come out of him!" ²⁶The evil spirit shook the man violently and came out of him with a shriek.

²⁷The people were all so amazed that they asked each other, "What is this? A new teaching—and with authority! He even gives orders to evil spirits and they obey him." ²⁸News about him spread quickly over the whole region of Galilee.

Jesus Heals Many

²⁹As soon as they left the synagogue, they went with James and John to the home of Simon and Andrew. ³⁰Simon's mother-in-law was in bed with a fever, and they told Jesus about her. ³¹So he went to her, took her hand and helped her up. The fever left her and she began to wait on them.

³²That evening after sunset the people brought to Jesus all the sick and demon-possessed. ³³The whole town gathered at the door, ³⁴and Jesus healed many who had various diseases. He also drove out many demons, but he would not let the demons speak because they knew who he was.

Jesus Prays in a Solitary Place

³⁵Very early in the morning, while it was still dark, Jesus got up, left the house and went off to a solitary place, where he prayed. ³⁶Simon and his companions went to look for him, ³⁷and when they found him, they exclaimed: "Everyone is looking for you!"

³⁸Jesus replied, "Let us go somewhere else—to the nearby villages—so I can preach there also. That is why I have come." ³⁹So he traveled throughout Galilee, preaching in their synagogues and driving out demons.

A Man With Leprosy

⁴⁰A man with leprosy^b came to him and begged him on his knees, "If you are willing, you can make me clean."

⁴¹Filled with compassion, Jesus reached out his hand and touched the man. "I am willing," he said. "Be clean!" ⁴²Immediately the leprosy left him and he was cured.

⁴³Jesus sent him away at once with a strong warning: ⁴⁴"See that you don't tell this to anyone. But go, show yourself to the priest and offer the sacrifices that Moses commanded for your cleansing, as a testimony to them." ⁴⁵Instead he went out and began to talk freely, spreading the news.

---

^a23 Greek *unclean*; also in verses 26 and 27   ^b40 The Greek word was used for various diseases affecting the skin—not necessarily leprosy.

As a result, Jesus could no longer enter a town openly but stayed outside in lonely places. Yet the people still came to him from everywhere.

Jesus Heals a Paralytic

2 A few days later, when Jesus again entered Capernaum, the people heard that he had come home. ²So many gathered that there was no room left, not even outside the door, and he preached the word to them. ³Some men came, bringing to him a paralytic, carried by four of them. ⁴Since they could not get him to Jesus because of the crowd, they made an opening in the roof above Jesus and, after digging through it, lowered the mat the paralyzed man was lying on. ⁵When Jesus saw their faith, he said to the paralytic, "Son, your sins are forgiven."

⁶Now some teachers of the law were sitting there, thinking to themselves, ⁷"Why does this fellow talk like that? He's blaspheming! Who can forgive sins but God alone?"

⁸Immediately Jesus knew in his spirit that this was what they were thinking in their hearts, and he said to them, "Why are you thinking these things? ⁹Which is easier: to say to the paralytic, 'Your sins are forgiven,' or to say, 'Get up, take your mat and walk'? ¹⁰But that you may know that the Son of Man has authority on earth to forgive sins . . . ." He said to the paralytic, ¹¹"I tell you, get up, take your mat and go home." ¹²He got up, took his mat and walked out in full view of them all. This amazed everyone and they praised God, saying, "We have never seen anything like this!"

The Calling of Levi

¹³Once again Jesus went out beside the lake. A large crowd came to him, and he began to teach them. ¹⁴As he walked along, he saw Levi son of Alphaeus sitting at the tax collector's booth. "Follow me," Jesus told him, and Levi got up and followed him.

¹⁵While Jesus was having dinner at Levi's house, many tax collectors and "sinners" were eating with him and his disciples, for there were many who followed him. ¹⁶When the teachers of the law who were Pharisees saw him eating with the "sinners" and tax collectors, they asked his disciples: "Why does he eat with tax collectors and 'sinners'?"

¹⁷On hearing this, Jesus said to them, "It is not the healthy who need a doctor, but the sick. I have not come to call the righteous, but sinners."

Jesus Questioned About Fasting

¹⁸Now John's disciples and the Pharisees were fasting. Some people came and asked Jesus, "How is it that John's disciples and the disciples of the Pharisees are fasting, but yours are not?"

¹⁹Jesus answered, "How can the guests of the bridegroom fast while he is with them? They cannot, so long as they have him with them. ²⁰But the time will come when the bridegroom will be taken from them, and on that day they will fast.

²¹"No one sews a patch of unshrunk cloth on an old garment. If he

does, the new piece will pull away from the old, making the tear worse. ²²And no one pours new wine into old wineskins. If he does, the wine will burst the skins, and both the wine and the wineskins will be ruined. No, he pours new wine into new wineskins.''

Lord of the Sabbath

²³One Sabbath Jesus was going through the grainfields, and as his disciples walked along, they began to pick some heads of grain. ²⁴The Pharisees said to him, ''Look, why are they doing what is unlawful on the Sabbath?''

²⁵He answered, ''Have you never read what David did when he and his companions were hungry and in need? ²⁶In the days of Abiathar the high priest, he entered the house of God and ate the consecrated bread, which is lawful only for priests to eat. And he also gave some to his companions.''

²⁷Then he said to them, ''The Sabbath was made for man, not man for the Sabbath. ²⁸So the Son of Man is Lord even of the Sabbath.''

3 Another time he went into the synagogue, and a man with a shriveled hand was there. ²Some of them were looking for a reason to accuse Jesus, so they watched him closely to see if he would heal him on the Sabbath. ³Jesus said to the man with the shriveled hand, ''Stand up in front of everyone.''

⁴Then Jesus asked them, ''Which is lawful on the Sabbath: to do good or to do evil, to save life or to kill?'' But they remained silent. ⁵He looked around at them in anger and, deeply distressed at their stubborn hearts, said to the man, ''Stretch out your hand.'' He stretched it out, and his hand was completely restored. ⁶Then the Pharisees went out and began to plot with the Herodians how they might kill Jesus.

Crowds Follow Jesus

⁷Jesus withdrew with his disciples to the lake, and a large crowd from Galilee followed. ⁸When they heard all he was doing, many people came to him from Judea, Jerusalem, Idumea, and the regions across the Jordan and around Tyre and Sidon. ⁹Because of the crowd he told his disciples to have a small boat ready for him, to keep the people from crowding him. ¹⁰For he had healed many, so that those with diseases were pushing forward to touch him. ¹¹Whenever the evil[a] spirits saw him, they fell down before him and cried out, ''You are the Son of God.'' ¹²But he gave them strict orders not to tell who he was.

The Appointing of the Twelve Apostles

¹³Jesus went up on a mountainside and called to him those he wanted, and they came to him. ¹⁴He appointed twelve—designating them apostles[b] —that they might be with him and that he might send them out to preach ¹⁵and to have authority to drive out demons. ¹⁶These are the twelve he appointed: Simon (to whom he gave the name Peter); ¹⁷James son of Zebe-

---

[a]11 Greek unclean; also in verse 30   [b]14 Some manuscripts do not have designating them apostles.

dee and his brother John (to them he gave the name Boanerges, which means Sons of Thunder); [18]Andrew, Philip, Bartholomew, Matthew, Thomas, James son of Alphaeus, Thaddaeus, Simon the Zealot [19]and Judas Iscariot, who betrayed him.

Jesus and Beelzebub

[20]Then Jesus entered a house, and again a crowd gathered, so that he and his disciples were not even able to eat. [21]When his family heard about this, they went to take charge of him, for they said, "He is out of his mind."

[22]And the teachers of the law who came down from Jerusalem said, "He is possessed by Beelzebub[a]! By the prince of demons he is driving out demons."

[23]So Jesus called them and spoke to them in parables: "How can Satan drive out Satan? [24]If a kingdom is divided against itself, that kingdom cannot stand. [25]If a house is divided against itself, that house cannot stand. [26]And if Satan opposes himself and is divided, he cannot stand; his end has come. [27]In fact, no one can enter a strong man's house and carry off his possessions unless he first ties up the strong man. Then he can rob his house. [28]I tell you the truth, all the sins and blasphemies of men will be forgiven them. [29]But whoever blasphemes against the Holy Spirit will never be forgiven; he is guilty of an eternal sin."

[30]He said this because they were saying, "He has an evil spirit."

Jesus' Mother and Brothers

[31]Then Jesus' mother and brothers arrived. Standing outside, they sent someone in to call him. [32]A crowd was sitting around him, and they told him, "Your mother and brothers are outside looking for you."

[33]"Who are my mother and my brothers?" he asked.

[34]Then he looked at those seated in a circle around him and said, "Here are my mother and my brothers! [35]Whoever does God's will is my brother and sister and mother."

The Parable of the Sower

4 Again Jesus began to teach by the lake. The crowd that gathered around him was so large that he got into a boat and sat in it out on the lake, while all the people were along the shore at the water's edge. [2]He taught them many things by parables, and in his teaching said: [3]"Listen! A farmer went out to sow his seed. [4]As he was scattering the seed, some fell along the path, and the birds came and ate it up. [5]Some fell on rocky places, where it did not have much soil. It sprang up quickly, because the soil was shallow. [6]But when the sun came up, the plants were scorched, and they withered because they had no root. [7]Other seed fell among thorns, which grew up and choked the plants, so that they did not bear grain. [8]Still other seed fell on good soil. It came up, grew and produced a crop, multiplying thirty, sixty, or even a hundred times."

[a]22 Greek Beezeboul or Beelzeboul

⁹Then Jesus said, "He who has ears to hear, let him hear."

¹⁰When he was alone, the Twelve and the others around him asked him about the parables. ¹¹He told them, "The secret of the kingdom of God has been given to you. But to those on the outside everything is said in parables ¹²so that,

> " 'they may be ever seeing but never perceiving,
>   and ever hearing but never understanding;
>   otherwise they might turn and be forgiven!'ᵃ"

¹³Then Jesus said to them, "Don't you understand this parable? How then will you understand any parable? ¹⁴The farmer sows the word. ¹⁵Some people are like seed along the path, where the word is sown. As soon as they hear it, Satan comes and takes away the word that was sown in them. ¹⁶Others, like seed sown on rocky places, hear the word and at once receive it with joy. ¹⁷But since they have no root, they last only a short time. When trouble or persecution comes because of the word, they quickly fall away. ¹⁸Still others, like seed sown among thorns, hear the word; ¹⁹but the worries of this life, the deceitfulness of wealth and the desires for other things come in and choke the word, making it unfruitful. ²⁰Others, like seed sown on good soil, hear the word, accept it, and produce a crop—thirty, sixty or even a hundred times what was sown."

A Lamp on a Stand

²¹He said to them, "Do you bring in a lamp to put it under a bowl or a bed? Instead, don't you put it on its stand? ²²For whatever is hidden is meant to be disclosed, and whatever is concealed is meant to be brought out into the open. ²³If anyone has ears to hear, let him hear."

²⁴"Consider carefully what you hear," he continued. "With the measure you use, it will be measured to you—and even more. ²⁵Whoever has will be given more; whoever does not have, even what he has will be taken from him."

The Parable of the Growing Seed

²⁶He also said, "This is what the kingdom of God is like. A man scatters seed on the ground. ²⁷Night and day, whether he sleeps or gets up, the seed sprouts and grows, though he does not know how. ²⁸All by itself the soil produces grain—first the stalk, then the head, then the full kernel in the head. ²⁹As soon as the grain is ripe, he puts the sickle to it, because the harvest has come."

The Parable of the Mustard Seed

³⁰Again he said, "What shall we say the kingdom of God is like, or what parable shall we use to describe it? ³¹It is like a mustard seed, which is the smallest seed you plant in the ground. ³²Yet when planted, it grows and

ᵃ12 Isaiah 6:9,10

becomes the largest of all garden plants, with such big branches that the birds of the air can perch in its shade."

³³With many similar parables Jesus spoke the word to them, as much as they could understand. ³⁴He did not say anything to them without using a parable. But when he was alone with his own disciples, he explained everything.

Jesus Calms the Storm

³⁵That day when evening came, he said to his disciples, "Let us go over to the other side." ³⁶Leaving the crowd behind, they took him along, just as he was, in the boat. There were also other boats with him. ³⁷A furious squall came up, and the waves broke over the boat, so that it was nearly swamped. ³⁸Jesus was in the stern, sleeping on a cushion. The disciples woke him and said to him, "Teacher, don't you care if we drown?"

³⁹He got up, rebuked the wind and said to the waves, "Quiet! Be still!" Then the wind died down and it was completely calm.

⁴⁰He said to his disciples, "Why are you so afraid? Do you still have no faith?"

⁴¹They were terrified and asked each other, "Who is this? Even the wind and the waves obey him!"

The Healing of a Demon-possessed Man

5 They went across the lake to the region of the Gerasenes.^a ²When Jesus got out of the boat, a man with an evil^b spirit came from the tombs to meet him. ³This man lived in the tombs, and no one could bind him any more, not even with a chain. ⁴For he had often been chained hand and foot, but he tore the chains apart and broke the irons on his feet. No one was strong enough to subdue him. ⁵Night and day among the tombs and in the hills he would cry out and cut himself with stones.

⁶When he saw Jesus from a distance, he ran and fell on his knees in front of him. ⁷He shouted at the top of his voice, "What do you want with me, Jesus, Son of the Most High God? Swear to God that you won't torture me!" ⁸For Jesus had said to him, "Come out of this man, you evil spirit!"

⁹Then Jesus asked him, "What is your name?"

"My name is Legion," he replied, "for we are many." ¹⁰And he begged Jesus again and again not to send them out of the area.

¹¹A large herd of pigs was feeding on the nearby hillside. ¹²The demons begged Jesus, "Send us among the pigs; allow us to go into them." ¹³He gave them permission, and the evil spirits came out and went into the pigs. The herd, about two thousand in number, rushed down the steep bank into the lake and were drowned.

¹⁴Those tending the pigs ran off and reported this in the town and countryside, and the people went out to see what had happened. ¹⁵When they came to Jesus, they saw the man who had been possessed by the legion

^a1 Some manuscripts *Gadarenes*; other manuscripts *Gergesenes*   ^b2 Greek *unclean*; also in verses 8 and 13

of demons, sitting there, dressed and in his right mind; and they were afraid. [16]Those who had seen it told the people what had happened to the demon-possessed man—and told about the pigs as well. [17]Then the people began to plead with Jesus to leave their region.

[18]As Jesus was getting into the boat, the man who had been demon-possessed begged to go with him. [19]Jesus did not let him, but said, "Go home to your family and tell them how much the Lord has done for you, and how he has had mercy on you." [20]So the man went away and began to tell in the Decapolis[a] how much Jesus had done for him. And all the people were amazed.

A Dead Girl and a Sick Woman

[21]When Jesus had again crossed over by boat to the other side of the lake, a large crowd gathered around him while he was by the lake. [22]Then one of the synagogue rulers, named Jairus, came there. Seeing Jesus, he fell at his feet [23]and pleaded earnestly with him, "My little daughter is dying. Please come and put your hands on her so that she will be healed and live." [24]So Jesus went with him.

A large crowd followed and pressed around him. [25]And a woman was there who had been subject to bleeding for twelve years. [26]She had suffered a great deal under the care of many doctors and had spent all she had, yet instead of getting better she grew worse. [27]When she heard about Jesus, she came up behind him in the crowd and touched his cloak, [28]because she thought, "If I just touch his clothes, I will be healed." [29]Immediately her bleeding stopped and she felt in her body that she was freed from her suffering.

[30]At once Jesus realized that power had gone out from him. He turned around in the crowd and asked, "Who touched my clothes?"

[31]"You see the people crowding against you," his disciples answered, "and yet you can ask, 'Who touched me?' "

[32]But Jesus kept looking around to see who had done it. [33]Then the woman, knowing what had happened to her, came and fell at his feet and, trembling with fear, told him the whole truth. [34]He said to her, "Daughter, your faith has healed you. Go in peace and be freed from your suffering."

[35]While Jesus was still speaking, some men came from the house of Jairus, the synagogue ruler. "Your daughter is dead," they said. "Why bother the teacher any more?"

[36]Ignoring what they said, Jesus told the synagogue ruler, "Don't be afraid; just believe."

[37]He did not let anyone follow him except Peter, James and John the brother of James. [38]When they came to the home of the synagogue ruler, Jesus saw a commotion, with people crying and wailing loudly. [39]He went in and said to them, "Why all this commotion and wailing? The child is not dead but asleep." [40]But they laughed at him.

After he put them all out, he took the child's father and mother and

[a]20 That is, the Ten Cities

the disciples who were with him, and went in where the child was. ⁴¹He took her by the hand and said to her, *"Talitha koum!"* (which means, "Little girl, I say to you, get up!"). ⁴²Immediately the girl stood up and walked around (she was twelve years old). At this they were completely astonished. ⁴³He gave strict orders not to let anyone know about this, and told them to give her something to eat.

A Prophet Without Honor

6 Jesus left there and went to his hometown, accompanied by his disciples. ²When the Sabbath came, he began to teach in the synagogue, and many who heard him were amazed.

"Where did this man get these things?" they asked. "What's this wisdom that has been given him, that he even does miracles! ³Isn't this the carpenter? Isn't this Mary's son and the brother of James, Joseph,ᵃ Judas and Simon? Aren't his sisters here with us?" And they took offense at him.

⁴Jesus said to them, "Only in his hometown, among his relatives and in his own house is a prophet without honor." ⁵He could not do any miracles there, except lay his hands on a few sick people and heal them. ⁶And he was amazed at their lack of faith.

Jesus Sends Out the Twelve

Then Jesus went around teaching from village to village. ⁷Calling the Twelve to him, he sent them out two by two and gave them authority over evilᵇ spirits.

⁸These were his instructions: "Take nothing for the journey except a staff—no bread, no bag, no money in your belts. ⁹Wear sandals but not an extra tunic. ¹⁰Whenever you enter a house, stay there until you leave that town. ¹¹And if any place will not welcome you or listen to you, shake the dust off your feet when you leave, as a testimony against them."

¹²They went out and preached that people should repent. ¹³They drove out many demons and anointed many sick people with oil and healed them.

John the Baptist Beheaded

¹⁴King Herod heard about this, for Jesus' name had become well known. Some were saying,ᶜ "John the Baptist has been raised from the dead, and that is why miraculous powers are at work in him."

¹⁵Others said, "He is Elijah."

And still others claimed, "He is a prophet, like one of the prophets of long ago."

¹⁶But when Herod heard this, he said, "John, the man I beheaded, has been raised from the dead!"

¹⁷For Herod himself had given orders to have John arrested, and he had him bound and put in prison. He did this because of Herodias, his brother Philip's wife, whom he had married. ¹⁸For John had been saying to Herod, "It is not lawful for you to have your brother's wife." ¹⁹So Herodias nursed

---

ᵃ3 Greek *Joses*, a variant of *Joseph*   ᵇ7 Greek *unclean*   ᶜ14 Some early manuscripts *He was saying* a grudge against John and wanted to kill him. But she was not able to, ²⁰because Herod feared John and protected him, knowing him to be a righteous and holy man. When Herod heard John, he was greatly puzzled^a; yet he liked to listen to him.

²¹Finally the opportune time came. On his birthday Herod gave a banquet for his high officials and military commanders and the leading men of Galilee. ²²When the daughter of Herodias came in and danced, she pleased Herod and his dinner guests.

The king said to the girl, "Ask me for anything you want, and I'll give it to you." ²³And he promised her with an oath, "Whatever you ask I will give you, up to half my kingdom."

²⁴She went out and said to her mother, "What shall I ask for?"

"The head of John the Baptist," she answered.

²⁵At once the girl hurried in to the king with the request: "I want you to give me right now the head of John the Baptist on a platter."

²⁶The king was greatly distressed, but because of his oaths and his dinner guests, he did not want to refuse her. ²⁷So he immediately sent an executioner with orders to bring John's head. The man went, beheaded John in the prison, ²⁸and brought back his head on a platter. He presented it to the girl, and she gave it to her mother. ²⁹On hearing of this, John's disciples came and took his body and laid it in a tomb.

Jesus Feeds the Five Thousand

³⁰The apostles gathered around Jesus and reported to him all they had done and taught. ³¹Then, because so many people were coming and going that they did not even have a chance to eat, he said to them, "Come with me by yourselves to a quiet place and get some rest."

³²So they went away by themselves in a boat to a solitary place. ³³But many who saw them leaving recognized them and ran on foot from all the towns and got there ahead of them. ³⁴When Jesus landed and saw a large crowd, he had compassion on them, because they were like sheep without a shepherd. So he began teaching them many things.

³⁵By this time it was late in the day, so his disciples came to him. "This is a remote place," they said, "and it's already very late. ³⁶Send the people away so they can go to the surrounding countryside and villages and buy themselves something to eat."

³⁷But he answered, "You give them something to eat."

They said to him, "That would take eight months of a man's wages^b! Are we to go and spend that much on bread and give it to them to eat?"

³⁸"How many loaves do you have?" he asked. "Go and see."

When they found out, they said, "Five—and two fish."

³⁹Then Jesus directed them to have all the people sit down in groups on the green grass. ⁴⁰So they sat down in groups of hundreds and fifties. ⁴¹Taking the five loaves and the two fish and looking up to heaven, he gave thanks and broke the loaves. Then he gave them to his disciples to set before

---

^a20 Some early manuscripts *he did many things*   ^b37 Greek *take two hundred denarii*

the people. He also divided the two fish among them all. ⁴²They all ate and were satisfied, ⁴³and the disciples picked up twelve basketfuls of broken pieces of bread and fish. ⁴⁴The number of the men who had eaten was five thousand.

Jesus Walks on the Water

⁴⁵Immediately Jesus made his disciples get into the boat and go on ahead of him to Bethsaida, while he dismissed the crowd. ⁴⁶After leaving them, he went up on a mountainside to pray.

⁴⁷When evening came, the boat was in the middle of the lake, and he was alone on land. ⁴⁸He saw the disciples straining at the oars, because the wind was against them. About the fourth watch of the night he went out to them, walking on the lake. He was about to pass by them, ⁴⁹but when they saw him walking on the lake, they thought he was a ghost. They cried out, ⁵⁰because they all saw him and were terrified.

Immediately he spoke to them and said, "Take courage! It is I. Don't be afraid." ⁵¹Then he climbed into the boat with them, and the wind died down. They were completely amazed, ⁵²for they had not understood about the loaves; their hearts were hardened.

⁵³When they had crossed over, they landed at Gennesaret and anchored there. ⁵⁴As soon as they got out of the boat, people recognized Jesus. ⁵⁵They ran throughout that whole region and carried the sick on mats to wherever they heard he was. ⁵⁶And wherever he went—into villages, towns or countryside—they placed the sick in the marketplaces. They begged him to let them touch even the edge of his cloak, and all who touched him were healed.

Clean and Unclean

7 The Pharisees and some of the teachers of the law who had come from Jerusalem gathered around Jesus and ²saw some of his disciples eating food with hands that were "unclean," that is, unwashed. ³(The Pharisees and all the Jews do not eat unless they give their hands a ceremonial washing, holding to the tradition of the elders. ⁴When they come from the marketplace they do not eat unless they wash. And they observe many other traditions, such as the washing of cups, pitchers and kettles.ᵃ)

⁵So the Pharisees and teachers of the law asked Jesus, "Why don't your disciples live according to the tradition of the elders instead of eating their food with 'unclean' hands?"

⁶He replied, "Isaiah was right when he prophesied about you hypocrites; as it is written:

> " 'These people honor me with their lips,
>   but their hearts are far from me.
> ⁷They worship me in vain;
>   their teachings are but rules taught by men.'ᵇ

ᵃ4 Some early manuscripts *pitchers, kettles and dining couches*   ᵇ6,7 Isaiah 29:13

[8]You have let go of the commands of God and are holding on to the traditions of men."

[9]And he said to them: "You have a fine way of setting aside the commands of God in order to observe[a] your own traditions! [10]For Moses said, 'Honor your father and your mother,'[b] and, 'Anyone who curses his father or mother must be put to death.'[c] [11]But you say that if a man says to his father or mother: 'Whatever help you might otherwise have received from me is Corban' (that is, a gift devoted to God), [12]then you no longer let him do anything for his father or mother. [13]Thus you nullify the word of God by your tradition that you have handed down. And you do many things like that."

[14]Again Jesus called the crowd to him and said, "Listen to me, everyone, and understand this. [15]Nothing outside a man can make him 'unclean' by going into him. Rather, it is what comes out of a man that makes him 'unclean.'[d]"

[17]After he had left the crowd and entered the house, his disciples asked him about this parable. [18]"Are you so dull?" he asked. "Don't you see that nothing that enters a man from the outside can make him 'unclean'? [19]For it doesn't go into his heart but into his stomach, and then out of his body." (In saying this, Jesus declared all foods "clean.")

[20]He went on: "What comes out of a man is what makes him 'unclean.' [21]For from within, out of men's hearts, come evil thoughts, sexual immorality, theft, murder, adultery, [22]greed, malice, deceit, lewdness, envy, slander, arrogance and folly. [23]All these evils come from inside and make a man 'unclean.' "

The Faith of a Syrophoenician Woman

[24]Jesus left that place and went to the vicinity of Tyre.[e] He entered a house and did not want anyone to know it; yet he could not keep his presence secret. [25]In fact, as soon as she heard about him, a woman whose little daughter was possessed by an evil[f] spirit came and fell at his feet. [26]The woman was a Greek, born in Syrian Phoenicia. She begged Jesus to drive the demon out of her daughter.

[27]"First let the children eat all they want," he told her, "for it is not right to take the children's bread and toss it to their dogs."

[28]"Yes, Lord," she replied, "but even the dogs under the table eat the children's crumbs."

[29]Then he told her, "For such a reply, you may go; the demon has left your daughter."

[30]She went home and found her child lying on the bed, and the demon gone.

---

[a]9 Some manuscripts *set up*   [b]10 Exodus 20:12; Deut. 5:16   [c]10 Exodus 21:17; Lev. 20:9
[d]15 Some early manuscripts *'unclean.'* [16]*If anyone has ears to hear, let him hear.*   [e]24 Many early manuscripts *Tyre and Sidon*   [f]25 Greek *unclean*

The Healing of a Deaf and Mute Man

[31]Then Jesus left the vicinity of Tyre and went through Sidon, down to the Sea of Galilee and into the region of the Decapolis. [a] [32]There some people brought to him a man who was deaf and could hardly talk, and they begged him to place his hand on the man.

[33]After he took him aside, away from the crowd, Jesus put his fingers into the man's ears. Then he spit and touched the man's tongue. [34]He looked up to heaven and with a deep sigh said to him, *"Ephphatha!"* (which means, "Be opened!"). [35]At this, the man's ears were opened, his tongue was loosened and he began to speak plainly.

[36]Jesus commanded them not to tell anyone. But the more he did so, the more they kept talking about it. [37]People were overwhelmed with amazement. "He has done everything well," they said. "He even makes the deaf hear and the mute speak."

Jesus Feeds the Four Thousand

8 During those days another large crowd gathered. Since they had nothing to eat, Jesus called his disciples to him and said, [2]"I have compassion for these people; they have already been with me three days and have nothing to eat. [3]If I send them home hungry, they will collapse on the way, because some of them have come a long distance."

[4]His disciples answered, "But where in this remote place can anyone get enough bread to feed them?"

[5]"How many loaves do you have?" Jesus asked.

"Seven," they replied.

[6]He told the crowd to sit down on the ground. When he had taken the seven loaves and given thanks, he broke them and gave them to his disciples to set before the people, and they did so. [7]They had a few small fish as well; he gave thanks for them also and told the disciples to distribute them. [8]The people ate and were satisfied. Afterward the disciples picked up seven basketfuls of broken pieces that were left over. [9]About four thousand men were present. And having sent them away, [10]he got into the boat with his disciples and went to the region of Dalmanutha.

[11]The Pharisees came and began to question Jesus. To test him, they asked him for a sign from heaven. [12]He sighed deeply and said, "Why does this generation ask for a miraculous sign? I tell you the truth, no sign will be given to it." [13]Then he left them, got back into the boat and crossed to the other side.

The Yeast of the Pharisees and Herod

[14]The disciples had forgotten to bring bread, except for one loaf they had with them in the boat. [15]"Be careful," Jesus warned them. "Watch out for the yeast of the Pharisees and that of Herod."

[a]31 That is, the Ten Cities

¹⁶They discussed this with one another and said, "It is because we have no bread."

¹⁷Aware of their discussion, Jesus asked them: "Why are you talking about having no bread? Do you still not see or understand? Are your hearts hardened? ¹⁸Do you have eyes but fail to see, and ears but fail to hear? And don't you remember? ¹⁹When I broke the five loaves for the five thousand, how many basketfuls of pieces did you pick up?"

"Twelve," they replied.

²⁰"And when I broke the seven loaves for the four thousand, how many basketfuls of pieces did you pick up?"

They answered, "Seven."

²¹He said to them, "Do you still not understand?"

The Healing of a Blind Man at Bethsaida

²²They came to Bethsaida, and some people brought a blind man and begged Jesus to touch him. ²³He took the blind man by the hand and led him outside the village. When he had spit on the man's eyes and put his hands on him, Jesus asked, "Do you see anything?"

²⁴He looked up and said, "I see people; they look like trees walking around."

²⁵Once more Jesus put his hands on the man's eyes. Then his eyes were opened, his sight was restored, and he saw everything clearly. ²⁶Jesus sent him home, saying, "Don't go into the village.ᵃ"

Peter's Confession of Christ

²⁷Jesus and his disciples went on to the villages around Caesarea Philippi. On the way he asked them, "Who do people say I am?"

²⁸They replied, "Some say John the Baptist; others say Elijah; and still others, one of the prophets."

²⁹"But what about you?" he asked. "Who do you say I am?"

Peter answered, "You are the Christ.ᵇ"

³⁰Jesus warned them not to tell anyone about him.

Jesus Predicts His Death

³¹He then began to teach them that the Son of Man must suffer many things and be rejected by the elders, chief priests and teachers of the law, and that he must be killed and after three days rise again. ³²He spoke plainly about this, and Peter took him aside and began to rebuke him.

³³But when Jesus turned and looked at his disciples, he rebuked Peter. "Get behind me, Satan!" he said. "You do not have in mind the things of God, but the things of men."

³⁴Then he called the crowd to him along with his disciples and said: "If anyone would come after me, he must deny himself and take up his cross

---

ᵃ26 Some manuscripts *Don't go and tell anyone in the village*   ᵇ29 Or *Messiah*. "The Christ" (Greek) and "the Messiah" (Hebrew) both mean "the Anointed One."

and follow me. [35]For whoever wants to save his life[a] will lose it, but whoever loses his life for me and for the gospel will save it. [36]What good is it for a man to gain the whole world, yet forfeit his soul? [37]Or what can a man give in exchange for his soul? [38]If anyone is ashamed of me and my words in this adulterous and sinful generation, the Son of Man will be ashamed of him when he comes in his Father's glory with the holy angels."

9 And he said to them, "I tell you the truth, some who are standing here will not taste death before they see the kingdom of God come with power."

The Transfiguration

[2]After six days Jesus took Peter, James and John with him and led them up a high mountain, where they were all alone. There he was transfigured before them. [3]His clothes became dazzling white, whiter than anyone in the world could bleach them. [4]And there appeared before them Elijah and Moses, who were talking with Jesus.

[5]Peter said to Jesus, "Rabbi, it is good for us to be here. Let us put up three shelters—one for you, one for Moses and one for Elijah." [6](He did not know what to say, they were so frightened.)

[7]Then a cloud appeared and enveloped them, and a voice came from the cloud: "This is my Son, whom I love. Listen to him!"

[8]Suddenly, when they looked around, they no longer saw anyone with them except Jesus.

[9]As they were coming down the mountain, Jesus gave them orders not to tell anyone what they had seen until the Son of Man had risen from the dead. [10]They kept the matter to themselves, discussing what "rising from the dead" meant.

[11]And they asked him, "Why do the teachers of the law say that Elijah must come first?"

[12]Jesus replied, "To be sure, Elijah does come first, and restores all things. Why then is it written that the Son of Man must suffer much and be rejected? [13]But I tell you, Elijah has come, and they have done to him everything they wished, just as it is written about him."

The Healing of a Boy With an Evil Spirit

[14]When they came to the other disciples, they saw a large crowd around them and the teachers of the law arguing with them. [15]As soon as all the people saw Jesus, they were overwhelmed with wonder and ran to greet him.

[16]"What are you arguing with them about?" he asked.

[17]A man in the crowd answered, "Teacher, I brought you my son, who is possessed by a spirit that has robbed him of speech. [18]Whenever it seizes him, it throws him to the ground. He foams at the mouth, gnashes his teeth and becomes rigid. I asked your disciples to drive out the spirit, but they could not."

[a]35 The Greek word means either *life* or *soul*; also in verse 36.

¹⁹"O unbelieving generation," Jesus replied, "how long shall I stay with you? How long shall I put up with you? Bring the boy to me."

²⁰So they brought him. When the spirit saw Jesus, it immediately threw the boy into a convulsion. He fell to the ground and rolled around, foaming at the mouth.

²¹Jesus asked the boy's father, "How long has he been like this?"

"From childhood," he answered. ²²"It has often thrown him into fire or water to kill him. But if you can do anything, take pity on us and help us."

²³" 'If you can'?" said Jesus. "Everything is possible for him who believes."

²⁴Immediately the boy's father exclaimed, "I do believe; help me overcome my unbelief!"

²⁵When Jesus saw that a crowd was running to the scene, he rebuked the evil[a] spirit. "You deaf and mute spirit," he said, "I command you, come out of him and never enter him again."

²⁶The spirit shrieked, convulsed him violently and came out. The boy looked so much like a corpse that many said, "He's dead." ²⁷But Jesus took him by the hand and lifted him to his feet, and he stood up.

²⁸After Jesus had gone indoors, his disciples asked him privately, "Why couldn't we drive it out?"

²⁹He replied, "This kind can come out only by prayer.[b]"

³⁰They left that place and passed through Galilee. Jesus did not want anyone to know where they were, ³¹because he was teaching his disciples. He said to them, "The Son of Man is going to be betrayed into the hands of men. They will kill him, and after three days he will rise." ³²But they did not understand what he meant and were afraid to ask him about it.

Who Is the Greatest?

³³They came to Capernaum. When he was in the house, he asked them, "What were you arguing about on the road?" ³⁴But they kept quiet because on the way they had argued about who was the greatest.

³⁵Sitting down, Jesus called the Twelve and said, "If anyone wants to be first, he must be the very last, and the servant of all."

³⁶He took a little child and had him stand among them. Taking him in his arms, he said to them, ³⁷"Whoever welcomes one of these little children in my name welcomes me; and whoever welcomes me does not welcome me but the one who sent me."

Whoever Is Not Against Us Is for Us

³⁸"Teacher," said John, "we saw a man driving out demons in your name and we told him to stop, because he was not one of us."

³⁹"Do not stop him," Jesus said. "No one who does a miracle in my name can in the next moment say anything bad about me, ⁴⁰for whoever is not against us is for us. ⁴¹I tell you the truth, anyone who gives you a cup

---

[a]25 Greek *unclean*   [b]29 Some manuscripts *prayer and fasting*

of water in my name because you belong to Christ will certainly not lose his reward.

Causing to Sin

[42]"And if anyone causes one of these little ones who believe in me to sin, it would be better for him to be thrown into the sea with a large millstone tied around his neck. [43]If your hand causes you to sin, cut it off. It is better for you to enter life maimed than with two hands to go into hell, where the fire never goes out. [a] [45]And if your foot causes you to sin, cut it off. It is better for you to enter life crippled than to have two feet and be thrown into hell. [b] [47]And if your eye causes you to sin, pluck it out. It is better for you to enter the kingdom of God with one eye than to have two eyes and be thrown into hell, [48]where

> " 'their worm does not die,
> and the fire is not quenched.'[c]

[49]Everyone will be salted with fire.

[50]"Salt is good, but if it loses its saltiness, how can you make it salty again? Have salt in yourselves, and be at peace with each other."

Divorce

10 Jesus then left that place and went into the region of Judea and across the Jordan. Again crowds of people came to him, and as was his custom, he taught them.

[2]Some Pharisees came and tested him by asking, "Is it lawful for a man to divorce his wife?"

[3]"What did Moses command you?" he replied.

[4]They said, "Moses permitted a man to write a certificate of divorce and send her away."

[5]"It was because your hearts were hard that Moses wrote you this law," Jesus replied. [6]"But at the beginning of creation God 'made them male and female.'[d] [7]'For this reason a man will leave his father and mother and be united to his wife,[e] [8]and the two will become one flesh.'[f] So they are no longer two, but one. [9]Therefore what God has joined together, let man not separate."

[10]When they were in the house again, the disciples asked Jesus about this. [11]He answered, "Anyone who divorces his wife and marries another woman commits adultery against her. [12]And if she divorces her husband and marries another man, she commits adultery."

The Little Children and Jesus

[13]People were bringing little children to Jesus to have him touch them,

---

[a]43 Some manuscripts *out,* [44]*where I* " *'their worm does not die, I and the fire is not quenched.'*
[b]45 Some manuscripts *hell,* [46]*where I* " *'their worm does not die, I and the fire is not quenched.'*
[c]48 Isaiah 66:24   [d]6 Gen. 1:27   [e]7 Some early manuscripts do not have *and be united to his wife.*
[f]8 Gen. 2:24

but the disciples rebuked them. [14]When Jesus saw this, he was indignant. He said to them, "Let the little children come to me, and do not hinder them, for the kingdom of God belongs to such as these. [15]I tell you the truth, anyone who will not receive the kingdom of God like a little child will never enter it." [16]And he took the children in his arms, put his hands on them and blessed them.

The Rich Young Man

[17]As Jesus started on his way, a man ran up to him and fell on his knees before him. "Good teacher," he asked, "what must I do to inherit eternal life?"

[18]"Why do you call me good?" Jesus answered. "No one is good— except God alone. [19]You know the commandments: 'Do not murder, do not commit adultery, do not steal, do not give false testimony, do not defraud, honor your father and mother.'[a]"

[20]"Teacher," he declared, "all these I have kept since I was a boy."

[21]Jesus looked at him and loved him. "One thing you lack," he said. "Go, sell everything you have and give to the poor, and you will have treasure in heaven. Then come, follow me."

[22]At this the man's face fell. He went away sad, because he had great wealth.

[23]Jesus looked around and said to his disciples, "How hard it is for the rich to enter the kingdom of God!"

[24]The disciples were amazed at his words. But Jesus said again, "Children, how hard it is[b] to enter the kingdom of God! [25]It is easier for a camel to go through the eye of a needle than for a rich man to enter the kingdom of God."

[26]The disciples were even more amazed, and said to each other, "Who then can be saved?"

[27]Jesus looked at them and said, "With man this is impossible, but not with God; all things are possible with God."

[28]Peter said to him, "We have left everything to follow you!"

[29]"I tell you the truth," Jesus replied, "no one who has left home or brothers or sisters or mother or father or children or fields for me and the gospel [30]will fail to receive a hundred times as much in this present age (homes, brothers, sisters, mothers, children and fields—and with them, persecutions) and in the age to come, eternal life. [31]But many who are first will be last, and the last first."

Jesus Again Predicts His Death

[32]They were on their way up to Jerusalem, with Jesus leading the way, and the disciples were astonished, while those who followed were afraid. Again he took the Twelve aside and told them what was going to happen to him. [33]"We are going up to Jerusalem," he said, "and the Son of Man will be betrayed to the chief priests and teachers of the law. They will

[a]19 Exodus 20:12-16; Deut. 5:16-20   [b]24 Some manuscripts *is for those who trust in riches*

condemn him to death and will hand him over to the Gentiles, ³⁴who will mock him and spit on him, flog him and kill him. Three days later he will rise."

The Request of James and John

³⁵Then James and John, the sons of Zebedee, came to him. "Teacher," they said, "we want you to do for us whatever we ask."

³⁶"What do you want me to do for you?" he asked.

³⁷They replied, "Let one of us sit at your right and the other at your left in your glory."

³⁸"You don't know what you are asking," Jesus said. "Can you drink the cup I drink or be baptized with the baptism I am baptized with?"

³⁹"We can," they answered.

Jesus said to them, "You will drink the cup I drink and be baptized with the baptism I am baptized with, ⁴⁰but to sit at my right or left is not for me to grant. These places belong to those for whom they have been prepared."

⁴¹When the ten heard about this, they became indignant with James and John. ⁴²Jesus called them together and said, "You know that those who are regarded as rulers of the Gentiles lord it over them, and their high officials exercise authority over them. ⁴³Not so with you. Instead, whoever wants to become great among you must be your servant, ⁴⁴and whoever wants to be first must be slave of all. ⁴⁵For even the Son of Man did not come to be served, but to serve, and to give his life as a ransom for many."

Blind Bartimaeus Receives His Sight

⁴⁶Then they came to Jericho. As Jesus and his disciples, together with a large crowd, were leaving the city, a blind man, Bartimaeus (that is, the Son of Timaeus), was sitting by the roadside begging. ⁴⁷When he heard that it was Jesus of Nazareth, he began to shout, "Jesus, Son of David, have mercy on me!"

⁴⁸Many rebuked him and told him to be quiet, but he shouted all the more, "Son of David, have mercy on me!"

⁴⁹Jesus stopped and said, "Call him."

So they called to the blind man, "Cheer up! On your feet! He's calling you." ⁵⁰Throwing his cloak aside, he jumped to his feet and came to Jesus.

⁵¹"What do you want me to do for you?" Jesus asked him.

The blind man said, "Rabbi, I want to see."

⁵²"Go," said Jesus, "your faith has healed you." Immediately he received his sight and followed Jesus along the road.

The Triumphal Entry

11 As they approached Jerusalem and came to Bethphage and Bethany at the Mount of Olives, Jesus sent two of his disciples, ²saying to them, "Go to the village ahead of you, and just as you enter it, you will find a colt tied there, which no one has ever ridden. Untie it and bring it here.

³If anyone asks you, 'Why are you doing this?' tell him, 'The Lord needs it and will send it back here shortly.' "

⁴They went and found a colt outside in the street, tied at a doorway. As they untied it, ⁵some people standing there asked, "What are you doing, untying that colt?" ⁶They answered as Jesus had told them to, and the people let them go. ⁷When they brought the colt to Jesus and threw their cloaks over it, he sat on it. ⁸Many people spread their cloaks on the road, while others spread branches they had cut in the fields. ⁹Those who went ahead and those who followed shouted,

"Hosanna!ᵃ"

"Blessed is he who comes in the name of the Lord!"ᵇ

¹⁰"Blessed is the coming kingdom of our father David!"

"Hosanna in the highest!"

¹¹Jesus entered Jerusalem and went to the temple. He looked around at everything, but since it was already late, he went out to Bethany with the Twelve.

Jesus Clears the Temple

¹²The next day as they were leaving Bethany, Jesus was hungry. ¹³Seeing in the distance a fig tree in leaf, he went to find out if it had any fruit. When he reached it, he found nothing but leaves, because it was not the season for figs. ¹⁴Then he said to the tree, "May no one ever eat fruit from you again." And his disciples heard him say it.

¹⁵On reaching Jerusalem, Jesus entered the temple area and began driving out those who were buying and selling there. He overturned the tables of the money changers and the benches of those selling doves, ¹⁶and would not allow anyone to carry merchandise through the temple courts. ¹⁷And as he taught them, he said, "Is it not written:

" 'My house will be called
a house of prayer for all nations'ᶜ?

But you have made it 'a den of robbers.'ᵈ"

¹⁸The chief priests and the teachers of the law heard this and began looking for a way to kill him, for they feared him, because the whole crowd was amazed at his teaching.

¹⁹When evening came, theyᵉ went out of the city.

The Withered Fig Tree

²⁰In the morning, as they went along, they saw the fig tree withered from the roots. ²¹Peter remembered and said to Jesus, "Rabbi, look! The fig tree you cursed has withered!"

ᵃ9 A Hebrew expression meaning "Save!" which became an exclamation of praise; also in verse 10
ᵇ9 Psalm 118:25,26   ᶜ17 Isaiah 56:7   ᵈ17 Jer. 7:11   ᵉ19 Some early manuscripts *he*

²²"Have*ᵃ* faith in God," Jesus answered. ²³"I tell you the truth, if anyone says to this mountain, 'Go, throw yourself into the sea,' and does not doubt in his heart but believes that what he says will happen, it will be done for him. ²⁴Therefore I tell you, whatever you ask for in prayer, believe that you have received it, and it will be yours. ²⁵And when you stand praying, if you hold anything against anyone, forgive him, so that your Father in heaven may forgive you your sins. *ᵇ*"

The Authority of Jesus Questioned

²⁷They arrived again in Jerusalem, and while Jesus was walking in the temple courts, the chief priests, the teachers of the law and the elders came to him. ²⁸"By what authority are you doing these things?" they asked. "And who gave you authority to do this?"

²⁹Jesus replied, "I will ask you one question. Answer me, and I will tell you by what authority I am doing these things. ³⁰John's baptism—was it from heaven, or from men? Tell me!"

³¹They discussed it among themselves and said, "If we say, 'From heaven,' he will ask, 'Then why didn't you believe him?' ³²But if we say, 'From men' . . . ." (They feared the people, for everyone held that John really was a prophet.)

³³So they answered Jesus, "We don't know."

Jesus said, "Neither will I tell you by what authority I am doing these things."

The Parable of the Tenants

12 He then began to speak to them in parables: "A man planted a vineyard. He put a wall around it, dug a pit for the winepress and built a watchtower. Then he rented the vineyard to some farmers and went away on a journey. ²At harvest time he sent a servant to the tenants to collect from them some of the fruit of the vineyard. ³But they seized him, beat him and sent him away empty-handed. ⁴Then he sent another servant to them; they struck this man on the head and treated him shamefully. ⁵He sent still another, and that one they killed. He sent many others; some of them they beat, others they killed.

⁶"He had one left to send, a son, whom he loved. He sent him last of all, saying, 'They will respect my son.'

⁷"But the tenants said to one another, 'This is the heir. Come, let's kill him, and the inheritance will be ours.' ⁸So they took him and killed him, and threw him out of the vineyard.

⁹"What then will the owner of the vineyard do? He will come and kill those tenants and give the vineyard to others. ¹⁰Haven't you read this scripture:

" 'The stone the builders rejected

ᵃ22 Some early manuscripts If you have   ᵇ25 Some manuscripts sins. ²⁶But if you do not forgive, neither will your Father who is in heaven forgive your sins.

> has become the capstone[a];
> [11]the Lord has done this,
> and it is marvelous in our eyes'[b]?''

[12]Then they looked for a way to arrest him because they knew he had spoken the parable against them. But they were afraid of the crowd; so they left him and went away.

Paying Taxes to Caesar

[13]Later they sent some of the Pharisees and Herodians to Jesus to catch him in his words. [14]They came to him and said, "Teacher, we know you are a man of integrity. You aren't swayed by men, because you pay no attention to who they are; but you teach the way of God in accordance with the truth. Is it right to pay taxes to Caesar or not? [15]Should we pay or shouldn't we?''

But Jesus knew their hypocrisy. "Why are you trying to trap me?" he asked. "Bring me a denarius and let me look at it." [16]They brought the coin, and he asked them, "Whose portrait is this? And whose inscription?"

"Caesar's," they replied.

[17]Then Jesus said to them, "Give to Caesar what is Caesar's and to God what is God's."

And they were amazed at him.

Marriage at the Resurrection

[18]Then the Sadducees, who say there is no resurrection, came to him with a question. [19]"Teacher," they said, "Moses wrote for us that if a man's brother dies and leaves a wife but no children, the man must marry the widow and have children for his brother. [20]Now there were seven brothers. The first one married and died without leaving any children. [21]The second one married the widow, but he also died, leaving no child. It was the same with the third. [22]In fact, none of the seven left any children. Last of all, the woman died too. [23]At the resurrection[c] whose wife will she be, since the seven were married to her?''

[24]Jesus replied, "Are you not in error because you do not know the Scriptures or the power of God? [25]When the dead rise, they will neither marry nor be given in marriage; they will be like the angels in heaven. [26]Now about the dead rising—have you not read in the book of Moses, in the account of the bush, how God said to him, 'I am the God of Abraham, the God of Isaac, and the God of Jacob'[d]? [27]He is not the God of the dead, but of the living. You are badly mistaken!''

The Greatest Commandment

[28]One of the teachers of the law came and heard them debating. Noticing that Jesus had given them a good answer, he asked him, "Of all the commandments, which is the most important?''

---

[a]10 Or *cornerstone*   [b]11 Psalm 118:22,23   [c]23 Some manuscripts *resurrection, when men rise from the dead,*   [d]26 Exodus 3:6

29"The most important one," answered Jesus, "is this: 'Hear, O Israel, the Lord our God, the Lord is one.ᵃ 30Love the Lord your God with all your heart and with all your soul and with all your mind and with all your strength.'ᵇ 31The second is this: 'Love your neighbor as yourself.'ᶜ There is no commandment greater than these."

32"Well said, teacher," the man replied. "You are right in saying that God is one and there is no other but him. 33To love him with all your heart, with all your understanding and with all your strength, and to love your neighbor as yourself is more important than all burnt offerings and sacrifices."

34When Jesus saw that he had answered wisely, he said to him, "You are not far from the kingdom of God." And from then on no one dared ask him any more questions.

Whose Son Is the Christ?

35While Jesus was teaching in the temple courts, he asked, "How is it that the teachers of the law say that the Christᵈ is the son of David? 36David himself, speaking by the Holy Spirit, declared:

" 'The Lord said to my Lord:
"Sit at my right hand
until I put your enemies
under your feet." 'ᵉ

37David himself calls him 'Lord.' How then can he be his son?"

The large crowd listened to him with delight.

38As he taught, Jesus said, "Watch out for the teachers of the law. They like to walk around in flowing robes and be greeted in the marketplaces, 39and have the most important seats in the synagogues and the places of honor at banquets. 40They devour widows' houses and for a show make lengthy prayers. Such men will be punished most severely."

The Widow's Offering

41Jesus sat down opposite the place where the offerings were put and watched the crowd putting their money into the temple treasury. Many rich people threw in large amounts. 42But a poor widow came and put in two very small copper coins,ᶠ worth only a fraction of a penny.ᵍ

43Calling his disciples to him, Jesus said, "I tell you the truth, this poor widow has put more into the treasury than all the others. 44They all gave out of their wealth; but she, out of her poverty, put in everything—all she had to live on."

Signs of the End of the Age

13 As he was leaving the temple, one of his disciples said to him, "Look, Teacher! What massive stones! What magnificent buildings!"

ᵃ29 Or *the Lord our God is one Lord*   ᵇ30 Deut. 6:4,5   ᶜ31 Lev. 19:18   ᵈ35 Or *Messiah*
ᵉ36 Psalm 110:1   ᶠ42 Greek *two lepta*   ᵍ42 Greek *kodrantes*

2"Do you see all these great buildings?" replied Jesus. "Not one stone here will be left on another; every one will be thrown down."

3As Jesus was sitting on the Mount of Olives opposite the temple, Peter, James, John and Andrew asked him privately, 4"Tell us, when will these things happen? And what will be the sign that they are all about to be fulfilled?"

5Jesus said to them: "Watch out that no one deceives you. 6Many will come in my name, claiming, 'I am he,' and will deceive many. 7When you hear of wars and rumors of wars, do not be alarmed. Such things must happen, but the end is still to come. 8Nation will rise against nation, and kingdom against kingdom. There will be earthquakes in various places, and famines. These are the beginning of birth pains.

9"You must be on your guard. You will be handed over to the local councils and flogged in the synagogues. On account of me you will stand before governors and kings as witnesses to them. 10And the gospel must first be preached to all nations. 11Whenever you are arrested and brought to trial, do not worry beforehand about what to say. Just say whatever is given you at the time, for it is not you speaking, but the Holy Spirit.

12"Brother will betray brother to death, and a father his child. Children will rebel against their parents and have them put to death. 13All men will hate you because of me, but he who stands firm to the end will be saved.

14"When you see 'the abomination that causes desolation'ᵃ standing where itᵇ does not belong—let the reader understand—then let those who are in Judea flee to the mountains. 15Let no one on the roof of his house go down or enter the house to take anything out. 16Let no one in the field go back to get his cloak. 17How dreadful it will be in those days for pregnant women and nursing mothers! 18Pray that this will not take place in winter, 19because those will be days of distress unequaled from the beginning, when God created the world, until now—and never to be equaled again. 20If the Lord had not cut short those days, no one would survive. But for the sake of the elect, whom he has chosen, he has shortened them. 21At that time if anyone says to you, 'Look, here is the Christᶜ!' or, 'Look, there he is!' do not believe it. 22For false Christs and false prophets will appear and perform signs and miracles to deceive the elect—if that were possible. 23So be on your guard; I have told you everything ahead of time.

24"But in those days, following that distress,

> " 'the sun will be darkened,
>   and the moon will not give its light;
> 25the stars will fall from the sky,
>   and the heavenly bodies will be shaken.'ᵈ

26"At that time men will see the Son of Man coming in clouds with great power and glory. 27And he will send his angels and gather his elect from the four winds, from the ends of the earth to the ends of the heavens.

ᵃ14 Daniel 9:27; 11:31; 12:11   ᵇ14 Or *he*; also in verse 29   ᶜ21 Or *Messiah*   ᵈ25 Isaiah 13:10; 34:4

²⁸"Now learn this lesson from the fig tree: As soon as its twigs get tender and its leaves come out, you know that summer is near. ²⁹Even so, when you see these things happening, you know that it is near, right at the door. ³⁰I tell you the truth, this generation^a will certainly not pass away until all these things have happened. ³¹Heaven and earth will pass away, but my words will never pass away.

The Day and Hour Unknown

³²"No one knows about that day or hour, not even the angels in heaven, nor the Son, but only the Father. ³³Be on guard! Be alert^b! You do not know when that time will come. ³⁴It's like a man going away: He leaves his house and puts his servants in charge, each with his assigned task, and tells the one at the door to keep watch.

³⁵"Therefore keep watch because you do not know when the owner of the house will come back—whether in the evening, or at midnight, or when the rooster crows, or at dawn. ³⁶If he comes suddenly, do not let him find you sleeping. ³⁷What I say to you, I say to everyone: 'Watch!'"

Jesus Anointed at Bethany

14 Now the Passover and the Feast of Unleavened Bread were only two days away, and the chief priests and the teachers of the law were looking for some sly way to arrest Jesus and kill him. ²"But not during the Feast," they said, "or the people may riot."

³While he was in Bethany, reclining at the table in the home of a man known as Simon the Leper, a woman came with an alabaster jar of very expensive perfume, made of pure nard. She broke the jar and poured the perfume on his head.

⁴Some of those present were saying indignantly to one another, "Why this waste of perfume? ⁵It could have been sold for more than a year's wages^c and the money given to the poor." And they rebuked her harshly.

⁶"Leave her alone," said Jesus. "Why are you bothering her? She has done a beautiful thing to me. ⁷The poor you will always have with you, and you can help them any time you want. But you will not always have me. ⁸She did what she could. She poured perfume on my body beforehand to prepare for my burial. ⁹I tell you the truth, wherever the gospel is preached throughout the world, what she has done will also be told, in memory of her."

¹⁰Then Judas Iscariot, one of the Twelve, went to the chief priests to betray Jesus to them. ¹¹They were delighted to hear this and promised to give him money. So he watched for an opportunity to hand him over.

The Lord's Supper

¹²On the first day of the Feast of Unleavened Bread, when it was customary to sacrifice the Passover lamb, Jesus' disciples asked him,

^a30 Or *race*   ^b33 Some manuscripts *alert and pray*   ^c5 Greek *than three hundred denarii*

"Where do you want us to go and make preparations for you to eat the Passover?"

¹³So he sent two of his disciples, telling them, "Go into the city, and a man carrying a jar of water will meet you. Follow him. ¹⁴Say to the owner of the house he enters, 'The Teacher asks: Where is my guest room, where I may eat the Passover with my disciples?' ¹⁵He will show you a large upper room, furnished and ready. Make preparations for us there."

¹⁶The disciples left, went into the city and found things just as Jesus had told them. So they prepared the Passover.

¹⁷When evening came, Jesus arrived with the Twelve. ¹⁸While they were reclining at the table eating, he said, "I tell you the truth, one of you will betray me—one who is eating with me."

¹⁹They were saddened, and one by one they said to him, "Surely not I?"

²⁰"It is one of the Twelve," he replied, "one who dips bread into the bowl with me. ²¹The Son of Man will go just as it is written about him. But woe to that man who betrays the Son of Man! It would be better for him if he had not been born."

²²While they were eating, Jesus took bread, gave thanks and broke it, and gave it to his disciples, saying, "Take it; this is my body."

²³Then he took the cup, gave thanks and offered it to them, and they all drank from it.

²⁴"This is my blood of the[a] covenant, which is poured out for many," he said to them. ²⁵"I tell you the truth, I will not drink again of the fruit of the vine until that day when I drink it anew in the kingdom of God."

²⁶When they had sung a hymn, they went out to the Mount of Olives.

Jesus Predicts Peter's Denial

²⁷"You will all fall away," Jesus told them, "for it is written:

" 'I will strike the shepherd,
and the sheep will be scattered.'[b]

²⁸But after I have risen, I will go ahead of you into Galilee."

²⁹Peter declared, "Even if all fall away, I will not."

³⁰"I tell you the truth," Jesus answered, "today—yes, tonight—before the rooster crows twice[c] you yourself will disown me three times."

³¹But Peter insisted emphatically, "Even if I have to die with you, I will never disown you." And all the others said the same.

Gethsemane

³²They went to a place called Gethsemane, and Jesus said to his disciples, "Sit here while I pray." ³³He took Peter, James and John along with him, and he began to be deeply distressed and troubled. ³⁴"My soul is overwhelmed with sorrow to the point of death," he said to them. "Stay here and keep watch."

a24 Some manuscripts the new   *b27 Zech. 13:7*   *c30 Some early manuscripts do not have twice.*

³⁵Going a little farther, he fell to the ground and prayed that if possible the hour might pass from him. ³⁶"*Abba*,^a Father," he said, "everything is possible for you. Take this cup from me. Yet not what I will, but what you will."

³⁷Then he returned to his disciples and found them sleeping. "Simon," he said to Peter, "are you asleep? Could you not keep watch for one hour? ³⁸Watch and pray so that you will not fall into temptation. The spirit is willing, but the body is weak."

³⁹Once more he went away and prayed the same thing. ⁴⁰When he came back, he again found them sleeping, because their eyes were heavy. They did not know what to say to him.

⁴¹Returning the third time, he said to them, "Are you still sleeping and resting? Enough! The hour has come. Look, the Son of Man is betrayed into the hands of sinners. ⁴²Rise! Let us go! Here comes my betrayer!"

Jesus Arrested

⁴³Just as he was speaking, Judas, one of the Twelve, appeared. With him was a crowd armed with swords and clubs, sent from the chief priests, the teachers of the law, and the elders.

⁴⁴Now the betrayer had arranged a signal with them: "The one I kiss is the man; arrest him and lead him away under guard." ⁴⁵Going at once to Jesus, Judas said, "Rabbi!" and kissed him. ⁴⁶The men seized Jesus and arrested him. ⁴⁷Then one of those standing near drew his sword and struck the servant of the high priest, cutting off his ear.

⁴⁸"Am I leading a rebellion," said Jesus, "that you have come out with swords and clubs to capture me? ⁴⁹Every day I was with you, teaching in the temple courts, and you did not arrest me. But the Scriptures must be fulfilled." ⁵⁰Then everyone deserted him and fled.

⁵¹A young man, wearing nothing but a linen garment, was following Jesus. When they seized him, ⁵²he fled naked, leaving his garment behind.

Before the Sanhedrin

⁵³They took Jesus to the high priest, and all the chief priests, elders and teachers of the law came together. ⁵⁴Peter followed him at a distance, right into the courtyard of the high priest. There he sat with the guards and warmed himself at the fire.

⁵⁵The chief priests and the whole Sanhedrin were looking for evidence against Jesus so that they could put him to death, but they did not find any. ⁵⁶Many testified falsely against him, but their statements did not agree.

⁵⁷Then some stood up and gave this false testimony against him: ⁵⁸"We heard him say, 'I will destroy this man-made temple and in three days will build another, not made by man.' " ⁵⁹Yet even then their testimony did not agree.

⁶⁰Then the high priest stood up before them and asked Jesus, "Are you

^a36 Aramaic for *Father*

not going to answer? What is this testimony that these men are bringing against you?" ⁶¹But Jesus remained silent and gave no answer.

Again the high priest asked him, "Are you the Christ,ᵃ the Son of the Blessed One?"

⁶²"I am," said Jesus. "And you will see the Son of Man sitting at the right hand of the Mighty One and coming on the clouds of heaven."

⁶³The high priest tore his clothes. "Why do we need any more witnesses?" he asked. ⁶⁴"You have heard the blasphemy. What do you think?"

They all condemned him as worthy of death. ⁶⁵Then some began to spit at him; they blindfolded him, struck him with their fists, and said, "Prophesy!" And the guards took him and beat him.

Peter Disowns Jesus

⁶⁶While Peter was below in the courtyard, one of the servant girls of the high priest came by. ⁶⁷When she saw Peter warming himself, she looked closely at him.

"You also were with that Nazarene, Jesus," she said.

⁶⁸But he denied it. "I don't know or understand what you're talking about," he said, and went out into the entryway.ᵇ

⁶⁹When the servant girl saw him there, she said again to those standing around, "This fellow is one of them." ⁷⁰Again he denied it.

After a little while, those standing near said to Peter, "Surely you are one of them, for you are a Galilean."

⁷¹He began to call down curses on himself, and he swore to them, "I don't know this man you're talking about."

⁷²Immediately the rooster crowed the second time.ᶜ Then Peter remembered the word Jesus had spoken to him: "Before the rooster crows twiceᵈ you will disown me three times." And he broke down and wept.

Jesus Before Pilate

15 Very early in the morning, the chief priests, with the elders, the teachers of the law and the whole Sanhedrin, reached a decision. They bound Jesus, led him away and handed him over to Pilate.

²"Are you the king of the Jews?" asked Pilate.

"Yes, it is as you say," Jesus replied.

³The chief priests accused him of many things. ⁴So again Pilate asked him, "Aren't you going to answer? See how many things they are accusing you of."

⁵But Jesus still made no reply, and Pilate was amazed.

⁶Now it was the custom at the Feast to release a prisoner whom the people requested. ⁷A man called Barabbas was in prison with the insurrectionists who had committed murder in the uprising. ⁸The crowd came up and asked Pilate to do for them what he usually did.

⁹"Do you want me to release to you the king of the Jews?" asked Pilate,

---

ᵃ61 Or *Messiah*   ᵇ68 Some early manuscripts *entryway and the rooster crowed*   ᶜ72 Some early manuscripts do not have *the second time.*   ᵈ72 Some early manuscripts do not have *twice.*

[10]knowing it was out of envy that the chief priests had handed Jesus over to him. [11]But the chief priests stirred up the crowd to have Pilate release Barabbas instead.

[12]"What shall I do, then, with the one you call the king of the Jews?" Pilate asked them.

[13]"Crucify him!" they shouted.

[14]"Why? What crime has he committed?" asked Pilate.

But they shouted all the louder, "Crucify him!"

[15]Wanting to satisfy the crowd, Pilate released Barabbas to them. He had Jesus flogged, and handed him over to be crucified.

The Soldiers Mock Jesus

[16]The soldiers led Jesus away into the palace (that is, the Praetorium) and called together the whole company of soldiers. [17]They put a purple robe on him, then twisted together a crown of thorns and set it on him. [18]And they began to call out to him, "Hail, king of the Jews!" [19]Again and again they struck him on the head with a staff and spit on him. Falling on their knees, they paid homage to him. [20]And when they had mocked him, they took off the purple robe and put his own clothes on him. Then they led him out to crucify him.

The Crucifixion

[21]A certain man from Cyrene, Simon, the father of Alexander and Rufus, was passing by on his way in from the country, and they forced him to carry the cross. [22]They brought Jesus to the place called Golgotha (which means The Place of the Skull). [23]Then they offered him wine mixed with myrrh, but he did not take it. [24]And they crucified him. Dividing up his clothes, they cast lots to see what each would get.

[25]It was the third hour when they crucified him. [26]The written notice of the charge against him read: THE KING OF THE JEWS. [27]They crucified two robbers with him, one on his right and one on his left.[a] [29]Those who passed by hurled insults at him, shaking their heads and saying, "So! You who are going to destroy the temple and build it in three days, [30]come down from the cross and save yourself!"

[31]In the same way the chief priests and the teachers of the law mocked him among themselves. "He saved others," they said, "but he can't save himself! [32]Let this Christ,[b] this King of Israel, come down now from the cross, that we may see and believe." Those crucified with him also heaped insults on him.

The Death of Jesus

[33]At the sixth hour darkness came over the whole land until the ninth hour. [34]And at the ninth hour Jesus cried out in a loud voice, "Eloi, Eloi, lama

---

[a]27 Some manuscripts left, [28]and the scripture was fulfilled which says, "He was counted with the lawless ones" (Isaiah 53:12) [b]32 Or Messiah

sabachthani?"—which means, "My God, my God, why have you forsaken me?"*[a]*

[35]When some of those standing near heard this, they said, "Listen, he's calling Elijah."

[36]One man ran, filled a sponge with wine vinegar, put it on a stick, and offered it to Jesus to drink. "Now leave him alone. Let's see if Elijah comes to take him down," he said.

[37]With a loud cry, Jesus breathed his last.

[38]The curtain of the temple was torn in two from top to bottom. [39]And when the centurion, who stood there in front of Jesus, heard his cry and*[b]* saw how he died, he said, "Surely this man was the Son*[c]* of God!"

[40]Some women were watching from a distance. Among them were Mary Magdalene, Mary the mother of James the younger and of Joses, and Salome. [41]In Galilee these women had followed him and cared for his needs. Many other women who had come up with him to Jerusalem were also there.

The Burial of Jesus

[42]It was Preparation Day (that is, the day before the Sabbath). So as evening approached, [43]Joseph of Arimathea, a prominent member of the Council, who was himself waiting for the kingdom of God, went boldly to Pilate and asked for Jesus' body. [44]Pilate was surprised to hear that he was already dead. Summoning the centurion, he asked him if Jesus had already died. [45]When he learned from the centurion that it was so, he gave the body to Joseph. [46]So Joseph bought some linen cloth, took down the body, wrapped it in the linen, and placed it in a tomb cut out of rock. Then he rolled a stone against the entrance of the tomb. [47]Mary Magdalene and Mary the mother of Joses saw where he was laid.

The Resurrection

16 When the Sabbath was over, Mary Magdalene, Mary the mother of James, and Salome bought spices so that they might go to anoint Jesus' body. [2]Very early on the first day of the week, just after sunrise, they were on their way to the tomb [3]and they asked each other, "Who will roll the stone away from the entrance of the tomb?"

[4]But when they looked up, they saw that the stone, which was very large, had been rolled away. [5]As they entered the tomb, they saw a young man dressed in a white robe sitting on the right side, and they were alarmed.

[6]"Don't be alarmed," he said. "You are looking for Jesus the Nazarene, who was crucified. He has risen! He is not here. See the place where they laid him. [7]But go, tell his disciples and Peter, 'He is going ahead of you into Galilee. There you will see him, just as he told you.' "

[8]Trembling and bewildered, the women went out and fled from the tomb. They said nothing to anyone, because they were afraid.

---

*[a]*34 Psalm 22:1   *[b]*39 Some manuscripts do not have *heard his cry and*.   *[c]*39 Or *a son*

[The most reliable early manuscripts and other ancient witnesses do not have Mark 16:9–20.]

⁹When Jesus rose early on the first day of the week, he appeared first to Mary Magdalene, out of whom he had driven seven demons. ¹⁰She went and told those who had been with him and who were mourning and weeping. ¹¹When they heard that Jesus was alive and that she had seen him, they did not believe it.

¹²Afterward Jesus appeared in a different form to two of them while they were walking in the country. ¹³These returned and reported it to the rest; but they did not believe them either.

¹⁴Later Jesus appeared to the Eleven as they were eating; he rebuked them for their lack of faith and their stubborn refusal to believe those who had seen him after he had risen.

¹⁵He said to them, "Go into all the world and preach the good news to all creation. ¹⁶Whoever believes and is baptized will be saved, but whoever does not believe will be condemned. ¹⁷And these signs will accompany those who believe: In my name they will drive out demons; they will speak in new tongues; ¹⁸they will pick up snakes with their hands; and when they drink deadly poison, it will not hurt them at all; they will place their hands on sick people, and they will get well."

¹⁹After the Lord Jesus had spoken to them, he was taken up into heaven and he sat at the right hand of God. ²⁰Then the disciples went out and preached everywhere, and the Lord worked with them and confirmed his word by the signs that accompanied it.

Luke

INTRODUCTION

Tradition identifies Luke with the physician and companion to Paul (Phlm 24; Col 4:14; 2 Tim 4:11), but this is not certain, nor is it of crucial importance, for we know much about this inspired writer from internal evidence. Luke was a Gentile Christian, well versed in Hellenistic culture and in the Greek Old Testament, a person of great sensitivity and compassion. He lived outside Palestine, probably in Antioch of Syria, and wrote about 80–90 A.D.

Luke addressed both his Gospel and Acts to Theophilus (Lk 1:3; Acts 1:1), possibly a Roman official. His audience was primarily composed of Gentile Christians, and Luke wrote to reassure them that their Church was truly founded on the words and deeds of Jesus (Lk 1:4; Acts 1:1–2), the one and only Savior of mankind (Lk 2:11; Acts 4:12).

In composing the Gospel, Luke did much research (1:1–4) and used several sources, primarily the Gospel according to Mark, whose outline he generally followed (with minor changes and with an important insertion, the "journey to Jerusalem," Lk 9:51—18:14). A second major source was a collection of the sayings of Jesus found also in Matthew (e.g., Mt 3:7–10/Lk 3:7–9; Mt 11:25–27/Lk 10:21–22; Mt 23:37–39/Lk 13:34–35). Finally, there is a considerable amount of material which appears only in Luke, such as the correlation of the life of Jesus with secular history (2:1–2; 3:1–2), the woes to the rich (6:24–26), the widow of Nain (7:11–17), the sinful woman in the house of the Pharisee (7:36–50), the good Samaritan (10:29–37), the importunate friend at midnight (11:5–8), the crippled woman on the sabbath (13:10–17), the lost son (15:11–32), the rich man and Lazarus (16:19–31), the ten lepers (17:11–19), the persistent widow (18:1–8), the Pharisee and the tax collector (18:9–14), Zacchaeus (19:1–10), the trial before Herod (23:6–12), and the appearance of Jesus on the road to Emmaus (24:13–35).

Several concerns of Luke are readily apparent from the listing of his special material and of his changes in Mark: linkage of Jesus to secular history, emphasis on the city of Jerusalem, trust in God's mercy, care for the poor and needy, humility, and perseverance in prayer. Luke stresses not only God's mercy and forgiveness, but contrasts it with human hardness of heart—Jesus forgives the sinful woman while Simon despises her (7:36–50); the Father pardons his lost son with joy, but the brother refuses to take part in the celebration (15:11–32); the tax collector is justified while the Pharisee looks down upon him in prayer (18:9–14); Zacchaeus is saved in the presence of a murmuring crowd (19:1–10). Connected with this is the general framework of the humbling of the proud and the lifting up of the lowly (1:52; 2:34; 3:5–6; 14:11; 16:15; 16:19–31; 18:14).

Luke intended to strengthen his readers' faith in the continuity of their Church with Jesus the Savior, Messiah, and risen Lord. That continuity is well expressed by Luke's portrayal of the movement of Jesus toward Jerusalem, the ancient city of David where he was to suffer, die, and rise again (9:51; 13:33; 18:31; 19:41; 24:1ff), but from which the good news of salvation was to spread to the ends of the earth, symbolized by Rome, the capital of the Mediterranean world (Lk 24:47; Acts 1:8; 23:11; 28:14). It was also accomplished by dividing history into three periods: the Old Testament promise of salvation, its fulfillment in Jesus (Lk 4:21; 24:27), and its continuation in the Church (Lk 16:16; Acts 1:1ff).

A subordinate theme is the toning down of some traditional expressions that implied an imminent coming of the parousia (Lk 19:11; 12:45–46). There is a corresponding stress on the present as the time of salvation (4:21; 11:3; 19:9; 23:43); it is aptly summed up in the proclamation that "the kingdom of God is within you" (17:21).

Luke's Gospel may be outlined as follows:

Prologue (1:1–4)
Infancy Narrative (1:5—2:52)
Preparation for Public Ministry (3:1—4:13)
Ministry in Galilee (4:14—9:50)
Journey to Jerusalem (9:51—19:27)
Ministry in Jerusalem (19:28—21:38)
Passion Narrative (22:1—23:56)
Resurrection and Ascension (24:1–53)

JOSEPH F. WIMMER, O.S.A.

Points for Reflection

1. As I marvel at the beauty of Mary's vocation and of her unassuming willingness to serve (1:26–56), am I aware of my own high calling as a child of God and do I joyfully reach out to others in humble service?
2. When I hear the woes against the rich (6:24–26) do I reflect on my own attitude toward the goods of this world?
3. When I hear of sinners who turn to Christ and are saved, such as the woman in the house of Simon (7:36–50), the lost son (15:11–32), and Zacchaeus the tax collector (19:1–10), do I despise them? Am I not rather encouraged to cry out to the Lord for mercy?
4. The words "today" and "daily" (4:21; 11:3; 19:9; 23:43) urge me to accept and live out my salvation now. How do I respond?
5. The two disciples on the road to Emmaus recognized their exalted companion in the breaking of the bread after they had urged him to stay with them (24:28–32). How can I recognize Jesus?

Introduction

1 Many have undertaken to draw up an account of the things that have been fulfilled[a] among us, [2]just as they were handed down to us by those who from the first were eyewitnesses and servants of the word. [3]Therefore, since I myself have carefully investigated everything from the beginning, it seemed good also to me to write an orderly account for you, most excellent Theophilus, [4]so that you may know the certainty of the things you have been taught.

The Birth of John the Baptist Foretold

[5]In the time of Herod king of Judea there was a priest named Zechariah, who belonged to the priestly division of Abijah; his wife Elizabeth was also a descendant of Aaron. [6]Both of them were upright in the sight of God, observing all the Lord's commandments and regulations blamelessly. [7]But they had no children, because Elizabeth was barren; and they were both well along in years.

[8]Once when Zechariah's division was on duty and he was serving as priest before God, [9]he was chosen by lot, according to the custom of the priesthood, to go into the temple of the Lord and burn incense. [10]And when the time for the burning of incense came, all the assembled worshipers were praying outside.

[11]Then an angel of the Lord appeared to him, standing at the right side of the altar of incense. [12]When Zechariah saw him, he was startled and was gripped with fear. [13]But the angel said to him: "Do not be afraid, Zechariah; your prayer has been heard. Your wife Elizabeth will bear you a son, and you are to give him the name John. [14]He will be a joy and delight to you, and many will rejoice because of his birth, [15]for he will be great in the sight of the Lord. He is never to take wine or other fermented drink, and he will be filled with the Holy Spirit even from birth.[b] [16]Many of the people of Israel will he bring back to the Lord their God. [17]And he will go on before the Lord, in the spirit and power of Elijah, to turn the hearts of the fathers to their children and the disobedient to the wisdom of the righteous—to make ready a people prepared for the Lord."

[18]Zechariah asked the angel, "How can I be sure of this? I am an old man and my wife is well along in years."

[19]The angel answered, "I am Gabriel. I stand in the presence of God, and I have been sent to speak to you and to tell you this good news. [20]And now you will be silent and not able to speak until the day this happens, because you did not believe my words, which will come true at their proper time."

[21]Meanwhile, the people were waiting for Zechariah and wondering why he stayed so long in the temple. [22]When he came out, he could not speak to them. They realized he had seen a vision in the temple, for he kept making signs to them but remained unable to speak.

---

[a]1 Or *been surely believed*   [b]15 Or *from his mother's womb*

²³When his time of service was completed, he returned home. ²⁴After this his wife Elizabeth became pregnant and for five months remained in seclusion. ²⁵"The Lord has done this for me," she said. "In these days he has shown his favor and taken away my disgrace among the people."

The Birth of Jesus Foretold

²⁶In the sixth month, God sent the angel Gabriel to Nazareth, a town in Galilee, ²⁷to a virgin pledged to be married to a man named Joseph, a descendant of David. The virgin's name was Mary. ²⁸The angel went to her and said, "Greetings, you who are highly favored! The Lord is with you."

²⁹Mary was greatly troubled at his words and wondered what kind of greeting this might be. ³⁰But the angel said to her, "Do not be afraid, Mary, you have found favor with God. ³¹You will be with child and give birth to a son, and you are to give him the name Jesus. ³²He will be great and will be called the Son of the Most High. The Lord God will give him the throne of his father David, ³³and he will reign over the house of Jacob forever; his kingdom will never end."

³⁴"How will this be," Mary asked the angel, "since I am a virgin?"

³⁵The angel answered, "The Holy Spirit will come upon you, and the power of the Most High will overshadow you. So the holy one to be born will be called ᵃ the Son of God. ³⁶Even Elizabeth your relative is going to have a child in her old age, and she who was said to be barren is in her sixth month. ³⁷For nothing is impossible with God."

³⁸"I am the Lord's servant," Mary answered. "May it be to me as you have said." Then the angel left her.

Mary Visits Elizabeth

³⁹At that time Mary got ready and hurried to a town in the hill country of Judea, ⁴⁰where she entered Zechariah's home and greeted Elizabeth. ⁴¹When Elizabeth heard Mary's greeting, the baby leaped in her womb, and Elizabeth was filled with the Holy Spirit. ⁴²In a loud voice she exclaimed: "Blessed are you among women, and blessed is the child you will bear! ⁴³But why am I so favored, that the mother of my Lord should come to me? ⁴⁴As soon as the sound of your greeting reached my ears, the baby in my womb leaped for joy. ⁴⁵Blessed is she who has believed that what the Lord has said to her will be accomplished!"

Mary's Song

⁴⁶And Mary said:

> "My soul glorifies the Lord
> ⁴⁷   and my spirit rejoices in God my Savior,
> ⁴⁸for he has been mindful
>   of the humble state of his servant.
>   From now on all generations will call me blessed,

ᵃ35 Or *So the child to be born will be called holy,*

⁴⁹ for the Mighty One has done great things for me—
holy is his name.
⁵⁰His mercy extends to those who fear him,
from generation to generation.
⁵¹He has performed mighty deeds with his arm;
he has scattered those who are proud in their inmost
thoughts.
⁵²He has brought down rulers from their thrones
but has lifted up the humble.
⁵³He has filled the hungry with good things
but has sent the rich away empty.
⁵⁴He has helped his servant Israel,
remembering to be merciful
⁵⁵to Abraham and his descendants forever,
even as he said to our fathers."

⁵⁶Mary stayed with Elizabeth for about three months and then returned home.

The Birth of John the Baptist

⁵⁷When it was time for Elizabeth to have her baby, she gave birth to a son. ⁵⁸Her neighbors and relatives heard that the Lord had shown her great mercy, and they shared her joy.

⁵⁹On the eighth day they came to circumcise the child, and they were going to name him after his father Zechariah, ⁶⁰but his mother spoke up and said, "No! He is to be called John."

⁶¹They said to her, "There is no one among your relatives who has that name."

⁶²Then they made signs to his father, to find out what he would like to name the child. ⁶³He asked for a writing tablet, and to everyone's astonishment he wrote, "His name is John." ⁶⁴Immediately his mouth was opened and his tongue was loosed, and he began to speak, praising God. ⁶⁵The neighbors were all filled with awe, and throughout the hill country of Judea people were talking about all these things. ⁶⁶Everyone who heard this wondered about it, asking, "What then is this child going to be?" For the Lord's hand was with him.

Zechariah's Song

⁶⁷His father Zechariah was filled with the Holy Spirit and prophesied:

⁶⁸"Praise be to the Lord, the God of Israel,
because he has come and has redeemed his people.
⁶⁹He has raised up a horn^a of salvation for us
in the house of his servant David
⁷⁰(as he said through his holy prophets of long ago),
⁷¹salvation from our enemies

^a69 Horn here symbolizes strength.

and from the hand of all who hate us—
⁷²to show mercy to our fathers
and to remember his holy covenant,
⁷³ the oath he swore to our father Abraham:
⁷⁴to rescue us from the hand of our enemies,
and to enable us to serve him without fear
⁷⁵ in holiness and righteousness before him all our days.

⁷⁶And you, my child, will be called a prophet of the Most
High;
for you will go on before the Lord to prepare the way for
him,
⁷⁷to give his people the knowledge of salvation
through the forgiveness of their sins,
⁷⁸because of the tender mercy of our God,
by which the rising sun will come to us from heaven
⁷⁹to shine on those living in darkness
and in the shadow of death,
to guide our feet into the path of peace."

⁸⁰And the child grew and became strong in spirit; and he lived in the desert until he appeared publicly to Israel.

The Birth of Jesus

2 In those days Caesar Augustus issued a decree that a census should be taken of the entire Roman world. ²(This was the first census that took place while Quirinius was governor of Syria.) ³And everyone went to his own town to register.

⁴So Joseph also went up from the town of Nazareth in Galilee to Judea, to Bethlehem the town of David, because he belonged to the house and line of David. ⁵He went there to register with Mary, who was pledged to be married to him and was expecting a child. ⁶While they were there, the time came for the baby to be born, ⁷and she gave birth to her firstborn, a son. She wrapped him in cloths and placed him in a manger, because there was no room for them in the inn.

The Shepherds and the Angels

⁸And there were shepherds living out in the fields nearby, keeping watch over their flocks at night. ⁹An angel of the Lord appeared to them, and the glory of the Lord shone around them, and they were terrified. ¹⁰But the angel said to them, "Do not be afraid. I bring you good news of great joy that will be for all the people. ¹¹Today in the town of David a Savior has been born to you; he is Christ*ᵃ* the Lord. ¹²This will be a sign to you: You will find a baby wrapped in cloths and lying in a manger."

ᵃ11 Or *Messiah.* "The Christ" (Greek) and "the Messiah" (Hebrew) both mean "the Anointed One"; also in verse 26.

[13]Suddenly a great company of the heavenly host appeared with the angel, praising God and saying,

[14]"Glory to God in the highest,
  and on earth peace to men on whom his favor rests."

[15]When the angels had left them and gone into heaven, the shepherds said to one another, "Let's go to Bethlehem and see this thing that has happened, which the Lord has told us about."

[16]So they hurried off and found Mary and Joseph, and the baby, who was lying in the manger. [17]When they had seen him, they spread the word concerning what had been told them about this child, [18]and all who heard it were amazed at what the shepherds said to them. [19]But Mary treasured up all these things and pondered them in her heart. [20]The shepherds returned, glorifying and praising God for all the things they had heard and seen, which were just as they had been told.

Jesus Presented in the Temple

[21]On the eighth day, when it was time to circumcise him, he was named Jesus, the name the angel had given him before he had been conceived.

[22]When the time of their purification according to the Law of Moses had been completed, Joseph and Mary took him to Jerusalem to present him to the Lord [23](as it is written in the Law of the Lord, "Every firstborn male is to be consecrated to the Lord"[a]), [24]and to offer a sacrifice in keeping with what is said in the Law of the Lord: "a pair of doves or two young pigeons."[b]

[25]Now there was a man in Jerusalem called Simeon, who was righteous and devout. He was waiting for the consolation of Israel, and the Holy Spirit was upon him. [26]It had been revealed to him by the Holy Spirit that he would not die before he had seen the Lord's Christ. [27]Moved by the Spirit, he went into the temple courts. When the parents brought in the child Jesus to do for him what the custom of the Law required, [28]Simeon took him in his arms and praised God, saying:

[29]"Sovereign Lord, as you have promised,
  you now dismiss[c] your servant in peace.
[30]For my eyes have seen your salvation,
[31] which you have prepared in the sight of all people,
[32]a light for revelation to the Gentiles
  and for glory to your people Israel."

[33]The child's father and mother marveled at what was said about him. [34]Then Simeon blessed them and said to Mary, his mother: "This child is destined to cause the falling and rising of many in Israel, and to be a sign that will be spoken against, [35]so that the thoughts of many hearts will be revealed. And a sword will pierce your own soul too."

[36]There was also a prophetess, Anna, the daughter of Phanuel, of the tribe of Asher. She was very old; she had lived with her husband seven

---

[a]23 Exodus 13:2,12   [b]24 Lev. 12:8   [c]29 Or *promised, / now dismiss*

years after her marriage, ³⁷and then was a widow until she was eighty-four. ^a
She never left the temple but worshiped night and day, fasting and praying.
³⁸Coming up to them at that very moment, she gave thanks to God and
spoke about the child to all who were looking forward to the redemption
of Jerusalem.

³⁹When Joseph and Mary had done everything required by the Law of
the Lord, they returned to Galilee to their own town of Nazareth. ⁴⁰And the
child grew and became strong; he was filled with wisdom, and the grace
of God was upon him.

The Boy Jesus at the Temple

⁴¹Every year his parents went to Jerusalem for the Feast of the Passover.
⁴²When he was twelve years old, they went up to the Feast, according to
the custom. ⁴³After the Feast was over, while his parents were returning
home, the boy Jesus stayed behind in Jerusalem, but they were unaware
of it. ⁴⁴Thinking he was in their company, they traveled on for a day. Then
they began looking for him among their relatives and friends. ⁴⁵When they
did not find him, they went back to Jerusalem to look for him. ⁴⁶After three
days they found him in the temple courts, sitting among the teachers,
listening to them and asking them questions. ⁴⁷Everyone who heard him
was amazed at his understanding and his answers. ⁴⁸When his parents saw
him, they were astonished. His mother said to him, "Son, why have you
treated us like this? Your father and I have been anxiously searching for
you."

⁴⁹"Why were you searching for me?" he asked. "Didn't you know I had
to be in my Father's house?" ⁵⁰But they did not understand what he was
saying to them.

⁵¹Then he went down to Nazareth with them and was obedient to them.
But his mother treasured all these things in her heart. ⁵²And Jesus grew in
wisdom and stature, and in favor with God and men.

John the Baptist Prepares the Way

3 In the fifteenth year of the reign of Tiberius Caesar—when Pontius
Pilate was governor of Judea, Herod tetrarch of Galilee, his brother
Philip tetrarch of Iturea and Traconitis, and Lysanias tetrarch of Abilene—
²during the high priesthood of Annas and Caiaphas, the word of God came
to John son of Zechariah in the desert. ³He went into all the country around
the Jordan, preaching a baptism of repentance for the forgiveness of sins.
⁴As is written in the book of the words of Isaiah the prophet:

> "A voice of one calling in the desert,
> 'Prepare the way for the Lord,
>   make straight paths for him.
> ⁵Every valley shall be filled in,
>   every mountain and hill made low.

---

^a37 Or *widow for eighty-four years*

The crooked roads shall become straight,
the rough ways smooth.
⁶And all mankind will see God's salvation.' "ᵃ

⁷John said to the crowds coming out to be baptized by him, "You brood of vipers! Who warned you to flee from the coming wrath? ⁸Produce fruit in keeping with repentance. And do not begin to say to yourselves, 'We have Abraham as our father.' For I tell you that out of these stones God can raise up children for Abraham. ⁹The ax is already at the root of the trees, and every tree that does not produce good fruit will be cut down and thrown into the fire."

¹⁰"What should we do then?" the crowd asked.

¹¹John answered, "The man with two tunics should share with him who has none, and the one who has food should do the same."

¹²Tax collectors also came to be baptized. "Teacher," they asked, "what should we do?"

¹³"Don't collect any more than you are required to," he told them.

¹⁴Then some soldiers asked him, "And what should we do?"

He replied, "Don't extort money and don't accuse people falsely—be content with your pay."

¹⁵The people were waiting expectantly and were all wondering in their hearts if John might possibly be the Christ.ᵇ ¹⁶John answered them all, "I baptize you withᶜ water. But one more powerful than I will come, the thongs of whose sandals I am not worthy to untie. He will baptize you with the Holy Spirit and with fire. ¹⁷His winnowing fork is in his hand to clear his threshing floor and to gather the wheat into his barn, but he will burn up the chaff with unquenchable fire." ¹⁸And with many other words John exhorted the people and preached the good news to them.

¹⁹But when John rebuked Herod the tetrarch because of Herodias, his brother's wife, and all the other evil things he had done, ²⁰Herod added this to them all: He locked John up in prison.

The Baptism and Genealogy of Jesus

²¹When all the people were being baptized, Jesus was baptized too. And as he was praying, heaven was opened ²²and the Holy Spirit descended on him in bodily form like a dove. And a voice came from heaven: "You are my Son, whom I love; with you I am well pleased."

²³Now Jesus himself was about thirty years old when he began his ministry. He was the son, so it was thought, of Joseph,

the son of Heli, ²⁴the son of Matthat,
the son of Levi, the son of Melki,
the son of Jannai, the son of Joseph,
²⁵the son of Mattathias, the son of Amos,
the son of Nahum, the son of Esli,
the son of Naggai, ²⁶the son of Maath,

ᵃ6 Isaiah 40:3-5   ᵇ15 Or Messiah   ᶜ16 Or in

the son of Mattathias, the son of Semein,
the son of Josech, the son of Joda,
²⁷the son of Joanan, the son of Rhesa,
the son of Zerubbabel, the son of Shealtiel,
the son of Neri, ²⁸the son of Melki,
the son of Addi, the son of Cosam,
the son of Elmadam, the son of Er,
²⁹the son of Joshua, the son of Eliezer,
the son of Jorim, the son of Matthat,
the son of Levi, ³⁰the son of Simeon,
the son of Judah, the son of Joseph,
the son of Jonam, the son of Eliakim,
³¹the son of Melea, the son of Menna,
the son of Mattatha, the son of Nathan,
the son of David, ³²the son of Jesse,
the son of Obed, the son of Boaz,
the son of Salmon, ᵃ the son of Nahshon,
³³the son of Amminadab, the son of Ram, ᵇ
the son of Hezron, the son of Perez,
the son of Judah, ³⁴the son of Jacob,
the son of Isaac, the son of Abraham,
the son of Terah, the son of Nahor,
³⁵the son of Serug, the son of Reu,
the son of Peleg, the son of Eber,
the son of Shelah, ³⁶the son of Cainan,
the son of Arphaxad, the son of Shem,
the son of Noah, the son of Lamech,
³⁷the son of Methuselah, the son of Enoch,
the son of Jared, the son of Mahalalel,
the son of Kenan, ³⁸the son of Enosh,
the son of Seth, the son of Adam,
the son of God.

The Temptation of Jesus

4 Jesus, full of the Holy Spirit, returned from the Jordan and was led by the Spirit in the desert, ²where for forty days he was tempted by the devil. He ate nothing during those days, and at the end of them he was hungry.

³The devil said to him, "If you are the Son of God, tell this stone to become bread."

⁴Jesus answered, "It is written: 'Man does not live on bread alone.'ᶜ"

⁵The devil led him up to a high place and showed him in an instant all the kingdoms of the world. ⁶And he said to him, "I will give you all their

---

ᵃ32 Some early manuscripts *Sala*   ᵇ33 Some manuscripts *Amminadab, the son of Admin, the son of Arni*; other manuscripts vary widely.   ᶜ4 Deut. 8:3

authority and splendor, for it has been given to me, and I can give it to anyone I want to. ⁷So if you worship me, it will all be yours."

⁸Jesus answered, "It is written: 'Worship the Lord your God and serve him only.'ᵃ"

⁹The devil led him to Jerusalem and had him stand on the highest point of the temple. "If you are the Son of God," he said, "throw yourself down from here. ¹⁰For it is written:

" 'He will command his angels concerning you
  to guard you carefully;
¹¹they will lift you up in their hands,
  so that you will not strike your foot against a stone.'ᵇ"

¹²Jesus answered, "It says: 'Do not put the Lord your God to the test.'ᶜ"

¹³When the devil had finished all this tempting, he left him until an opportune time.

Jesus Rejected at Nazareth

¹⁴Jesus returned to Galilee in the power of the Spirit, and news about him spread through the whole countryside. ¹⁵He taught in their synagogues, and everyone praised him.

¹⁶He went to Nazareth, where he had been brought up, and on the Sabbath day he went into the synagogue, as was his custom. And he stood up to read. ¹⁷The scroll of the prophet Isaiah was handed to him. Unrolling it, he found the place where it is written:

¹⁸"The Spirit of the Lord is on me,
  because he has anointed me
  to preach good news to the poor.
He has sent me to proclaim freedom for the prisoners
  and recovery of sight for the blind,
  to release the oppressed,
¹⁹   to proclaim the year of the Lord's favor."ᵈ

²⁰Then he rolled up the scroll, gave it back to the attendant and sat down. The eyes of everyone in the synagogue were fastened on him, ²¹and he began by saying to them, "Today this scripture is fulfilled in your hearing."

²²All spoke well of him and were amazed at the gracious words that came from his lips. "Isn't this Joseph's son?" they asked.

²³Jesus said to them, "Surely you will quote this proverb to me: 'Physician, heal yourself! Do here in your hometown what we have heard that you did in Capernaum.' "

²⁴"I tell you the truth," he continued, "no prophet is accepted in his hometown. ²⁵I assure you that there were many widows in Israel in Elijah's time, when the sky was shut for three and a half years and there was a severe famine throughout the land. ²⁶Yet Elijah was not sent to any of them,

ᵃ8 Deut. 6:13   ᵇ11 Psalm 91:11,12   ᶜ12 Deut. 6:16   ᵈ19 Isaiah 61:1,2 but to a widow in Zarephath in the region of Sidon. ²⁷And there were many in Israel with leprosy*ᵃ* in the time of Elisha the prophet, yet not one of them was cleansed—only Naaman the Syrian.''

²⁸All the people in the synagogue were furious when they heard this. ²⁹They got up, drove him out of the town, and took him to the brow of the hill on which the town was built, in order to throw him down the cliff. ³⁰But he walked right through the crowd and went on his way.

Jesus Drives Out an Evil Spirit

³¹Then he went down to Capernaum, a town in Galilee, and on the Sabbath began to teach the people. ³²They were amazed at his teaching, because his message had authority.

³³In the synagogue there was a man possessed by a demon, an evil*ᵇ* spirit. He cried out at the top of his voice, ³⁴''Ha! What do you want with us, Jesus of Nazareth? Have you come to destroy us? I know who you are— the Holy One of God!''

³⁵''Be quiet!'' Jesus said sternly. ''Come out of him!'' Then the demon threw the man down before them all and came out without injuring him.

³⁶All the people were amazed and said to each other, ''What is this teaching? With authority and power he gives orders to evil spirits and they come out!'' ³⁷And the news about him spread throughout the surrounding area.

Jesus Heals Many

³⁸Jesus left the synagogue and went to the home of Simon. Now Simon's mother-in-law was suffering from a high fever, and they asked Jesus to help her. ³⁹So he bent over her and rebuked the fever, and it left her. She got up at once and began to wait on them.

⁴⁰When the sun was setting, the people brought to Jesus all who had various kinds of sickness, and laying his hands on each one, he healed them. ⁴¹Moreover, demons came out of many people, shouting, ''You are the Son of God!'' But he rebuked them and would not allow them to speak, because they knew he was the Christ.*ᶜ*

⁴²At daybreak Jesus went out to a solitary place. The people were looking for him and when they came to where he was, they tried to keep him from leaving them. ⁴³But he said, ''I must preach the good news of the kingdom of God to the other towns also, because that is why I was sent.'' ⁴⁴And he kept on preaching in the synagogues of Judea.*ᵈ*

The Calling of the First Disciples

5 One day as Jesus was standing by the Lake of Gennesaret,*ᵉ* with the people crowding around him and listening to the word of God, ²he saw at the water's edge two boats, left there by the fishermen, who were

---

ᵃ27 The Greek word was used for various diseases affecting the skin—not necessarily leprosy.
ᵇ33 Greek *unclean*; also in verse 36   *ᶜ41* Or *Messiah*   *ᵈ44* Or *the land of the Jews*; some manuscripts *Galilee*   *ᵉ1* That is, Sea of Galilee

washing their nets. ³He got into one of the boats, the one belonging to Simon, and asked him to put out a little from shore. Then he sat down and taught the people from the boat.

⁴When he had finished speaking, he said to Simon, "Put out into deep water, and let down* the nets for a catch."

⁵Simon answered, "Master, we've worked hard all night and haven't caught anything. But because you say so, I will let down the nets."

⁶When they had done so, they caught such a large number of fish that their nets began to break. ⁷So they signaled their partners in the other boat to come and help them, and they came and filled both boats so full that they began to sink.

⁸When Simon Peter saw this, he fell at Jesus' knees and said, "Go away from me, Lord; I am a sinful man!" ⁹For he and all his companions were astonished at the catch of fish they had taken, ¹⁰and so were James and John, the sons of Zebedee, Simon's partners.

Then Jesus said to Simon, "Don't be afraid; from now on you will catch men." ¹¹So they pulled their boats up on shore, left everything and followed him.

The Man With Leprosy

¹²While Jesus was in one of the towns, a man came along who was covered with leprosy.ᵇ When he saw Jesus, he fell with his face to the ground and begged him, "Lord, if you are willing, you can make me clean."

¹³Jesus reached out his hand and touched the man. "I am willing," he said. "Be clean!" And immediately the leprosy left him.

¹⁴Then Jesus ordered him, "Don't tell anyone, but go, show yourself to the priest and offer the sacrifices that Moses commanded for your cleansing, as a testimony to them."

¹⁵Yet the news about him spread all the more, so that crowds of people came to hear him and to be healed of their sicknesses. ¹⁶But Jesus often withdrew to lonely places and prayed.

Jesus Heals a Paralytic

¹⁷One day as he was teaching, Pharisees and teachers of the law, who had come from every village of Galilee and from Judea and Jerusalem, were sitting there. And the power of the Lord was present for him to heal the sick. ¹⁸Some men came carrying a paralytic on a mat and tried to take him into the house to lay him before Jesus. ¹⁹When they could not find a way to do this because of the crowd, they went up on the roof and lowered him on his mat through the tiles into the middle of the crowd, right in front of Jesus.

²⁰When Jesus saw their faith, he said, "Friend, your sins are forgiven."

²¹The Pharisees and the teachers of the law began thinking to them-

---

ᵃ4 The Greek verb is plural.   ᵇ12 The Greek word was used for various diseases affecting the skin—not necessarily leprosy.

selves, "Who is this fellow who speaks blasphemy? Who can forgive sins but God alone?"

²²Jesus knew what they were thinking and asked, "Why are you thinking these things in your hearts? ²³Which is easier: to say, 'Your sins are forgiven,' or to say, 'Get up and walk'? ²⁴But that you may know that the Son of Man has authority on earth to forgive sins. . . .'' He said to the paralyzed man, "I tell you, get up, take your mat and go home." ²⁵Immediately he stood up in front of them, took what he had been lying on and went home praising God. ²⁶Everyone was amazed and gave praise to God. They were filled with awe and said, "We have seen remarkable things today."

The Calling of Levi

²⁷After this, Jesus went out and saw a tax collector by the name of Levi sitting at his tax booth. "Follow me," Jesus said to him, ²⁸and Levi got up, left everything and followed him.

²⁹Then Levi held a great banquet for Jesus at his house, and a large crowd of tax collectors and others were eating with them. ³⁰But the Pharisees and the teachers of the law who belonged to their sect complained to his disciples, "Why do you eat and drink with tax collectors and 'sinners'?"

³¹Jesus answered them, "It is not the healthy who need a doctor, but the sick. ³²I have not come to call the righteous, but sinners to repentance."

Jesus Questioned About Fasting

³³They said to him, "John's disciples often fast and pray, and so do the disciples of the Pharisees, but yours go on eating and drinking."

³⁴Jesus answered, "Can you make the guests of the bridegroom fast while he is with them? ³⁵But the time will come when the bridegroom will be taken from them; in those days they will fast."

³⁶He told them this parable: "No one tears a patch from a new garment and sews it on an old one. If he does, he will have torn the new garment, and the patch from the new will not match the old. ³⁷And no one pours new wine into old wineskins. If he does, the new wine will burst the skins, the wine will run out and the wineskins will be ruined. ³⁸No, new wine must be poured into new wineskins. ³⁹And no one after drinking old wine wants the new, for he says, 'The old is better.' "

Lord of the Sabbath

6 One Sabbath Jesus was going through the grainfields, and his disciples began to pick some heads of grain, rub them in their hands and eat the kernels. ²Some of the Pharisees asked, "Why are you doing what is unlawful on the Sabbath?"

³Jesus answered them, "Have you never read what David did when he and his companions were hungry? ⁴He entered the house of God, and taking the consecrated bread, he ate what is lawful only for priests to eat. And he also gave some to his companions." ⁵Then Jesus said to them, "The Son of Man is Lord of the Sabbath."

⁶On another Sabbath he went into the synagogue and was teaching, and a man was there whose right hand was shriveled. ⁷The Pharisees and the teachers of the law were looking for a reason to accuse Jesus, so they watched him closely to see if he would heal on the Sabbath. ⁸But Jesus knew what they were thinking and said to the man with the shriveled hand, "Get up and stand in front of everyone." So he got up and stood there.

⁹Then Jesus said to them, "I ask you, which is lawful on the Sabbath: to do good or to do evil, to save life or to destroy it?"

¹⁰He looked around at them all, and then said to the man, "Stretch out your hand." He did so, and his hand was completely restored. ¹¹But they were furious and began to discuss with one another what they might do to Jesus.

The Twelve Apostles

¹²One of those days Jesus went out to a mountainside to pray, and spent the night praying to God. ¹³When morning came, he called his disciples to him and chose twelve of them, whom he also designated apostles: ¹⁴Simon (whom he named Peter), his brother Andrew, James, John, Philip, Bartholomew, ¹⁵Matthew, Thomas, James son of Alphaeus, Simon who was called the Zealot, ¹⁶Judas son of James, and Judas Iscariot, who became a traitor.

Blessings and Woes

¹⁷He went down with them and stood on a level place. A large crowd of his disciples was there and a great number of people from all over Judea, from Jerusalem, and from the coast of Tyre and Sidon, ¹⁸who had come to hear him and to be healed of their diseases. Those troubled by evil*ᵃ* spirits were cured, ¹⁹and the people all tried to touch him, because power was coming from him and healing them all.

²⁰Looking at his disciples, he said:

> "Blessed are you who are poor,
>   for yours is the kingdom of God.
> ²¹Blessed are you who hunger now,
>   for you will be satisfied.
> Blessed are you who weep now,
>   for you will laugh.
> ²²Blessed are you when men hate you,
>   when they exclude you and insult you
>   and reject your name as evil,
>   because of the Son of Man.

²³"Rejoice in that day and leap for joy, because great is your reward in heaven. For that is how their fathers treated the prophets.

²⁴"But woe to you who are rich,

ᵃ18 Greek unclean

for you have already received your comfort.
²⁵Woe to you who are well fed now,
for you will go hungry.
Woe to you who laugh now,
for you will mourn and weep.
²⁶Woe to you when all men speak well of you,
for that is how their fathers treated the false prophets.

Love for Enemies

²⁷"But I tell you who hear me: Love your enemies, do good to those who hate you, ²⁸bless those who curse you, pray for those who mistreat you. ²⁹If someone strikes you on one cheek, turn to him the other also. If someone takes your cloak, do not stop him from taking your tunic. ³⁰Give to everyone who asks you, and if anyone takes what belongs to you, do not demand it back. ³¹Do to others as you would have them do to you.

³²"If you love those who love you, what credit is that to you? Even 'sinners' love those who love them. ³³And if you do good to those who are good to you, what credit is that to you? Even 'sinners' do that. ³⁴And if you lend to those from whom you expect repayment, what credit is that to you? Even 'sinners' lend to 'sinners,' expecting to be repaid in full. ³⁵But love your enemies, do good to them, and lend to them without expecting to get anything back. Then your reward will be great, and you will be sons of the Most High, because he is kind to the ungrateful and wicked. ³⁶Be merciful, just as your Father is merciful.

Judging Others

³⁷"Do not judge, and you will not be judged. Do not condemn, and you will not be condemned. Forgive, and you will be forgiven. ³⁸Give, and it will be given to you. A good measure, pressed down, shaken together and running over, will be poured into your lap. For with the measure you use, it will be measured to you."

³⁹He also told them this parable: "Can a blind man lead a blind man? Will they not both fall into a pit? ⁴⁰A student is not above his teacher, but everyone who is fully trained will be like his teacher.

⁴¹"Why do you look at the speck of sawdust in your brother's eye and pay no attention to the plank in your own eye? ⁴²How can you say to your brother, 'Brother, let me take the speck out of your eye,' when you yourself fail to see the plank in your own eye? You hypocrite, first take the plank out of your eye, and then you will see clearly to remove the speck from your brother's eye.

A Tree and Its Fruit

⁴³"No good tree bears bad fruit, nor does a bad tree bear good fruit. ⁴⁴Each tree is recognized by its own fruit. People do not pick figs from thornbushes, or grapes from briers. ⁴⁵The good man brings good things out of the good stored up in his heart, and the evil man brings evil things out

of the evil stored up in his heart. For out of the overflow of his heart his mouth speaks.

The Wise and Foolish Builders

⁴⁶"Why do you call me, 'Lord, Lord,' and do not do what I say? ⁴⁷I will show you what he is like who comes to me and hears my words and puts them into practice. ⁴⁸He is like a man building a house, who dug down deep and laid the foundation on rock. When a flood came, the torrent struck that house but could not shake it, because it was well built. ⁴⁹But the one who hears my words and does not put them into practice is like a man who built a house on the ground without a foundation. The moment the torrent struck that house, it collapsed and its destruction was complete."

The Faith of the Centurion

7 When Jesus had finished saying all this in the hearing of the people, he entered Capernaum. ²There a centurion's servant, whom his master valued highly, was sick and about to die. ³The centurion heard of Jesus and sent some elders of the Jews to him, asking him to come and heal his servant. ⁴When they came to Jesus, they pleaded earnestly with him, "This man deserves to have you do this, ⁵because he loves our nation and has built our synagogue." ⁶So Jesus went with them.

He was not far from the house when the centurion sent friends to say to him: "Lord, don't trouble yourself, for I do not deserve to have you come under my roof. ⁷That is why I did not even consider myself worthy to come to you. But say the word, and my servant will be healed. ⁸For I myself am a man under authority, with soldiers under me. I tell this one, 'Go,' and he goes; and that one, 'Come,' and he comes. I say to my servant, 'Do this,' and he does it."

⁹When Jesus heard this, he was amazed at him, and turning to the crowd following him, he said, "I tell you, I have not found such great faith even in Israel." ¹⁰Then the men who had been sent returned to the house and found the servant well.

Jesus Raises a Widow's Son

¹¹Soon afterward, Jesus went to a town called Nain, and his disciples and a large crowd went along with him. ¹²As he approached the town gate, a dead person was being carried out—the only son of his mother, and she was a widow. And a large crowd from the town was with her. ¹³When the Lord saw her, his heart went out to her and he said, "Don't cry."

¹⁴Then he went up and touched the coffin, and those carrying it stood still. He said, "Young man, I say to you, get up!" ¹⁵The dead man sat up and began to talk, and Jesus gave him back to his mother.

¹⁶They were all filled with awe and praised God. "A great prophet has appeared among us," they said. "God has come to help his people." ¹⁷This news about Jesus spread throughout Judea*a* and the surrounding country.

*a*17 Or *the land of the Jews*

Jesus and John the Baptist

[18]John's disciples told him about all these things. Calling two of them, [19]he sent them to the Lord to ask, "Are you the one who was to come, or should we expect someone else?"

[20]When the men came to Jesus, they said, "John the Baptist sent us to you to ask, 'Are you the one who was to come, or should we expect someone else?' "

[21]At that very time Jesus cured many who had diseases, sicknesses and evil spirits, and gave sight to many who were blind. [22]So he replied to the messengers, "Go back and report to John what you have seen and heard: The blind receive sight, the lame walk, those who have leprosy[a] are cured, the deaf hear, the dead are raised, and the good news is preached to the poor. [23]Blessed is the man who does not fall away on account of me."

[24]After John's messengers left, Jesus began to speak to the crowd about John: "What did you go out into the desert to see? A reed swayed by the wind? [25]If not, what did you go out to see? A man dressed in fine clothes? No, those who wear expensive clothes and indulge in luxury are in palaces. [26]But what did you go out to see? A prophet? Yes, I tell you, and more than a prophet. [27]This is the one about whom it is written:

> " 'I will send my messenger ahead of you,
>   who will prepare your way before you.'[b]

[28]I tell you, among those born of women there is no one greater than John; yet the one who is least in the kingdom of God is greater than he."

[29](All the people, even the tax collectors, when they heard Jesus' words, acknowledged that God's way was right, because they had been baptized by John. [30]But the Pharisees and experts in the law rejected God's purpose for themselves, because they had not been baptized by John.)

[31]"To what, then, can I compare the people of this generation? What are they like? [32]They are like children sitting in the marketplace and calling out to each other:

> " 'We played the flute for you,
>   and you did not dance;
> we sang a dirge,
>   and you did not cry.'

[33]For John the Baptist came neither eating bread nor drinking wine, and you say, 'He has a demon.' [34]The Son of Man came eating and drinking, and you say, 'Here is a glutton and a drunkard, a friend of tax collectors and "sinners." ' [35]But wisdom is proved right by all her children."

Jesus Anointed by a Sinful Woman

[36]Now one of the Pharisees invited Jesus to have dinner with him, so

---

[a]22 The Greek word was used for various diseases affecting the skin—not necessarily leprosy.
[b]27 Mal. 3:1

he went to the Pharisee's house and reclined at the table. 37When a woman who had lived a sinful life in that town learned that Jesus was eating at the Pharisee's house, she brought an alabaster jar of perfume, 38and as she stood behind him at his feet weeping, she began to wet his feet with her tears. Then she wiped them with her hair, kissed them and poured perfume on them.

39When the Pharisee who had invited him saw this, he said to himself, "If this man were a prophet, he would know who is touching him and what kind of woman she is—that she is a sinner."

40Jesus answered him, "Simon, I have something to tell you."

"Tell me, teacher," he said.

41"Two men owed money to a certain moneylender. One owed him five hundred denarii,ᵃ and the other fifty. 42Neither of them had the money to pay him back, so he canceled the debts of both. Now which of them will love him more?"

43Simon replied, "I suppose the one who had the bigger debt canceled."

"You have judged correctly," Jesus said.

44Then he turned toward the woman and said to Simon, "Do you see this woman? I came into your house. You did not give me any water for my feet, but she wet my feet with her tears and wiped them with her hair. 45You did not give me a kiss, but this woman, from the time I entered, has not stopped kissing my feet. 46You did not put oil on my head, but she has poured perfume on my feet. 47Therefore, I tell you, her many sins have been forgiven—for she loved much. But he who has been forgiven little loves little."

48Then Jesus said to her, "Your sins are forgiven."

49The other guests began to say among themselves, "Who is this who even forgives sins?"

50Jesus said to the woman, "Your faith has saved you; go in peace."

The Parable of the Sower

8 After this, Jesus traveled about from one town and village to another, proclaiming the good news of the kingdom of God. The Twelve were with him, 2and also some women who had been cured of evil spirits and diseases: Mary (called Magdalene) from whom seven demons had come out; 3Joanna the wife of Cuza, the manager of Herod's household; Susanna; and many others. These women were helping to support them out of their own means.

4While a large crowd was gathering and people were coming to Jesus from town after town, he told this parable: 5"A farmer went out to sow his seed. As he was scattering the seed, some fell along the path; it was trampled on, and the birds of the air ate it up. 6Some fell on rock, and when it came up, the plants withered because they had no moisture. 7Other seed fell among thorns, which grew up with it and choked the plants. 8Still other

---

ᵃ41 A denarius was a coin worth about a day's wages.

seed fell on good soil. It came up and yielded a crop, a hundred times more than was sown."

When he said this, he called out, "He who has ears to hear, let him hear."

⁹His disciples asked him what this parable meant. ¹⁰He said, "The knowledge of the secrets of the kingdom of God has been given to you, but to others I speak in parables, so that,

" 'though seeing, they may not see;
though hearing, they may not understand.'ᵃ

¹¹"This is the meaning of the parable: The seed is the word of God. ¹²Those along the path are the ones who hear, and then the devil comes and takes away the word from their hearts, so that they may not believe and be saved. ¹³Those on the rock are the ones who receive the word with joy when they hear it, but they have no root. They believe for a while, but in the time of testing they fall away. ¹⁴The seed that fell among thorns stands for those who hear, but as they go on their way they are choked by life's worries, riches and pleasures, and they do not mature. ¹⁵But the seed on good soil stands for those with a noble and good heart, who hear the word, retain it, and by persevering produce a crop.

A Lamp on a Stand

¹⁶"No one lights a lamp and hides it in a jar or puts it under a bed. Instead, he puts it on a stand, so that those who come in can see the light. ¹⁷For there is nothing hidden that will not be disclosed, and nothing concealed that will not be known or brought out into the open. ¹⁸Therefore consider carefully how you listen. Whoever has will be given more; whoever does not have, even what he thinks he has will be taken from him."

Jesus' Mother and Brothers

¹⁹Now Jesus' mother and brothers came to see him, but they were not able to get near him because of the crowd. ²⁰Someone told him, "Your mother and brothers are standing outside, wanting to see you."

²¹He replied, "My mother and brothers are those who hear God's word and put it into practice."

Jesus Calms the Storm

²²One day Jesus said to his disciples, "Let's go over to the other side of the lake." So they got into a boat and set out. ²³As they sailed, he fell asleep. A squall came down on the lake, so that the boat was being swamped, and they were in great danger.

²⁴The disciples went and woke him, saying, "Master, Master, we're going to drown!"

He got up and rebuked the wind and the raging waters; the storm subsided, and all was calm. ²⁵"Where is your faith?" he asked his disciples.

ᵃ10 Isaiah 6:9

114

In fear and amazement they asked one another, "Who is this? He commands even the winds and the water, and they obey him."

The Healing of a Demon-possessed Man

²⁶They sailed to the region of the Gerasenes,ᵃ which is across the lake from Galilee. ²⁷When Jesus stepped ashore, he was met by a demon-possessed man from the town. For a long time this man had not worn clothes or lived in a house, but had lived in the tombs. ²⁸When he saw Jesus, he cried out and fell at his feet, shouting at the top of his voice, "What do you want with me, Jesus, Son of the Most High God? I beg you, don't torture me!" ²⁹For Jesus had commanded the evilᵇ spirit to come out of the man. Many times it had seized him, and though he was chained hand and foot and kept under guard, he had broken his chains and had been driven by the demon into solitary places.

³⁰Jesus asked him, "What is your name?"

"Legion," he replied, because many demons had gone into him. ³¹And they begged him repeatedly not to order them to go into the Abyss.

³²A large herd of pigs was feeding there on the hillside. The demons begged Jesus to let them go into them, and he gave them permission. ³³When the demons came out of the man, they went into the pigs, and the herd rushed down the steep bank into the lake and was drowned.

³⁴When those tending the pigs saw what had happened, they ran off and reported this in the town and countryside, ³⁵and the people went out to see what had happened. When they came to Jesus, they found the man from whom the demons had gone out, sitting at Jesus' feet, dressed and in his right mind; and they were afraid. ³⁶Those who had seen it told the people how the demon-possessed man had been cured. ³⁷Then all the people of the region of the Gerasenes asked Jesus to leave them, because they were overcome with fear. So he got into the boat and left.

³⁸The man from whom the demons had gone out begged to go with him, but Jesus sent him away, saying, ³⁹"Return home and tell how much God has done for you." So the man went away and told all over town how much Jesus had done for him.

A Dead Girl and a Sick Woman

⁴⁰Now when Jesus returned, a crowd welcomed him, for they were all expecting him. ⁴¹Then a man named Jairus, a ruler of the synagogue, came and fell at Jesus' feet, pleading with him to come to his house ⁴²because his only daughter, a girl of about twelve, was dying.

As Jesus was on his way, the crowds almost crushed him. ⁴³And a woman was there who had been subject to bleeding for twelve years,ᶜ but no one could heal her. ⁴⁴She came up behind him and touched the edge of his cloak, and immediately her bleeding stopped.

⁴⁵"Who touched me?" Jesus asked.

ᵃ26 Some manuscripts *Gadarenes*; other manuscripts *Gergesenes*; also in verse 37   ᵇ29 Greek *unclean*
ᶜ43 Many manuscripts *years, and she had spent all she had on doctors*

When they all denied it, Peter said, "Master, the people are crowding and pressing against you."

⁴⁶But Jesus said, "Someone touched me; I know that power has gone out from me."

⁴⁷Then the woman, seeing that she could not go unnoticed, came trembling and fell at his feet. In the presence of all the people, she told why she had touched him and how she had been instantly healed. ⁴⁸Then he said to her, "Daughter, your faith has healed you. Go in peace."

⁴⁹While Jesus was still speaking, someone came from the house of Jairus, the synagogue ruler. "Your daughter is dead," he said. "Don't bother the teacher any more."

⁵⁰Hearing this, Jesus said to Jairus, "Don't be afraid; just believe, and she will be healed."

⁵¹When he arrived at the house of Jairus, he did not let anyone go in with him except Peter, John and James, and the child's father and mother. ⁵²Meanwhile, all the people were wailing and mourning for her. "Stop wailing," Jesus said. "She is not dead but asleep."

⁵³They laughed at him, knowing that she was dead. ⁵⁴But he took her by the hand and said, "My child, get up!" ⁵⁵Her spirit returned, and at once she stood up. Then Jesus told them to give her something to eat. ⁵⁶Her parents were astonished, but he ordered them not to tell anyone what had happened.

Jesus Sends Out the Twelve

9 When Jesus had called the Twelve together, he gave them power and authority to drive out all demons and to cure diseases, ²and he sent them out to preach the kingdom of God and to heal the sick. ³He told them: "Take nothing for the journey—no staff, no bag, no bread, no money, no extra tunic. ⁴Whatever house you enter, stay there until you leave that town. ⁵If people do not welcome you, shake the dust off your feet when you leave their town, as a testimony against them." ⁶So they set out and went from village to village, preaching the gospel and healing people everywhere.

⁷Now Herod the tetrarch heard about all that was going on. And he was perplexed, because some were saying that John had been raised from the dead, ⁸others that Elijah had appeared, and still others that one of the prophets of long ago had come back to life. ⁹But Herod said, "I beheaded John. Who, then, is this I hear such things about?" And he tried to see him.

Jesus Feeds the Five Thousand

¹⁰When the apostles returned, they reported to Jesus what they had done. Then he took them with him and they withdrew by themselves to a town called Bethsaida, ¹¹but the crowds learned about it and followed him. He welcomed them and spoke to them about the kingdom of God, and healed those who needed healing.

¹²Late in the afternoon the Twelve came to him and said, "Send the

crowd away so they can go to the surrounding villages and countryside and find food and lodging, because we are in a remote place here."

[13]He replied, "You give them something to eat."

They answered, "We have only five loaves of bread and two fish—unless we go and buy food for all this crowd." [14](About five thousand men were there.)

But he said to his disciples, "Have them sit down in groups of about fifty each." [15]The disciples did so, and everybody sat down. [16]Taking the five loaves and the two fish and looking up to heaven, he gave thanks and broke them. Then he gave them to the disciples to set before the people. [17]They all ate and were satisfied, and the disciples picked up twelve basketfuls of broken pieces that were left over.

Peter's Confession of Christ

[18]Once when Jesus was praying in private and his disciples were with him, he asked them, "Who do the crowds say I am?"

[19]They replied, "Some say John the Baptist; others say Elijah; and still others, that one of the prophets of long ago has come back to life."

[20]"But what about you?" he asked. "Who do you say I am?"

Peter answered, "The Christ[a] of God."

[21]Jesus strictly warned them not to tell this to anyone. [22]And he said, "The Son of Man must suffer many things and be rejected by the elders, chief priests and teachers of the law, and he must be killed and on the third day be raised to life."

[23]Then he said to them all: "If anyone would come after me, he must deny himself and take up his cross daily and follow me. [24]For whoever wants to save his life will lose it, but whoever loses his life for me will save it. [25]What good is it for a man to gain the whole world, and yet lose or forfeit his very self? [26]If anyone is ashamed of me and my words, the Son of Man will be ashamed of him when he comes in his glory and in the glory of the Father and of the holy angels. [27]I tell you the truth, some who are standing here will not taste death before they see the kingdom of God."

The Transfiguration

[28]About eight days after Jesus said this, he took Peter, John and James with him and went up onto a mountain to pray. [29]As he was praying, the appearance of his face changed, and his clothes became as bright as a flash of lightning. [30]Two men, Moses and Elijah, [31]appeared in glorious splendor, talking with Jesus. They spoke about his departure, which he was about to bring to fulfillment at Jerusalem. [32]Peter and his companions were very sleepy, but when they became fully awake, they saw his glory and the two men standing with him. [33]As the men were leaving Jesus, Peter said to him, "Master, it is good for us to be here. Let us put up three shelters—one for you, one for Moses and one for Elijah." (He did not know what he was saying.)

[a]20 Or Messiah

[34]While he was speaking, a cloud appeared and enveloped them, and they were afraid as they entered the cloud. [35]A voice came from the cloud, saying, "This is my Son, whom I have chosen; listen to him." [36]When the voice had spoken, they found that Jesus was alone. The disciples kept this to themselves, and told no one at that time what they had seen.

The Healing of a Boy With an Evil Spirit

[37]The next day, when they came down from the mountain, a large crowd met him. [38]A man in the crowd called out, "Teacher, I beg you to look at my son, for he is my only child. [39]A spirit seizes him and he suddenly screams; it throws him into convulsions so that he foams at the mouth. It scarcely ever leaves him and is destroying him. [40]I begged your disciples to drive it out, but they could not."

[41]"O unbelieving and perverse generation," Jesus replied, "how long shall I stay with you and put up with you? Bring your son here."

[42]Even while the boy was coming, the demon threw him to the ground in a convulsion. But Jesus rebuked the evil[a] spirit, healed the boy and gave him back to his father. [43]And they were all amazed at the greatness of God.

While everyone was marveling at all that Jesus did, he said to his disciples, [44]"Listen carefully to what I am about to tell you: The Son of Man is going to be betrayed into the hands of men." [45]But they did not understand what this meant. It was hidden from them, so that they did not grasp it, and they were afraid to ask him about it.

Who Will Be the Greatest?

[46]An argument started among the disciples as to which of them would be the greatest. [47]Jesus, knowing their thoughts, took a little child and had him stand beside him. [48]Then he said to them, "Whoever welcomes this little child in my name welcomes me; and whoever welcomes me welcomes the one who sent me. For he who is least among you all—he is the greatest."

[49]"Master," said John, "we saw a man driving out demons in your name and we tried to stop him, because he is not one of us."

[50]"Do not stop him," Jesus said, "for whoever is not against you is for you."

Samaritan Opposition

[51]As the time approached for him to be taken up to heaven, Jesus resolutely set out for Jerusalem. [52]And he sent messengers on ahead, who went into a Samaritan village to get things ready for him; [53]but the people there did not welcome him, because he was heading for Jerusalem. [54]When the disciples James and John saw this, they asked, "Lord, do you want us to call fire down from heaven to destroy them[b]?" [55]But Jesus turned and rebuked them, [56]and[c] they went to another village.

---

[a]42 Greek unclean   [b]54 Some manuscripts them, even as Elijah did   [c]55,56 Some manuscripts them. And he said, "You do not know what kind of spirit you are of, for the Son of Man did not come to destroy men's lives, but to save them." [56]And

The Cost of Following Jesus

⁵⁷As they were walking along the road, a man said to him, "I will follow you wherever you go."

⁵⁸Jesus replied, "Foxes have holes and birds of the air have nests, but the Son of Man has no place to lay his head."

⁵⁹He said to another man, "Follow me."

But the man replied, "Lord, first let me go and bury my father."

⁶⁰Jesus said to him, "Let the dead bury their own dead, but you go and proclaim the kingdom of God."

⁶¹Still another said, "I will follow you, Lord; but first let me go back and say good-by to my family."

⁶²Jesus replied, "No one who puts his hand to the plow and looks back is fit for service in the kingdom of God."

Jesus Sends Out the Seventy-two

10 After this the Lord appointed seventy-two*a* others and sent them two by two ahead of him to every town and place where he was about to go. ²He told them, "The harvest is plentiful, but the workers are few. Ask the Lord of the harvest, therefore, to send out workers into his harvest field. ³Go! I am sending you out like lambs among wolves. ⁴Do not take a purse or bag or sandals; and do not greet anyone on the road.

⁵"When you enter a house, first say, 'Peace to this house.' ⁶If a man of peace is there, your peace will rest on him; if not, it will return to you. ⁷Stay in that house, eating and drinking whatever they give you, for the worker deserves his wages. Do not move around from house to house.

⁸"When you enter a town and are welcomed, eat what is set before you. ⁹Heal the sick who are there and tell them, 'The kingdom of God is near you.' ¹⁰But when you enter a town and are not welcomed, go into its streets and say, ¹¹'Even the dust of your town that sticks to our feet we wipe off against you. Yet be sure of this: The kingdom of God is near.' ¹²I tell you, it will be more bearable on that day for Sodom than for that town.

¹³"Woe to you, Korazin! Woe to you, Bethsaida! For if the miracles that were performed in you had been performed in Tyre and Sidon, they would have repented long ago, sitting in sackcloth and ashes. ¹⁴But it will be more bearable for Tyre and Sidon at the judgment than for you. ¹⁵And you, Capernaum, will you be lifted up to the skies? No, you will go down to the depths.*b*

¹⁶"He who listens to you listens to me; he who rejects you rejects me; but he who rejects me rejects him who sent me."

¹⁷The seventy-two returned with joy and said, "Lord, even the demons submit to us in your name."

¹⁸He replied, "I saw Satan fall like lightning from heaven. ¹⁹I have given you authority to trample on snakes and scorpions and to overcome all the power of the enemy; nothing will harm you. ²⁰However, do not rejoice that

---

*a*1 Some manuscripts *seventy*; also in verse 17   *b*15 Greek *Hades* the spirits submit to you, but rejoice that your names are written in heaven."

²¹At that time Jesus, full of joy through the Holy Spirit, said, "I praise you, Father, Lord of heaven and earth, because you have hidden these things from the wise and learned, and revealed them to little children. Yes, Father, for this was your good pleasure.

²²"All things have been committed to me by my Father. No one knows who the Son is except the Father, and no one knows who the Father is except the Son and those to whom the Son chooses to reveal him."

²³Then he turned to his disciples and said privately, "Blessed are the eyes that see what you see. ²⁴For I tell you that many prophets and kings wanted to see what you see but did not see it, and to hear what you hear but did not hear it."

The Parable of the Good Samaritan

²⁵On one occasion an expert in the law stood up to test Jesus. "Teacher," he asked, "what must I do to inherit eternal life?"

²⁶"What is written in the Law?" he replied. "How do you read it?"

²⁷He answered: " 'Love the Lord your God with all your heart and with all your soul and with all your strength and with all your mind'ᵃ; and, 'Love your neighbor as yourself.'ᵇ"

²⁸"You have answered correctly," Jesus replied. "Do this and you will live."

²⁹But he wanted to justify himself, so he asked Jesus, "And who is my neighbor?"

³⁰In reply Jesus said: "A man was going down from Jerusalem to Jericho, when he fell into the hands of robbers. They stripped him of his clothes, beat him and went away, leaving him half dead. ³¹A priest happened to be going down the same road, and when he saw the man, he passed by on the other side. ³²So too, a Levite, when he came to the place and saw him, passed by on the other side. ³³But a Samaritan, as he traveled, came where the man was; and when he saw him, he took pity on him. ³⁴He went to him and bandaged his wounds, pouring on oil and wine. Then he put the man on his own donkey, took him to an inn and took care of him. ³⁵The next day he took out two silver coinsᶜ and gave them to the innkeeper. 'Look after him,' he said, 'and when I return, I will reimburse you for any extra expense you may have.'

³⁶"Which of these three do you think was a neighbor to the man who fell into the hands of robbers?"

³⁷The expert in the law replied, "The one who had mercy on him."
Jesus told him, "Go and do likewise."

At the Home of Martha and Mary

³⁸As Jesus and his disciples were on their way, he came to a village where a woman named Martha opened her home to him. ³⁹She had a sister

ᵃ27 Deut. 6:5   ᵇ27 Lev. 19:18   ᶜ35 Greek *two denarii*

called Mary, who sat at the Lord's feet listening to what he said. ⁴⁰But Martha was distracted by all the preparations that had to be made. She came to him and asked, "Lord, don't you care that my sister has left me to do the work by myself? Tell her to help me!"

⁴¹"Martha, Martha," the Lord answered, "you are worried and upset about many things, ⁴²but only one thing is needed.ᵃ Mary has chosen what is better, and it will not be taken away from her."

Jesus' Teaching on Prayer

11 One day Jesus was praying in a certain place. When he finished, one of his disciples said to him, "Lord, teach us to pray, just as John taught his disciples."

²He said to them, "When you pray, say:

" 'Father,ᵇ
hallowed be your name,
your kingdom come.ᶜ
³Give us each day our daily bread.
⁴Forgive us our sins,
     for we also forgive everyone who sins against us.ᵈ
And lead us not into temptation.ᵉ' "

⁵Then he said to them, "Suppose one of you has a friend, and he goes to him at midnight and says, 'Friend, lend me three loaves of bread, ⁶because a friend of mine on a journey has come to me, and I have nothing to set before him.'

⁷"Then the one inside answers, 'Don't bother me. The door is already locked, and my children are with me in bed. I can't get up and give you anything.' ⁸I tell you, though he will not get up and give him the bread because he is his friend, yet because of the man's boldnessᶠ he will get up and give him as much as he needs.

⁹"So I say to you: Ask and it will be given to you; seek and you will find; knock and the door will be opened to you. ¹⁰For everyone who asks receives; he who seeks finds; and to him who knocks, the door will be opened.

¹¹"Which of you fathers, if your son asks forᵍ a fish, will give him a snake instead? ¹²Or if he asks for an egg, will give him a scorpion? ¹³If you then, though you are evil, know how to give good gifts to your children, how much more will your Father in heaven give the Holy Spirit to those who ask him!"

Jesus and Beelzebub

¹⁴Jesus was driving out a demon that was mute. When the demon left,

---

ᵃ42 Some manuscripts *but few things are needed—or only one*   ᵇ2 Some manuscripts *Our Father in heaven*   ᶜ2 Some manuscripts *come. May your will be done on earth as it is in heaven.*   ᵈ4 Greek *everyone who is indebted to us*   ᵉ4 Some manuscripts *temptation but deliver us from the evil one*   ᶠ8 Or *persistence*   ᵍ11 Some manuscripts *for bread, will give him a stone; or if he asks for* the man who had been mute spoke, and the crowd was amazed. [15]But some of them said, "By Beelzebub,[a] the prince of demons, he is driving out demons." [16]Others tested him by asking for a sign from heaven.

[17]Jesus knew their thoughts and said to them: "Any kingdom divided against itself will be ruined, and a house divided against itself will fall. [18]If Satan is divided against himself, how can his kingdom stand? I say this because you claim that I drive out demons by Beelzebub. [19]Now if I drive out demons by Beelzebub, by whom do your followers drive them out? So then, they will be your judges. [20]But if I drive out demons by the finger of God, then the kingdom of God has come to you.

[21]"When a strong man, fully armed, guards his own house, his possessions are safe. [22]But when someone stronger attacks and overpowers him, he takes away the armor in which the man trusted and divides up the spoils.

[23]"He who is not with me is against me, and he who does not gather with me, scatters.

[24]"When an evil[b] spirit comes out of a man, it goes through arid places seeking rest and does not find it. Then it says, 'I will return to the house I left.' [25]When it arrives, it finds the house swept clean and put in order. [26]Then it goes and takes seven other spirits more wicked than itself, and they go in and live there. And the final condition of that man is worse than the first."

[27]As Jesus was saying these things, a woman in the crowd called out, "Blessed is the mother who gave you birth and nursed you."

[28]He replied, "Blessed rather are those who hear the word of God and obey it."

The Sign of Jonah

[29]As the crowds increased, Jesus said, "This is a wicked generation. It asks for a miraculous sign, but none will be given it except the sign of Jonah. [30]For as Jonah was a sign to the Ninevites, so also will the Son of Man be to this generation. [31]The Queen of the South will rise at the judgment with the men of this generation and condemn them; for she came from the ends of the earth to listen to Solomon's wisdom, and now one[c] greater than Solomon is here. [32]The men of Nineveh will stand up at the judgment with this generation and condemn it; for they repented at the preaching of Jonah, and now one greater than Jonah is here.

The Lamp of the Body

[33]"No one lights a lamp and puts it in a place where it will be hidden, or under a bowl. Instead he puts it on its stand, so that those who come in may see the light. [34]Your eye is the lamp of your body. When your eyes are good, your whole body also is full of light. But when they are bad, your body also is full of darkness. [35]See to it, then, that the light within you is not darkness. [36]Therefore, if your whole body is full of light, and no part

[a]15 Greek *Beezeboul* or *Beelzeboul*; also in verses 18 and 19   [b]24 Greek *unclean*   [c]31 Or *something*; also in verse 32

of it dark, it will be completely lighted, as when the light of a lamp shines on you."

Six Woes

[37]When Jesus had finished speaking, a Pharisee invited him to eat with him; so he went in and reclined at the table. [38]But the Pharisee, noticing that Jesus did not first wash before the meal, was surprised.

[39]Then the Lord said to him, "Now then, you Pharisees clean the outside of the cup and dish, but inside you are full of greed and wickedness. [40]You foolish people! Did not the one who made the outside make the inside also? [41]But give what is inside ˻the dish˼[a] to the poor, and everything will be clean for you.

[42]"Woe to you Pharisees, because you give God a tenth of your mint, rue and all other kinds of garden herbs, but you neglect justice and the love of God. You should have practiced the latter without leaving the former undone.

[43]"Woe to you Pharisees, because you love the most important seats in the synagogues and greetings in the marketplaces.

[44]"Woe to you, because you are like unmarked graves, which men walk over without knowing it."

[45]One of the experts in the law answered him, "Teacher, when you say these things, you insult us also."

[46]Jesus replied, "And you experts in the law, woe to you, because you load people down with burdens they can hardly carry, and you yourselves will not lift one finger to help them.

[47]"Woe to you, because you build tombs for the prophets, and it was your forefathers who killed them. [48]So you testify that you approve of what your forefathers did; they killed the prophets, and you build their tombs. [49]Because of this, God in his wisdom said, 'I will send them prophets and apostles, some of whom they will kill and others they will persecute.' [50]Therefore this generation will be held responsible for the blood of all the prophets that has been shed since the beginning of the world, [51]from the blood of Abel to the blood of Zechariah, who was killed between the altar and the sanctuary. Yes, I tell you, this generation will be held responsible for it all.

[52]"Woe to you experts in the law, because you have taken away the key to knowledge. You yourselves have not entered, and you have hindered those who were entering."

[53]When Jesus left there, the Pharisees and the teachers of the law began to oppose him fiercely and to besiege him with questions, [54]waiting to catch him in something he might say.

Warnings and Encouragements

12 Meanwhile, when a crowd of many thousands had gathered, so that they were trampling on one another, Jesus began to speak first to his

[a]41 Or *what you have*

disciples, saying: "Be on your guard against the yeast of the Pharisees, which is hypocrisy. ²There is nothing concealed that will not be disclosed, or hidden that will not be made known. ³What you have said in the dark will be heard in the daylight, and what you have whispered in the ear in the inner rooms will be proclaimed from the roofs.

⁴"I tell you, my friends, do not be afraid of those who kill the body and after that can do no more. ⁵But I will show you whom you should fear: Fear him who, after the killing of the body, has power to throw you into hell. Yes, I tell you, fear him. ⁶Are not five sparrows sold for two pennies[a]? Yet not one of them is forgotten by God. ⁷Indeed, the very hairs of your head are all numbered. Don't be afraid; you are worth more than many sparrows.

⁸"I tell you, whoever acknowledges me before men, the Son of Man will also acknowledge him before the angels of God. ⁹But he who disowns me before men will be disowned before the angels of God. ¹⁰And everyone who speaks a word against the Son of Man will be forgiven, but anyone who blasphemes against the Holy Spirit will not be forgiven.

¹¹"When you are brought before synagogues, rulers and authorities, do not worry about how you will defend yourselves or what you will say, ¹²for the Holy Spirit will teach you at that time what you should say."

The Parable of the Rich Fool

¹³Someone in the crowd said to him, "Teacher, tell my brother to divide the inheritance with me."

¹⁴Jesus replied, "Man, who appointed me a judge or an arbiter between you?" ¹⁵Then he said to them, "Watch out! Be on your guard against all kinds of greed; a man's life does not consist in the abundance of his possessions."

¹⁶And he told them this parable: "The ground of a certain rich man produced a good crop. ¹⁷He thought to himself, 'What shall I do? I have no place to store my crops.'

¹⁸"Then he said, 'This is what I'll do. I will tear down my barns and build bigger ones, and there I will store all my grain and my goods. ¹⁹And I'll say to myself, "You have plenty of good things laid up for many years. Take life easy; eat, drink and be merry." '

²⁰"But God said to him, 'You fool! This very night your life will be demanded from you. Then who will get what you have prepared for yourself?'

²¹"This is how it will be with anyone who stores up things for himself but is not rich toward God."

Do Not Worry

²²Then Jesus said to his disciples: "Therefore I tell you, do not worry about your life, what you will eat; or about your body, what you will wear. ²³Life is more than food, and the body more than clothes. ²⁴Consider the ravens: They do not sow or reap, they have no storeroom or barn; yet God

[a]6 Greek *two assaria*

feeds them. And how much more valuable you are than birds! ²⁵Who of you by worrying can add a single hour to his life^a? ²⁶Since you cannot do this very little thing, why do you worry about the rest?

²⁷"Consider how the lilies grow. They do not labor or spin. Yet I tell you, not even Solomon in all his splendor was dressed like one of these. ²⁸If that is how God clothes the grass of the field, which is here today, and tomorrow is thrown into the fire, how much more will he clothe you, O you of little faith! ²⁹And do not set your heart on what you will eat or drink; do not worry about it. ³⁰For the pagan world runs after all such things, and your Father knows that you need them. ³¹But seek his kingdom, and these things will be given to you as well.

³²"Do not be afraid, little flock, for your Father has been pleased to give you the kingdom. ³³Sell your possessions and give to the poor. Provide purses for yourselves that will not wear out, a treasure in heaven that will not be exhausted, where no thief comes near and no moth destroys. ³⁴For where your treasure is, there your heart will be also.

Watchfulness

³⁵"Be dressed ready for service and keep your lamps burning, ³⁶like men waiting for their master to return from a wedding banquet, so that when he comes and knocks they can immediately open the door for him. ³⁷It will be good for those servants whose master finds them watching when he comes. I tell you the truth, he will dress himself to serve, will have them recline at the table and will come and wait on them. ³⁸It will be good for those servants whose master finds them ready, even if he comes in the second or third watch of the night. ³⁹But understand this: If the owner of the house had known at what hour the thief was coming, he would not have let his house be broken into. ⁴⁰You also must be ready, because the Son of Man will come at an hour when you do not expect him."

⁴¹Peter asked, "Lord, are you telling this parable to us, or to everyone?"

⁴²The Lord answered, "Who then is the faithful and wise manager, whom the master puts in charge of his servants to give them their food allowance at the proper time? ⁴³It will be good for that servant whom the master finds doing so when he returns. ⁴⁴I tell you the truth, he will put him in charge of all his possessions. ⁴⁵But suppose the servant says to himself, 'My master is taking a long time in coming,' and he then begins to beat the menservants and maidservants and to eat and drink and get drunk. ⁴⁶The master of that servant will come on a day when he does not expect him and at an hour he is not aware of. He will cut him to pieces and assign him a place with the unbelievers.

⁴⁷"That servant who knows his master's will and does not get ready or does not do what his master wants will be beaten with many blows. ⁴⁸But the one who does not know and does things deserving punishment will be beaten with few blows. From everyone who has been given much, much

a25 Or *single cubit to his height*

will be demanded; and from the one who has been entrusted with much, much more will be asked.

Not Peace but Division

[49]"I have come to bring fire on the earth, and how I wish it were already kindled! [50]But I have a baptism to undergo, and how distressed I am until it is completed! [51]Do you think I came to bring peace on earth? No, I tell you, but division. [52]From now on there will be five in one family divided against each other, three against two and two against three. [53]They will be divided, father against son and son against father, mother against daughter and daughter against mother, mother-in-law against daughter-in-law and daughter-in-law against mother-in-law."

Interpreting the Times

[54]He said to the crowd: "When you see a cloud rising in the west, immediately you say, 'It's going to rain,' and it does. [55]And when the south wind blows, you say, 'It's going to be hot,' and it is. [56]Hypocrites! You know how to interpret the appearance of the earth and the sky. How is it that you don't know how to interpret this present time?

[57]"Why don't you judge for yourselves what is right? [58]As you are going with your adversary to the magistrate, try hard to be reconciled to him on the way, or he may drag you off to the judge, and the judge turn you over to the officer, and the officer throw you into prison. [59]I tell you, you will not get out until you have paid the last penny.[a]"

Repent or Perish

13 Now there were some present at that time who told Jesus about the Galileans whose blood Pilate had mixed with their sacrifices. [2]Jesus answered, "Do you think that these Galileans were worse sinners than all the other Galileans because they suffered this way? [3]I tell you, no! But unless you repent, you too will all perish. [4]Or those eighteen who died when the tower in Siloam fell on them—do you think they were more guilty than all the others living in Jerusalem? [5]I tell you, no! But unless you repent, you too will all perish."

[6]Then he told this parable: "A man had a fig tree, planted in his vineyard, and he went to look for fruit on it, but did not find any. [7]So he said to the man who took care of the vineyard, 'For three years now I've been coming to look for fruit on this fig tree and haven't found any. Cut it down! Why should it use up the soil?'

[8]"'Sir,' the man replied, 'leave it alone for one more year, and I'll dig around it and fertilize it. [9]If it bears fruit next year, fine! If not, then cut it down.'"

A Crippled Woman Healed on the Sabbath

[10]On a Sabbath Jesus was teaching in one of the synagogues, [11]and a

[a]59 Greek lepton

woman was there who had been crippled by a spirit for eighteen years. She was bent over and could not straighten up at all. [12]When Jesus saw her, he called her forward and said to her, "Woman, you are set free from your infirmity." [13]Then he put his hands on her, and immediately she straightened up and praised God.

[14]Indignant because Jesus had healed on the Sabbath, the synagogue ruler said to the people, "There are six days for work. So come and be healed on those days, not on the Sabbath."

[15]The Lord answered him, "You hypocrites! Doesn't each of you on the Sabbath untie his ox or donkey from the stall and lead it out to give it water? [16]Then should not this woman, a daughter of Abraham, whom Satan has kept bound for eighteen long years, be set free on the Sabbath day from what bound her?"

[17]When he said this, all his opponents were humiliated, but the people were delighted with all the wonderful things he was doing.

The Parables of the Mustard Seed and the Yeast

[18]Then Jesus asked, "What is the kingdom of God like? What shall I compare it to? [19]It is like a mustard seed, which a man took and planted in his garden. It grew and became a tree, and the birds of the air perched in its branches."

[20]Again he asked, "What shall I compare the kingdom of God to? [21]It is like yeast that a woman took and mixed into a large amount[a] of flour until it worked all through the dough."

The Narrow Door

[22]Then Jesus went through the towns and villages, teaching as he made his way to Jerusalem. [23]Someone asked him, "Lord, are only a few people going to be saved?"

He said to them, [24]"Make every effort to enter through the narrow door, because many, I tell you, will try to enter and will not be able to. [25]Once the owner of the house gets up and closes the door, you will stand outside knocking and pleading, 'Sir, open the door for us.'

"But he will answer, 'I don't know you or where you come from.'

[26]"Then you will say, 'We ate and drank with you, and you taught in our streets.'

[27]"But he will reply, 'I don't know you or where you come from. Away from me, all you evildoers!'

[28]"There will be weeping there, and gnashing of teeth, when you see Abraham, Isaac and Jacob and all the prophets in the kingdom of God, but you yourselves thrown out. [29]People will come from east and west and north and south, and will take their places at the feast in the kingdom of God. [30]Indeed there are those who are last who will be first, and first who will be last."

---

[a]21 Greek three satas (probably about 1/2 bushel or 22 liters)

Jesus' Sorrow for Jerusalem

³¹At that time some Pharisees came to Jesus and said to him, "Leave this place and go somewhere else. Herod wants to kill you."

³²He replied, "Go tell that fox, 'I will drive out demons and heal people today and tomorrow, and on the third day I will reach my goal.' ³³In any case, I must keep going today and tomorrow and the next day—for surely no prophet can die outside Jerusalem!

³⁴"O Jerusalem, Jerusalem, you who kill the prophets and stone those sent to you, how often I have longed to gather your children together, as a hen gathers her chicks under her wings, but you were not willing! ³⁵Look, your house is left to you desolate. I tell you, you will not see me again until you say, 'Blessed is he who comes in the name of the Lord.'ᵃ"

Jesus at a Pharisee's House

14 One Sabbath, when Jesus went to eat in the house of a prominent Pharisee, he was being carefully watched. ²There in front of him was a man suffering from dropsy. ³Jesus asked the Pharisees and experts in the law, "Is it lawful to heal on the Sabbath or not?" ⁴But they remained silent. So taking hold of the man, he healed him and sent him away.

⁵Then he asked them, "If one of you has a sonᵇ or an ox that falls into a well on the Sabbath day, will you not immediately pull him out?" ⁶And they had nothing to say.

⁷When he noticed how the guests picked the places of honor at the table, he told them this parable: ⁸"When someone invites you to a wedding feast, do not take the place of honor, for a person more distinguished than you may have been invited. ⁹If so, the host who invited both of you will come and say to you, 'Give this man your seat.' Then, humiliated, you will have to take the least important place. ¹⁰But when you are invited, take the lowest place, so that when your host comes, he will say to you, 'Friend, move up to a better place.' Then you will be honored in the presence of all your fellow guests. ¹¹For everyone who exalts himself will be humbled, and he who humbles himself will be exalted."

¹²Then Jesus said to his host, "When you give a luncheon or dinner, do not invite your friends, your brothers or relatives, or your rich neighbors; if you do, they may invite you back and so you will be repaid. ¹³But when you give a banquet, invite the poor, the crippled, the lame, the blind, ¹⁴and you will be blessed. Although they cannot repay you, you will be repaid at the resurrection of the righteous."

The Parable of the Great Banquet

¹⁵When one of those at the table with him heard this, he said to Jesus, "Blessed is the man who will eat at the feast in the kingdom of God."

¹⁶Jesus replied: "A certain man was preparing a great banquet and

ᵃ35 Psalm 118:26   ᵇ5 Some manuscripts *donkey*

invited many guests. [17]At the time of the banquet he sent his servant to tell those who had been invited, 'Come, for everything is now ready.'

[18]"But they all alike began to make excuses. The first said, 'I have just bought a field, and I must go and see it. Please excuse me.'

[19]"Another said, 'I have just bought five yoke of oxen, and I'm on my way to try them out. Please excuse me.'

[20]"Still another said, 'I just got married, so I can't come.'

[21]"The servant came back and reported this to his master. Then the owner of the house became angry and ordered his servant, 'Go out quickly into the streets and alleys of the town and bring in the poor, the crippled, the blind and the lame.'

[22]" 'Sir,' the servant said, 'what you ordered has been done, but there is still room.'

[23]"Then the master told his servant, 'Go out to the roads and country lanes and make them come in, so that my house will be full. [24]I tell you, not one of those men who were invited will get a taste of my banquet.' "

The Cost of Being a Disciple

[25]Large crowds were traveling with Jesus, and turning to them he said: [26]"If anyone comes to me and does not hate his father and mother, his wife and children, his brothers and sisters—yes, even his own life—he cannot be my disciple. [27]And anyone who does not carry his cross and follow me cannot be my disciple.

[28]"Suppose one of you wants to build a tower. Will he not first sit down and estimate the cost to see if he has enough money to complete it? [29]For if he lays the foundation and is not able to finish it, everyone who sees it will ridicule him, [30]saying, 'This fellow began to build and was not able to finish.'

[31]"Or suppose a king is about to go to war against another king. Will he not first sit down and consider whether he is able with ten thousand men to oppose the one coming against him with twenty thousand? [32]If he is not able, he will send a delegation while the other is still a long way off and will ask for terms of peace. [33]In the same way, any of you who does not give up everything he has cannot be my disciple.

[34]"Salt is good, but if it loses its saltiness, how can it be made salty again? [35]It is fit neither for the soil nor for the manure pile; it is thrown out.

"He who has ears to hear, let him hear."

The Parable of the Lost Sheep

15 Now the tax collectors and "sinners" were all gathering around to hear him. [2]But the Pharisees and the teachers of the law muttered, "This man welcomes sinners and eats with them."

[3]Then Jesus told them this parable: [4]"Suppose one of you has a hundred sheep and loses one of them. Does he not leave the ninety-nine in the open country and go after the lost sheep until he finds it? [5]And when he finds it, he joyfully puts it on his shoulders [6]and goes home. Then he calls his

friends and neighbors together and says, 'Rejoice with me; I have found my lost sheep.' 7I tell you that in the same way there will be more rejoicing in heaven over one sinner who repents than over ninety-nine righteous persons who do not need to repent.

The Parable of the Lost Coin

8"Or suppose a woman has ten silver coins*a* and loses one. Does she not light a lamp, sweep the house and search carefully until she finds it? 9And when she finds it, she calls her friends and neighbors together and says, 'Rejoice with me; I have found my lost coin.' 10In the same way, I tell you, there is rejoicing in the presence of the angels of God over one sinner who repents."

The Parable of the Lost Son

11Jesus continued: "There was a man who had two sons. 12The younger one said to his father, 'Father, give me my share of the estate.' So he divided his property between them.

13"Not long after that, the younger son got together all he had, set off for a distant country and there squandered his wealth in wild living. 14After he had spent everything, there was a severe famine in that whole country, and he began to be in need. 15So he went and hired himself out to a citizen of that country, who sent him to his fields to feed pigs. 16He longed to fill his stomach with the pods that the pigs were eating, but no one gave him anything.

17"When he came to his senses, he said, 'How many of my father's hired men have food to spare, and here I am starving to death! 18I will set out and go back to my father and say to him: Father, I have sinned against heaven and against you. 19I am no longer worthy to be called your son; make me like one of your hired men.' 20So he got up and went to his father.

"But while he was still a long way off, his father saw him and was filled with compassion for him; he ran to his son, threw his arms around him and kissed him.

21"The son said to him, 'Father, I have sinned against heaven and against you. I am no longer worthy to be called your son.*b*'

22"But the father said to his servants, 'Quick! Bring the best robe and put it on him. Put a ring on his finger and sandals on his feet. 23Bring the fattened calf and kill it. Let's have a feast and celebrate. 24For this son of mine was dead and is alive again; he was lost and is found.' So they began to celebrate.

25"Meanwhile, the older son was in the field. When he came near the house, he heard music and dancing. 26So he called one of the servants and asked him what was going on. 27'Your brother has come,' he replied, 'and your father has killed the fattened calf because he has him back safe and sound.'

---

*a*8 Greek *ten drachmas,* each worth about a day's wages   *b*21 Some early manuscripts *son. Make me like one of your hired men.*

28"The older brother became angry and refused to go in. So his father went out and pleaded with him. 29But he answered his father, 'Look! All these years I've been slaving for you and never disobeyed your orders. Yet you never gave me even a young goat so I could celebrate with my friends. 30But when this son of yours who has squandered your property with prostitutes comes home, you kill the fattened calf for him!'

31" 'My son,' the father said, 'you are always with me, and everything I have is yours. 32But we had to celebrate and be glad, because this brother of yours was dead and is alive again; he was lost and is found.' "

The Parable of the Shrewd Manager

16 Jesus told his disciples: "There was a rich man whose manager was accused of wasting his possessions. 2So he called him in and asked him, 'What is this I hear about you? Give an account of your management, because you cannot be manager any longer.'

3"The manager said to himself, 'What shall I do now? My master is taking away my job. I'm not strong enough to dig, and I'm ashamed to beg— 4I know what I'll do so that, when I lose my job here, people will welcome me into their houses.'

5"So he called in each one of his master's debtors. He asked the first, 'How much do you owe my master?'

6" 'Eight hundred gallons*a* of olive oil,' he replied.

"The manager told him, 'Take your bill, sit down quickly, and make it four hundred.'

7"Then he asked the second, 'And how much do you owe?'

" 'A thousand bushels*b* of wheat,' he replied.

"He told him, 'Take your bill and make it eight hundred.'

8"The master commended the dishonest manager because he had acted shrewdly. For the people of this world are more shrewd in dealing with their own kind than are the people of the light. 9I tell you, use worldly wealth to gain friends for yourselves, so that when it is gone, you will be welcomed into eternal dwellings.

10"Whoever can be trusted with very little can also be trusted with much, and whoever is dishonest with very little will also be dishonest with much. 11So if you have not been trustworthy in handling worldly wealth, who will trust you with true riches? 12And if you have not been trustworthy with someone else's property, who will give you property of your own?

13"No servant can serve two masters. Either he will hate the one and love the other, or he will be devoted to the one and despise the other. You cannot serve both God and Money."

14The Pharisees, who loved money, heard all this and were sneering at Jesus. 15He said to them, "You are the ones who justify yourselves in the eyes of men, but God knows your hearts. What is highly valued among men is detestable in God's sight.

---

*a*6 Greek *one hundred batous* (probably about 3 kiloliters)   *b*7 Greek *one hundred korous* (probably about 35 kiloliters)

Additional Teachings

16"The Law and the Prophets were proclaimed until John. Since that time, the good news of the kingdom of God is being preached, and everyone is forcing his way into it. 17It is easier for heaven and earth to disappear than for the least stroke of a pen to drop out of the Law.

18"Anyone who divorces his wife and marries another woman commits adultery, and the man who marries a divorced woman commits adultery.

The Rich Man and Lazarus

19"There was a rich man who was dressed in purple and fine linen and lived in luxury every day. 20At his gate was laid a beggar named Lazarus, covered with sores 21and longing to eat what fell from the rich man's table. Even the dogs came and licked his sores.

22"The time came when the beggar died and the angels carried him to Abraham's side. The rich man also died and was buried. 23In hell,ᵃ where he was in torment, he looked up and saw Abraham far away, with Lazarus by his side. 24So he called to him, 'Father Abraham, have pity on me and send Lazarus to dip the tip of his finger in water and cool my tongue, because I am in agony in this fire.'

25"But Abraham replied, 'Son, remember that in your lifetime you received your good things, while Lazarus received bad things, but now he is comforted here and you are in agony. 26And besides all this, between us and you a great chasm has been fixed, so that those who want to go from here to you cannot, nor can anyone cross over from there to us.'

27"He answered, 'Then I beg you, father, send Lazarus to my father's house, 28for I have five brothers. Let him warn them, so that they will not also come to this place of torment.'

29"Abraham replied, 'They have Moses and the Prophets; let them listen to them.'

30" 'No, father Abraham,' he said, 'but if someone from the dead goes to them, they will repent.'

31"He said to him, 'If they do not listen to Moses and the Prophets, they will not be convinced even if someone rises from the dead.' "

Sin, Faith, Duty

17 Jesus said to his disciples: "Things that cause people to sin are bound to come, but woe to that person through whom they come. 2It would be better for him to be thrown into the sea with a millstone tied around his neck than for him to cause one of these little ones to sin. 3So watch yourselves.

"If your brother sins, rebuke him, and if he repents, forgive him. 4If he sins against you seven times in a day, and seven times comes back to you and says, 'I repent,' forgive him."

5The apostles said to the Lord, "Increase our faith!"

ᵃ23 Greek *Hades*

⁶He replied, "If you have faith as small as a mustard seed, you can say to this mulberry tree, 'Be uprooted and planted in the sea,' and it will obey you.

⁷"Suppose one of you had a servant plowing or looking after the sheep. Would he say to the servant when he comes in from the field, 'Come along now and sit down to eat'? ⁸Would he not rather say, 'Prepare my supper, get yourself ready and wait on me while I eat and drink; after that you may eat and drink'? ⁹Would he thank the servant because he did what he was told to do? ¹⁰So you also, when you have done everything you were told to do, should say, 'We are unworthy servants; we have only done our duty.' "

Ten Healed of Leprosy

¹¹Now on his way to Jerusalem, Jesus traveled along the border between Samaria and Galilee. ¹²As he was going into a village, ten men who had leprosy[a] met him. They stood at a distance ¹³and called out in a loud voice, "Jesus, Master, have pity on us!"

¹⁴When he saw them, he said, "Go, show yourselves to the priests." And as they went, they were cleansed.

¹⁵One of them, when he saw he was healed, came back, praising God in a loud voice. ¹⁶He threw himself at Jesus' feet and thanked him—and he was a Samaritan.

¹⁷Jesus asked, "Were not all ten cleansed? Where are the other nine? ¹⁸Was no one found to return and give praise to God except this foreigner?" ¹⁹Then he said to him, "Rise and go; your faith has made you well."

The Coming of the Kingdom of God

²⁰Once, having been asked by the Pharisees when the kingdom of God would come, Jesus replied, "The kingdom of God does not come with your careful observation, ²¹nor will people say, 'Here it is,' or 'There it is,' because the kingdom of God is within[b] you."

²²Then he said to his disciples, "The time is coming when you will long to see one of the days of the Son of Man, but you will not see it. ²³Men will tell you, 'There he is!' or 'Here he is!' Do not go running off after them. ²⁴For the Son of Man in his day[c] will be like the lightning, which flashes and lights up the sky from one end to the other. ²⁵But first he must suffer many things and be rejected by this generation.

²⁶"Just as it was in the days of Noah, so also will it be in the days of the Son of Man. ²⁷People were eating, drinking, marrying and being given in marriage up to the day Noah entered the ark. Then the flood came and destroyed them all.

²⁸"It was the same in the days of Lot. People were eating and drinking, buying and selling, planting and building. ²⁹But the day Lot left Sodom, fire and sulfur rained down from heaven and destroyed them all.

a12 The Greek word was used for various diseases affecting the skin—not necessarily leprosy. b21 Or among c24 Some manuscripts do not have in his day.

[30]"It will be just like this on the day the Son of Man is revealed. [31]On that day no one who is on the roof of his house, with his goods inside, should go down to get them. Likewise, no one in the field should go back for anything. [32]Remember Lot's wife! [33]Whoever tries to keep his life will lose it, and whoever loses his life will preserve it. [34]I tell you, on that night two people will be in one bed; one will be taken and the other left. [35]Two women will be grinding grain together; one will be taken and the other left. [a]"

[37]"Where, Lord?" they asked.

He replied, "Where there is a dead body, there the vultures will gather."

The Parable of the Persistent Widow

18 Then Jesus told his disciples a parable to show them that they should always pray and not give up. [2]He said: "In a certain town there was a judge who neither feared God nor cared about men. [3]And there was a widow in that town who kept coming to him with the plea, 'Grant me justice against my adversary.'

[4]"For some time he refused. But finally he said to himself, 'Even though I don't fear God or care about men, [5]yet because this widow keeps bothering me, I will see that she gets justice, so that she won't eventually wear me out with her coming!' "

[6]And the Lord said, "Listen to what the unjust judge says. [7]And will not God bring about justice for his chosen ones, who cry out to him day and night? Will he keep putting them off? [8]I tell you, he will see that they get justice, and quickly. However, when the Son of Man comes, will he find faith on the earth?"

The Parable of the Pharisee and the Tax Collector

[9]To some who were confident of their own righteousness and looked down on everybody else, Jesus told this parable: [10]"Two men went up to the temple to pray, one a Pharisee and the other a tax collector. [11]The Pharisee stood up and prayed about[b] himself: 'God, I thank you that I am not like other men—robbers, evildoers, adulterers—or even like this tax collector. [12]I fast twice a week and give a tenth of all I get.'

[13]"But the tax collector stood at a distance. He would not even look up to heaven, but beat his breast and said, 'God, have mercy on me, a sinner.'

[14]"I tell you that this man, rather than the other, went home justified before God. For everyone who exalts himself will be humbled, and he who humbles himself will be exalted."

The Little Children and Jesus

[15]People were also bringing babies to Jesus to have him touch them. When the disciples saw this, they rebuked them. [16]But Jesus called the children to him and said, "Let the little children come to me, and do not

---

a35 Some manuscripts *left.* 36*Two men will be in the field; one will be taken and the other left.*   b11 Or *to* hinder them, for the kingdom of God belongs to such as these. [17]I tell you the truth, anyone who will not receive the kingdom of God like a little child will never enter it."

The Rich Ruler

[18]A certain ruler asked him, "Good teacher, what must I do to inherit eternal life?"

[19]"Why do you call me good?" Jesus answered. "No one is good— except God alone. [20]You know the commandments: 'Do not commit adultery, do not murder, do not steal, do not give false testimony, honor your father and mother.'[a]"

[21]"All these I have kept since I was a boy," he said.

[22]When Jesus heard this, he said to him, "You still lack one thing. Sell everything you have and give to the poor, and you will have treasure in heaven. Then come, follow me."

[23]When he heard this, he became very sad, because he was a man of great wealth. [24]Jesus looked at him and said, "How hard it is for the rich to enter the kingdom of God! [25]Indeed, it is easier for a camel to go through the eye of a needle than for a rich man to enter the kingdom of God."

[26]Those who heard this asked, "Who then can be saved?"

[27]Jesus replied, "What is impossible with men is possible with God."

[28]Peter said to him, "We have left all we had to follow you!"

[29]"I tell you the truth," Jesus said to them, "no one who has left home or wife or brothers or parents or children for the sake of the kingdom of God [30]will fail to receive many times as much in this age and, in the age to come, eternal life."

Jesus Again Predicts His Death

[31]Jesus took the Twelve aside and told them, "We are going up to Jerusalem, and everything that is written by the prophets about the Son of Man will be fulfilled. [32]He will be handed over to the Gentiles. They will mock him, insult him, spit on him, flog him and kill him. [33]On the third day he will rise again."

[34]The disciples did not understand any of this. Its meaning was hidden from them, and they did not know what he was talking about.

A Blind Beggar Receives His Sight

[35]As Jesus approached Jericho, a blind man was sitting by the roadside begging. [36]When he heard the crowd going by, he asked what was happening. [37]They told him, "Jesus of Nazareth is passing by."

[38]He called out, "Jesus, Son of David, have mercy on me!"

[39]Those who led the way rebuked him and told him to be quiet, but he shouted all the more, "Son of David, have mercy on me!"

[40]Jesus stopped and ordered the man to be brought to him. When he came near, Jesus asked him, [41]"What do you want me to do for you?"

[a]20 Exodus 20:12-16; Deut. 5:16-20

"Lord, I want to see," he replied.

⁴²Jesus said to him, "Receive your sight; your faith has healed you."
⁴³Immediately he received his sight and followed Jesus, praising God. When
all the people saw it, they also praised God.

Zacchaeus the Tax Collector

19 Jesus entered Jericho and was passing through. ²A man was there by
the name of Zacchaeus; he was a chief tax collector and was wealthy.
³He wanted to see who Jesus was, but being a short man he could not,
because of the crowd. ⁴So he ran ahead and climbed a sycamore-fig tree to
see him, since Jesus was coming that way.

⁵When Jesus reached the spot, he looked up and said to him, "Zacchaeus, come down immediately. I must stay at your house today." ⁶So he
came down at once and welcomed him gladly.

⁷All the people saw this and began to mutter, "He has gone to be the
guest of a 'sinner.' "

⁸But Zacchaeus stood up and said to the Lord, "Look, Lord! Here and
now I give half of my possessions to the poor, and if I have cheated anybody
out of anything, I will pay back four times the amount."

⁹Jesus said to him, "Today salvation has come to this house, because
this man, too, is a son of Abraham. ¹⁰For the Son of Man came to seek and
to save what was lost."

The Parable of the Ten Minas

¹¹While they were listening to this, he went on to tell them a parable,
because he was near Jerusalem and the people thought that the kingdom
of God was going to appear at once. ¹²He said: "A man of noble birth went
to a distant country to have himself appointed king and then to return. ¹³So
he called ten of his servants and gave them ten minas.ᵃ 'Put this money to
work,' he said, 'until I come back.'

¹⁴"But his subjects hated him and sent a delegation after him to say, 'We
don't want this man to be our king.'

¹⁵"He was made king, however, and returned home. Then he sent for
the servants to whom he had given the money, in order to find out what
they had gained with it.

¹⁶"The first one came and said, 'Sir, your mina has earned ten more.'

¹⁷" 'Well done, my good servant!' his master replied. 'Because you have
been trustworthy in a very small matter, take charge of ten cities.'

¹⁸"The second came and said, 'Sir, your mina has earned five more.'

¹⁹"His master answered, 'You take charge of five cities.'

²⁰"Then another servant came and said, 'Sir, here is your mina; I have
kept it laid away in a piece of cloth. ²¹I was afraid of you, because you are
a hard man. You take out what you did not put in and reap what you did
not sow.'

²²"His master replied, 'I will judge you by your own words, you wicked

ᵃ13 A mina was about three months' wages.

servant! You knew, did you, that I am a hard man, taking out what I did not put in, and reaping what I did not sow? ²³Why then didn't you put my money on deposit, so that when I came back, I could have collected it with interest?'

²⁴"Then he said to those standing by, 'Take his mina away from him and give it to the one who has ten minas.'

²⁵"'Sir,' they said, 'he already has ten!'

²⁶"He replied, 'I tell you that to everyone who has, more will be given, but as for the one who has nothing, even what he has will be taken away. ²⁷But those enemies of mine who did not want me to be king over them—bring them here and kill them in front of me.' "

The Triumphal Entry

²⁸After Jesus had said this, he went on ahead, going up to Jerusalem. ²⁹As he approached Bethphage and Bethany at the hill called the Mount of Olives, he sent two of his disciples, saying to them, ³⁰"Go to the village ahead of you, and as you enter it, you will find a colt tied there, which no one has ever ridden. Untie it and bring it here. ³¹If anyone asks you, 'Why are you untying it?' tell him, 'The Lord needs it.' "

³²Those who were sent ahead went and found it just as he had told them. ³³As they were untying the colt, its owners asked them, "Why are you untying the colt?"

³⁴They replied, "The Lord needs it."

³⁵They brought it to Jesus, threw their cloaks on the colt and put Jesus on it. ³⁶As he went along, people spread their cloaks on the road.

³⁷When he came near the place where the road goes down the Mount of Olives, the whole crowd of disciples began joyfully to praise God in loud voices for all the miracles they had seen:

³⁸"Blessed is the king who comes in the name of the Lord!"[a]

"Peace in heaven and glory in the highest!"

³⁹Some of the Pharisees in the crowd said to Jesus, "Teacher, rebuke your disciples!"

⁴⁰"I tell you," he replied, "if they keep quiet, the stones will cry out."

⁴¹As he approached Jerusalem and saw the city, he wept over it ⁴²and said, "If you, even you, had only known on this day what would bring you peace—but now it is hidden from your eyes. ⁴³The days will come upon you when your enemies will build an embankment against you and encircle you and hem you in on every side. ⁴⁴They will dash you to the ground, you and the children within your walls. They will not leave one stone on another, because you did not recognize the time of God's coming to you."

Jesus at the Temple

⁴⁵Then he entered the temple area and began driving out those who

a38 Psalm 118:26

were selling. ⁴⁶"It is written," he said to them, " 'My house will be a house of prayer'ᵃ; but you have made it 'a den of robbers.'ᵇ"

⁴⁷Every day he was teaching at the temple. But the chief priests, the teachers of the law and the leaders among the people were trying to kill him. ⁴⁸Yet they could not find any way to do it, because all the people hung on his words.

The Authority of Jesus Questioned

20 One day as he was teaching the people in the temple courts and preaching the gospel, the chief priests and the teachers of the law, together with the elders, came up to him. ²"Tell us by what authority you are doing these things," they said. "Who gave you this authority?"

³He replied, "I will also ask you a question. Tell me, ⁴John's baptism— was it from heaven, or from men?"

⁵They discussed it among themselves and said, "If we say, 'From heaven,' he will ask, 'Why didn't you believe him?' ⁶But if we say, 'From men,' all the people will stone us, because they are persuaded that John was a prophet."

⁷So they answered, "We don't know where it was from."

⁸Jesus said, "Neither will I tell you by what authority I am doing these things."

The Parable of the Tenants

⁹He went on to tell the people this parable: "A man planted a vineyard, rented it to some farmers and went away for a long time. ¹⁰At harvest time he sent a servant to the tenants so they would give him some of the fruit of the vineyard. But the tenants beat him and sent him away empty-handed. ¹¹He sent another servant, but that one also they beat and treated shamefully and sent away empty-handed. ¹²He sent still a third, and they wounded him and threw him out.

¹³"Then the owner of the vineyard said, 'What shall I do? I will send my son, whom I love; perhaps they will respect him.'

¹⁴"But when the tenants saw him, they talked the matter over. 'This is the heir,' they said. 'Let's kill him, and the inheritance will be ours.' ¹⁵So they threw him out of the vineyard and killed him.

"What then will the owner of the vineyard do to them? ¹⁶He will come and kill those tenants and give the vineyard to others."

When the people heard this, they said, "May this never be!"

¹⁷Jesus looked directly at them and asked, "Then what is the meaning of that which is written:

" 'The stone the builders rejected
has become the capstoneᶜ ᵈ?

¹⁸Everyone who falls on that stone will be broken to pieces, but he on whom it falls will be crushed."

ᵃ46 Isaiah 56:7   ᵇ46 Jer. 7:11   ᶜ17 Or *cornerstone*   ᵈ17 Psalm 118:22

[19]The teachers of the law and the chief priests looked for a way to arrest him immediately, because they knew he had spoken this parable against them. But they were afraid of the people.

Paying Taxes to Caesar

[20]Keeping a close watch on him, they sent spies, who pretended to be honest. They hoped to catch Jesus in something he said so that they might hand him over to the power and authority of the governor. [21]So the spies questioned him: "Teacher, we know that you speak and teach what is right, and that you do not show partiality but teach the way of God in accordance with the truth. [22]Is it right for us to pay taxes to Caesar or not?"

[23]He saw through their duplicity and said to them, [24]"Show me a denarius. Whose portrait and inscription are on it?"

[25]"Caesar's," they replied.

He said to them, "Then give to Caesar what is Caesar's, and to God what is God's."

[26]They were unable to trap him in what he had said there in public. And astonished by his answer, they became silent.

The Resurrection and Marriage

[27]Some of the Sadducees, who say there is no resurrection, came to Jesus with a question. [28]"Teacher," they said, "Moses wrote for us that if a man's brother dies and leaves a wife but no children, the man must marry the widow and have children for his brother. [29]Now there were seven brothers. The first one married a woman and died childless. [30]The second [31]and then the third married her, and in the same way the seven died, leaving no children. [32]Finally, the woman died too. [33]Now then, at the resurrection whose wife will she be, since the seven were married to her?"

[34]Jesus replied, "The people of this age marry and are given in marriage. [35]But those who are considered worthy of taking part in that age and in the resurrection from the dead will neither marry nor be given in marriage, [36]and they can no longer die; for they are like the angels. They are God's children, since they are children of the resurrection. [37]But in the account of the bush, even Moses showed that the dead rise, for he calls the Lord 'the God of Abraham, and the God of Isaac, and the God of Jacob.'[a] [38]He is not the God of the dead, but of the living, for to him all are alive."

[39]Some of the teachers of the law responded, "Well said, teacher!" [40]And no one dared to ask him any more questions.

Whose Son Is the Christ?

[41]Then Jesus said to them, "How is it that they say the Christ[b] is the Son of David? [42]David himself declares in the Book of Psalms:

> " 'The Lord said to my Lord:
> "Sit at my right hand

[a]37 Exodus 3:6   [b]41 Or Messiah

> [43] until I make your enemies
> a footstool for your feet.' " [a]

[44] David calls him 'Lord.' How then can he be his son?"

[45] While all the people were listening, Jesus said to his disciples, [46] "Beware of the teachers of the law. They like to walk around in flowing robes and love to be greeted in the marketplaces and have the most important seats in the synagogues and the places of honor at banquets. [47] They devour widows' houses and for a show make lengthy prayers. Such men will be punished most severely."

The Widow's Offering

21 As he looked up, Jesus saw the rich putting their gifts into the temple treasury. [2] He also saw a poor widow put in two very small copper coins. [b] [3] "I tell you the truth," he said, "this poor widow has put in more than all the others. [4] All these people gave their gifts out of their wealth; but she out of her poverty put in all she had to live on."

Signs of the End of the Age

[5] Some of his disciples were remarking about how the temple was adorned with beautiful stones and with gifts dedicated to God. But Jesus said, [6] "As for what you see here, the time will come when not one stone will be left on another; every one of them will be thrown down."

[7] "Teacher," they asked, "when will these things happen? And what will be the sign that they are about to take place?"

[8] He replied: "Watch out that you are not deceived. For many will come in my name, claiming, 'I am he,' and, 'The time is near.' Do not follow them. [9] When you hear of wars and revolutions, do not be frightened. These things must happen first, but the end will not come right away."

[10] Then he said to them: "Nation will rise against nation, and kingdom against kingdom. [11] There will be great earthquakes, famines and pestilences in various places, and fearful events and great signs from heaven.

[12] "But before all this, they will lay hands on you and persecute you. They will deliver you to synagogues and prisons, and you will be brought before kings and governors, and all on account of my name. [13] This will result in your being witnesses to them. [14] But make up your mind not to worry beforehand how you will defend yourselves. [15] For I will give you words and wisdom that none of your adversaries will be able to resist or contradict. [16] You will be betrayed even by parents, brothers, relatives and friends, and they will put some of you to death. [17] All men will hate you because of me. [18] But not a hair of your head will perish. [19] By standing firm you will gain life.

[20] "When you see Jerusalem being surrounded by armies, you will know that its desolation is near. [21] Then let those who are in Judea flee to the mountains, let those in the city get out, and let those in the country not

[a] 43 Psalm 110:1   [b] 2 Greek two lepta

enter the city. ²²For this is the time of punishment in fulfillment of all that has been written. ²³How dreadful it will be in those days for pregnant women and nursing mothers! There will be great distress in the land and wrath against this people. ²⁴They will fall by the sword and will be taken as prisoners to all the nations. Jerusalem will be trampled on by the Gentiles until the times of the Gentiles are fulfilled.

²⁵"There will be signs in the sun, moon and stars. On the earth, nations will be in anguish and perplexity at the roaring and tossing of the sea. ²⁶Men will faint from terror, apprehensive of what is coming on the world, for the heavenly bodies will be shaken. ²⁷At that time they will see the Son of Man coming in a cloud with power and great glory. ²⁸When these things begin to take place, stand up and lift up your heads, because your redemption is drawing near."

²⁹He told them this parable: "Look at the fig tree and all the trees. ³⁰When they sprout leaves, you can see for yourselves and know that summer is near. ³¹Even so, when you see these things happening, you know that the kingdom of God is near.

³²"I tell you the truth, this generation*ᵃ* will certainly not pass away until all these things have happened. ³³Heaven and earth will pass away, but my words will never pass away.

³⁴"Be careful, or your hearts will be weighed down with dissipation, drunkenness and the anxieties of life, and that day will close on you unexpectedly like a trap. ³⁵For it will come upon all those who live on the face of the whole earth. ³⁶Be always on the watch, and pray that you may be able to escape all that is about to happen, and that you may be able to stand before the Son of Man."

³⁷Each day Jesus was teaching at the temple, and each evening he went out to spend the night on the hill called the Mount of Olives, ³⁸and all the people came early in the morning to hear him at the temple.

Judas Agrees to Betray Jesus

22 Now the Feast of Unleavened Bread, called the Passover, was approaching, ²and the chief priests and the teachers of the law were looking for some way to get rid of Jesus, for they were afraid of the people. ³Then Satan entered Judas, called Iscariot, one of the Twelve. ⁴And Judas went to the chief priests and the officers of the temple guard and discussed with them how he might betray Jesus. ⁵They were delighted and agreed to give him money. ⁶He consented, and watched for an opportunity to hand Jesus over to them when no crowd was present.

The Last Supper

⁷Then came the day of Unleavened Bread on which the Passover lamb had to be sacrificed. ⁸Jesus sent Peter and John, saying, "Go and make preparations for us to eat the Passover."

⁹"Where do you want us to prepare for it?" they asked.

ᵃ32 Or *race*

141

¹⁰He replied, "As you enter the city, a man carrying a jar of water will meet you. Follow him to the house that he enters, ¹¹and say to the owner of the house, 'The Teacher asks: Where is the guest room, where I may eat the Passover with my disciples?' ¹²He will show you a large upper room, all furnished. Make preparations there."

¹³They left and found things just as Jesus had told them. So they prepared the Passover.

¹⁴When the hour came, Jesus and his apostles reclined at the table. ¹⁵And he said to them, "I have eagerly desired to eat this Passover with you before I suffer. ¹⁶For I tell you, I will not eat it again until it finds fulfillment in the kingdom of God."

¹⁷After taking the cup, he gave thanks and said, "Take this and divide it among you. ¹⁸For I tell you I will not drink again of the fruit of the vine until the kingdom of God comes."

¹⁹And he took bread, gave thanks and broke it, and gave it to them, saying, "This is my body given for you; do this in remembrance of me."

²⁰In the same way, after the supper he took the cup, saying, "This cup is the new covenant in my blood, which is poured out for you. ²¹But the hand of him who is going to betray me is with mine on the table. ²²The Son of Man will go as it has been decreed, but woe to that man who betrays him." ²³They began to question among themselves which of them it might be who would do this.

²⁴Also a dispute arose among them as to which of them was considered to be greatest. ²⁵Jesus said to them, "The kings of the Gentiles lord it over them; and those who exercise authority over them call themselves Benefactors. ²⁶But you are not to be like that. Instead, the greatest among you should be like the youngest, and the one who rules like the one who serves. ²⁷For who is greater, the one who is at the table or the one who serves? Is it not the one who is at the table? But I am among you as one who serves. ²⁸You are those who have stood by me in my trials. ²⁹And I confer on you a kingdom, just as my Father conferred one on me, ³⁰so that you may eat and drink at my table in my kingdom and sit on thrones, judging the twelve tribes of Israel.

³¹"Simon, Simon, Satan has asked to sift you[a] as wheat. ³²But I have prayed for you, Simon, that your faith may not fail. And when you have turned back, strengthen your brothers."

³³But he replied, "Lord, I am ready to go with you to prison and to death."

³⁴Jesus answered, "I tell you, Peter, before the rooster crows today, you will deny three times that you know me."

³⁵Then Jesus asked them, "When I sent you without purse, bag or sandals, did you lack anything?"

"Nothing," they answered.

³⁶He said to them, "But now if you have a purse, take it, and also a bag; and if you don't have a sword, sell your cloak and buy one. ³⁷It is written:

a31 The Greek is plural.

'And he was numbered with the transgressors'*a*; and I tell you that this must be fulfilled in me. Yes, what is written about me is reaching its fulfillment."
[38]The disciples said, "See, Lord, here are two swords."
"That is enough," he replied.

Jesus Prays on the Mount of Olives

[39]Jesus went out as usual to the Mount of Olives, and his disciples followed him. [40]On reaching the place, he said to them, "Pray that you will not fall into temptation." [41]He withdrew about a stone's throw beyond them, knelt down and prayed, [42]"Father, if you are willing, take this cup from me; yet not my will, but yours be done." [43]An angel from heaven appeared to him and strengthened him. [44]And being in anguish, he prayed more earnestly, and his sweat was like drops of blood falling to the ground. *b*

[45]When he rose from prayer and went back to the disciples, he found them asleep, exhausted from sorrow. [46]"Why are you sleeping?" he asked them. "Get up and pray so that you will not fall into temptation."

Jesus Arrested

[47]While he was still speaking a crowd came up, and the man who was called Judas, one of the Twelve, was leading them. He approached Jesus to kiss him, [48]but Jesus asked him, "Judas, are you betraying the Son of Man with a kiss?"
[49]When Jesus' followers saw what was going to happen, they said, "Lord, should we strike with our swords?" [50]And one of them struck the servant of the high priest, cutting off his right ear.
[51]But Jesus answered, "No more of this!" And he touched the man's ear and healed him.
[52]Then Jesus said to the chief priests, the officers of the temple guard, and the elders, who had come for him, "Am I leading a rebellion, that you have come with swords and clubs? [53]Every day I was with you in the temple courts, and you did not lay a hand on me. But this is your hour—when darkness reigns."

Peter Disowns Jesus

[54]Then seizing him, they led him away and took him into the house of the high priest. Peter followed at a distance. [55]But when they had kindled a fire in the middle of the courtyard and had sat down together, Peter sat down with them. [56]A servant girl saw him seated there in the firelight. She looked closely at him and said, "This man was with him."
[57]But he denied it. "Woman, I don't know him," he said.
[58]A little later someone else saw him and said, "You also are one of them."
"Man, I am not!" Peter replied.
[59]About an hour later another asserted, "Certainly this fellow was with him, for he is a Galilean."

*a*37 Isaiah 53:12   *b*44 Some early manuscripts do not have verses 43 and 44.

⁶⁰Peter replied, "Man, I don't know what you're talking about!" Just as he was speaking, the rooster crowed. ⁶¹The Lord turned and looked straight at Peter. Then Peter remembered the word the Lord had spoken to him: "Before the rooster crows today, you will disown me three times." ⁶²And he went outside and wept bitterly.

The Soldiers Mock Jesus

⁶³The men who were guarding Jesus began mocking and beating him. ⁶⁴They blindfolded him and demanded, "Prophesy! Who hit you?" ⁶⁵And they said many other insulting things to him.

Jesus Before Pilate and Herod

⁶⁶At daybreak the council of the elders of the people, both the chief priests and teachers of the law, met together, and Jesus was led before them. ⁶⁷"If you are the Christ,ᵃ" they said, "tell us."

Jesus answered, "If I tell you, you will not believe me, ⁶⁸and if I asked you, you would not answer. ⁶⁹But from now on, the Son of Man will be seated at the right hand of the mighty God."

⁷⁰They all asked, "Are you then the Son of God?"

He replied, "You are right in saying I am."

⁷¹Then they said, "Why do we need any more testimony? We have heard it from his own lips."

23 Then the whole assembly rose and led him off to Pilate. ²And they began to accuse him, saying, "We have found this man subverting our nation. He opposes payment of taxes to Caesar and claims to be Christ,ᵇ a king."

³So Pilate asked Jesus, "Are you the king of the Jews?"

"Yes, it is as you say," Jesus replied.

⁴Then Pilate announced to the chief priests and the crowd, "I find no basis for a charge against this man."

⁵But they insisted, "He stirs up the people all over Judeaᶜ by his teaching. He started in Galilee and has come all the way here."

⁶On hearing this, Pilate asked if the man was a Galilean. ⁷When he learned that Jesus was under Herod's jurisdiction, he sent him to Herod, who was also in Jerusalem at that time.

⁸When Herod saw Jesus, he was greatly pleased, because for a long time he had been wanting to see him. From what he had heard about him, he hoped to see him perform some miracle. ⁹He plied him with many questions, but Jesus gave him no answer. ¹⁰The chief priests and the teachers of the law were standing there, vehemently accusing him. ¹¹Then Herod and his soldiers ridiculed and mocked him. Dressing him in an elegant robe, they sent him back to Pilate. ¹²That day Herod and Pilate became friends—before this they had been enemies.

¹³Pilate called together the chief priests, the rulers and the people, ¹⁴and said to them, "You brought me this man as one who was inciting the people

ᵃ67 Or Messiah   ᵇ2 Or Messiah; also in verses 35 and 39   ᶜ5 Or over the land of the Jews to rebellion. I have examined him in your presence and have found no basis for your charges against him. [15]Neither has Herod, for he sent him back to us; as you can see, he has done nothing to deserve death. [16]Therefore, I will punish him and then release him. [a]"

[18]With one voice they cried out, "Away with this man! Release Barabbas to us!" [19](Barabbas had been thrown into prison for an insurrection in the city, and for murder.)

[20]Wanting to release Jesus, Pilate appealed to them again. [21]But they kept shouting, "Crucify him! Crucify him!"

[22]For the third time he spoke to them: "Why? What crime has this man committed? I have found in him no grounds for the death penalty. Therefore I will have him punished and then release him."

[23]But with loud shouts they insistently demanded that he be crucified, and their shouts prevailed. [24]So Pilate decided to grant their demand. [25]He released the man who had been thrown into prison for insurrection and murder, the one they asked for, and surrendered Jesus to their will.

The Crucifixion

[26]As they led him away, they seized Simon from Cyrene, who was on his way in from the country, and put the cross on him and made him carry it behind Jesus. [27]A large number of people followed him, including women who mourned and wailed for him. [28]Jesus turned and said to them, "Daughters of Jerusalem, do not weep for me; weep for yourselves and for your children. [29]For the time will come when you will say, 'Blessed are the barren women, the wombs that never bore and the breasts that never nursed!' [30]Then

> " 'they will say to the mountains, "Fall on us!"
> and to the hills, "Cover us!" ' [b]

[31]For if men do these things when the tree is green, what will happen when it is dry?"

[32]Two other men, both criminals, were also led out with him to be executed. [33]When they came to the place called the Skull, there they crucified him, along with the criminals—one on his right, the other on his left. [34]Jesus said, "Father, forgive them, for they do not know what they are doing." [c] And they divided up his clothes by casting lots.

[35]The people stood watching, and the rulers even sneered at him. They said, "He saved others; let him save himself if he is the Christ of God, the Chosen One."

[36]The soldiers also came up and mocked him. They offered him wine vinegar [37]and said, "If you are the king of the Jews, save yourself."

[38]There was a written notice above him, which read: THIS IS THE KING OF THE JEWS.

[a]16 Some manuscripts him." [17]Now he was obliged to release one man to them at the Feast.   [b]30 Hosea 10:8   [c]34 Some early manuscripts do not have this sentence.

³⁹One of the criminals who hung there hurled insults at him: "Aren't you the Christ? Save yourself and us!"

⁴⁰But the other criminal rebuked him. "Don't you fear God," he said, "since you are under the same sentence? ⁴¹We are punished justly, for we are getting what our deeds deserve. But this man has done nothing wrong."

⁴²Then he said, "Jesus, remember me when you come into your kingdom.^a"

⁴³Jesus answered him, "I tell you the truth, today you will be with me in paradise."

Jesus' Death

⁴⁴It was now about the sixth hour, and darkness came over the whole land until the ninth hour, ⁴⁵for the sun stopped shining. And the curtain of the temple was torn in two. ⁴⁶Jesus called out with a loud voice, "Father, into your hands I commit my spirit." When he had said this, he breathed his last.

⁴⁷The centurion, seeing what had happened, praised God and said, "Surely this was a righteous man." ⁴⁸When all the people who had gathered to witness this sight saw what took place, they beat their breasts and went away. ⁴⁹But all those who knew him, including the women who had followed him from Galilee, stood at a distance, watching these things.

Jesus' Burial

⁵⁰Now there was a man named Joseph, a member of the Council, a good and upright man, ⁵¹who had not consented to their decision and action. He came from the Judean town of Arimathea and he was waiting for the kingdom of God. ⁵²Going to Pilate, he asked for Jesus' body. ⁵³Then he took it down, wrapped it in linen cloth and placed it in a tomb cut in the rock, one in which no one had yet been laid. ⁵⁴It was Preparation Day, and the Sabbath was about to begin.

⁵⁵The women who had come with Jesus from Galilee followed Joseph and saw the tomb and how his body was laid in it. ⁵⁶Then they went home and prepared spices and perfumes. But they rested on the Sabbath in obedience to the commandment.

The Resurrection

24 On the first day of the week, very early in the morning, the women took the spices they had prepared and went to the tomb. ²They found the stone rolled away from the tomb, ³but when they entered, they did not find the body of the Lord Jesus. ⁴While they were wondering about this, suddenly two men in clothes that gleamed like lightning stood beside them. ⁵In their fright the women bowed down with their faces to the ground, but the men said to them, "Why do you look for the living among the dead? ⁶He is not here; he has risen! Remember how he told you, while he was still with you in Galilee: ⁷'The Son of Man must be delivered into the hands of

^a42 Some manuscripts *come with your kingly power*

sinful men, be crucified and on the third day be raised again.' " ⁸Then they remembered his words.

⁹When they came back from the tomb, they told all these things to the Eleven and to all the others. ¹⁰It was Mary Magdalene, Joanna, Mary the mother of James, and the others with them who told this to the apostles. ¹¹But they did not believe the women, because their words seemed to them like nonsense. ¹²Peter, however, got up and ran to the tomb. Bending over, he saw the strips of linen lying by themselves, and he went away, wondering to himself what had happened.

On the Road to Emmaus

¹³Now that same day two of them were going to a village called Emmaus, about seven miles*a* from Jerusalem. ¹⁴They were talking with each other about everything that had happened. ¹⁵As they talked and discussed these things with each other, Jesus himself came up and walked along with them; ¹⁶but they were kept from recognizing him.

¹⁷He asked them, "What are you discussing together as you walk along?"

They stood still, their faces downcast. ¹⁸One of them, named Cleopas, asked him, "Are you only a visitor to Jerusalem and do not know the things that have happened there in these days?"

¹⁹"What things?" he asked.

"About Jesus of Nazareth," they replied. "He was a prophet, powerful in word and deed before God and all the people. ²⁰The chief priests and our rulers handed him over to be sentenced to death, and they crucified him; ²¹but we had hoped that he was the one who was going to redeem Israel. And what is more, it is the third day since all this took place. ²²In addition, some of our women amazed us. They went to the tomb early this morning ²³but didn't find his body. They came and told us that they had seen a vision of angels, who said he was alive. ²⁴Then some of our companions went to the tomb and found it just as the women had said, but him they did not see."

²⁵He said to them, "How foolish you are, and how slow of heart to believe all that the prophets have spoken! ²⁶Did not the Christ*b* have to suffer these things and then enter his glory?" ²⁷And beginning with Moses and all the Prophets, he explained to them what was said in all the Scriptures concerning himself.

²⁸As they approached the village to which they were going, Jesus acted as if he were going farther. ²⁹But they urged him strongly, "Stay with us, for it is nearly evening; the day is almost over." So he went in to stay with them.

³⁰When he was at the table with them, he took bread, gave thanks, broke it and began to give it to them. ³¹Then their eyes were opened and they recognized him, and he disappeared from their sight. ³²They asked

---

a13 Greek *sixty stadia* (about 11 kilometers)   *b26* Or *Messiah*; also in verse 46 each other, "Were not our hearts burning within us while he talked with us on the road and opened the Scriptures to us?"

³³They got up and returned at once to Jerusalem. There they found the Eleven and those with them, assembled together ³⁴and saying, "It is true! The Lord has risen and has appeared to Simon." ³⁵Then the two told what had happened on the way, and how Jesus was recognized by them when he broke the bread.

Jesus Appears to the Disciples

³⁶While they were still talking about this, Jesus himself stood among them and said to them, "Peace be with you."

³⁷They were startled and frightened, thinking they saw a ghost. ³⁸He said to them, "Why are you troubled, and why do doubts rise in your minds? ³⁹Look at my hands and my feet. It is I myself! Touch me and see; a ghost does not have flesh and bones, as you see I have."

⁴⁰When he had said this, he showed them his hands and feet. ⁴¹And while they still did not believe it because of joy and amazement, he asked them, "Do you have anything here to eat?" ⁴²They gave him a piece of broiled fish, ⁴³and he took it and ate it in their presence.

⁴⁴He said to them, "This is what I told you while I was still with you: Everything must be fulfilled that is written about me in the Law of Moses, the Prophets and the Psalms."

⁴⁵Then he opened their minds so they could understand the Scriptures. ⁴⁶He told them, "This is what is written: The Christ will suffer and rise from the dead on the third day, ⁴⁷and repentance and forgiveness of sins will be preached in his name to all nations, beginning at Jerusalem. ⁴⁸You are witnesses of these things. ⁴⁹I am going to send you what my Father has promised; but stay in the city until you have been clothed with power from on high."

The Ascension

⁵⁰When he had led them out to the vicinity of Bethany, he lifted up his hands and blessed them. ⁵¹While he was blessing them, he left them and was taken up into heaven. ⁵²Then they worshiped him and returned to Jerusalem with great joy. ⁵³And they stayed continually at the temple, praising God.

John

INTRODUCTION

The Gospel of John addresses the word of God to believers today. We gain insights into our common Christian heritage and receive guidance for personal religious life. Like the Synoptic Gospels, the Fourth Gospel tells of the life and death of the Lord but also has many distinctive approaches which separate it from the other Gospels. This introduction will not offer to the reader a complete analysis of the Gospel, but, rather, certain ideas, elements, and themes will be chosen to give assistance as the reader actually opens the book, studies and prays over this most unusual testimony of the Lord Jesus.

The actual origin and early history of the Gospel remains in shadows. A growing consensus discovers a collection of miracle stories and possibly a collection of homilies delivered by the Beloved Disciple to his Christian community. All will agree that the actual Gospel went through various stages of development before it reached its final form known to us. No theory is complete and thus need not occupy the attention of the reader other than that it might be useful to be aware of a long history of development in both an oral and written form.

The identity of the author also remains in shadows. More current opinion recognizes the Beloved Disciple, that interesting and somewhat mysterious unnamed figure who has an important role in the Fourth Gospel but does not appear elsewhere in the New Testament, as not being one of the twelve, nor John, the son of Zebedee, but still probably an eye-witness to the Jesus event. It seems that the Beloved Disciple was the founder of the community from which the Fourth Gospel arose. He must have been an eye-witness and not just another follower of Jesus because only thus could the Johannine community receive credibility as being a true and proper approach to the Jesus tradition. The Beloved Disciple as the founder of the community and source of its teaching and follower of the historical Jesus protected the community from rejection and misunderstanding by other Christian groups.

Although the Beloved Disciple was the ultimate source behind the Gospel, we should not necessarily infer that he was the actual author.

He may have been responsible for the early stage of the development but today scholars widely accept the presence of several hands in the final composition. The comparison of chapter twenty with chapter twenty-one shows two endings evidencing at least a final editor responsible for the last chapter. This editor may also be responsible for the prologue and some other insertions within the Gospel.

Most commentators place the Gospel's origin toward the end of the first century, probably in Syria. No one can pinpoint the exact time or place, but provided that an elastic time period of approximately fifteen years from 85 A.D. to 100 A.D. is accepted, the general reader may feel satisfied. In the history of interpretation several locations have been suggested: Ephesus, Alexandria and Antioch in Syria. Today many tend toward Antioch because of the cosmopolitan character of the city and the fact that it was a flourishing Christian center.

Certain themes run throughout the Gospel of John, making it truly distinct from the other Gospels. The author seems to have wanted to emphasize not the future world, but this world and the present reality, along with its human relationships. The Synoptics and Paul speak often of future hopes and expectations and the eternal life that will come. For this Gospel, salvation and eternal life are now: "This is eternal life: that they may know you, the only true God, and Jesus Christ, whom you have sent" (Jn 17:3). "I tell you the truth, whoever hears my word and believes him who sent me has eternal life and will not be condemned; he has crossed over

from death to life" (Jn 5:24).

The Synoptics emphasize the twofold love of God and neighbor as the fundamental commandments of Jesus (Mk 12:30; Mt 22:34-40; Lk 20:39-40). The Gospel of John speaks only of the new commandment, the love of the brethren (Jn 13:34). If people love one another, then they have fulfilled the command of the Lord.

The usual understanding of the Christian Church presupposes an ecclesiastical authority as well as the celebration of the sacraments. The Gospel of John shows little interest in either. In this Gospel Jesus does not send out his disciple with his authority as found in the Synoptics (Mt 10:5; Lk 9:1). The only true leader is Jesus the Good Shepherd and the only one who shares in this ministry, up to chapter twenty one, is the Spirit of the Paraclete.

In chapter twenty-one Peter shares in the pastoral ministry of Jesus but this chapter is a later addition to the Gospel, the result of the changing needs of the community. But no matter what opinion one may follow with regard to this chapter, when the reader compares this gospel with the Synoptics or the pastoral epistles, it becomes evident that this Gospel de-emphasizes the authority in the Church.

The author of John also seems to de-emphasize the sacraments of baptism and the Eucharist. He omits the baptism of Jesus and even in chapter three which has a reference to "water and the spirit" the emphasis is on the rebirth through the Spirit and not through water. This Gospel also contains the longest section on the Last Supper but nevertheless omits the institution of the Eucharist.

Throughout the Gospel the author concentrates on the two characteristics of Johannine Christianity: the personal faith commitment to the Lord and the love of the brethren. This fascinating interpretation of the meaning of Jesus will always give guidance and light to the Christian Church of every age. The Gospel remains the final testimony of the Beloved Disciple and his community to the Church. The careful reading of this testimony can only enrich the follower of the Lord.

JOHN F. O'GRADY

Points for Reflection

1. This Gospel stresses the centrality of the personal faith commitment to the Lord and the love of the brethren. How do I express this commitment and love? In what ways can I further develop these virtues?
2. The fullness of this living faith commitment is accomplished with the Holy Spirit. How does John describe the relationship between the Lord and the Holy Spirit? What else does the Spirit or Paraclete help us accomplish in our spiritual lives?
3. Contrast the manner in which baptismal and Eucharistic teachings are presented in this Gospel with the manner presented in the Synoptics.
4. The emphasis here is on the present life, or in theological terms, "realized eschatology." How can this emphasis bring me to terms with the world I live in, especially since I live with the threat of total annihilation through nuclear war?
5. "I and the Father are one." This is one example of how Jesus expressed his relationship with God. What are the other statements of Christ that describe this relationship? How does this compare with the ones presented in the Synoptics?
6. Mary, the Mother of God, the Beloved Disciple, and the Samaritan woman are representatives of ideal believers. How can modern believers use these representatives as role models?
7. Mary is also an Intercessor for us to the Lord. In your spiritual life does she play a role? Is she meaningful to you? What do you think of Mary's role in the Church today?

The Word Became Flesh

1 In the beginning was the Word, and the Word was with God, and the Word was God. ²He was with God in the beginning.

³Through him all things were made; without him nothing was made that has been made. ⁴In him was life, and that life was the light of men. ⁵The light shines in the darkness, but the darkness has not understood* it.

⁶There came a man who was sent from God; his name was John. ⁷He came as a witness to testify concerning that light, so that through him all men might believe. ⁸He himself was not the light; he came only as a witness to the light. ⁹The true light that gives light to every man was coming into the world.*

¹⁰He was in the world, and though the world was made through him, the world did not recognize him. ¹¹He came to that which was his own, but his own did not receive him. ¹²Yet to all who received him, to those who believed in his name, he gave the right to become children of God— ¹³children born not of natural descent,* nor of human decision or a husband's will, but born of God.

¹⁴The Word became flesh and made his dwelling among us. We have seen his glory, the glory of the One and Only,* who came from the Father, full of grace and truth.

¹⁵John testifies concerning him. He cries out, saying, "This was he of whom I said, 'He who comes after me has surpassed me because he was before me.'" ¹⁶From the fullness of his grace we have all received one blessing after another. ¹⁷For the law was given through Moses; grace and truth came through Jesus Christ. ¹⁸No one has ever seen God, but God the One and Only,* *who is at the Father's side, has made him known.

John the Baptist Denies Being the Christ

¹⁹Now this was John's testimony when the Jews of Jerusalem sent priests and Levites to ask him who he was. ²⁰He did not fail to confess, but confessed freely, "I am not the Christ.*"

²¹They asked him, "Then who are you? Are you Elijah?"

He said, "I am not."

"Are you the Prophet?"

He answered, "No."

²²Finally they said, "Who are you? Give us an answer to take back to those who sent us. What do you say about yourself?"

²³John replied in the words of Isaiah the prophet, "I am the voice of one calling in the desert, 'Make straight the way for the Lord.'"*

²⁴Now some Pharisees who had been sent ²⁵questioned him, "Why then do you baptize if you are not the Christ, nor Elijah, nor the Prophet?"

*a*5 Or *darkness, and the darkness has not overcome*   *b*9 Or *This was the true light that gives light to every man who comes into the world*   *c*13 Greek *of bloods*   *d*14,18 Or *the Only Begotten*   *e*18 Some manuscripts *but the only (or only begotten) Son*   *f*20 Or *Messiah*. "The Christ" (Greek) and "the Messiah" (Hebrew) both mean "the Anointed One"; also in verse 25.   *g*23 Isaiah 40:3

26"I baptize with^a water," John replied, "but among you stands one you do not know. 27He is the one who comes after me, the thongs of whose sandals I am not worthy to untie."

28This all happened at Bethany on the other side of the Jordan, where John was baptizing.

Jesus the Lamb of God

29The next day John saw Jesus coming toward him and said, "Look, the Lamb of God, who takes away the sin of the world! 30This is the one I meant when I said, 'A man who comes after me has surpassed me because he was before me.' 31I myself did not know him, but the reason I came baptizing with water was that he might be revealed to Israel."

32Then John gave this testimony: "I saw the Spirit come down from heaven as a dove and remain on him. 33I would not have known him, except that the one who sent me to baptize with water told me, 'The man on whom you see the Spirit come down and remain is he who will baptize with the Holy Spirit.' 34I have seen and I testify that this is the Son of God."

Jesus' First Disciples

35The next day John was there again with two of his disciples. 36When he saw Jesus passing by, he said, "Look, the Lamb of God!"

37When the two disciples heard him say this, they followed Jesus. 38Turning around, Jesus saw them following and asked, "What do you want?"

They said, "Rabbi" (which means Teacher), "where are you staying?"

39"Come," he replied, "and you will see."

So they went and saw where he was staying, and spent that day with him. It was about the tenth hour.

40Andrew, Simon Peter's brother, was one of the two who heard what John had said and who had followed Jesus. 41The first thing Andrew did was to find his brother Simon and tell him, "We have found the Messiah" (that is, the Christ). 42And he brought him to Jesus.

Jesus looked at him and said, "You are Simon son of John. You will be called Cephas" (which, when translated, is Peter^b).

Jesus Calls Philip and Nathanael

43The next day Jesus decided to leave for Galilee. Finding Philip, he said to him, "Follow me."

44Philip, like Andrew and Peter, was from the town of Bethsaida. 45Philip found Nathanael and told him, "We have found the one Moses wrote about in the Law, and about whom the prophets also wrote—Jesus of Nazareth, the son of Joseph."

46"Nazareth! Can anything good come from there?" Nathanael asked.

"Come and see," said Philip.

^a26 Or in; also in verses 31 and 33   ^b42 Both Cephas (Aramaic) and Peter (Greek) mean rock.

⁴⁷When Jesus saw Nathanael approaching, he said of him, "Here is a true Israelite, in whom there is nothing false."

⁴⁸"How do you know me?" Nathanael asked.

Jesus answered, "I saw you while you were still under the fig tree before Philip called you."

⁴⁹Then Nathanael declared, "Rabbi, you are the Son of God; you are the King of Israel."

⁵⁰Jesus said, "You believe*ᵃ* because I told you I saw you under the fig tree. You shall see greater things than that." ⁵¹He then added, "I tell you*ᵇ* the truth, you*ᵇ* shall see heaven open, and the angels of God ascending and descending on the Son of Man."

Jesus Changes Water to Wine

2 On the third day a wedding took place at Cana in Galilee. Jesus' mother was there, ²and Jesus and his disciples had also been invited to the wedding. ³When the wine was gone, Jesus' mother said to him, "They have no more wine."

⁴"Dear woman, why do you involve me?" Jesus replied, "My time has not yet come."

⁵His mother said to the servants, "Do whatever he tells you."

⁶Nearby stood six stone water jars, the kind used by the Jews for ceremonial washing, each holding from twenty to thirty gallons.*ᶜ*

⁷Jesus said to the servants, "Fill the jars with water"; so they filled them to the brim.

⁸Then he told them, "Now draw some out and take it to the master of the banquet."

They did so, ⁹and the master of the banquet tasted the water that had been turned into wine. He did not realize where it had come from, though the servants who had drawn the water knew. Then he called the bridegroom aside ¹⁰and said, "Everyone brings out the choice wine first and then the cheaper wine after the guests have had too much to drink; but you have saved the best till now."

¹¹This, the first of his miraculous signs, Jesus performed in Cana of Galilee. He thus revealed his glory, and his disciples put their faith in him.

Jesus Clears the Temple

¹²After this he went down to Capernaum with his mother and brothers and his disciples. There they stayed for a few days.

¹³When it was almost time for the Jewish Passover, Jesus went up to Jerusalem. ¹⁴In the temple courts he found men selling cattle, sheep and doves, and others sitting at tables exchanging money. ¹⁵So he made a whip out of cords, and drove all from the temple area, both sheep and cattle; he scattered the coins of the money changers and overturned their tables. ¹⁶To

---

*ᵃ50 Or Do you believe . . . ?   *ᵇ51 The Greek is plural.   *ᶜ6 Greek two to three metretes (probably about 75 to 115 liters) those who sold doves he said, "Get these out of here! How dare you turn my Father's house into a market!"

¹⁷His disciples remembered that it is written: "Zeal for your house will consume me."ᵃ

¹⁸Then the Jews demanded of him, "What miraculous sign can you show us to prove your authority to do all this?"

¹⁹Jesus answered them, "Destroy this temple, and I will raise it again in three days."

²⁰The Jews replied, "It has taken forty-six years to build this temple, and you are going to raise it in three days?" ²¹But the temple he had spoken of was his body. ²²After he was raised from the dead, his disciples recalled what he had said. Then they believed the Scripture and the words that Jesus had spoken.

²³Now while he was in Jerusalem at the Passover Feast, many people saw the miraculous signs he was doing and believed in his name.ᵇ ²⁴But Jesus would not entrust himself to them, for he knew all men. ²⁵He did not need man's testimony about man, for he knew what was in a man.

Jesus Teaches Nicodemus

3 Now there was a man of the Pharisees named Nicodemus, a member of the Jewish ruling council. ²He came to Jesus at night and said, "Rabbi, we know you are a teacher who has come from God. For no one could perform the miraculous signs you are doing if God were not with him."

³In reply Jesus declared, "I tell you the truth, no one can see the kingdom of God unless he is born again.ᶜ"

⁴"How can a man be born when he is old?" Nicodemus asked. "Surely he cannot enter a second time into his mother's womb to be born!"

⁵Jesus answered, "I tell you the truth, no one can enter the kingdom of God unless he is born of water and the Spirit. ⁶Flesh gives birth to flesh, but the Spiritᵈ gives birth to spirit. ⁷You should not be surprised at my saying, 'Youᵉ must be born again.' ⁸The wind blows wherever it pleases. You hear its sound, but you cannot tell where it comes from or where it is going. So it is with everyone born of the Spirit."

⁹"How can this be?" Nicodemus asked.

¹⁰"You are Israel's teacher," said Jesus, "and do you not understand these things? ¹¹I tell you the truth, we speak of what we know, and we testify to what we have seen, but still you people do not accept our testimony. ¹²I have spoken to you of earthly things and you do not believe; how then will you believe if I speak of heavenly things? ¹³No one has ever gone into heaven except the one who came from heaven—the Son of Man.ᶠ ¹⁴Just as Moses lifted up the snake in the desert, so the Son of Man must be lifted up, ¹⁵that everyone who believes in him may have eternal life.ᵍ

¹⁶"For God so loved the world that he gave his one and only Son,ʰ that

ᵃ17 Psalm 69:9   ᵇ23 Or *and believed in him*   ᶜ3 Or *born from above*; also in verse 7   ᵈ6 Or *but spirit*   ᵉ7 The Greek is plural.   ᶠ13 Some manuscripts *Man, who is in heaven*   ᵍ15 Or *believes may have eternal life in him*   ʰ16 Or *his only begotten Son*

155

whoever believes in him shall not perish but have eternal life. [17]For God did not send his Son into the world to condemn the world, but to save the world through him. [18]Whoever believes in him is not condemned, but whoever does not believe stands condemned already because he has not believed in the name of God's one and only Son.[a] [19]This is the verdict: Light has come into the world, but men loved darkness instead of light because their deeds were evil. [20]Everyone who does evil hates the light, and will not come into the light for fear that his deeds will be exposed. [21]But whoever lives by the truth comes into the light, so that it may be seen plainly that what he has done has been done through God."[b]

John the Baptist's Testimony About Jesus

[22]After this, Jesus and his disciples went out into the Judean country-side, where he spent some time with them, and baptized. [23]Now John also was baptizing at Aenon near Salim, because there was plenty of water, and people were constantly coming to be baptized. [24](This was before John was put in prison.) [25]An argument developed between some of John's disciples and a certain Jew[c] over the matter of ceremonial washing. [26]They came to John and said to him, "Rabbi, that man who was with you on the other side of the Jordan—the one you testified about—well, he is baptizing, and everyone is going to him."

[27]To this John replied, "A man can receive only what is given him from heaven. [28]You yourselves can testify that I said, 'I am not the Christ[d] but am sent ahead of him.' [29]The bride belongs to the bridegroom. The friend who attends the bridegroom waits and listens for him, and is full of joy when he hears the bridegroom's voice. That joy is mine, and it is now complete. [30]He must become greater; I must become less.

[31]"The one who comes from above is above all; the one who is from the earth belongs to the earth, and speaks as one from the earth. The one who comes from heaven is above all. [32]He testifies to what he has seen and heard, but no one accepts his testimony. [33]The man who has accepted it has certified that God is truthful. [34]For the one whom God has sent speaks the words of God, for God[e] gives the Spirit without limit. [35]The Father loves the Son and has placed everything in his hands. [36]Whoever believes in the Son has eternal life, but whoever rejects the Son will not see life, for God's wrath remains on him."[f]

Jesus Talks With a Samaritan Woman

4 The Pharisees heard that Jesus was gaining and baptizing more disciples than John, [2]although in fact it was not Jesus who baptized, but his disciples. [3]When the Lord learned of this, he left Judea and went back once more to Galilee.

[4]Now he had to go through Samaria. [5]So he came to a town in Samaria

---

[a]18 Or *God's only begotten Son*   [b]21 Some interpreters end the quotation after verse 15.
[c]25 Some manuscripts *and certain Jews*   [d]28 Or *Messiah*   [e]34 Greek *he*   [f]36 Some interpreters end the quotation after verse 30.

called Sychar, near the plot of ground Jacob had given to his son Joseph. [6]Jacob's well was there, and Jesus, tired as he was from the journey, sat down by the well. It was about the sixth hour.

[7]When a Samaritan woman came to draw water, Jesus said to her, "Will you give me a drink?" [8](His disciples had gone into the town to buy food.)

[9]The Samaritan woman said to him, "You are a Jew and I am a Samaritan woman. How can you ask me for a drink?" (For Jews do not associate with Samaritans. [a])

[10]Jesus answered her, "If you knew the gift of God and who it is that asks you for a drink, you would have asked him and he would have given you living water."

[11]"Sir," the woman said, "you have nothing to draw with and the well is deep. Where can you get this living water? [12]Are you greater than our father Jacob, who gave us the well and drank from it himself, as did also his sons and his flocks and herds?"

[13]Jesus answered, "Everyone who drinks this water will be thirsty again, [14]but whoever drinks the water I give him will never thirst. Indeed, the water I give him will become in him a spring of water welling up to eternal life."

[15]The woman said to him, "Sir, give me this water so that I won't get thirsty and have to keep coming here to draw water."

[16]He told her, "Go, call your husband and come back."

[17]"I have no husband," she replied.

Jesus said to her, "You are right when you say you have no husband. [18]The fact is, you have had five husbands, and the man you now have is not your husband. What you have just said is quite true."

[19]"Sir," the woman said, "I can see that you are a prophet. [20]Our fathers worshiped on this mountain, but you Jews claim that the place where we must worship is in Jerusalem."

[21]Jesus declared, "Believe me, woman, a time is coming when you will worship the Father neither on this mountain nor in Jerusalem. [22]You Samaritans worship what you do not know; we worship what we do know, for salvation is from the Jews. [23]Yet a time is coming and has now come when the true worshipers will worship the Father in spirit and truth, for they are the kind of worshipers the Father seeks. [24]God is spirit, and his worshipers must worship in spirit and in truth."

[25]The woman said, "I know that Messiah" (called Christ) "is coming. When he comes, he will explain everything to us."

[26]Then Jesus declared, "I who speak to you am he."

The Disciples Rejoin Jesus

[27]Just then his disciples returned and were surprised to find him talking with a woman. But no one asked, "What do you want?" or "Why are you talking with her?"

[28]Then, leaving her water jar, the woman went back to the town and

[a]9 Or *do not use dishes Samaritans have used*

said to the people, ²⁹"Come, see a man who told me everything I ever did. Could this be the Christ*?" ³⁰They came out of the town and made their way toward him.

³¹Meanwhile his disciples urged him, "Rabbi, eat something."

³²But he said to them, "I have food to eat that you know nothing about."

³³Then his disciples said to each other, "Could someone have brought him food?"

³⁴"My food," said Jesus, "is to do the will of him who sent me and to finish his work. ³⁵Do you not say, 'Four months more and then the harvest'? I tell you, open your eyes and look at the fields! They are ripe for harvest. ³⁶Even now the reaper draws his wages, even now he harvests the crop for eternal life, so that the sower and the reaper may be glad together. ³⁷Thus the saying 'One sows and another reaps' is true. ³⁸I sent you to reap what you have not worked for. Others have done the hard work, and you have reaped the benefits of their labor."

Many Samaritans Believe

³⁹Many of the Samaritans from that town believed in him because of the woman's testimony, "He told me everything I ever did." ⁴⁰So when the Samaritans came to him, they urged him to stay with them, and he stayed two days. ⁴¹And because of his words many more became believers.

⁴²They said to the woman, "We no longer believe just because of what you said; now we have heard for ourselves, and we know that this man really is the Savior of the world."

Jesus Heals the Official's Son

⁴³After the two days he left for Galilee. ⁴⁴(Now Jesus himself had pointed out that a prophet has no honor in his own country.) ⁴⁵When he arrived in Galilee, the Galileans welcomed him. They had seen all that he had done in Jerusalem at the Passover Feast, for they also had been there.

⁴⁶Once more he visited Cana in Galilee, where he had turned the water into wine. And there was a certain royal official whose son lay sick at Capernaum. ⁴⁷When this man heard that Jesus had arrived in Galilee from Judea, he went to him and begged him to come and heal his son, who was close to death.

⁴⁸"Unless you people see miraculous signs and wonders," Jesus told him, "you will never believe."

⁴⁹The royal official said, "Sir, come down before my child dies."

⁵⁰Jesus replied, "You may go. Your son will live."

The man took Jesus at his word and departed. ⁵¹While he was still on the way, his servants met him with the news that his boy was living. ⁵²When he inquired as to the time when his son got better, they said to him, "The fever left him yesterday at the seventh hour."

⁵³Then the father realized that this was the exact time at which Jesus

*29 Or *Messiah*

had said to him, "Your son will live." So he and all his household believed.

⁵⁴This was the second miraculous sign that Jesus performed, having come from Judea to Galilee.

The Healing at the Pool

5 Some time later, Jesus went up to Jerusalem for a feast of the Jews. ²Now there is in Jerusalem near the Sheep Gate a pool, which in Aramaic is called Bethesda*a* and which is surrounded by five covered colonnades. ³Here a great number of disabled people used to lie—the blind, the lame, the paralyzed.*b* ⁵One who was there had been an invalid for thirty-eight years. ⁶When Jesus saw him lying there and learned that he had been in this condition for a long time, he asked him, "Do you want to get well?"

⁷"Sir," the invalid replied, "I have no one to help me into the pool when the water is stirred. While I am trying to get in, someone else goes down ahead of me."

⁸Then Jesus said to him, "Get up! Pick up your mat and walk." ⁹At once the man was cured; he picked up his mat and walked.

The day on which this took place was a Sabbath, ¹⁰and so the Jews said to the man who had been healed, "It is the Sabbath; the law forbids you to carry your mat."

¹¹But he replied, "The man who made me well said to me, 'Pick up your mat and walk.'"

¹²So they asked him, "Who is this fellow who told you to pick it up and walk?"

¹³The man who was healed had no idea who it was, for Jesus had slipped away into the crowd that was there.

¹⁴Later Jesus found him at the temple and said to him, "See, you are well again. Stop sinning or something worse may happen to you." ¹⁵The man went away and told the Jews that it was Jesus who had made him well.

Life Through the Son

¹⁶So, because Jesus was doing these things on the Sabbath, the Jews persecuted him. ¹⁷Jesus said to them, "My Father is always at his work to this very day, and I, too, am working." ¹⁸For this reason the Jews tried all the harder to kill him; not only was he breaking the Sabbath, but he was even calling God his own Father, making himself equal with God.

¹⁹Jesus gave them this answer: "I tell you the truth, the Son can do nothing by himself; he can do only what he sees his Father doing, because whatever the Father does the Son also does. ²⁰For the Father loves the Son and shows him all he does. Yes, to your amazement he will show him even greater things than these. ²¹For just as the Father raises the dead and gives them life, even so the Son gives life to whom he is pleased to give it.

---

a2 Some manuscripts *Bethzatha*; other manuscripts *Bethsaida*   *b3* Some less important manuscripts *paralyzed—and they waited for the moving of the waters. ⁴From time to time an angel of the Lord would come down and stir up the waters. The first one into the pool after each such disturbance would be cured of whatever disease he had.*

²²Moreover, the Father judges no one, but has entrusted all judgment to the Son, ²³that all may honor the Son just as they honor the Father. He who does not honor the Son does not honor the Father, who sent him.

²⁴"I tell you the truth, whoever hears my word and believes him who sent me has eternal life and will not be condemned; he has crossed over from death to life. ²⁵I tell you the truth, a time is coming and has now come when the dead will hear the voice of the Son of God and those who hear will live. ²⁶For as the Father has life in himself, so he has granted the Son to have life in himself. ²⁷And he has given him authority to judge because he is the Son of Man.

²⁸"Do not be amazed at this, for a time is coming when all who are in their graves will hear his voice ²⁹and come out—those who have done good will rise to live, and those who have done evil will rise to be condemned. ³⁰By myself I can do nothing; I judge only as I hear, and my judgment is just, for I seek not to please myself but him who sent me.

Testimonies About Jesus

³¹"If I testify about myself, my testimony is not valid. ³²There is another who testifies in my favor, and I know that his testimony about me is valid.

³³"You have sent to John and he has testified to the truth. ³⁴Not that I accept human testimony; but I mention it that you may be saved. ³⁵John was a lamp that burned and gave light, and you chose for a time to enjoy his light.

³⁶"I have testimony weightier than that of John. For the very work that the Father has given me to finish, and which I am doing, testifies that the Father has sent me. ³⁷And the Father who sent me has himself testified concerning me. You have never heard his voice nor seen his form, ³⁸nor does his word dwell in you, for you do not believe the one he sent. ³⁹You diligently study^a the Scriptures because you think that by them you possess eternal life. These are the Scriptures that testify about me, ⁴⁰yet you refuse to come to me to have life.

⁴¹"I do not accept praise from men, ⁴²but I know you. I know that you do not have the love of God in your hearts. ⁴³I have come in my Father's name, and you do not accept me; but if someone else comes in his own name, you will accept him. ⁴⁴How can you believe if you accept praise from one another, yet make no effort to obtain the praise that comes from the only God^b?

⁴⁵"But do not think I will accuse you before the Father. Your accuser is Moses, on whom your hopes are set. ⁴⁶If you believed Moses, you would believe me, for he wrote about me. ⁴⁷But since you do not believe what he wrote, how are you going to believe what I say?"

Jesus Feeds the Five Thousand

6 Some time after this, Jesus crossed to the far shore of the Sea of Galilee (that is, the Sea of Tiberias), ²and a great crowd of people followed him

---

^{a}39 Or Study diligently (the imperative) ^{b}44 Some early manuscripts the Only One because they saw the miraculous signs he had performed on the sick. ³Then Jesus went up on a mountainside and sat down with his disciples. ⁴The Jewish Passover Feast was near.

⁵When Jesus looked up and saw a great crowd coming toward him, he said to Philip, "Where shall we buy bread for these people to eat?" ⁶He asked this only to test him, for he already had in mind what he was going to do.

⁷Philip answered him, "Eight months' wages*ᵃ* would not buy enough bread for each one to have a bite!"

⁸Another of his disciples, Andrew, Simon Peter's brother, spoke up, ⁹"Here is a boy with five small barley loaves and two small fish, but how far will they go among so many?"

¹⁰Jesus said, "Have the people sit down." There was plenty of grass in that place, and the men sat down, about five thousand of them. ¹¹Jesus then took the loaves, gave thanks, and distributed to those who were seated as much as they wanted. He did the same with the fish.

¹²When they had all had enough to eat, he said to his disciples, "Gather the pieces that are left over. Let nothing be wasted." ¹³So they gathered them and filled twelve baskets with the pieces of the five barley loaves left over by those who had eaten.

¹⁴After the people saw the miraculous sign that Jesus did, they began to say, "Surely this is the Prophet who is to come into the world." ¹⁵Jesus, knowing that they intended to come and make him king by force, withdrew again to a mountain by himself.

Jesus Walks on the Water

¹⁶When evening came, his disciples went down to the lake, ¹⁷where they got into a boat and set off across the lake for Capernaum. By now it was dark, and Jesus had not yet joined them. ¹⁸A strong wind was blowing and the waters grew rough. ¹⁹When they had rowed three or three and a half miles,*ᵇ* they saw Jesus approaching the boat, walking on the water; and they were terrified. ²⁰But he said to them, "It is I; don't be afraid." ²¹Then they were willing to take him into the boat, and immediately the boat reached the shore where they were heading.

²²The next day the crowd that had stayed on the opposite shore of the lake realized that only one boat had been there, and that Jesus had not entered it with his disciples, but that they had gone away alone. ²³Then some boats from Tiberias landed near the place where the people had eaten the bread after the Lord had given thanks. ²⁴Once the crowd realized that neither Jesus nor his disciples were there, they got into the boats and went to Capernaum in search of Jesus.

Jesus the Bread of Life

²⁵When they found him on the other side of the lake, they asked him, "Rabbi, when did you get here?"

---

*ᵃ*7 Greek *two hundred denarii*   *ᵇ*19 Greek *rowed twenty-five or thirty stadia* (about 5 or 6 kilometers)

²⁶Jesus answered, "I tell you the truth, you are looking for me, not because you saw miraculous signs but because you ate the loaves and had your fill. ²⁷Do not work for food that spoils, but for food that endures to eternal life, which the Son of Man will give you. On him God the Father has placed his seal of approval."

²⁸Then they asked him, "What must we do to do the works God requires?"

²⁹Jesus answered, "The work of God is this: to believe in the one he has sent."

³⁰So they asked him, "What miraculous sign then will you give that we may see it and believe you? What will you do? ³¹Our forefathers ate the manna in the desert; as it is written: 'He gave them bread from heaven to eat.'ᵃ"

³²Jesus said to them, "I tell you the truth, it is not Moses who has given you the bread from heaven, but it is my Father who gives you the true bread from heaven. ³³For the bread of God is he who comes down from heaven and gives life to the world."

³⁴"Sir," they said, "from now on give us this bread."

³⁵Then Jesus declared, "I am the bread of life. He who comes to me will never go hungry, and he who believes in me will never be thirsty. ³⁶But as I told you, you have seen me and still you do not believe. ³⁷All that the Father gives me will come to me, and whoever comes to me I will never drive away. ³⁸For I have come down from heaven not to do my will but to do the will of him who sent me. ³⁹And this is the will of him who sent me, that I shall lose none of all that he has given me, but raise them up at the last day. ⁴⁰For my Father's will is that everyone who looks to the Son and believes in him shall have eternal life, and I will raise him up at the last day."

⁴¹At this the Jews began to grumble about him because he said, "I am the bread that came down from heaven." ⁴²They said, "Is this not Jesus, the son of Joseph, whose father and mother we know? How can he now say, 'I came down from heaven'?"

⁴³"Stop grumbling among yourselves," Jesus answered. ⁴⁴"No one can come to me unless the Father who sent me draws him, and I will raise him up at the last day. ⁴⁵It is written in the Prophets: 'They will all be taught by God.'ᵇ Everyone who listens to the Father and learns from him comes to me. ⁴⁶No one has seen the Father except the one who is from God; only he has seen the Father. ⁴⁷I tell you the truth, he who believes has everlasting life. ⁴⁸I am the bread of life. ⁴⁹Your forefathers ate the manna in the desert, yet they died. ⁵⁰But here is the bread that comes down from heaven, which a man may eat and not die. ⁵¹I am the living bread that came down from heaven. If anyone eats of this bread, he will live forever. This bread is my flesh, which I will give for the life of the world."

⁵²Then the Jews began to argue sharply among themselves, "How can this man give us his flesh to eat?"

⁵³Jesus said to them, "I tell you the truth, unless you eat the flesh of

ᵃ31 Exodus 16:4; Neh. 9:15; Psalm 78:24,25   ᵇ45 Isaiah 54:13

the Son of Man and drink his blood, you have no life in you. ⁵⁴Whoever eats my flesh and drinks my blood has eternal life, and I will raise him up at the last day. ⁵⁵For my flesh is real food and my blood is real drink. ⁵⁶Whoever eats my flesh and drinks my blood remains in me, and I in him. ⁵⁷Just as the living Father sent me and I live because of the Father, so the one who feeds on me will live because of me. ⁵⁸This is the bread that came down from heaven. Your forefathers ate manna and died, but he who feeds on this bread will live forever." ⁵⁹He said this while teaching in the synagogue in Capernaum.

Many Disciples Desert Jesus

⁶⁰On hearing it, many of his disciples said, "This is a hard teaching. Who can accept it?"

⁶¹Aware that his disciples were grumbling about this, Jesus said to them, "Does this offend you? ⁶²What if you see the Son of Man ascend to where he was before! ⁶³The Spirit gives life; the flesh counts for nothing. The words I have spoken to you are spirit*a* and they are life. ⁶⁴Yet there are some of you who do not believe." For Jesus had known from the beginning which of them did not believe and who would betray him. ⁶⁵He went on to say, "This is why I told you that no one can come to me unless the Father has enabled him."

⁶⁶From this time many of his disciples turned back and no longer followed him.

⁶⁷"You do not want to leave too, do you?" Jesus asked the Twelve.

⁶⁸Simon Peter answered him, "Lord, to whom shall we go? You have the words of eternal life. ⁶⁹We believe and know that you are the Holy One of God."

⁷⁰Then Jesus replied, "Have I not chosen you, the Twelve? Yet one of you is a devil!" ⁷¹(He meant Judas, the son of Simon Iscariot, who, though one of the Twelve, was later to betray him.)

Jesus Goes to the Feast of Tabernacles

7 After this, Jesus went around in Galilee, purposely staying away from Judea because the Jews there were waiting to take his life. ²But when the Jewish Feast of Tabernacles was near, ³Jesus' brothers said to him, "You ought to leave here and go to Judea, so that your disciples may see the miracles you do. ⁴No one who wants to become a public figure acts in secret. Since you are doing these things, show yourself to the world." ⁵For even his own brothers did not believe in him.

⁶Therefore Jesus told them, "The right time for me has not yet come; for you any time is right. ⁷The world cannot hate you, but it hates me because I testify that what it does is evil. ⁸You go to the Feast. I am not yet*b* going up to this Feast, because for me the right time has not yet come." ⁹Having said this, he stayed in Galilee.

¹⁰However, after his brothers had left for the Feast, he went also, not

---

*a*63 Or *Spirit*   *b*8 Some early manuscripts do not have *yet*.

publicly, but in secret. [11]Now at the Feast the Jews were watching for him and asking, "Where is that man?"

[12]Among the crowds there was widespread whispering about him. Some said, "He is a good man."

Others replied, "No, he deceives the people." [13]But no one would say anything publicly about him for fear of the Jews.

Jesus Teaches at the Feast

[14]Not until halfway through the Feast did Jesus go up to the temple courts and begin to teach. [15]The Jews were amazed and asked, "How did this man get such learning without having studied?"

[16]Jesus answered, "My teaching is not my own. It comes from him who sent me. [17]If anyone chooses to do God's will, he will find out whether my teaching comes from God or whether I speak on my own. [18]He who speaks on his own does so to gain honor for himself, but he who works for the honor of the one who sent him is a man of truth; there is nothing false about him. [19]Has not Moses given you the law? Yet not one of you keeps the law. Why are you trying to kill me?"

[20]"You are demon-possessed," the crowd answered. "Who is trying to kill you?"

[21]Jesus said to them, "I did one miracle, and you are all astonished. [22]Yet, because Moses gave you circumcision (though actually it did not come from Moses, but from the patriarchs), you circumcise a child on the Sabbath. [23]Now if a child can be circumcised on the Sabbath so that the law of Moses may not be broken, why are you angry with me for healing the whole man on the Sabbath? [24]Stop judging by mere appearances, and make a right judgment."

Is Jesus the Christ?

[25]At that point some of the people of Jerusalem began to ask, "Isn't this the man they are trying to kill? [26]Here he is, speaking publicly, and they are not saying a word to him. Have the authorities really concluded that he is the Christ[a]? [27]But we know where this man is from; when the Christ comes, no one will know where he is from."

[28]Then Jesus, still teaching in the temple courts, cried out, "Yes, you know me, and you know where I am from. I am not here on my own, but he who sent me is true. You do not know him, [29]but I know him because I am from him and he sent me."

[30]At this they tried to seize him, but no one laid a hand on him, because his time had not yet come. [31]Still, many in the crowd put their faith in him. They said, "When the Christ comes, will he do more miraculous signs than this man?"

[32]The Pharisees heard the crowd whispering such things about him. Then the chief priests and the Pharisees sent temple guards to arrest him.

[33]Jesus said, "I am with you for only a short time, and then I go to the

[a]26 Or *Messiah*; also in verses 27, 31, 41 and 42

one who sent me. ³⁴You will look for me, but you will not find me; and where I am, you cannot come."

³⁵The Jews said to one another, "Where does this man intend to go that we cannot find him? Will he go where our people live scattered among the Greeks, and teach the Greeks? ³⁶What did he mean when he said, 'You will look for me, but you will not find me,' and 'Where I am, you cannot come'?"

³⁷On the last and greatest day of the Feast, Jesus stood and said in a loud voice, "If anyone is thirsty, let him come to me and drink. ³⁸Whoever believes in me, as*a* the Scripture has said, streams of living water will flow from within him." ³⁹By this he meant the Spirit, whom those who believed in him were later to receive. Up to that time the Spirit had not been given, since Jesus had not yet been glorified.

⁴⁰On hearing his words, some of the people said, "Surely this man is the Prophet."

⁴¹Others said, "He is the Christ."

Still others asked, "How can the Christ come from Galilee? ⁴²Does not the Scripture say that the Christ will come from David's family*b* and from Bethlehem, the town where David lived?" ⁴³Thus the people were divided because of Jesus. ⁴⁴Some wanted to seize him, but no one laid a hand on him.

Unbelief of the Jewish Leaders

⁴⁵Finally the temple guards went back to the chief priests and Pharisees, who asked them, "Why didn't you bring him in?"

⁴⁶"No one ever spoke the way this man does," the guards declared.

⁴⁷"You mean he has deceived you also?" the Pharisees retorted. ⁴⁸"Has any of the rulers or of the Pharisees believed in him? ⁴⁹No! But this mob that knows nothing of the law—there is a curse on them."

⁵⁰Nicodemus, who had gone to Jesus earlier and who was one of their own number, asked, ⁵¹"Does our law condemn anyone without first hearing him to find out what he is doing?"

⁵²They replied, "Are you from Galilee, too? Look into it, and you will find that a prophet*c* does not come out of Galilee."

[The earliest and most reliable manuscripts and other ancient witnesses do not have John 7:53–8:11.]

⁵³Then each went to his own home.

8 But Jesus went to the Mount of Olives. ²At dawn he appeared again in the temple courts, where all the people gathered around him, and he sat down to teach them. ³The teachers of the law and the Pharisees brought in a woman caught in adultery. They made her stand before the group ⁴and

a37,38 Or / If anyone is thirsty, let him come to me. / And let him drink, ³⁸who believes in me. / As
b42 Greek seed   *c52 Two early manuscripts the Prophet*

said to Jesus, "Teacher, this woman was caught in the act of adultery. ⁵In the Law Moses commanded us to stone such women. Now what do you say?" ⁶They were using this question as a trap, in order to have a basis for accusing him.

But Jesus bent down and started to write on the ground with his finger. ⁷When they kept on questioning him, he straightened up and said to them, "If any one of you is without sin, let him be the first to throw a stone at her." ⁸Again he stooped down and wrote on the ground.

⁹At this, those who heard began to go away one at a time, the older ones first, until only Jesus was left, with the woman still standing there. ¹⁰Jesus straightened up and asked her, "Woman, where are they? Has no one condemned you?"

¹¹"No one, sir," she said.

"Then neither do I condemn you," Jesus declared. "Go now and leave your life of sin."

The Validity of Jesus' Testimony

¹²When Jesus spoke again to the people, he said, "I am the light of the world. Whoever follows me will never walk in darkness, but will have the light of life."

¹³The Pharisees challenged him, "Here you are, appearing as your own witness; your testimony is not valid."

¹⁴Jesus answered, "Even if I testify on my own behalf, my testimony is valid, for I know where I came from and where I am going. But you have no idea where I come from or where I am going. ¹⁵You judge by human standards; I pass judgment on no one. ¹⁶But if I do judge, my decisions are right, because I am not alone. I stand with the Father, who sent me. ¹⁷In your own Law it is written that the testimony of two men is valid. ¹⁸I am one who testifies for myself; my other witness is the Father, who sent me."

¹⁹Then they asked him, "Where is your father?"

"You do not know me or my Father," Jesus replied. "If you knew me, you would know my Father also." ²⁰He spoke these words while teaching in the temple area near the place where the offerings were put. Yet no one seized him, because his time had not yet come.

²¹Once more Jesus said to them, "I am going away, and you will look for me, and you will die in your sin. Where I go, you cannot come."

²²This made the Jews ask, "Will he kill himself? Is that why he says, 'Where I go, you cannot come'?"

²³But he continued, "You are from below; I am from above. You are of this world; I am not of this world. ²⁴I told you that you would die in your sins; if you do not believe that I am ⌊the one I claim to be⌋,ᵃ you will indeed die in your sins."

ᵃ24 Or *I am he*; also in verse 28

²⁵"Who are you?" they asked.

"Just what I have been claiming all along," Jesus replied. ²⁶"I have much to say in judgment of you. But he who sent me is reliable, and what I have heard from him I tell the world."

²⁷They did not understand that he was telling them about his Father. ²⁸So Jesus said, "When you have lifted up the Son of Man, then you will know that I am ˌthe one I claim to beˌ and that I do nothing on my own but speak just what the Father has taught me. ²⁹The one who sent me is with me; he has not left me alone, for I always do what pleases him." ³⁰Even as he spoke, many put their faith in him.

The Children of Abraham

³¹To the Jews who had believed him, Jesus said, "If you hold to my teaching, you are really my disciples. ³²Then you will know the truth, and the truth will set you free."

³³They answered him, "We are Abraham's descendants^a and have never been slaves of anyone. How can you say that we shall be set free?"

³⁴Jesus replied, "I tell you the truth, everyone who sins is a slave to sin. ³⁵Now a slave has no permanent place in the family, but a son belongs to it forever. ³⁶So if the Son sets you free, you will be free indeed. ³⁷I know you are Abraham's descendants. Yet you are ready to kill me, because you have no room for my word. ³⁸I am telling you what I have seen in the Father's presence, and you do what you have heard from your father.^b"

³⁹"Abraham is our father," they answered.

"If you were Abraham's children," said Jesus, "then you would^c do the things Abraham did. ⁴⁰As it is, you are determined to kill me, a man who has told you the truth that I heard from God. Abraham did not do such things. ⁴¹You are doing the things your own father does."

"We are not illegitimate children," they protested. "The only Father we have is God himself."

The Children of the Devil

⁴²Jesus said to them, "If God were your Father, you would love me, for I came from God and now am here. I have not come on my own; but he sent me. ⁴³Why is my language not clear to you? Because you are unable to hear what I say. ⁴⁴You belong to your father, the devil, and you want to carry out your father's desire. He was a murderer from the beginning, not holding to the truth, for there is no truth in him. When he lies, he speaks his native language, for he is a liar and the father of lies. ⁴⁵Yet because I tell the truth, you do not believe me! ⁴⁶Can any of you prove me guilty of sin? If I am telling the truth, why don't you believe me? ⁴⁷He who belongs to God hears what God says. The reason you do not hear is that you do not belong to God."

---

^a33 Greek seed; also in verse 37   ^b38 Or presence. Therefore do what you have heard from the Father.
^c39 Some early manuscripts "If you are Abraham's children," said Jesus, "then

The Claims of Jesus About Himself

⁴⁸The Jews answered him, "Aren't we right in saying that you are a Samaritan and demon-possessed?"

⁴⁹"I am not possessed by a demon," said Jesus, "but I honor my Father and you dishonor me. ⁵⁰I am not seeking glory for myself; but there is one who seeks it, and he is the judge. ⁵¹I tell you the truth, if anyone keeps my word, he will never see death."

⁵²At this the Jews exclaimed, "Now we know that you are demon-possessed! Abraham died and so did the prophets, yet you say that if anyone keeps your word, he will never taste death. ⁵³Are you greater than our father Abraham? He died, and so did the prophets. Who do you think you are?"

⁵⁴Jesus replied, "If I glorify myself, my glory means nothing. My Father, whom you claim as your God, is the one who glorifies me. ⁵⁵Though you do not know him, I know him. If I said I did not, I would be a liar like you, but I do know him and keep his word. ⁵⁶Your father Abraham rejoiced at the thought of seeing my day; he saw it and was glad."

⁵⁷"You are not yet fifty years old," the Jews said to him, "and you have seen Abraham!"

⁵⁸"I tell you the truth," Jesus answered, "before Abraham was born, I am!" ⁵⁹At this, they picked up stones to stone him, but Jesus hid himself, slipping away from the temple grounds.

Jesus Heals a Man Born Blind

9 As he went along, he saw a man blind from birth. ²His disciples asked him, "Rabbi, who sinned, this man or his parents, that he was born blind?"

³"Neither this man nor his parents sinned," said Jesus, "but this happened so that the work of God might be displayed in his life. ⁴As long as it is day, we must do the work of him who sent me. Night is coming, when no one can work. ⁵While I am in the world, I am the light of the world."

⁶Having said this, he spit on the ground, made some mud with the saliva, and put it on the man's eyes. ⁷"Go," he told him, "wash in the Pool of Siloam" (this word means Sent). So the man went and washed, and came home seeing.

⁸His neighbors and those who had formerly seen him begging asked, "Isn't this the same man who used to sit and beg?" ⁹Some claimed that he was.

Others said, "No, he only looks like him."

But he himself insisted, "I am the man."

¹⁰"How then were your eyes opened?" they demanded.

¹¹He replied, "The man they call Jesus made some mud and put it on my eyes. He told me to go to Siloam and wash. So I went and washed, and then I could see."

¹²"Where is this man?" they asked him.

"I don't know," he said.

The Pharisees Investigate the Healing

[13]They brought to the Pharisees the man who had been blind. [14]Now the day on which Jesus had made the mud and opened the man's eyes was a Sabbath. [15]Therefore the Pharisees also asked him how he had received his sight. "He put mud on my eyes," the man replied, "and I washed, and now I see."

[16]Some of the Pharisees said, "This man is not from God, for he does not keep the Sabbath."

But others asked, "How can a sinner do such miraculous signs?" So they were divided.

[17]Finally they turned again to the blind man, "What have you to say about him? It was your eyes he opened."

The man replied, "He is a prophet."

[18]The Jews still did not believe that he had been blind and had received his sight until they sent for the man's parents. [19]"Is this your son?" they asked. "Is this the one you say was born blind? How is it that now he can see?"

[20]"We know he is our son," the parents answered, "and we know he was born blind. [21]But how he can see now, or who opened his eyes, we don't know. Ask him. He is of age; he will speak for himself." [22]His parents said this because they were afraid of the Jews, for already the Jews had decided that anyone who acknowledged that Jesus was the Christ[a] would be put out of the synagogue. [23]That was why his parents said, "He is of age; ask him."

[24]A second time they summoned the man who had been blind. "Give glory to God,[b]" they said. "We know this man is a sinner."

[25]He replied, "Whether he is a sinner or not, I don't know. One thing I do know. I was blind but now I see!"

[26]Then they asked him, "What did he do to you? How did he open your eyes?"

[27]He answered, "I have told you already and you did not listen. Why do you want to hear it again? Do you want to become his disciples, too?"

[28]Then they hurled insults at him and said, "You are this fellow's disciple! We are disciples of Moses! [29]We know that God spoke to Moses, but as for this fellow, we don't even know where he comes from."

[30]The man answered, "Now that is remarkable! You don't know where he comes from, yet he opened my eyes. [31]We know that God does not listen to sinners. He listens to the godly man who does his will. [32]Nobody has ever heard of opening the eyes of a man born blind. [33]If this man were not from God, he could do nothing."

[34]To this they replied, "You were steeped in sin at birth; how dare you lecture us!" And they threw him out.

[a]22 Or *Messiah*   [b]24 A solemn charge to tell the truth (see Joshua 7:19)

Spiritual Blindness

³⁵Jesus heard that they had thrown him out, and when he found him, he said, "Do you believe in the Son of Man?"

³⁶"Who is he, sir?" the man asked. "Tell me so that I may believe in him."

³⁷Jesus said, "You have now seen him; in fact, he is the one speaking with you."

³⁸Then the man said, "Lord, I believe," and he worshiped him.

³⁹Jesus said, "For judgment I have come into this world, so that the blind will see and those who see will become blind."

⁴⁰Some Pharisees who were with him heard him say this and asked, "What? Are we blind too?"

⁴¹Jesus said, "If you were blind, you would not be guilty of sin; but now that you claim you can see, your guilt remains.

The Shepherd and His Flock

10 "I tell you the truth, the man who does not enter the sheep pen by the gate, but climbs in by some other way, is a thief and a robber. ²The man who enters by the gate is the shepherd of his sheep. ³The watchman opens the gate for him, and the sheep listen to his voice. He calls his own sheep by name and leads them out. ⁴When he has brought out all his own, he goes on ahead of them, and his sheep follow him because they know his voice. ⁵But they will never follow a stranger; in fact, they will run away from him because they do not recognize a stranger's voice." ⁶Jesus used this figure of speech, but they did not understand what he was telling them.

⁷Therefore Jesus said again, "I tell you the truth, I am the gate for the sheep. ⁸All who ever came before me were thieves and robbers, but the sheep did not listen to them. ⁹I am the gate; whoever enters through me will be saved.ᵃ He will come in and go out, and find pasture. ¹⁰The thief comes only to steal and kill and destroy; I have come that they may have life, and have it to the full.

¹¹"I am the good shepherd. The good shepherd lays down his life for the sheep. ¹²The hired hand is not the shepherd who owns the sheep. So when he sees the wolf coming, he abandons the sheep and runs away. Then the wolf attacks the flock and scatters it. ¹³The man runs away because he is a hired hand and cares nothing for the sheep.

¹⁴"I am the good shepherd; I know my sheep and my sheep know me— ¹⁵just as the Father knows me and I know the Father—and I lay down my life for the sheep. ¹⁶I have other sheep that are not of this sheep pen. I must bring them also. They too will listen to my voice, and there shall be one flock and one shepherd. ¹⁷The reason my Father loves me is that I lay down my life—only to take it up again. ¹⁸No one takes it from me, but I lay it down

ᵃ9 Or *kept safe*

of my own accord. I have authority to lay it down and authority to take it up again. This command I received from my Father."

[19]At these words the Jews were again divided. [20]Many of them said, "He is demon-possessed and raving mad. Why listen to him?"

[21]But others said, "These are not the sayings of a man possessed by a demon. Can a demon open the eyes of the blind?"

The Unbelief of the Jews

[22]Then came the Feast of Dedication[a] at Jerusalem. It was winter, [23]and Jesus was in the temple area walking in Solomon's Colonnade. [24]The Jews gathered around him, saying, "How long will you keep us in suspense? If you are the Christ,[b] tell us plainly."

[25]Jesus answered, "I did tell you, but you do not believe. The miracles I do in my Father's name speak for me, [26]but you do not believe because you are not my sheep. [27]My sheep listen to my voice; I know them, and they follow me. [28]I give them eternal life, and they shall never perish; no one can snatch them out of my hand. [29]My Father, who has given them to me, is greater than all[c]; no one can snatch them out of my Father's hand. [30]I and the Father are one."

[31]Again the Jews picked up stones to stone him, [32]but Jesus said to them, "I have shown you many great miracles from the Father. For which of these do you stone me?"

[33]"We are not stoning you for any of these," replied the Jews, "but for blasphemy, because you, a mere man, claim to be God."

[34]Jesus answered them, "Is it not written in your Law, 'I have said you are gods'[d]? [35]If he called them 'gods,' to whom the word of God came—and the Scripture cannot be broken— [36]what about the one whom the Father set apart as his very own and sent into the world? Why then do you accuse me of blasphemy because I said, 'I am God's Son'? [37]Do not believe me unless I do what my Father does. [38]But if I do it, even though you do not believe me, believe the miracles, that you may know and understand that the Father is in me, and I in the Father." [39]Again they tried to seize him, but he escaped their grasp.

[40]Then Jesus went back across the Jordan to the place where John had been baptizing in the early days. Here he stayed [41]and many people came to him. They said, "Though John never performed a miraculous sign, all that John said about this man was true." [42]And in that place many believed in Jesus.

The Death of Lazarus

11 Now a man named Lazarus was sick. He was from Bethany, the village of Mary and her sister Martha. [2]This Mary, whose brother Lazarus now lay sick, was the same one who poured perfume on the Lord

---

[a]22 That is, Hanukkah   [b]24 Or *Messiah*   [c]29 Many early manuscripts *What my Father has given me is greater than all*   [d]34 Psalm 82:6

and wiped his feet with her hair. ³So the sisters sent word to Jesus, "Lord, the one you love is sick."

⁴When he heard this, Jesus said, "This sickness will not end in death. No, it is for God's glory so that God's Son may be glorified through it." ⁵Jesus loved Martha and her sister and Lazarus. ⁶Yet when he heard that Lazarus was sick, he stayed where he was two more days.

⁷Then he said to his disciples, "Let us go back to Judea."

⁸"But Rabbi," they said, "a short while ago the Jews tried to stone you, and yet you are going back there?"

⁹Jesus answered, "Are there not twelve hours of daylight? A man who walks by day will not stumble, for he sees by this world's light. ¹⁰It is when he walks by night that he stumbles, for he has no light."

¹¹After he had said this, he went on to tell them, "Our friend Lazarus has fallen asleep; but I am going there to wake him up."

¹²His disciples replied, "Lord, if he sleeps, he will get better." ¹³Jesus had been speaking of his death, but his disciples thought he meant natural sleep.

¹⁴So then he told them plainly, "Lazarus is dead, ¹⁵and for your sake I am glad I was not there, so that you may believe. But let us go to him."

¹⁶Then Thomas (called Didymus) said to the rest of the disciples, "Let us also go, that we may die with him."

Jesus Comforts the Sisters

¹⁷On his arrival, Jesus found that Lazarus had already been in the tomb for four days. ¹⁸Bethany was less than two miles[a] from Jerusalem, ¹⁹and many Jews had come to Martha and Mary to comfort them in the loss of their brother. ²⁰When Martha heard that Jesus was coming, she went out to meet him, but Mary stayed at home.

²¹"Lord," Martha said to Jesus, "if you had been here, my brother would not have died. ²²But I know that even now God will give you whatever you ask."

²³Jesus said to her, "Your brother will rise again."

²⁴Martha answered, "I know he will rise again in the resurrection at the last day."

²⁵Jesus said to her, "I am the resurrection and the life. He who believes in me will live, even though he dies; ²⁶and whoever lives and believes in me will never die. Do you believe this?"

²⁷"Yes, Lord," she told him, "I believe that you are the Christ,[b] the Son of God, who was to come into the world."

²⁸And after she had said this, she went back and called her sister Mary aside. "The Teacher is here," she said, "and is asking for you." ²⁹When Mary heard this, she got up quickly and went to him. ³⁰Now Jesus had not yet entered the village, but was still at the place where Martha had met him. ³¹When the Jews who had been with Mary in the house, comforting her,

---

a18 Greek *fifteen stadia* (about 3 kilometers)   b27 Or *Messiah* noticed how quickly she got up and went out, they followed her, supposing she was going to the tomb to mourn there.

[32]When Mary reached the place where Jesus was and saw him, she fell at his feet and said, "Lord, if you had been here, my brother would not have died."

[33]When Jesus saw her weeping, and the Jews who had come along with her also weeping, he was deeply moved in spirit and troubled. [34]"Where have you laid him?" he asked.

"Come and see, Lord," they replied.

[35]Jesus wept.

[36]Then the Jews said, "See how he loved him!"

[37]But some of them said, "Could not he who opened the eyes of the blind man have kept this man from dying?"

Jesus Raises Lazarus From the Dead

[38]Jesus, once more deeply moved, came to the tomb. It was a cave with a stone laid across the entrance. [39]"Take away the stone," he said.

"But, Lord," said Martha, the sister of the dead man, "by this time there is a bad odor, for he has been there four days."

[40]Then Jesus said, "Did I not tell you that if you believed, you would see the glory of God?"

[41]So they took away the stone. Then Jesus looked up and said, "Father, I thank you that you have heard me. [42]I knew that you always hear me, but I said this for the benefit of the people standing here, that they may believe that you sent me."

[43]When he had said this, Jesus called in a loud voice, "Lazarus, come out!" [44]The dead man came out, his hands and feet wrapped with strips of linen, and a cloth around his face.

Jesus said to them, "Take off the grave clothes and let him go."

The Plot to Kill Jesus

[45]Therefore many of the Jews who had come to visit Mary, and had seen what Jesus did, put their faith in him. [46]But some of them went to the Pharisees and told them what Jesus had done. [47]Then the chief priests and the Pharisees called a meeting of the Sanhedrin.

"What are we accomplishing?" they asked. "Here is this man performing many miraculous signs. [48]If we let him go on like this, everyone will believe in him, and then the Romans will come and take away both our place[a] and our nation."

[49]Then one of them, named Caiaphas, who was high priest that year, spoke up, "You know nothing at all! [50]You do not realize that it is better for you that one man die for the people than that the whole nation perish."

[51]He did not say this on his own, but as high priest that year he prophesied that Jesus would die for the Jewish nation, [52]and not only for that nation but also for the scattered children of God, to bring them together

[a]48 Or temple

and make them one. ⁵³So from that day on they plotted to take his life.

⁵⁴Therefore Jesus no longer moved about publicly among the Jews. Instead he withdrew to a region near the desert, to a village called Ephraim, where he stayed with his disciples.

⁵⁵When it was almost time for the Jewish Passover, many went up from the country to Jerusalem for their ceremonial cleansing before the Passover. ⁵⁶They kept looking for Jesus, and as they stood in the temple area they asked one another, "What do you think? Isn't he coming to the Feast at all?" ⁵⁷But the chief priests and Pharisees had given orders that if anyone found out where Jesus was, he should report it so that they might arrest him.

Jesus Anointed at Bethany

12 Six days before the Passover, Jesus arrived at Bethany, where Lazarus lived, whom Jesus had raised from the dead. ²Here a dinner was given in Jesus' honor. Martha served, while Lazarus was among those reclining at the table with him. ³Then Mary took about a pint*ᵃ* of pure nard, an expensive perfume; she poured it on Jesus' feet and wiped his feet with her hair. And the house was filled with the fragrance of the perfume.

⁴But one of his disciples, Judas Iscariot, who was later to betray him, objected, ⁵"Why wasn't this perfume sold and the money given to the poor? It was worth a year's wages.*ᵇ*" ⁶He did not say this because he cared about the poor but because he was a thief; as keeper of the money bag, he used to help himself to what was put into it.

⁷"Leave her alone," Jesus replied. "It was intended that she should save this perfume for the day of my burial. ⁸You will always have the poor among you, but you will not always have me."

⁹Meanwhile a large crowd of Jews found out that Jesus was there and came, not only because of him but also to see Lazarus, whom he had raised from the dead. ¹⁰So the chief priests made plans to kill Lazarus as well, ¹¹for on account of him many of the Jews were going over to Jesus and putting their faith in him.

The Triumphal Entry

¹²The next day the great crowd that had come for the Feast heard that Jesus was on his way to Jerusalem. ¹³They took palm branches and went out to meet him, shouting,

> "Hosanna!*ᶜ*"

> "Blessed is he who comes in the name of the Lord!"*ᵈ*

> "Blessed is the King of Israel!"

¹⁴Jesus found a young donkey and sat upon it, as it is written,

> ¹⁵"Do not be afraid, O Daughter of Zion;

ᵃ3 Greek *a litra* (probably about 0.5 liter)   *ᵇ5* Greek *three hundred denarii*   *ᶜ13* A Hebrew expression meaning "Save!" which became an exclamation of praise   *ᵈ13* Psalm 118:25, 26

see, your king is coming,
seated on a donkey's colt."[a]

[16]At first his disciples did not understand all this. Only after Jesus was glorified did they realize that these things had been written about him and that they had done these things to him.

[17]Now the crowd that was with him when he called Lazarus from the tomb and raised him from the dead continued to spread the word. [18]Many people, because they had heard that he had given this miraculous sign, went out to meet him. [19]So the Pharisees said to one another, "See, this is getting us nowhere. Look how the whole world has gone after him!"

Jesus Predicts His Death

[20]Now there were some Greeks among those who went up to worship at the Feast. [21]They came to Philip, who was from Bethsaida in Galilee, with a request. "Sir," they said, "we would like to see Jesus." [22]Philip went to tell Andrew; Andrew and Philip in turn told Jesus.

[23]Jesus replied, "The hour has come for the Son of Man to be glorified. [24]I tell you the truth, unless a kernel of wheat falls to the ground and dies, it remains only a single seed. But if it dies, it produces many seeds. [25]The man who loves his life will lose it, while the man who hates his life in this world will keep it for eternal life. [26]Whoever serves me must follow me; and where I am, my servant also will be. My Father will honor the one who serves me.

[27]"Now my heart is troubled, and what shall I say? 'Father, save me from this hour'? No, it was for this very reason I came to this hour. [28]Father, glorify your name!"

Then a voice came from heaven, "I have glorified it, and will glorify it again." [29]The crowd that was there and heard it said it had thundered; others said an angel had spoken to him.

[30]Jesus said, "This voice was for your benefit, not mine. [31]Now is the time for judgment on this world; now the prince of this world will be driven out. [32]But I, when I am lifted up from the earth, will draw all men to myself." [33]He said this to show the kind of death he was going to die.

[34]The crowd spoke up, "We have heard from the Law that the Christ[b] will remain forever, so how can you say, 'The Son of Man must be lifted up'? Who is this 'Son of Man'?"

[35]Then Jesus told them, "You are going to have the light just a little while longer. Walk while you have the light, before darkness overtakes you. The man who walks in the dark does not know where he is going. [36]Put your trust in the light while you have it, so that you may become sons of light." When he had finished speaking, Jesus left and hid himself from them.

The Jews Continue in Their Unbelief

[37]Even after Jesus had done all these miraculous signs in their presence,

[a]15 Zech. 9:9   [b]34 Or Messiah

they still would not believe in him. [38]This was to fulfill the word of Isaiah the prophet:

> "Lord, who has believed our message
> and to whom has the arm of the Lord been revealed?"[a]

[39]For this reason they could not believe, because, as Isaiah says elsewhere:

> [40]"He has blinded their eyes
> and deadened their hearts,
> so they can neither see with their eyes,
> nor understand with their hearts,
> nor turn—and I would heal them."[b]

[41]Isaiah said this because he saw Jesus' glory and spoke about him.

[42]Yet at the same time many even among the leaders believed in him. But because of the Pharisees they would not confess their faith for fear they would be put out of the synagogue; [43]for they loved praise from men more than praise from God.

[44]Then Jesus cried out, "When a man believes in me, he does not believe in me only, but in the one who sent me. [45]When he looks at me, he sees the one who sent me. [46]I have come into the world as a light, so that no one who believes in me should stay in darkness.

[47]"As for the person who hears my words but does not keep them, I do not judge him. For I did not come to judge the world, but to save it. [48]There is a judge for the one who rejects me and does not accept my words; that very word which I spoke will condemn him at the last day. [49]For I did not speak of my own accord, but the Father who sent me commanded me what to say and how to say it. [50]I know that his command leads to eternal life. So whatever I say is just what the Father has told me to say."

Jesus Washes His Disciples' Feet

13 It was just before the Passover Feast. Jesus knew that the time had come for him to leave this world and go to the Father. Having loved his own who were in the world, he now showed them the full extent of his love.[c]

[2]The evening meal was being served, and the devil had already prompted Judas Iscariot, son of Simon, to betray Jesus. [3]Jesus knew that the Father had put all things under his power, and that he had come from God and was returning to God; [4]so he got up from the meal, took off his outer clothing, and wrapped a towel around his waist. [5]After that, he poured water into a basin and began to wash his disciples' feet, drying them with the towel that was wrapped around him.

[6]He came to Simon Peter, who said to him, "Lord, are you going to wash my feet?"

---

[a]38 Isaiah 53:1   [b]40 Isaiah 6:10   [c]1 Or *he loved them to the last*

[7]Jesus replied, "You do not realize now what I am doing, but later you will understand."

[8]"No," said Peter, "you shall never wash my feet."

Jesus answered, "Unless I wash you, you have no part with me."

[9]"Then, Lord," Simon Peter replied, "not just my feet but my hands and my head as well!"

[10]Jesus answered, "A person who has had a bath needs only to wash his feet; his whole body is clean. And you are clean, though not every one of you." [11]For he knew who was going to betray him, and that was why he said not every one was clean.

[12]When he had finished washing their feet, he put on his clothes and returned to his place. "Do you understand what I have done for you?" he asked them. [13]"You call me 'Teacher' and 'Lord,' and rightly so, for that is what I am. [14]Now that I, your Lord and Teacher, have washed your feet, you also should wash one another's feet. [15]I have set you an example that you should do as I have done for you. [16]I tell you the truth, no servant is greater than his master, nor is a messenger greater than the one who sent him. [17]Now that you know these things, you will be blessed if you do them.

Jesus Predicts His Betrayal

[18]"I am not referring to all of you; I know those I have chosen. But this is to fulfill the scripture: 'He who shares my bread has lifted up his heel against me.'[a]

[19]"I am telling you now before it happens, so that when it does happen you will believe that I am He. [20]I tell you the truth, whoever accepts anyone I send accepts me; and whoever accepts me accepts the one who sent me."

[21]After he had said this, Jesus was troubled in spirit and testified, "I tell you the truth, one of you is going to betray me."

[22]His disciples stared at one another, at a loss to know which of them he meant. [23]One of them, the disciple whom Jesus loved, was reclining next to him. [24]Simon Peter motioned to this disciple and said, "Ask him which one he means."

[25]Leaning back against Jesus, he asked him, "Lord, who is it?"

[26]Jesus answered, "It is the one to whom I will give this piece of bread when I have dipped it in the dish." Then, dipping the piece of bread, he gave it to Judas Iscariot, son of Simon. [27]As soon as Judas took the bread, Satan entered into him.

"What you are about to do, do quickly," Jesus told him, [28]but no one at the meal understood why Jesus said this to him. [29]Since Judas had charge of the money, some thought Jesus was telling him to buy what was needed for the Feast, or to give something to the poor. [30]As soon as Judas had taken the bread, he went out. And it was night.

Jesus Predicts Peter's Denial

[31]When he was gone, Jesus said, "Now is the Son of Man glorified and

[a]18 Psalm 41:9

God is glorified in him. [32]If God is glorified in him,[a] God will glorify the Son in himself, and will glorify him at once.

[33]"My children, I will be with you only a little longer. You will look for me, and just as I told the Jews, so I tell you now: Where I am going, you cannot come.

[34]"A new command I give you: Love one another. As I have loved you, so you must love one another. [35]By this all men will know that you are my disciples, if you love one another."

[36]Simon Peter asked him, "Lord, where are you going?"

Jesus replied, "Where I am going, you cannot follow now, but you will follow later."

[37]Peter asked, "Lord, why can't I follow you now? I will lay down my life for you."

[38]Then Jesus answered, "Will you really lay down your life for me? I tell you the truth, before the rooster crows, you will disown me three times!

Jesus Comforts His Disciples

14 "Do not let your hearts be troubled. Trust in God[b]; trust also in me. [2]In my Father's house are many rooms; if it were not so, I would have told you. I am going there to prepare a place for you. [3]And if I go and prepare a place for you, I will come back and take you to be with me that you also may be where I am. [4]You know the way to the place where I am going."

Jesus the Way to the Father

[5]Thomas said to him, "Lord, we don't know where you are going, so how can we know the way?"

[6]Jesus answered, "I am the way and the truth and the life. No one comes to the Father except through me. [7]If you really knew me, you would know[c] my Father as well. From now on, you do know him and have seen him."

[8]Philip said, "Lord, show us the Father and that will be enough for us."

[9]Jesus answered: "Don't you know me, Philip, even after I have been among you such a long time? Anyone who has seen me has seen the Father. How can you say, 'Show us the Father'? [10]Don't you believe that I am in the Father, and that the Father is in me? The words I say to you are not just my own. Rather, it is the Father, living in me, who is doing his work. [11]Believe me when I say that I am in the Father and the Father is in me; or at least believe on the evidence of the miracles themselves. [12]I tell you the truth, anyone who has faith in me will do what I have been doing. He will do even greater things than these, because I am going to the Father. [13]And I will do whatever you ask in my name, so that the Son may bring glory to the Father. [14]You may ask me for anything in my name, and I will do it.

---

[a]32 Many early manuscripts do not have *If God is glorified in him.*   [b]1 Or *You trust in God*
[c]7 Some early manuscripts *If you really have known me, you will know*

Jesus Promises the Holy Spirit

15"If you love me, you will obey what I command. 16And I will ask the Father, and he will give you another Counselor to be with you forever— 17the Spirit of truth. The world cannot accept him, because it neither sees him nor knows him. But you know him, for he lives with you and will be*a* in you. 18I will not leave you as orphans; I will come to you. 19Before long, the world will not see me anymore, but you will see me. Because I live, you also will live. 20On that day you will realize that I am in my Father, and you are in me, and I am in you. 21Whoever has my commands and obeys them, he is the one who loves me. He who loves me will be loved by my Father, and I too will love him and show myself to him."

22Then Judas (not Judas Iscariot) said, "But, Lord, why do you intend to show yourself to us and not to the world?"

23Jesus replied, "If anyone loves me, he will obey my teaching. My Father will love him, and we will come to him and make our home with him. 24He who does not love me will not obey my teaching. These words you hear are not my own; they belong to the Father who sent me.

25"All this I have spoken while still with you. 26But the Counselor, the Holy Spirit, whom the Father will send in my name, will teach you all things and will remind you of everything I have said to you. 27Peace I leave with you; my peace I give you. I do not give to you as the world gives. Do not let your hearts be troubled and do not be afraid.

28"You heard me say, 'I am going away and I am coming back to you.' If you loved me, you would be glad that I am going to the Father, for the Father is greater than I. 29I have told you now before it happens, so that when it does happen you will believe. 30I will not speak with you much longer, for the prince of this world is coming. He has no hold on me, 31but the world must learn that I love the Father and that I do exactly what my Father has commanded me.

"Come now; let us leave.

The Vine and the Branches

15 "I am the true vine, and my Father is the gardener. 2He cuts off every branch in me that bears no fruit, while every branch that does bear fruit he prunes*b* so that it will be even more fruitful. 3You are already clean because of the word I have spoken to you. 4Remain in me, and I will remain in you. No branch can bear fruit by itself; it must remain in the vine. Neither can you bear fruit unless you remain in me.

5"I am the vine; you are the branches. If a man remains in me and I in him, he will bear much fruit; apart from me you can do nothing. 6If anyone does not remain in me, he is like a branch that is thrown away and withers; such branches are picked up, thrown into the fire and burned. 7If you remain in me and my words remain in you, ask whatever you wish, and

---

*a17 Some early manuscripts *and is*   *b2 The Greek for *prunes* also means *cleans.*

it will be given you. [8]This is to my Father's glory, that you bear much fruit, showing yourselves to be my disciples.

[9]"As the Father has loved me, so have I loved you. Now remain in my love. [10]If you obey my commands, you will remain in my love, just as I have obeyed my Father's commands and remain in his love. [11]I have told you this so that my joy may be in you and that your joy may be complete. [12]My command is this: Love each other as I have loved you. [13]Greater love has no one than this, that he lay down his life for his friends. [14]You are my friends if you do what I command. [15]I no longer call you servants, because a servant does not know his master's business. Instead, I have called you friends, for everything that I learned from my Father I have made known to you. [16]You did not choose me, but I chose you and appointed you to go and bear fruit—fruit that will last. Then the Father will give you whatever you ask in my name. [17]This is my command: Love each other.

The World Hates the Disciples

[18]"If the world hates you, keep in mind that it hated me first. [19]If you belonged to the world, it would love you as its own. As it is, you do not belong to the world, but I have chosen you out of the world. That is why the world hates you. [20]Remember the words I spoke to you: 'No servant is greater than his master.'[a] If they persecuted me, they will persecute you also. If they obeyed my teaching, they will obey yours also. [21]They will treat you this way because of my name, for they do not know the One who sent me. [22]If I had not come and spoken to them, they would not be guilty of sin. Now, however, they have no excuse for their sin. [23]He who hates me hates my Father as well. [24]If I had not done among them what no one else did, they would not be guilty of sin. But now they have seen these miracles, and yet they have hated both me and my Father. [25]But this is to fulfill what is written in their Law: 'They hated me without reason.'[b]

[26]"When the Counselor comes, whom I will send to you from the Father, the Spirit of truth who goes out from the Father, he will testify about me. [27]And you also must testify, for you have been with me from the beginning.

16 "All this I have told you so that you will not go astray. [2]They will put you out of the synagogue; in fact, a time is coming when anyone who kills you will think he is offering a service to God. [3]They will do such things because they have not known the Father or me. [4]I have told you this, so that when the time comes you will remember that I warned you. I did not tell you this at first because I was with you.

The Work of the Holy Spirit

[5]"Now I am going to him who sent me, yet none of you asks me, 'Where are you going?' [6]Because I have said these things, you are filled with grief. [7]But I tell you the truth: It is for your good that I am going away. Unless I go away, the Counselor will not come to you; but if I go, I will send

[a]20 John 13:16   [b]25 Psalms 35:19; 69:4

him to you. [8]When he comes, he will convict the world of guilt[a] in regard to sin and righteousness and judgment: [9]in regard to sin, because men do not believe in me; [10]in regard to righteousness, because I am going to the Father, where you can see me no longer; [11]and in regard to judgment, because the prince of this world now stands condemned.

[12]"I have much more to say to you, more than you can now bear. [13]But when he, the Spirit of truth, comes, he will guide you into all truth. He will not speak on his own; he will speak only what he hears, and he will tell you what is yet to come. [14]He will bring glory to me by taking from what is mine and making it known to you. [15]All that belongs to the Father is mine. That is why I said the Spirit will take from what is mine and make it known to you.

[16]"In a little while you will see me no more, and then after a little while you will see me."

The Disciples' Grief Will Turn to Joy

[17]Some of his disciples said to one another, "What does he mean by saying, 'In a little while you will see me no more, and then after a little while you will see me,' and 'Because I am going to the Father'?" [18]They kept asking, "What does he mean by 'a little while'? We don't understand what he is saying."

[19]Jesus saw that they wanted to ask him about this, so he said to them, "Are you asking one another what I meant when I said, 'In a little while you will see me no more, and then after a little while you will see me'? [20]I tell you the truth, you will weep and mourn while the world rejoices. You will grieve, but your grief will turn to joy. [21]A woman giving birth to a child has pain because her time has come; but when her baby is born she forgets the anguish because of her joy that a child is born into the world. [22]So with you: Now is your time of grief, but I will see you again and you will rejoice, and no one will take away your joy. [23]In that day you will no longer ask me anything. I tell you the truth, my Father will give you whatever you ask in my name. [24]Until now you have not asked for anything in my name. Ask and you will receive, and your joy will be complete.

[25]"Though I have been speaking figuratively, a time is coming when I will no longer use this kind of language but will tell you plainly about my Father. [26]In that day you will ask in my name. I am not saying that I will ask the Father on your behalf. [27]No, the Father himself loves you because you have loved me and have believed that I came from God. [28]I came from the Father and entered the world; now I am leaving the world and going back to the Father."

[29]Then Jesus' disciples said, "Now you are speaking clearly and without figures of speech. [30]Now we can see that you know all things and that you do not even need to have anyone ask you questions. This makes us believe that you came from God."

[31]"You believe at last!"[b] Jesus answered. [32]"But a time is coming, and

[a]8 Or will expose the guilt of the world   [b]31 Or "Do you now believe?"

has come, when you will be scattered, each to his own home. You will leave me all alone. Yet I am not alone, for my Father is with me.

[33]"I have told you these things, so that in me you may have peace. In this world you will have trouble. But take heart! I have overcome the world."

Jesus Prays for Himself

17 After Jesus said this, he looked toward heaven and prayed:

"Father, the time has come. Glorify your Son, that your Son may glorify you. [2]For you granted him authority over all people that he might give eternal life to all those you have given him. [3]Now this is eternal life: that they may know you, the only true God, and Jesus Christ, whom you have sent. [4]I have brought you glory on earth by completing the work you gave me to do. [5]And now, Father, glorify me in your presence with the glory I had with you before the world began.

Jesus Prays for His Disciples

[6]"I have revealed you[a] to those whom you gave me out of the world. They were yours; you gave them to me and they have obeyed your word. [7]Now they know that everything you have given me comes from you. [8]For I gave them the words you gave me and they accepted them. They knew with certainty that I came from you, and they believed that you sent me. [9]I pray for them. I am not praying for the world, but for those you have given me, for they are yours. [10]All I have is yours, and all you have is mine. And glory has come to me through them. [11]I will remain in the world no longer, but they are still in the world, and I am coming to you. Holy Father, protect them by the power of your name—the name you gave me—so that they may be one as we are one. [12]While I was with them, I protected them and kept them safe by that name you gave me. None has been lost except the one doomed to destruction so that Scripture would be fulfilled.

[13]"I am coming to you now, but I say these things while I am still in the world, so that they may have the full measure of my joy within them. [14]I have given them your word and the world has hated them, for they are not of the world any more than I am of the world. [15]My prayer is not that you take them out of the world but that you protect them from the evil one. [16]They are not of the world, even as I am not of it. [17]Sanctify[b] them by the truth; your word is truth. [18]As you sent me into the world, I have sent them into the world. [19]For them I sanctify myself, that they too may be truly sanctified.

Jesus Prays for All Believers

[20]"My prayer is not for them alone. I pray also for those who will

---

[a]6 Greek *your name*; also in verse 26   [b]17 Greek *hagiazo* (set apart for sacred use or make holy); also in verse 19

believe in me through their message, [21]that all of them may be one, Father, just as you are in me and I am in you. May they also be in us so that the world may believe that you have sent me. [22]I have given them the glory that you gave me, that they may be one as we are one: [23]I in them and you in me. May they be brought to complete unity to let the world know that you sent me and have loved them even as you have loved me.

[24]"Father, I want those you have given me to be with me where I am, and to see my glory, the glory you have given me because you loved me before the creation of the world.

[25]"Righteous Father, though the world does not know you, I know you, and they know that you have sent me. [26]I have made you known to them, and will continue to make you known in order that the love you have for me may be in them and that I myself may be in them."

Jesus Arrested

18 When he had finished praying, Jesus left with his disciples and crossed the Kidron Valley. On the other side there was an olive grove, and he and his disciples went into it.

[2]Now Judas, who betrayed him, knew the place, because Jesus had often met there with his disciples. [3]So Judas came to the grove, guiding a detachment of soldiers and some officials from the chief priests and Pharisees. They were carrying torches, lanterns and weapons.

[4]Jesus, knowing all that was going to happen to him, went out and asked them, "Who is it you want?"

[5]"Jesus of Nazareth," they replied.

"I am he," Jesus said. (And Judas the traitor was standing there with them.) [6]When Jesus said, "I am he," they drew back and fell to the ground.

[7]Again he asked them, "Who is it you want?"

And they said, "Jesus of Nazareth."

[8]"I told you that I am he," Jesus answered. "If you are looking for me, then let these men go." [9]This happened so that the words he had spoken would be fulfilled: "I have not lost one of those you gave me."[a]

[10]Then Simon Peter, who had a sword, drew it and struck the high priest's servant, cutting off his right ear. (The servant's name was Malchus.)

[11]Jesus commanded Peter, "Put your sword away! Shall I not drink the cup the Father has given me?"

Jesus Taken to Annas

[12]Then the detachment of soldiers with its commander and the Jewish officials arrested Jesus. They bound him [13]and brought him first to Annas, who was the father-in-law of Caiaphas, the high priest that year. [14]Caiaphas was the one who had advised the Jews that it would be good if one man died for the people.

[a]9 John 6:39

Peter's First Denial

¹⁵Simon Peter and another disciple were following Jesus. Because this disciple was known to the high priest, he went with Jesus into the high priest's courtyard, ¹⁶but Peter had to wait outside at the door. The other disciple, who was known to the high priest, came back, spoke to the girl on duty there and brought Peter in.

¹⁷"You are not one of his disciples, are you?" the girl at the door asked Peter.

He replied, "I am not."

¹⁸It was cold, and the servants and officials stood around a fire they had made to keep warm. Peter also was standing with them, warming himself.

The High Priest Questions Jesus

¹⁹Meanwhile, the high priest questioned Jesus about his disciples and his teaching.

²⁰"I have spoken openly to the world," Jesus replied. "I always taught in synagogues or at the temple, where all the Jews come together. I said nothing in secret. ²¹Why question me? Ask those who heard me. Surely they know what I said."

²²When Jesus said this, one of the officials nearby struck him in the face. "Is this the way you answer the high priest?" he demanded.

²³"If I said something wrong," Jesus replied, "testify as to what is wrong. But if I spoke the truth, why did you strike me?" ²⁴Then Annas sent him, still bound, to Caiaphas the high priest.ᵃ

Peter's Second and Third Denials

²⁵As Simon Peter stood warming himself, he was asked, "You are not one of his disciples, are you?"

He denied it, saying, "I am not."

²⁶One of the high priest's servants, a relative of the man whose ear Peter had cut off, challenged him, "Didn't I see you with him in the olive grove?" ²⁷Again Peter denied it, and at that moment a rooster began to crow.

Jesus Before Pilate

²⁸Then the Jews led Jesus from Caiaphas to the palace of the Roman governor. By now it was early morning, and to avoid ceremonial uncleanness the Jews did not enter the palace; they wanted to be able to eat the Passover. ²⁹So Pilate came out to them and asked, "What charges are you bringing against this man?"

³⁰"If he were not a criminal," they replied, "we would not have handed him over to you."

³¹Pilate said, "Take him yourselves and judge him by your own law."

"But we have no right to execute anyone," the Jews objected. ³²This

ᵃ24 Or *(Now Annas had sent him, still bound, to Caiaphas the high priest.)*

happened so that the words Jesus had spoken indicating the kind of death he was going to die would be fulfilled.

³³Pilate then went back inside the palace, summoned Jesus and asked him, "Are you the king of the Jews?"

³⁴"Is that your own idea," Jesus asked, "or did others talk to you about me?"

³⁵"Am I a Jew?" Pilate replied. "It was your people and your chief priests who handed you over to me. What is it you have done?"

³⁶Jesus said, "My kingdom is not of this world. If it were, my servants would fight to prevent my arrest by the Jews. But now my kingdom is from another place."

³⁷"You are a king, then!" said Pilate.

Jesus answered, "You are right in saying I am a king. In fact, for this reason I was born, and for this I came into the world, to testify to the truth. Everyone on the side of truth listens to me."

³⁸"What is truth?" Pilate asked. With this he went out again to the Jews and said, "I find no basis for a charge against him. ³⁹But it is your custom for me to release to you one prisoner at the time of the Passover. Do you want me to release 'the king of the Jews'?"

⁴⁰They shouted back, "No, not him! Give us Barabbas!" Now Barabbas had taken part in a rebellion.

Jesus Sentenced to be Crucified

19 Then Pilate took Jesus and had him flogged. ²The soldiers twisted together a crown of thorns and put it on his head. They clothed him in a purple robe ³and went up to him again and again, saying, "Hail, king of the Jews!" And they struck him in the face.

⁴Once more Pilate came out and said to the Jews, "Look, I am bringing him out to you to let you know that I find no basis for a charge against him." ⁵When Jesus came out wearing the crown of thorns and the purple robe, Pilate said to them, "Here is the man!"

⁶As soon as the chief priests and their officials saw him, they shouted, "Crucify! Crucify!"

But Pilate answered, "You take him and crucify him. As for me, I find no basis for a charge against him."

⁷The Jews insisted, "We have a law, and according to that law he must die, because he claimed to be the Son of God."

⁸When Pilate heard this, he was even more afraid, ⁹and he went back inside the palace. "Where do you come from?" he asked Jesus, but Jesus gave him no answer. ¹⁰"Do you refuse to speak to me?" Pilate said. "Don't you realize I have power either to free you or to crucify you?"

¹¹Jesus answered, "You would have no power over me if it were not given to you from above. Therefore the one who handed me over to you is guilty of a greater sin."

¹²From then on, Pilate tried to set Jesus free, but the Jews kept shouting,

"If you let this man go, you are no friend of Caesar. Anyone who claims to be a king opposes Caesar."

¹³When Pilate heard this, he brought Jesus out and sat down on the judge's seat at a place known as the Stone Pavement (which in Aramaic is Gabbatha). ¹⁴It was the day of Preparation of Passover Week, about the sixth hour.

"Here is your king," Pilate said to the Jews.

¹⁵But they shouted, "Take him away! Take him away! Crucify him!"

"Shall I crucify your king?" Pilate asked.

"We have no king but Caesar," the chief priests answered.

¹⁶Finally Pilate handed him over to them to be crucified.

The Crucifixion

So the soldiers took charge of Jesus. ¹⁷Carrying his own cross, he went out to the place of the Skull (which in Aramaic is called Golgotha). ¹⁸Here they crucified him, and with him two others—one on each side and Jesus in the middle.

¹⁹Pilate had a notice prepared and fastened to the cross. It read: JESUS OF NAZARETH, THE KING OF THE JEWS. ²⁰Many of the Jews read this sign, for the place where Jesus was crucified was near the city, and the sign was written in Aramaic, Latin and Greek. ²¹The chief priests of the Jews protested to Pilate, "Do not write 'The King of the Jews,' but that this man claimed to be king of the Jews."

²²Pilate answered, "What I have written, I have written."

²³When the soldiers crucified Jesus, they took his clothes, dividing them into four shares, one for each of them, with the undergarment remaining. This garment was seamless, woven in one piece from top to bottom.

²⁴"Let's not tear it," they said to one another. "Let's decide by lot who will get it."

This happened that the scripture might be fulfilled which said,

> "They divided my garments among them
>   and cast lots for my clothing."[a]

So this is what the soldiers did.

²⁵Near the cross of Jesus stood his mother, his mother's sister, Mary the wife of Clopas, and Mary Magdalene. ²⁶When Jesus saw his mother there, and the disciple whom he loved standing nearby, he said to his mother, "Dear woman, here is your son," ²⁷and to the disciple, "Here is your mother." From that time on, this disciple took her into his home.

The Death of Jesus

²⁸Later, knowing that all was now completed, and so that the Scripture would be fulfilled, Jesus said, "I am thirsty." ²⁹A jar of wine vinegar was there, so they soaked a sponge in it, put the sponge on a stalk of the hyssop plant, and lifted it to Jesus' lips. ³⁰When he had received the drink, Jesus

<hr />

a24 Psalm 22:18

said, "It is finished." With that, he bowed his head and gave up his spirit.

³¹Now it was the day of Preparation, and the next day was to be a special Sabbath. Because the Jews did not want the bodies left on the crosses during the Sabbath, they asked Pilate to have the legs broken and the bodies taken down. ³²The soldiers therefore came and broke the legs of the first man who had been crucified with Jesus, and then those of the other. ³³But when they came to Jesus and found that he was already dead, they did not break his legs. ³⁴Instead, one of the soldiers pierced Jesus' side with a spear, bringing a sudden flow of blood and water. ³⁵The man who saw it has given testimony, and his testimony is true. He knows that he tells the truth, and he testifies so that you also may believe. ³⁶These things happened so that the scripture would be fulfilled: "Not one of his bones will be broken,"[a] ³⁷and, as another scripture says, "They will look on the one they have pierced."[b]

The Burial of Jesus

³⁸Later, Joseph of Arimathea asked Pilate for the body of Jesus. Now Joseph was a disciple of Jesus, but secretly because he feared the Jews. With Pilate's permission, he came and took the body away. ³⁹He was accompanied by Nicodemus, the man who earlier had visited Jesus at night. Nicodemus brought a mixture of myrrh and aloes, about seventy-five pounds.[c] ⁴⁰Taking Jesus' body, the two of them wrapped it, with the spices, in strips of linen. This was in accordance with Jewish burial customs. ⁴¹At the place where Jesus was crucified, there was a garden, and in the garden a new tomb, in which no one had ever been laid. ⁴²Because it was the Jewish day of Preparation and since the tomb was nearby, they laid Jesus there.

The Empty Tomb

20 Early on the first day of the week, while it was still dark, Mary Magdalene went to the tomb and saw that the stone had been removed from the entrance. ²So she came running to Simon Peter and the other disciple, the one Jesus loved, and said, "They have taken the Lord out of the tomb, and we don't know where they have put him!"

³So Peter and the other disciple started for the tomb. ⁴Both were running, but the other disciple outran Peter and reached the tomb first. ⁵He bent over and looked in at the strips of linen lying there but did not go in. ⁶Then Simon Peter, who was behind him, arrived and went into the tomb. He saw the strips of linen lying there, ⁷as well as the burial cloth that had been around Jesus' head. The cloth was folded up by itself, separate from the linen. ⁸Finally the other disciple, who had reached the tomb first, also went inside. He saw and believed. ⁹(They still did not understand from Scripture that Jesus had to rise from the dead.)

[a]36 Exodus 12:46; Num. 9:12; Psalm 34:20   [b]37 Zech. 12:10   [c]39 Greek *a hundred litrai* (about 34 kilograms)

Jesus Appears to Mary Magdalene

¹⁰Then the disciples went back to their homes, ¹¹but Mary stood outside the tomb crying. As she wept, she bent over to look into the tomb ¹²and saw two angels in white, seated where Jesus' body had been, one at the head and the other at the foot.

¹³They asked her, "Woman, why are you crying?"

"They have taken my Lord away," she said, "and I don't know where they have put him." ¹⁴At this, she turned around and saw Jesus standing there, but she did not realize that it was Jesus.

¹⁵"Woman," he said, "why are you crying? Who is it you are looking for?"

Thinking he was the gardener, she said, "Sir, if you have carried him away, tell me where you have put him, and I will get him."

¹⁶Jesus said to her, "Mary."

She turned toward him and cried out in Aramaic, "Rabboni!" (which means Teacher).

¹⁷Jesus said, "Do not hold on to me, for I have not yet returned to the Father. Go instead to my brothers and tell them, 'I am returning to my Father and your Father, to my God and your God.'"

¹⁸Mary Magdalene went to the disciples with the news: "I have seen the Lord!" And she told them that he had said these things to her.

Jesus Appears to His Disciples

¹⁹On the evening of that first day of the week, when the disciples were together, with the doors locked for fear of the Jews, Jesus came and stood among them and said, "Peace be with you!" ²⁰After he said this, he showed them his hands and side. The disciples were overjoyed when they saw the Lord.

²¹Again Jesus said, "Peace be with you! As the Father has sent me, I am sending you." ²²And with that he breathed on them and said, "Receive the Holy Spirit. ²³If you forgive anyone his sins, they are forgiven; if you do not forgive them, they are not forgiven."

Jesus Appears to Thomas

²⁴Now Thomas (called Didymus), one of the Twelve, was not with the disciples when Jesus came. ²⁵So the other disciples told him, "We have seen the Lord!"

But he said to them, "Unless I see the nail marks in his hands and put my finger where the nails were, and put my hand into his side, I will not believe it."

²⁶A week later his disciples were in the house again, and Thomas was with them. Though the doors were locked, Jesus came and stood among them and said, "Peace be with you!" ²⁷Then he said to Thomas, "Put your finger here; see my hands. Reach out your hand and put it into my side. Stop doubting and believe."

²⁸Thomas said to him, "My Lord and my God!"

²⁹Then Jesus told him, "Because you have seen me, you have believed; blessed are those who have not seen and yet have believed."

³⁰Jesus did many other miraculous signs in the presence of his disciples, which are not recorded in this book. ³¹But these are written that you may*ᵃ* believe that Jesus is the Christ, the Son of God, and that by believing you may have life in his name.

Jesus and the Miraculous Catch of Fish

21 Afterward Jesus appeared again to his disciples, by the Sea of Tiberias.*ᵇ* It happened this way: ²Simon Peter, Thomas (called Didymus), Nathanael from Cana in Galilee, the sons of Zebedee, and two other disciples were together. ³"I'm going out to fish," Simon Peter told them, and they said, "We'll go with you." So they went out and got into the boat, but that night they caught nothing.

⁴Early in the morning, Jesus stood on the shore, but the disciples did not realize that it was Jesus.

⁵He called out to them, "Friends, haven't you any fish?"

"No," they answered.

⁶He said, "Throw your net on the right side of the boat and you will find some." When they did, they were unable to haul the net in because of the large number of fish.

⁷Then the disciple whom Jesus loved said to Peter, "It is the Lord!" As soon as Simon Peter heard him say, "It is the Lord," he wrapped his outer garment around him (for he had taken it off) and jumped into the water. ⁸The other disciples followed in the boat, towing the net full of fish, for they were not far from shore, about a hundred yards.*ᶜ* ⁹When they landed, they saw a fire of burning coals there with fish on it, and some bread.

¹⁰Jesus said to them, "Bring some of the fish you have just caught."

¹¹Simon Peter climbed aboard and dragged the net ashore. It was full of large fish, 153, but even with so many the net was not torn. ¹²Jesus said to them, "Come and have breakfast." None of the disciples dared ask him, "Who are you?" They knew it was the Lord. ¹³Jesus came, took the bread and gave it to them, and did the same with the fish. ¹⁴This was now the third time Jesus appeared to his disciples after he was raised from the dead.

Jesus Reinstates Peter

¹⁵When they had finished eating, Jesus said to Simon Peter, "Simon son of John, do you truly love me more than these?"

"Yes, Lord," he said, "you know that I love you."

Jesus said, "Feed my lambs."

¹⁶Again Jesus said, "Simon son of John, do you truly love me?"

He answered, "Yes, Lord, you know that I love you."

Jesus said, "Take care of my sheep."

¹⁷The third time he said to him, "Simon son of John, do you love me?"

---

*ᵃ*31 Some manuscripts *may continue to*   *ᵇ*1 That is, Sea of Galilee   *ᶜ*8 Greek *about two hundred cubits* (about 90 meters)

Peter was hurt because Jesus asked him the third time, "Do you love me?" He said, "Lord, you know all things; you know that I love you."

Jesus said, "Feed my sheep. [18]I tell you the truth, when you were younger you dressed yourself and went where you wanted; but when you are old you will stretch out your hands, and someone else will dress you and lead you where you do not want to go." [19]Jesus said this to indicate the kind of death by which Peter would glorify God. Then he said to him, "Follow me!"

[20]Peter turned and saw that the disciple whom Jesus loved was following them. (This was the one who had leaned back against Jesus at the supper and had said, "Lord, who is going to betray you?") [21]When Peter saw him, he asked, "Lord, what about him?"

[22]Jesus answered, "If I want him to remain alive until I return, what is that to you? You must follow me." [23]Because of this, the rumor spread among the brothers that this disciple would not die. But Jesus did not say that he would not die; he only said, "If I want him to remain alive until I return, what is that to you?"

[24]This is the disciple who testifies to these things and who wrote them down. We know that his testimony is true.

[25]Jesus did many other things as well. If every one of them were written down, I suppose that even the whole world would not have room for the books that would be written.

Acts

INTRODUCTION

Scholars agree with tradition that Acts was written by the author of the Gospel according to Luke and is its continuation (cf. Lk 1:3; Acts 1:1, and the correlation between Lk 24:46–53 and Acts 1:4–9). It was composed some time after the Gospel, probably around 85–90 A.D., before the letters of Paul had become a literary corpus available to the author, and before the fierce persecution of Christians by Domitian which began toward the end of his reign (81–96 A.D.).

Acts illustrates the growth of the Church and shows how, under the guidance of the Holy Spirit, salvation in Jesus was made available from Jerusalem to the whole world through special witnesses who had been with the Lord "beginning from John's baptism to the time Jesus was taken up from us" (Acts 1:22; see 1:2–11). The structure of the book follows the geographical plan given in Acts 1:8 and carried forward in 23:11 (see Lk 24:47). It is as follows:

Introduction (1:1–26)
Witness in Jerusalem (2:1—5:42)
Witness in Judea and Samaria;
First Mission to Gentiles

(6:1—15:35)
Witness to the Ends of the
Earth, Rome (15:35—28:31)

Within this theological framework much reliable historical information can be found. Certain incidents can be approximately dated from external evidence, such as the death of Agrippa (12:20–23), the expulsion of the Jews from Rome by Claudius (18:2), Gallio's tenure as proconsul of Achaia (18:12), and the succession of Felix by Porcius Festus as governor of Caesarea (24:27). As a result, a reasonably accurate chronology of the events recounted in Acts can be drawn up:

A.D. 30 death of Jesus
31/32 conversion of Paul
34/35 Paul's first journey to Jerusalem
45–49 first missionary journey to Syria and Cilicia
48/49 Council of Jerusalem
49–53 second missionary journey
53–58 third missionary journey
57/58 imprisonment of Paul in Jerusalem
59/60 transfer of Paul to Rome

Luke's purpose in writing Acts was to show the continuity of the tradition about Jesus from the beginning (as described in his Gospel) up to his own time, the late 80's. He emphasized the identity of the preaching of the apostles with the teaching of Jesus (Acts 1:3).

This also meant that the question of the parousia was effectively postponed to the indefinite future. The apostles were warned not to worry about "times or dates" (Acts 1:7), and were instead commissioned to be witnesses of Jesus from Jerusalem to the ends of the earth (1:7–8). Jesus would indeed return again (1:11), but no one could say when.

A major concern of Acts is salvation through Jesus, exalted by the Father as Savior "that he might give repentance and forgiveness of sins to Israel" (Acts 5:31); through his grace both Jews and Gentiles are to be saved (Acts 15:11; see 16:31; also 11:14; 13:26,47; 16:17; 26:17–18; 28:28), "for there is no other name under heaven . . . by which we must be saved" (Acts 4:12).

Equally important is the presence of the Holy Spirit in the Church. The Spirit is the gift of power from the Father through Jesus to the disciples (1:8; 2:38; 10:45), especially in baptism (1:5; 11:16; 19:5 –6). He actively guided the early missionary efforts (1:8; 8:29,39; 10:19; 13:2–4; 16:6–7; 20:22–23), and even assisted in preaching (6:10; 7:51; see Lk 12:12).

Generous sharing of one's resources is another theme developed by Luke. He presented an idealized picture of how the early Christians held everything in common and gave to anyone in need (Acts 2:44–45; 4:32–35). Note the charity of the Christians of Antioch for the famine victims in Judea (11:28–30; 24:17). Luke is the only New Testament writer to record the word of the Lord that "it is more blessed to give than to receive" (Acts 20:35).

Acts continues Luke's special awareness of women in the early Church: their presence at Pentecost (1:13–14: 2:1), Tabitha (9:36–42), Damaris (17:34), Lydia (16:14–15), Priscilla (18:2ff), and the four daughters of Philip who prophesied (21:7).

JOSEPH F. WIMMER, O.S.A.

Points for Reflection

1. Jesus is the only Savior in the world. Is he mine?
2. The early Christians were profoundly aware of the presence of the Holy Spirit in their lives. Is that my experience? How can I deepen it?
3. "It is more blessed to give than to receive." Do I believe this and act on it?
4. Paul's imprisonment in Rome was an effective stage for bearing witness to Jesus. Do I properly utilize the many opportunities I am granted to bear witness to him?
5. Jesus will return to judge the world. Will I be ready when he comes?

Jesus Taken Up Into Heaven

1 In my former book, Theophilus, I wrote about all that Jesus began to do and to teach [2]until the day he was taken up to heaven, after giving instructions through the Holy Spirit to the apostles he had chosen. [3]After his suffering, he showed himself to these men and gave many convincing proofs that he was alive. He appeared to them over a period of forty days and spoke about the kingdom of God. [4]On one occasion, while he was eating with them, he gave them this command: "Do not leave Jerusalem, but wait for the gift my Father promised, which you have heard me speak about. [5]For John baptized with[a] water, but in a few days you will be baptized with the Holy Spirit."

[6]So when they met together, they asked him, "Lord, are you at this time going to restore the kingdom to Israel?"

[7]He said to them: "It is not for you to know the times or dates the Father has set by his own authority. [8]But you will receive power when the Holy Spirit comes on you; and you will be my witnesses in Jerusalem, and in all Judea and Samaria, and to the ends of the earth."

[9]After he said this, he was taken up before their very eyes, and a cloud hid him from their sight.

[10]They were looking intently up into the sky as he was going, when suddenly two men dressed in white stood beside them. [11]"Men of Galilee," they said, "why do you stand here looking into the sky? This same Jesus, who has been taken from you into heaven, will come back in the same way you have seen him go into heaven."

Matthias Chosen to Replace Judas

[12]Then they returned to Jerusalem from the hill called the Mount of Olives, a Sabbath day's walk[b] from the city. [13]When they arrived, they went upstairs to the room where they were staying. Those present were Peter, John, James and Andrew; Philip and Thomas, Bartholomew and Matthew; James son of Alphaeus and Simon the Zealot, and Judas son of James. [14]They all joined together constantly in prayer, along with the women and Mary the mother of Jesus, and with his brothers.

[15]In those days Peter stood up among the believers[c] (a group numbering about a hundred and twenty) [16]and said, "Brothers, the Scripture had to be fulfilled which the Holy Spirit spoke long ago through the mouth of David concerning Judas, who served as guide for those who arrested Jesus —[17]he was one of our number and shared in this ministry."

[18](With the reward he got for his wickedness, Judas bought a field; there he fell headlong, his body burst open and all his intestines spilled out. [19]Everyone in Jerusalem heard about this, so they called that field in their language Akeldama, that is, Field of Blood.)

[20]"For," said Peter, "it is written in the book of Psalms,

" 'May his place be deserted;

[a]5 Or *in*   [b]12 That is, about 3/4 mile (about 1,100 meters)   [c]15 Greek *brothers*

let there be no one to dwell in it,'[a]

and,

" 'May another take his place of leadership.'[b]

[21]Therefore it is necessary to choose one of the men who have been with us the whole time the Lord Jesus went in and out among us, [22]beginning from John's baptism to the time when Jesus was taken up from us. For one of these must become a witness with us of his resurrection."

[23]So they proposed two men: Joseph called Barsabbas (also known as Justus) and Matthias. [24]Then they prayed, "Lord, you know everyone's heart. Show us which of these two you have chosen [25]to take over this apostolic ministry, which Judas left to go where he belongs." [26]Then they cast lots, and the lot fell to Matthias; so he was added to the eleven apostles.

The Holy Spirit Comes at Pentecost

2 When the day of Pentecost came, they were all together in one place. [2]Suddenly a sound like the blowing of a violent wind came from heaven and filled the whole house where they were sitting. [3]They saw what seemed to be tongues of fire that separated and came to rest on each of them. [4]All of them were filled with the Holy Spirit and began to speak in other tongues[c] as the Spirit enabled them.

[5]Now there were staying in Jerusalem God-fearing Jews from every nation under heaven. [6]When they heard this sound, a crowd came together in bewilderment, because each one heard them speaking in his own language. [7]Utterly amazed, they asked: "Are not all these men who are speaking Galileans? [8]Then how is it that each of us hears them in his own native language? [9]Parthians, Medes and Elamites; residents of Mesopotamia, Judea and Cappadocia, Pontus and Asia, [10]Phrygia and Pamphylia, Egypt and the parts of Libya near Cyrene; visitors from Rome [11](both Jews and converts to Judaism); Cretans and Arabs—we hear them declaring the wonders of God in our own tongues!" [12]Amazed and perplexed, they asked one another, "What does this mean?"

[13]Some, however, made fun of them and said, "They have had too much wine.[d]"

Peter Addresses the Crowd

[14]Then Peter stood up with the Eleven, raised his voice and addressed the crowd: "Fellow Jews and all of you who live in Jerusalem, let me explain this to you; listen carefully to what I say. [15]These men are not drunk, as you suppose. It's only nine in the morning! [16]No, this is what was spoken by the prophet Joel:

[17]" 'In the last days, God says,
I will pour out my Spirit on all people.
Your sons and daughters will prophesy,

[a]20 Psalm 69:25   [b]20 Psalm 109:8   [c]4 Or *languages*; also in verse 11   [d]13 Or *sweet wine*

your young men will see visions,
    your old men will dream dreams.
[18]Even on my servants, both men and women,
    I will pour out my Spirit in those days,
    and they will prophesy.
[19]I will show wonders in the heaven above
    and signs on the earth below,
    blood and fire and billows of smoke.
[20]The sun will be turned to darkness
    and the moon to blood
    before the coming of the great and glorious day of the
        Lord.
[21]And everyone who calls
    on the name of the Lord will be saved.'[a]

[22]"Men of Israel, listen to this: Jesus of Nazareth was a man accredited by God to you by miracles, wonders and signs, which God did among you through him, as you yourselves know. [23]This man was handed over to you by God's set purpose and foreknowledge; and you, with the help of wicked men,[b] put him to death by nailing him to the cross. [24]But God raised him from the dead, freeing him from the agony of death, because it was impossible for death to keep its hold on him. [25]David said about him:

" 'I saw the Lord always before me.
    Because he is at my right hand,
    I will not be shaken.
[26]Therefore my heart is glad and my tongue rejoices;
    my body also will live in hope,
[27]because you will not abandon me to the grave,
    nor will you let your Holy One see decay.
[28]You have made known to me the paths of life;
    you will fill me with joy in your presence.'[c]

[29]"Brothers, I can tell you confidently that the patriarch David died and was buried, and his tomb is here to this day. [30]But he was a prophet and knew that God had promised him on oath that he would place one of his descendants on his throne. [31]Seeing what was ahead, he spoke of the resurrection of the Christ,[d] that he was not abandoned to the grave, nor did his body see decay. [32]God has raised this Jesus to life, and we are all witnesses of the fact. [33]Exalted to the right hand of God, he has received from the Father the promised Holy Spirit and has poured out what you now see and hear. [34]For David did not ascend to heaven, and yet he said,

" 'The Lord said to my Lord:
    "Sit at my right hand

[a]21 Joel 2:28-32   [b]23 Or of those not having the law (that is, Gentiles)   [c]28 Psalm 16:8-11
[d]31 Or Messiah. "The Christ" (Greek) and "the Messiah" (Hebrew) both mean "the Anointed One";
also in verse 36.

35until I make your enemies
 a footstool for your feet." '[a]

36"Therefore let all Israel be assured of this: God has made this Jesus, whom you crucified, both Lord and Christ."

37When the people heard this, they were cut to the heart and said to Peter and the other apostles, "Brothers, what shall we do?"

38Peter replied, "Repent and be baptized, every one of you, in the name of Jesus Christ for the forgiveness of your sins. And you will receive the gift of the Holy Spirit. 39The promise is for you and your children and for all who are far off—for all whom the Lord our God will call."

40With many other words he warned them; and he pleaded with them, "Save yourselves from this corrupt generation." 41Those who accepted his message were baptized, and about three thousand were added to their number that day.

The Fellowship of the Believers

42They devoted themselves to the apostles' teaching and to the fellowship, to the breaking of bread and to prayer. 43Everyone was filled with awe, and many wonders and miraculous signs were done by the apostles. 44All the believers were together and had everything in common. 45Selling their possessions and goods, they gave to anyone as he had need. 46Every day they continued to meet together in the temple courts. They broke bread in their homes and ate together with glad and sincere hearts, 47praising God and enjoying the favor of all the people. And the Lord added to their number daily those who were being saved.

Peter Heals the Crippled Beggar

3 One day Peter and John were going up to the temple at the time of prayer—at three in the afternoon. 2Now a man crippled from birth was being carried to the temple gate called Beautiful, where he was put every day to beg from those going into the temple courts. 3When he saw Peter and John about to enter, he asked them for money. 4Peter looked straight at him, as did John. Then Peter said, "Look at us!" 5So the man gave them his attention, expecting to get something from them.

6Then Peter said, "Silver or gold I do not have, but what I have I give you. In the name of Jesus Christ of Nazareth, walk." 7Taking him by the right hand, he helped him up, and instantly the man's feet and ankles became strong. 8He jumped to his feet and began to walk. Then he went with them into the temple courts, walking and jumping, and praising God. 9When all the people saw him walking and praising God, 10they recognized him as the same man who used to sit begging at the temple gate called Beautiful, and they were filled with wonder and amazement at what had happened to him.

[a]35 Psalm 110:1

Peter Speaks to the Onlookers

[11]While the beggar held on to Peter and John, all the people were astonished and came running to them in the place called Solomon's Colonnade. [12]When Peter saw this, he said to them: "Men of Israel, why does this surprise you? Why do you stare at us as if by our own power or godliness we had made this man walk? [13]The God of Abraham, Isaac and Jacob, the God of our fathers, has glorified his servant Jesus. You handed him over to be killed, and you disowned him before Pilate, though he had decided to let him go. [14]You disowned the Holy and Righteous One and asked that a murderer be released to you. [15]You killed the author of life, but God raised him from the dead. We are witnesses of this. [16]By faith in the name of Jesus, this man whom you see and know was made strong. It is Jesus' name and the faith that comes through him that has given this complete healing to him, as you can all see.

[17]"Now, brothers, I know that you acted in ignorance, as did your leaders. [18]But this is how God fulfilled what he had foretold through all the prophets, saying that his Christ[a] would suffer. [19]Repent, then, and turn to God, so that your sins may be wiped out, that times of refreshing may come from the Lord, [20]and that he may send the Christ, who has been appointed for you—even Jesus. [21]He must remain in heaven until the time comes for God to restore everything, as he promised long ago through his holy prophets. [22]For Moses said, 'The Lord your God will raise up for you a prophet like me from among your own people; you must listen to everything he tells you. [23]Anyone who does not listen to him will be completely cut off from among his people.'[b]

[24]"Indeed, all the prophets from Samuel on, as many as have spoken, have foretold these days. [25]And you are heirs of the prophets and of the covenant God made with your fathers. He said to Abraham, 'Through your offspring all peoples on earth will be blessed.'[c] [26]When God raised up his servant, he sent him first to you to bless you by turning each of you from your wicked ways."

Peter and John Before the Sanhedrin

4 The priests and the captain of the temple guard and the Sadducees came up to Peter and John while they were speaking to the people. [2]They were greatly disturbed because the apostles were teaching the people and proclaiming in Jesus the resurrection of the dead. [3]They seized Peter and John, and because it was evening, they put them in jail until the next day. [4]But many who heard the message believed, and the number of men grew to about five thousand.

[5]The next day the rulers, elders and teachers of the law met in Jerusalem. [6]Annas the high priest was there, and so were Caiaphas, John, Alexander and the other men of the high priest's family. [7]They had Peter and John

[a]18 Or Messiah; also in verse 20   [b]23 Deut. 18:15,18,19   [c]25 Gen. 22:18; 26:4

brought before them and began to question them: "By what power or what name did you do this?"

⁸Then Peter, filled with the Holy Spirit, said to them: "Rulers and elders of the people! ⁹If we are being called to account today for an act of kindness shown to a cripple and are asked how he was healed, ¹⁰then know this, you and all the people of Israel: It is by the name of Jesus Christ of Nazareth, whom you crucified but whom God raised from the dead, that this man stands before you healed. ¹¹He is

> " 'the stone you builders rejected,
> which has become the capstone. ᵃ' ᵇ

¹²Salvation is found in no one else, for there is no other name under heaven given to men by which we must be saved."

¹³When they saw the courage of Peter and John and realized that they were unschooled, ordinary men, they were astonished and they took note that these men had been with Jesus. ¹⁴But since they could see the man who had been healed standing there with them, there was nothing they could say. ¹⁵So they ordered them to withdraw from the Sanhedrin and then conferred together. ¹⁶"What are we going to do with these men?" they asked. "Everybody living in Jerusalem knows they have done an outstanding miracle, and we cannot deny it. ¹⁷But to stop this thing from spreading any further among the people, we must warn these men to speak no longer to anyone in this name."

¹⁸Then they called them in again and commanded them not to speak or teach at all in the name of Jesus. ¹⁹But Peter and John replied, "Judge for yourselves whether it is right in God's sight to obey you rather than God. ²⁰For we cannot help speaking about what we have seen and heard."

²¹After further threats they let them go. They could not decide how to punish them, because all the people were praising God for what had happened. ²²For the man who was miraculously healed was over forty years old.

The Believers' Prayer

²³On their release, Peter and John went back to their own people and reported all that the chief priests and elders had said to them. ²⁴When they heard this, they raised their voices together in prayer to God. "Sovereign Lord," they said, "you made the heaven and the earth and the sea, and everything in them. ²⁵You spoke by the Holy Spirit through the mouth of your servant, our father David:

> " 'Why do the nations rage
> and the peoples plot in vain?
> ²⁶The kings of the earth take their stand
> and the rulers gather together
> against the Lord

ᵃ11 Or *cornerstone*   ᵇ11 Psalm 118:22

and against his Anointed One. *ᵃ ᵇ*

²⁷Indeed Herod and Pontius Pilate met together with the Gentiles and the people*ᶜ* of Israel in this city to conspire against your holy servant Jesus, whom you anointed. ²⁸They did what your power and will had decided beforehand should happen. ²⁹Now, Lord, consider their threats and enable your servants to speak your word with great boldness. ³⁰Stretch out your hand to heal and perform miraculous signs and wonders through the name of your holy servant Jesus."

³¹After they prayed, the place where they were meeting was shaken. And they were all filled with the Holy Spirit and spoke the word of God boldly.

The Believers Share Their Possessions

³²All the believers were one in heart and mind. No one claimed that any of his possessions was his own, but they shared everything they had. ³³With great power the apostles continued to testify to the resurrection of the Lord Jesus, and much grace was upon them all. ³⁴There were no needy persons among them. For from time to time those who owned lands or houses sold them, brought the money from the sales ³⁵and put it at the apostles' feet, and it was distributed to anyone as he had need.

³⁶Joseph, a Levite from Cyprus, whom the apostles called Barnabas (which means Son of Encouragement), ³⁷sold a field he owned and brought the money and put it at the apostles' feet.

Ananias and Sapphira

5 Now a man named Ananias, together with his wife Sapphira, also sold a piece of property. ²With his wife's full knowledge he kept back part of the money for himself, but brought the rest and put it at the apostles' feet.

³Then Peter said, "Ananias, how is it that Satan has so filled your heart that you have lied to the Holy Spirit and have kept for yourself some of the money you received for the land? ⁴Didn't it belong to you before it was sold? And after it was sold, wasn't the money at your disposal? What made you think of doing such a thing? You have not lied to men but to God."

⁵When Ananias heard this, he fell down and died. And great fear seized all who heard what had happened. ⁶Then the young men came forward, wrapped up his body, and carried him out and buried him.

⁷About three hours later his wife came in, not knowing what had happened. ⁸Peter asked her, "Tell me, is this the price you and Ananias got for the land?"

"Yes," she said, "that is the price."

⁹Peter said to her, "How could you agree to test the Spirit of the Lord? Look! The feet of the men who buried your husband are at the door, and they will carry you out also."

ᵃ26 That is, Christ or Messiah   ᵇ26 Psalm 2:1,2   ᶜ27 The Greek is plural.

[10]At that moment she fell down at his feet and died. Then the young men came in and, finding her dead, carried her out and buried her beside her husband. [11]Great fear seized the whole church and all who heard about these events.

The Apostles Heal Many

[12]The apostles performed many miraculous signs and wonders among the people. And all the believers used to meet together in Solomon's Colonnade. [13]No one else dared join them, even though they were highly regarded by the people. [14]Nevertheless, more and more men and women believed in the Lord and were added to their number. [15]As a result, people brought the sick into the streets and laid them on beds and mats so that at least Peter's shadow might fall on some of them as he passed by. [16]Crowds gathered also from the towns around Jerusalem, bringing their sick and those tormented by evil[a] spirits, and all of them were healed.

The Apostles Persecuted

[17]Then the high priest and all his associates, who were members of the party of the Sadducees, were filled with jealousy. [18]They arrested the apostles and put them in the public jail. [19]But during the night an angel of the Lord opened the doors of the jail and brought them out. [20]"Go, stand in the temple courts," he said, "and tell the people the full message of this new life."

[21]At daybreak they entered the temple courts, as they had been told, and began to teach the people.

When the high priest and his associates arrived, they called together the Sanhedrin—the full assembly of the elders of Israel—and sent to the jail for the apostles. [22]But on arriving at the jail, the officers did not find them there. So they went back and reported, [23]"We found the jail securely locked, with the guards standing at the doors; but when we opened them, we found no one inside." [24]On hearing this report, the captain of the temple guard and the chief priests were puzzled, wondering what would come of this.

[25]Then someone came and said, "Look! The men you put in jail are standing in the temple courts teaching the people." [26]At that, the captain went with his officers and brought the apostles. They did not use force, because they feared that the people would stone them.

[27]Having brought the apostles, they made them appear before the Sanhedrin to be questioned by the high priest. [28]"We gave you strict orders not to teach in this name," he said. "Yet you have filled Jerusalem with your teaching and are determined to make us guilty of this man's blood."

[29]Peter and the other apostles replied: "We must obey God rather than men! [30]The God of our fathers raised Jesus from the dead—whom you had killed by hanging him on a tree. [31]God exalted him to his own right hand as Prince and Savior that he might give repentance and forgiveness of sins

[a]16 Greek *unclean*

to Israel. ³²We are witnesses of these things, and so is the Holy Spirit, whom God has given to those who obey him."

³³When they heard this, they were furious and wanted to put them to death. ³⁴But a Pharisee named Gamaliel, a teacher of the law, who was honored by all the people, stood up in the Sanhedrin and ordered that the men be put outside for a little while. ³⁵Then he addressed them: "Men of Israel, consider carefully what you intend to do to these men. ³⁶Some time ago Theudas appeared, claiming to be somebody, and about four hundred men rallied to him. He was killed, all his followers were dispersed, and it all came to nothing. ³⁷After him, Judas the Galilean appeared in the days of the census and led a band of people in revolt. He too was killed, and all his followers were scattered. ³⁸Therefore, in the present case I advise you: Leave these men alone! Let them go! For if their purpose or activity is of human origin, it will fail. ³⁹But if it is from God, you will not be able to stop these men; you will only find yourselves fighting against God."

⁴⁰His speech persuaded them. They called the apostles in and had them flogged. Then they ordered them not to speak in the name of Jesus, and let them go.

⁴¹The apostles left the Sanhedrin, rejoicing because they had been counted worthy of suffering disgrace for the Name. ⁴²Day after day, in the temple courts and from house to house, they never stopped teaching and proclaiming the good news that Jesus is the Christ.ᵃ

The Choosing of the Seven

6 In those days when the number of disciples was increasing, the Grecian Jews among them complained against the Hebraic Jews because their widows were being overlooked in the daily distribution of food. ²So the Twelve gathered all the disciples together and said, "It would not be right for us to neglect the ministry of the word of God in order to wait on tables. ³Brothers, choose seven men from among you who are known to be full of the Spirit and wisdom. We will turn this responsibility over to them ⁴and will give our attention to prayer and the ministry of the word."

⁵This proposal pleased the whole group. They chose Stephen, a man full of faith and of the Holy Spirit; also Philip, Procorus, Nicanor, Timon, Parmenas, and Nicolas from Antioch, a convert to Judaism. ⁶They presented these men to the apostles, who prayed and laid their hands on them.

⁷So the word of God spread. The number of disciples in Jerusalem increased rapidly, and a large number of priests became obedient to the faith.

Stephen Seized

⁸Now Stephen, a man full of God's grace and power, did great wonders and miraculous signs among the people. ⁹Opposition arose, however, from members of the Synagogue of the Freedmen (as it was called)—Jews of

ᵃ42 Or *Messiah*

Cyrene and Alexandria as well as the provinces of Cilicia and Asia. These men began to argue with Stephen, [10]but they could not stand up against his wisdom or the Spirit by whom he spoke.

[11]Then they secretly persuaded some men to say, "We have heard Stephen speak words of blasphemy against Moses and against God."

[12]So they stirred up the people and the elders and the teachers of the law. They seized Stephen and brought him before the Sanhedrin. [13]They produced false witnesses, who testified, "This fellow never stops speaking against this holy place and against the law. [14]For we have heard him say that this Jesus of Nazareth will destroy this place and change the customs Moses handed down to us."

[15]All who were sitting in the Sanhedrin looked intently at Stephen, and they saw that his face was like the face of an angel.

Stephen's Speech to the Sanhedrin

7 Then the high priest asked him, "Are these charges true?" [2]To this he replied: "Brothers and fathers, listen to me! The God of glory appeared to our father Abraham while he was still in Mesopotamia, before he lived in Haran. [3]'Leave your country and your people,' God said, 'and go to the land I will show you.'[a]

[4]"So he left the land of the Chaldeans and settled in Haran. After the death of his father, God sent him to this land where you are now living. [5]He gave him no inheritance here, not even a foot of ground. But God promised him that he and his descendants after him would possess the land, even though at that time Abraham had no child. [6]God spoke to him in this way: 'Your descendants will be strangers in a country not their own, and they will be enslaved and mistreated four hundred years. [7]But I will punish the nation they serve as slaves,' God said, 'and afterward they will come out of that country and worship me in this place.'[b] [8]Then he gave Abraham the covenant of circumcision. And Abraham became the father of Isaac and circumcised him eight days after his birth. Later Isaac became the father of Jacob, and Jacob became the father of the twelve patriarchs.

[9]"Because the patriarchs were jealous of Joseph, they sold him as a slave into Egypt. But God was with him [10]and rescued him from all his troubles. He gave Joseph wisdom and enabled him to gain the goodwill of Pharaoh king of Egypt; so he made him ruler over Egypt and all his palace.

[11]"Then a famine struck all Egypt and Canaan, bringing great suffering, and our fathers could not find food. [12]When Jacob heard that there was grain in Egypt, he sent our fathers on their first visit. [13]On their second visit, Joseph told his brothers who he was, and Pharaoh learned about Joseph's family. [14]After this, Joseph sent for his father Jacob and his whole family, seventy-five in all. [15]Then Jacob went down to Egypt, where he and our fathers died. [16]Their bodies were brought back to Shechem and placed in the tomb that Abraham had bought from the sons of Hamor at Shechem for a certain sum of money.

[a]3 Gen. 12:1   [b]7 Gen. 15:13,14

[17]"As the time drew near for God to fulfill his promise to Abraham, the number of our people in Egypt greatly increased. [18]Then another king, who knew nothing about Joseph, became ruler of Egypt. [19]He dealt treacherously with our people and oppressed our forefathers by forcing them to throw out their newborn babies so that they would die.

[20]"At that time Moses was born, and he was no ordinary child.[a] For three months he was cared for in his father's house. [21]When he was placed outside, Pharaoh's daughter took him and brought him up as her own son. [22]Moses was educated in all the wisdom of the Egyptians and was powerful in speech and action.

[23]"When Moses was forty years old, he decided to visit his fellow Israelites. [24]He saw one of them being mistreated by an Egyptian, so he went to his defense and avenged him by killing the Egyptian. [25]Moses thought that his own people would realize that God was using him to rescue them, but they did not. [26]The next day Moses came upon two Israelites who were fighting. He tried to reconcile them by saying, 'Men, you are brothers; why do you want to hurt each other?'

[27]"But the man who was mistreating the other pushed Moses aside and said, 'Who made you ruler and judge over us? [28]Do you want to kill me as you killed the Egyptian yesterday?'[b] [29]When Moses heard this, he fled to Midian, where he settled as a foreigner and had two sons.

[30]"After forty years had passed, an angel appeared to Moses in the flames of a burning bush in the desert near Mount Sinai. [31]When he saw this, he was amazed at the sight. As he went over to look more closely, he heard the Lord's voice: [32]'I am the God of your fathers, the God of Abraham, Isaac and Jacob.'[c] Moses trembled with fear and did not dare to look.

[33]"Then the Lord said to him, 'Take off your sandals; the place where you are standing is holy ground. [34]I have indeed seen the oppression of my people in Egypt. I have heard their groaning and have come down to set them free. Now come, I will send you back to Egypt.'[d]

[35]"This is the same Moses whom they had rejected with the words, 'Who made you ruler and judge?' He was sent to be their ruler and deliverer by God himself, through the angel who appeared to him in the bush. [36]He led them out of Egypt and did wonders and miraculous signs in Egypt, at the Red Sea[e] and for forty years in the desert.

[37]"This is that Moses who told the Israelites, 'God will send you a prophet like me from your own people.'[f] [38]He was in the assembly in the desert, with the angel who spoke to him on Mount Sinai, and with our fathers; and he received living words to pass on to us.

[39]"But our fathers refused to obey him. Instead, they rejected him and in their hearts turned back to Egypt. [40]They told Aaron, 'Make us gods who will go before us. As for this fellow Moses who led us out of Egypt—we don't know what has happened to him!'[g] [41]That was the time they made an idol in the form of a calf. They brought sacrifices to it and held a celebration

---

[a]20 Or *was fair in the sight of God*   [b]28 Exodus 2:14   [c]32 Exodus 3:6   [d]34 Exodus 3:5,7,8,10
[e]36 That is, Sea of Reeds   [f]37 Deut. 18:15   [g]40 Exodus 32:1

in honor of what their hands had made. ⁴²But God turned away and gave them over to the worship of the heavenly bodies. This agrees with what is written in the book of the prophets:

> " 'Did you bring me sacrifices and offerings
> forty years in the desert, O house of Israel?
> ⁴³You have lifted up the shrine of Molech
> and the star of your god Rephan,
> the idols you made to worship.
> Therefore I will send you into exile'ᵃ beyond Babylon.

⁴⁴"Our forefathers had the tabernacle of the Testimony with them in the desert. It had been made as God directed Moses, according to the pattern he had seen. ⁴⁵Having received the tabernacle, our fathers under Joshua brought it with them when they took the land from the nations God drove out before them. It remained in the land until the time of David, ⁴⁶who enjoyed God's favor and asked that he might provide a dwelling place for the God of Jacob.ᵇ ⁴⁷But it was Solomon who built the house for him.

⁴⁸"However, the Most High does not live in houses made by men. As the prophet says:

> ⁴⁹" 'Heaven is my throne,
> and the earth is my footstool.
> What kind of house will you build for me?
>
> says the Lord.
>
> Or where will my resting place be?
> ⁵⁰Has not my hand made all these things?'ᶜ

⁵¹"You stiff-necked people, with uncircumcised hearts and ears! You are just like your fathers: You always resist the Holy Spirit! ⁵²Was there ever a prophet your fathers did not persecute? They even killed those who predicted the coming of the Righteous One. And now you have betrayed and murdered him— ⁵³you who have received the law that was put into effect through angels but have not obeyed it."

The Stoning of Stephen

⁵⁴When they heard this, they were furious and gnashed their teeth at him. ⁵⁵But Stephen, full of the Holy Spirit, looked up to heaven and saw the glory of God, and Jesus standing at the right hand of God. ⁵⁶"Look," he said, "I see heaven open and the Son of Man standing at the right hand of God."

⁵⁷At this they covered their ears and, yelling at the top of their voices, they all rushed at him, ⁵⁸dragged him out of the city and began to stone him. Meanwhile, the witnesses laid their clothes at the feet of a young man named Saul.

⁵⁹While they were stoning him, Stephen prayed, "Lord Jesus, receive

---

ᵃ43 Amos 5:25-27   ᵇ46 Some early manuscripts *the house of Jacob*   ᶜ50 Isaiah 66:1,2 my spirit." ⁶⁰Then he fell on his knees and cried out, "Lord, do not hold this sin against them." When he had said this, he fell asleep.

8 And Saul was there, giving approval to his death.

The Church Persecuted and Scattered

On that day a great persecution broke out against the church at Jerusalem, and all except the apostles were scattered throughout Judea and Samaria. ²Godly men buried Stephen and mourned deeply for him. ³But Saul began to destroy the church. Going from house to house, he dragged off men and women and put them in prison.

Philip in Samaria

⁴Those who had been scattered preached the word wherever they went. ⁵Philip went down to a city in Samaria and proclaimed the Christ*ᵃ* there. ⁶When the crowds heard Philip and saw the miraculous signs he did, they all paid close attention to what he said. ⁷With shrieks, evil*ᵇ* spirits came out of many, and many paralytics and cripples were healed. ⁸So there was great joy in that city.

Simon the Sorcerer

⁹Now for some time a man named Simon had practiced sorcery in the city and amazed all the people of Samaria. He boasted that he was someone great, ¹⁰and all the people, both high and low, gave him their attention and exclaimed, "This man is the divine power known as the Great Power." ¹¹They followed him because he had amazed them for a long time with his magic. ¹²But when they believed Philip as he preached the good news of the kingdom of God and the name of Jesus Christ, they were baptized, both men and women. ¹³Simon himself believed and was baptized. And he followed Philip everywhere, astonished by the great signs and miracles he saw.

¹⁴When the apostles in Jerusalem heard that Samaria had accepted the word of God, they sent Peter and John to them. ¹⁵When they arrived, they prayed for them that they might receive the Holy Spirit, ¹⁶because the Holy Spirit had not yet come upon any of them; they had simply been baptized into*ᶜ* the name of the Lord Jesus. ¹⁷Then Peter and John placed their hands on them, and they received the Holy Spirit.

¹⁸When Simon saw that the Spirit was given at the laying on of the apostles' hands, he offered them money ¹⁹and said, "Give me also this ability so that everyone on whom I lay my hands may receive the Holy Spirit."

²⁰Peter answered: "May your money perish with you, because you thought you could buy the gift of God with money! ²¹You have no part or share in this ministry, because your heart is not right before God. ²²Repent of this wickedness and pray to the Lord. Perhaps he will forgive you for

---

ᵃ5 Or *Messiah*   *ᵇ7* Greek *unclean*   *ᶜ16* Or *in*

having such a thought in your heart. ²³For I see that you are full of bitterness and captive to sin."

²⁴Then Simon answered, "Pray to the Lord for me so that nothing you have said may happen to me."

²⁵When they had testified and proclaimed the word of the Lord, Peter and John returned to Jerusalem, preaching the gospel in many Samaritan villages.

Philip and the Ethiopian

²⁶Now an angel of the Lord said to Philip, "Go south to the road—the desert road—that goes down from Jerusalem to Gaza." ²⁷So he started out, and on his way he met an Ethiopian[a] eunuch, an important official in charge of all the treasury of Candace, queen of the Ethiopians. This man had gone to Jerusalem to worship, ²⁸and on his way home was sitting in his chariot reading the book of Isaiah the prophet. ²⁹The Spirit told Philip, "Go to that chariot and stay near it."

³⁰Then Philip ran up to the chariot and heard the man reading Isaiah the prophet. "Do you understand what you are reading?" Philip asked.

³¹"How can I," he said, "unless someone explains it to me?" So he invited Philip to come up and sit with him.

³²The eunuch was reading this passage of Scripture:

> "He was led like a sheep to the slaughter,
>   and as a lamb before the shearer is silent,
>   so he did not open his mouth.
> ³³In his humiliation he was deprived of justice.
>   Who can speak of his descendants?
>   For his life was taken from the earth."[b]

³⁴The eunuch asked Philip, "Tell me, please, who is the prophet talking about, himself or someone else?" ³⁵Then Philip began with that very passage of Scripture and told him the good news about Jesus.

³⁶As they traveled along the road, they came to some water and the eunuch said, "Look, here is water. Why shouldn't I be baptized?"[c] ³⁸And he gave orders to stop the chariot. Then both Philip and the eunuch went down into the water and Philip baptized him. ³⁹When they came up out of the water, the Spirit of the Lord suddenly took Philip away, and the eunuch did not see him again, but went on his way rejoicing. ⁴⁰Philip, however, appeared at Azotus and traveled about, preaching the gospel in all the towns until he reached Caesarea.

Saul's Conversion

9 Meanwhile, Saul was still breathing out murderous threats against the Lord's disciples. He went to the high priest ²and asked him for letters

---

[a]27 That is, from the upper Nile region   [b]33 Isaiah 53:7,8   [c]36 Some late manuscripts *baptized?"*
[d]37Philip said, "If you believe with all your heart, you may." The eunuch answered, "I believe that Jesus Christ is the Son of God."

to the synagogues in Damascus, so that if he found any there who belonged to the Way, whether men or women, he might take them as prisoners to Jerusalem. [3]As he neared Damascus on his journey, suddenly a light from heaven flashed around him. [4]He fell to the ground and heard a voice say to him, "Saul, Saul, why do you persecute me?"

[5]"Who are you, Lord?" Saul asked.

"I am Jesus, whom you are persecuting," he replied. [6]"Now get up and go into the city, and you will be told what you must do."

[7]The men traveling with Saul stood there speechless; they heard the sound but did not see anyone. [8]Saul got up from the ground, but when he opened his eyes he could see nothing. So they led him by the hand into Damascus. [9]For three days he was blind, and did not eat or drink anything.

[10]In Damascus there was a disciple named Ananias. The Lord called to him in a vision, "Ananias!"

"Yes, Lord," he answered.

[11]The Lord told him, "Go to the house of Judas on Straight Street and ask for a man from Tarsus named Saul, for he is praying. [12]In a vision he has seen a man named Ananias come and place his hands on him to restore his sight."

[13]"Lord," Ananias answered, "I have heard many reports about this man and all the harm he has done to your saints in Jerusalem. [14]And he has come here with authority from the chief priests to arrest all who call on your name."

[15]But the Lord said to Ananias, "Go! This man is my chosen instrument to carry my name before the Gentiles and their kings and before the people of Israel. [16]I will show him how much he must suffer for my name."

[17]Then Ananias went to the house and entered it. Placing his hands on Saul, he said, "Brother Saul, the Lord—Jesus, who appeared to you on the road as you were coming here—has sent me so that you may see again and be filled with the Holy Spirit." [18]Immediately, something like scales fell from Saul's eyes, and he could see again. He got up and was baptized, [19]and after taking some food, he regained his strength.

Saul in Damascus and Jerusalem

Saul spent several days with the disciples in Damascus. [20]At once he began to preach in the synagogues that Jesus is the Son of God. [21]All those who heard him were astonished and asked, "Isn't he the man who raised havoc in Jerusalem among those who call on this name? And hasn't he come here to take them as prisoners to the chief priests?" [22]Yet Saul grew more and more powerful and baffled the Jews living in Damascus by proving that Jesus is the Christ.[a]

[23]After many days had gone by, the Jews conspired to kill him, [24]but Saul learned of their plan. Day and night they kept close watch on the city gates in order to kill him. [25]But his followers took him by night and lowered him in a basket through an opening in the wall.

[a]22 Or Messiah

²⁶When he came to Jerusalem, he tried to join the disciples, but they were all afraid of him, not believing that he really was a disciple. ²⁷But Barnabas took him and brought him to the apostles. He told them how Saul on his journey had seen the Lord and that the Lord had spoken to him, and how in Damascus he had preached fearlessly in the name of Jesus. ²⁸So Saul stayed with them and moved about freely in Jerusalem, speaking boldly in the name of the Lord. ²⁹He talked and debated with the Grecian Jews, but they tried to kill him. ³⁰When the brothers learned of this, they took him down to Caesarea and sent him off to Tarsus.

³¹Then the church throughout Judea, Galilee and Samaria enjoyed a time of peace. It was strengthened; and encouraged by the Holy Spirit, it grew in numbers, living in the fear of the Lord.

Aeneas and Dorcas

³²As Peter traveled about the country, he went to visit the saints in Lydda. ³³There he found a man named Aeneas, a paralytic who had been bedridden for eight years. ³⁴"Aeneas," Peter said to him, "Jesus Christ heals you. Get up and take care of your mat." Immediately Aeneas got up. ³⁵All those who lived in Lydda and Sharon saw him and turned to the Lord.

³⁶In Joppa there was a disciple named Tabitha (which, when translated, is Dorcas*ᵃ*), who was always doing good and helping the poor. ³⁷About that time she became sick and died, and her body was washed and placed in an upstairs room. ³⁸Lydda was near Joppa; so when the disciples heard that Peter was in Lydda, they sent two men to him and urged him, "Please come at once!"

³⁹Peter went with them, and when he arrived he was taken upstairs to the room. All the widows stood around him, crying and showing him the robes and other clothing that Dorcas had made while she was still with them.

⁴⁰Peter sent them all out of the room; then he got down on his knees and prayed. Turning toward the dead woman, he said, "Tabitha, get up." She opened her eyes, and seeing Peter she sat up. ⁴¹He took her by the hand and helped her to her feet. Then he called the believers and the widows and presented her to them alive. ⁴²This became known all over Joppa, and many people believed in the Lord. ⁴³Peter stayed in Joppa for some time with a tanner named Simon.

Cornelius Calls for Peter

10 At Caesarea there was a man named Cornelius, a centurion in what was known as the Italian Regiment. ²He and all his family were devout and God-fearing; he gave generously to those in need and prayed to God regularly. ³One day at about three in the afternoon he had a vision. He distinctly saw an angel of God, who came to him and said, "Cornelius!"

⁴Cornelius stared at him in fear. "What is it, Lord?" he asked.

The angel answered, "Your prayers and gifts to the poor have come up

ᵃ36 Both *Tabitha* (Aramaic) and *Dorcas* (Greek) mean *gazelle.*

as a memorial offering before God. ⁵Now send men to Joppa to bring back a man named Simon who is called Peter. ⁶He is staying with Simon the tanner, whose house is by the sea."

⁷When the angel who spoke to him had gone, Cornelius called two of his servants and a devout soldier who was one of his attendants. ⁸He told them everything that had happened and sent them to Joppa.

Peter's Vision

⁹About noon the following day as they were on their journey and approaching the city, Peter went up on the roof to pray. ¹⁰He became hungry and wanted something to eat, and while the meal was being prepared, he fell into a trance. ¹¹He saw heaven opened and something like a large sheet being let down to earth by its four corners. ¹²It contained all kinds of four-footed animals, as well as reptiles of the earth and birds of the air. ¹³Then a voice told him, "Get up, Peter. Kill and eat."

¹⁴"Surely not, Lord!" Peter replied. "I have never eaten anything impure or unclean."

¹⁵The voice spoke to him a second time, "Do not call anything impure that God has made clean."

¹⁶This happened three times, and immediately the sheet was taken back to heaven.

¹⁷While Peter was wondering about the meaning of the vision, the men sent by Cornelius found out where Simon's house was and stopped at the gate. ¹⁸They called out, asking if Simon who was known as Peter was staying there.

¹⁹While Peter was still thinking about the vision, the Spirit said to him, "Simon, three*a* men are looking for you. ²⁰So get up and go downstairs. Do not hesitate to go with them, for I have sent them."

²¹Peter went down and said to the men, "I'm the one you're looking for. Why have you come?"

²²The men replied, "We have come from Cornelius the centurion. He is a righteous and God-fearing man, who is respected by all the Jewish people. A holy angel told him to have you come to his house so that he could hear what you have to say." ²³Then Peter invited the men into the house to be his guests.

Peter at Cornelius' House

The next day Peter started out with them, and some of the brothers from Joppa went along. ²⁴The following day he arrived in Caesarea. Cornelius was expecting them and had called together his relatives and close friends. ²⁵As Peter entered the house, Cornelius met him and fell at his feet in reverence. ²⁶But Peter made him get up. "Stand up," he said, "I am only a man myself."

²⁷Talking with him, Peter went inside and found a large gathering of people. ²⁸He said to them: "You are well aware that it is against our law for

---

a19 One early manuscript *two;* other manuscripts do not have the number.

a Jew to associate with a Gentile or visit him. But God has shown me that I should not call any man impure or unclean. ²⁹So when I was sent for, I came without raising any objection. May I ask why you sent for me?"

³⁰Cornelius answered: "Four days ago I was in my house praying at this hour, at three in the afternoon. Suddenly a man in shining clothes stood before me ³¹and said, 'Cornelius, God has heard your prayer and remembered your gifts to the poor. ³²Send to Joppa for Simon who is called Peter. He is a guest in the home of Simon the tanner, who lives by the sea.' ³³So I sent for you immediately, and it was good of you to come. Now we are all here in the presence of God to listen to everything the Lord has commanded you to tell us."

³⁴Then Peter began to speak: "I now realize how true it is that God does not show favoritism ³⁵but accepts men from every nation who fear him and do what is right. ³⁶You know the message God sent to the people of Israel, telling the good news of peace through Jesus Christ, who is Lord of all. ³⁷You know what has happened throughout Judea, beginning in Galilee after the baptism that John preached— ³⁸how God anointed Jesus of Nazareth with the Holy Spirit and power, and how he went around doing good and healing all who were under the power of the devil, because God was with him.

³⁹"We are witnesses of everything he did in the country of the Jews and in Jerusalem. They killed him by hanging him on a tree, ⁴⁰but God raised him from the dead on the third day and caused him to be seen. ⁴¹He was not seen by all the people, but by witnesses whom God had already chosen —by us who ate and drank with him after he rose from the dead. ⁴²He commanded us to preach to the people and to testify that he is the one whom God appointed as judge of the living and the dead. ⁴³All the prophets testify about him that everyone who believes in him receives forgiveness of sins through his name."

⁴⁴While Peter was still speaking these words, the Holy Spirit came on all who heard the message. ⁴⁵The circumcised believers who had come with Peter were astonished that the gift of the Holy Spirit had been poured out even on the Gentiles. ⁴⁶For they heard them speaking in tongues[a] and praising God.

Then Peter said, ⁴⁷"Can anyone keep these people from being baptized with water? They have received the Holy Spirit just as we have." ⁴⁸So he ordered that they be baptized in the name of Jesus Christ. Then they asked Peter to stay with them for a few days.

Peter Explains His Actions

11 The apostles and the brothers throughout Judea heard that the Gentiles also had received the word of God. ²So when Peter went up to Jerusalem, the circumcised believers criticized him ³and said, "You went into the house of uncircumcised men and ate with them."

⁴Peter began and explained everything to them precisely as it had

---

ᵃ46 Or *other languages*

happened: [5]"I was in the city of Joppa praying, and in a trance I saw a vision. I saw something like a large sheet being let down from heaven by its four corners, and it came down to where I was. [6]I looked into it and saw four-footed animals of the earth, wild beasts, reptiles, and birds of the air. [7]Then I heard a voice telling me, 'Get up, Peter. Kill and eat.'

[8]"I replied, 'Surely not, Lord! Nothing impure or unclean has ever entered my mouth.'

[9]"The voice spoke from heaven a second time, 'Do not call anything impure that God has made clean.' [10]This happened three times, and then it was all pulled up to heaven again.

[11]"Right then three men who had been sent to me from Caesarea stopped at the house where I was staying. [12]The Spirit told me to have no hesitation about going with them. These six brothers also went with me, and we entered the man's house. [13]He told us how he had seen an angel appear in his house and say, 'Send to Joppa for Simon who is called Peter. [14]He will bring you a message through which you and all your household will be saved.'

[15]"As I began to speak, the Holy Spirit came on them as he had come on us at the beginning. [16]Then I remembered what the Lord had said: 'John baptized with[a] water, but you will be baptized with the Holy Spirit.' [17]So if God gave them the same gift as he gave us, who believed in the Lord Jesus Christ, who was I to think that I could oppose God?"

[18]When they heard this, they had no further objections and praised God, saying, "So then, God has granted even the Gentiles repentance unto life."

The Church in Antioch

[19]Now those who had been scattered by the persecution in connection with Stephen traveled as far as Phoenicia, Cyprus and Antioch, telling the message only to Jews. [20]Some of them, however, men from Cyprus and Cyrene, went to Antioch and began to speak to Greeks also, telling them the good news about the Lord Jesus. [21]The Lord's hand was with them, and a great number of people believed and turned to the Lord.

[22]News of this reached the ears of the church at Jerusalem, and they sent Barnabas to Antioch. [23]When he arrived and saw the evidence of the grace of God, he was glad and encouraged them all to remain true to the Lord with all their hearts. [24]He was a good man, full of the Holy Spirit and faith, and a great number of people were brought to the Lord.

[25]Then Barnabas went to Tarsus to look for Saul, [26]and when he found him, he brought him to Antioch. So for a whole year Barnabas and Saul met with the church and taught great numbers of people. The disciples were called Christians first at Antioch.

[27]During this time some prophets came down from Jerusalem to Antioch. [28]One of them, named Agabus, stood up and through the Spirit predicted that a severe famine would spread over the entire Roman world.

[a]16 Or in

211

(This happened during the reign of Claudius.) ²⁹The disciples, each according to his ability, decided to provide help for the brothers living in Judea. ³⁰This they did, sending their gift to the elders by Barnabas and Saul.

Peter's Miraculous Escape From Prison

12 It was about this time that King Herod arrested some who belonged to the church, intending to persecute them. ²He had James, the brother of John, put to death with the sword. ³When he saw that this pleased the Jews, he proceeded to seize Peter also. This happened during the Feast of Unleavened Bread. ⁴After arresting him, he put him in prison, handing him over to be guarded by four squads of four soldiers each. Herod intended to bring him out for public trial after the Passover.

⁵So Peter was kept in prison, but the church was earnestly praying to God for him.

⁶The night before Herod was to bring him to trial, Peter was sleeping between two soldiers, bound with two chains, and sentries stood guard at the entrance. ⁷Suddenly an angel of the Lord appeared and a light shone in the cell. He struck Peter on the side and woke him up. "Quick, get up!" he said, and the chains fell off Peter's wrists.

⁸Then the angel said to him, "Put on your clothes and sandals." And Peter did so. "Wrap your cloak around you and follow me," the angel told him. ⁹Peter followed him out of the prison, but he had no idea that what the angel was doing was really happening; he thought he was seeing a vision. ¹⁰They passed the first and second guards and came to the iron gate leading to the city. It opened for them by itself, and they went through it. When they had walked the length of one street, suddenly the angel left him.

¹¹Then Peter came to himself and said, "Now I know without a doubt that the Lord sent his angel and rescued me from Herod's clutches and from everything the Jewish people were anticipating."

¹²When this had dawned on him, he went to the house of Mary the mother of John, also called Mark, where many people had gathered and were praying. ¹³Peter knocked at the outer entrance, and a servant girl named Rhoda came to answer the door. ¹⁴When she recognized Peter's voice, she was so overjoyed she ran back without opening it and exclaimed, "Peter is at the door!"

¹⁵"You're out of your mind," they told her. When she kept insisting that it was so, they said, "It must be his angel."

¹⁶But Peter kept on knocking, and when they opened the door and saw him, they were astonished. ¹⁷Peter motioned with his hand for them to be quiet and described how the Lord had brought him out of prison. "Tell James and the brothers about this," he said, and then he left for another place.

¹⁸In the morning, there was no small commotion among the soldiers as to what had become of Peter. ¹⁹After Herod had a thorough search made for him and did not find him, he cross-examined the guards and ordered that they be executed.

Herod's Death

Then Herod went from Judea to Caesarea and stayed there a while.
[20]He had been quarreling with the people of Tyre and Sidon; they now joined together and sought an audience with him. Having secured the support of Blastus, a trusted personal servant of the king, they asked for peace, because they depended on the king's country for their food supply.

[21]On the appointed day Herod, wearing his royal robes, sat on his throne and delivered a public address to the people. [22]They shouted, "This is the voice of a god, not of a man." [23]Immediately, because Herod did not give praise to God, an angel of the Lord struck him down, and he was eaten by worms and died.

[24]But the word of God continued to increase and spread.

[25]When Barnabas and Saul had finished their mission, they returned from[a] Jerusalem, taking with them John, also called Mark.

Barnabas and Saul Sent Off

13 In the church at Antioch there were prophets and teachers: Barnabas, Simeon called Niger, Lucius of Cyrene, Manaen (who had been brought up with Herod the tetrarch) and Saul. [2]While they were worshiping the Lord and fasting, the Holy Spirit said, "Set apart for me Barnabas and Saul for the work to which I have called them." [3]So after they had fasted and prayed, they placed their hands on them and sent them off.

On Cyprus

[4]The two of them, sent on their way by the Holy Spirit, went down to Seleucia and sailed from there to Cyprus. [5]When they arrived at Salamis, they proclaimed the word of God in the Jewish synagogues. John was with them as their helper.

[6]They traveled through the whole island until they came to Paphos. There they met a Jewish sorcerer and false prophet named Bar-Jesus, [7]who was an attendant of the proconsul, Sergius Paulus. The proconsul, an intelligent man, sent for Barnabas and Saul because he wanted to hear the word of God. [8]But Elymas the sorcerer (for that is what his name means) opposed them and tried to turn the proconsul from the faith. [9]Then Saul, who was also called Paul, filled with the Holy Spirit, looked straight at Elymas and said, [10]"You are a child of the devil and an enemy of everything that is right! You are full of all kinds of deceit and trickery. Will you never stop perverting the right ways of the Lord? [11]Now the hand of the Lord is against you. You are going to be blind, and for a time you will be unable to see the light of the sun."

Immediately mist and darkness came over him, and he groped about, seeking someone to lead him by the hand. [12]When the proconsul saw what had happened, he believed, for he was amazed at the teaching about the Lord.

[a]25 Some manuscripts *to*

In Pisidian Antioch

¹³From Paphos, Paul and his companions sailed to Perga in Pamphylia, where John left them to return to Jerusalem. ¹⁴From Perga they went on to Pisidian Antioch. On the Sabbath they entered the synagogue and sat down. ¹⁵After the reading from the Law and the Prophets, the synagogue rulers sent word to them, saying, "Brothers, if you have a message of encouragement for the people, please speak."

¹⁶Standing up, Paul motioned with his hand and said: "Men of Israel and you Gentiles who worship God, listen to me! ¹⁷The God of the people of Israel chose our fathers; he made the people prosper during their stay in Egypt, with mighty power he led them out of that country, ¹⁸he endured their conduct*a* for about forty years in the desert, ¹⁹he overthrew seven nations in Canaan and gave their land to his people as their inheritance. ²⁰All this took about 450 years.

"After this, God gave them judges until the time of Samuel the prophet. ²¹Then the people asked for a king, and he gave them Saul son of Kish, of the tribe of Benjamin, who ruled forty years. ²²After removing Saul, he made David their king. He testified concerning him: 'I have found David son of Jesse a man after my own heart; he will do everything I want him to do.'

²³"From this man's descendants God has brought to Israel the Savior Jesus, as he promised. ²⁴Before the coming of Jesus, John preached repentance and baptism to all the people of Israel. ²⁵As John was completing his work, he said: 'Who do you think I am? I am not that one. No, but he is coming after me, whose sandals I am not worthy to untie.'

²⁶"Brothers, children of Abraham, and you God-fearing Gentiles, it is to us that this message of salvation has been sent. ²⁷The people of Jerusalem and their rulers did not recognize Jesus, yet in condemning him they fulfilled the words of the prophets that are read every Sabbath. ²⁸Though they found no proper ground for a death sentence, they asked Pilate to have him executed. ²⁹When they had carried out all that was written about him, they took him down from the tree and laid him in a tomb. ³⁰But God raised him from the dead, ³¹and for many days he was seen by those who had traveled with him from Galilee to Jerusalem. They are now his witnesses to our people.

³²"We tell you the good news: What God promised our fathers ³³he has fulfilled for us, their children, by raising up Jesus. As it is written in the second Psalm:

" 'You are my Son;
    today I have become your Father.*b/ c*

³⁴The fact that God raised him from the dead, never to decay, is stated in these words:

---

a18 Some manuscripts *and cared for them*   *b33* Or *have begotten you*   *c33* Psalm 2:7

" 'I will give you the holy and sure blessings promised to
David.'[a]

35So it is stated elsewhere:

" 'You will not let your Holy One see decay.'[b]

36"For when David had served God's purpose in his own generation,
he fell asleep; he was buried with his fathers and his body decayed. 37But
the one whom God raised from the dead did not see decay.

38"Therefore, my brothers, I want you to know that through Jesus the
forgiveness of sins is proclaimed to you. 39Through him everyone who
believes is justified from everything you could not be justified from by the
law of Moses. 40Take care that what the prophets have said does not happen
to you:

41" 'Look, you scoffers,
   wonder and perish,
for I am going to do something in your days
   that you would never believe,
   even if someone told you.'[c]"

42As Paul and Barnabas were leaving the synagogue, the people invited
them to speak further about these things on the next Sabbath. 43When the
congregation was dismissed, many of the Jews and devout converts to
Judaism followed Paul and Barnabas, who talked with them and urged
them to continue in the grace of God.

44On the next Sabbath almost the whole city gathered to hear the word
of the Lord. 45When the Jews saw the crowds, they were filled with jealousy
and talked abusively against what Paul was saying.

46Then Paul and Barnabas answered them boldly: "We had to speak the
word of God to you first. Since you reject it and do not consider yourselves
worthy of eternal life, we now turn to the Gentiles. 47For this is what the
Lord has commanded us:

" 'I have made you[d] a light for the Gentiles,
   that you[d] may bring salvation to the ends of the earth.'[e]"

48When the Gentiles heard this, they were glad and honored the word
of the Lord; and all who were appointed for eternal life believed.

49The word of the Lord spread through the whole region. 50But the Jews
incited the God-fearing women of high standing and the leading men of the
city. They stirred up persecution against Paul and Barnabas, and expelled
them from their region. 51So they shook the dust from their feet in protest
against them and went to Iconium. 52And the disciples were filled with joy
and with the Holy Spirit.

---

[a]34 Isaiah 55:3   [b]35 Psalm 16:10   [c]41 Hab. 1:5   [d]47 The Greek is singular.   [e]47 Isaiah
49:6

215

In Iconium

14 At Iconium Paul and Barnabas went as usual into the Jewish synagogue. There they spoke so effectively that a great number of Jews and Gentiles believed. ²But the Jews who refused to believe stirred up the Gentiles and poisoned their minds against the brothers. ³So Paul and Barnabas spent considerable time there, speaking boldly for the Lord, who confirmed the message of his grace by enabling them to do miraculous signs and wonders. ⁴The people of the city were divided; some sided with the Jews, others with the apostles. ⁵There was a plot afoot among the Gentiles and Jews, together with their leaders, to mistreat them and stone them. ⁶But they found out about it and fled to the Lycaonian cities of Lystra and Derbe and to the surrounding country, ⁷where they continued to preach the good news.

In Lystra and Derbe

⁸In Lystra there sat a man crippled in his feet, who was lame from birth and had never walked. ⁹He listened to Paul as he was speaking. Paul looked directly at him, saw that he had faith to be healed ¹⁰and called out, "Stand up on your feet!" At that, the man jumped up and began to walk.

¹¹When the crowd saw what Paul had done, they shouted in the Lycaonian language, "The gods have come down to us in human form!" ¹²Barnabas they called Zeus, and Paul they called Hermes because he was the chief speaker. ¹³The priest of Zeus, whose temple was just outside the city, brought bulls and wreaths to the city gates because he and the crowd wanted to offer sacrifices to them.

¹⁴But when the apostles Barnabas and Paul heard of this, they tore their clothes and rushed out into the crowd, shouting: ¹⁵"Men, why are you doing this? We too are only men, human like you. We are bringing you good news, telling you to turn from these worthless things to the living God, who made heaven and earth and sea and everything in them. ¹⁶In the past, he let all nations go their own way. ¹⁷Yet he has not left himself without testimony: He has shown kindness by giving you rain from heaven and crops in their seasons; he provides you with plenty of food and fills your hearts with joy." ¹⁸Even with these words, they had difficulty keeping the crowd from sacrificing to them.

¹⁹Then some Jews came from Antioch and Iconium and won the crowd over. They stoned Paul and dragged him outside the city, thinking he was dead. ²⁰But after the disciples had gathered around him, he got up and went back into the city. The next day he and Barnabas left for Derbe.

The Return to Antioch in Syria

²¹They preached the good news in that city and won a large number of disciples. Then they returned to Lystra, Iconium and Antioch, ²²strengthening the disciples and encouraging them to remain true to the faith. "We must go through many hardships to enter the kingdom of God," they said.

²³Paul and Barnabas appointed elders^a for them in each church and, with prayer and fasting, committed them to the Lord, in whom they had put their trust. ²⁴After going through Pisidia, they came into Pamphylia, ²⁵and when they had preached the word in Perga, they went down to Attalia.

²⁶From Attalia they sailed back to Antioch, where they had been committed to the grace of God for the work they had now completed. ²⁷On arriving there, they gathered the church together and reported all that God had done through them and how he had opened the door of faith to the Gentiles. ²⁸And they stayed there a long time with the disciples.

The Council at Jerusalem

15 Some men came down from Judea to Antioch and were teaching the brothers: "Unless you are circumcised, according to the custom taught by Moses, you cannot be saved." ²This brought Paul and Barnabas into sharp dispute and debate with them. So Paul and Barnabas were appointed, along with some other believers, to go up to Jerusalem to see the apostles and elders about this question. ³The church sent them on their way, and as they traveled through Phoenicia and Samaria, they told how the Gentiles had been converted. This news made all the brothers very glad. ⁴When they came to Jerusalem, they were welcomed by the church and the apostles and elders, to whom they reported everything God had done through them.

⁵Then some of the believers who belonged to the party of the Pharisees stood up and said, "The Gentiles must be circumcised and required to obey the law of Moses."

⁶The apostles and elders met to consider this question. ⁷After much discussion, Peter got up and addressed them: "Brothers, you know that some time ago God made a choice among you that the Gentiles might hear from my lips the message of the gospel and believe. ⁸God, who knows the heart, showed that he accepted them by giving the Holy Spirit to them, just as he did to us. ⁹He made no distinction between us and them, for he purified their hearts by faith. ¹⁰Now then, why do you try to test God by putting on the necks of the disciples a yoke that neither we nor our fathers have been able to bear? ¹¹No! We believe it is through the grace of our Lord Jesus that we are saved, just as they are."

¹²The whole assembly became silent as they listened to Barnabas and Paul telling about the miraculous signs and wonders God had done among the Gentiles through them. ¹³When they finished, James spoke up: "Brothers, listen to me. ¹⁴Simon^b has described to us how God at first showed his concern by taking from the Gentiles a people for himself. ¹⁵The words of the prophets are in agreement with this, as it is written:

> ¹⁶" 'After this I will return
> and rebuild David's fallen tent.

^a23 Or *Barnabas ordained elders*; or *Barnabas had elders elected* that is, Peter   ^b14 Greek *Simeon*, a variant of *Simon*;

> Its ruins I will rebuild,
>   and I will restore it,
> [17]that the remnant of men may seek the Lord,
>   and all the Gentiles who bear my name,
> says the Lord, who does these things'[a]
> [18] that have been known for ages.[b]

[19]"It is my judgment, therefore, that we should not make it difficult for the Gentiles who are turning to God. [20]Instead we should write to them, telling them to abstain from food polluted by idols, from sexual immorality, from the meat of strangled animals and from blood. [21]For Moses has been preached in every city from the earliest times and is read in the synagogues on every Sabbath."

The Council's Letter to Gentile Believers

[22]Then the apostles and elders, with the whole church, decided to choose some of their own men and send them to Antioch with Paul and Barnabas. They chose Judas (called Barsabbas) and Silas, two men who were leaders among the brothers. [23]With them they sent the following letter:

The apostles and elders, your brothers,

To the Gentile believers in Antioch, Syria and Cilicia:

Greetings.

[24]We have heard that some went out from us without our authorization and disturbed you, troubling your minds by what they said. [25]So we all agreed to choose some men and send them to you with our dear friends Barnabas and Paul— [26]men who have risked their lives for the name of our Lord Jesus Christ. [27]Therefore we are sending Judas and Silas to confirm by word of mouth what we are writing. [28]It seemed good to the Holy Spirit and to us not to burden you with anything beyond the following requirements: [29]You are to abstain from food sacrificed to idols, from blood, from the meat of strangled animals and from sexual immorality. You will do well to avoid these things.

Farewell.

[30]The men were sent off and went down to Antioch, where they gathered the church together and delivered the letter. [31]The people read it and were glad for its encouraging message. [32]Judas and Silas, who themselves were prophets, said much to encourage and strengthen the brothers. [33]After spending some time there, they were sent off by the brothers with the blessing of peace to return to those who had sent them.[c] [35]But Paul and

---

[a]17 Amos 9:11,12   [b]17,18 Some manuscripts *things'—* / [18]*known to the Lord for ages is his work*
[c]33 Some manuscripts *them,* [34]*but Silas decided to remain there*

Barnabas remained in Antioch, where they and many others taught and preached the word of the Lord.

Disagreement Between Paul and Barnabas

³⁶Some time later Paul said to Barnabas, "Let us go back and visit the brothers in all the towns where we preached the word of the Lord and see how they are doing." ³⁷Barnabas wanted to take John, also called Mark, with them, ³⁸but Paul did not think it wise to take him, because he had deserted them in Pamphylia and had not continued with them in the work. ³⁹They had such a sharp disagreement that they parted company. Barnabas took Mark and sailed for Cyprus, ⁴⁰but Paul chose Silas and left, commended by the brothers to the grace of the Lord. ⁴¹He went through Syria and Cilicia, strengthening the churches.

Timothy Joins Paul and Silas

16 He came to Derbe and then to Lystra, where a disciple named Timothy lived, whose mother was a Jewess and a believer, but whose father was a Greek. ²The brothers at Lystra and Iconium spoke well of him. ³Paul wanted to take him along on the journey, so he circumcised him because of the Jews who lived in that area, for they all knew that his father was a Greek. ⁴As they traveled from town to town, they delivered the decisions reached by the apostles and elders in Jerusalem for the people to obey. ⁵So the churches were strengthened in the faith and grew daily in numbers.

Paul's Vision of the Man of Macedonia

⁶Paul and his companions traveled throughout the region of Phrygia and Galatia, having been kept by the Holy Spirit from preaching the word in the province of Asia. ⁷When they came to the border of Mysia, they tried to enter Bithynia, but the Spirit of Jesus would not allow them to. ⁸So they passed by Mysia and went down to Troas. ⁹During the night Paul had a vision of a man of Macedonia standing and begging him, "Come over to Macedonia and help us." ¹⁰After Paul had seen the vision, we got ready at once to leave for Macedonia, concluding that God had called us to preach the gospel to them.

Lydia's Conversion in Philippi

¹¹From Troas we put out to sea and sailed straight for Samothrace, and the next day on to Neapolis. ¹²From there we traveled to Philippi, a Roman colony and the leading city of that district of Macedonia. And we stayed there several days.

¹³On the Sabbath we went outside the city gate to the river, where we expected to find a place of prayer. We sat down and began to speak to the women who had gathered there. ¹⁴One of those listening was a woman named Lydia, a dealer in purple cloth from the city of Thyatira, who was a worshiper of God. The Lord opened her heart to respond to Paul's

message. ¹⁵When she and the members of her household were baptized, she invited us to her home. "If you consider me a believer in the Lord," she said, "come and stay at my house." And she persuaded us.

Paul and Silas in Prison

¹⁶Once when we were going to the place of prayer, we were met by a slave girl who had a spirit by which she predicted the future. She earned a great deal of money for her owners by fortune-telling. ¹⁷This girl followed Paul and the rest of us, shouting, "These men are servants of the Most High God, who are telling you the way to be saved." ¹⁸She kept this up for many days. Finally Paul became so troubled that he turned around and said to the spirit, "In the name of Jesus Christ I command you to come out of her!" At that moment the spirit left her.

¹⁹When the owners of the slave girl realized that their hope of making money was gone, they seized Paul and Silas and dragged them into the marketplace to face the authorities. ²⁰They brought them before the magistrates and said, "These men are Jews, and are throwing our city into an uproar ²¹by advocating customs unlawful for us Romans to accept or practice."

²²The crowd joined in the attack against Paul and Silas, and the magistrates ordered them to be stripped and beaten. ²³After they had been severely flogged, they were thrown into prison, and the jailer was commanded to guard them carefully. ²⁴Upon receiving such orders, he put them in the inner cell and fastened their feet in the stocks.

²⁵About midnight Paul and Silas were praying and singing hymns to God, and the other prisoners were listening to them. ²⁶Suddenly there was such a violent earthquake that the foundations of the prison were shaken. At once all the prison doors flew open, and everybody's chains came loose. ²⁷The jailer woke up, and when he saw the prison doors open, he drew his sword and was about to kill himself because he thought the prisoners had escaped. ²⁸But Paul shouted, "Don't harm yourself! We are all here!"

²⁹The jailer called for lights, rushed in and fell trembling before Paul and Silas. ³⁰He then brought them out and asked, "Sirs, what must I do to be saved?"

³¹They replied, "Believe in the Lord Jesus, and you will be saved—you and your household." ³²Then they spoke the word of the Lord to him and to all the others in his house. ³³At that hour of the night the jailer took them and washed their wounds; then immediately he and all his family were baptized. ³⁴The jailer brought them into his house and set a meal before them; he was filled with joy because he had come to believe in God—he and his whole family.

³⁵When it was daylight, the magistrates sent their officers to the jailer with the order: "Release those men." ³⁶The jailer told Paul, "The magistrates have ordered that you and Silas be released. Now you can leave. Go in peace."

³⁷But Paul said to the officers: "They beat us publicly without a trial,

even though we are Roman citizens, and threw us into prison. And now do they want to get rid of us quietly? No! Let them come themselves and escort us out."

[38]The officers reported this to the magistrates, and when they heard that Paul and Silas were Roman citizens, they were alarmed. [39]They came to appease them and escorted them from the prison, requesting them to leave the city. [40]After Paul and Silas came out of the prison, they went to Lydia's house, where they met with the brothers and encouraged them. Then they left.

In Thessalonica

17 When they had passed through Amphipolis and Apollonia, they came to Thessalonica, where there was a Jewish synagogue. [2]As his custom was, Paul went into the synagogue, and on three Sabbath days he reasoned with them from the Scriptures, [3]explaining and proving that the Christ[a] had to suffer and rise from the dead. "This Jesus I am proclaiming to you is the Christ,[a]" he said. [4]Some of the Jews were persuaded and joined Paul and Silas, as did a large number of God-fearing Greeks and not a few prominent women.

[5]But the Jews were jealous; so they rounded up some bad characters from the marketplace, formed a mob and started a riot in the city. They rushed to Jason's house in search of Paul and Silas in order to bring them out to the crowd.[b] [6]But when they did not find them, they dragged Jason and some other brothers before the city officials, shouting: "These men who have caused trouble all over the world have now come here, [7]and Jason has welcomed them into his house. They are all defying Caesar's decrees, saying that there is another king, one called Jesus." [8]When they heard this, the crowd and the city officials were thrown into turmoil. [9]Then they made Jason and the others post bond and let them go.

In Berea

[10]As soon as it was night, the brothers sent Paul and Silas away to Berea. On arriving there, they went to the Jewish synagogue. [11]Now the Bereans were of more noble character than the Thessalonians, for they received the message with great eagerness and examined the Scriptures every day to see if what Paul said was true. [12]Many of the Jews believed, as did also a number of prominent Greek women and many Greek men.

[13]When the Jews in Thessalonica learned that Paul was preaching the word of God at Berea, they went there too, agitating the crowds and stirring them up. [14]The brothers immediately sent Paul to the coast, but Silas and Timothy stayed at Berea. [15]The men who escorted Paul brought him to Athens and then left with instructions for Silas and Timothy to join him as soon as possible.

[a]3 Or Messiah   [b]5 Or the assembly of the people

In Athens

¹⁶While Paul was waiting for them in Athens, he was greatly distressed to see that the city was full of idols. ¹⁷So he reasoned in the synagogue with the Jews and the God-fearing Greeks, as well as in the marketplace day by day with those who happened to be there. ¹⁸A group of Epicurean and Stoic philosophers began to dispute with him. Some of them asked, "What is this babbler trying to say?" Others remarked, "He seems to be advocating foreign gods." They said this because Paul was preaching the good news about Jesus and the resurrection. ¹⁹Then they took him and brought him to a meeting of the Areopagus, where they said to him, "May we know what this new teaching is that you are presenting? ²⁰You are bringing some strange ideas to our ears, and we want to know what they mean." ²¹(All the Athenians and the foreigners who lived there spent their time doing nothing but talking about and listening to the latest ideas.)

²²Paul then stood up in the meeting of the Areopagus and said: "Men of Athens! I see that in every way you are very religious. ²³For as I walked around and looked carefully at your objects of worship, I even found an altar with this inscription: TO AN UNKNOWN GOD. Now what you worship as something unknown I am going to proclaim to you.

²⁴"The God who made the world and everything in it is the Lord of heaven and earth and does not live in temples built by hands. ²⁵And he is not served by human hands, as if he needed anything, because he himself gives all men life and breath and everything else. ²⁶From one man he made every nation of men, that they should inhabit the whole earth; and he determined the times set for them and the exact places where they should live. ²⁷God did this so that men would seek him and perhaps reach out for him and find him, though he is not far from each one of us. ²⁸'For in him we live and move and have our being.' As some of your own poets have said, 'We are his offspring.'

²⁹"Therefore since we are God's offspring, we should not think that the divine being is like gold or silver or stone—an image made by man's design and skill. ³⁰In the past God overlooked such ignorance, but now he commands all people everywhere to repent. ³¹For he has set a day when he will judge the world with justice by the man he has appointed. He has given proof of this to all men by raising him from the dead."

³²When they heard about the resurrection of the dead, some of them sneered, but others said, "We want to hear you again on this subject." ³³At that, Paul left the Council. ³⁴A few men became followers of Paul and believed. Among them was Dionysius, a member of the Areopagus, also a woman named Damaris, and a number of others.

In Corinth

18 After this, Paul left Athens and went to Corinth. ²There he met a Jew named Aquila, a native of Pontus, who had recently come from Italy with his wife Priscilla, because Claudius had ordered all the Jews to leave Rome. Paul went to see them, ³and because he was a tentmaker as they were, he stayed and worked with them. ⁴Every Sabbath he reasoned in the synagogue, trying to persuade Jews and Greeks.

⁵When Silas and Timothy came from Macedonia, Paul devoted himself exclusively to preaching, testifying to the Jews that Jesus was the Christ.ᵃ ⁶But when the Jews opposed Paul and became abusive, he shook out his clothes in protest and said to them, "Your blood be on your own heads! I am clear of my responsibility. From now on I will go to the Gentiles."

⁷Then Paul left the synagogue and went next door to the house of Titius Justus, a worshiper of God. ⁸Crispus, the synagogue ruler, and his entire household believed in the Lord; and many of the Corinthians who heard him believed and were baptized.

⁹One night the Lord spoke to Paul in a vision: "Do not be afraid; keep on speaking, do not be silent. ¹⁰For I am with you, and no one is going to attack and harm you, because I have many people in this city." ¹¹So Paul stayed for a year and a half, teaching them the word of God.

¹²While Gallio was proconsul of Achaia, the Jews made a united attack on Paul and brought him into court. ¹³"This man," they charged, "is persuading the people to worship God in ways contrary to the law."

¹⁴Just as Paul was about to speak, Gallio said to the Jews, "If you Jews were making a complaint about some misdemeanor or serious crime, it would be reasonable for me to listen to you. ¹⁵But since it involves questions about words and names and your own law—settle the matter yourselves. I will not be a judge of such things." ¹⁶So he had them ejected from the court. ¹⁷Then they all turned on Sosthenes the synagogue ruler and beat him in front of the court. But Gallio showed no concern whatever.

Priscilla, Aquila and Apollos

¹⁸Paul stayed on in Corinth for some time. Then he left the brothers and sailed for Syria, accompanied by Priscilla and Aquila. Before he sailed, he had his hair cut off at Cenchrea because of a vow he had taken. ¹⁹They arrived at Ephesus, where Paul left Priscilla and Aquila. He himself went into the synagogue and reasoned with the Jews. ²⁰When they asked him to spend more time with them, he declined. ²¹But as he left, he promised, "I will come back if it is God's will." Then he set sail from Ephesus. ²²When he landed at Caesarea, he went up and greeted the church and then went down to Antioch.

²³After spending some time in Antioch, Paul set out from there and traveled from place to place throughout the region of Galatia and Phrygia, strengthening all the disciples.

²⁴Meanwhile a Jew named Apollos, a native of Alexandria, came to Ephesus. He was a learned man, with a thorough knowledge of the Scriptures. ²⁵He had been instructed in the way of the Lord, and he spoke with great fervorᵇ and taught about Jesus accurately, though he knew only the baptism of John. ²⁶He began to speak boldly in the synagogue. When

ᵃ5 Or *Messiah;* also in verse 28   ᵇ25 Or *with fervor in the Spirit*

Priscilla and Aquila heard him, they invited him to their home and explained to him the way of God more adequately.

²⁷When Apollos wanted to go to Achaia, the brothers encouraged him and wrote to the disciples there to welcome him. On arriving, he was a great help to those who by grace had believed. ²⁸For he vigorously refuted the Jews in public debate, proving from the Scriptures that Jesus was the Christ.

Paul in Ephesus

19 While Apollos was at Corinth, Paul took the road through the interior and arrived at Ephesus. There he found some disciples ²and asked them, "Did you receive the Holy Spirit when*ᵃ* you believed?"

They answered, "No, we have not even heard that there is a Holy Spirit."

³So Paul asked, "Then what baptism did you receive?"

"John's baptism," they replied.

⁴Paul said, "John's baptism was a baptism of repentance. He told the people to believe in the one coming after him, that is, in Jesus." ⁵On hearing this, they were baptized into*ᵇ* the name of the Lord Jesus. ⁶When Paul placed his hands on them, the Holy Spirit came on them, and they spoke in tongues*ᶜ* and prophesied. ⁷There were about twelve men in all.

⁸Paul entered the synagogue and spoke boldly there for three months, arguing persuasively about the kingdom of God. ⁹But some of them became obstinate; they refused to believe and publicly maligned the Way. So Paul left them. He took the disciples with him and had discussions daily in the lecture hall of Tyrannus. ¹⁰This went on for two years, so that all the Jews and Greeks who lived in the province of Asia heard the word of the Lord.

¹¹God did extraordinary miracles through Paul, ¹²so that even handkerchiefs and aprons that had touched him were taken to the sick, and their illnesses were cured and the evil spirits left them.

¹³Some Jews who went around driving out evil spirits tried to invoke the name of the Lord Jesus over those who were demon-possessed. They would say, "In the name of Jesus, whom Paul preaches, I command you to come out." ¹⁴Seven sons of Sceva, a Jewish chief priest, were doing this. ¹⁵One day, the evil spirit answered them, "Jesus I know, and I know about Paul, but who are you?" ¹⁶Then the man who had the evil spirit jumped on them and overpowered them all. He gave them such a beating that they ran out of the house naked and bleeding.

¹⁷When this became known to the Jews and Greeks living in Ephesus, they were all seized with fear, and the name of the Lord Jesus was held in high honor. ¹⁸Many of those who believed now came and openly confessed their evil deeds. ¹⁹A number who had practiced sorcery brought their scrolls together and burned them publicly. When they calculated the value of the scrolls, the total came to fifty thousand drachmas.*ᵈ* ²⁰In this way the word of the Lord spread widely and grew in power.

ᵃ2 Or *after*   *ᵇ5* Or *in*   *ᶜ6* Or *other languages*   *ᵈ19* A drachma was a silver coin worth about a day's wages.

²¹After all this had happened, Paul decided to go to Jerusalem, passing through Macedonia and Achaia. "After I have been there," he said, "I must visit Rome also." ²²He sent two of his helpers, Timothy and Erastus, to Macedonia, while he stayed in the province of Asia a little longer.

The Riot in Ephesus

²³About that time there arose a great disturbance about the Way. ²⁴A silversmith named Demetrius, who made silver shrines of Artemis, brought in no little business for the craftsmen. ²⁵He called them together, along with the workmen in related trades, and said: "Men, you know we receive a good income from this business. ²⁶And you see and hear how this fellow Paul has convinced and led astray large numbers of people here in Ephesus and in practically the whole province of Asia. He says that man-made gods are no gods at all. ²⁷There is danger not only that our trade will lose its good name, but also that the temple of the great goddess Artemis will be discredited, and the goddess herself, who is worshiped throughout the province of Asia and the world, will be robbed of her divine majesty."

²⁸When they heard this, they were furious and began shouting: "Great is Artemis of the Ephesians!" ²⁹Soon the whole city was in an uproar. The people seized Gaius and Aristarchus, Paul's traveling companions from Macedonia, and rushed as one man into the theater. ³⁰Paul wanted to appear before the crowd, but the disciples would not let him. ³¹Even some of the officials of the province, friends of Paul, sent him a message begging him not to venture into the theater.

³²The assembly was in confusion: Some were shouting one thing, some another. Most of the people did not even know why they were there. ³³The Jews pushed Alexander to the front, and some of the crowd shouted instructions to him. He motioned for silence in order to make a defense before the people. ³⁴But when they realized he was a Jew, they all shouted in unison for about two hours: "Great is Artemis of the Ephesians!"

³⁵The city clerk quieted the crowd and said: "Men of Ephesus, doesn't all the world know that the city of Ephesus is the guardian of the temple of the great Artemis and of her image, which fell from heaven? ³⁶Therefore, since these facts are undeniable, you ought to be quiet and not do anything rash. ³⁷You have brought these men here, though they have neither robbed temples nor blasphemed our goddess. ³⁸If, then, Demetrius and his fellow craftsmen have a grievance against anybody, the courts are open and there are proconsuls. They can press charges. ³⁹If there is anything further you want to bring up, it must be settled in a legal assembly. ⁴⁰As it is, we are in danger of being charged with rioting because of today's events. In that case we would not be able to account for this commotion, since there is no reason for it." ⁴¹After he had said this, he dismissed the assembly.

Through Macedonia and Greece

20 When the uproar had ended, Paul sent for the disciples and, after encouraging them, said good-by and set out for Macedonia. ²He traveled through that area, speaking many words of encouragement to the people, and finally arrived in Greece, ³where he stayed three months. Because the Jews made a plot against him just as he was about to sail for Syria, he decided to go back through Macedonia. ⁴He was accompanied by Sopater son of Pyrrhus from Berea, Aristarchus and Secundus from Thessalonica, Gaius from Derbe, Timothy also, and Tychicus and Trophimus from the province of Asia. ⁵These men went on ahead and waited for us at Troas. ⁶But we sailed from Philippi after the Feast of Unleavened Bread, and five days later joined the others at Troas, where we stayed seven days.

Eutychus Raised From the Dead at Troas

⁷On the first day of the week we came together to break bread. Paul spoke to the people and, because he intended to leave the next day, kept on talking until midnight. ⁸There were many lamps in the upstairs room where we were meeting. ⁹Seated in a window was a young man named Eutychus, who was sinking into a deep sleep as Paul talked on and on. When he was sound asleep, he fell to the ground from the third story and was picked up dead. ¹⁰Paul went down, threw himself on the young man and put his arms around him. "Don't be alarmed," he said. "He's alive!" ¹¹Then he went upstairs again and broke bread and ate. After talking until daylight, he left. ¹²The people took the young man home alive and were greatly comforted.

Paul's Farewell to the Ephesian Elders

¹³We went on ahead to the ship and sailed for Assos, where we were going to take Paul aboard. He had made this arrangement because he was going there on foot. ¹⁴When he met us at Assos, we took him aboard and went on to Mitylene. ¹⁵The next day we set sail from there and arrived off Kios. The day after that we crossed over to Samos, and on the following day arrived at Miletus. ¹⁶Paul had decided to sail past Ephesus to avoid spending time in the province of Asia, for he was in a hurry to reach Jerusalem, if possible, by the day of Pentecost.

¹⁷From Miletus, Paul sent to Ephesus for the elders of the church. ¹⁸When they arrived, he said to them: "You know how I lived the whole time I was with you, from the first day I came into the province of Asia. ¹⁹I served the Lord with great humility and with tears, although I was severely tested by the plots of the Jews. ²⁰You know that I have not hesitated to preach anything that would be helpful to you but have taught you publicly and from house to house. ²¹I have declared to both Jews and Greeks that they must turn to God in repentance and have faith in our Lord Jesus.

²²"And now, compelled by the Spirit, I am going to Jerusalem, not knowing what will happen to me there. ²³I only know that in every city the Holy Spirit warns me that prison and hardships are facing me. ²⁴However, I consider my life worth nothing to me, if only I may finish the race and complete the task the Lord Jesus has given me—the task of testifying to the gospel of God's grace.

²⁵"Now I know that none of you among whom I have gone about preaching the kingdom will ever see me again. ²⁶Therefore, I declare to you today that I am innocent of the blood of all men. ²⁷For I have not hesitated to proclaim to you the whole will of God. ²⁸Keep watch over yourselves and all the flock of which the Holy Spirit has made you overseers.^a Be shepherds of the church of God,^b which he bought with his own blood. ²⁹I know that after I leave, savage wolves will come in among you and will not spare the flock. ³⁰Even from your own number men will arise and distort the truth in order to draw away disciples after them. ³¹So be on your guard! Remember that for three years I never stopped warning each of you night and day with tears.

³²"Now I commit you to God and to the word of his grace, which can build you up and give you an inheritance among all those who are sanctified. ³³I have not coveted anyone's silver or gold or clothing. ³⁴You yourselves know that these hands of mine have supplied my own needs and the needs of my companions. ³⁵In everything I did, I showed you that by this kind of hard work we must help the weak, remembering the words the Lord Jesus himself said: 'It is more blessed to give than to receive.' "

³⁶When he had said this, he knelt down with all of them and prayed. ³⁷They all wept as they embraced him and kissed him. ³⁸What grieved them most was his statement that they would never see his face again. Then they accompanied him to the ship.

On to Jerusalem

21 After we had torn ourselves away from them, we put out to sea and sailed straight to Cos. The next day we went to Rhodes and from there to Patara. ²We found a ship crossing over to Phoenicia, went on board and set sail. ³After sighting Cyprus and passing to the south of it, we sailed on to Syria. We landed at Tyre, where our ship was to unload its cargo. ⁴Finding the disciples there, we stayed with them seven days. Through the Spirit they urged Paul not to go on to Jerusalem. ⁵But when our time was up, we left and continued on our way. All the disciples and their wives and children accompanied us out of the city, and there on the beach we knelt to pray. ⁶After saying good-by to each other, we went aboard the ship, and they returned home.

⁷We continued our voyage from Tyre and landed at Ptolemais, where we greeted the brothers and stayed with them for a day. ⁸Leaving the next day, we reached Caesarea and stayed at the house of Philip the evangelist, one of the Seven. ⁹He had four unmarried daughters who prophesied.

¹⁰After we had been there a number of days, a prophet named Agabus came down from Judea. ¹¹Coming over to us, he took Paul's belt, tied his own hands and feet with it and said, "The Holy Spirit says, 'In this way the Jews of Jerusalem will bind the owner of this belt and will hand him over to the Gentiles.' "

¹²When we heard this, we and the people there pleaded with Paul not

---

a28 Traditionally *bishops*   *b28* Many manuscripts *of the Lord* to go up to Jerusalem. [13]Then Paul answered, "Why are you weeping and breaking my heart? I am ready not only to be bound, but also to die in Jerusalem for the name of the Lord Jesus." [14]When he would not be dissuaded, we gave up and said, "The Lord's will be done."

[15]After this, we got ready and went up to Jerusalem. [16]Some of the disciples from Caesarea accompanied us and brought us to the home of Mnason, where we were to stay. He was a man from Cyprus and one of the early disciples.

Paul's Arrival at Jerusalem

[17]When we arrived at Jerusalem, the brothers received us warmly. [18]The next day Paul and the rest of us went to see James, and all the elders were present. [19]Paul greeted them and reported in detail what God had done among the Gentiles through his ministry.

[20]When they heard this, they praised God. Then they said to Paul: "You see, brother, how many thousands of Jews have believed, and all of them are zealous for the law. [21]They have been informed that you teach all the Jews who live among the Gentiles to turn away from Moses, telling them not to circumcise their children or live according to our customs. [22]What shall we do? They will certainly hear that you have come, [23]so do what we tell you. There are four men with us who have made a vow. [24]Take these men, join in their purification rites and pay their expenses, so that they can have their heads shaved. Then everybody will know there is no truth in these reports about you, but that you yourself are living in obedience to the law. [25]As for the Gentile believers, we have written to them our decision that they should abstain from food sacrificed to idols, from blood, from the meat of strangled animals and from sexual immorality."

[26]The next day Paul took the men and purified himself along with them. Then he went to the temple to give notice of the date when the days of purification would end and the offering would be made for each of them.

Paul Arrested

[27]When the seven days were nearly over, some Jews from the province of Asia saw Paul at the temple. They stirred up the whole crowd and seized him, [28]shouting, "Men of Israel, help us! This is the man who teaches all men everywhere against our people and our law and this place. And besides, he has brought Greeks into the temple area and defiled this holy place." [29](They had previously seen Trophimus the Ephesian in the city with Paul and assumed that Paul had brought him into the temple area.)

[30]The whole city was aroused, and the people came running from all directions. Seizing Paul, they dragged him from the temple, and immediately the gates were shut. [31]While they were trying to kill him, news reached the commander of the Roman troops that the whole city of Jerusalem was in an uproar. [32]He at once took some officers and soldiers and ran down to the crowd. When the rioters saw the commander and his soldiers, they stopped beating Paul.

[33]The commander came up and arrested him and ordered him to be bound with two chains. Then he asked who he was and what he had done. [34]Some in the crowd shouted one thing and some another, and since the commander could not get at the truth because of the uproar, he ordered that Paul be taken into the barracks. [35]When Paul reached the steps, the violence of the mob was so great he had to be carried by the soldiers. [36]The crowd that followed kept shouting, "Away with him!"

Paul Speaks to the Crowd

[37]As the soldiers were about to take Paul into the barracks, he asked the commander, "May I say something to you?"

"Do you speak Greek?" he replied. [38]"Aren't you the Egyptian who started a revolt and led four thousand terrorists out into the desert some time ago?"

[39]Paul answered, "I am a Jew, from Tarsus in Cilicia, a citizen of no ordinary city. Please let me speak to the people."

[40]Having received the commander's permission, Paul stood on the steps and motioned to the crowd. When they were all silent, he said to them

22 in Aramaic[a]: [1]"Brothers and fathers, listen now to my defense." [2]When they heard him speak to them in Aramaic, they became very quiet.

Then Paul said: [3]"I am a Jew, born in Tarsus of Cilicia, but brought up in this city. Under Gamaliel I was thoroughly trained in the law of our fathers and was just as zealous for God as any of you are today. [4]I persecuted the followers of this Way to their death, arresting both men and women and throwing them into prison, [5]as also the high priest and all the Council can testify. I even obtained letters from them to their brothers in Damascus, and went there to bring these people as prisoners to Jerusalem to be punished.

[6]"About noon as I came near Damascus, suddenly a bright light from heaven flashed around me. [7]I fell to the ground and heard a voice say to me, 'Saul! Saul! Why do you persecute me?'

[8]" 'Who are you, Lord?' I asked.

" 'I am Jesus of Nazareth, whom you are persecuting,' he replied. [9]My companions saw the light, but they did not understand the voice of him who was speaking to me.

[10]" 'What shall I do, Lord?' I asked.

" 'Get up,' the Lord said, 'and go into Damascus. There you will be told all that you have been assigned to do.' [11]My companions led me by the hand into Damascus, because the brilliance of the light had blinded me.

[12]"A man named Ananias came to see me. He was a devout observer of the law and highly respected by all the Jews living there. [13]He stood beside me and said, 'Brother Saul, receive your sight!' And at that very moment I was able to see him.

[14]"Then he said: 'The God of our fathers has chosen you to know his

---

[a]40 Or possibly *Hebrew*; also in 22:2

will and to see the Righteous One and to hear words from his mouth. ¹⁵You will be his witness to all men of what you have seen and heard. ¹⁶And now what are you waiting for? Get up, be baptized and wash your sins away, calling on his name.'

¹⁷"When I returned to Jerusalem and was praying at the temple, I fell into a trance ¹⁸and saw the Lord speaking. 'Quick!' he said to me. 'Leave Jerusalem immediately, because they will not accept your testimony about me.'

¹⁹" 'Lord,' I replied, 'these men know that I went from one synagogue to another to imprison and beat those who believe in you. ²⁰And when the blood of your martyr[a] Stephen was shed, I stood there giving my approval and guarding the clothes of those who were killing him.'

²¹"Then the Lord said to me, 'Go; I will send you far away to the Gentiles.' "

Paul the Roman Citizen

²²The crowd listened to Paul until he said this. Then they raised their voices and shouted, "Rid the earth of him! He's not fit to live!"

²³As they were shouting and throwing off their cloaks and flinging dust into the air, ²⁴the commander ordered Paul to be taken into the barracks. He directed that he be flogged and questioned in order to find out why the people were shouting at him like this. ²⁵As they stretched him out to flog him, Paul said to the centurion standing there, "Is it legal for you to flog a Roman citizen who hasn't even been found guilty?"

²⁶When the centurion heard this, he went to the commander and reported it. "What are you going to do?" he asked. "This man is a Roman citizen."

²⁷The commander went to Paul and asked, "Tell me, are you a Roman citizen?"

"Yes, I am," he answered.

²⁸Then the commander said, "I had to pay a big price for my citizenship."

"But I was born a citizen," Paul replied.

²⁹Those who were about to question him withdrew immediately. The commander himself was alarmed when he realized that he had put Paul, a Roman citizen, in chains.

Before the Sanhedrin

³⁰The next day, since the commander wanted to find out exactly why Paul was being accused by the Jews, he released him and ordered the chief priests and all the Sanhedrin to assemble. Then he brought Paul and had him stand before them.

23 Paul looked straight at the Sanhedrin and said, "My brothers, I have fulfilled my duty to God in all good conscience to this day." ²At this the high priest Ananias ordered those standing near Paul to strike him on

[a]20 Or witness

the mouth. ³Then Paul said to him, "God will strike you, you whitewashed wall! You sit there to judge me according to the law, yet you yourself violate the law by commanding that I be struck!"

⁴Those who were standing near Paul said, "You dare to insult God's high priest?"

⁵Paul replied, "Brothers, I did not realize that he was the high priest; for it is written: 'Do not speak evil about the ruler of your people.'ᵃ"

⁶Then Paul, knowing that some of them were Sadducees and the others Pharisees, called out in the Sanhedrin, "My brothers, I am a Pharisee, the son of a Pharisee. I stand on trial because of my hope in the resurrection of the dead." ⁷When he said this, a dispute broke out between the Pharisees and the Sadducees, and the assembly was divided. ⁸(The Sadducees say that there is no resurrection, and that there are neither angels nor spirits, but the Pharisees acknowledge them all.)

⁹There was a great uproar, and some of the teachers of the law who were Pharisees stood up and argued vigorously. "We find nothing wrong with this man," they said. "What if a spirit or an angel has spoken to him?" ¹⁰The dispute became so violent that the commander was afraid Paul would be torn to pieces by them. He ordered the troops to go down and take him away from them by force and bring him into the barracks.

¹¹The following night the Lord stood near Paul and said, "Take courage! As you have testified about me in Jerusalem, so you must also testify in Rome."

The Plot to Kill Paul

¹²The next morning the Jews formed a conspiracy and bound themselves with an oath not to eat or drink until they had killed Paul. ¹³More than forty men were involved in this plot. ¹⁴They went to the chief priests and elders and said, "We have taken a solemn oath not to eat anything until we have killed Paul. ¹⁵Now then, you and the Sanhedrin petition the commander to bring him before you on the pretext of wanting more accurate information about his case. We are ready to kill him before he gets here."

¹⁶But when the son of Paul's sister heard of this plot, he went into the barracks and told Paul.

¹⁷Then Paul called one of the centurions and said, "Take this young man to the commander; he has something to tell him." ¹⁸So he took him to the commander.

The centurion said, "Paul, the prisoner, sent for me and asked me to bring this young man to you because he has something to tell you."

¹⁹The commander took the young man by the hand, drew him aside and asked, "What is it you want to tell me?"

²⁰He said: "The Jews have agreed to ask you to bring Paul before the Sanhedrin tomorrow on the pretext of wanting more accurate information about him. ²¹Don't give in to them, because more than forty of them are waiting in ambush for him. They have taken an oath not to eat or drink until

ᵃ5 Exodus 22:28

they have killed him. They are ready now, waiting for your consent to their request."

²²The commander dismissed the young man and cautioned him, "Don't tell anyone that you have reported this to me."

Paul Transferred to Caesarea

²³Then he called two of his centurions and ordered them, "Get ready a detachment of two hundred soldiers, seventy horsemen and two hundred spearmen*ᵃ* to go to Caesarea at nine tonight. ²⁴Provide mounts for Paul so that he may be taken safely to Governor Felix."

²⁵He wrote a letter as follows:

²⁶Claudius Lysias,

To His Excellency, Governor Felix:

Greetings.

²⁷This man was seized by the Jews and they were about to kill him, but I came with my troops and rescued him, for I had learned that he is a Roman citizen. ²⁸I wanted to know why they were accusing him, so I brought him to their Sanhedrin. ²⁹I found that the accusation had to do with questions about their law, but there was no charge against him that deserved death or imprisonment. ³⁰When I was informed of a plot to be carried out against the man, I sent him to you at once. I also ordered his accusers to present to you their case against him.

³¹So the soldiers, carrying out their orders, took Paul with them during the night and brought him as far as Antipatris. ³²The next day they let the cavalry go on with him, while they returned to the barracks. ³³When the cavalry arrived in Caesarea, they delivered the letter to the governor and handed Paul over to him. ³⁴The governor read the letter and asked what province he was from. Learning that he was from Cilicia, ³⁵he said, "I will hear your case when your accusers get here." Then he ordered that Paul be kept under guard in Herod's palace.

The Trial Before Felix

24 Five days later the high priest Ananias went down to Caesarea with some of the elders and a lawyer named Tertullus, and they brought their charges against Paul before the governor. ²When Paul was called in, Tertullus presented his case before Felix: "We have enjoyed a long period of peace under you, and your foresight has brought about reforms in this nation. ³Everywhere and in every way, most excellent Felix, we acknowledge this with profound gratitude. ⁴But in order not to weary you further, I would request that you be kind enough to hear us briefly.

⁵"We have found this man to be a troublemaker, stirring up riots among

ᵃ23 The meaning of the Greek for this word is uncertain.

the Jews all over the world. He is a ringleader of the Nazarene sect ⁶and even tried to desecrate the temple; so we seized him. ⁸By ᵃ examining him yourself you will be able to learn the truth about all these charges we are bringing against him."

⁹The Jews joined in the accusation, asserting that these things were true.

¹⁰When the governor motioned for him to speak, Paul replied: "I know that for a number of years you have been a judge over this nation; so I gladly make my defense. ¹¹You can easily verify that no more than twelve days ago I went up to Jerusalem to worship. ¹²My accusers did not find me arguing with anyone at the temple, or stirring up a crowd in the synagogues or anywhere else in the city. ¹³And they cannot prove to you the charges they are now making against me. ¹⁴However, I admit that I worship the God of our fathers as a follower of the Way, which they call a sect. I believe everything that agrees with the Law and that is written in the Prophets, ¹⁵and I have the same hope in God as these men, that there will be a resurrection of both the righteous and the wicked. ¹⁶So I strive always to keep my conscience clear before God and man.

¹⁷"After an absence of several years, I came to Jerusalem to bring my people gifts for the poor and to present offerings. ¹⁸I was ceremonially clean when they found me in the temple courts doing this. There was no crowd with me, nor was I involved in any disturbance. ¹⁹But there are some Jews from the province of Asia, who ought to be here before you and bring charges if they have anything against me. ²⁰Or these who are here should state what crime they found in me when I stood before the Sanhedrin— ²¹unless it was this one thing I shouted as I stood in their presence: 'It is concerning the resurrection of the dead that I am on trial before you today.' "

²²Then Felix, who was well acquainted with the Way, adjourned the proceedings. "When Lysias the commander comes," he said, "I will decide your case." ²³He ordered the centurion to keep Paul under guard but to give him some freedom and permit his friends to take care of his needs.

²⁴Several days later Felix came with his wife Drusilla, who was a Jewess. He sent for Paul and listened to him as he spoke about faith in Christ Jesus. ²⁵As Paul discoursed on righteousness, self-control and the judgment to come, Felix was afraid and said, "That's enough for now! You may leave. When I find it convenient, I will send for you." ²⁶At the same time he was hoping that Paul would offer him a bribe, so he sent for him frequently and talked with him.

²⁷When two years had passed, Felix was succeeded by Porcius Festus, but because Felix wanted to grant a favor to the Jews, he left Paul in prison.

ᵃ6-8 Some manuscripts *him and wanted to judge him according to our law.* ⁷*But the commander, Lysias, came and with the use of much force snatched him from our hands* ⁸*and ordered his accusers to come before you. By*

The Trial Before Festus

25 Three days after arriving in the province, Festus went up from Caesarea to Jerusalem, [2]where the chief priests and Jewish leaders appeared before him and presented the charges against Paul. [3]They urgently requested Festus, as a favor to them, to have Paul transferred to Jerusalem, for they were preparing an ambush to kill him along the way. [4]Festus answered, "Paul is being held at Caesarea, and I myself am going there soon. [5]Let some of your leaders come with me and press charges against the man there, if he has done anything wrong."

[6]After spending eight or ten days with them, he went down to Caesarea, and the next day he convened the court and ordered that Paul be brought before him. [7]When Paul appeared, the Jews who had come down from Jerusalem stood around him, bringing many serious charges against him, which they could not prove.

[8]Then Paul made his defense: "I have done nothing wrong against the law of the Jews or against the temple or against Caesar."

[9]Festus, wishing to do the Jews a favor, said to Paul, "Are you willing to go up to Jerusalem and stand trial before me there on these charges?"

[10]Paul answered: "I am now standing before Caesar's court, where I ought to be tried. I have not done any wrong to the Jews, as you yourself know very well. [11]If, however, I am guilty of doing anything deserving death, I do not refuse to die. But if the charges brought against me by these Jews are not true, no one has the right to hand me over to them. I appeal to Caesar!"

[12]After Festus had conferred with his council, he declared: "You have appealed to Caesar. To Caesar you will go!"

Festus Consults King Agrippa

[13]A few days later King Agrippa and Bernice arrived at Caesarea to pay their respects to Festus. [14]Since they were spending many days there, Festus discussed Paul's case with the king. He said: "There is a man here whom Felix left as a prisoner. [15]When I went to Jerusalem, the chief priests and elders of the Jews brought charges against him and asked that he be condemned.

[16]"I told them that it is not the Roman custom to hand over any man before he has faced his accusers and has had an opportunity to defend himself against their charges. [17]When they came here with me, I did not delay the case, but convened the court the next day and ordered the man to be brought in. [18]When his accusers got up to speak, they did not charge him with any of the crimes I had expected. [19]Instead, they had some points of dispute with him about their own religion and about a dead man named Jesus who Paul claimed was alive. [20]I was at a loss how to investigate such matters; so I asked if he would be willing to go to Jerusalem and stand trial there on these charges. [21]When Paul made his appeal to be held over for the Emperor's decision, I ordered him held until I could send him to Caesar."

²²Then Agrippa said to Festus, "I would like to hear this man myself." He replied, "Tomorrow you will hear him."

Paul Before Agrippa

²³The next day Agrippa and Bernice came with great pomp and entered the audience room with the high ranking officers and the leading men of the city. At the command of Festus, Paul was brought in. ²⁴Festus said: "King Agrippa, and all who are present with us, you see this man! The whole Jewish community has petitioned me about him in Jerusalem and here in Caesarea, shouting that he ought not to live any longer. ²⁵I found he had done nothing deserving of death, but because he made his appeal to the Emperor I decided to send him to Rome. ²⁶But I have nothing definite to write to His Majesty about him. Therefore I have brought him before all of you, and especially before you, King Agrippa, so that as a result of this investigation I may have something to write. ²⁷For I think it is unreasonable to send on a prisoner without specifying the charges against him."

26 Then Agrippa said to Paul, "You have permission to speak for yourself."

So Paul motioned with his hand and began his defense: ²"King Agrippa, I consider myself fortunate to stand before you today as I make my defense against all the accusations of the Jews, ³and especially so because you are well acquainted with all the Jewish customs and controversies. Therefore, I beg you to listen to me patiently.

⁴"The Jews all know the way I have lived ever since I was a child, from the beginning of my life in my own country, and also in Jerusalem. ⁵They have known me for a long time and can testify, if they are willing, that according to the strictest sect of our religion, I lived as a Pharisee. ⁶And now it is because of my hope in what God has promised our fathers that I am on trial today. ⁷This is the promise our twelve tribes are hoping to see fulfilled as they earnestly serve God day and night. O king, it is because of this hope that the Jews are accusing me. ⁸Why should any of you consider it incredible that God raises the dead?

⁹"I too was convinced that I ought to do all that was possible to oppose the name of Jesus of Nazareth. ¹⁰And that is just what I did in Jerusalem. On the authority of the chief priests I put many of the saints in prison, and when they were put to death, I cast my vote against them. ¹¹Many a time I went from one synagogue to another to have them punished, and I tried to force them to blaspheme. In my obsession against them, I even went to foreign cities to persecute them.

¹²"On one of these journeys I was going to Damascus with the authority and commission of the chief priests. ¹³About noon, O king, as I was on the road, I saw a light from heaven, brighter than the sun, blazing around me and my companions. ¹⁴We all fell to the ground, and I heard a voice saying to me in Aramaic,ᵃ 'Saul, Saul, why do you persecute me? It is hard for you to kick against the goads.'

ᵃ14 Or *Hebrew*

¹⁵"Then I asked, 'Who are you, Lord?'

" 'I am Jesus, whom you are persecuting,' the Lord replied. ¹⁶'Now get up and stand on your feet. I have appeared to you to appoint you as a servant and as a witness of what you have seen of me and what I will show you. ¹⁷I will rescue you from your own people and from the Gentiles. I am sending you to them ¹⁸to open their eyes and turn them from darkness to light, and from the power of Satan to God, so that they may receive forgiveness of sins and a place among those who are sanctified by faith in me.'

¹⁹"So then, King Agrippa, I was not disobedient to the vision from heaven. ²⁰First to those in Damascus, then to those in Jerusalem and in all Judea, and to the Gentiles also, I preached that they should repent and turn to God and prove their repentance by their deeds. ²¹That is why the Jews seized me in the temple courts and tried to kill me. ²²But I have had God's help to this very day, and so I stand here and testify to small and great alike. I am saying nothing beyond what the prophets and Moses said would happen— ²³that the Christ*ᵃ* would suffer and, as the first to rise from the dead, would proclaim light to his own people and to the Gentiles."

²⁴At this point Festus interrupted Paul's defense. "You are out of your mind, Paul!" he shouted. "Your great learning is driving you insane."

²⁵"I am not insane, most excellent Festus," Paul replied. "What I am saying is true and reasonable. ²⁶The king is familiar with these things, and I can speak freely to him. I am convinced that none of this has escaped his notice, because it was not done in a corner. ²⁷King Agrippa, do you believe the prophets? I know you do."

²⁸Then Agrippa said to Paul, "Do you think that in such a short time you can persuade me to be a Christian?"

²⁹Paul replied, "Short time or long—I pray God that not only you but all who are listening to me today may become what I am, except for these chains."

³⁰The king rose, and with him the governor and Bernice and those sitting with them. ³¹They left the room, and while talking with one another, they said, "This man is not doing anything that deserves death or imprisonment."

³²Agrippa said to Festus, "This man could have been set free if he had not appealed to Caesar."

Paul Sails for Rome

27 When it was decided that we would sail for Italy, Paul and some other prisoners were handed over to a centurion named Julius, who belonged to the Imperial Regiment. ²We boarded a ship from Adramyttium about to sail for ports along the coast of the province of Asia, and we put out to sea. Aristarchus, a Macedonian from Thessalonica, was with us.

³The next day we landed at Sidon; and Julius, in kindness to Paul, allowed him to go to his friends so they might provide for his needs. ⁴From there we put out to sea again and passed to the lee of Cyprus because the

ᵃ23 Or *Messiah*

winds were against us. [5]When we had sailed across the open sea off the coast of Cilicia and Pamphylia, we landed at Myra in Lycia. [6]There the centurion found an Alexandrian ship sailing for Italy and put us on board. [7]We made slow headway for many days and had difficulty arriving off Cnidus. When the wind did not allow us to hold our course, we sailed to the lee of Crete, opposite Salmone. [8]We moved along the coast with difficulty and came to a place called Fair Havens, near the town of Lasea.

[9]Much time had been lost, and sailing had already become dangerous because by now it was after the Fast.[a] So Paul warned them, [10]"Men, I can see that our voyage is going to be disastrous and bring great loss to ship and cargo, and to our own lives also." [11]But the centurion, instead of listening to what Paul said, followed the advice of the pilot and of the owner of the ship. [12]Since the harbor was unsuitable to winter in, the majority decided that we should sail on, hoping to reach Phoenix and winter there. This was a harbor in Crete, facing both southwest and northwest.

The Storm

[13]When a gentle south wind began to blow, they thought they had obtained what they wanted; so they weighed anchor and sailed along the shore of Crete. [14]Before very long, a wind of hurricane force, called the "northeaster," swept down from the island. [15]The ship was caught by the storm and could not head into the wind; so we gave way to it and were driven along. [16]As we passed to the lee of a small island called Cauda, we were hardly able to make the lifeboat secure. [17]When the men had hoisted it aboard, they passed ropes under the ship itself to hold it together. Fearing that they would run aground on the sandbars of Syrtis, they lowered the sea anchor and let the ship be driven along. [18]We took such a violent battering from the storm that the next day they began to throw the cargo overboard. [19]On the third day, they threw the ship's tackle overboard with their own hands. [20]When neither sun nor stars appeared for many days and the storm continued raging, we finally gave up all hope of being saved.

[21]After the men had gone a long time without food, Paul stood up before them and said: "Men, you should have taken my advice not to sail from Crete; then you would have spared yourselves this damage and loss. [22]But now I urge you to keep up your courage, because not one of you will be lost; only the ship will be destroyed. [23]Last night an angel of the God whose I am and whom I serve stood beside me [24]and said, 'Do not be afraid, Paul. You must stand trial before Caesar; and God has graciously given you the lives of all who sail with you.' [25]So keep up your courage, men, for I have faith in God that it will happen just as he told me. [26]Nevertheless, we must run aground on some island."

The Shipwreck

[27]On the fourteenth night we were still being driven across the Adriatic[b]

_____

[a]9 That is, the Day of Atonement (Yom Kippur)   [b]27 In ancient times the name referred to an area extending well south of Italy.

Sea, when about midnight the sailors sensed they were approaching land. [28]They took soundings and found that the water was a hundred and twenty feet[a] deep. A short time later they took soundings again and found it was ninety feet[b] deep. [29]Fearing that we would be dashed against the rocks, they dropped four anchors from the stern and prayed for daylight. [30]In an attempt to escape from the ship, the sailors let the lifeboat down into the sea, pretending they were going to lower some anchors from the bow. [31]Then Paul said to the centurion and the soldiers, "Unless these men stay with the ship, you cannot be saved." [32]So the soldiers cut the ropes that held the lifeboat and let it fall away.

[33]Just before dawn Paul urged them all to eat. "For the last fourteen days," he said, "you have been in constant suspense and have gone without food—you haven't eaten anything. [34]Now I urge you to take some food. You need it to survive. Not one of you will lose a single hair from his head." [35]After he said this, he took some bread and gave thanks to God in front of them all. Then he broke it and began to eat. [36]They were all encouraged and ate some food themselves. [37]Altogether there were 276 of us on board. [38]When they had eaten as much as they wanted, they lightened the ship by throwing the grain into the sea.

[39]When daylight came, they did not recognize the land, but they saw a bay with a sandy beach, where they decided to run the ship aground if they could. [40]Cutting loose the anchors, they left them in the sea and at the same time untied the ropes that held the rudders. Then they hoisted the foresail to the wind and made for the beach. [41]But the ship struck a sandbar and ran aground. The bow stuck fast and would not move, and the stern was broken to pieces by the pounding of the surf.

[42]The soldiers planned to kill the prisoners to prevent any of them from swimming away and escaping. [43]But the centurion wanted to spare Paul's life and kept them from carrying out their plan. He ordered those who could swim to jump overboard first and get to land. [44]The rest were to get there on planks or on pieces of the ship. In this way everyone reached land in safety.

Ashore on Malta

28 Once safely on shore, we found out that the island was called Malta. [2]The islanders showed us unusual kindness. They built a fire and welcomed us all because it was raining and cold. [3]Paul gathered a pile of brushwood and, as he put it on the fire, a viper, driven out by the heat, fastened itself on his hand. [4]When the islanders saw the snake hanging from his hand, they said to each other, "This man must be a murderer; for though he escaped from the sea, Justice has not allowed him to live." [5]But Paul shook the snake off into the fire and suffered no ill effects. [6]The people expected him to swell up or suddenly fall dead, but after waiting a long time and seeing nothing unusual happen to him, they changed their minds and said he was a god.

[a]28 Greek *twenty orguias* (about 37 meters)   [b]28 Greek *fifteen orguias* (about 27 meters)

7There was an estate nearby that belonged to Publius, the chief official of the island. He welcomed us to his home and for three days entertained us hospitably. 8His father was sick in bed, suffering from fever and dysentery. Paul went in to see him and, after prayer, placed his hands on him and healed him. 9When this had happened, the rest of the sick on the island came and were cured. 10They honored us in many ways and when we were ready to sail, they furnished us with the supplies we needed.

Arrival at Rome

11After three months we put out to sea in a ship that had wintered in the island. It was an Alexandrian ship with the figurehead of the twin gods Castor and Pollux. 12We put in at Syracuse and stayed there three days. 13From there we set sail and arrived at Rhegium. The next day the south wind came up, and on the following day we reached Puteoli. 14There we found some brothers who invited us to spend a week with them. And so we came to Rome. 15The brothers there had heard that we were coming, and they traveled as far as the Forum of Appius and the Three Taverns to meet us. At the sight of these men Paul thanked God and was encouraged. 16When we got to Rome, Paul was allowed to live by himself, with a soldier to guard him.

Paul Preaches at Rome Under Guard

17Three days later he called together the leaders of the Jews. When they had assembled, Paul said to them: "My brothers, although I have done nothing against our people or against the customs of our ancestors, I was arrested in Jerusalem and handed over to the Romans. 18They examined me and wanted to release me, because I was not guilty of any crime deserving death. 19But when the Jews objected, I was compelled to appeal to Caesar—not that I had any charge to bring against my own people. 20For this reason I have asked to see you and talk with you. It is because of the hope of Israel that I am bound with this chain."

21They replied, "We have not received any letters from Judea concerning you, and none of the brothers who have come from there has reported or said anything bad about you. 22But we want to hear what your views are, for we know that people everywhere are talking against this sect."

23They arranged to meet Paul on a certain day, and came in even larger numbers to the place where he was staying. From morning till evening he explained and declared to them the kingdom of God and tried to convince them about Jesus from the Law of Moses and from the Prophets. 24Some were convinced by what he said, but others would not believe. 25They disagreed among themselves and began to leave after Paul had made this final statement: "The Holy Spirit spoke the truth to your forefathers when he said through Isaiah the prophet:

26" 'Go to this people and say,
  "You will be ever hearing but never understanding;
   you will be ever seeing but never perceiving."

²⁷For this people's heart has become calloused;
> they hardly hear with their ears,
> and they have closed their eyes.
Otherwise they might see with their eyes,
> hear with their ears,
> understand with their hearts
and turn, and I would heal them.'^a

²⁸"Therefore I want you to know that God's salvation has been sent to the Gentiles, and they will listen!"^b

³⁰For two whole years Paul stayed there in his own rented house and welcomed all who came to see him. ³¹Boldly and without hindrance he preached the kingdom of God and taught about the Lord Jesus Christ.

---

^a27 Isaiah 6:9,10   ^b28 Some manuscripts *listen!"* ²⁹*After he said this, the Jews left, arguing vigorously among themselves.*

Romans

INTRODUCTION

Romans was probably the last of Paul's letters, written from Corinth around the year 57 A.D. during Paul's last visit to that city. Romans is unique among Paul's letters not only because it is the most profoundly theological but also because it is written to a community that Paul had never even visited. A question often raised about this letter is whether it deals with specific problems of the community addressed or with universal concerns of the Chruch everywhere. The answer can probably be given in terms of Paul's intended itinerary: Jerusalem, Rome, Spain. Paul was planning to go to Jerusalem to deliver the money he had collected for the poor (cf. 2 Cor 8—9) and then set out on a missionary journey to Spain stopping off at Rome on the way (15:28). The letter paved the way for Paul's visit. Serious accusations had been leveled against Paul, i.e., that he was not a genuine apostle and that his preaching of justification by faith alone and of Christian liberty was an invitation to licentiousness. The detailed explanation of his Gospel would assure the Romans of the legitimacy of his apostleship and Paul could

therefore expect to receive their support and assistance in carrying his Gospel to the ends of the earth, i.e., to Spain. The letter also provided Paul with an opportunity to rehearse, in writing, the defense of his understanding of the Gospel that he would soon have to present before the elders in Jerusalem. Confidence in the support of the prestigious Roman community would aid Paul in his dealings with the Jerusalem community.

A third and final purpose of the letter was to address a real need of this Roman community. A problem had recently arisen in that community between the strong and the weak, most likely a conflict between Gentile Christians who saw no need for Jewish legal observances and Jewish Christians who had only recently returned to Rome under Nero after having been expelled around 49 A.D. by Claudius. Paul was especially competent to deal with this problem because it was similar to problems he had recently encountered in Galatia (Judaizing influence) and Corinth (factions).

The first eleven chapters, while relevant to the specific problem at Rome, deal with humanity in

241

general. Paul is concerned with the authenticity of his Gospel which he states first in traditional terms (1:2–4) and then in his own controversial form (1:16–17). His overriding concern, however, is with the Jewish-Gentile problem. Paul begins the main body of the letter by showing how Jews and Gentiles are both sinful, both descended from Adam, both under the same condemnation (1:18—3:20). He then goes on to show how all are saved by faith alone (3:21—4:25). The continuing significance of the law of Moses, however, remained a problem and in three carefully nuanced chapters (5–7) Paul both defends himself against the charge of promoting licentiousness and shows how the law, though good, was incapable of saving mankind and therefore only had the effect of increasing human guilt. The climax of the letter is reached in chapter 8 in a celebration of the new life of the Spirit that comes through faith in Jesus. Chapters 9–11 return to the question of the Jews, affirming the continuing validity of God's promises and Paul's confidence in their eventual salvation.

Having dealt with the general theological problems surrounding his ministry Paul turns his attention, in the final chapters, to the needs of the community at Rome. General exhortations to live out in their daily lives the faith they profess (12:1—13:14) are followed by directives concerning the specific Roman problem of the strong and the weak (14:1—15:13). Just as the letter began by asserting the unity of mankind under the condemnation of sin (3:9), so the letter draws to its conclusion by encouraging unity and mutual acceptance within the Roman Christian community (15:5–7).

TERENCE J. KEEGAN, O.P.

Points for Reflection

1. The Letter to the Romans is profoundly theological and yet it addresses needs and concerns that touch the daily lives of every Christian. Do we strive to please God and then become discouraged over our failures? Can we accept our inability to please God, confess our guilt and then receive the free gift of God's justifying grace through Jesus (3:23f)?
2. We all experience suffering, but do we understand our suffering as essential to our eventual sharing in the glory of God (5:1–5)?
3. Do we really appreciate what Jesus means for us at every moment of our lives, i.e., that he has already done for us what we could never do for ourselves (8:3f) and that by the gift of his Spirit he had made us children of God enabling us to address God as "*Abba*, Father" (8:15f)? If we can appreciate the impact of Romans on our daily lives then we can see how the substance of this complex theological masterpiece is summed up in the simple advice: "He who loves his fellowman has fulfilled the law" (13:8).

1 Paul, a servant of Christ Jesus, called to be an apostle and set apart for the gospel of God— [2]the gospel he promised beforehand through his prophets in the Holy Scriptures [3]regarding his Son, who as to his human nature was a descendant of David, [4]and who through the Spirit[a] of holiness was declared with power to be the Son of God[b] by his resurrection from the dead: Jesus Christ our Lord. [5]Through him and for his name's sake, we received grace and apostleship to call people from among all the Gentiles to the obedience that comes from faith. [6]And you also are among those who are called to belong to Jesus Christ.

[7]To all in Rome who are loved by God and called to be saints:

Grace and peace to you from God our Father and from the Lord Jesus Christ.

Paul's Longing to Visit Rome

[8]First, I thank my God through Jesus Christ for all of you, because your faith is being reported all over the world. [9]God, whom I serve with my whole heart in preaching the gospel of his Son, is my witness how constantly I remember you [10]in my prayers at all times; and I pray that now at last by God's will the way may be opened for me to come to you.

[11]I long to see you so that I may impart to you some spiritual gift to make you strong— [12]that is, that you and I may be mutually encouraged by each other's faith. [13]I do not want you to be unaware, brothers, that I planned many times to come to you (but have been prevented from doing so until now) in order that I might have a harvest among you, just as I have had among the other Gentiles.

[14]I am obligated both to Greeks and non-Greeks, both to the wise and the foolish. [15]That is why I am so eager to preach the gospel also to you who are at Rome.

[16]I am not ashamed of the gospel, because it is the power of God for the salvation of everyone who believes: first for the Jew, then for the Gentile. [17]For in the gospel a righteousness from God is revealed, a righteousness that is by faith from first to last,[c] just as it is written: "The righteous will live by faith."[d]

God's Wrath Against Mankind

[18]The wrath of God is being revealed from heaven against all the godlessness and wickedness of men who suppress the truth by their wickedness, [19]since what may be known about God is plain to them, because God has made it plain to them. [20]For since the creation of the world God's invisible qualities—his eternal power and divine nature—have been clearly seen, being understood from what has been made, so that men are without excuse.

[21]For although they knew God, they neither glorified him as God nor

a4 Or who as to his spirit   b4 Or was appointed to be the Son of God with power   c17 Or is from faith to faith   d17 Hab. 2:4

gave thanks to him, but their thinking became futile and their foolish hearts were darkened. [22]Although they claimed to be wise, they became fools [23]and exchanged the glory of the immortal God for images made to look like mortal man and birds and animals and reptiles.

[24]Therefore God gave them over in the sinful desires of their hearts to sexual impurity for the degrading of their bodies with one another. [25]They exchanged the truth of God for a lie, and worshiped and served created things rather than the Creator—who is forever praised. Amen.

[26]Because of this, God gave them over to shameful lusts. Even their women exchanged natural relations for unnatural ones. [27]In the same way the men also abandoned natural relations with women and were inflamed with lust for one another. Men committed indecent acts with other men, and received in themselves the due penalty for their perversion.

[28]Furthermore, since they did not think it worthwhile to retain the knowledge of God, he gave them over to a depraved mind, to do what ought not to be done. [29]They have become filled with every kind of wickedness, evil, greed and depravity. They are full of envy, murder, strife, deceit and malice. They are gossips, [30]slanderers, God-haters, insolent, arrogant and boastful; they invent ways of doing evil; they disobey their parents; [31]they are senseless, faithless, heartless, ruthless. [32]Although they know God's righteous decree that those who do such things deserve death, they not only continue to do these very things but also approve of those who practice them.

God's Righteous Judgment

2 You, therefore, have no excuse, you who pass judgment on someone else, for at whatever point you judge the other, you are condemning yourself, because you who pass judgment do the same things. [2]Now we know that God's judgment against those who do such things is based on truth. [3]So when you, a mere man, pass judgment on them and yet do the same things, do you think you will escape God's judgment? [4]Or do you show contempt for the riches of his kindness, tolerance and patience, not realizing that God's kindness leads you toward repentance?

[5]But because of your stubbornness and your unrepentant heart, you are storing up wrath against yourself for the day of God's wrath, when his righteous judgment will be revealed. [6]God "will give to each person according to what he has done."[a] [7]To those who by persistence in doing good seek glory, honor and immortality, he will give eternal life. [8]But for those who are self-seeking and who reject the truth and follow evil, there will be wrath and anger. [9]There will be trouble and distress for every human being who does evil: first for the Jew, then for the Gentile; [10]but glory, honor and peace for everyone who does good: first for the Jew, then for the Gentile. [11]For God does not show favoritism.

[12]All who sin apart from the law will also perish apart from the law, and all who sin under the law will be judged by the law. [13]For it is not those who

[a]6 Psalm 62:12; Prov. 24:12

244

hear the law who are righteous in God's sight, but it is those who obey the law who will be declared righteous. [14](Indeed, when Gentiles, who do not have the law, do by nature things required by the law, they are a law for themselves, even though they do not have the law, [15]since they show that the requirements of the law are written on their hearts, their consciences also bearing witness, and their thoughts now accusing, now even defending them.) [16]This will take place on the day when God will judge men's secrets through Jesus Christ, as my gospel declares.

The Jews and the Law

[17]Now you, if you call yourself a Jew; if you rely on the law and brag about your relationship to God; [18]if you know his will and approve of what is superior because you are instructed by the law; [19]if you are convinced that you are a guide for the blind, a light for those who are in the dark, [20]an instructor of the foolish, a teacher of infants, because you have in the law the embodiment of knowledge and truth— [21]you, then, who teach others, do you not teach yourself? You who preach against stealing, do you steal? [22]You who say that people should not commit adultery, do you commit adultery? You who abhor idols, do you rob temples? [23]You who brag about the law, do you dishonor God by breaking the law? [24]As it is written: "God's name is blasphemed among the Gentiles because of you."[a]

[25]Circumcision has value if you observe the law, but if you break the law, you have become as though you had not been circumcised. [26]If those who are not circumcised keep the law's requirements, will they not be regarded as though they were circumcised? [27]The one who is not circumcised physically and yet obeys the law will condemn you who, even though you have the[b] written code and circumcision, are a lawbreaker.

[28]A man is not a Jew if he is only one outwardly, nor is circumcision merely outward and physical. [29]No, a man is a Jew if he is one inwardly; and circumcision is circumcision of the heart, by the Spirit, not by the written code. Such a man's praise is not from men, but from God.

God's Faithfulness

3 What advantage, then, is there in being a Jew, or what value is there in circumcision? [2]Much in every way! First of all, they have been entrusted with the very words of God.

[3]What if some did not have faith? Will their lack of faith nullify God's faithfulness? [4]Not at all! Let God be true, and every man a liar. As it is written:

> "So that you may be proved right when you speak
> and prevail when you judge."[c]

[5]But if our unrighteousness brings out God's righteousness more clearly, what shall we say? That God is unjust in bringing his wrath on us? (I am using a human argument.) [6]Certainly not! If that were so, how could

[a]24 Isaiah 52:5; Ezek. 36:22   [b]27 Or *who, by means of a*   [c]4 Psalm 51:4

God judge the world? [7]Someone might argue, "If my falsehood enhances God's truthfulness and so increases his glory, why am I still condemned as a sinner?" [8]Why not say—as we are being slanderously reported as saying and as some claim that we say—"Let us do evil that good may result"? Their condemnation is deserved.

No One Is Righteous

[9]What shall we conclude then? Are we any better[a]? Not at all! We have already made the charge that Jews and Gentiles alike are all under sin. [10]As it is written:

> "There is no one righteous, not even one;
> [11] there is no one who understands,
>   no one who seeks God.
> [12]All have turned away,
>   they have together become worthless;
> there is no one who does good,
>   not even one."[b]
> [13]"Their throats are open graves;
>   their tongues practice deceit."[c]
> "The poison of vipers is on their lips."[d]
> [14] "Their mouths are full of cursing and bitterness."[e]
> [15]"Their feet are swift to shed blood;
> [16] ruin and misery mark their ways,
> [17]and the way of peace they do not know."[f]
> [18] "There is no fear of God before their eyes."[g]

[19]Now we know that whatever the law says, it says to those who are under the law, so that every mouth may be silenced and the whole world held accountable to God. [20]Therefore no one will be declared righteous in his sight by observing the law; rather, through the law we become conscious of sin.

Righteousness Through Faith

[21]But now a righteousness from God, apart from law, has been made known, to which the Law and the Prophets testify. [22]This righteousness from God comes through faith in Jesus Christ to all who believe. There is no difference, [23]for all have sinned and fall short of the glory of God, [24]and are justified freely by his grace through the redemption that came by Christ Jesus. [25]God presented him as a sacrifice of atonement,[h] through faith in his blood. He did this to demonstrate his justice, because in his forbearance he had left the sins committed beforehand unpunished— [26]he did it to demonstrate his justice at the present time, so as to be just and the one who justifies those who have faith in Jesus.

---

[a]9 Or worse   [b]12 Psalms 14:1-3; 53:1-3; Eccles. 7:20   [c]13 Psalm 5:9   [d]13 Psalm 140:3
[e]14 Psalm 10:7   [f]17 Isaiah 59:7,8   [g]18 Psalm 36:1   [h]25 Or as the one who would turn aside his wrath, taking away sin

[27]Where, then, is boasting? It is excluded. On what principle? On that of observing the law? No, but on that of faith. [28]For we maintain that a man is justified by faith apart from observing the law. [29]Is God the God of Jews only? Is he not the God of Gentiles too? Yes, of Gentiles too, [30]since there is only one God, who will justify the circumcised by faith and the uncircumcised through that same faith. [31]Do we, then, nullify the law by this faith? Not at all! Rather, we uphold the law.

Abraham Justified by Faith

4 What then shall we say that Abraham, our forefather, discovered in this matter? [2]If, in fact, Abraham was justified by works, he had something to boast about—but not before God. [3]What does the Scripture say? "Abraham believed God, and it was credited to him as righteousness."[a]

[4]Now when a man works, his wages are not credited to him as a gift, but as an obligation. [5]However, to the man who does not work but trusts God who justifies the wicked, his faith is credited as righteousness. [6]David says the same thing when he speaks of the blessedness of the man to whom God credits righteousness apart from works:

[7]"Blessed are they
    whose transgressions are forgiven,
    whose sins are covered.
[8]Blessed is the man
    whose sin the Lord will never count against him."[b]

[9]Is this blessedness only for the circumcised, or also for the uncircumcised? We have been saying that Abraham's faith was credited to him as righteousness. [10]Under what circumstances was it credited? Was it after he was circumcised, or before? It was not after, but before! [11]And he received the sign of circumcision, a seal of the righteousness that he had by faith while he was still uncircumcised. So then, he is the father of all who believe but have not been circumcised, in order that righteousness might be credited to them. [12]And he is also the father of the circumcised who not only are circumcised but who also walk in the footsteps of the faith that our father Abraham had before he was circumcised.

[13]It was not through law that Abraham and his offspring received the promise that he would be heir of the world, but through the righteousness that comes by faith. [14]For if those who live by law are heirs, faith has no value and the promise is worthless, [15]because law brings wrath. And where there is no law there is no transgression.

[16]Therefore, the promise comes by faith, so that it may be by grace and may be guaranteed to all Abraham's offspring—not only to those who are of the law but also to those who are of the faith of Abraham. He is the father of us all. [17]As it is written: "I have made you a father of many nations."[c] He is our father in the sight of God, in whom he believed—the God who gives life to the dead and calls things that are not as though they were.

[a]3 Gen. 15:6; also in verse 22   [b]8 Psalm 32:1,2   [c]17 Gen. 17:5

[18]Against all hope, Abraham in hope believed and so became the father of many nations, just as it had been said to him, "So shall your offspring be."[a] [19]Without weakening in his faith, he faced the fact that his body was as good as dead—since he was about a hundred years old—and that Sarah's womb was also dead. [20]Yet he did not waver through unbelief regarding the promise of God, but was strengthened in his faith and gave glory to God, [21]being fully persuaded that God had power to do what he had promised. [22]This is why "it was credited to him as righteousness." [23]The words "it was credited to him" were written not for him alone, [24]but also for us, to whom God will credit righteousness—for us who believe in him who raised Jesus our Lord from the dead. [25]He was delivered over to death for our sins and was raised to life for our justification.

Peace and Joy

5 Therefore, since we have been justified through faith, we[b] have peace with God through our Lord Jesus Christ, [2]through whom we have gained access by faith into this grace in which we now stand. And we[b] rejoice in the hope of the glory of God. [3]Not only so, but we[b] also rejoice in our sufferings, because we know that suffering produces perseverance; [4]perseverance, character; and character, hope. [5]And hope does not disappoint us, because God has poured out his love into our hearts by the Holy Spirit, whom he has given us.

[6]You see, at just the right time, when we were still powerless, Christ died for the ungodly. [7]Very rarely will anyone die for a righteous man, though for a good man someone might possibly dare to die. [8]But God demonstrates his own love for us in this: While we were still sinners, Christ died for us.

[9]Since we have now been justified by his blood, how much more shall we be saved from God's wrath through him! [10]For if, when we were God's enemies, we were reconciled to him through the death of his Son, how much more, having been reconciled, shall we be saved through his life! [11]Not only is this so, but we also rejoice in God through our Lord Jesus Christ, through whom we have now received reconciliation.

Death Through Adam, Life Through Christ

[12]Therefore, just as sin entered the world through one man, and death through sin, and in this way death came to all men, because all sinned— [13]for before the law was given, sin was in the world. But sin is not taken into account when there is no law. [14]Nevertheless, death reigned from the time of Adam to the time of Moses, even over those who did not sin by breaking a command, as did Adam, who was a pattern of the one to come.

[15]But the gift is not like the trespass. For if the many died by the trespass of the one man, how much more did God's grace and the gift that came by the grace of the one man, Jesus Christ, overflow to the many! [16]Again, the gift of God is not like the result of the one man's sin: The judgment followed

---

[a]18 Gen. 15:5   [b]1,2,3 Or let us

one sin and brought condemnation, but the gift followed many trespasses and brought justification. ¹⁷For if, by the trespass of the one man, death reigned through that one man, how much more will those who receive God's abundant provision of grace and of the gift of righteousness reign in life through the one man, Jesus Christ.

¹⁸Consequently, just as the result of one trespass was condemnation for all men, so also the result of one act of righteousness was justification that brings life for all men. ¹⁹For just as through the disobedience of the one man the many were made sinners, so also through the obedience of the one man the many will be made righteous.

²⁰The law was added so that the trespass might increase. But where sin increased, grace increased all the more, ²¹so that, just as sin reigned in death, so also grace might reign through righteousness to bring eternal life through Jesus Christ our Lord.

Dead to Sin, Alive in Christ

6 What shall we say, then? Shall we go on sinning so that grace may increase? ²By no means! We died to sin; how can we live in it any longer? ³Or don't you know that all of us who were baptized into Christ Jesus were baptized into his death? ⁴We were therefore buried with him through baptism into death in order that, just as Christ was raised from the dead through the glory of the Father, we too may live a new life.

⁵If we have been united with him like this in his death, we will certainly also be united with him in his resurrection. ⁶For we know that our old self was crucified with him so that the body of sin might be done away with,^a that we should no longer be slaves to sin— ⁷because anyone who has died has been freed from sin.

⁸Now if we died with Christ, we believe that we will also live with him. ⁹For we know that since Christ was raised from the dead, he cannot die again; death no longer has mastery over him. ¹⁰The death he died, he died to sin once for all; but the life he lives, he lives to God.

¹¹In the same way, count yourselves dead to sin but alive to God in Christ Jesus. ¹²Therefore do not let sin reign in your mortal body so that you obey its evil desires. ¹³Do not offer the parts of your body to sin, as instruments of wickedness, but rather offer yourselves to God, as those who have been brought from death to life; and offer the parts of your body to him as instruments of righteousness. ¹⁴For sin shall not be your master, because you are not under law, but under grace.

Slaves to Righteousness

¹⁵What then? Shall we sin because we are not under law but under grace? By no means! ¹⁶Don't you know that when you offer yourselves to someone to obey him as slaves, you are slaves to the one whom you obey— whether you are slaves to sin, which leads to death, or to obedience, which leads to righteousness? ¹⁷But thanks be to God that, though you used to be

^a6 Or *be rendered powerless*

slaves to sin, you wholeheartedly obeyed the form of teaching to which you were entrusted. [18]You have been set free from sin and have become slaves to righteousness.

[19]I put this in human terms because you are weak in your natural selves. Just as you used to offer the parts of your body in slavery to impurity and to ever-increasing wickedness, so now offer them in slavery to righteousness leading to holiness. [20]When you were slaves to sin, you were free from the control of righteousness. [21]What benefit did you reap at that time from the things you are now ashamed of? Those things result in death! [22]But now that you have been set free from sin and have become slaves to God, the benefit you reap leads to holiness, and the result is eternal life. [23]For the wages of sin is death, but the gift of God is eternal life in[a] Christ Jesus our Lord.

An Illustration From Marriage

7 Do you not know, brothers—for I am speaking to men who know the law—that the law has authority over a man only as long as he lives? [2]For example, by law a married woman is bound to her husband as long as he is alive, but if her husband dies, she is released from the law of marriage. [3]So then, if she marries another man while her husband is still alive, she is called an adulteress. But if her husband dies, she is released from that law and is not an adulteress, even though she marries another man.

[4]So, my brothers, you also died to the law through the body of Christ, that you might belong to another, to him who was raised from the dead, in order that we might bear fruit to God. [5]For when we were controlled by the sinful nature,[b] the sinful passions aroused by the law were at work in our bodies, so that we bore fruit for death. [6]But now, by dying to what once bound us, we have been released from the law so that we serve in the new way of the Spirit, and not in the old way of the written code.

Struggling With Sin

[7]What shall we say, then? Is the law sin? Certainly not! Indeed I would not have known what sin was except through the law. For I would not have known what coveting really was if the law had not said, "Do not covet."[c] [8]But sin, seizing the opportunity afforded by the commandment, produced in me every kind of covetous desire. For apart from law, sin is dead. [9]Once I was alive apart from law; but when the commandment came, sin sprang to life and I died. [10]I found that the very commandment that was intended to bring life actually brought death. [11]For sin, seizing the opportunity afforded by the commandment, deceived me, and through the commandment put me to death. [12]So then, the law is holy, and the commandment is holy, righteous and good.

[13]Did that which is good, then, become death to me? By no means! But in order that sin might be recognized as sin, it produced death in me

[a]23 Or through   [b]5 Or the flesh; also in verse 25   [c]7 Exodus 20:17; Deut. 5:21

through what was good, so that through the commandment sin might become utterly sinful.

[14]We know that the law is spiritual; but I am unspiritual, sold as a slave to sin. [15]I do not understand what I do. For what I want to do I do not do, but what I hate I do. [16]And if I do what I do not want to do, I agree that the law is good. [17]As it is, it is no longer I myself who do it, but it is sin living in me. [18]I know that nothing good lives in me, that is, in my sinful nature.[a] For I have the desire to do what is good, but I cannot carry it out. [19]For what I do is not the good I want to do; no, the evil I do not want to do—this I keep on doing. [20]Now if I do what I do not want to do, it is no longer I who do it, but it is sin living in me that does it.

[21]So I find this law at work: When I want to do good, evil is right there with me. [22]For in my inner being I delight in God's law; [23]but I see another law at work in the members of my body, waging war against the law of my mind and making me a prisoner of the law of sin at work within my members. [24]What a wretched man I am! Who will rescue me from this body of death? [25]Thanks be to God—through Jesus Christ our Lord!

So then, I myself in my mind am a slave to God's law, but in the sinful nature a slave to the law of sin.

Life Through the Spirit

8 Therefore, there is now no condemnation for those who are in Christ Jesus,[b] [2]because through Christ Jesus the law of the Spirit of life set me free from the law of sin and death. [3]For what the law was powerless to do in that it was weakened by the sinful nature,[c] God did by sending his own Son in the likeness of sinful man to be a sin offering.[d] And so he condemned sin in sinful man,[e] [4]in order that the righteous requirements of the law might be fully met in us, who do not live according to the sinful nature but according to the Spirit.

[5]Those who live according to the sinful nature have their minds set on what that nature desires; but those who live in accordance with the Spirit have their minds set on what the Spirit desires. [6]The mind of sinful man[f] is death, but the mind controlled by the Spirit is life and peace; [7]the sinful mind[g] is hostile to God. It does not submit to God's law, nor can it do so. [8]Those controlled by the sinful nature cannot please God.

[9]You, however, are controlled not by the sinful nature but by the Spirit, if the Spirit of God lives in you. And if anyone does not have the Spirit of Christ, he does not belong to Christ. [10]But if Christ is in you, your body is dead because of sin, yet your spirit is alive because of righteousness. [11]And if the Spirit of him who raised Jesus from the dead is living in you, he who raised Christ from the dead will also give life to your mortal bodies through his Spirit, who lives in you.

[12]Therefore, brothers, we have an obligation—but it is not to the sinful

[a]18 Or my flesh   [b]1 Some later manuscripts Jesus, who do not live according to the sinful nature but according to the Spirit,   [c]3 Or the flesh; also in verses 4, 5, 8, 9, 12 and 13   [d]3 Or man, for sin   [e]3 Or in the flesh   [f]6 Or mind set on the flesh   [g]7 Or the mind set on the flesh

nature, to live according to it. [13]For if you live according to the sinful nature, you will die; but if by the Spirit you put to death the misdeeds of the body, you will live, [14]because those who are led by the Spirit of God are sons of God. [15]For you did not receive a spirit that makes you a slave again to fear, but you received the Spirit of sonship. [a] And by him we cry, "Abba, [b] Father." [16]The Spirit himself testifies with our spirit that we are God's children. [17]Now if we are children, then we are heirs—heirs of God and co-heirs with Christ, if indeed we share in his sufferings in order that we may also share in his glory.

Future Glory

[18]I consider that our present sufferings are not worth comparing with the glory that will be revealed in us. [19]The creation waits in eager expectation for the sons of God to be revealed. [20]For the creation was subjected to frustration, not by its own choice, but by the will of the one who subjected it, in hope [21]that[c] the creation itself will be liberated from its bondage to decay and brought into the glorious freedom of the children of God.

[22]We know that the whole creation has been groaning as in the pains of childbirth right up to the present time. [23]Not only so, but we ourselves, who have the firstfruits of the Spirit, groan inwardly as we wait eagerly for our adoption as sons, the redemption of our bodies. [24]For in this hope we were saved. But hope that is seen is no hope at all. Who hopes for what he already has? [25]But if we hope for what we do not yet have, we wait for it patiently.

[26]In the same way, the Spirit helps us in our weakness. We do not know what we ought to pray for, but the Spirit himself intercedes for us with groans that words cannot express. [27]And he who searches our hearts knows the mind of the Spirit, because the Spirit intercedes for the saints in accordance with God's will.

More Than Conquerors

[28]And we know that in all things God works for the good of those who love him, [d] who[e] have been called according to his purpose. [29]For those God foreknew he also predestined to be conformed to the likeness of his Son, that he might be the firstborn among many brothers. [30]And those he predestined, he also called; those he called, he also justified; those he justified, he also glorified.

[31]What, then, shall we say in response to this? If God is for us, who can be against us? [32]He who did not spare his own Son, but gave him up for us all—how will he not also, along with him, graciously give us all things? [33]Who will bring any charge against those whom God has chosen? It is God who justifies. [34]Who is he that condemns? Christ Jesus, who died—more than that, who was raised to life—is at the right hand of God and is also

---

[a]15 Or adoption   [b]15 Aramaic for Father   [c]20,21 Or subjected it in hope. [21]For   [d]28 Some manuscripts And we know that all things work together for good to those who love God   [e]28 Or works together with those who love him to bring about what is good—with those who

interceding for us. ³⁵Who shall separate us from the love of Christ? Shall trouble or hardship or persecution or famine or nakedness or danger or sword? ³⁶As it is written:

> "For your sake we face death all day long;
>   we are considered as sheep to be slaughtered."ᵃ

³⁷No, in all these things we are more than conquerors through him who loved us. ³⁸For I am convinced that neither death nor life, neither angels nor demons,ᵇ neither the present nor the future, nor any powers, ³⁹neither height nor depth, nor anything else in all creation, will be able to separate us from the love of God that is in Christ Jesus our Lord.

God's Sovereign Choice

9 I speak the truth in Christ—I am not lying, my conscience confirms it in the Holy Spirit— ²I have great sorrow and unceasing anguish in my heart. ³For I could wish that I myself were cursed and cut off from Christ for the sake of my brothers, those of my own race, ⁴the people of Israel. Theirs is the adoption as sons; theirs the divine glory, the covenants, the receiving of the law, the temple worship and the promises. ⁵Theirs are the patriarchs, and from them is traced the human ancestry of Christ, who is God over all, forever praised!ᶜ Amen.

⁶It is not as though God's word had failed. For not all who are descended from Israel are Israel. ⁷Nor because they are his descendants are they all Abraham's children. On the contrary, "It is through Isaac that your offspring will be reckoned."ᵈ ⁸In other words, it is not the natural children who are God's children, but it is the children of the promise who are regarded as Abraham's offspring. ⁹For this was how the promise was stated: "At the appointed time I will return, and Sarah will have a son."ᵉ

¹⁰Not only that, but Rebekah's children had one and the same father, our father Isaac. ¹¹Yet, before the twins were born or had done anything good or bad—in order that God's purpose in election might stand: ¹²not by works but by him who calls—she was told, "The older will serve the younger."ᶠ ¹³Just as it is written: "Jacob I loved, but Esau I hated."ᵍ

¹⁴What then shall we say? Is God unjust? Not at all! ¹⁵For he says to Moses,

> "I will have mercy on whom I have mercy,
>   and I will have compassion on whom I have
>   compassion."ʰ

¹⁶It does not, therefore, depend on man's desire or effort, but on God's mercy. ¹⁷For the Scripture says to Pharaoh: "I raised you up for this very purpose, that I might display my power in you and that my name might

---

ᵃ36 Psalm 44:22   ᵇ38 Or *nor heavenly rulers*   ᶜ5 Or *Christ, who is over all. God be forever praised!* Or *Christ. God who is over all be forever praised!*   ᵈ7 Gen. 21:12   ᵉ9 Gen. 18:10,14   ᶠ12 Gen. 25:23   ᵍ13 Mal. 1:2,3   ʰ15 Exodus 33:19

be proclaimed in all the earth."[a] [18]Therefore God has mercy on whom he wants to have mercy, and he hardens whom he wants to harden.

[19]One of you will say to me: "Then why does God still blame us? For who resists his will?" [20]But who are you, O man, to talk back to God? "Shall what is formed say to him who formed it, 'Why did you make me like this?' "[b] [21]Does not the potter have the right to make out of the same lump of clay some pottery for noble purposes and some for common use?

[22]What if God, choosing to show his wrath and make his power known, bore with great patience the objects of his wrath—prepared for destruction? [23]What if he did this to make the riches of his glory known to the objects of his mercy, whom he prepared in advance for glory— [24]even us, whom he also called, not only from the Jews but also from the Gentiles? [25]As he says in Hosea:

> "I will call them 'my people' who are not my people;
>   and I will call her 'my loved one' who is not my loved
>   one,"[c]

[26]and,

> "It will happen that in the very place where it was said to
>   them,
>   'You are not my people,'
> they will be called 'sons of the living God.' "[d]

[27]Isaiah cries out concerning Israel:

> "Though the number of the Israelites be like the sand by the
>   sea,
>   only the remnant will be saved.
> [28]For the Lord will carry out
>   his sentence on earth with speed and finality."[e]

[29]It is just as Isaiah said previously:

> "Unless the Lord Almighty
>   had left us descendants,
> we would have become like Sodom,
>   we would have been like Gomorrah."[f]

Israel's Unbelief

[30]What then shall we say? That the Gentiles, who did not pursue righteousness, have obtained it, a righteousness that is by faith; [31]but Israel, who pursued a law of righteousness, has not attained it. [32]Why not? Because they pursued it not by faith but as if it were by works. They stumbled over the "stumbling stone." [33]As it is written:

> "See, I lay in Zion a stone that causes men to stumble

[a]17 Exodus 9:16   [b]20 Isaiah 29:16; 45:9   [c]25 Hosea 2:23   [d]26 Hosea 1:10
[e]28 Isaiah 10:22,23   [f]29 Isaiah 1:9

nourishing sap from the olive root, [18]do not boast over those branches. If you do, consider this: You do not support the root, but the root supports you. [19]You will say then, "Branches were broken off so that I could be grafted in." [20]Granted. But they were broken off because of unbelief, and you stand by faith. Do not be arrogant, but be afraid. [21]For if God did not spare the natural branches, he will not spare you either.

[22]Consider therefore the kindness and sternness of God: sternness to those who fell, but kindness to you, provided that you continue in his kindness. Otherwise, you also will be cut off. [23]And if they do not persist in unbelief, they will be grafted in, for God is able to graft them in again. [24]After all, if you were cut out of an olive tree that is wild by nature, and contrary to nature were grafted into a cultivated olive tree, how much more readily will these, the natural branches, be grafted into their own olive tree!

All Israel Will Be Saved

[25]I do not want you to be ignorant of this mystery, brothers, so that you may not be conceited: Israel has experienced a hardening in part until the full number of the Gentiles has come in. [26]And so all Israel will be saved, as it is written:

> "The deliverer will come from Zion;
>   he will turn godlessness away from Jacob.
> [27]And this is[a] my covenant with them
>   when I take away their sins."[b]

[28]As far as the gospel is concerned, they are enemies on your account; but as far as election is concerned, they are loved on account of the patriarchs, [29]for God's gifts and his call are irrevocable. [30]Just as you who were at one time disobedient to God have now received mercy as a result of their disobedience, [31]so they too have now become disobedient in order that they too may now[c] receive mercy as a result of God's mercy to you. [32]For God has bound all men over to disobedience so that he may have mercy on them all.

Doxology

> [33]Oh, the depth of the riches of the wisdom and[d] knowledge
>   of God!
>   How unsearchable his judgments,
>   and his paths beyond tracing out!
> [34]"Who has known the mind of the Lord?
>   Or who has been his counselor?"[e]
> [35]"Who has ever given to God,
>   that God should repay him?"[f]
> [36]For from him and through him and to him are all things.
>   To him be the glory forever! Amen.

---

[a]27 Or will be   [b]27 Isaiah 59:20,21; 27:9; Jer. 31:33,34   [c]31 Some manuscripts do not have now.
[d]33 Or riches and the wisdom and the   [e]34 Isaiah 40:13   [f]35 Job 41:11

Living Sacrifices

12 Therefore, I urge you, brothers, in view of God's mercy, to offer your bodies as living sacrifices, holy and pleasing to God—this is your spiritual[a] act of worship. [2]Do not conform any longer to the pattern of this world, but be transformed by the renewing of your mind. Then you will be able to test and approve what God's will is—his good, pleasing and perfect will.

[3]For by the grace given me I say to every one of you: Do not think of yourself more highly than you ought, but rather think of yourself with sober judgment, in accordance with the measure of faith God has given you. [4]Just as each of us has one body with many members, and these members do not all have the same function, [5]so in Christ we who are many form one body, and each member belongs to all the others. [6]We have different gifts, according to the grace given us. If a man's gift is prophesying, let him use it in proportion to his[b] faith. [7]If it is serving, let him serve; if it is teaching, let him teach; [8]if it is encouraging, let him encourage; if it is contributing to the needs of others, let him give generously; if it is leadership, let him govern diligently; if it is showing mercy, let him do it cheerfully.

Love

[9]Love must be sincere. Hate what is evil; cling to what is good. [10]Be devoted to one another in brotherly love. Honor one another above yourselves. [11]Never be lacking in zeal, but keep your spiritual fervor, serving the Lord. [12]Be joyful in hope, patient in affliction, faithful in prayer. [13]Share with God's people who are in need. Practice hospitality.

[14]Bless those who persecute you; bless and do not curse. [15]Rejoice with those who rejoice; mourn with those who mourn. [16]Live in harmony with one another. Do not be proud, but be willing to associate with people of low position.[c] Do not be conceited.

[17]Do not repay anyone evil for evil. Be careful to do what is right in the eyes of everybody. [18]If it is possible, as far as it depends on you, live at peace with everyone. [19]Do not take revenge, my friends, but leave room for God's wrath, for it is written: "It is mine to avenge; I will repay,"[d] says the Lord. [20]On the contrary:

> "If your enemy is hungry, feed him;
>   if he is thirsty, give him something to drink.
> In doing this, you will heap burning coals on his head."[e]

[21]Do not be overcome by evil, but overcome evil with good.

Submission to the Authorities

13 Everyone must submit himself to the governing authorities, for there is no authority except that which God has established. The authori-

[a]1 Or *reasonable*   [b]6 Or *in agreement with the*   [c]16 Or *willing to do menial work*   [d]19 Deut. 32:35
[e]20 Prov. 25:21,22

ties that exist have been established by God. [2]Consequently, he who rebels against the authority is rebelling against what God has instituted, and those who do so will bring judgment on themselves. [3]For rulers hold no terror for those who do right, but for those who do wrong. Do you want to be free from fear of the one in authority? Then do what is right and he will commend you. [4]For he is God's servant to do you good. But if you do wrong, be afraid, for he does not bear the sword for nothing. He is God's servant, an agent of wrath to bring punishment on the wrongdoer. [5]Therefore, it is necessary to submit to the authorities, not only because of possible punishment but also because of conscience.

[6]This is also why you pay taxes, for the authorities are God's servants, who give their full time to governing. [7]Give everyone what you owe him: If you owe taxes, pay taxes; if revenue, then revenue; if respect, then respect; if honor, then honor.

Love, for the Day Is Near

[8]Let no debt remain outstanding, except the continuing debt to love one another, for he who loves his fellowman has fulfilled the law. [9]The commandments, "Do not commit adultery," "Do not murder," "Do not steal," "Do not covet,"[a] and whatever other commandment there may be, are summed up in this one rule: "Love your neighbor as yourself."[b] [10]Love does no harm to its neighbor. Therefore love is the fulfillment of the law.

[11]And do this, understanding the present time. The hour has come for you to wake up from your slumber, because our salvation is nearer now than when we first believed. [12]The night is nearly over; the day is almost here. So let us put aside the deeds of darkness and put on the armor of light. [13]Let us behave decently, as in the daytime, not in orgies and drunkenness, not in sexual immorality and debauchery, not in dissension and jealousy. [14]Rather, clothe yourselves with the Lord Jesus Christ, and do not think about how to gratify the desires of the sinful nature.[c]

The Weak and the Strong

14 Accept him whose faith is weak, without passing judgment on disputable matters. [1]One man's faith allows him to eat everything, but another man, whose faith is weak, eats only vegetables. [3]The man who eats everything must not look down on him who does not, and the man who does not eat everything must not condemn the man who does, for God has accepted him. [4]Who are you to judge someone else's servant? To his own master he stands or falls. And he will stand, for the Lord is able to make him stand.

[5]One man considers one day more sacred than another; another man considers every day alike. Each one should be fully convinced in his own mind. [6]He who regards one day as special, does so to the Lord. He who eats meat, eats to the Lord, for he gives thanks to God; and he who abstains, does so to the Lord and gives thanks to God. [7]For none of us lives to himself

[a]9 Exodus 20:13-15,17; Deut. 5:17-19,21   [b]9 Lev. 19:18   [c]14 Or *the flesh*

alone and none of us dies to himself alone. [8]If we live, we live to the Lord; and if we die, we die to the Lord. So, whether we live or die, we belong to the Lord.

[9]For this very reason, Christ died and returned to life so that he might be the Lord of both the dead and the living. [10]You, then, why do you judge your brother? Or why do you look down on your brother? For we will all stand before God's judgment seat. [11]It is written:

" 'As surely as I live,' says the Lord,
'every knee will bow before me;
    every tongue will confess to God.' "[a]

[12]So then, each of us will give an account of himself to God.

[13]Therefore let us stop passing judgment on one another. Instead, make up your mind not to put any stumbling block or obstacle in your brother's way. [14]As one who is in the Lord Jesus, I am fully convinced that no food[b] is unclean in itself. But if anyone regards something as unclean, then for him it is unclean. [15]If your brother is distressed because of what you eat, you are no longer acting in love. Do not by your eating destroy your brother for whom Christ died. [16]Do not allow what you consider good to be spoken of as evil. [17]For the kingdom of God is not a matter of eating and drinking, but of righteousness, peace and joy in the Holy Spirit, [18]because anyone who serves Christ in this way is pleasing to God and approved by men.

[19]Let us therefore make every effort to do what leads to peace and to mutual edification. [20]Do not destroy the work of God for the sake of food. All food is clean, but it is wrong for a man to eat anything that causes someone else to stumble. [21]It is better not to eat meat or drink wine or to do anything else that will cause your brother to fall.

[22]So whatever you believe about these things keep between yourself and God. Blessed is the man who does not condemn himself by what he approves. [23]But the man who has doubts is condemned if he eats, because his eating is not from faith; and everything that does not come from faith is sin.

15 We who are strong ought to bear with the failings of the weak and not to please ourselves. [2]Each of us should please his neighbor for his good, to build him up. [3]For even Christ did not please himself but, as it is written: "The insults of those who insult you have fallen on me."[c] [4]For everything that was written in the past was written to teach us, so that through endurance and the encouragement of the Scriptures we might have hope.

[5]May the God who gives endurance and encouragement give you a spirit of unity among yourselves as you follow Christ Jesus, [6]so that with one heart and mouth you may glorify the God and Father of our Lord Jesus Christ.

[7]Accept one another, then, just as Christ accepted you, in order to bring praise to God. [8]For I tell you that Christ has become a servant of the Jews[d]

[a]11 Isaiah 45:23   [b]14 Or that nothing   [c]3 Psalm 69:9   [d]8 Greek circumcision

on behalf of God's truth, to confirm the promises made to the patriarchs
[9]so that the Gentiles may glorify God for his mercy, as it is written:

> "Therefore I will praise you among the Gentiles;
>   I will sing hymns to your name."[a]

[10]Again, it says,

> "Rejoice, O Gentiles, with his people."[b]

[11]And again,

> "Praise the Lord, all you Gentiles,
>   and sing praises to him, all you peoples."[c]

[12]And again, Isaiah says,

> "The Root of Jesse will spring up,
>   one who will arise to rule over the nations;
> the Gentiles will hope in him."[d]

[13]May the God of hope fill you with all joy and peace as you trust in
him, so that you may overflow with hope by the power of the Holy Spirit.

Paul the Minister to the Gentiles

[14]I myself am convinced, my brothers, that you yourselves are full of
goodness, complete in knowledge and competent to instruct one another.
[15]I have written you quite boldly on some points, as if to remind you of them
again, because of the grace God gave me [16]to be a minister of Christ Jesus
to the Gentiles with the priestly duty of proclaiming the gospel of God, so
that the Gentiles might become an offering acceptable to God, sanctified by
the Holy Spirit.

[17]Therefore I glory in Christ Jesus in my service to God. [18]I will not
venture to speak of anything except what Christ has accomplished through
me in leading the Gentiles to obey God by what I have said and done— [19]by
the power of signs and miracles, through the power of the Spirit. So from
Jerusalem all the way around to Illyricum, I have fully proclaimed the
gospel of Christ. [20]It has always been my ambition to preach the gospel
where Christ was not known, so that I would not be building on someone
else's foundation. [21]Rather, as it is written:

> "Those who were not told about him will see,
>   and those who have not heard will understand."[e]

[22]This is why I have often been hindered from coming to you.

Paul's Plan to Visit Rome

[23]But now that there is no more place for me to work in these regions,
and since I have been longing for many years to see you, [24]I plan to do so

[a]9 2 Samuel 22:50; Psalm 18:49   [b]10 Deut. 32:43   [c]11 Psalm 117:1   [d]12 Isaiah 11:10
[e]21 Isaiah 52:15

when I go to Spain. I hope to visit you while passing through and to have you assist me on my journey there, after I have enjoyed your company for a while. ²⁵Now, however, I am on my way to Jerusalem in the service of the saints there. ²⁶For Macedonia and Achaia were pleased to make a contribution for the poor among the saints in Jerusalem. ²⁷They were pleased to do it, and indeed they owe it to them. For if the Gentiles have shared in the Jews' spiritual blessings, they owe it to the Jews to share with them their material blessings. ²⁸So after I have completed this task and have made sure that they have received this fruit, I will go to Spain and visit you on the way. ²⁹I know that when I come to you, I will come in the full measure of the blessing of Christ.

³⁰I urge you, brothers, by our Lord Jesus Christ and by the love of the Spirit, to join me in my struggle by praying to God for me. ³¹Pray that I may be rescued from the unbelievers in Judea and that my service in Jerusalem may be acceptable to the saints there, ³²so that by God's will I may come to you with joy and together with you be refreshed. ³³The God of peace be with you all. Amen.

Personal Greetings

16 I commend to you our sister Phoebe, a servant[a] of the church in Cenchrea. ²I ask you to receive her in the Lord in a way worthy of the saints and to give her any help she may need from you, for she has been a great help to many people, including me.

³Greet Priscilla[b] and Aquila, my fellow workers in Christ Jesus. ⁴They risked their lives for me. Not only I but all the churches of the Gentiles are grateful to them.

⁵Greet also the church that meets at their house.

Greet my dear friend Epenetus, who was the first convert to Christ in the province of Asia.

⁶Greet Mary, who worked very hard for you.

⁷Greet Andronicus and Junias, my relatives who have been in prison with me. They are outstanding among the apostles, and they were in Christ before I was.

⁸Greet Ampliatus, whom I love in the Lord.

⁹Greet Urbanus, our fellow worker in Christ, and my dear friend Stachys.

¹⁰Greet Apelles, tested and approved in Christ.

Greet those who belong to the household of Aristobulus.

¹¹Greet Herodion, my relative.

Greet those in the household of Narcissus who are in the Lord.

¹²Greet Tryphena and Tryphosa, those women who work hard in the Lord.

Greet my dear friend Persis, another woman who has worked very hard in the Lord.

¹³Greet Rufus, chosen in the Lord, and his mother, who has been a mother to me, too.

---

[a]1 Or *deaconess*   [b]3 Greek *Prisca*, a variant of *Priscilla*

[14]Greet Asyncritus, Phlegon, Hermes, Patrobas, Hermas and the brothers with them.

[15]Greet Philologus, Julia, Nereus and his sister, and Olympas and all the saints with them.

[16]Greet one another with a holy kiss.

All the churches of Christ send greetings.

[17]I urge you, brothers, to watch out for those who cause divisions and put obstacles in your way that are contrary to the teaching you have learned. Keep away from them. [18]For such people are not serving our Lord Christ, but their own appetites. By smooth talk and flattery they deceive the minds of naive people. [19]Everyone has heard about your obedience, so I am full of joy over you; but I want you to be wise about what is good, and innocent about what is evil.

[20]The God of peace will soon crush Satan under your feet.

The grace of our Lord Jesus be with you.

[21]Timothy, my fellow worker, sends his greetings to you, as do Lucius, Jason and Sosipater, my relatives.

[22]I, Tertius, who wrote down this letter, greet you in the Lord.

[23]Gaius, whose hospitality I and the whole church here enjoy, sends you his greetings.

Erastus, who is the city's director of public works, and our brother Quartus send you their greetings. [a]

[25]Now to him who is able to establish you by my gospel and the proclamation of Jesus Christ, according to the revelation of the mystery hidden for long ages past, [26]but now revealed and made known through the prophetic writings by the command of the eternal God, so that all nations might believe and obey him— [27]to the only wise God be glory forever through Jesus Christ! Amen.

---

[a]23 Some manuscripts *their greetings.* [24]*May the grace of our Lord Jesus Christ be with all of you. Amen.*

1 Corinthians

INTRODUCTION

Paul was devoted to the Corinthian community. His visits were of considerable duration and even when he was away from Corinth he agonized over its problems and carried on an extensive correspondence, receiving and writing letters (he wrote at least four), receiving and sending messengers. Corinth could be described as the sin city of the ancient world. It had a population of a half million, was the seat of the Roman governor of Achaia, a port city, a trade center, and a meeting place for international travelers. An enormous amount of wealth poured through the city and a proportionate amount of sensuous entertainment was available for the traveling merchants, seamen and diplomats.

Men and women of Corinth, immersed in the cultural and intellectual traditions of Greece as well as in the licentious living of their cosmopolitan city, had converted to Jesus. The radical change wrought by their conversions resulted in an enthusiasm for the Gospel rivaling that of Paul himself. It was an enthusiasm, however, which resulted in numerous problems as the Corinthians went from one extreme to another.

After Paul had written at least twice to the Corinthians (the letter mentioned in 1 Cor 5:9, and 1 Cor itself), he visited the community (as promised in 1 Cor 16:1ff) and found the community in open revolt. Some shocking incident occurred (2 Cor 2:1 –9) which caused Paul to alter his plans. He had intended to return to Corinth after visiting the churches of Macedonia (2 Cor 1:15—2:4) but instead returned to Ephesus and wrote his "letter of tears" (2 Cor 2:3f). Some feel that parts of this letter are preserved in 2 Corinthians 10–13. After the situation had improved Paul wrote still another letter which probably included much of 2 Corinthians 1–7.

The Corinthians had initially received the Gospel which Paul preached everywhere, the Gospel of freedom based on the new life in the Spirit won by the death and resurrection of Jesus. The Corinthians, however, carried their enthusiasm for freedom in the Spirit to extremes resulting in an array of problems brought to the attention of Paul by letters and messengers while he was in Ephesus (1 Cor 1:11; 7:1ff; 16:15ff) and prompting him to write 1 Corinthians. Various factions in Corinth were each insisting on their own understandings being correct. Pride had entered in everywhere causing difficulties even in the celebration of the Eucharist, the sacrament of unity, and in the prayer meetings where the gifts of the Spirit were most manifest. In the main body of 1 Corinthians Paul handles each specific problem in its turn but develops an increasingly clear central image by which to enable the Corinthians to recognize their pride and deal with their problems, the image of the body of Christ: "Now you are the body of Christ, and each one of you is a part of it" (1 Cor 12:27). There was one gift, however, that was beyond the reach of pride, i.e., love. Chapter 13, one of the most familiar and beautiful passages of the Bible, deals with the perfection of love.

Behind the ethical problems dealt with in this letter was a more serious doctrinal problem, the problem of the resurrection. Many of the enthusiastic Corinthians had become so engrossed in the new life of the Spirit that they already enjoyed that they had effectively denied the future resurrection, the object of Christian hope. The presumed fullness of what they already enjoyed led to the pride which puffs up rather than the love which builds up the body of Christ (cf. 8:1; 14:12). Paul, therefore, framed his letter with an insistence, at the beginning, on the necessity of viewing present Christian existence in terms of the foolish and scandalous cross of Christ, and at the end on a correct understanding of the resurrection. The resurrection has already occurred with Jesus but is yet to come for Christians. It is the object of hope and expectation, a future assurance which makes present life under the cross both meaningful and possible for Christians.

TERENCE J. KEEGAN, O.P.

Points for Reflection

1. It is significant that in a letter concerned with moral problems Paul avoids motivating ethical behavior by external compulsion. He relies instead on fostering a deeper awareness of the nature of God's grace in Christ, recognizing that authentic goodness arises out of the heart as a free response to that grace. As we read 1 Corinthians we can ask what the death and resurrection of Jesus means in our own lives. Have we been radically changed by the cross of Christ? Do we live in eager expectation of the fulfillment to come in the resurrection? Do we take pride in our present Christian existence?
2. Is it a selfish pride or do we boast only in the cross of Jesus? Are we aware of the gifts of the Spirit in our lives? Do we use these gifts to build up the body of Christ, the Church?

1 Paul, called to be an apostle of Christ Jesus by the will of God, and our brother Sosthenes,

²To the church of God in Corinth, to those sanctified in Christ Jesus and called to be holy, together with all those everywhere who call on the name of our Lord Jesus Christ—their Lord and ours:

³Grace and peace to you from God our Father and the Lord Jesus Christ.

Thanksgiving

⁴I always thank God for you because of his grace given you in Christ Jesus. ⁵For in him you have been enriched in every way—in all your speaking and in all your knowledge— ⁶because our testimony about Christ was confirmed in you. ⁷Therefore you do not lack any spiritual gift as you eagerly wait for our Lord Jesus Christ to be revealed. ⁸He will keep you strong to the end, so that you will be blameless on the day of our Lord Jesus Christ. ⁹God, who has called you into fellowship with his Son Jesus Christ our Lord, is faithful.

Divisions in the Church

¹⁰I appeal to you, brothers, in the name of our Lord Jesus Christ, that all of you agree with one another so that there may be no divisions among you and that you may be perfectly united in mind and thought. ¹¹My brothers, some from Chloe's household have informed me that there are quarrels among you. ¹²What I mean is this: One of you says, "I follow Paul"; another, "I follow Apollos"; another, "I follow Cephas[a]"; still another, "I follow Christ."

¹³Is Christ divided? Was Paul crucified for you? Were you baptized into[b] the name of Paul? ¹⁴I am thankful that I did not baptize any of you except Crispus and Gaius, ¹⁵so no one can say that you were baptized into my name. ¹⁶(Yes, I also baptized the household of Stephanas; beyond that, I don't remember if I baptized anyone else.) ¹⁷For Christ did not send me to baptize, but to preach the gospel—not with words of human wisdom, lest the cross of Christ be emptied of its power.

Christ the Wisdom and Power of God

¹⁸For the message of the cross is foolishness to those who are perishing, but to us who are being saved it is the power of God. ¹⁹For it is written:

"I will destroy the wisdom of the wise;
    the intelligence of the intelligent I will frustrate."[c]

²⁰Where is the wise man? Where is the scholar? Where is the philosopher of this age? Has not God made foolish the wisdom of the world? ²¹For since in the wisdom of God the world through its wisdom did not know him, God was pleased through the foolishness of what was preached to save those who believe. ²²Jews demand miraculous signs and Greeks look

---

a12 That is, Peter   *b13* Or *in;* also in verse 15   *c19* Isaiah 29:14

for wisdom, [23]but we preach Christ crucified: a stumbling block to Jews and foolishness to Gentiles, [24]but to those whom God has called, both Jews and Greeks, Christ the power of God and the wisdom of God. [25]For the foolishness of God is wiser than man's wisdom, and the weakness of God is stronger than man's strength.

[26]Brothers, think of what you were when you were called. Not many of you were wise by human standards; not many were influential; not many were of noble birth. [27]But God chose the foolish things of the world to shame the wise; God chose the weak things of the world to shame the strong. [28]He chose the lowly things of this world and the despised things—and the things that are not—to nullify the things that are, [29]so that no one may boast before him. [30]It is because of him that you are in Christ Jesus, who has become for us wisdom from God—that is, our righteousness, holiness and redemption. [31]Therefore, as it is written: "Let him who boasts boast in the Lord."[a]

2 When I came to you, brothers, I did not come with eloquence or superior wisdom as I proclaimed to you the testimony about God.[b] [2]For I resolved to know nothing while I was with you except Jesus Christ and him crucified. [3]I came to you in weakness and fear, and with much trembling. [4]My message and my preaching were not with wise and persuasive words, but with a demonstration of the Spirit's power, [5]so that your faith might not rest on men's wisdom, but on God's power.

Wisdom From the Spirit

[6]We do, however, speak a message of wisdom among the mature, but not the wisdom of this age or of the rulers of this age, who are coming to nothing. [7]No, we speak of God's secret wisdom, a wisdom that has been hidden and that God destined for our glory before time began. [8]None of the rulers of this age understood it, for if they had, they would not have crucified the Lord of glory. [9]However, as it is written:

> "No eye has seen,
>   no ear has heard,
>   no mind has conceived
>   what God has prepared for those who love him"[c]—

[10]but God has revealed it to us by his Spirit.

The Spirit searches all things, even the deep things of God. [11]For who among men knows the thoughts of a man except the man's spirit within him? In the same way no one knows the thoughts of God except the Spirit of God. [12]We have not received the spirit of the world but the Spirit who is from God, that we may understand what God has freely given us. [13]This is what we speak, not in words taught us by human wisdom but in words taught by the Spirit, expressing spiritual truths in spiritual words.[d] [14]The man without the Spirit does not accept the things that come from the Spirit

[a]31 Jer. 9:24   [b]1 Some manuscripts *as I proclaimed to you God's mystery*   [c]9 Isaiah 64:4   [d]13 Or *Spirit, interpreting spiritual truths to spiritual men*

of God, for they are foolishness to him, and he cannot understand them, because they are spiritually discerned. [15]The spiritual man makes judgments about all things, but he himself is not subject to any man's judgment:

> [16]"For who has known the mind of the Lord
> that he may instruct him?"[a]

But we have the mind of Christ.

On Divisions in the Church

3 Brothers, I could not address you as spiritual but as worldly—mere infants in Christ. [2]I gave you milk, not solid food, for you were not yet ready for it. Indeed, you are still not ready. [3]You are still worldly. For since there is jealousy and quarreling among you, are you not worldly? Are you not acting like mere men? [4]For when one says, "I follow Paul," and another, "I follow Apollos," are you not mere men?

[5]What, after all, is Apollos? And what is Paul? Only servants, through whom you came to believe—as the Lord has assigned to each his task. [6]I planted the seed, Apollos watered it, but God made it grow. [7]So neither he who plants nor he who waters is anything, but only God, who makes things grow. [8]The man who plants and the man who waters have one purpose, and each will be rewarded according to his own labor. [9]For we are God's fellow workers; you are God's field, God's building.

[10]By the grace God has given me, I laid a foundation as an expert builder, and someone else is building on it. But each one should be careful how he builds. [11]For no one can lay any foundation other than the one already laid, which is Jesus Christ. [12]If any man builds on this foundation using gold, silver, costly stones, wood, hay or straw, [13]his work will be shown for what it is, because the Day will bring it to light. It will be revealed with fire, and the fire will test the quality of each man's work. [14]If what he has built survives, he will receive his reward. [15]If it is burned up, he will suffer loss; he himself will be saved, but only as one escaping through the flames.

[16]Don't you know that you yourselves are God's temple and that God's Spirit lives in you? [17]If anyone destroys God's temple, God will destroy him; for God's temple is sacred, and you are that temple.

[18]Do not deceive yourselves. If any one of you thinks he is wise by the standards of this age, he should become a "fool" so that he may become wise. [19]For the wisdom of this world is foolishness in God's sight. As it is written: "He catches the wise in their craftiness"[b]; [20]and again, "The Lord knows that the thoughts of the wise are futile."[c] [21]So then, no more boasting about men! All things are yours, [22]whether Paul or Apollos or Cephas[d] or the world or life or death or the present or the future—all are yours, [23]and you are of Christ, and Christ is of God.

[a]16 Isaiah 40:13   [b]19 Job 5:13   [c]20 Psalm 94:11   [d]22 That is, Peter

Apostles of Christ

4 So then, men ought to regard us as servants of Christ and as those entrusted with the secret things of God. ²Now it is required that those who have been given a trust must prove faithful. ³I care very little if I am judged by you or by any human court; indeed, I do not even judge myself. ⁴My conscience is clear, but that does not make me innocent. It is the Lord who judges me. ⁵Therefore judge nothing before the appointed time; wait till the Lord comes. He will bring to light what is hidden in darkness and will expose the motives of men's hearts. At that time each will receive his praise from God.

⁶Now, brothers, I have applied these things to myself and Apollos for your benefit, so that you may learn from us the meaning of the saying, "Do not go beyond what is written." Then you will not take pride in one man over against another. ⁷For who makes you different from anyone else? What do you have that you did not receive? And if you did receive it, why do you boast as though you did not?

⁸Already you have all you want! Already you have become rich! You have become kings—and that without us! How I wish that you really had become kings so that we might be kings with you! ⁹For it seems to me that God has put us apostles on display at the end of the procession, like men condemned to die in the arena. We have been made a spectacle to the whole universe, to angels as well as to men. ¹⁰We are fools for Christ, but you are so wise in Christ! We are weak, but you are strong! You are honored, we are dishonored! ¹¹To this very hour we go hungry and thirsty, we are in rags, we are brutally treated, we are homeless. ¹²We work hard with our own hands. When we are cursed, we bless; when we are persecuted, we endure it; ¹³when we are slandered, we answer kindly. Up to this moment we have become the scum of the earth, the refuse of the world.

¹⁴I am not writing this to shame you, but to warn you, as my dear children. ¹⁵Even though you have ten thousand guardians in Christ, you do not have many fathers, for in Christ Jesus I became your father through the gospel. ¹⁶Therefore I urge you to imitate me. ¹⁷For this reason I am sending to you Timothy, my son whom I love, who is faithful in the Lord. He will remind you of my way of life in Christ Jesus, which agrees with what I teach everywhere in every church.

¹⁸Some of you have become arrogant, as if I were not coming to you. ¹⁹But I will come to you very soon, if the Lord is willing, and then I will find out not only how these arrogant people are talking, but what power they have. ²⁰For the kingdom of God is not a matter of talk but of power. ²¹What do you prefer? Shall I come to you with a whip, or in love and with a gentle spirit?

Expel the Immoral Brother!

5 It is actually reported that there is sexual immorality among you, and of a kind that does not occur even among pagans: A man has his father's wife. ²And you are proud! Shouldn't you rather have been filled with grief

and have put out of your fellowship the man who did this? ³Even though I am not physically present, I am with you in spirit. And I have already passed judgment on the one who did this, just as if I were present. ⁴When you are assembled in the name of our Lord Jesus and I am with you in spirit, and the power of our Lord Jesus is present, ⁵hand this man over to Satan, so that the sinful nature*ᵃ* may be destroyed and his spirit saved on the day of the Lord.

⁶Your boasting is not good. Don't you know that a little yeast works through the whole batch of dough? ⁷Get rid of the old yeast that you may be a new batch without yeast—as you really are. For Christ, our Passover lamb, has been sacrificed. ⁸Therefore let us keep the Festival, not with the old yeast, the yeast of malice and wickedness, but with bread without yeast, the bread of sincerity and truth.

⁹I have written you in my letter not to associate with sexually immoral people— ¹⁰not at all meaning the people of this world who are immoral, or the greedy and swindlers, or idolaters. In that case you would have to leave this world. ¹¹But now I am writing you that you must not associate with anyone who calls himself a brother but is sexually immoral or greedy, an idolater or a slanderer, a drunkard or a swindler. With such a man do not even eat.

¹²What business is it of mine to judge those outside the church? Are you not to judge those inside? ¹³God will judge those outside. "Expel the wicked man from among you."*ᵇ*

Lawsuits Among Believers

6 If any of you has a dispute with another, dare he take it before the ungodly for judgment instead of before the saints? ²Do you not know that the saints will judge the world? And if you are to judge the world, are you not competent to judge trivial cases? ³Do you not know that we will judge angels? How much more the things of this life! ⁴Therefore, if you have disputes about such matters, appoint as judges even men of little account in the church!*ᶜ* ⁵I say this to shame you. Is it possible that there is nobody among you wise enough to judge a dispute between believers? ⁶But instead, one brother goes to law against another—and this in front of unbelievers!

⁷The very fact that you have lawsuits among you means you have been completely defeated already. Why not rather be wronged? Why not rather be cheated? ⁸Instead, you yourselves cheat and do wrong, and you do this to your brothers.

⁹Do you not know that the wicked will not inherit the kingdom of God? Do not be deceived: Neither the sexually immoral nor idolaters nor adulterers nor male prostitutes nor homosexual offenders ¹⁰nor thieves nor the greedy nor drunkards nor slanderers nor swindlers will inherit the kingdom of God. ¹¹And that is what some of you were. But you were washed, you

ᵃ5 Or *that his body; or that the flesh*   *ᵇ13* Deut. 17:7; 19:19; 21:21; 22:21,24; 24:7   *ᶜ4* Or *matters, do you appoint as judges men of little account in the church?*

were sanctified, you were justified in the name of the Lord Jesus Christ and by the Spirit of our God.

Sexual Immorality

12"Everything is permissible for me"—but not everything is beneficial. "Everything is permissible for me"—but I will not be mastered by anything. 13"Food for the stomach and the stomach for food"—but God will destroy them both. The body is not meant for sexual immorality, but for the Lord, and the Lord for the body. 14By his power God raised the Lord from the dead, and he will raise us also. 15Do you not know that your bodies are members of Christ himself? Shall I then take the members of Christ and unite them with a prostitute? Never! 16Do you not know that he who unites himself with a prostitute is one with her in body? For it is said, "The two will become one flesh."*a* 17But he who unites himself with the Lord is one with him in spirit.

18Flee from sexual immorality. All other sins a man commits are outside his body, but he who sins sexually sins against his own body. 19Do you not know that your body is a temple of the Holy Spirit, who is in you, whom you have received from God? You are not your own; 20you were bought at a price. Therefore honor God with your body.

Marriage

7 Now for the matters you wrote about: It is good for a man not to marry.*b* 2But since there is so much immorality, each man should have his own wife, and each woman her own husband. 3The husband should fulfill his marital duty to his wife, and likewise the wife to her husband. 4The wife's body does not belong to her alone but also to her husband. In the same way, the husband's body does not belong to him alone but also to his wife. 5Do not deprive each other except by mutual consent and for a time, so that you may devote yourselves to prayer. Then come together again so that Satan will not tempt you because of your lack of self-control. 6I say this as a concession, not as a command. 7I wish that all men were as I am. But each man has his own gift from God; one has this gift, another has that.

8Now to the unmarried and the widows I say: It is good for them to stay unmarried, as I am. 9But if they cannot control themselves, they should marry, for it is better to marry than to burn with passion.

10To the married I give this command (not I, but the Lord): A wife must not separate from her husband. 11But if she does, she must remain unmarried or else be reconciled to her husband. And a husband must not divorce his wife.

12To the rest I say this (I, not the Lord): If any brother has a wife who is not a believer and she is willing to live with him, he must not divorce her. 13And if a woman has a husband who is not a believer and he is willing to live with her, she must not divorce him. 14For the unbelieving husband has been sanctified through his wife, and the unbelieving wife has been sancti-

a16 Gen. 2:24   b1 Or "It is good for a man not to have sexual relations with a woman."

fied through her believing husband. Otherwise your children would be unclean, but as it is, they are holy.

¹⁵But if the unbeliever leaves, let him do so. A believing man or woman is not bound in such circumstances; God has called us to live in peace. ¹⁶How do you know, wife, whether you will save your husband? Or, how do you know, husband, whether you will save your wife?

¹⁷Nevertheless, each one should retain the place in life that the Lord assigned to him and to which God has called him. This is the rule I lay down in all the churches. ¹⁸Was a man already circumcised when he was called? He should not become uncircumcised. Was a man uncircumcised when he was called? He should not be circumcised. ¹⁹Circumcision is nothing and uncircumcision is nothing. Keeping God's commands is what counts. ²⁰Each one should remain in the situation which he was in when God called him. ²¹Were you a slave when you were called? Don't let it trouble you— although if you can gain your freedom, do so. ²²For he who was a slave when he was called by the Lord is the Lord's freedman; similarly, he who was a free man when he was called is Christ's slave. ²³You were bought at a price; do not become slaves of men. ²⁴Brothers, each man, as responsible to God, should remain in the situation God called him to.

²⁵Now about virgins: I have no command from the Lord, but I give a judgment as one who by the Lord's mercy is trustworthy. ²⁶Because of the present crisis, I think that it is good for you to remain as you are. ²⁷Are you married? Do not seek a divorce. Are you unmarried? Do not look for a wife. ²⁸But if you do marry, you have not sinned; and if a virgin marries, she has not sinned. But those who marry will face many troubles in this life, and I want to spare you this.

²⁹What I mean, brothers, is that the time is short. From now on those who have wives should live as if they had none; ³⁰those who mourn, as if they did not; those who are happy, as if they were not; those who buy something, as if it were not theirs to keep; ³¹those who use the things of the world, as if not engrossed in them. For this world in its present form is passing away.

³²I would like you to be free from concern. An unmarried man is concerned about the Lord's affairs—how he can please the Lord. ³³But a married man is concerned about the affairs of this world—how he can please his wife— ³⁴and his interests are divided. An unmarried woman or virgin is concerned about the Lord's affairs: Her aim is to be devoted to the Lord in both body and spirit. But a married woman is concerned about the affairs of this world—how she can please her husband. ³⁵I am saying this for your own good, not to restrict you, but that you may live in a right way in undivided devotion to the Lord.

³⁶If anyone thinks he is acting improperly toward the virgin he is engaged to, and if she is getting along in years and he feels he ought to marry, he should do as he wants. He is not sinning. They should get married. ³⁷But the man who has settled the matter in his own mind, who is under no compulsion but has control over his own will, and who has

made up his mind not to marry the virgin—this man also does the right thing. [38]So then, he who marries the virgin does right, but he who does not marry her does even better.[a]

[39]A woman is bound to her husband as long as he lives. But if her husband dies, she is free to marry anyone she wishes, but he must belong to the Lord. [40]In my judgment, she is happier if she stays as she is—and I think that I too have the Spirit of God.

Food Sacrificed to Idols

8 Now about food sacrificed to idols: We know that we all possess knowledge.[b] Knowledge puffs up, but love builds up. [2]The man who thinks he knows something does not yet know as he ought to know. [3]But the man who loves God is known by God.

[4]So then, about eating food sacrificed to idols: We know that an idol is nothing at all in the world and that there is no God but one. [5]For even if there are so-called gods, whether in heaven or on earth (as indeed there are many "gods" and many "lords"), [6]yet for us there is but one God, the Father, from whom all things came and for whom we live; and there is but one Lord, Jesus Christ, through whom all things came and through whom we live.

[7]But not everyone knows this. Some people are still so accustomed to idols that when they eat such food they think of it as having been sacrificed to an idol, and since their conscience is weak, it is defiled. [8]But food does not bring us near to God; we are no worse if we do not eat, and no better if we do.

[9]Be careful, however, that the exercise of your freedom does not become a stumbling block to the weak. [10]For if anyone with a weak conscience sees you who have this knowledge eating in an idol's temple, won't he be emboldened to eat what has been sacrificed to idols? [11]So this weak brother, for whom Christ died, is destroyed by your knowledge. [12]When you sin against your brothers in this way and wound their weak conscience, you sin against Christ. [13]Therefore, if what I eat causes my brother to fall into sin, I will never eat meat again, so that I will not cause him to fall.

The Rights of an Apostle

9 Am I not free? Am I not an apostle? Have I not seen Jesus our Lord? Are you not the result of my work in the Lord? [2]Even though I may not be an apostle to others, surely I am to you! For you are the seal of my apostleship in the Lord.

[3]This is my defense to those who sit in judgment on me. [4]Don't we have the right to food and drink? [5]Don't we have the right to take a believing wife

---

[a]36-38 Or [36]*If anyone thinks he is not treating his daughter properly, and if she is getting along in years, and he feels she ought to marry, he should do as he wants. He is not sinning. He should let her get married.* [37]*But the man who has settled the matter in his own mind, who is under no compulsion but has control over his own will, and who has made up his mind to keep the virgin unmarried—this man also does the right thing.* [38]*So then, he who gives his virgin in marriage does right, but he who does not give her in marriage does even better.*
[b]1 Or *"We all possess knowledge,"* as you say

along with us, as do the other apostles and the Lord's brothers and Cephas[a]? [6]Or is it only I and Barnabas who must work for a living?

[7]Who serves as a soldier at his own expense? Who plants a vineyard and does not eat of its grapes? Who tends a flock and does not drink of the milk? [8]Do I say this merely from a human point of view? Doesn't the Law say the same thing? [9]For it is written in the Law of Moses: "Do not muzzle an ox while it is treading out the grain."[b] Is it about oxen that God is concerned? [10]Surely he says this for us, doesn't he? Yes, this was written for us, because when the plowman plows and the thresher threshes, they ought to do so in the hope of sharing in the harvest. [11]If we have sown spiritual seed among you, is it too much if we reap a material harvest from you? [12]If others have this right of support from you, shouldn't we have it all the more?

But we did not use this right. On the contrary, we put up with anything rather than hinder the gospel of Christ. [13]Don't you know that those who work in the temple get their food from the temple, and those who serve at the altar share in what is offered on the altar? [14]In the same way, the Lord has commanded that those who preach the gospel should receive their living from the gospel.

[15]But I have not used any of these rights. And I am not writing this in the hope that you will do such things for me. I would rather die than have anyone deprive me of this boast. [16]Yet when I preach the gospel, I cannot boast, for I am compelled to preach. Woe to me if I do not preach the gospel! [17]If I preach voluntarily, I have a reward; if not voluntarily, I am simply discharging the trust committed to me. [18]What then is my reward? Just this: that in preaching the gospel I may offer it free of charge, and so not make use of my rights in preaching it.

[19]Though I am free and belong to no man, I make myself a slave to everyone, to win as many as possible. [20]To the Jews I became like a Jew, to win the Jews. To those under the law I became like one under the law (though I myself am not under the law), so as to win those under the law. [21]To those not having the law I became like one not having the law (though I am not free from God's law but am under Christ's law), so as to win those not having the law. [22]To the weak I became weak, to win the weak. I have become all things to all men so that by all possible means I might save some. [23]I do all this for the sake of the gospel, that I may share in its blessings.

[24]Do you not know that in a race all the runners run, but only one gets the prize? Run in such a way as to get the prize. [25]Everyone who competes in the games goes into strict training. They do it to get a crown that will not last; but we do it to get a crown that will last forever. [26]Therefore I do not run like a man running aimlessly; I do not fight like a man beating the air. [27]No, I beat my body and make it my slave so that after I have preached to others, I myself will not be disqualified for the prize.

[a]5 That is, Peter   [b]9 Deut. 25:4

Warnings From Israel's History

10 For I do not want you to be ignorant of the fact, brothers, that our forefathers were all under the cloud and that they all passed through the sea. ²They were all baptized into Moses in the cloud and in the sea. ³They all ate the same spiritual food ⁴and drank the same spiritual drink; for they drank from the spiritual rock that accompanied them, and that rock was Christ. ⁵Nevertheless, God was not pleased with most of them; their bodies were scattered over the desert.

⁶Now these things occurred as examples[a] to keep us from setting our hearts on evil things as they did. ⁷Do not be idolaters, as some of them were; as it is written: "The people sat down to eat and drink and got up to indulge in pagan revelry."[b] ⁸We should not commit sexual immorality, as some of them did—and in one day twenty-three thousand of them died. ⁹We should not test the Lord, as some of them did—and were killed by snakes. ¹⁰And do not grumble, as some of them did—and were killed by the destroying angel.

¹¹These things happened to them as examples and were written down as warnings for us, on whom the fulfillment of the ages has come. ¹²So, if you think you are standing firm, be careful that you don't fall! ¹³No temptation has seized you except what is common to man. And God is faithful; he will not let you be tempted beyond what you can bear. But when you are tempted, he will also provide a way out so that you can stand up under it.

Idol Feasts and the Lord's Supper

¹⁴Therefore, my dear friends, flee from idolatry. ¹⁵I speak to sensible people; judge for yourselves what I say. ¹⁶Is not the cup of thanksgiving for which we give thanks a participation in the blood of Christ? And is not the bread that we break a participation in the body of Christ? ¹⁷Because there is one loaf, we, who are many, are one body, for we all partake of the one loaf.

¹⁸Consider the people of Israel: Do not those who eat the sacrifices participate in the altar? ¹⁹Do I mean then that a sacrifice offered to an idol is anything, or that an idol is anything? ²⁰No, but the sacrifices of pagans are offered to demons, not to God, and I do not want you to be participants with demons. ²¹You cannot drink the cup of the Lord and the cup of demons too; you cannot have a part in both the Lord's table and the table of demons. ²²Are we trying to arouse the Lord's jealousy? Are we stronger than he?

The Believer's Freedom

²³"Everything is permissible"—but not everything is beneficial. "Everything is permissible"—but not everything is constructive. ²⁴Nobody should seek his own good, but the good of others.

a6 Or *types*; also in verse 11   b7 Exodus 32:6

[25]Eat anything sold in the meat market without raising questions of conscience, [26]for, "The earth is the Lord's, and everything in it."[a]

[27]If some unbeliever invites you to a meal and you want to go, eat whatever is put before you without raising questions of conscience. [28]But if anyone says to you, "This has been offered in sacrifice," then do not eat it, both for the sake of the man who told you and for conscience' sake[b]— [29]the other man's conscience, I mean, not yours. For why should my freedom be judged by another's conscience? [30]If I take part in the meal with thankfulness, why am I denounced because of something I thank God for?

[31]So whether you eat or drink or whatever you do, do it all for the glory of God. [32]Do not cause anyone to stumble, whether Jews, Greeks or the church of God— [33]even as I try to please everybody in every way. For I am not seeking my own good but the good of many, so that they may be saved.

11
[1]Follow my example, as I follow the example of Christ.

Propriety in Worship

[2]I praise you for remembering me in everything and for holding to the teachings,[c] just as I passed them on to you.

[3]Now I want you to realize that the head of every man is Christ, and the head of the woman is man, and the head of Christ is God. [4]Every man who prays or prophesies with his head covered dishonors his head. [5]And every woman who prays or prophesies with her head uncovered dishonors her head—it is just as though her head were shaved. [6]If a woman does not cover her head, she should have her hair cut off; and if it is a disgrace for a woman to have her hair cut or shaved off, she should cover her head. [7]A man ought not to cover his head,[d] since he is the image and glory of God; but the woman is the glory of man. [8]For man did not come from woman, but woman from man; [9]neither was man created for woman, but woman for man. [10]For this reason, and because of the angels, the woman ought to have a sign of authority on her head.

[11]In the Lord, however, woman is not independent of man, nor is man independent of woman. [12]For as woman came from man, so also man is born of woman. But everything comes from God. [13]Judge for yourselves: Is it proper for a woman to pray to God with her head uncovered? [14]Does not the very nature of things teach you that if a man has long hair, it is a disgrace to him, [15]but that if a woman has long hair, it is her glory? For long hair is given to her as a covering. [16]If anyone wants to be contentious about this, we have no other practice—nor do the churches of God.

The Lord's Supper

[17]In the following directives I have no praise for you, for your meetings

---

[a]26 Psalm 24:1   [b]28 Some manuscripts *conscience' sake, for "the earth is the Lord's and everything in it"*
[c]2 Or *traditions*   [d]4-7 Or [4]*Every man who prays or prophesies with long hair dishonors his head.* [5]*And every woman who prays or prophesies with no covering of hair on her head dishonors her head—she is just like one of the "shorn women."* [6]*If a woman has no covering, let her be for now with short hair, but since it is a disgrace for a woman to have her hair shorn or shaved, she should grow it again.* [7]*A man ought not to have long hair*

do more harm than good. [18]In the first place, I hear that when you come together as a church, there are divisions among you, and to some extent I believe it. [19]No doubt there have to be differences among you to show which of you have God's approval. [20]When you come together, it is not the Lord's Supper you eat, [21]for as you eat, each of you goes ahead without waiting for anybody else. One remains hungry, another gets drunk. [22]Don't you have homes to eat and drink in? Or do you despise the church of God and humiliate those who have nothing? What shall I say to you? Shall I praise you for this? Certainly not!

[23]For I received from the Lord what I also passed on to you: The Lord Jesus, on the night he was betrayed, took bread, [24]and when he had given thanks, he broke it and said, "This is my body, which is for you; do this in remembrance of me." [25]In the same way, after supper he took the cup, saying, "This cup is the new covenant in my blood; do this, whenever you drink it, in remembrance of me." [26]For whenever you eat this bread and drink this cup, you proclaim the Lord's death until he comes.

[27]Therefore, whoever eats the bread or drinks the cup of the Lord in an unworthy manner will be guilty of sinning against the body and blood of the Lord. [28]A man ought to examine himself before he eats of the bread and drinks of the cup. [29]For anyone who eats and drinks without recognizing the body of the Lord eats and drinks judgment on himself. [30]That is why many among you are weak and sick, and a number of you have fallen asleep. [31]But if we judged ourselves, we would not come under judgment. [32]When we are judged by the Lord, we are being disciplined so that we will not be condemned with the world.

[33]So then, my brothers, when you come together to eat, wait for each other. [34]If anyone is hungry, he should eat at home, so that when you meet together it may not result in judgment.

And when I come I will give further directions.

Spiritual Gifts

12 Now about spiritual gifts, brothers, I do not want you to be ignorant. [2]You know that when you were pagans, somehow or other you were influenced and led astray to mute idols. [3]Therefore I tell you that no one who is speaking by the Spirit of God says, "Jesus be cursed," and no one can say, "Jesus is Lord," except by the Holy Spirit.

[4]There are different kinds of gifts, but the same Spirit. [5]There are different kinds of service, but the same Lord. [6]There are different kinds of working, but the same God works all of them in all men.

[7]Now to each one the manifestation of the Spirit is given for the common good. [8]To one there is given through the Spirit the message of wisdom, to another the message of knowledge by means of the same Spirit, [9]to another faith by the same Spirit, to another gifts of healing by that one Spirit, [10]to another miraculous powers, to another prophecy, to another distinguishing between spirits, to another speaking in different kinds of

tongues,ᵃ and to still another the interpretation of tongues.ᵃ ¹¹All these are the work of one and the same Spirit, and he gives them to each one, just as he determines.

One Body, Many Parts

¹²The body is a unit, though it is made up of many parts; and though all its parts are many, they form one body. So it is with Christ. ¹³For we were all baptized byᵇ one Spirit into one body—whether Jews or Greeks, slave or free—and we were all given the one Spirit to drink.

¹⁴Now the body is not made up of one part but of many. ¹⁵If the foot should say, "Because I am not a hand, I do not belong to the body," it would not for that reason cease to be part of the body. ¹⁶And if the ear should say, "Because I am not an eye, I do not belong to the body," it would not for that reason cease to be part of the body. ¹⁷If the whole body were an eye, where would the sense of hearing be? If the whole body were an ear, where would the sense of smell be? ¹⁸But in fact God has arranged the parts in the body, every one of them, just as he wanted them to be. ¹⁹If they were all one part, where would the body be? ²⁰As it is, there are many parts, but one body.

²¹The eye cannot say to the hand, "I don't need you!" And the head cannot say to the feet, "I don't need you!" ²²On the contrary, those parts of the body that seem to be weaker are indispensable, ²³and the parts that we think are less honorable we treat with special honor. And the parts that are unpresentable are treated with special modesty, ²⁴while our presentable parts need no special treatment. But God has combined the members of the body and has given greater honor to the parts that lacked it, ²⁵so that there should be no division in the body, but that its parts should have equal concern for each other. ²⁶If one part suffers, every part suffers with it; if one part is honored, every part rejoices with it.

²⁷Now you are the body of Christ, and each one of you is a part of it. ²⁸And in the church God has appointed first of all apostles, second prophets, third teachers, then workers of miracles, also those having gifts of healing, those able to help others, those with gifts of administration, and those speaking in different kinds of tongues. ²⁹Are all apostles? Are all prophets? Are all teachers? Do all work miracles? ³⁰Do all have gifts of healing? Do all speak in tonguesᶜ? Do all interpret? ³¹But eagerly desireᵈ the greater gifts.

Love

And now I will show you the most excellent way.

13 If I speak in the tonguesᵉ of men and of angels, but have not love, I am only a resounding gong or a clanging cymbal. ²If I have the gift of prophecy and can fathom all mysteries and all knowledge, and if I have a faith that can move mountains, but have not love, I am nothing. ³If I give

ᵃ10 Or languages; also in verse 28   ᵇ13 Or with; or in   ᶜ30 Or other languages   ᵈ31 Or But you are eagerly desiring   ᵉ1 Or languages all I possess to the poor and surrender my body to the flames,^a but have not love, I gain nothing.

⁴Love is patient, love is kind. It does not envy, it does not boast, it is not proud. ⁵It is not rude, it is not self-seeking, it is not easily angered, it keeps no record of wrongs. ⁶Love does not delight in evil but rejoices with the truth. ⁷It always protects, always trusts, always hopes, always perseveres.

⁸Love never fails. But where there are prophecies, they will cease; where there are tongues, they will be stilled; where there is knowledge, it will pass away. ⁹For we know in part and we prophesy in part, ¹⁰but when perfection comes, the imperfect disappears. ¹¹When I was a child, I talked like a child, I thought like a child, I reasoned like a child. When I became a man, I put childish ways behind me. ¹²Now we see but a poor reflection as in a mirror; then we shall see face to face. Now I know in part; then I shall know fully, even as I am fully known.

¹³And now these three remain: faith, hope and love. But the greatest of these is love.

Gifts of Prophecy and Tongues

14 Follow the way of love and eagerly desire spiritual gifts, especially the gift of prophecy. ²For anyone who speaks in a tongue^b does not speak to men but to God. Indeed, no one understands him; he utters mysteries with his spirit. ^c ³But everyone who prophesies speaks to men for their strengthening, encouragement and comfort. ⁴He who speaks in a tongue edifies himself, but he who prophesies edifies the church. ⁵I would like every one of you to speak in tongues,^d but I would rather have you prophesy. He who prophesies is greater than one who speaks in tongues,^d unless he interprets, so that the church may be edified.

⁶Now, brothers, if I come to you and speak in tongues, what good will I be to you, unless I bring you some revelation or knowledge or prophecy or word of instruction? ⁷Even in the case of lifeless things that make sounds, such as the flute or harp, how will anyone know what tune is being played unless there is a distinction in the notes? ⁸Again, if the trumpet does not sound a clear call, who will get ready for battle? ⁹So it is with you. Unless you speak intelligible words with your tongue, how will anyone know what you are saying? You will just be speaking into the air. ¹⁰Undoubtedly there are all sorts of languages in the world, yet none of them is without meaning. ¹¹If then I do not grasp the meaning of what someone is saying, I am a foreigner to the speaker, and he is a foreigner to me. ¹²So it is with you. Since you are eager to have spiritual gifts, try to excel in gifts that build up the church.

¹³For this reason anyone who speaks in a tongue should pray that he may interpret what he says. ¹⁴For if I pray in a tongue, my spirit prays, but my mind is unfruitful. ¹⁵So what shall I do? I will pray with my spirit, but

^a3 Some early manuscripts *body that I may boast*   ^b2 Or *another language; also in verses 4, 13, 14, 19, 26 and 27*   ^c2 Or *by the Spirit*   ^d5 Or *other languages; also in verses 6, 18, 22, 23 and 39*

I will also pray with my mind; I will sing with my spirit, but I will also sing with my mind. [16]If you are praising God with your spirit, how can one who finds himself among those who do not understand[a] say "Amen" to your thanksgiving, since he does not know what you are saying? [17]You may be giving thanks well enough, but the other man is not edified.

[18]I thank God that I speak in tongues more than all of you. [19]But in the church I would rather speak five intelligible words to instruct others than ten thousand words in a tongue.

[20]Brothers, stop thinking like children. In regard to evil be infants, but in your thinking be adults. [21]In the Law it is written:

> "Through men of strange tongues
>   and through the lips of foreigners
> I will speak to this people,
>   but even then they will not listen to me,"[b]

says the Lord.

[22]Tongues, then, are a sign, not for believers but for unbelievers; prophecy, however, is for believers, not for unbelievers. [23]So if the whole church comes together and everyone speaks in tongues, and some who do not understand[c] or some unbelievers come in, will they not say that you are out of your mind? [24]But if an unbeliever or someone who does not understand[d] comes in while everybody is prophesying, he will be convinced by all that he is a sinner and will be judged by all, [25]and the secrets of his heart will be laid bare. So he will fall down and worship God, exclaiming, "God is really among you!"

Orderly Worship

[26]What then shall we say, brothers? When you come together, everyone has a hymn, or a word of instruction, a revelation, a tongue or an interpretation. All of these must be done for the strengthening of the church. [27]If anyone speaks in a tongue, two—or at the most three—should speak, one at a time, and someone must interpret. [28]If there is no interpreter, the speaker should keep quiet in the church and speak to himself and God.

[29]Two or three prophets should speak, and the others should weigh carefully what is said. [30]And if a revelation comes to someone who is sitting down, the first speaker should stop. [31]For you can all prophesy in turn so that everyone may be instructed and encouraged. [32]The spirits of prophets are subject to the control of prophets. [33]For God is not a God of disorder but of peace.

As in all the congregations of the saints, [34]women should remain silent in the churches. They are not allowed to speak, but must be in submission, as the Law says. [35]If they want to inquire about something, they should ask their own husbands at home; for it is disgraceful for a woman to speak in the church.

[36]Did the word of God originate with you? Or are you the only people

---

[a]16 Or *among the inquirers*   [b]21 Isaiah 28:11,12   [c]23 Or *some inquirers*   [d]24 Or *or some inquirer*

it has reached? [37]If anybody thinks he is a prophet or spiritually gifted, let him acknowledge that what I am writing to you is the Lord's command. [38]If he ignores this, he himself will be ignored.[a]

[39]Therefore, my brothers, be eager to prophesy, and do not forbid speaking in tongues. [40]But everything should be done in a fitting and orderly way.

The Resurrection of Christ

15 Now, brothers, I want to remind you of the gospel I preached to you, which you received and on which you have taken your stand. [2]By this gospel you are saved, if you hold firmly to the word I preached to you. Otherwise, you have believed in vain.

[3]For what I received I passed on to you as of first importance[b]: that Christ died for our sins according to the Scriptures, [4]that he was buried, that he was raised on the third day according to the Scriptures, [5]and that he appeared to Peter,[c] and then to the Twelve. [6]After that, he appeared to more than five hundred of the brothers at the same time, most of whom are still living, though some have fallen asleep. [7]Then he appeared to James, then to all the apostles, [8]and last of all he appeared to me also, as to one abnormally born.

[9]For I am the least of the apostles and do not even deserve to be called an apostle, because I persecuted the church of God. [10]But by the grace of God I am what I am, and his grace to me was not without effect. No, I worked harder than all of them—yet not I, but the grace of God that was with me. [11]Whether, then, it was I or they, this is what we preach, and this is what you believed.

The Resurrection of the Dead

[12]But if it is preached that Christ has been raised from the dead, how can some of you say that there is no resurrection of the dead? [13]If there is no resurrection of the dead, then not even Christ has been raised. [14]And if Christ has not been raised, our preaching is useless and so is your faith. [15]More than that, we are then found to be false witnesses about God, for we have testified about God that he raised Christ from the dead. But he did not raise him if in fact the dead are not raised. [16]For if the dead are not raised, then Christ has not been raised either. [17]And if Christ has not been raised, your faith is futile; you are still in your sins. [18]Then those also who have fallen asleep in Christ are lost. [19]If only for this life we have hope in Christ, we are to be pitied more than all men.

[20]But Christ has indeed been raised from the dead, the firstfruits of those who have fallen asleep. [21]For since death came through a man, the resurrection of the dead comes also through a man. [22]For as in Adam all die, so in Christ all will be made alive. [23]But each in his own turn: Christ, the firstfruits; then, when he comes, those who belong to him. [24]Then the end

[a]38 Some manuscripts *If he is ignorant of this, let him be ignorant*   [b]3 Or *you at the first*   [c]5 Greek *Cephas*

will come, when he hands over the kingdom to God the Father after he has destroyed all dominion, authority and power. ²⁵For he must reign until he has put all his enemies under his feet. ²⁶The last enemy to be destroyed is death. ²⁷For he "has put everything under his feet."ᵃ Now when it says that "everything" has been put under him, it is clear that this does not include God himself, who put everything under Christ. ²⁸When he has done this, then the Son himself will be made subject to him who put everything under him, so that God may be all in all.

²⁹Now if there is no resurrection, what will those do who are baptized for the dead? If the dead are not raised at all, why are people baptized for them? ³⁰And as for us, why do we endanger ourselves every hour? ³¹I die every day—I mean that, brothers—just as surely as I glory over you in Christ Jesus our Lord. ³²If I fought wild beasts in Ephesus for merely human reasons, what have I gained? If the dead are not raised,

> "Let us eat and drink,
> for tomorrow we die."ᵇ

³³Do not be misled: "Bad company corrupts good character." ³⁴Come back to your senses as you ought, and stop sinning; for there are some who are ignorant of God—I say this to your shame.

The Resurrection Body

³⁵But someone may ask, "How are the dead raised? With what kind of body will they come?" ³⁶How foolish! What you sow does not come to life unless it dies. ³⁷When you sow, you do not plant the body that will be, but just a seed, perhaps of wheat or of something else. ³⁸But God gives it a body as he has determined, and to each kind of seed he gives its own body. ³⁹All flesh is not the same: Men have one kind of flesh, animals have another, birds another and fish another. ⁴⁰There are also heavenly bodies and there are earthly bodies; but the splendor of the heavenly bodies is one kind, and the splendor of the earthly bodies is another. ⁴¹The sun has one kind of splendor, the moon another and the stars another; and star differs from star in splendor.

⁴²So will it be with the resurrection of the dead. The body that is sown is perishable, it is raised imperishable; ⁴³it is sown in dishonor, it is raised in glory; it is sown in weakness, it is raised in power; ⁴⁴it is sown a natural body, it is raised a spiritual body.

If there is a natural body, there is also a spiritual body. ⁴⁵So it is written: "The first man Adam became a living being"ᶜ; the last Adam, a life-giving spirit. ⁴⁶The spiritual did not come first, but the natural, and after that the spiritual. ⁴⁷The first man was of the dust of the earth, the second man from heaven. ⁴⁸As was the earthly man, so are those who are of the earth; and as is the man from heaven, so also are those who are of heaven. ⁴⁹And just as we have borne the likeness of the earthly man, so shall weᵈ bear the likeness of the man from heaven.

ᵃ27 Psalm 8:6   ᵇ32 Isaiah 22:13   ᶜ45 Gen. 2:7   ᵈ49 Some early manuscripts *so let us*

⁵⁰I declare to you, brothers, that flesh and blood cannot inherit the kingdom of God, nor does the perishable inherit the imperishable. ⁵¹Listen, I tell you a mystery: We will not all sleep, but we will all be changed— ⁵²in a flash, in the twinkling of an eye, at the last trumpet. For the trumpet will sound, the dead will be raised imperishable, and we will be changed. ⁵³For the perishable must clothe itself with the imperishable, and the mortal with immortality. ⁵⁴When the perishable has been clothed with the imperishable, and the mortal with immortality, then the saying that is written will come true: "Death has been swallowed up in victory."ᵃ

⁵⁵"Where, O death, is your victory?
Where, O death, is your sting?"ᵇ

⁵⁶The sting of death is sin, and the power of sin is the law. ⁵⁷But thanks be to God! He gives us the victory through our Lord Jesus Christ.

⁵⁸Therefore, my dear brothers, stand firm. Let nothing move you. Always give yourselves fully to the work of the Lord, because you know that your labor in the Lord is not in vain.

The Collection for God's People

16 Now about the collection for God's people: Do what I told the Galatian churches to do. ²On the first day of every week, each one of you should set aside a sum of money in keeping with his income, saving it up, so that when I come no collections will have to be made. ³Then, when I arrive, I will give letters of introduction to the men you approve and send them with your gift to Jerusalem. ⁴If it seems advisable for me to go also, they will accompany me.

Personal Requests

⁵After I go through Macedonia, I will come to you—for I will be going through Macedonia. ⁶Perhaps I will stay with you awhile, or even spend the winter, so that you can help me on my journey, wherever I go. ⁷I do not want to see you now and make only a passing visit; I hope to spend some time with you, if the Lord permits. ⁸But I will stay on at Ephesus until Pentecost, ⁹because a great door for effective work has opened to me, and there are many who oppose me.

¹⁰If Timothy comes, see to it that he has nothing to fear while he is with you, for he is carrying on the work of the Lord, just as I am. ¹¹No one, then, should refuse to accept him. Send him on his way in peace so that he may return to me. I am expecting him along with the brothers.

¹²Now about our brother Apollos: I strongly urged him to go to you with the brothers. He was quite unwilling to go now, but he will go when he has the opportunity.

¹³Be on your guard; stand firm in the faith; be men of courage; be strong. ¹⁴Do everything in love.

¹⁵You know that the household of Stephanas were the first converts in

ᵃ54 Isaiah 25:8   ᵇ55 Hosea 13:14

Achaia, and they have devoted themselves to the service of the saints. I urge you, brothers, [16]to submit to such as these and to everyone who joins in the work, and labors at it. [17]I was glad when Stephanas, Fortunatus and Achaicus arrived, because they have supplied what was lacking from you. [18]For they refreshed my spirit and yours also. Such men deserve recognition.

Final Greetings

[19]The churches in the province of Asia send you greetings. Aquila and Priscilla[a] greet you warmly in the Lord, and so does the church that meets at their house. [20]All the brothers here send you greetings. Greet one another with a holy kiss.

[21]I, Paul, write this greeting in my own hand.

[22]If anyone does not love the Lord—a curse be on him. Come, O Lord[b]!

[23]The grace of the Lord Jesus be with you.

[24]My love to all of you in Christ Jesus. Amen.[c]

[a]19 Greek *Prisca*, a variant of *Priscilla*   [b]22 In Aramaic the expression *Come, O Lord* is *Marana tha.*
[c]24 Some manuscripts do not have *Amen.*

2 Corinthians

INTRODUCTION

Second Corinthians is an arrangement of portions of Paul's subsequent correspondence with the Corinthians. After 1 Corinthians had been sent, other missionaries had turned the community against Paul by claiming that they and their miracle-working stood in continuity with the powerful words and deeds of the historical Jesus. Whereas in 1 Corinthians Paul had emphasized the "not yet" aspect of Christian existence, in 2 Corinthians he refutes these "super apostles" by emphasizing the already transformed nature of present Christian existence: "If anyone is in Christ, he is a new creation; the old has gone, the new has come!" (5:17). This emphasis on transformed existence is followed by an appeal to respond to God's generosity by financially assisting the needy Christians in Jerusalem (chaps. 8–9). Second Corinthians concludes with an explanation of the true nature of the continuity that exists with Jesus (chaps. 10–13). The true apostle is not one who is ostentatiously powerful in word and deed, but one who, for Christ's sake, delights "in weaknesses, in insults, in hardships, in persecutions, in difficulties" (12:10).

TERENCE J. KEEGAN, O.P.

Points for Reflection

1. One of the most outstanding features of this letter is the loving forgiveness it manifests. Can we respond to rejection at the hands of people we have devoted ourselves to the way Paul did?
2. Paul could respond as he did because he was not concerned with external platitudes or tangible measures of success. For him true success was measured by fidelity to the cross of Jesus. Do we see our true identity as members of the new creation in the same light?

1 Paul, an apostle of Christ Jesus by the will of God, and Timothy our brother,

To the church of God in Corinth, together with all the saints throughout Achaia:

²Grace and peace to you from God our Father and the Lord Jesus Christ.

The God of All Comfort

³Praise be to the God and Father of our Lord Jesus Christ, the Father of compassion and the God of all comfort, ⁴who comforts us in all our troubles, so that we can comfort those in any trouble with the comfort we ourselves have received from God. ⁵For just as the sufferings of Christ flow over into our lives, so also through Christ our comfort overflows. ⁶If we are distressed, it is for your comfort and salvation; if we are comforted, it is for your comfort, which produces in you patient endurance of the same sufferings we suffer. ⁷And our hope for you is firm, because we know that just as you share in our sufferings, so also you share in our comfort.

⁸We do not want you to be uninformed, brothers, about the hardships we suffered in the province of Asia. We were under great pressure, far beyond our ability to endure, so that we despaired even of life. ⁹Indeed, in our hearts we felt the sentence of death. But this happened that we might not rely on ourselves but on God, who raises the dead. ¹⁰He has delivered us from such a deadly peril, and he will deliver us. On him we have set our hope that he will continue to deliver us, ¹¹as you help us by your prayers. Then many will give thanks on our[a] behalf for the gracious favor granted us in answer to the prayers of many.

Paul's Change of Plans

¹²Now this is our boast: Our conscience testifies that we have conducted ourselves in the world, and especially in our relations with you, in the holiness and sincerity that are from God. We have done so not according to worldly wisdom but according to God's grace. ¹³For we do not write you anything you cannot read or understand. And I hope that, ¹⁴as you have understood us in part, you will come to understand fully that you can boast of us just as we will boast of you in the day of the Lord Jesus.

¹⁵Because I was confident of this, I planned to visit you first so that you might benefit twice. ¹⁶I planned to visit you on my way to Macedonia and to come back to you from Macedonia, and then to have you send me on my way to Judea. ¹⁷When I planned this, did I do it lightly? Or do I make my plans in a worldly manner so that in the same breath I say, "Yes, yes" and "No, no"?

¹⁸But as surely as God is faithful, our message to you is not "Yes" and "No." ¹⁹For the Son of God, Jesus Christ, who was preached among you by me and Silas[b] and Timothy, was not "Yes" and "No," but in him it has always been "Yes." ²⁰For no matter how many promises God has made,

a11 Many manuscripts your   _b19 Greek Silvanus, a variant of Silas_ they are "Yes" in Christ. And so through him the "Amen" is spoken by us to the glory of God. [21]Now it is God who makes both us and you stand firm in Christ. He anointed us, [22]set his seal of ownership on us, and put his Spirit in our hearts as a deposit, guaranteeing what is to come.

[23]I call God as my witness that it was in order to spare you that I did not return to Corinth. [24]Not that we lord it over your faith, but we work with you for your joy, because it is by faith you stand firm. [1]So I made up my mind that I would not make another painful visit to you. [2]For if I grieve you, who is left to make me glad but you whom I have grieved? [3]I wrote as I did so that when I came I should not be distressed by those who ought to make me rejoice. I had confidence in all of you, that you would all share my joy. [4]For I wrote you out of great distress and anguish of heart and with many tears, not to grieve you but to let you know the depth of my love for you.

Forgiveness for the Sinner

[5]If anyone has caused grief, he has not so much grieved me as he has grieved all of you, to some extent—not to put it too severely. [6]The punishment inflicted on him by the majority is sufficient for him. [7]Now instead, you ought to forgive and comfort him, so that he will not be overwhelmed by excessive sorrow. [8]I urge you, therefore, to reaffirm your love for him. [9]The reason I wrote you was to see if you would stand the test and be obedient in everything. [10]If you forgive anyone, I also forgive him. And what I have forgiven—if there was anything to forgive—I have forgiven in the sight of Christ for your sake, [11]in order that Satan might not outwit us. For we are not unaware of his schemes.

Ministers of the New Covenant

[12]Now when I went to Troas to preach the gospel of Christ and found that the Lord had opened a door for me, [13]I still had no peace of mind, because I did not find my brother Titus there. So I said good-by to them and went on to Macedonia.

[14]But thanks be to God, who always leads us in triumphal procession in Christ and through us spreads everywhere the fragrance of the knowledge of him. [15]For we are to God the aroma of Christ among those who are being saved and those who are perishing. [16]To the one we are the smell of death; to the other, the fragrance of life. And who is equal to such a task? [17]Unlike so many, we do not peddle the word of God for profit. On the contrary, in Christ we speak before God with sincerity, like men sent from God.

[1] Are we beginning to commend ourselves again? Or do we need, like some people, letters of recommendation to you or from you? [2]You yourselves are our letter, written on our hearts, known and read by everybody. [3]You show that you are a letter from Christ, the result of our ministry, written not with ink but with the Spirit of the living God, not on tablets of stone but on tablets of human hearts.

⁴Such confidence as this is ours through Christ before God. ⁵Not that we are competent in ourselves to claim anything for ourselves, but our competence comes from God. ⁶He has made us competent as ministers of a new covenant—not of the letter but of the Spirit; for the letter kills, but the Spirit gives life.

The Glory of the New Covenant

⁷Now if the ministry that brought death, which was engraved in letters on stone, came with glory, so that the Israelites could not look steadily at the face of Moses because of its glory, fading though it was, ⁸will not the ministry of the Spirit be even more glorious? ⁹If the ministry that condemns men is glorious, how much more glorious is the ministry that brings righteousness! ¹⁰For what was glorious has no glory now in comparison with the surpassing glory. ¹¹And if what was fading away came with glory, how much greater is the glory of that which lasts!

¹²Therefore, since we have such a hope, we are very bold. ¹³We are not like Moses, who would put a veil over his face to keep the Israelites from gazing at it while the radiance was fading away. ¹⁴But their minds were made dull, for to this day the same veil remains when the old covenant is read. It has not been removed, because only in Christ is it taken away. ¹⁵Even to this day when Moses is read, a veil covers their hearts. ¹⁶But whenever anyone turns to the Lord, the veil is taken away. ¹⁷Now the Lord is the Spirit, and where the Spirit of the Lord is, there is freedom. ¹⁸And we, who with unveiled faces all reflect[a] the Lord's glory, are being transformed into his likeness with ever-increasing glory, which comes from the Lord, who is the Spirit.

Treasures in Jars of Clay

4 Therefore, since through God's mercy we have this ministry, we do not lose heart. ²Rather, we have renounced secret and shameful ways; we do not use deception, nor do we distort the word of God. On the contrary, by setting forth the truth plainly we commend ourselves to every man's conscience in the sight of God. ³And even if our gospel is veiled, it is veiled to those who are perishing. ⁴The god of this age has blinded the minds of unbelievers, so that they cannot see the light of the gospel of the glory of Christ, who is the image of God. ⁵For we do not preach ourselves, but Jesus Christ as Lord, and ourselves as your servants for Jesus' sake. ⁶For God, who said, "Let light shine out of darkness,"[b] made his light shine in our hearts to give us the light of the knowledge of the glory of God in the face of Christ.

⁷But we have this treasure in jars of clay to show that this all-surpassing power is from God and not from us. ⁸We are hard pressed on every side, but not crushed; perplexed, but not in despair; ⁹persecuted, but not abandoned; struck down, but not destroyed. ¹⁰We always carry around in our body the death of Jesus, so that the life of Jesus may also be revealed in our

---

[a]18 Or *contemplate*   [b]6 Gen. 1:3

body. [11]For we who are alive are always being given over to death for Jesus' sake, so that his life may be revealed in our mortal body. [12]So then, death is at work in us, but life is at work in you.

[13]It is written: "I believed; therefore I have spoken."[a] With that same spirit of faith we also believe and therefore speak, [14]because we know that the one who raised the Lord Jesus from the dead will also raise us with Jesus and present us with you in his presence. [15]All this is for your benefit, so that the grace that is reaching more and more people may cause thanksgiving to overflow to the glory of God.

[16]Therefore we do not lose heart. Though outwardly we are wasting away, yet inwardly we are being renewed day by day. [17]For our light and momentary troubles are achieving for us an eternal glory that far outweighs them all. [18]So we fix our eyes not on what is seen, but on what is unseen. For what is seen is temporary, but what is unseen is eternal.

Our Heavenly Dwelling

5 Now we know that if the earthly tent we live in is destroyed, we have a building from God, an eternal house in heaven, not built by human hands. [2]Meanwhile we groan, longing to be clothed with our heavenly dwelling, [3]because when we are clothed, we will not be found naked. [4]For while we are in this tent, we groan and are burdened, because we do not wish to be unclothed but to be clothed with our heavenly dwelling, so that what is mortal may be swallowed up by life. [5]Now it is God who has made us for this very purpose and has given us the Spirit as a deposit, guaranteeing what is to come.

[6]Therefore we are always confident and know that as long as we are at home in the body we are away from the Lord. [7]We live by faith, not by sight. [8]We are confident, I say, and would prefer to be away from the body and at home with the Lord. [9]So we make it our goal to please him, whether we are at home in the body or away from it. [10]For we must all appear before the judgment seat of Christ, that each one may receive what is due him for the things done while in the body, whether good or bad.

The Ministry of Reconciliation

[11]Since, then, we know what it is to fear the Lord, we try to persuade men. What we are is plain to God, and I hope it is also plain to your conscience. [12]We are not trying to commend ourselves to you again, but are giving you an opportunity to take pride in us, so that you can answer those who take pride in what is seen rather than in what is in the heart. [13]If we are out of our mind, it is for the sake of God; if we are in our right mind, it is for you. [14]For Christ's love compels us, because we are convinced that one died for all, and therefore all died. [15]And he died for all, that those who live should no longer live for themselves but for him who died for them and was raised again.

[16]So from now on we regard no one from a worldly point of view.

[a]13 Psalm 116:10

Though we once regarded Christ in this way, we do so no longer. [17]Therefore, if anyone is in Christ, he is a new creation; the old has gone, the new has come! [18]All this is from God, who reconciled us to himself through Christ and gave us the ministry of reconciliation: [19]that God was reconciling the world to himself in Christ, not counting men's sins against them. And he has committed to us the message of reconciliation. [20]We are therefore Christ's ambassadors, as though God were making his appeal through us. We implore you on Christ's behalf: Be reconciled to God. [21]God made him who had. no sin to be sin[a] for us, so that in him we might become the righteousness of God.

6 As God's fellow workers we urge you not to receive God's grace in vain. [2]For he says,

> "In the time of my favor I heard you,
>   and in the day of salvation I helped you."[b]

I tell you, now is the time of God's favor, now is the day of salvation.

Paul's Hardships

[3]We put no stumbling block in anyone's path, so that our ministry will not be discredited. [4]Rather, as servants of God we commend ourselves in every way: in great endurance; in troubles, hardships and distresses; [5]in beatings, imprisonments and riots; in hard work, sleepless nights and hunger; [6]in purity, understanding, patience and kindness; in the Holy Spirit and in sincere love; [7]in truthful speech and in the power of God; with weapons of righteousness in the right hand and in the left; [8]through glory and dishonor, bad report and good report; genuine, yet regarded as impostors; [9]known, yet regarded as unknown; dying, and yet we live on; beaten, and yet not killed; [10]sorrowful, yet always rejoicing; poor, yet making many rich; having nothing, and yet possessing everything.

[11]We have spoken freely to you, Corinthians, and opened wide our hearts to you. [12]We are not withholding our affection from you, but you are withholding yours from us. [13]As a fair exchange—I speak as to my children —open wide your hearts also.

Do Not Be Yoked With Unbelievers

[14]Do not be yoked together with unbelievers. For what do righteousness and wickedness have in common? Or what fellowship can light have with darkness? [15]What harmony is there between Christ and Belial[c]? What does a believer have in common with an unbeliever? [16]What agreement is there between the temple of God and idols? For we are the temple of the living God. As God has said: "I will live with them and walk among them, and I will be their God, and they will be my people."[d]

[17]"Therefore come out from them

---

[a]21 Or *be a sin offering*   [b]2 Isaiah 49:8   [c]15 Greek *Beliar*, a variant of *Belial*   [d]16 Lev. 26:12; Jer. 32:38; Ezek. 37:27

and be separate,

says the Lord.

Touch no unclean thing,
and I will receive you."[a]
18"I will be a Father to you,
and you will be my sons and daughters,

says the Lord Almighty."[b]

7 Since we have these promises, dear friends, let us purify ourselves from everything that contaminates body and spirit, perfecting holiness out of reverence for God.

Paul's Joy

[2]Make room for us in your hearts. We have wronged no one, we have corrupted no one, we have exploited no one. [3]I do not say this to condemn you; I have said before that you have such a place in our hearts that we would live or die with you. [4]I have great confidence in you; I take great pride in you. I am greatly encouraged; in all our troubles my joy knows no bounds.

[5]For when we came into Macedonia, this body of ours had no rest, but we were harassed at every turn—conflicts on the outside, fears within. [6]But God, who comforts the downcast, comforted us by the coming of Titus, [7]and not only by his coming but also by the comfort you had given him. He told us about your longing for me, your deep sorrow, your ardent concern for me, so that my joy was greater than ever.

[8]Even if I caused you sorrow by my letter, I do not regret it. Though I did regret it—I see that my letter hurt you, but only for a little while— [9]yet now I am happy, not because you were made sorry, but because your sorrow led you to repentance. For you became sorrowful as God intended and so were not harmed in any way by us. [10]Godly sorrow brings repentance that leads to salvation and leaves no regret, but worldly sorrow brings death. [11]See what this godly sorrow has produced in you: what earnestness, what eagerness to clear yourselves, what indignation, what alarm, what longing, what concern, what readiness to see justice done. At every point you have proved yourselves to be innocent in this matter. [12]So even though I wrote to you, it was not on account of the one who did the wrong or of the injured party, but rather that before God you could see for yourselves how devoted to us you are. [13]By all this we are encouraged.

In addition to our own encouragement, we were especially delighted to see how happy Titus was, because his spirit has been refreshed by all of you. [14]I had boasted to him about you, and you have not embarrassed me. But just as everything we said to you was true, so our boasting about you to Titus has proved to be true as well. [15]And his affection for you is all the greater when he remembers that you were all obedient, receiving him with fear and trembling. [16]I am glad I can have complete confidence in you.

[a]17 Isaiah 52:11; Ezek. 20:34,41   [b]18 2 Samuel 7:14; 7:8

293

Generosity Encouraged

8 And now, brothers, we want you to know about the grace that God has given the Macedonian churches. [2]Out of the most severe trial, their overflowing joy and their extreme poverty welled up in rich generosity. [3]For I testify that they gave as much as they were able, and even beyond their ability. Entirely on their own, [4]they urgently pleaded with us for the privilege of sharing in this service to the saints. [5]And they did not do as we expected, but they gave themselves first to the Lord and then to us in keeping with God's will. [6]So we urged Titus, since he had earlier made a beginning, to bring also to completion this act of grace on your part. [7]But just as you excel in everything—in faith, in speech, in knowledge, in complete earnestness and in your love for us[a]—see that you also excel in this grace of giving.

[8]I am not commanding you, but I want to test the sincerity of your love by comparing it with the earnestness of others. [9]For you know the grace of our Lord Jesus Christ, that though he was rich, yet for your sakes he became poor, so that you through his poverty might become rich.

[10]And here is my advice about what is best for you in this matter: Last year you were the first not only to give but also to have the desire to do so. [11]Now finish the work, so that your eager willingness to do it may be matched by your completion of it, according to your means. [12]For if the willingness is there, the gift is acceptable according to what one has, not according to what he does not have.

[13]Our desire is not that others might be relieved while you are hard pressed, but that there might be equality. [14]At the present time your plenty will supply what they need, so that in turn their plenty will supply what you need. Then there will be equality, [15]as it is written: "He who gathered much did not have too much, and he who gathered little did not have too little."[b]

Titus Sent to Corinth

[16]I thank God, who put into the heart of Titus the same concern I have for you. [17]For Titus not only welcomed our appeal, but he is coming to you with much enthusiasm and on his own initiative. [18]And we are sending along with him the brother who is praised by all the churches for his service to the gospel. [19]What is more, he was chosen by the churches to accompany us as we carry the offering, which we administer in order to honor the Lord himself and to show our eagerness to help. [20]We want to avoid any criticism of the way we administer this liberal gift. [21]For we are taking pains to do what is right, not only in the eyes of the Lord but also in the eyes of men.

[22]In addition, we are sending with them our brother who has often proved to us in many ways that he is zealous, and now even more so because of his great confidence in you. [23]As for Titus, he is my partner and fellow worker among you; as for our brothers, they are representatives of

---

[a]7 Some manuscripts *in our love for you*   [b]15 Exodus 16:18

the churches and an honor to Christ. [24]Therefore show these men the proof of your love and the reason for our pride in you, so that the churches can see it.

9 There is no need for me to write to you about this service to the saints. [2]For I know your eagerness to help, and I have been boasting about it to the Macedonians, telling them that since last year you in Achaia were ready to give; and your enthusiasm has stirred most of them to action. [3]But I am sending the brothers in order that our boasting about you in this matter should not prove hollow, but that you may be ready, as I said you would be. [4]For if any Macedonians come with me and find you unprepared, we—not to say anything about you—would be ashamed of having been so confident. [5]So I thought it necessary to urge the brothers to visit you in advance and finish the arrangements for the generous gift you had promised. Then it will be ready as a generous gift, not as one grudgingly given.

Sowing Generously

[6]Remember this: Whoever sows sparingly will also reap sparingly, and whoever sows generously will also reap generously. [7]Each man should give what he has decided in his heart to give, not reluctantly or under compulsion, for God loves a cheerful giver. [8]And God is able to make all grace abound to you, so that in all things at all times, having all that you need, you will abound in every good work. [9]As it is written:

> "He has scattered abroad his gifts to the poor;
> his righteousness endures forever."[a]

[10]Now he who supplies seed to the sower and bread for food will also supply and increase your store of seed and will enlarge the harvest of your righteousness. [11]You will be made rich in every way so that you can be generous on every occasion, and through us your generosity will result in thanksgiving to God.

[12]This service that you perform is not only supplying the needs of God's people but is also overflowing in many expressions of thanks to God. [13]Because of the service by which you have proved yourselves, men will praise God for the obedience that accompanies your confession of the gospel of Christ, and for your generosity in sharing with them and with everyone else. [14]And in their prayers for you their hearts will go out to you, because of the surpassing grace God has given you. [15]Thanks be to God for his indescribable gift!

Paul's Defense of His Ministry

10 By the meekness and gentleness of Christ, I appeal to you—I, Paul, who am "timid" when face to face with you, but "bold" when away! [2]I beg you that when I come I may not have to be as bold as I expect to be toward some people who think that we live by the standards of this world. [3]For though we live in the world, we do not wage war as the world does.

[a]9 Psalm 112:9

[4]The weapons we fight with are not the weapons of the world. On the contrary, they have divine power to demolish strongholds. [5]We demolish arguments and every pretension that sets itself up against the knowledge of God, and we take captive every thought to make it obedient to Christ. [6]And we will be ready to punish every act of disobedience, once your obedience is complete.

[7]You are looking only on the surface of things.[a] If anyone is confident that he belongs to Christ, he should consider again that we belong to Christ just as much as he. [8]For even if I boast somewhat freely about the authority the Lord gave us for building you up rather than pulling you down, I will not be ashamed of it. [9]I do not want to seem to be trying to frighten you with my letters. [10]For some say, "His letters are weighty and forceful, but in person he is unimpressive and his speaking amounts to nothing." [11]Such people should realize that what we are in our letters when we are absent, we will be in our actions when we are present.

[12]We do not dare to classify or compare ourselves with some who commend themselves. When they measure themselves by themselves and compare themselves with themselves, they are not wise. [13]We, however, will not boast beyond proper limits, but will confine our boasting to the field God has assigned to us, a field that reaches even to you. [14]We are not going too far in our boasting, as would be the case if we had not come to you, for we did get as far as you with the gospel of Christ. [15]Neither do we go beyond our limits by boasting of work done by others.[b] Our hope is that, as your faith continues to grow, our area of activity among you will greatly expand, [16]so that we can preach the gospel in the regions beyond you. For we do not want to boast about work already done in another man's territory. [17]But, "Let him who boasts boast in the Lord."[c] [18]For it is not the one who commends himself who is approved, but the one whom the Lord commends.

Paul and the False Apostles

11 I hope you will put up with a little of my foolishness; but you are already doing that. [2]I am jealous for you with a godly jealousy. I promised you to one husband, to Christ, so that I might present you as a pure virgin to him. [3]But I am afraid that just as Eve was deceived by the serpent's cunning, your minds may somehow be led astray from your sincere and pure devotion to Christ. [4]For if someone comes to you and preaches a Jesus other than the Jesus we preached, or if you receive a different spirit from the one you received, or a different gospel from the one you accepted, you put up with it easily enough. [5]But I do not think I am in the least inferior to those "super-apostles." [6]I may not be a trained

[a]7 Or Look at the obvious facts   [b]13-15 Or [13]We, however, will not boast about things that cannot be measured, but we will boast according to the standard of measurement that the God of measure has assigned us—a measurement that relates even to you. [14] . . . . [15]Neither do we boast about things that cannot be measured in regard to the work done by others.   [c]17 Jer. 9:24

speaker, but I do have knowledge. We have made this perfectly clear to you in every way.

⁷Was it a sin for me to lower myself in order to elevate you by preaching the gospel of God to you free of charge? ⁸I robbed other churches by receiving support from them so as to serve you. ⁹And when I was with you and needed something, I was not a burden to anyone, for the brothers who came from Macedonia supplied what I needed. I have kept myself from being a burden to you in any way, and will continue to do so. ¹⁰As surely as the truth of Christ is in me, nobody in the regions of Achaia will stop this boasting of mine. ¹¹Why? Because I do not love you? God knows I do! ¹²And I will keep on doing what I am doing in order to cut the ground from under those who want an opportunity to be considered equal with us in the things they boast about.

¹³For such men are false apostles, deceitful workmen, masquerading as apostles of Christ. ¹⁴And no wonder, for Satan himself masquerades as an angel of light. ¹⁵It is not surprising, then, if his servants masquerade as servants of righteousness. Their end will be what their actions deserve.

Paul Boasts About His Sufferings

¹⁶I repeat: Let no one take me for a fool. But if you do, then receive me just as you would a fool, so that I may do a little boasting. ¹⁷In this self-confident boasting I am not talking as the Lord would, but as a fool. ¹⁸Since many are boasting in the way the world does, I too will boast. ¹⁹You gladly put up with fools since you are so wise! ²⁰In fact, you even put up with anyone who enslaves you or exploits you or takes advantage of you or pushes himself forward or slaps you in the face. ²¹To my shame I admit that we were too weak for that!

What anyone else dares to boast about—I am speaking as a fool—I also dare to boast about. ²²Are they Hebrews? So am I. Are they Israelites? So am I. Are they Abraham's descendants? So am I. ²³Are they servants of Christ? (I am out of my mind to talk like this.) I am more. I have worked much harder, been in prison more frequently, been flogged more severely, and been exposed to death again and again. ²⁴Five times I received from the Jews the forty lashes minus one. ²⁵Three times I was beaten with rods, once I was stoned, three times I was shipwrecked, I spent a night and a day in the open sea, ²⁶I have been constantly on the move. I have been in danger from rivers, in danger from bandits, in danger from my own countrymen, in danger from Gentiles; in danger in the city, in danger in the country, in danger at sea; and in danger from false brothers. ²⁷I have labored and toiled and have often gone without sleep; I have known hunger and thirst and have often gone without food; I have been cold and naked. ²⁸Besides everything else, I face daily the pressure of my concern for all the churches. ²⁹Who is weak, and I do not feel weak? Who is led into sin, and I do not inwardly burn?

³⁰If I must boast, I will boast of the things that show my weakness. ³¹The God and Father of the Lord Jesus, who is to be praised forever, knows that

I am not lying. ³²In Damascus the governor under King Aretas had the city of the Damascenes guarded in order to arrest me. ³³But I was lowered in a basket from a window in the wall and slipped through his hands.

Paul's Vision and His Thorn

12 I must go on boasting. Although there is nothing to be gained, I will go on to visions and revelations from the Lord. ²I know a man in Christ who fourteen years ago was caught up to the third heaven. Whether it was in the body or out of the body I do not know—God knows. ³And I know that this man—whether in the body or apart from the body I do not know, but God knows— ⁴was caught up to paradise. He heard inexpressible things, things that man is not permitted to tell. ⁵I will boast about a man like that, but I will not boast about myself, except about my weaknesses. ⁶Even if I should choose to boast, I would not be a fool, because I would be speaking the truth. But I refrain, so no one will think more of me than is warranted by what I do or say.

⁷To keep me from becoming conceited because of these surpassingly great revelations, there was given me a thorn in my flesh, a messenger of Satan, to torment me. ⁸Three times I pleaded with the Lord to take it away from me. ⁹But he said to me, "My grace is sufficient for you, for my power is made perfect in weakness." Therefore I will boast all the more gladly about my weaknesses, so that Christ's power may rest on me. ¹⁰That is why, for Christ's sake, I delight in weaknesses, in insults, in hardships, in persecutions, in difficulties. For when I am weak, then I am strong.

Paul's Concern for the Corinthians

¹¹I have made a fool of myself, but you drove me to it. I ought to have been commended by you, for I am not in the least inferior to the "super-apostles," even though I am nothing. ¹²The things that mark an apostle—signs, wonders and miracles—were done among you with great perseverance. ¹³How were you inferior to the other churches, except that I was never a burden to you? Forgive me this wrong!

¹⁴Now I am ready to visit you for the third time, and I will not be a burden to you, because what I want is not your possessions but you. After all, children should not have to save up for their parents, but parents for their children. ¹⁵So I will very gladly spend for you everything I have and expend myself as well. If I love you more, will you love me less? ¹⁶Be that as it may, I have not been a burden to you. Yet, crafty fellow that I am, I caught you by trickery! ¹⁷Did I exploit you through any of the men I sent you? ¹⁸I urged Titus to go to you and I sent our brother with him. Titus did not exploit you, did he? Did we not act in the same spirit and follow the same course?

¹⁹Have you been thinking all along that we have been defending ourselves to you? We have been speaking in the sight of God as those in Christ; and everything we do, dear friends, is for your strengthening. ²⁰For I am afraid that when I come I may not find you as I want you to be, and you

may not find me as you want me to be. I fear that there may be quarreling, jealousy, outbursts of anger, factions, slander, gossip, arrogance and disorder. [21]I am afraid that when I come again my God will humble me before you, and I will be grieved over many who have sinned earlier and have not repented of the impurity, sexual sin and debauchery in which they have indulged.

Final Warnings

13 This will be my third visit to you. "Every matter must be established by the testimony of two or three witnesses."[a] [2]I already gave you a warning when I was with you the second time. I now repeat it while absent: On my return I will not spare those who sinned earlier or any of the others, [3]since you are demanding proof that Christ is speaking through me. He is not weak in dealing with you, but is powerful among you. [4]For to be sure, he was crucified in weakness, yet he lives by God's power. Likewise, we are weak in him, yet by God's power we will live with him to serve you.

[5]Examine yourselves to see whether you are in the faith; test yourselves. Do you not realize that Christ Jesus is in you—unless, of course, you fail the test? [6]And I trust that you will discover that we have not failed the test. [7]Now we pray to God that you will not do anything wrong. Not that people will see that we have stood the test but that you will do what is right even though we may seem to have failed. [8]For we cannot do anything against the truth, but only for the truth. [9]We are glad whenever we are weak but you are strong; and our prayer is for your perfection. [10]This is why I write these things when I am absent, that when I come I may not have to be harsh in my use of authority—the authority the Lord gave me for building you up, not for tearing you down.

Final Greetings

[11]Finally, brothers, good-by. Aim for perfection, listen to my appeal, be of one mind, live in peace. And the God of love and peace will be with you.

[12]Greet one another with a holy kiss. [13]All the saints send their greetings.

[14]May the grace of the Lord Jesus Christ, and the love of God, and the fellowship of the Holy Spirit be with you all.

[a]1 Deut. 19:15

Galatians

INTRODUCTION

While the central message of Galatians, Christian freedom, is clear and easy to identify, other details of this letter are not so clear. The recipients of this letter are pagan converts to Christianity now under attack by Jewish converts to Christianity. But exactly where they are located in Galatia (north or south) is not known. Paul traveled and missionized in both areas, but on two different journeys; hence the date of the letter is also difficult to determine with accuracy. It is safe to say that he wrote the letter during the middle years of his missionary work, sometime in the early 50's, perhaps 53 or 54 A.D.

The heated polemic nature of the letter is clear to even the most superficial reader as is the rather large amount of autobiographical information. Once again it is important to take Paul at his word in this letter (e.g., Gal 2:1–10) and avoid imposing upon it any "corrective" from Acts 15:6–12. In ironing out the differences, Paul's statements must be respected.

Christian freedom is the dominant theme of Galatians, and its special feature is that it entails (literally) "slave service" to others. True Christian freedom must be protected against external restrictions as well as unbridled selfishness.

Freedom must never rupture Christian unity, a related theme in this letter. Paul is incensed over the attempts of Jewish converts to Christianity who want to restore some former beliefs and practices as a supplement to the Christian life.

JOHN J. PILCH

Points for Reflection

1. Conversion to Christ or to deeper life in Christ often meets with uncomfortable reactions from others. What lessons do Paul's experiences offer on this matter?
2. Considering Peter his equal, Paul boldly challenged his compromising behavior. Would this work in your experience? Why or why not?
3. Paul's impressive use of Scripture in chapters 3 and 4 was typical of Jewish interpretations in his day. What are some typical uses of Scripture that you make in daily life?

4. Paul teaches that the Torah as law only had a temporary value. What religious beliefs or values in your life have had temporary value? Lasting value? Is Paul persuasive to you on this point?
5. Some scholars believe that the reference to "principles of the world" (4:3,9) reflects a belief in astrology. What is so appealing about astrology that causes it to get in the way of one's intimate relationship with God?
6. Paul offers both personal example (4:12) as well as instruction (5:1–15) for the guidance of his readers. How have you been able to benefit from both?

1 Paul, an apostle—sent not from men nor by man, but by Jesus Christ and God the Father, who raised him from the dead— ²and all the brothers with me,

To the churches in Galatia:

³Grace and peace to you from God our Father and the Lord Jesus Christ, ⁴who gave himself for our sins to rescue us from the present evil age, according to the will of our God and Father, ⁵to whom be glory for ever and ever. Amen.

No Other Gospel

⁶I am astonished that you are so quickly deserting the one who called you by the grace of Christ and are turning to a different gospel— ⁷which is really no gospel at all. Evidently some people are throwing you into confusion and are trying to pervert the gospel of Christ. ⁸But even if we or an angel from heaven should preach a gospel other than the one we preached to you, let him be eternally condemned! ⁹As we have already said, so now I say again: If anybody is preaching to you a gospel other than what you accepted, let him be eternally condemned!

¹⁰Am I now trying to win the approval of men, or of God? Or am I trying to please men? If I were still trying to please men, I would not be a servant of Christ.

Paul Called by God

¹¹I want you to know, brothers, that the gospel I preached is not something that man made up. ¹²I did not receive it from any man, nor was I taught it; rather, I received it by revelation from Jesus Christ.

¹³For you have heard of my previous way of life in Judaism, how intensely I persecuted the church of God and tried to destroy it. ¹⁴I was advancing in Judaism beyond many Jews of my own age and was extremely zealous for the traditions of my fathers. ¹⁵But when God, who set me apart from birth*a* and called me by his grace, was pleased ¹⁶to reveal his Son in me so that I might preach him among the Gentiles, I did not consult any man, ¹⁷nor did I go up to Jerusalem to see those who were apostles before I was, but I went immediately into Arabia and later returned to Damascus.

¹⁸Then after three years, I went up to Jerusalem to get acquainted with Peter*b* and stayed with him fifteen days. ¹⁹I saw none of the other apostles— only James, the Lord's brother. ²⁰I assure you before God that what I am writing you is no lie. ²¹Later I went to Syria and Cilicia. ²²I was personally unknown to the churches of Judea that are in Christ. ²³They only heard the report: "The man who formerly persecuted us is now preaching the faith he once tried to destroy." ²⁴And they praised God because of me.

*a*15 Or *from my mother's womb*   *b*18 Greek *Cephas*

Paul Accepted by the Apostles

2 Fourteen years later I went up again to Jerusalem, this time with Barnabas. I took Titus along also. [2]I went in response to a revelation and set before them the gospel that I preach among the Gentiles. But I did this privately to those who seemed to be leaders, for fear that I was running or had run my race in vain. [3]Yet not even Titus, who was with me, was compelled to be circumcised, even though he was a Greek. [4]This matter arose, because some false brothers had infiltrated our ranks to spy on the freedom we have in Christ Jesus and to make us slaves. [5]We did not give in to them for a moment, so that the truth of the gospel might remain with you.

[6]As for those who seemed to be important—whatever they were makes no difference to me; God does not judge by external appearance—those men added nothing to my message. [7]On the contrary, they saw that I had been entrusted with the task of preaching the gospel to the Gentiles,[a] just as Peter had been to the Jews.[b] [8]For God, who was at work in the ministry of Peter as an apostle to the Jews, was also at work in my ministry as an apostle to the Gentiles. [9]James, Peter[c] and John, those reputed to be pillars, gave me and Barnabas the right hand of fellowship when they recognized the grace given to me. They agreed that we should go to the Gentiles, and they to the Jews. [10]All they asked was that we should continue to remember the poor, the very thing I was eager to do.

Paul Opposes Peter

[11]When Peter came to Antioch, I opposed him to his face, because he was clearly in the wrong. [12]Before certain men came from James, he used to eat with the Gentiles. But when they arrived, he began to draw back and separate himself from the Gentiles because he was afraid of those who belonged to the circumcision group. [13]The other Jews joined him in his hypocrisy, so that by their hypocrisy even Barnabas was led astray.

[14]When I saw that they were not acting in line with the truth of the gospel, I said to Peter in front of them all, "You are a Jew, yet you live like a Gentile and not like a Jew. How is it, then, that you force Gentiles to follow Jewish customs?

[15]"We who are Jews by birth and not 'Gentile sinners' [16]know that a man is not justified by observing the law, but by faith in Jesus Christ. So we, too, have put our faith in Christ Jesus that we may be justified by faith in Christ and not by observing the law, because by observing the law no one will be justified.

[17]"If, while we seek to be justified in Christ, it becomes evident that we ourselves are sinners, does that mean that Christ promotes sin? Absolutely not! [18]If I rebuild what I destroyed, I prove that I am a lawbreaker. [19]For through the law I died to the law so that I might live for God. [20]I have been

---

[a]7 Greek uncircumcised   [b]7 Greek circumcised; also in verses 8 and 9   [c]9 Greek Cephas; also in verses 11 and 14

crucified with Christ and I no longer live, but Christ lives in me. The life I live in the body, I live by faith in the Son of God, who loved me and gave himself for me. ²¹I do not set aside the grace of God, for if righteousness could be gained through the law, Christ died for nothing!"ᵃ

Faith or Observance of the Law

3 You foolish Galatians! Who has bewitched you? Before your very eyes Jesus Christ was clearly portrayed as crucified. ²I would like to learn just one thing from you: Did you receive the Spirit by observing the law, or by believing what you heard? ³Are you so foolish? After beginning with the Spirit, are you now trying to attain your goal by human effort? ⁴Have you suffered so much for nothing—if it really was for nothing? ⁵Does God give you his Spirit and work miracles among you because you observe the law, or because you believe what you heard?

⁶Consider Abraham: "He believed God, and it was credited to him as righteousness."ᵇ ⁷Understand, then, that those who believe are children of Abraham. ⁸The Scripture foresaw that God would justify the Gentiles by faith, and announced the gospel in advance to Abraham: "All nations will be blessed through you."ᶜ ⁹So those who have faith are blessed along with Abraham, the man of faith.

¹⁰All who rely on observing the law are under a curse, for it is written: "Cursed is everyone who does not continue to do everything written in the Book of the Law."ᵈ ¹¹Clearly no one is justified before God by the law, because, "The righteous will live by faith."ᵉ ¹²The law is not based on faith; on the contrary, "The man who does these things will live by them."ᶠ ¹³Christ redeemed us from the curse of the law by becoming a curse for us, for it is written: "Cursed is everyone who is hung on a tree."ᵍ ¹⁴He redeemed us in order that the blessing given to Abraham might come to the Gentiles through Christ Jesus, so that by faith we might receive the promise of the Spirit.

The Law and the Promise

¹⁵Brothers, let me take an example from everyday life. Just as no one can set aside or add to a human covenant that has been duly established, so it is in this case. ¹⁶The promises were spoken to Abraham and to his seed. The Scripture does not say "and to seeds," meaning many people, but "and to your seed,"ʰ meaning one person, who is Christ. ¹⁷What I mean is this: The law, introduced 430 years later, does not set aside the covenant previously established by God and thus do away with the promise. ¹⁸For if the inheritance depends on the law, then it no longer depends on a promise; but God in his grace gave it to Abraham through a promise.

¹⁹What, then, was the purpose of the law? It was added because of transgressions until the Seed to whom the promise referred had come. The

---

ᵃ21 Some interpreters end the quotation after verse 14.   ᵇ6 Gen. 15:6   ᶜ8 Gen. 12:3; 18:18; 22:18
ᵈ10 Deut. 27:26   ᵉ11 Hab. 2:4   ᶠ12 Lev. 18:5   ᵍ13 Deut. 21:23   ʰ16 Gen. 12:7; 13:15; 24:7

law was put into effect through angels by a mediator. [20]A mediator, however, does not represent just one party; but God is one.

[21]Is the law, therefore, opposed to the promises of God? Absolutely not! For if a law had been given that could impart life, then righteousness would certainly have come by the law. [22]But the Scripture declares that the whole world is a prisoner of sin, so that what was promised, being given through faith in Jesus Christ, might be given to those who believe.

[23]Before this faith came, we were held prisoners by the law, locked up until faith should be revealed. [24]So the law was put in charge to lead us to Christ[a] that we might be justified by faith. [25]Now that faith has come, we are no longer under the supervision of the law.

Sons of God

[26]You are all sons of God through faith in Christ Jesus, [27]for all of you who were baptized into Christ have clothed yourselves with Christ. [28]There is neither Jew nor Greek, slave nor free, male nor female, for you are all one in Christ Jesus. [29]If you belong to Christ, then you are Abraham's seed, and heirs according to the promise.

4 What I am saying is that as long as the heir is a child, he is no different from a slave, although he owns the whole estate. [2]He is subject to guardians and trustees until the time set by his father. [3]So also, when we were children, we were in slavery under the basic principles of the world. [4]But when the time had fully come, God sent his Son, born of a woman, born under law, [5]to redeem those under law, that we might receive the full rights of sons. [6]Because you are sons, God sent the Spirit of his Son into our hearts, the Spirit who calls out, "Abba,[b] Father." [7]So you are no longer a slave, but a son; and since you are a son, God has made you also an heir.

Paul's Concern for the Galatians

[8]Formerly, when you did not know God, you were slaves to those who by nature are not gods. [9]But now that you know God—or rather are known by God—how is it that you are turning back to those weak and miserable principles? Do you wish to be enslaved by them all over again? [10]You are observing special days and months and seasons and years! [11]I fear for you, that somehow I have wasted my efforts on you.

[12]I plead with you, brothers, become like me, for I became like you. You have done me no wrong. [13]As you know, it was because of an illness that I first preached the gospel to you. [14]Even though my illness was a trial to you, you did not treat me with contempt or scorn. Instead, you welcomed me as if I were an angel of God, as if I were Christ Jesus himself. [15]What has happened to all your joy? I can testify that, if you could have done so, you would have torn out your eyes and given them to me. [16]Have I now become your enemy by telling you the truth?

[17]Those people are zealous to win you over, but for no good. What they want is to alienate you ⌞from us⌟, so that you may be zealous for them. [18]It

[a]24 Or *charge until Christ came*   [b]6 Aramaic for *Father*

is fine to be zealous, provided the purpose is good, and to be so always and not just when I am with you. [19]My dear children, for whom I am again in the pains of childbirth until Christ is formed in you, [20]how I wish I could be with you now and change my tone, because I am perplexed about you!

Hagar and Sarah

[21]Tell me, you who want to be under the law, are you not aware of what the law says? [22]For it is written that Abraham had two sons, one by the slave woman and the other by the free woman. [23]His son by the slave woman was born in the ordinary way; but his son by the free woman was born as the result of a promise.

[24]These things may be taken figuratively, for the women represent two covenants. One covenant is from Mount Sinai and bears children who are to be slaves: This is Hagar. [25]Now Hagar stands for Mount Sinai in Arabia and corresponds to the present city of Jerusalem, because she is in slavery with her children. [26]But the Jerusalem that is above is free, and she is our mother. [27]For it is written:

> "Be glad, O barren woman,
>   who bears no children;
> break forth and cry aloud,
>   you who have no labor pains;
> because more are the children of the desolate woman
>   than of her who has a husband."[a]

[28]Now you, brothers, like Isaac, are children of promise. [29]At that time the son born in the ordinary way persecuted the son born by the power of the Spirit. It is the same now. [30]But what does the Scripture say? "Get rid of the slave woman and her son, for the slave woman's son will never share in the inheritance with the free woman's son."[b] [31]Therefore, brothers, we are not children of the slave woman, but of the free woman.

Freedom in Christ

5 It is for freedom that Christ has set us free. Stand firm, then, and do not let yourselves be burdened again by a yoke of slavery.

[2]Mark my words! I, Paul, tell you that if you let yourselves be circumcised, Christ will be of no value to you at all. [3]Again I declare to every man who lets himself be circumcised that he is obligated to obey the whole law. [4]You who are trying to be justified by law have been alienated from Christ; you have fallen away from grace. [5]But by faith we eagerly await through the Spirit the righteousness for which we hope. [6]For in Christ Jesus neither circumcision nor uncircumcision has any value. The only thing that counts is faith expressing itself through love.

[7]You were running a good race. Who cut in on you and kept you from obeying the truth? [8]That kind of persuasion does not come from the one who calls you. [9]"A little yeast works through the whole batch of dough."

[a]27 Isaiah 54:1   [b]30 Gen. 21:10

[10]I am confident in the Lord that you will take no other view. The one who is throwing you into confusion will pay the penalty, whoever he may be. [11]Brothers, if I am still preaching circumcision, why am I still being persecuted? In that case the offense of the cross has been abolished. [12]As for those agitators, I wish they would go the whole way and emasculate themselves!

[13]You, my brothers, were called to be free. But do not use your freedom to indulge the sinful nature[a]; rather, serve one another in love. [14]The entire law is summed up in a single command: "Love your neighbor as yourself."[b] [15]If you keep on biting and devouring each other, watch out or you will be destroyed by each other.

Life by the Spirit

[16]So I say, live by the Spirit, and you will not gratify the desires of the sinful nature. [17]For the sinful nature desires what is contrary to the Spirit, and the Spirit what is contrary to the sinful nature. They are in conflict with each other, so that you do not do what you want. [18]But if you are led by the Spirit, you are not under law.

[19]The acts of the sinful nature are obvious: sexual immorality, impurity and debauchery; [20]idolatry and witchcraft; hatred, discord, jealousy, fits of rage, selfish ambition, dissensions, factions [21]and envy; drunkenness, orgies, and the like. I warn you, as I did before, that those who live like this will not inherit the kingdom of God.

[22]But the fruit of the Spirit is love, joy, peace, patience, kindness, goodness, faithfulness, [23]gentleness and self-control. Against such things there is no law. [24]Those who belong to Christ Jesus have crucified the sinful nature with its passions and desires. [25]Since we live by the Spirit, let us keep in step with the Spirit. [26]Let us not become conceited, provoking and envying each other.

Doing Good to All

6 Brothers, if someone is caught in a sin, you who are spiritual should restore him gently. But watch yourself, or you also may be tempted. [2]Carry each other's burdens, and in this way you will fulfill the law of Christ. [3]If anyone thinks he is something when he is nothing, he deceives himself. [4]Each one should test his own actions. Then he can take pride in himself, without comparing himself to somebody else, [5]for each one should carry his own load.

[6]Anyone who receives instruction in the word must share all good things with his instructor.

[7]Do not be deceived: God cannot be mocked. A man reaps what he sows. [8]The one who sows to please his sinful nature, from that nature[c] will reap destruction; the one who sows to please the Spirit, from the Spirit will reap eternal life. [9]Let us not become weary in doing good, for at the proper time we will reap a harvest if we do not give up. [10]Therefore, as we have

---

[a]13 Or *the flesh*; also in verses 16, 17, 19 and 24   [b]14 Lev. 19:18   [c]8 Or *his flesh, from the flesh*

opportunity, let us do good to all people, especially to those who belong to the family of believers.

Not Circumcision but a New Creation

[11]See what large letters I use as I write to you with my own hand!

[12]Those who want to make a good impression outwardly are trying to compel you to be circumcised. The only reason they do this is to avoid being persecuted for the cross of Christ. [13]Not even those who are circumcised obey the law, yet they want you to be circumcised that they may boast about your flesh. [14]May I never boast except in the cross of our Lord Jesus Christ, through which[a] the world has been crucified to me, and I to the world. [15]Neither circumcision nor uncircumcision means anything; what counts is a new creation. [16]Peace and mercy to all who follow this rule, even to the Israel of God.

[17]Finally, let no one cause me trouble, for I bear on my body the marks of Jesus.

[18]The grace of our Lord Jesus Christ be with your spirit, brothers. Amen.

[a]14 Or *whom*

Ephesians

INTRODUCTION

One writer called this work "the swan song of Paul the theologian." Indeed, it is less a letter than a song of faith with a long ethical exhortation added. The apostle Paul spent a long period of time at Ephesus, the capital of the Roman province of Asia in what is now western Asia Minor. If he had occasion to write a letter to that community, it would have been more personal and specific than this document. These facts, plus the absence of the name of the city of Ephesus in the best manuscripts, are some reasons why most scholars now attribute Ephesians to a disciple of Paul. Its purpose is to preserve in cultic language and poetic images the Pauline vision of God's universal saving plan.

The first half (omitting 3:1–14) is a carefully structured liturgy. It opens with a lofty hymn of thanks, celebrating the divine plan or sacred economy of universal salvation in Christ. The tone is one of sacred awe; the style is solemn and reflective (1:3–14). Then comes an intercessory prayer to appreciate the gifts that come with being a member of the Church, the body of Christ (1:15–23). How generously God has dealt with humanity is celebrated in the twofold narrative of remembering (2:1–22). On the one hand, God's grace has given new life to his chosen Jewish people. On the other hand, God has incorporated the Gentiles into the body of Christ to make one new people.

Once again the author breaks into a prayer of intercession, asking the Father to make Christ and his love dwell in all hearts (3:14–19). A doxology to God, who alone can grant these petitions, closes the first part of the letter (3:20–21). Into that liturgy is inserted a sketch of Paul's life in the form of an autobiography (3:1–14). He is the apostle of the plan revealed by God "in Christ"—the phrase that summarizes the mystery of God's saving will. This passage explains the Pauline origin of the teaching expressed here in cultic language.

In accord with the structure of a Pauline letter, an exhortation is added. It instructs the community about how to act as a cell of the body of Christ. This exhortation, similar to that of the Letter to the Colossians, is twofold: to unity (4:1–16) and to moral integrity (4:17—6:9). The sources of unity are

311

principally the Holy Spirit, the Lord Jesus and God the Father. The body-Eucharist, baptism and faith are included. Leaders like apostles, prophets and teachers make the body of Christ more responsive to Christ her Head or heavenly Spouse. From the risen Christ flow all the graces that are pictured like cosmic bonds linking the Church to the heavenly sphere to make her members grow in mutual love.

A long ethical code dominates the final exhortation (5:1—6:9). It is an appeal to carry out in personal relationships the cosmic reconciliation accomplished by Jesus. The code reflects but transforms similar instructions of Greek moral philosophers. It roots Christian moral conduct in the sacrificial love of Jesus. The song of faith ends with a famous description of the spiritual combat against the devil (6:10–20).

JAMES M. REESE, O.S.F.S.

Points for Reflection

1. A basic theme of this letter is unity of the faith. How is this unity accomplished (Eph 4)? A basic goal of the ecumenical movement is the unity of the Church. What is the common bond of Christians? How can I bridge the gap between my fellow Christians of other denominations?

2. "Be completely humble" (Eph 4:2). What is humility? How do I differentiate between being humble and being one who "tries to please everyone"?

3. Eph 4:30 urges: "Do not grieve the Holy Spirit." Have I grieved the Holy Spirit by my carelessness, negligence, or self-indulgence?

4. In 5:21—6:9, St. Paul describes the relationships in the Christian family. One description is the relationship between wives and husbands. How does God's relation to the world and to Israel, and Christ's relation to the Church supply a model and example for marriage?

5. "Be strong in the Lord," in order to combat against the devil. ". . . Take your stand against the devil's schemes." These exhortations are strongly stated by St. Paul. What evil forces do I meet with in my daily life that require a "full armor of God"? How have I "taken a stand against the devil's schemes," and allowed this evil influence to take hold of my life?

6. We are called to give thanks for everything (Eph 5:20). How can I be thankful to God while suffering loss and pain? Perhaps, we should look to the saints to be our models for this attitude.

7. We are exhorted to "put off your old self . . . and put on the new self." What steps can I take to become "like God in true righteousness and holiness"?

1 Paul, an apostle of Christ Jesus by the will of God,

To the saints in Ephesus,[a] the faithful[b] in Christ Jesus:

[2]Grace and peace to you from God our Father and the Lord Jesus Christ.

Spiritual Blessings in Christ

[3]Praise be to the God and Father of our Lord Jesus Christ, who has blessed us in the heavenly realms with every spiritual blessing in Christ. [4]For he chose us in him before the creation of the world to be holy and blameless in his sight. In love [5]he[c] predestined us to be adopted as his sons through Jesus Christ, in accordance with his pleasure and will— [6]to the praise of his glorious grace, which he has freely given us in the One he loves. [7]In him we have redemption through his blood, the forgiveness of sins, in accordance with the riches of God's grace [8]that he lavished on us with all wisdom and understanding. [9]And he[d] made known to us the mystery of his will according to his good pleasure, which he purposed in Christ, [10]to be put into effect when the times will have reached their fulfillment—to bring all things in heaven and on earth together under one head, even Christ.

[11]In him we were also chosen,[e] having been predestined according to the plan of him who works out everything in conformity with the purpose of his will, [12]in order that we, who were the first to hope in Christ, might be for the praise of his glory. [13]And you also were included in Christ when you heard the word of truth, the gospel of your salvation. Having believed, you were marked in him with a seal, the promised Holy Spirit, [14]who is a deposit guaranteeing our inheritance until the redemption of those who are God's possession—to the praise of his glory.

Thanksgiving and Prayer

[15]For this reason, ever since I heard about your faith in the Lord Jesus and your love for all the saints, [16]I have not stopped giving thanks for you, remembering you in my prayers. [17]I keep asking that the God of our Lord Jesus Christ, the glorious Father, may give you the Spirit[f] of wisdom and revelation, so that you may know him better. [18]I pray also that the eyes of your heart may be enlightened in order that you may know the hope to which he has called you, the riches of his glorious inheritance in the saints, [19]and his incomparably great power for us who believe. That power is like the working of his mighty strength, [20]which he exerted in Christ when he raised him from the dead and seated him at his right hand in the heavenly realms, [21]far above all rule and authority, power and dominion, and every title that can be given, not only in the present age but also in the one to come. [22]And God placed all things under his feet and appointed him to be head over everything for the church, [23]which is his body, the fullness of him who fills everything in every way.

---

[a]1 Some early manuscripts do not have *in Ephesus.*   [b]1 Or *believers who are*   [c]4,5 Or *sight in love.*
[5]*He*   [d]8,9 Or *us. With all wisdom and understanding,* [9]*he*   [e]11 Or *were made heirs*   [f]17 Or *a spirit*

Made Alive in Christ

2 As for you, you were dead in your transgressions and sins, [2]in which you used to live when you followed the ways of this world and of the ruler of the kingdom of the air, the spirit who is now at work in those who are disobedient. [3]All of us also lived among them at one time, gratifying the cravings of our sinful nature[a] and following its desires and thoughts. Like the rest, we were by nature objects of wrath. [4]But because of his great love for us, God, who is rich in mercy, [5]made us alive with Christ even when we were dead in transgressions—it is by grace you have been saved. [6]And God raised us up with Christ and seated us with him in the heavenly realms in Christ Jesus, [7]in order that in the coming ages he might show the incomparable riches of his grace, expressed in his kindness to us in Christ Jesus. [8]For it is by grace you have been saved, through faith—and this not from yourselves, it is the gift of God— [9]not by works, so that no one can boast. [10]For we are God's workmanship, created in Christ Jesus to do good works, which God prepared in advance for us to do.

One in Christ

[11]Therefore, remember that formerly you who are Gentiles by birth and called "uncircumcised" by those who call themselves "the circumcision" (that done in the body by the hands of men)— [12]remember that at that time you were separate from Christ, excluded from citizenship in Israel and foreigners to the covenants of the promise, without hope and without God in the world. [13]But now in Christ Jesus you who once were far away have been brought near through the blood of Christ.

[14]For he himself is our peace, who has made the two one and has destroyed the barrier, the dividing wall of hostility, [15]by abolishing in his flesh the law with its commandments and regulations. His purpose was to create in himself one new man out of the two, thus making peace, [16]and in this one body to reconcile both of them to God through the cross, by which he put to death their hostility. [17]He came and preached peace to you who were far away and peace to those who were near. [18]For through him we both have access to the Father by one Spirit.

[19]Consequently, you are no longer foreigners and aliens, but fellow citizens with God's people and members of God's household, [20]built on the foundation of the apostles and prophets, with Christ Jesus himself as the chief cornerstone. [21]In him the whole building is joined together and rises to become a holy temple in the Lord. [22]And in him you too are being built together to become a dwelling in which God lives by his Spirit.

Paul the Preacher to the Gentiles

3 For this reason I, Paul, the prisoner of Christ Jesus for the sake of you Gentiles—

[2]Surely you have heard about the administration of God's grace that

---

[a]3 Or *our flesh*

was given to me for you, ³that is, the mystery made known to me by revelation, as I have already written briefly. ⁴In reading this, then, you will be able to understand my insight into the mystery of Christ, ⁵which was not made known to men in other generations as it has now been revealed by the Spirit to God's holy apostles and prophets. ⁶This mystery is that through the gospel the Gentiles are heirs together with Israel, members together of one body, and sharers together in the promise in Christ Jesus.

⁷I became a servant of this gospel by the gift of God's grace given me through the working of his power. ⁸Although I am less than the least of all God's people, this grace was given me: to preach to the Gentiles the unsearchable riches of Christ, ⁹and to make plain to everyone the administration of this mystery, which for ages past was kept hidden in God, who created all things. ¹⁰His intent was that now, through the church, the manifold wisdom of God should be made known to the rulers and authorities in the heavenly realms, ¹¹according to his eternal purpose which he accomplished in Christ Jesus our Lord. ¹²In him and through faith in him we may approach God with freedom and confidence. ¹³I ask you, therefore, not to be discouraged because of my sufferings for you, which are your glory.

A Prayer for the Ephesians

¹⁴For this reason I kneel before the Father, ¹⁵from whom his whole family*ᵃ* in heaven and on earth derives its name. ¹⁶I pray that out of his glorious riches he may strengthen you with power through his Spirit in your inner being, ¹⁷so that Christ may dwell in your hearts through faith. And I pray that you, being rooted and established in love, ¹⁸may have power, together with all the saints, to grasp how wide and long and high and deep is the love of Christ, ¹⁹and to know this love that surpasses knowledge—that you may be filled to the measure of all the fullness of God.

²⁰Now to him who is able to do immeasurably more than all we ask or imagine, according to his power that is at work within us, ²¹to him be glory in the church and in Christ Jesus throughout all generations, for ever and ever! Amen.

Unity in the Body of Christ

4 As a prisoner for the Lord, then, I urge you to live a life worthy of the calling you have received. ²Be completely humble and gentle; be patient, bearing with one another in love. ³Make every effort to keep the unity of the Spirit through the bond of peace. ⁴There is one body and one Spirit— just as you were called to one hope when you were called— ⁵one Lord, one faith, one baptism; ⁶one God and Father of all, who is over all and through all and in all.

⁷But to each one of us grace has been given as Christ apportioned it. ⁸This is why it*ᵇ* says:

ᵃ15 Or whom all fatherhood   *ᵇ8 Or God*

> "When he ascended on high,
> he led captives in his train
> and gave gifts to men."[a]

[9](What does "he ascended" mean except that he also descended to the lower, earthly regions[b]? [10]He who descended is the very one who ascended higher than all the heavens, in order to fill the whole universe.) [11]It was he who gave some to be apostles, some to be prophets, some to be evangelists, and some to be pastors and teachers, [12]to prepare God's people for works of service, so that the body of Christ may be built up [13]until we all reach unity in the faith and in the knowledge of the Son of God and become mature, attaining to the whole measure of the fullness of Christ.

[14]Then we will no longer be infants, tossed back and forth by the waves, and blown here and there by every wind of teaching and by the cunning and craftiness of men in their deceitful scheming. [15]Instead, speaking the truth in love, we will in all things grow up into him who is the Head, that is, Christ. [16]From him the whole body, joined and held together by every supporting ligament, grows and builds itself up in love, as each part does its work.

Living as Children of Light

[17]So I tell you this, and insist on it in the Lord, that you must no longer live as the Gentiles do, in the futility of their thinking. [18]They are darkened in their understanding and separated from the life of God because of the ignorance that is in them due to the hardening of their hearts. [19]Having lost all sensitivity, they have given themselves over to sensuality so as to indulge in every kind of impurity, with a continual lust for more.

[20]You, however, did not come to know Christ that way. [21]Surely you heard of him and were taught in him in accordance with the truth that is in Jesus. [22]You were taught, with regard to your former way of life, to put off your old self, which is being corrupted by its deceitful desires; [23]to be made new in the attitude of your minds; [24]and to put on the new self, created to be like God in true righteousness and holiness.

[25]Therefore each of you must put off falsehood and speak truthfully to his neighbor, for we are all members of one body. [26]"In your anger do not sin"[c]: Do not let the sun go down while you are still angry, [27]and do not give the devil a foothold. [28]He who has been stealing must steal no longer, but must work, doing something useful with his own hands, that he may have something to share with those in need.

[29]Do not let any unwholesome talk come out of your mouths, but only what is helpful for building others up according to their needs, that it may benefit those who listen. [30]And do not grieve the Holy Spirit of God, with whom you were sealed for the day of redemption. [31]Get rid of all bitterness, rage and anger, brawling and slander, along with every form of malice. [32]Be

[a]8 Psalm 68:18   [b]9 Or *the depths of the earth*   [c]26 Psalm 4:4

kind and compassionate to one another, forgiving each other, just as in Christ God forgave you.

5 Be imitators of God, therefore, as dearly loved children [2]and live a life of love, just as Christ loved us and gave himself up for us as a fragrant offering and sacrifice to God.

[3]But among you there must not be even a hint of sexual immorality, or of any kind of impurity, or of greed, because these are improper for God's holy people. [4]Nor should there be obscenity, foolish talk or coarse joking, which are out of place, but rather thanksgiving. [5]For of this you can be sure: No immoral, impure or greedy person—such a man is an idolater—has any inheritance in the kingdom of Christ and of God.[a] [6]Let no one deceive you with empty words, for because of such things God's wrath comes on those who are disobedient. [7]Therefore do not be partners with them.

[8]For you were once darkness, but now you are light in the Lord. Live as children of light [9](for the fruit of the light consists in all goodness, righteousness and truth) [10]and find out what pleases the Lord. [11]Have nothing to do with the fruitless deeds of darkness, but rather expose them. [12]For it is shameful even to mention what the disobedient do in secret. [13]But everything exposed by the light becomes visible, [14]for it is light that makes everything visible. This is why it is said:

> "Wake up, O sleeper,
> rise from the dead,
> and Christ will shine on you."

[15]Be very careful, then, how you live—not as unwise but as wise, [16]making the most of every opportunity, because the days are evil. [17]Therefore do not be foolish, but understand what the Lord's will is. [18]Do not get drunk on wine, which leads to debauchery. Instead, be filled with the Spirit. [19]Speak to one another with psalms, hymns and spiritual songs. Sing and make music in your heart to the Lord, [20]always giving thanks to God the Father for everything, in the name of our Lord Jesus Christ.

[21]Submit to one another out of reverence for Christ.

Wives and Husbands

[22]Wives, submit to your husbands as to the Lord. [23]For the husband is the head of the wife as Christ is the head of the church, his body, of which he is the Savior. [24]Now as the church submits to Christ, so also wives should submit to their husbands in everything.

[25]Husbands, love your wives, just as Christ loved the church and gave himself up for her [26]to make her holy, cleansing[b] her by the washing with water through the word, [27]and to present her to himself as a radiant church, without stain or wrinkle or any other blemish, but holy and blameless. [28]In this same way, husbands ought to love their wives as their own bodies. He who loves his wife loves himself. [29]After all, no one ever hated his own body, but he feeds and cares for it, just as Christ does the church— [30]for

---

a5 Or *kingdom of the Christ and God*   *b26* Or *having cleansed* we are members of his body. [31]"For this reason a man will leave his father and mother and be united to his wife, and the two will become one flesh."[a] [32]This is a profound mystery—but I am talking about Christ and the church. [33]However, each one of you also must love his wife as he loves himself, and the wife must respect her husband.

Children and Parents

6 Children, obey your parents in the Lord, for this is right. [2]"Honor your father and mother"—which is the first commandment with a promise— [3]"that it may go well with you and that you may enjoy long life on the earth."[b]

[4]Fathers, do not exasperate your children; instead, bring them up in the training and instruction of the Lord.

Slaves and Masters

[5]Slaves, obey your earthly masters with respect and fear, and with sincerity of heart, just as you would obey Christ. [6]Obey them not only to win their favor when their eye is on you, but like slaves of Christ, doing the will of God from your heart. [7]Serve wholeheartedly, as if you were serving the Lord, not men, [8]because you know that the Lord will reward everyone for whatever good he does, whether he is slave or free.

[9]And masters, treat your slaves in the same way. Do not threaten them, since you know that he who is both their Master and yours is in heaven, and there is no favoritism with him.

The Armor of God

[10]Finally, be strong in the Lord and in his mighty power. [11]Put on the full armor of God so that you can take your stand against the devil's schemes. [12]For our struggle is not against flesh and blood, but against the rulers, against the authorities, against the powers of this dark world and against the spiritual forces of evil in the heavenly realms. [13]Therefore put on the full armor of God, so that when the day of evil comes, you may be able to stand your ground, and after you have done everything, to stand. [14]Stand firm then, with the belt of truth buckled around your waist, with the breastplate of righteousness in place, [15]and with your feet fitted with the readiness that comes from the gospel of peace. [16]In addition to all this, take up the shield of faith, with which you can extinguish all the flaming arrows of the evil one. [17]Take the helmet of salvation and the sword of the Spirit, which is the word of God. [18]And pray in the Spirit on all occasions with all kinds of prayers and requests. With this in mind, be alert and always keep on praying for all the saints.

[19]Pray also for me, that whenever I open my mouth, words may be given me so that I will fearlessly make known the mystery of the gospel, [20]for which I am an ambassador in chains. Pray that I may declare it fearlessly, as I should.

[a]31 Gen. 2:24   [b]3 Deut. 5:16

Final Greetings

[21]Tychicus, the dear brother and faithful servant in the Lord, will tell you everything, so that you also may know how I am and what I am doing. [22]I am sending him to you for this very purpose, that you may know how we are, and that he may encourage you.

[23]Peace to the brothers, and love with faith from God the Father and the Lord Jesus Christ. [24]Grace to all who love our Lord Jesus Christ with an undying love.

Philippians

INTRODUCTION

During the course of his second missionary journey Paul crossed to Philippi and finally entered the Western orbit, standing on another missionary frontier. Evidently he touched the heart of Lydia (Acts 16:14–15) and thus began his special mission and attachment to the people of Philippi. No one knows how long he preached there but we do know that the Church of Philippi would always remain loyal to Paul. Like their teacher, the Christians of Philippi would suffer (Phil 1:29–30) and out of this suffering, perhaps, was forged the closest of bonds between apostle and converts. Though reluctant to receive remuneration from other churches, Paul often accepted help from Philippi (Phil 4:15–16). He also held them up to the Corinthians as an example of generosity (2 Cor 8:1–5), and as a church they lived their faith united, with the presence of bishops and deacons suggesting an established order. The Christians at Philippi afforded Paul his deepest consolation, for they were his joy and his crown (Phil 4:1) and thus his letter to them reflects his great satisfaction with their commitment to the Lord.

The occasion of the letter was an expression of gratitude on the part of Paul for their most recent sign of affection and loyalty which they had offered through Epaphroditus (Phil 2:25; 4:18). In the letter, however, he also attacks Judaizers in language reminiscent of Galatians. The abrupt introduction of those who disparage the cross after an apparent farewell has led some commentators to ask whether our canonical letter to the Philippians is actually a combination of two or even three letters. The reader need not, however, be concerned with such an issue. Rather, the reader should listen to the words of Paul as addressed personally and be enveloped in the deep affection that existed between the preacher and the believers.

As Paul suffered, he became aware of the power of the resurrection and looked forward to heaven and transfiguration (Phil 3:20 –21). The hymn in the second chapter illuminates the entire letter and the teaching (kerygma) of Paul: the abasement of Jesus and his ultimate exaltation. Paul cautions the Philippians to work out their personal salvation with Christ, with "fear and trembling" (Phil 2:12). Then they too shall share in the exaltation.

The Philippians did not disparage the cross but Paul evidently knew that there were some enemies of the cross and wanted his favorites to be aware of the evil. The specter of the Judaizers shadowed Paul in his mission to the Gentiles but in espousing the crucified Christ, the Philippians joyfully espoused the cross.

The peace and joy and the saving presence of the Spirit would pervade their hearts and minds and would deepen as their trust in God increased (Phil 4:6). As they had been a source of joy to Paul, he cherished their association with him in spreading the happy news of salvation. Jesus is the Lord and to him all powers will offer their obeisance as the triumphant risen Lord.

JOHN F. O'GRADY

Points for Reflection

1. Find the passages where the apostle speaks of joy. Have I ever experienced this joy? What is the difference between Christian joy and happiness? Am I able to rejoice in the Lord when things are not going the way I had hoped they would?
2. Harmony and peace are characteristics of believers. Do I strive for these qualities in my family, in my parish? Do I try to find peace and understanding with those who have differing opinions and beliefs?
3. Gratitude is another characteristic of a Christian community. Am I thankful for God's blessings, even for the ones I do not see? Is my parish?
4. This letter conveys the message that the future offers salvation to all who believe. Do I really agree with this? "For to me, to live is Christ" (Phil 1:21) can only be announced when one has "let go" and "let God" take control. How do I allow Christ to live in me? Is there room for Christ in my life?
5. The apostle states that the enemies of the cross fail to see how the cross brings a share in the glory of Jesus. Do I fully understand this myself? Do I rejoice in suffering and pain, realizing that this is exactly what our Lord experienced and then three days later was resurrected in glory?
6. "I can do everything through him who gives me strength" (Phil 4:13). Have I found this to be a true statement? Have there been times when I felt that I could not endure or accomplish something but somehow found the strength to see it through?
7. Prayer was very central to St. Paul's life, and this letter expresses this. Is prayer central to my life? When I am anxious do I commit what is bothering me to prayer?
8. The letter concludes with greetings to all the saints or "holy ones" of the Church. Do I believe that I am called to be a saint? How does this calling affect the way I choose to live?

1 Paul and Timothy, servants of Christ Jesus,

To all the saints in Christ Jesus at Philippi, together with the overseers[a] and deacons:

[2]Grace and peace to you from God our Father and the Lord Jesus Christ.

Thanksgiving and Prayer

[3]I thank my God every time I remember you. [4]In all my prayers for all of you, I always pray with joy [5]because of your partnership in the gospel from the first day until now, [6]being confident of this, that he who began a good work in you will carry it on to completion until the day of Christ Jesus.

[7]It is right for me to feel this way about all of you, since I have you in my heart; for whether I am in chains or defending and confirming the gospel, all of you share in God's grace with me. [8]God can testify how I long for all of you with the affection of Christ Jesus.

[9]And this is my prayer: that your love may abound more and more in knowledge and depth of insight, [10]so that you may be able to discern what is best and may be pure and blameless until the day of Christ, [11]filled with the fruit of righteousness that comes through Jesus Christ—to the glory and praise of God.

Paul's Chains Advance the Gospel

[12]Now I want you to know, brothers, that what has happened to me has really served to advance the gospel. [13]As a result, it has become clear throughout the whole palace guard[b] and to everyone else that I am in chains for Christ. [14]Because of my chains, most of the brothers in the Lord have been encouraged to speak the word of God more courageously and fearlessly.

[15]It is true that some preach Christ out of envy and rivalry, but others out of goodwill. [16]The latter do so in love, knowing that I am put here for the defense of the gospel. [17]The former preach Christ out of selfish ambition, not sincerely, supposing that they can stir up trouble for me while I am in chains.[c] [18]But what does it matter? The important thing is that in every way, whether from false motives or true, Christ is preached. And because of this I rejoice.

Yes, and I will continue to rejoice, [19]for I know that through your prayers and the help given by the Spirit of Jesus Christ, what has happened to me will turn out for my deliverance.[d] [20]I eagerly expect and hope that I will in no way be ashamed, but will have sufficient courage so that now as always Christ will be exalted in my body, whether by life or by death. [21]For to me, to live is Christ and to die is gain. [22]If I am to go on living in the body, this will mean fruitful labor for me. Yet what shall I choose? I do not know! [23]I am torn between the two: I desire to depart and be with Christ, which

---

[a]1 Traditionally *bishops*   [b]13 Or *whole palace*   [c]16,17 Some late manuscripts have verses 16 and 17 in reverse order.   [d]19 Or *salvation*

is better by far; [24]but it is more necessary for you that I remain in the body. [25]Convinced of this, I know that I will remain, and I will continue with all of you for your progress and joy in the faith, [26]so that through my being with you again your joy in Christ Jesus will overflow on account of me.

[27]Whatever happens, conduct yourselves in a manner worthy of the gospel of Christ. Then, whether I come and see you or only hear about you in my absence, I will know that you stand firm in one spirit, contending as one man for the faith of the gospel [28]without being frightened in any way by those who oppose you. This is a sign to them that they will be destroyed, but that you will be saved—and that by God. [29]For it has been granted to you on behalf of Christ not only to believe on him, but also to suffer for him, [30]since you are going through the same struggle you saw I had, and now hear that I still have.

Imitating Christ's Humility

2 If you have any encouragement from being united with Christ, if any comfort from his love, if any fellowship with the Spirit, if any tenderness and compassion, [2]then make my joy complete by being like-minded, having the same love, being one in spirit and purpose. [3]Do nothing out of selfish ambition or vain conceit, but in humility consider others better than yourselves. [4]Each of you should look not only to your own interests, but also to the interests of others.

[5]Your attitude should be the same as that of Christ Jesus:

> [6]Who, being in very nature[a] God,
>   did not consider equality with God something to be
>   grasped,
> [7]but made himself nothing,
>   taking the very nature[b] of a servant,
>   being made in human likeness.
> [8]And being found in appearance as a man,
>   he humbled himself
>   and became obedient to death—
>   even death on a cross!
> [9]Therefore God exalted him to the highest place
>   and gave him the name that is above every name,
> [10]that at the name of Jesus every knee should bow,
>   in heaven and on earth and under the earth,
> [11]and every tongue confess that Jesus Christ is Lord,
>   to the glory of God the Father.

Shining as Stars

[12]Therefore, my dear friends, as you have always obeyed—not only in my presence, but now much more in my absence—continue to work out

[a]6 Or *in the form of*   [b]7 Or *the form*

your salvation with fear and trembling, [13]for it is God who works in you to will and to act according to his good purpose.

[14]Do everything without complaining or arguing, [15]so that you may become blameless and pure, children of God without fault in a crooked and depraved generation, in which you shine like stars in the universe [16]as you hold out[a] the word of life—in order that I may boast on the day of Christ that I did not run or labor for nothing. [17]But even if I am being poured out like a drink offering on the sacrifice and service coming from your faith, I am glad and rejoice with all of you. [18]So you too should be glad and rejoice with me.

Timothy and Epaphroditus

[19]I hope in the Lord Jesus to send Timothy to you soon, that I also may be cheered when I receive news about you. [20]I have no one else like him, who takes a genuine interest in your welfare. [21]For everyone looks out for his own interests, not those of Jesus Christ. [22]But you know that Timothy has proved himself, because as a son with his father he has served with me in the work of the gospel. [23]I hope, therefore, to send him as soon as I see how things go with me. [24]And I am confident in the Lord that I myself will come soon.

[25]But I think it is necessary to send back to you Epaphroditus, my brother, fellow worker and fellow soldier, who is also your messenger, whom you sent to take care of my needs. [26]For he longs for all of you and is distressed because you heard he was ill. [27]Indeed he was ill, and almost died. But God had mercy on him, and not on him only but also on me, to spare me sorrow upon sorrow. [28]Therefore I am all the more eager to send him, so that when you see him again you may be glad and I may have less anxiety. [29]Welcome him in the Lord with great joy, and honor men like him, [30]because he almost died for the work of Christ, risking his life to make up for the help you could not give me.

No Confidence in the Flesh

3 Finally, my brothers, rejoice in the Lord! It is no trouble for me to write the same things to you again, and it is a safeguard for you.

[2]Watch out for those dogs, those men who do evil, those mutilators of the flesh. [3]For it is we who are the circumcision, we who worship by the Spirit of God, who glory in Christ Jesus, and who put no confidence in the flesh— [4]though I myself have reasons for such confidence.

If anyone else thinks he has reasons to put confidence in the flesh, I have more: [5]circumcised on the eighth day, of the people of Israel, of the tribe of Benjamin, a Hebrew of Hebrews; in regard to the law, a Pharisee; [6]as for zeal, persecuting the church; as for legalistic righteousness, faultless.

[7]But whatever was to my profit I now consider loss for the sake of Christ. [8]What is more, I consider everything a loss compared to the surpassing greatness of knowing Christ Jesus my Lord, for whose sake I have lost

[a]16 Or hold on to

all things. I consider them rubbish, that I may gain Christ [9]and be found in him, not having a righteousness of my own that comes from the law, but that which is through faith in Christ—the righteousness that comes from God and is by faith. [10]I want to know Christ and the power of his resurrection and the fellowship of sharing in his sufferings, becoming like him in his death, [11]and so, somehow, to attain to the resurrection from the dead.

Pressing on Toward the Goal

[12]Not that I have already obtained all this, or have already been made perfect, but I press on to take hold of that for which Christ Jesus took hold of me. [13]Brothers, I do not consider myself yet to have taken hold of it. But one thing I do: Forgetting what is behind and straining toward what is ahead, [14]I press on toward the goal to win the prize for which God has called me heavenward in Christ Jesus.

[15]All of us who are mature should take such a view of things. And if on some point you think differently, that too God will make clear to you. [16]Only let us live up to what we have already attained.

[17]Join with others in following my example, brothers, and take note of those who live according to the pattern we gave you. [18]For, as I have often told you before and now say again even with tears, many live as enemies of the cross of Christ. [19]Their destiny is destruction, their god is their stomach, and their glory is in their shame. Their mind is on earthly things. [20]But our citizenship is in heaven. And we eagerly await a Savior from there, the Lord Jesus Christ, [21]who, by the power that enables him to bring everything under his control, will transform our lowly bodies so that they will be like his glorious body.

4 Therefore, my brothers, you whom I love and long for, my joy and crown, that is how you should stand firm in the Lord, dear friends!

Exhortations

[2]I plead with Euodia and I plead with Syntyche to agree with each other in the Lord. [3]Yes, and I ask you, loyal yokefellow,[a] help these women who have contended at my side in the cause of the gospel, along with Clement and the rest of my fellow workers, whose names are in the book of life.

[4]Rejoice in the Lord always. I will say it again: Rejoice! [5]Let your gentleness be evident to all. The Lord is near. [6]Do not be anxious about anything, but in everything, by prayer and petition, with thanksgiving, present your requests to God. [7]And the peace of God, which transcends all understanding, will guard your hearts and your minds in Christ Jesus.

[8]Finally, brothers, whatever is true, whatever is noble, whatever is right, whatever is pure, whatever is lovely, whatever is admirable—if anything is excellent or praiseworthy—think about such things. [9]Whatever you have learned or received or heard from me, or seen in me—put it into practice. And the God of peace will be with you.

[a]3 Or loyal Syzygus

Thanks for Their Gifts

[10]I rejoice greatly in the Lord that at last you have renewed your concern for me. Indeed, you have been concerned, but you had no opportunity to show it. [11]I am not saying this because I am in need, for I have learned to be content whatever the circumstances. [12]I know what it is to be in need, and I know what it is to have plenty. I have learned the secret of being content in any and every situation, whether well fed or hungry, whether living in plenty or in want. [13]I can do everything through him who gives me strength.

[14]Yet it was good of you to share in my troubles. [15]Moreover, as you Philippians know, in the early days of your acquaintance with the gospel, when I set out from Macedonia, not one church shared with me in the matter of giving and receiving, except you only; [16]for even when I was in Thessalonica, you sent me aid again and again when I was in need. [17]Not that I am looking for a gift, but I am looking for what may be credited to your account. [18]I have received full payment and even more; I am amply supplied, now that I have received from Epaphroditus the gifts you sent. They are a fragrant offering, an acceptable sacrifice, pleasing to God. [19]And my God will meet all your needs according to his glorious riches in Christ Jesus.

[20]To our God and Father be glory for ever and ever. Amen.

Final Greetings

[21]Greet all the saints in Christ Jesus. The brothers who are with me send greetings. [22]All the saints send you greetings, especially those who belong to Caesar's household.

[23]The grace of the Lord Jesus Christ be with your spirit. Amen. [a]

---

[a]23 Some manuscripts do not have *Amen.*

327

Colossians

INTRODUCTION

If the Letter to the Colossians does not read like a personal letter, the circumstances of its origin explain why. Paul was not the founder of this community in Asia Minor, and so what he knows about it comes from hearsay (1:4). Epaphras, mentioned in 1:7 and 4:12, first proclaimed the Gospel there. Now, about the year 60 A.D., he comes to the imprisoned Paul for help: how is he to instruct this community whose faith is threatened?

The letter is Paul's way of warning Christians at Colossae not to abandon their belief in the divine mission of Jesus Christ. This is more an essay than a letter; indeed, it is one of the most tightly structured writings of the New Testament. It is also one of the most difficult for modern readers to understand because we know almost nothing about the nature of this challenge to the role of Jesus Christ in the mystery of God's saving plan of salvation.

What complicates our reading is that Paul incorporates some of the cultic and ascetic terminology of rival teachers into these instructions. That is not surprising because he wanted to show how their teachings were contrary to true faith. Yet Paul's references make reading difficult for us who are neither familiar with this dispute nor with the prevailing apocalyptic atmosphere, that is, with the strong feeling that the final age of the world was at hand.

In proclaiming Jesus as unique reconciler, Paul penned the most lofty summary of his Christology—a hymn linking the place of Christ in creation, the first outpouring of God's saving grace, and in bringing eternal salvation to all (1:15–20). In two parallel stanzas Paul portrays this twofold mission of Jesus Christ: he is firstborn of God's creation, and he is firstborn from the dead. At the first stage, the pre-existing Christ was God's principal agent in creating, for God used him as model to create all creatures, not only on earth but in the heavenly places. In Christ were created even the spiritual powers that these rival teachers want the Colossians to worship. Paul rejects any cult of these powers, who are completely subordinate to Christ.

More important for Paul is Christ's role in humanity's reconciliation with God. As firstborn from the dead, Jesus is sole cause of our resurrection and model for all who will enter God's kingdom to share in divine glory. The earthly mission of Jesus was to reconcile all creation to the heavenly Father through his obedient and voluntary self-sacrifice on the cross.

Paul elaborates on this hymn in a profoundly theological instruction about the mystery of the reconciling work of Jesus (1:21—2:15). Paul is not content with abstractions. The mystery of Christ is a call to prayerful and wholehearted devotion to Jesus and to his body, the Church. Paul holds up his own zeal as a model of response for believers.

In his concluding directives Paul encourages vibrant and creative liturgies. He urges all members of the extended household to be responsible. He warns against stirring up social unrest. The mark of Christian responsibility is to act with Christ-like compassion and ethical integrity.

JAMES M. REESE, O.S.F.S.

Points for Reflection

1. The basic theme of Colossians is the supremacy of Christ over all things. Is Christ supreme in my life? Do I compromise my faith in Christ?
2. "See to it that no one takes you captive through hollow and deceptive philosophy" (Col 2:8). Is there any practice in my life that keeps me from living a Christian life?
3. The apostle's zeal for the faith is a model for all of us to follow. Are there any role models today either in my community or in the world for me to follow? How could I become a role model for my family? My parish?
4. "Forgive as the Lord forgave you" (Col 3:13). Is it easy for me to forgive those who have grieved and wronged me?
5. What does the letter say about prayer? Do I pray for others? Do I see how my prayers can affect other people's lives?

1 Paul, an apostle of Christ Jesus by the will of God, and Timothy our brother,

²To the holy and faithful*a* brothers in Christ at Colosse:

Grace and peace to you from God our Father.*b*

Thanksgiving and Prayer

³We always thank God, the Father of our Lord Jesus Christ, when we pray for you, ⁴because we have heard of your faith in Christ Jesus and of the love you have for all the saints— ⁵the faith and love that spring from the hope that is stored up for you in heaven and that you have already heard about in the word of truth, the gospel ⁶that has come to you. All over the world this gospel is bearing fruit and growing, just as it has been doing among you since the day you heard it and understood God's grace in all its truth. ⁷You learned it from Epaphras, our dear fellow servant, who is a faithful minister of Christ on our*c* behalf, ⁸and who also told us of your love in the Spirit.

⁹For this reason, since the day we heard about you, we have not stopped praying for you and asking God to fill you with the knowledge of his will through all spiritual wisdom and understanding. ¹⁰And we pray this in order that you may live a life worthy of the Lord and may please him in every way: bearing fruit in every good work, growing in the knowledge of God, ¹¹being strengthened with all power according to his glorious might so that you may have great endurance and patience, and joyfully ¹²giving thanks to the Father, who has qualified you*d* to share in the inheritance of the saints in the kingdom of light. ¹³For he has rescued us from the dominion of darkness and brought us into the kingdom of the Son he loves, ¹⁴in whom we have redemption,*e* the forgiveness of sins.

The Supremacy of Christ

¹⁵He is the image of the invisible God, the firstborn over all creation. ¹⁶For by him all things were created: things in heaven and on earth, visible and invisible, whether thrones or powers or rulers or authorities; all things were created by him and for him. ¹⁷He is before all things, and in him all things hold together. ¹⁸And he is the head of the body, the church; he is the beginning and the firstborn from among the dead, so that in everything he might have the supremacy. ¹⁹For God was pleased to have all his fullness dwell in him, ²⁰and through him to reconcile to himself all things, whether things on earth or things in heaven, by making peace through his blood, shed on the cross.

²¹Once you were alienated from God and were enemies in your minds because of*f* your evil behavior. ²²But now he has reconciled you by Christ's physical body through death to present you holy in his sight, without

*a*2 Or *believing*   *b*2 Some manuscripts *Father and the Lord Jesus Christ*   *c*7 Some manuscripts *your*
*d*12 Some manuscripts *us*   *e*14 A few late manuscripts *redemption through his blood*   *f*21 Or *minds, as shown by*

blemish and free from accusation— ²³if you continue in your faith, established and firm, not moved from the hope held out in the gospel. This is the gospel that you heard and that has been proclaimed to every creature under heaven, and of which I, Paul, have become a servant.

Paul's Labor for the Church

²⁴Now I rejoice in what was suffered for you, and I fill up in my flesh what is still lacking in regard to Christ's afflictions, for the sake of his body, which is the church. ²⁵I have become its servant by the commission God gave me to present to you the word of God in its fullness— ²⁶the mystery that has been kept hidden for ages and generations, but is now disclosed to the saints. ²⁷To them God has chosen to make known among the Gentiles the glorious riches of this mystery, which is Christ in you, the hope of glory.

²⁸We proclaim him, admonishing and teaching everyone with all wisdom, so that we may present everyone perfect in Christ. ²⁹To this end I labor, struggling with all his energy, which so powerfully works in me.

2 I want you to know how much I am struggling for you and for those at Laodicea, and for all who have not met me personally. ²My purpose is that they may be encouraged in heart and united in love, so that they may have the full riches of complete understanding, in order that they may know the mystery of God, namely, Christ, ³in whom are hidden all the treasures of wisdom and knowledge. ⁴I tell you this so that no one may deceive you by fine-sounding arguments. ⁵For though I am absent from you in body, I am present with you in spirit and delight to see how orderly you are and how firm your faith in Christ is.

Freedom From Human Regulations Through Life With Christ

⁶So then, just as you received Christ Jesus as Lord, continue to live in him, ⁷rooted and built up in him, strengthened in the faith as you were taught, and overflowing with thankfulness.

⁸See to it that no one takes you captive through hollow and deceptive philosophy, which depends on human tradition and the basic principles of this world rather than on Christ.

⁹For in Christ all the fullness of the Deity lives in bodily form, ¹⁰and you have been given fullness in Christ, who is the head over every power and authority. ¹¹In him you were also circumcised, in the putting off of the sinful nature,ᵃ not with a circumcision done by the hands of men but with the circumcision done by Christ, ¹²having been buried with him in baptism and raised with him through your faith in the power of God, who raised him from the dead.

¹³When you were dead in your sins and in the uncircumcision of your sinful nature,ᵇ God made youᶜ alive with Christ. He forgave us all our sins, ¹⁴having canceled the written code, with its regulations, that was against us and that stood opposed to us; he took it away, nailing it to the cross. ¹⁵And

ᵃ11 Or *the flesh*   ᵇ13 Or *your flesh*   ᶜ13 Some manuscripts *us* having disarmed the powers and authorities, he made a public spectacle of them, triumphing over them by the cross.[a]

[16]Therefore do not let anyone judge you by what you eat or drink, or with regard to a religious festival, a New Moon celebration or a Sabbath day. [17]These are a shadow of the things that were to come; the reality, however, is found in Christ. [18]Do not let anyone who delights in false humility and the worship of angels disqualify you for the prize. Such a person goes into great detail about what he has seen, and his unspiritual mind puffs him up with idle notions. [19]He has lost connection with the Head, from whom the whole body, supported and held together by its ligaments and sinews, grows as God causes it to grow.

[20]Since you died with Christ to the basic principles of this world, why, as though you still belonged to it, do you submit to its rules: [21]"Do not handle! Do not taste! Do not touch!"? [22]These are all destined to perish with use, because they are based on human commands and teachings. [23]Such regulations indeed have an appearance of wisdom, with their self-imposed worship, their false humility and their harsh treatment of the body, but they lack any value in restraining sensual indulgence.

Rules for Holy Living

3 Since, then, you have been raised with Christ, set your hearts on things above, where Christ is seated at the right hand of God. [2]Set your minds on things above, not on earthly things. [3]For you died, and your life is now hidden with Christ in God. [4]When Christ, who is your[b] life, appears, then you also will appear with him in glory.

[5]Put to death, therefore, whatever belongs to your earthly nature: sexual immorality, impurity, lust, evil desires and greed, which is idolatry. [6]Because of these, the wrath of God is coming.[c] [7]You used to walk in these ways, in the life you once lived. [8]But now you must rid yourselves of all such things as these: anger, rage, malice, slander, and filthy language from your lips. [9]Do not lie to each other, since you have taken off your old self with its practices [10]and have put on the new self, which is being renewed in knowledge in the image of its Creator. [11]Here there is no Greek or Jew, circumcised or uncircumcised, barbarian, Scythian, slave or free, but Christ is all, and is in all.

[12]Therefore, as God's chosen people, holy and dearly loved, clothe yourselves with compassion, kindness, humility, gentleness and patience. [13]Bear with each other and forgive whatever grievances you may have against one another. Forgive as the Lord forgave you. [14]And over all these virtues put on love, which binds them all together in perfect unity.

[15]Let the peace of Christ rule in your hearts, since as members of one body you were called to peace. And be thankful. [16]Let the word of Christ dwell in you richly as you teach and admonish one another with all wisdom, and as you sing psalms, hymns and spiritual songs with gratitude in your

---

[a]15 Or *them in him*   [b]4 Some manuscripts *our*   [c]6 Some early manuscripts *coming on those who are disobedient*

hearts to God. [17]And whatever you do, whether in word or deed, do it all in the name of the Lord Jesus, giving thanks to God the Father through him.

Rules for Christian Households

[18]Wives, submit to your husbands, as is fitting in the Lord.

[19]Husbands, love your wives and do not be harsh with them.

[20]Children, obey your parents in everything, for this pleases the Lord.

[21]Fathers, do not embitter your children, or they will become discouraged.

[22]Slaves, obey your earthly masters in everything; and do it, not only when their eye is on you and to win their favor, but with sincerity of heart and reverence for the Lord. [23]Whatever you do, work at it with all your heart, as working for the Lord, not for men, [24]since you know that you will receive an inheritance from the Lord as a reward. It is the Lord Christ you are serving. [25]Anyone who does wrong will be repaid for his wrong, and there is no favoritism.

4 Masters, provide your slaves with what is right and fair, because you know that you also have a Master in heaven.

Further Instructions

[2]Devote yourselves to prayer, being watchful and thankful. [3]And pray for us, too, that God may open a door for our message, so that we may proclaim the mystery of Christ, for which I am in chains. [4]Pray that I may proclaim it clearly, as I should. [5]Be wise in the way you act toward outsiders; make the most of every opportunity. [6]Let your conversation be always full of grace, seasoned with salt, so that you may know how to answer everyone.

Final Greetings

[7]Tychicus will tell you all the news about me. He is a dear brother, a faithful minister and fellow servant in the Lord. [8]I am sending him to you for the express purpose that you may know about our[a] circumstances and that he may encourage your hearts. [9]He is coming with Onesimus, our faithful and dear brother, who is one of you. They will tell you everything that is happening here.

[10]My fellow prisoner Aristarchus sends you his greetings, as does Mark, the cousin of Barnabas. (You have received instructions about him; if he comes to you, welcome him.) [11]Jesus, who is called Justus, also sends greetings. These are the only Jews among my fellow workers for the kingdom of God, and they have proved a comfort to me. [12]Epaphras, who is one of you and a servant of Christ Jesus, sends greetings. He is always wrestling in prayer for you, that you may stand firm in all the will of God, mature and fully assured. [13]I vouch for him that he is working hard for you and for those at Laodicea and Hierapolis. [14]Our dear friend Luke, the doctor, and

a8 Some manuscripts that he may know about your

Demas send greetings. ¹⁵Give my greetings to the brothers at Laodicea, and to Nympha and the church in her house.

¹⁶After this letter has been read to you, see that it is also read in the church of the Laodiceans and that you in turn read the letter from Laodicea.

¹⁷Tell Archippus: "See to it that you complete the work you have received in the Lord."

¹⁸I, Paul, write this greeting in my own hand. Remember my chains. Grace be with you.

1 Thessalonians

INTRODUCTION

Paul established a Christian community in Thessalonica in 49 A.D. during a soujourn there on his second missionary journey. Shortly afterward in Athens he learned of their sufferings, sent Timothy to investigate, and, upon hearing of their steadfast faith, wrote this first letter to strengthen them.

A second letter to the Thessalonians seems somewhat similar to the first, yet a careful reading of both uncovers some puzzles. Why does Paul say he certifies all his letters (2 Thes 3:14) to a community which has already received an earlier, "uncertified" letter (see the ending)? Why would Paul spell out a timetable for the day of the Lord (2 Thes 2:1–13) and say "remember . . . I used to tell you these things" but fail to have mentioned it in the first letter (1 Thes 4:13–18)? Though 2 Thessalonians repeats many phrases from 1 Thessalonians, there are differences in vocabulary, style, and perspective significant enough to support the conclusion of scholars that Paul wrote 1 Thessalonians but a disciple wrote 2 Thessalonians.

Even in 1 Thessalonians the strongly anti-Semitic segment (2:13–16) is considered to have been inserted perhaps by a persecuted Christian in a moment of triumphalistic vengeance. Nowhere else in Paul's letters are such sentiments echoed.

Nevertheless, modern scholarship respects Paul's authentic letters as reliable firsthand sources of information that ought not be interpreted or "corrected" by the Acts of the Apostles which was written some twenty to thirty years later. Thus Paul's claim that Christians at Thessalonica were converts from paganism (1 Thes 1:9) is preferred to Luke's report in Acts 17:4 that they were converts from Judaism. In this oldest of all Christian documents Paul establishes a new form of Christian communication. Watch it develop in his other letters.

The chief themes of the letters are (1) Christian behavioral guidelines and (2) proper understanding of the "end." Paul discourages futile calculations of the end but rather encourages fidelity to his teaching. The suffering of an apostle is best understood in the context of Jesus' suffering. The image of God the Father overshadows that of the Son in this letter.

JOHN J. PILCH

1 THESSALONIANS

Points for Reflection

1. What personal lessons can you draw from Paul's exhortations to his converts to remain faithful to their conversion (3:1–13)?
2. Paul urges believers to "win the respect" of non-believers ("outsiders," 4:11 –12). How might a modern believer do that? What result might be expected?
3. The return of the Lord is not as central in today's theology as it is in this letter. What "encouragement" on that topic does Paul's comment in 4:13–18 give you?

1 Paul, Silas[a] and Timothy,

To the church of the Thessalonians in God the Father and the Lord Jesus Christ:

Grace and peace to you.[b]

Thanksgiving for the Thessalonians' Faith

[2]We always thank God for all of you, mentioning you in our prayers. [3]We continually remember before our God and Father your work produced by faith, your labor prompted by love, and your endurance inspired by hope in our Lord Jesus Christ.

[4]For we know, brothers loved by God, that he has chosen you, [5]because our gospel came to you not simply with words, but also with power, with the Holy Spirit and with deep conviction. You know how we lived among you for your sake. [6]You became imitators of us and of the Lord; in spite of severe suffering, you welcomed the message with the joy given by the Holy Spirit. [7]And so you became a model to all the believers in Macedonia and Achaia. [8]The Lord's message rang out from you not only in Macedonia and Achaia—your faith in God has become known everywhere. Therefore we do not need to say anything about it, [9]for they themselves report what kind of reception you gave us. They tell how you turned to God from idols to serve the living and true God, [10]and to wait for his Son from heaven, whom he raised from the dead—Jesus, who rescues us from the coming wrath.

Paul's Ministry in Thessalonica

2 You know, brothers, that our visit to you was not a failure. [2]We had previously suffered and been insulted in Philippi, as you know, but with the help of our God we dared to tell you his gospel in spite of strong opposition. [3]For the appeal we make does not spring from error or impure motives, nor are we trying to trick you. [4]On the contrary, we speak as men approved by God to be entrusted with the gospel. We are not trying to please men but God, who tests our hearts. [5]You know we never used flattery, nor did we put on a mask to cover up greed—God is our witness. [6]We were not looking for praise from men, not from you or anyone else.

As apostles of Christ we could have been a burden to you, [7]but we were gentle among you, like a mother caring for her little children. [8]We loved you so much that we were delighted to share with you not only the gospel of God but our lives as well, because you had become so dear to us. [9]Surely you remember, brothers, our toil and hardship; we worked night and day in order not to be a burden to anyone while we preached the gospel of God to you.

[10]You are witnesses, and so is God, of how holy, righteous and blameless we were among you who believed. [11]For you know that we dealt with each of you as a father deals with his own children, [12]encouraging, comfort-

---

[a]1 Greek *Silvanus*, a variant of *Silas* [b]1 Some early manuscripts *you from God our Father and the Lord Jesus Christ*

ing and urging you to live lives worthy of God, who calls you into his kingdom and glory.

[13]And we also thank God continually because, when you received the word of God, which you heard from us, you accepted it not as the word of men, but as it actually is, the word of God, which is at work in you who believe. [14]For you, brothers, became imitators of God's churches in Judea, which are in Christ Jesus: You suffered from your own countrymen the same things those churches suffered from the Jews, [15]who killed the Lord Jesus and the prophets and also drove us out. They displease God and are hostile to all men [16]in their effort to keep us from speaking to the Gentiles so that they may be saved. In this way they always heap up their sins to the limit. The wrath of God has come upon them at last.[a]

Paul's Longing to See the Thessalonians

[17]But, brothers, when we were torn away from you for a short time (in person, not in thought), out of our intense longing we made every effort to see you. [18]For we wanted to come to you—certainly I, Paul, did, again and again—but Satan stopped us. [19]For what is our hope, our joy, or the crown in which we will glory in the presence of our Lord Jesus when he comes? Is it not you? [20]Indeed, you are our glory and joy.

3 So when we could stand it no longer, we thought it best to be left by ourselves in Athens. [2]We sent Timothy, who is our brother and God's fellow worker[b] in spreading the gospel of Christ, to strengthen and encourage you in your faith, [3]so that no one would be unsettled by these trials. You know quite well that we were destined for them. [4]In fact, when we were with you, we kept telling you that we would be persecuted. And it turned out that way, as you well know. [5]For this reason, when I could stand it no longer, I sent to find out about your faith. I was afraid that in some way the tempter might have tempted you and our efforts might have been useless.

Timothy's Encouraging Report

[6]But Timothy has just now come to us from you and has brought good news about your faith and love. He has told us that you always have pleasant memories of us and that you long to see us, just as we also long to see you. [7]Therefore, brothers, in all our distress and persecution we were encouraged about you because of your faith. [8]For now we really live, since you are standing firm in the Lord. [9]How can we thank God enough for you in return for all the joy we have in the presence of our God because of you? [10]Night and day we pray most earnestly that we may see you again and supply what is lacking in your faith.

[11]Now may our God and Father himself and our Lord Jesus clear the way for us to come to you. [12]May the Lord make your love increase and overflow for each other and for everyone else, just as ours does for you.

---

[a]16 Or them fully   [b]2 Some manuscripts brother and fellow worker; other manuscripts brother and God's servant

¹³May he strengthen your hearts so that you will be blameless and holy in the presence of our God and Father when our Lord Jesus comes with all his holy ones.

Living to Please God

4 Finally, brothers, we instructed you how to live in order to please God, as in fact you are living. Now we ask you and urge you in the Lord Jesus to do this more and more. ²For you know what instructions we gave you by the authority of the Lord Jesus.

³It is God's will that you should be sanctified: that you should avoid sexual immorality; ⁴that each of you should learn to control his own body* in a way that is holy and honorable, ⁵not in passionate lust like the heathen, who do not know God; ⁶and that in this matter no one should wrong his brother or take advantage of him. The Lord will punish men for all such sins, as we have already told you and warned you. ⁷For God did not call us to be impure, but to live a holy life. ⁸Therefore, he who rejects this instruction does not reject man but God, who gives you his Holy Spirit.

⁹Now about brotherly love we do not need to write to you, for you yourselves have been taught by God to love each other. ¹⁰And in fact, you do love all the brothers throughout Macedonia. Yet we urge you, brothers, to do so more and more.

¹¹Make it your ambition to lead a quiet life, to mind your own business and to work with your hands, just as we told you, ¹²so that your daily life may win the respect of outsiders and so that you will not be dependent on anybody.

The Coming of the Lord

¹³Brothers, we do not want you to be ignorant about those who fall asleep, or to grieve like the rest of men, who have no hope. ¹⁴We believe that Jesus died and rose again and so we believe that God will bring with Jesus those who have fallen asleep in him. ¹⁵According to the Lord's own word, we tell you that we who are still alive, who are left till the coming of the Lord, will certainly not precede those who have fallen asleep. ¹⁶For the Lord himself will come down from heaven, with a loud command, with the voice of the archangel and with the trumpet call of God, and the dead in Christ will rise first. ¹⁷After that, we who are still alive and are left will be caught up together with them in the clouds to meet the Lord in the air. And so we will be with the Lord forever. ¹⁸Therefore encourage each other with these words.

5 Now, brothers, about times and dates we do not need to write to you, ²for you know very well that the day of the Lord will come like a thief in the night. ³While people are saying, "Peace and safety," destruction will come on them suddenly, as labor pains on a pregnant woman, and they will not escape.

⁴But you, brothers, are not in darkness so that this day should surprise

*4 Or *learn to live with his own wife;* or *learn to acquire a wife*

you like a thief. [5]You are all sons of the light and sons of the day. We do not belong to the night or to the darkness. [6]So then, let us not be like others, who are asleep, but let us be alert and self-controlled. [7]For those who sleep, sleep at night, and those who get drunk, get drunk at night. [8]But since we belong to the day, let us be self-controlled, putting on faith and love as a breastplate, and the hope of salvation as a helmet. [9]For God did not appoint us to suffer wrath but to receive salvation through our Lord Jesus Christ. [10]He died for us so that, whether we are awake or asleep, we may live together with him. [11]Therefore encourage one another and build each other up, just as in fact you are doing.

Final Instructions

[12]Now we ask you, brothers, to respect those who work hard among you, who are over you in the Lord and who admonish you. [13]Hold them in the highest regard in love because of their work. Live in peace with each other. [14]And we urge you, brothers, warn those who are idle, encourage the timid, help the weak, be patient with everyone. [15]Make sure that nobody pays back wrong for wrong, but always try to be kind to each other and to everyone else.

[16]Be joyful always; [17]pray continually; [18]give thanks in all circumstances, for this is God's will for you in Christ Jesus.

[19]Do not put out the Spirit's fire; [20]do not treat prophecies with contempt. [21]Test everything. Hold on to the good. [22]Avoid every kind of evil.

[23]May God himself, the God of peace, sanctify you through and through. May your whole spirit, soul and body be kept blameless at the coming of our Lord Jesus Christ. [24]The one who calls you is faithful and he will do it.

[25]Brothers, pray for us. [26]Greet all the brothers with a holy kiss. [27]I charge you before the Lord to have this letter read to all the brothers.

[28]The grace of our Lord Jesus Christ be with you.

2 Thessalonians

INTRODUCTION

The community to which this letter was addressed (likely not Thessalonica at all) was disturbed by those preaching that the day of the Lord had already arrived. Many had quit working and lost interest in the demands of day-to-day living. The author recalls that Paul had addressed a similar problem in Thessalonica, so he composes this "imitation" letter under Paul's name and addresses it to the troubled communities who know and respect Paul's authority, sometime after 70 A.D.

Only the authority of Paul could check the two major problems troubling this community after his death: persecution and suffering suggesting that the end had already dawned, and a consequent loss of interest in living. His argument in 2 Thessalonians 2:1–13 is that the end has NOT come; life must go on. He congratulates the believers for their growth in faith and their perseverance and urges them to continue steadfastly.

JOHN J. PILCH

Points for Reflection

1. This letter seeks to defend and explain Paul's authentic teaching (2:2; 3:17). How do you recognize authentic teaching and protect it from distortion?
2. Remember to read 2:1–13 and 3:6–13 together. How can 2:1–13 help evaluate idle speculations about the Lord's second coming?
3. Does 3:6–13 apply primarily to "end of the world" inspired idleness or to all times? How do you know?

1 Paul, Silas[a] and Timothy,

To the church of the Thessalonians in God our Father and the Lord Jesus Christ:

[2]Grace and peace to you from God the Father and the Lord Jesus Christ.

Thanksgiving and Prayer

[3]We ought always to thank God for you, brothers, and rightly so, because your faith is growing more and more, and the love every one of you has for each other is increasing. [4]Therefore, among God's churches we boast about your perseverance and faith in all the persecutions and trials you are enduring.

[5]All this is evidence that God's judgment is right, and as a result you will be counted worthy of the kingdom of God, for which you are suffering. [6]God is just: He will pay back trouble to those who trouble you [7]and give relief to you who are troubled, and to us as well. This will happen when the Lord Jesus is revealed from heaven in blazing fire with his powerful angels. [8]He will punish those who do not know God and do not obey the gospel of our Lord Jesus. [9]They will be punished with everlasting destruction and shut out from the presence of the Lord and from the majesty of his power [10]on the day he comes to be glorified in his holy people and to be marveled at among all those who have believed. This includes you, because you believed our testimony to you.

[11]With this in mind, we constantly pray for you, that our God may count you worthy of his calling, and that by his power he may fulfill every good purpose of yours and every act prompted by your faith. [12]We pray this so that the name of our Lord Jesus may be glorified in you, and you in him, according to the grace of our God and the Lord Jesus Christ.[b]

The Man of Lawlessness

2 Concerning the coming of our Lord Jesus Christ and our being gathered to him, we ask you, brothers, [2]not to become easily unsettled or alarmed by some prophecy, report or letter supposed to have come from us, saying that the day of the Lord has already come. [3]Don't let anyone deceive you in any way, for that day will not come, until the rebellion occurs and the man of lawlessness[c] is revealed, the man doomed to destruction. [4]He will oppose and will exalt himself over everything that is called God or is worshiped, so that he sets himself up in God's temple, proclaiming himself to be God.

[5]Don't you remember that when I was with you I used to tell you these things? [6]And now you know what is holding him back, so that he may be revealed at the proper time. [7]For the secret power of lawlessness is already at work; but the one who now holds it back will continue to do so till he is taken out of the way. [8]And then the lawless one will be revealed, whom the Lord Jesus will overthrow with the breath of his mouth and destroy by

---

[a]1 Greek *Silvanus*, a variant of *Silas*   [b]12 Or *God and Lord, Jesus Christ*   [c]3 Some manuscripts *sin*

the splendor of his coming. ⁹The coming of the lawless one will be in accordance with the work of Satan displayed in all kinds of counterfeit miracles, signs and wonders, ¹⁰and in every sort of evil that deceives those who are perishing. They perish because they refused to love the truth and so be saved. ¹¹For this reason God sends them a powerful delusion so that they will believe the lie ¹²and so that all will be condemned who have not believed the truth but have delighted in wickedness.

Stand Firm

¹³But we ought always to thank God for you, brothers loved by the Lord, because from the beginning God chose you*ᵃ* to be saved through the sanctifying work of the Spirit and through belief in the truth. ¹⁴He called you to this through our gospel, that you might share in the glory of our Lord Jesus Christ. ¹⁵So then, brothers, stand firm and hold to the teachings*ᵇ* we passed on to you, whether by word of mouth or by letter.

¹⁶May our Lord Jesus Christ himself and God our Father, who loved us and by his grace gave us eternal encouragement and good hope, ¹⁷encourage your hearts and strengthen you in every good deed and word.

Request for Prayer

3 Finally, brothers, pray for us that the message of the Lord may spread rapidly and be honored, just as it was with you. ²And pray that we may be delivered from wicked and evil men, for not everyone has faith. ³But the Lord is faithful, and he will strengthen and protect you from the evil one. ⁴We have confidence in the Lord that you are doing and will continue to do the things we command. ⁵May the Lord direct your hearts into God's love and Christ's perseverance.

Warning Against Idleness

⁶In the name of the Lord Jesus Christ, we command you, brothers, to keep away from every brother who is idle and does not live according to the teaching*ᶜ* you received from us. ⁷For you yourselves know how you ought to follow our example. We were not idle when we were with you, ⁸nor did we eat anyone's food without paying for it. On the contrary, we worked night and day, laboring and toiling so that we would not be a burden to any of you. ⁹We did this, not because we do not have the right to such help, but in order to make ourselves a model for you to follow. ¹⁰For even when we were with you, we gave you this rule: "If a man will not work, he shall not eat."

¹¹We hear that some among you are idle. They are not busy; they are busybodies. ¹²Such people we command and urge in the Lord Jesus Christ to settle down and earn the bread they eat. ¹³And as for you, brothers, never tire of doing what is right.

¹⁴If anyone does not obey our instruction in this letter, take special note

---

ᵃ13 Some manuscripts because God chose you as his firstfruits   *ᵇ15 Or traditions*   *ᶜ6 Or tradition* of him. Do not associate with him, in order that he may feel ashamed. [15]Yet do not regard him as an enemy, but warn him as a brother.

Final Greetings

[16]Now may the Lord of peace himself give you peace at all times and in every way. The Lord be with all of you.

[17]I, Paul, write this greeting in my own hand, which is the distinguishing mark in all my letters. This is how I write.

[18]The grace of our Lord Jesus Christ be with you all.

1 Timothy

THE PASTORAL EPISTLES: INTRODUCTION

Around the end of the first century A.D. an anonymous author composed the two letters to Timothy and the letter to Titus, documents intended to provide a solid, stable base for the developing Church of the post-apostolic age. Attributing books written at a later date to a great person of an earlier age was an accepted practice in the ancient world, a practice evident in many books of the Bible. What is most important about all of these books is not who their human author was but the fact that they are recognized as pertaining to the scriptural conversation between the Spirit and the Chruch.

The letters to Timothy and Titus, although addressed to individuals, deal not with private matters but with advice for those holding pastoral office and with rulings concerning the organization of the Church. For this reason these three letters are usually referred to as the "Pastoral Epistles."

The end of the first century was a time of transition. The apostles and even their immediate disciples had passed from the scene. Earlier controversies had long been settled, the parousia had not arrived and it was increasingly evident that the Church would be around for a long time. The author of the Pastorals, therefore, composed these three letters establishing Paul as the apostolic authority par excellence and having Paul address two of his closest disciples on the organization of Church life for future generations.

The first two letters are addressed to Timothy, Paul's most outstanding fellow worker (Phil 2:19f). Although Timothy, who coauthored most of Paul's letters including his first (1 Thes 1:1), would hardly have been young (1 Ti 4:2; cf. 2 Ti 2:22) at the time of their composition, a later anonymous author used the youthful Timothy as a symbol of the trusted Church leader who receives his authority from an apostle and hands it on to the leaders of the Church at the end of the first century. The first letter to Timothy is primarily concerned with instructions on "how people ought to conduct themselves in God's household, which is the church of the living God" (3:15). This letter presupposes the existence of an organized Christian community with overseers (or bishops) and deacons

(3:1–12). The letter contains instructions on the prayer life of the community (ch. 2), on how its leaders are to conduct themselves (ch.3) and also on the conduct of other members of the community (ch. 5). Pervading the entire letter is a concern with the disruptive influence of false teachers. They are to be refuted by Timothy and subsequent Church leaders by adhering to the "sound doctrine that conforms to the glorious gospel of the blessed God, which he entrusted to me," i.e., to Paul (1:10f).

TERENCE J. KEEGAN, O.P.

Points for Reflection

1. This letter was addressed to the Church of an earlier age but its stabilizing influence is needed by the Church of every age. Do the leaders and others in the Church today measure up to the high standards set by this letter?
2. Do we, as members of the Church, bear responsibility for problems in the Church today? Do we "promote controversies rather than God's work" (1:4)? Do we want to be teachers of the law not knowing what we are talking about (1:7)?
3. Has the love of money caused us to wander from the faith (4:10)?

1 Paul, an apostle of Christ Jesus by the command of God our Savior and of Christ Jesus our hope,

²To Timothy my true son in the faith:

Grace, mercy and peace from God the Father and Christ Jesus our Lord.

Warning Against False Teachers of the Law

³As I urged you when I went into Macedonia, stay there in Ephesus so that you may command certain men not to teach false doctrines any longer ⁴nor to devote themselves to myths and endless genealogies. These promote controversies rather than God's work—which is by faith. ⁵The goal of this command is love, which comes from a pure heart and a good conscience and a sincere faith. ⁶Some have wandered away from these and turned to meaningless talk. ⁷They want to be teachers of the law, but they do not know what they are talking about or what they so confidently affirm.

⁸We know that the law is good if one uses it properly. ⁹We also know that law[a] is made not for the righteous but for lawbreakers and rebels, the ungodly and sinful, the unholy and irreligious; for those who kill their fathers or mothers, for murderers, ¹⁰for adulterers and perverts, for slave traders and liars and perjurers—and for whatever else is contrary to the sound doctrine ¹¹that conforms to the glorious gospel of the blessed God, which he entrusted to me.

The Lord's Grace to Paul

¹²I thank Christ Jesus our Lord, who has given me strength, that he considered me faithful, appointing me to his service. ¹³Even though I was once a blasphemer and a persecutor and a violent man, I was shown mercy because I acted in ignorance and unbelief. ¹⁴The grace of our Lord was poured out on me abundantly, along with the faith and love that are in Christ Jesus.

¹⁵Here is a trustworthy saying that deserves full acceptance: Christ Jesus came into the world to save sinners—of whom I am the worst. ¹⁶But for that very reason I was shown mercy so that in me, the worst of sinners, Christ Jesus might display his unlimited patience as an example for those who would believe on him and receive eternal life. ¹⁷Now to the King eternal, immortal, invisible, the only God, be honor and glory for ever and ever. Amen.

¹⁸Timothy, my son, I give you this instruction in keeping with the prophecies once made about you, so that by following them you may fight the good fight, ¹⁹holding on to faith and a good conscience. Some have rejected these and so have shipwrecked their faith. ²⁰Among them are Hymenaeus and Alexander, whom I have handed over to Satan to be taught not to blaspheme.

[a]9 Or *that the law*

Instructions on Worship

2 I urge, then, first of all, that requests, prayers, intercession and thanks-giving be made for everyone— ²for kings and all those in authority, that we may live peaceful and quiet lives in all godliness and holiness. ³This is good, and pleases God our Savior, ⁴who wants all men to be saved and to come to a knowledge of the truth. ⁵For there is one God and one mediator between God and men, the man Christ Jesus, ⁶who gave himself as a ransom for all men—the testimony given in its proper time. ⁷And for this purpose I was appointed a herald and an apostle—I am telling the truth, I am not lying—and a teacher of the true faith to the Gentiles.

⁸I want men everywhere to lift up holy hands in prayer, without anger or disputing.

⁹I also want women to dress modestly, with decency and propriety, not with braided hair or gold or pearls or expensive clothes, ¹⁰but with good deeds, appropriate for women who profess to worship God.

¹¹A woman should learn in quietness and full submission. ¹²I do not permit a woman to teach or to have authority over a man; she must be silent. ¹³For Adam was formed first, then Eve. ¹⁴And Adam was not the one deceived; it was the woman who was deceived and became a sinner. ¹⁵But women*ᵃ* will be saved*ᵇ* through childbearing—if they continue in faith, love and holiness with propriety.

Overseers and Deacons

3 Here is a trustworthy saying: If anyone sets his heart on being an overseer,*ᶜ* he desires a noble task. ²Now the overseer must be above reproach, the husband of but one wife, temperate, self-controlled, respect-able, hospitable, able to teach, ³not given to drunkenness, not violent but gentle, not quarrelsome, not a lover of money. ⁴He must manage his own family well and see that his children obey him with proper respect. ⁵(If anyone does not know how to manage his own family, how can he take care of God's church?) ⁶He must not be a recent convert, or he may become conceited and fall under the same judgment as the devil. ⁷He must also have a good reputation with outsiders, so that he will not fall into disgrace and into the devil's trap.

⁸Deacons, likewise, are to be men worthy of respect, sincere, not in-dulging in much wine, and not pursuing dishonest gain. ⁹They must keep hold of the deep truths of the faith with a clear conscience. ¹⁰They must first be tested; and then if there is nothing against them, let them serve as deacons.

¹¹In the same way, their wives*ᵈ* are to be women worthy of respect, not malicious talkers but temperate and trustworthy in everything.

¹²A deacon must be the husband of but one wife and must manage his

---

ᵃ15 Greek *she*   *ᵇ15* Or *restored*   *ᶜ1* Traditionally *bishop;* also in verse 2   *ᵈ11* Or *way,* deaconesses children and his household well. [13]Those who have served well gain an excellent standing and great assurance in their faith in Christ Jesus.

[14]Although I hope to come to you soon, I am writing you these instructions so that, [15]if I am delayed, you will know how people ought to conduct themselves in God's household, which is the church of the living God, the pillar and foundation of the truth. [16]Beyond all question, the mystery of godliness is great:

> He[a] appeared in a body,[b]
>   was vindicated by the Spirit,
> was seen by angels,
>   was preached among the nations,
> was believed on in the world,
>   was taken up in glory.

Instructions to Timothy

4 The Spirit clearly says that in later times some will abandon the faith and follow deceiving spirits and things taught by demons. [2]Such teachings come through hypocritical liars, whose consciences have been seared as with a hot iron. [3]They forbid people to marry and order them to abstain from certain foods, which God created to be received with thanksgiving by those who believe and who know the truth. [4]For everything God created is good, and nothing is to be rejected if it is received with thanksgiving, [5]because it is consecrated by the word of God and prayer.

[6]If you point these things out to the brothers, you will be a good minister of Christ Jesus, brought up in the truths of the faith and of the good teaching that you have followed. [7]Have nothing to do with godless myths and old wives' tales; rather, train yourself to be godly. [8]For physical training is of some value, but godliness has value for all things, holding promise for both the present life and the life to come.

[9]This is a trustworthy saying that deserves full acceptance [10](and for this we labor and strive), that we have put our hope in the living God, who is the Savior of all men, and especially of those who believe.

[11]Command and teach these things. [12]Don't let anyone look down on you because you are young, but set an example for the believers in speech, in life, in love, in faith and in purity. [13]Until I come, devote yourself to the public reading of Scripture, to preaching and to teaching. [14]Do not neglect your gift, which was given you through a prophetic message when the body of elders laid their hands on you.

[15]Be diligent in these matters; give yourself wholly to them, so that everyone may see your progress. [16]Watch your life and doctrine closely. Persevere in them, because if you do, you will save both yourself and your hearers.

[a]16 Some manuscripts God   [b]16 Or in the flesh

Advice About Widows, Elders and Slaves

5 Do not rebuke an older man harshly, but exhort him as if he were your father. Treat younger men as brothers, [2]older women as mothers, and younger women as sisters, with absolute purity.

[3]Give proper recognition to those widows who are really in need. [4]But if a widow has children or grandchildren, these should learn first of all to put their religion into practice by caring for their own family and so repaying their parents and grandparents, for this is pleasing to God. [5]The widow who is really in need and left all alone puts her hope in God and continues night and day to pray and to ask God for help. [6]But the widow who lives for pleasure is dead even while she lives. [7]Give the people these instructions, too, so that no one may be open to blame. [8]If anyone does not provide for his relatives, and especially for his immediate family, he has denied the faith and is worse than an unbeliever.

[9]No widow may be put on the list of widows unless she is over sixty, has been faithful to her husband, [a] [10]and is well known for her good deeds, such as bringing up children, showing hospitality, washing the feet of the saints, helping those in trouble and devoting herself to all kinds of good deeds.

[11]As for younger widows, do not put them on such a list. For when their sensual desires overcome their dedication to Christ, they want to marry. [12]Thus they bring judgment on themselves, because they have broken their first pledge. [13]Besides, they get into the habit of being idle and going about from house to house. And not only do they become idlers, but also gossips and busybodies, saying things they ought not to. [14]So I counsel younger widows to marry, to have children, to manage their homes and to give the enemy no opportunity for slander. [15]Some have in fact already turned away to follow Satan.

[16]If any woman who is a believer has widows in her family, she should help them and not let the church be burdened with them, so that the church can help those widows who are really in need.

[17]The elders who direct the affairs of the church well are worthy of double honor, especially those whose work is preaching and teaching. [18]For the Scripture says, "Do not muzzle the ox while it is treading out the grain," [b] and "The worker deserves his wages." [c] [19]Do not entertain an accusation against an elder unless it is brought by two or three witnesses. [20]Those who sin are to be rebuked publicly, so that the others may take warning.

[21]I charge you, in the sight of God and Christ Jesus and the elect angels, to keep these instructions without partiality, and to do nothing out of favoritism.

[22]Do not be hasty in the laying on of hands, and do not share in the sins of others. Keep yourself pure.

[a]9 Or *has had but one husband*   [b]18 Deut. 25:4   [c]18 Luke 10:7

²³Stop drinking only water, and use a little wine because of your stomach and your frequent illnesses.

²⁴The sins of some men are obvious, reaching the place of judgment ahead of them; the sins of others trail behind them. ²⁵In the same way, good deeds are obvious, and even those that are not cannot be hidden.

6 All who are under the yoke of slavery should consider their masters worthy of full respect, so that God's name and our teaching may not be slandered. ²Those who have believing masters are not to show less respect for them because they are brothers. Instead, they are to serve them even better, because those who benefit from their service are believers, and dear to them. These are the things you are to teach and urge on them.

Love of Money

³If anyone teaches false doctrines and does not agree to the sound instruction of our Lord Jesus Christ and to godly teaching, ⁴he is conceited and understands nothing. He has an unhealthy interest in controversies and quarrels about words that result in envy, strife, malicious talk, evil suspicions ⁵and constant friction between men of corrupt mind, who have been robbed of the truth and who think that godliness is a means to financial gain.

⁶But godliness with contentment is great gain. ⁷For we brought nothing into the world, and we can take nothing out of it. ⁸But if we have food and clothing, we will be content with that. ⁹People who want to get rich fall into temptation and a trap and into many foolish and harmful desires that plunge men into ruin and destruction. ¹⁰For the love of money is a root of all kinds of evil. Some people, eager for money, have wandered from the faith and pierced themselves with many griefs.

Paul's Charge to Timothy

¹¹But you, man of God, flee from all this, and pursue righteousness, godliness, faith, love, endurance and gentleness. ¹²Fight the good fight of the faith. Take hold of the eternal life to which you were called when you made your good confession in the presence of many witnesses. ¹³In the sight of God, who gives life to everything, and of Christ Jesus, who while testifying before Pontius Pilate made the good confession, I charge you ¹⁴to keep this command without spot or blame until the appearing of our Lord Jesus Christ, ¹⁵which God will bring about in his own time—God, the blessed and only Ruler, the King of kings and Lord of lords, ¹⁶who alone is immortal and who lives in unapproachable light, whom no one has seen or can see. To him be honor and might forever. Amen.

¹⁷Command those who are rich in this present world not to be arrogant nor to put their hope in wealth, which is so uncertain, but to put their hope in God, who richly provides us with everything for our enjoyment. ¹⁸Command them to do good, to be rich in good deeds, and to be generous and willing to share. ¹⁹In this way they will lay up treasure for themselves as

a firm foundation for the coming age, so that they may take hold of the life that is truly life.

[20]Timothy, guard what has been entrusted to your care. Turn away from godless chatter and the opposing ideas of what is falsely called knowledge, [21]which some have professed and in so doing have wandered from the faith.

Grace be with you.

2 Timothy

INTRODUCTION

Second Timothy also addresses the needs of the Church at the end of the first century. While 1 Timothy gave instructions on organized Church life in the name and on the authority of the apostle Paul, 2 Timothy is more concerned with establishing the nature and legitimacy of that authority.

Second Timothy is the most personal of all three Pastoral Epistles. It goes to great lengths to present Paul as the apostle par excellence who labored and suffered for the Gospel. There is concern for the conduct of Church leaders but there is no mention of the overseers and deacons of 1 Timothy. Instead Timothy himself is presented as the model of future Church leaders and is urged to model his behavior on that of Paul (3:10—4:8). An important emphasis of this letter is the continuance of the sound teaching that Paul has entrusted to Timothy (1:13–14), a continuance that is made possible by Timothy, in his turn, entrusting it "to reliable men who will also be qualified to teach others" (2:2). This letter, more than any other in the New Testament, emphasizes the continuity that exists between the present-day Church and the life and teaching of the apostles.

TERENCE J. KEEGAN, O.P.

Points for Reflection

1. The concern of this letter is with Church life in the future. Can we in the Church today see ourselves in continuity with the life, teaching and ministry of Paul?
2. Are we filled with apostolic zeal? Are we ever "ashamed to testify about our Lord" (1:8)? Are we reluctant to suffer for the sake of the Gospel? Do we, instead, look for new teachers who will say what our "itching ears want to hear" (4:3)?

1 Paul, an apostle of Christ Jesus by the will of God, according to the promise of life that is in Christ Jesus,

²To Timothy, my dear son:

Grace, mercy and peace from God the Father and Christ Jesus our Lord.

Encouragement to Be Faithful

³I thank God, whom I serve, as my forefathers did, with a clear conscience, as night and day I constantly remember you in my prayers. ⁴Recalling your tears, I long to see you, so that I may be filled with joy. ⁵I have been reminded of your sincere faith, which first lived in your grandmother Lois and in your mother Eunice and, I am persuaded, now lives in you also. ⁶For this reason I remind you to fan into flame the gift of God, which is in you through the laying on of my hands. ⁷For God did not give us a spirit of timidity, but a spirit of power, of love and of self-discipline.

⁸So do not be ashamed to testify about our Lord, or ashamed of me his prisoner. But join with me in suffering for the gospel, by the power of God, ⁹who has saved us and called us to a holy life—not because of anything we have done but because of his own purpose and grace. This grace was given us in Christ Jesus before the beginning of time, ¹⁰but it has now been revealed through the appearing of our Savior, Christ Jesus, who has destroyed death and has brought life and immortality to light through the gospel. ¹¹And of this gospel I was appointed a herald and an apostle and a teacher. ¹²That is why I am suffering as I am. Yet I am not ashamed, because I know whom I have believed, and am convinced that he is able to guard what I have entrusted to him for that day.

¹³What you heard from me, keep as the pattern of sound teaching, with faith and love in Christ Jesus. ¹⁴Guard the good deposit that was entrusted to you—guard it with the help of the Holy Spirit who lives in us.

¹⁵You know that everyone in the province of Asia has deserted me, including Phygelus and Hermogenes.

¹⁶May the Lord show mercy to the household of Onesiphorus, because he often refreshed me and was not ashamed of my chains. ¹⁷On the contrary, when he was in Rome, he searched hard for me until he found me. ¹⁸May the Lord grant that he will find mercy from the Lord on that day! You know very well in how many ways he helped me in Ephesus.

2 You then, my son, be strong in the grace that is in Christ Jesus. ²And the things you have heard me say in the presence of many witnesses entrust to reliable men who will also be qualified to teach others. ³Endure hardship with us like a good soldier of Christ Jesus. ⁴No one serving as a soldier gets involved in civilian affairs—he wants to please his commanding officer. ⁵Similarly, if anyone competes as an athlete, he does not receive the victor's crown unless he competes according to the rules. ⁶The hardworking farmer should be the first to receive a share of the crops. ⁷Reflect on what I am saying, for the Lord will give you insight into all this.

⁸Remember Jesus Christ, raised from the dead, descended from David.

This is my gospel, [9]for which I am suffering even to the point of being chained like a criminal. But God's word is not chained. [10]Therefore I endure everything for the sake of the elect, that they too may obtain the salvation that is in Christ Jesus, with eternal glory.

[11]Here is a trustworthy saying:

> If we died with him,
> we will also live with him;
> [12]if we endure,
> we will also reign with him.
> If we disown him,
> he will also disown us;
> [13]if we are faithless,
> he will remain faithful,
> for he cannot disown himself.

A Workman Approved by God

[14]Keep reminding them of these things. Warn them before God against quarreling about words; it is of no value, and only ruins those who listen. [15]Do your best to present yourself to God as one approved, a workman who does not need to be ashamed and who correctly handles the word of truth. [16]Avoid godless chatter, because those who indulge in it will become more and more ungodly. [17]Their teaching will spread like gangrene. Among them are Hymenaeus and Philetus, [18]who have wandered away from the truth. They say that the resurrection has already taken place, and they destroy the faith of some. [19]Nevertheless, God's solid foundation stands firm, sealed with this inscription: "The Lord knows those who are his,"[a] and, "Everyone who confesses the name of the Lord must turn away from wickedness."

[20]In a large house there are articles not only of gold and silver, but also of wood and clay; some are for noble purposes and some for ignoble. [21]If a man cleanses himself from the latter, he will be an instrument for noble purposes, made holy, useful to the Master and prepared to do any good work.

[22]Flee the evil desires of youth, and pursue righteousness, faith, love and peace, along with those who call on the Lord out of a pure heart. [23]Don't have anything to do with foolish and stupid arguments, because you know they produce quarrels. [24]And the Lord's servant must not quarrel; instead, he must be kind to everyone, able to teach, not resentful. [25]Those who oppose him he must gently instruct, in the hope that God will grant them repentance leading them to a knowledge of the truth, [26]and that they will come to their senses and escape from the trap of the devil, who has taken them captive to do his will.

[a]19 Num. 16:5 (see Septuagint)

Godlessness in the Last Days

3 But mark this: There will be terrible times in the last days. ²People will be lovers of themselves, lovers of money, boastful, proud, abusive, disobedient to their parents, ungrateful, unholy, ³without love, unforgiving, slanderous, without self-control, brutal, not lovers of the good, ⁴treacherous, rash, conceited, lovers of pleasure rather than lovers of God— ⁵having a form of godliness but denying its power. Have nothing to do with them.

⁶They are the kind who worm their way into homes and gain control over weak-willed women, who are loaded down with sins and are swayed by all kinds of evil desires, ⁷always learning but never able to acknowledge the truth. ⁸Just as Jannes and Jambres opposed Moses, so also these men oppose the truth—men of depraved minds, who, as far as the faith is concerned, are rejected. ⁹But they will not get very far because, as in the case of those men, their folly will be clear to everyone.

Paul's Charge to Timothy

¹⁰You, however, know all about my teaching, my way of life, my purpose, faith, patience, love, endurance, ¹¹persecutions, sufferings—what kinds of things happened to me in Antioch, Iconium and Lystra, the persecutions I endured. Yet the Lord rescued me from all of them. ¹²In fact, everyone who wants to live a godly life in Christ Jesus will be persecuted, ¹³while evil men and impostors will go from bad to worse, deceiving and being deceived. ¹⁴But as for you, continue in what you have learned and have become convinced of, because you know those from whom you learned it, ¹⁵and how from infancy you have known the holy Scriptures, which are able to make you wise for salvation through faith in Christ Jesus. ¹⁶All Scripture is God-breathed and is useful for teaching, rebuking, correcting and training in righteousness, ¹⁷so that the man of God may be thoroughly equipped for every good work.

4 In the presence of God and of Christ Jesus, who will judge the living and the dead, and in view of his appearing and his kingdom, I give you this charge: ²Preach the Word; be prepared in season and out of season; correct, rebuke and encourage—with great patience and careful instruction. ³For the time will come when men will not put up with sound doctrine. Instead, to suit their own desires, they will gather around them a great number of teachers to say what their itching ears want to hear. ⁴They will turn their ears away from the truth and turn aside to myths. ⁵But you, keep your head in all situations, endure hardship, do the work of an evangelist, discharge all the duties of your ministry.

⁶For I am already being poured out like a drink offering, and the time has come for my departure. ⁷I have fought the good fight, I have finished the race, I have kept the faith. ⁸Now there is in store for me the crown of righteousness, which the Lord, the righteous Judge, will award to me on that day—and not only to me, but also to all who have longed for his appearing.

Personal Remarks

[9]Do your best to come to me quickly, [10]for Demas, because he loved this world, has deserted me and has gone to Thessalonica. Crescens has gone to Galatia, and Titus to Dalmatia. [11]Only Luke is with me. Get Mark and bring him with you, because he is helpful to me in my ministry. [12]I sent Tychicus to Ephesus. [13]When you come, bring the cloak that I left with Carpus at Troas, and my scrolls, especially the parchments.

[14]Alexander the metalworker did me a great deal of harm. The Lord will repay him for what he has done. [15]You too should be on your guard against him, because he strongly opposed our message.

[16]At my first defense, no one came to my support, but everyone deserted me. May it not be held against them. [17]But the Lord stood at my side and gave me strength, so that through me the message might be fully proclaimed and all the Gentiles might hear it. And I was delivered from the lion's mouth. [18]The Lord will rescue me from every evil attack and will bring me safely to his heavenly kingdom. To him be glory for ever and ever. Amen

Final Greetings

[19]Greet Priscilla[a] and Aquila and the household of Onesiphorus. [20]Erastus stayed in Corinth, and I left Trophimus sick in Miletus. [21]Do your best to get here before winter. Eubulus greets you, and so do Pudens, Linus, Claudia and all the brothers.

[22]The Lord be with your spirit. Grace be with you.

---

[a]19 Greek *Prisca*, a variant of *Priscilla*

Titus

INTRODUCTION

Titus was a trusted assistant who served as Paul's personal envoy to Corinth (2 Cor 7:6f). This letter, however, like those to Timothy, is actually addressed to the needs of the Church at the end of the first century. Where Timothy was instructed on how to maintain order in an established community, Titus is instructed on bringing organization to a more recently emerging community. Titus' first task is to appoint elders and/or overseers in each town, giving his communities the same kind of hierarchical organization that already exists in Timothy's. While the letter to Titus expresses many of the same concerns found in 1 Timothy there is a greater emphasis on the need for Christians to settle down into stable, responsible communities. Each member is to fulfill his or her state in life, including slaves, and the community as a whole is to respect civil authority.

TERENCE J. KEEGAN

Points for Reflection

1. The Pastoral Epistles, and especially Titus, encourage a hard-working, Martha-like approach to Christianity (cf. Lk 10:38–41). While the validity of a Spirit-filled, dynamic approach is never denied, the letter to Titus stresses the more mundane, stabilizing aspects of the church.
2. We can all reflect on how appreciative we are of those who serve the Church as Marthas, perhaps as sextons in parish churches and administrators in diocesan offices. We can also consider how we regard those Martha-like aspects of our own lives. Do we accept our state and status in life? Do we fulfill our ongoing obligations as Christians, e.g., daily prayer, financial support of the Church, fidelity to the sacraments?

1 Paul, a servant of God and an apostle of Jesus Christ for the faith of God's elect and the knowledge of the truth that leads to godliness— [2]a faith and knowledge resting on the hope of eternal life, which God, who does not lie, promised before the beginning of time, [3]and at his appointed season he brought his word to light through the preaching entrusted to me by the command of God our Savior,

[4]To Titus, my true son in our common faith:

Grace and peace from God the Father and Christ Jesus our Savior.

Titus' Task on Crete

[5]The reason I left you in Crete was that you might straighten out what was left unfinished and appoint[a] elders in every town, as I directed you. [6]An elder must be blameless, the husband of but one wife, a man whose children believe and are not open to the charge of being wild and disobedient. [7]Since an overseer[b] is entrusted with God's work, he must be blameless —not overbearing, not quick-tempered, not given to drunkenness, not violent, not pursuing dishonest gain. [8]Rather he must be hospitable, one who loves what is good, who is self-controlled, upright, holy and disciplined. [9]He must hold firmly to the trustworthy message as it has been taught, so that he can encourage others by sound doctrine and refute those who oppose it.

[10]For there are many rebellious people, mere talkers and deceivers, especially those of the circumcision group. [11]They must be silenced, because they are ruining whole households by teaching things they ought not to teach—and that for the sake of dishonest gain. [12]Even one of their own prophets has said, "Cretans are always liars, evil brutes, lazy gluttons." [13]This testimony is true. Therefore, rebuke them sharply, so that they will be sound in the faith [14]and will pay no attention to Jewish myths or to the commands of those who reject the truth. [15]To the pure, all things are pure, but to those who are corrupted and do not believe, nothing is pure. In fact, both their minds and consciences are corrupted. [16]They claim to know God, but by their actions they deny him. They are detestable, disobedient and unfit for doing anything good.

What Must Be Taught to Various Groups

2 You must teach what is in accord with sound doctrine. [2]Teach the older men to be temperate, worthy of respect, self-controlled, and sound in faith, in love and in endurance.

[3]Likewise, teach the older women to be reverent in the way they live, not to be slanderers or addicted to much wine, but to teach what is good. [4]Then they can train the younger women to love their husbands and children, [5]to be self-controlled and pure, to be busy at home, to be kind, and to be subject to their husbands, so that no one will malign the word of God.

[6]Similarly, encourage the young men to be self-controlled. [7]In every-

---

[a]5 Or *ordain*   [b]7 Traditionally *bishop*

thing set them an example by doing what is good. In your teaching show integrity, seriousness ⁸and soundness of speech that cannot be condemned, so that those who oppose you may be ashamed because they have nothing bad to say about us.

⁹Teach slaves to be subject to their masters in everything, to try to please them, not to talk back to them, ¹⁰and not to steal from them, but to show that they can be fully trusted, so that in every way they will make the teaching about God our Savior attractive.

¹¹For the grace of God that brings salvation has appeared to all men. ¹²It teaches us to say "No" to ungodliness and worldly passions, and to live self-controlled, upright and godly lives in this present age, ¹³while we wait for the blessed hope—the glorious appearing of our great God and Savior, Jesus Christ, ¹⁴who gave himself for us to redeem us from all wickedness and to purify for himself a people that are his very own, eager to do what is good.

¹⁵These, then, are the things you should teach. Encourage and rebuke with all authority. Do not let anyone despise you.

Doing What Is Good

3 Remind the people to be subject to rulers and authorities, to be obedient, to be ready to do whatever is good, ²to slander no one, to be peaceable and considerate, and to show true humility toward all men.

³At one time we too were foolish, disobedient, deceived and enslaved by all kinds of passions and pleasures. We lived in malice and envy, being hated and hating one another. ⁴But when the kindness and love of God our Savior appeared, ⁵he saved us, not because of righteous things we had done, but because of his mercy. He saved us through the washing of rebirth and renewal by the Holy Spirit, ⁶whom he poured out on us generously through Jesus Christ our Savior, ⁷so that, having been justified by his grace, we might become heirs having the hope of eternal life. ⁸This is a trustworthy saying. And I want you to stress these things, so that those who have trusted in God may be careful to devote themselves to doing what is good. These things are excellent and profitable for everyone.

⁹But avoid foolish controversies and genealogies and arguments and quarrels about the law, because these are unprofitable and useless. ¹⁰Warn a divisive person once, and then warn him a second time. After that, have nothing to do with him. ¹¹You may be sure that such a man is warped and sinful; he is self-condemned.

Final Remarks

¹²As soon as I send Artemas or Tychicus to you, do your best to come to me at Nicopolis, because I have decided to winter there. ¹³Do everything you can to help Zenas the lawyer and Apollos on their way and see that they have everything they need. ¹⁴Our people must learn to devote themselves to doing what is good, in order that they may provide for daily necessities and not live unproductive lives.

[15]Everyone with me sends you greetings. Greet those who love us in the faith.

Grace be with you all.

Philemon

INTRODUCTION

This intensely personal letter of Paul reveals his heart in a unique way. It helps us see why St. John Chrysostom exclaimed, "The heart of Paul is the heart of Christ!" We know little about the circumstances of this letter except that it is linked to Paul's letter to the Colossians. In both cases he is in prison in Rome about 60 A.D. and mentions the same five coworkers: Epaphras, Mark, Aristarchus, Demas and Luke. In both, Paul greets Archippus and speaks of the return of the slave Onesimus. The letter to Philemon is much shorter. The only activity it discusses is Paul's sending Onesimus back to Colossae.

The address of the letter creates problems because it mentions not only Philemon but also Apphia, called "sister" in the Christian sense of fellow believer, and Archippus, identified as a fellow soldier in the spread of the Gospel, and the local house church. The difficulty is this: who is the host of this Christian community, Philemon or Archippus? The answer bears on the situation of Onesimus: is he a runaway slave or a slave on loan from the community? Most commentators judge that Philemon was both the slave owner and host of the house church.

We can accept this traditional interpretation and reconstruct the situation as follows. While still a pagan, Onesimus belied his name (which means "useful"), robbed Philemon and ran away. After arriving at Rome, he became an employee of Paul, whose preaching drew him to embrace the Christian faith. Paul would now like to retain him.

In the thanksgiving section Paul expresses gratitude to God that Philemon's faith has borne fruit, especially in his love and compassion toward his fellow Christians. That reputation gives Paul courage to send Onesimus back as his own dear son, for he brought him into the faith. Rather than acting on his authority as Christ's ambassador to emancipate Onesimus, Paul places that responsibility on the shoulders of Philemon. Paul hopes that he will recognize Onesimus as a brother in Christ and deal with him as he would deal with Paul himself. If there is any financial loss to be met, Paul will assume full responsibility. He'll pick up the bill!

Most modern readers are

surprised at Paul's manner of acting in this situation. We would prefer that Paul issue a public condemnation of slavery in the name of Jesus, or at least demand that this Christian slave owner free Onesimus and any other believing slaves he owns. How can Paul tolerate this evil institution within a Christian house church? But we can learn a profound truth if we look at Paul's priorities. To exhort through love is better than to command through authority. Only when Christians act through love will life on earth change.

This short letter can help the Church today to nourish a Christ-like love by openness to the grace of God poured into the hearts of believers at baptism. Freedom in Christ is a total commitment to the cross that accepts the burdens of social and political responsibility with discernment. A Christian's basic witness is to live according to the mind of Christ.

JAMES M. REESE, O.S.F.S.

Points for Reflection

1. A possible title for this epistle could be: "Two Prisoners Found Free in Christ." St. Paul considered himself to be a slave of Christ; Onesimus was considered a slave of labor. Once Onesimus became a Christian he was no longer a slave but a brother in the Lord. Do I treat my brethren in Christ fairly and equally? Is it possible to treat everyone the same way? What does this letter tell us about our real status and position in life?
2. How does this letter reflect Paul's view of pastoral care?
3. Obedience is part of our free response to God. The more perfect our obedience, the more perfect our experience of God's love. How does being obedient to Christ, and being motivated by his love, contrast with obedience to people in our lives who have authority over us?
4. Is my obedience to the Lord out of fear or out of love?

¹Paul, a prisoner of Christ Jesus, and Timothy our brother,

To Philemon our dear friend and fellow worker, ²to Apphia our sister, to Archippus our fellow soldier and to the church that meets in your home:

³Grace to you and peace from God our Father and the Lord Jesus Christ.

Thanksgiving and Prayer

⁴I always thank my God as I remember you in my prayers, ⁵because I hear about your faith in the Lord Jesus and your love for all the saints. ⁶I pray that you may be active in sharing your faith, so that you will have a full understanding of every good thing we have in Christ. ⁷Your love has given me great joy and encouragement, because you, brother, have refreshed the hearts of the saints.

Paul's Plea for Onesimus

⁸Therefore, although in Christ I could be bold and order you to do what you ought to do, ⁹yet I appeal to you on the basis of love. I then, as Paul— an old man and now also a prisoner of Christ Jesus— ¹⁰I appeal to you for my son Onesimus,ᵃ who became my son while I was in chains. ¹¹Formerly he was useless to you, but now he has become useful both to you and to me.

¹²I am sending him—who is my very heart—back to you. ¹³I would have liked to keep him with me so that he could take your place in helping me while I am in chains for the gospel. ¹⁴But I did not want to do anything without your consent, so that any favor you do will be spontaneous and not forced. ¹⁵Perhaps the reason he was separated from you for a little while was that you might have him back for good— ¹⁶no longer as a slave, but better than a slave, as a dear brother. He is very dear to me but even dearer to you, both as a man and as a brother in the Lord.

¹⁷So if you consider me a partner, welcome him as you would welcome me. ¹⁸If he has done you any wrong or owes you anything, charge it to me. ¹⁹I, Paul, am writing this with my own hand. I will pay it back—not to mention that you owe me your very self. ²⁰I do wish, brother, that I may have some benefit from you in the Lord; refresh my heart in Christ. ²¹Confident of your obedience, I write to you, knowing that you will do even more than I ask.

²²And one thing more: Prepare a guest room for me, because I hope to be restored to you in answer to your prayers.

²³Epaphras, my fellow prisoner in Christ Jesus, sends you greetings. ²⁴And so do Mark, Aristarchus, Demas and Luke, my fellow workers.

²⁵The grace of the Lord Jesus Christ be with your spirit.

ᵃ10 Onesimus means useful.

Hebrews

INTRODUCTION

The exact identity of the author, the date and the circumstances of the origin of Hebrews remain unknown. From the fourth century in the West and from the end of the second century in Alexandria the inscription is given to Paul. The literary characteristics and theological movement are so markedly different from Paul that even Origen (d. 253–4) accepted its Pauline authorship only in a wide sense and few commentators today, based on critical scholarship, would attribute the letter to Paul.

The careful reading of the letter—if in fact it is a letter since no greeting opens the work—shows some similarity with Pauline thought, but whether an actual disciple of Paul was responsible for the letter or whether the unknown author drew upon a common tradition with Paul remains an unanswered question. Like many of the books of the New Testament, the author of Hebrews cannot be identified.

Probably the author was a Jewish Christian of Hellenistic background. He contrasts the heavenly and earthly spheres of reality, with the latter being a shadow of the former. Such terminology smacks of Platonic influence.

The letter might rightly be called an exhortation (Heb 13:22) presented to ward off apostasy. The author might well have prepared a homily, not necessarily to be delivered but to be read, and in this homily he presented the major theme of the priesthood of Christ in such a way as to respond to the problem of apostasy.

Most commentators favor a date later than the year 70 A.D. The problem with such dating is the absence of any reference to the destruction of Jerusalem. Since the author attempts to show that the old covenant with its cult has been superseded, a reference in some way to the loss of the Temple would strengthen his case. Thus, some will favor a date prior to 70 A.D.

The place of origin also is unknown. The reference to "those from Italy" (Heb 13:24) might imply an origin in Rome but also might merely imply greetings from the individuals in the author's company who were originally from Italy.

The letter contains many major themes: God the Father's initiative in salvation; the divinity, priesthood and sacrificial death of Christ; the new covenant and its liturgical character which will influence the Christian life; and the priesthood of the faithful with its call for a profound faith, hope and love. The letter also contains many minor themes: God's judgment, the power of the Word, the second coming of Christ. Both the major and minor themes, however, are not presented for their own sake but to exhort readers, by promise or threat, to rise from their complacency and to renew and intensify their commitment to Christ. This fundamental pastoral purpose is seen particularly with regard to the central theme of the priesthood of Christ. The author presents his theology of the priesthood of Christ directed to the faithful as an example of self-sacrifice meant to encourage the believers, to give them comfort and to offer them a basis for hope.

Of all the writings of the New Testament, with the possible exception of Revelation, Hebrews is the great riddle. With patience, however, the reader gains entrance into the mind of the author and finds the reward of a vision of the Christian mystery which transcends time, circumstances and culture. The word of God is indeed the two-edge sword which continues to speak through Jesus, God's Son.

JOHN F. O'GRADY

Points for Reflection

1. This letter conveys the message that individual believers must continue to recommit themselves to the teachings of Jesus. Why is this process of continual recommitment necessary?
2. A characteristic of Christian commitment is self-sacrifice. What sacrifices have I made and/or am I willing to make in my life for a fellow Christian? Is it truly a sacrifice or a tolerable inconvenience that I am willing to endure for a while?
3. Dogmatic themes serve a pastoral need throughout this letter. What are some of those themes?
4. Christian virtues of faithfulness, sincerity, confidence and perseverance give comfort to the believer and to others. Have I practiced these virtues in my life? Do I practice them even during times of struggle?
5. God's word always remains powerful. Is this true in my life? Whose voices do I listen to and consider powerful? Is one of those voices God's?
6. The liturgy is the source and culmination of the Christian life. Do I agree with this statement? Do I participate in and live the liturgy to its fullest?

The Son Superior to Angels

1 In the past God spoke to our forefathers through the prophets at many times and in various ways, ²but in these last days he has spoken to us by his Son, whom he appointed heir of all things, and through whom he made the universe. ³The Son is the radiance of God's glory and the exact representation of his being, sustaining all things by his powerful word. After he had provided purification for sins, he sat down at the right hand of the Majesty in heaven. ⁴So he became as much superior to the angels as the name he has inherited is superior to theirs.

⁵For to which of the angels did God ever say,

"You are my Son;
today I have become your Father*ᵃ*"ᵇ?

Or again,

"I will be his Father,
and he will be my Son"ᶜ?

⁶And again, when God brings his firstborn into the world, he says,

"Let all God's angels worship him."ᵈ

⁷In speaking of the angels he says,

"He makes his angels winds,
his servants flames of fire."ᵉ

⁸But about the Son he says,

"Your throne, O God, will last for ever and ever,
and righteousness will be the scepter of your kingdom.
⁹You have loved righteousness and hated wickedness;
therefore God, your God, has set you above your
companions
by anointing you with the oil of joy."ᶠ

¹⁰He also says,

"In the beginning, O Lord, you laid the foundations of the
earth,
and the heavens are the work of your hands.
¹¹They will perish, but you remain;
they will all wear out like a garment.
¹²You will roll them up like a robe;
like a garment they will be changed.
But you remain the same,
and your years will never end."ᵍ

ᵃ5 Or *have begotten you*   ᵇ5 Psalm 2:7   ᶜ5 2 Samuel 7:14; 1 Chron. 17:13   ᵈ6 Deut. 32:43 (see Dead Sea Scrolls and Septuagint)   ᵉ7 Psalm 104:4   ᶠ9 Psalm 45:6,7   ᵍ12 Psalm 102:25-27

[13]To which of the angels did God ever say,

> "Sit at my right hand
> until I make your enemies
> a footstool for your feet"[a]?

[14]Are not all angels ministering spirits sent to serve those who will inherit salvation?

Warning to Pay Attention

2 We must pay more careful attention, therefore, to what we have heard, so that we do not drift away. [2]For if the message spoken by angels was binding, and every violation and disobedience received its just punishment, [3]how shall we escape if we ignore such a great salvation? This salvation, which was first announced by the Lord, was confirmed to us by those who heard him. [4]God also testified to it by signs, wonders and various miracles, and gifts of the Holy Spirit distributed according to his will.

Jesus Made Like His Brothers

[5]It is not to angels that he has subjected the world to come, about which we are speaking. [6]But there is a place where someone has testified:

> "What is man that you are mindful of him,
> the son of man that you care for him?
> [7]You made him a little[b] lower than the angels;
> you crowned him with glory and honor
> 8 and put everything under his feet."[c]

In putting everything under him, God left nothing that is not subject to him. Yet at present we do not see everything subject to him. [9]But we see Jesus, who was made a little lower than the angels, now crowned with glory and honor because he suffered death, so that by the grace of God he might taste death for everyone.

[10]In bringing many sons to glory, it was fitting that God, for whom and through whom everything exists, should make the author of their salvation perfect through suffering. [11]Both the one who makes men holy and those who are made holy are of the same family. So Jesus is not ashamed to call them brothers. [12]He says,

> "I will declare your name to my brothers;
> in the presence of the congregation I will sing your
> praises."[d]

[13]And again,

> "I will put my trust in him."[e]

And again he says,

---

[a]13 Psalm 110:1   [b]7 Or *him for a little while*; also in verse 9   [c]8 Psalm 8:4-6   [d]12 Psalm 22:22
[e]13 Isaiah 8:17

"Here am I, and the children God has given me."[a]

¹⁴Since the children have flesh and blood, he too shared in their humanity so that by his death he might destroy him who holds the power of death—that is, the devil— ¹⁵and free those who all their lives were held in slavery by their fear of death. ¹⁶For surely it is not angels he helps, but Abraham's descendants. ¹⁷For this reason he had to be made like his brothers in every way, in order that he might become a merciful and faithful high priest in service to God, and that he might make atonement for[b] the sins of the people. ¹⁸Because he himself suffered when he was tempted, he is able to help those who are being tempted.

Jesus Greater Than Moses

3 Therefore, holy brothers, who share in the heavenly calling, fix your thoughts on Jesus, the apostle and high priest whom we confess. ²He was faithful to the one who appointed him, just as Moses was faithful in all God's house. ³Jesus has been found worthy of greater honor than Moses, just as the builder of a house has greater honor than the house itself. ⁴For every house is built by someone, but God is the builder of everything. ⁵Moses was faithful as a servant in all God's house, testifying to what would be said in the future. ⁶But Christ is faithful as a son over God's house. And we are his house, if we hold on to our courage and the hope of which we boast.

Warning Against Unbelief

⁷So, as the Holy Spirit says:

"Today, if you hear his voice,
⁸ do not harden your hearts
as you did in the rebellion,
    during the time of testing in the desert,
⁹where your fathers tested and tried me
    and for forty years saw what I did.
¹⁰That is why I was angry with that generation,
    and I said, 'Their hearts are always going astray,
    and they have not known my ways.'
¹¹So I declared on oath in my anger,
    'They shall never enter my rest.' "[c]

¹²See to it, brothers, that none of you has a sinful, unbelieving heart that turns away from the living God. ¹³But encourage one another daily, as long as it is called Today, so that none of you may be hardened by sin's deceitfulness. ¹⁴We have come to share in Christ if we hold firmly till the end the confidence we had at first. ¹⁵As has just been said:

"Today, if you hear his voice,
    do not harden your hearts

a13 Isaiah 8:18   b17 Or *and that he might turn aside God's wrath, taking away*   c11 Psalm 95:7-11 as you did in the rebellion."[a]

[16]Who were they who heard and rebelled? Were they not all those Moses led out of Egypt? [17]And with whom was he angry for forty years? Was it not with those who sinned, whose bodies fell in the desert? [18]And to whom did God swear that they would never enter his rest if not to those who disobeyed[b]? [19]So we see that they were not able to enter, because of their unbelief.

A Sabbath-Rest for the People of God

4 Therefore, since the promise of entering his rest still stands, let us be careful that none of you be found to have fallen short of it. [2]For we also have had the gospel preached to us, just as they did; but the message they heard was of no value to them, because those who heard did not combine it with faith.[c] [3]Now we who have believed enter that rest, just as God has said,

> "So I declared on oath in my anger,
> 'They shall never enter my rest.' "[d]

And yet his work has been finished since the creation of the world. [4]For somewhere he has spoken about the seventh day in these words: "And on the seventh day God rested from all his work."[e] [5]And again in the passage above he says, "They shall never enter my rest."

[6]It still remains that some will enter that rest, and those who formerly had the gospel preached to them did not go in, because of their disobedience. [7]Therefore God again set a certain day, calling it Today, when a long time later he spoke through David, as was said before:

> "Today, if you hear his voice,
> do not harden your hearts."[a]

[8]For if Joshua had given them rest, God would not have spoken later about another day. [9]There remains, then, a Sabbath-rest for the people of God; [10]for anyone who enters God's rest also rests from his own work, just as God did from his. [11]Let us, therefore, make every effort to enter that rest, so that no one will fall by following their example of disobedience.

[12]For the word of God is living and active. Sharper than any double-edged sword, it penetrates even to dividing soul and spirit, joints and marrow; it judges the thoughts and attitudes of the heart. [13]Nothing in all creation is hidden from God's sight Everything is uncovered and laid bare before the eyes of him to whom we must give account.

Jesus the Great High Priest

[14]Therefore, since we have a great high priest who has gone through the heavens,[f] Jesus the Son of God, let us hold firmly to the faith we profess.

---

[a]15,7 Psalm 95:7,8   [b]18 Or *disbelieved*   [c]2 Many manuscripts *because they did not share in the faith*
of those who obeyed   [d]3 Psalm 95:11; also in verse 5   [e]4 Gen. 2:2   [f]14 Or *gone into heaven*

[15]For we do not have a high priest who is unable to sympathize with our weaknesses, but we have one who has been tempted in every way, just as we are—yet was without sin. [16]Let us then approach the throne of grace with confidence, so that we may receive mercy and find grace to help us in our time of need.

5 Every high priest is selected from among men and is appointed to represent them in matters related to God, to offer gifts and sacrifices for sins. [2]He is able to deal gently with those who are ignorant and are going astray, since he himself is subject to weakness. [3]This is why he has to offer sacrifices for his own sins, as well as for the sins of the people.

[4]No one takes this honor upon himself; he must be called by God, just as Aaron was. [5]So Christ also did not take upon himself the glory of becoming a high priest. But God said to him,

> "You are my Son;
> today I have become your Father.[a]"[b]

[6]And he says in another place,

> "You are a priest forever,
> in the order of Melchizedek."[c]

[7]During the days of Jesus' life on earth, he offered up prayers and petitions with loud cries and tears to the one who could save him from death, and he was heard because of his reverent submission. [8]Although he was a son, he learned obedience from what he suffered [9]and, once made perfect, he became the source of eternal salvation for all who obey him [10]and was designated by God to be high priest in the order of Melchizedek.

Warning Against Falling Away

[11]We have much to say about this, but it is hard to explain because you are slow to learn. [12]In fact, though by this time you ought to be teachers, you need someone to teach you the elementary truths of God's word all over again. You need milk, not solid food! [13]Anyone who lives on milk, being still an infant, is not acquainted with the teaching about righteousness. [14]But solid food is for the mature, who by constant use have trained themselves to distinguish good from evil.

6 Therefore let us leave the elementary teachings about Christ and go on to maturity, not laying again the foundation of repentance from acts that lead to death,[d] and of faith in God, [2]instruction about baptisms, the laying on of hands, the resurrection of the dead, and eternal judgment. [3]And God permitting, we will do so.

[4]It is impossible for those who have once been enlightened, who have tasted the heavenly gift, who have shared in the Holy Spirit, [5]who have tasted the goodness of the word of God and the powers of the coming age, [6]if they fall away, to be brought back to repentance, because[e] to their loss

---

[a]5 Or *have begotten you*   [b]5 Psalm 2:7   [c]6 Psalm 110:4   [d]1 Or *from useless rituals*   [e]6 Or *repentance while*

they are crucifying the Son of God all over again and subjecting him to public disgrace.

⁷Land that drinks in the rain often falling on it and that produces a crop useful to those for whom it is farmed receives the blessing of God. ⁸But land that produces thorns and thistles is worthless and is in danger of being cursed. In the end it will be burned.

⁹Even though we speak like this, dear friends, we are confident of better things in your case—things that accompany salvation. ¹⁰God is not unjust; he will not forget your work and the love you have shown him as you have helped his people and continue to help them. ¹¹We want each of you to show this same diligence to the very end, in order to make your hope sure. ¹²We do not want you to become lazy, but to imitate those who through faith and patience inherit what has been promised.

The Certainty of God's Promise

¹³When God made his promise to Abraham, since there was no one greater for him to swear by, he swore by himself, ¹⁴saying, "I will surely bless you and give you many descendants."ᵃ ¹⁵And so after waiting patiently, Abraham received what was promised.

¹⁶Men swear by someone greater than themselves, and the oath confirms what is said and puts an end to all argument. ¹⁷Because God wanted to make the unchanging nature of his purpose very clear to the heirs of what was promised, he confirmed it with an oath. ¹⁸God did this so that, by two unchangeable things in which it is impossible for God to lie, we who have fled to take hold of the hope offered to us may be greatly encouraged. ¹⁹We have this hope as an anchor for the soul, firm and secure. It enters the inner sanctuary behind the curtain, ²⁰where Jesus, who went before us, has entered on our behalf. He has become a high priest forever, in the order of Melchizedek.

Melchizedek the Priest

7 This Melchizedek was king of Salem and priest of God Most High. He met Abraham returning from the defeat of the kings and blessed him, ²and Abraham gave him a tenth of everything. First, his name means "king of righteousness"; then also, "king of Salem" means "king of peace." ³Without father or mother, without genealogy, without beginning of days or end of life, like the Son of God he remains a priest forever.

⁴Just think how great he was: Even the patriarch Abraham gave him a tenth of the plunder! ⁵Now the law requires the descendants of Levi who become priests to collect a tenth from the people—that is, their brothers— even though their brothers are descended from Abraham. ⁶This man, however, did not trace his descent from Levi, yet he collected a tenth from Abraham and blessed him who had the promises. ⁷And without doubt the lesser person is blessed by the greater. ⁸In the one case, the tenth is collected by men who die; but in the other case, by him who is declared to be living.

ᵃ14 Gen. 22:17

[9]One might even say that Levi, who collects the tenth, paid the tenth through Abraham, [10]because when Melchizedek met Abraham, Levi was still in the body of his ancestor.

Jesus Like Melchizedek

[11]If perfection could have been attained through the Levitical priesthood (for on the basis of it the law was given to the people), why was there still need for another priest to come—one in the order of Melchizedek, not in the order of Aaron? [12]For when there is a change of the priesthood, there must also be a change of the law. [13]He of whom these things are said belonged to a different tribe, and no one from that tribe has ever served at the altar. [14]For it is clear that our Lord descended from Judah, and in regard to that tribe Moses said nothing about priests. [15]And what we have said is even more clear if another priest like Melchizedek appears, [16]one who has become a priest not on the basis of a regulation as to his ancestry but on the basis of the power of an indestructible life. [17]For it is declared:

> "You are a priest forever,
>   in the order of Melchizedek."[a]

[18]The former regulation is set aside because it was weak and useless [19](for the law made nothing perfect), and a better hope is introduced, by which we draw near to God.

[20]And it was not without an oath! Others became priests without any oath, [21]but he became a priest with an oath when God said to him:

> "The Lord has sworn
>   and will not change his mind:
> 'You are a priest forever.' "[a]

[22]Because of this oath, Jesus has become the guarantee of a better covenant.

[23]Now there have been many of those priests, since death prevented them from continuing in office; [24]but because Jesus lives forever, he has a permanent priesthood. [25]Therefore he is able to save completely[b] those who come to God through him, because he always lives to intercede for them.

[26]Such a high priest meets our need—one who is holy, blameless, pure, set apart from sinners, exalted above the heavens. [27]Unlike the other high priests, he does not need to offer sacrifices day after day, first for his own sins, and then for the sins of the people. He sacrificed for their sins once for all when he offered himself. [28]For the law appoints as high priests men who are weak; but the oath, which came after the law, appointed the Son, who has been made perfect forever.

The High Priest of a New Covenant

8 The point of what we are saying is this: We do have such a high priest, who sat down at the right hand of the throne of the Majesty in heaven,

[a]17,21 Psalm 110:4   [b]25 Or forever

²and who serves in the sanctuary, the true tabernacle set up by the Lord, not by man.

³Every high priest is appointed to offer both gifts and sacrifices, and so it was necessary for this one also to have something to offer. ⁴If he were on earth, he would not be a priest, for there are already men who offer the gifts prescribed by the law. ⁵They serve at a sanctuary that is a copy and shadow of what is in heaven. This is why Moses was warned when he was about to build the tabernacle: "See to it that you make everything according to the pattern shown you on the mountain."ᵃ ⁶But the ministry Jesus has received is as superior to theirs as the covenant of which he is mediator is superior to the old one, and it is founded on better promises.

⁷For if there had been nothing wrong with that first covenant, no place would have been sought for another. ⁸But God found fault with the people and saidᵇ:

> "The time is coming, declares the Lord,
>   when I will make a new covenant
> with the house of Israel
>   and with the house of Judah.
> ⁹It will not be like the covenant
>   I made with their forefathers
> when I took them by the hand
>   to lead them out of Egypt,
> because they did not remain faithful to my covenant,
>   and I turned away from them,
>   declares the Lord.
> ¹⁰This is the covenant I will make with the house of Israel
>   after that time, declares the Lord.
> I will put my laws in their minds
>   and write them on their hearts.
> I will be their God,
>   and they will be my people.
> ¹¹No longer will a man teach his neighbor,
>   or a man his brother, saying, 'Know the Lord,'
> because they will all know me,
>   from the least of them to the greatest.
> ¹²For I will forgive their wickedness
>   and will remember their sins no more."ᶜ

¹³By calling this covenant "new," he has made the first one obsolete; and what is obsolete and aging will soon disappear.

Worship in the Earthly Tabernacle

9 Now the first covenant had regulations for worship and also an earthly sanctuary. ²A tabernacle was set up. In its first room were the lamp-

---

ᵃ5 Exodus 25:40   ᵇ8 Some manuscripts may be translated *fault and said to the people.*
ᶜ12 Jer. 31:31-34

stand, the table and the consecrated bread; this was called the Holy Place. [3]Behind the second curtain was a room called the Most Holy Place, [4]which had the golden altar of incense and the gold-covered ark of the covenant. This ark contained the gold jar of manna, Aaron's staff that had budded, and the stone tablets of the covenant. [5]Above the ark were the cherubim of the Glory, overshadowing the atonement cover.[a] But we cannot discuss these things in detail now.

[6]When everything had been arranged like this, the priests entered regularly into the outer room to carry on their ministry. [7]But only the high priest entered the inner room, and that only once a year, and never without blood, which he offered for himself and for the sins the people had committed in ignorance. [8]The Holy Spirit was showing by this that the way into the Most Holy Place had not yet been disclosed as long as the first tabernacle was still standing. [9]This is an illustration for the present time, indicating that the gifts and sacrifices being offered were not able to clear the conscience of the worshiper. [10]They are only a matter of food and drink and various ceremonial washings—external regulations applying until the time of the new order.

The Blood of Christ

[11]When Christ came as high priest of the good things that are already here,[b] he went through the greater and more perfect tabernacle that is not man-made, that is to say, not a part of this creation. [12]He did not enter by means of the blood of goats and calves; but he entered the Most Holy Place once for all by his own blood, having obtained eternal redemption. [13]The blood of goats and bulls and the ashes of a heifer sprinkled on those who are ceremonially unclean sanctify them so that they are outwardly clean. [14]How much more, then, will the blood of Christ, who through the eternal Spirit offered himself unblemished to God, cleanse our consciences from acts that lead to death,[c] so that we may serve the living God!

[15]For this reason Christ is the mediator of a new covenant, that those who are called may receive the promised eternal inheritance—now that he has died as a ransom to set them free from the sins committed under the first covenant.

[16]In the case of a will,[d] it is necessary to prove the death of the one who made it, [17]because a will is in force only when somebody has died; it never takes effect while the one who made it is living. [18]This is why even the first covenant was not put into effect without blood. [19]When Moses had proclaimed every commandment of the law to all the people, he took the blood of calves, together with water, scarlet wool and branches of hyssop, and sprinkled the scroll and all the people. [20]He said, "This is the blood of the covenant, which God has commanded you to keep."[e] [21]In the same way, he sprinkled with the blood both the tabernacle and everything used in its ceremonies. [22]In fact, the law requires that nearly everything be cleansed

---

[a]5 Traditionally *the mercy seat*   [b]11 Some early manuscripts *are to come*   [c]14 Or *from useless rituals*
[d]16 Same Greek word as *covenant*; also in verse 17   [e]20 Exodus 24:8

with blood, and without the shedding of blood there is no forgiveness.
²³It was necessary, then, for the copies of the heavenly things to be purified with these sacrifices, but the heavenly things themselves with better sacrifices than these. ²⁴For Christ did not enter a man-made sanctuary that was only a copy of the true one; he entered heaven itself, now to appear for us in God's presence. ²⁵Nor did he enter heaven to offer himself again and again, the way the high priest enters the Most Holy Place every year with blood that is not his own. ²⁶Then Christ would have had to suffer many times since the creation of the world. But now he has appeared once for all at the end of the ages to do away with sin by the sacrifice of himself. ²⁷Just as man is destined to die once, and after that to face judgment, ²⁸so Christ was sacrificed once to take away the sins of many people; and he will appear a second time, not to bear sin, but to bring salvation to those who are waiting for him.

Christ's Sacrifice Once for All

10 The law is only a shadow of the good things that are coming—not the realities themselves. For this reason it can never, by the same sacrifices repeated endlessly year after year, make perfect those who draw near to worship. ²If it could, would they not have stopped being offered? For the worshipers would have been cleansed once for all, and would no longer have felt guilty for their sins. ³But those sacrifices are an annual reminder of sins, ⁴because it is impossible for the blood of bulls and goats to take away sins.

⁵Therefore, when Christ came into the world, he said:

> "Sacrifice and offering you did not desire,
>   but a body you prepared for me;
> ⁶with burnt offerings and sin offerings
>   you were not pleased.
> ⁷Then I said, 'Here I am—it is written about me in the
>   scroll—
> I have come to do your will, O God.' "ᵃ

⁸First he said, "Sacrifices and offerings, burnt offerings and sin offerings you did not desire, nor were you pleased with them" (although the law required them to be made). ⁹Then he said, "Here I am, I have come to do your will." He sets aside the first to establish the second. ¹⁰And by that will, we have been made holy through the sacrifice of the body of Jesus Christ once for all.

¹¹Day after day every priest stands and performs his religious duties; again and again he offers the same sacrifices, which can never take away sins. ¹²But when this priest had offered for all time one sacrifice for sins, he sat down at the right hand of God. ¹³Since that time he waits for his enemies to be made his footstool, ¹⁴because by one sacrifice he has made perfect forever those who are being made holy.

ᵃ7 Psalm 40:6-8 (see Septuagint)

[15]The Holy Spirit also testifies to us about this. First he says:

[16]"This is the covenant I will make with them
after that time, says the Lord.
I will put my laws in their hearts,
and I will write them on their minds."[a]

[17]Then he adds:

"Their sins and lawless acts
I will remember no more."[b]

[18]And where these have been forgiven, there is no longer any sacrifice for sin.

A Call to Persevere

[19]Therefore, brothers, since we have confidence to enter the Most Holy Place by the blood of Jesus, [20]by a new and living way opened for us through the curtain, that is, his body, [21]and since we have a great priest over the house of God, [22]let us draw near to God with a sincere heart in full assurance of faith, having our hearts sprinkled to cleanse us from a guilty conscience and having our bodies washed with pure water. [23]Let us hold unswervingly to the hope we profess, for he who promised is faithful. [24]And let us consider how we may spur one another on toward love and good deeds. [25]Let us not give up meeting together, as some are in the habit of doing, but let us encourage one another—and all the more as you see the Day approaching.

[26]If we deliberately keep on sinning after we have received the knowledge of the truth, no sacrifice for sins is left, [27]but only a fearful expectation of judgment and of raging fire that will consume the enemies of God. [28]Anyone who rejected the law of Moses died without mercy on the testimony of two or three witnesses. [29]How much more severely do you think a man deserves to be punished who has trampled the Son of God under foot, who has treated as an unholy thing the blood of the covenant that sanctified him, and who has insulted the Spirit of grace? [30]For we know him who said, "It is mine to avenge; I will repay,"[c] and again, "The Lord will judge his people."[d] [31]It is a dreadful thing to fall into the hands of the living God.

[32]Remember those earlier days after you had received the light, when you stood your ground in a great contest in the face of suffering. [33]Sometimes you were publicly exposed to insult and persecution; at other times you stood side by side with those who were so treated. [34]You sympathized with those in prison and joyfully accepted the confiscation of your property, because you knew that you yourselves had better and lasting possessions.

[35]So do not throw away your confidence; it will be richly rewarded. [36]You need to persevere so that when you have done the will of God, you will receive what he has promised. [37]For in just a very little while,

[a]16 Jer. 31:33   [b]17 Jer. 31:34   [c]30 Deut. 32:35   [d]30 Deut. 32:36; Psalm 135:14

"He who is coming will come and will not delay.
38   But my righteous one*a* will live by faith.
And if he shrinks back,
I will not be pleased with him."*b*

39But we are not of those who shrink back and are destroyed, but of those who believe and are saved.

By Faith

11 Now faith is being sure of what we hope for and certain of what we do not see. 2This is what the ancients were commended for.

3By faith we understand that the universe was formed at God's command, so that what is seen was not made out of what was visible.

4By faith Abel offered God a better sacrifice than Cain did. By faith he was commended as a righteous man, when God spoke well of his offerings. And by faith he still speaks, even though he is dead.

5By faith Enoch was taken from this life, so that he did not experience death; he could not be found, because God had taken him away. For before he was taken, he was commended as one who pleased God. 6And without faith it is impossible to please God, because anyone who comes to him must believe that he exists and that he rewards those who earnestly seek him.

7By faith Noah, when warned about things not yet seen, in holy fear built an ark to save his family. By his faith he condemned the world and became heir of the righteousness that comes by faith.

8By faith Abraham, when called to go to a place he would later receive as his inheritance, obeyed and went, even though he did not know where he was going. 9By faith he made his home in the promised land like a stranger in a foreign country; he lived in tents, as did Isaac and Jacob, who were heirs with him of the same promise. 10For he was looking forward to the city with foundations, whose architect and builder is God.

11By faith Abraham, even though he was past age—and Sarah herself was barren—was enabled to become a father because he*c* considered him faithful who had made the promise. 12And so from this one man, and he as good as dead, came descendants as numerous as the stars in the sky and as countless as the sand on the seashore.

13All these people were still living by faith when they died. They did not receive the things promised; they only saw them and welcomed them from a distance. And they admitted that they were aliens and strangers on earth. 14People who say such things show that they are looking for a country of their own. 15If they had been thinking of the country they had left, they would have had opportunity to return. 16Instead, they were longing for a better country—a heavenly one. Therefore God is not ashamed to be called their God, for he has prepared a city for them.

17By faith Abraham, when God tested him, offered Isaac as a sacrifice.

a38 One early manuscript *But the righteous*   *b38* Hab. 2:3,4   *c11* Or *By faith even Sarah, who was*
past age, was enabled to bear children because she

He who had received the promises was about to sacrifice his one and only son, [18]even though God had said to him, "It is through Isaac that your offspring[a] will be reckoned."[b] [19]Abraham reasoned that God could raise the dead, and figuratively speaking, he did receive Isaac back from death.

[20]By faith Isaac blessed Jacob and Esau in regard to their future.

[21]By faith Jacob, when he was dying, blessed each of Joseph's sons, and worshiped as he leaned on the top of his staff.

[22]By faith Joseph, when his end was near, spoke about the exodus of the Israelites from Egypt and gave instructions about his bones.

[23]By faith Moses' parents hid him for three months after he was born, because they saw he was no ordinary child, and they were not afraid of the king's edict.

[24]By faith Moses, when he had grown up, refused to be known as the son of Pharaoh's daughter. [25]He chose to be mistreated along with the people of God rather than to enjoy the pleasures of sin for a short time. [26]He regarded disgrace for the sake of Christ as of greater value than the treasures of Egypt, because he was looking ahead to his reward. [27]By faith he left Egypt, not fearing the king's anger; he persevered because he saw him who is invisible. [28]By faith he kept the Passover and the sprinkling of blood, so that the destroyer of the firstborn would not touch the firstborn of Israel.

[29]By faith the people passed through the Red Sea[c] as on dry land; but when the Egyptians tried to do so, they were drowned.

[30]By faith the walls of Jericho fell, after the people had marched around them for seven days.

[31]By faith the prostitute Rahab, because she welcomed the spies, was not killed with those who were disobedient.[d]

[32]And what more shall I say? I do not have time to tell about Gideon, Barak, Samson, Jephthah, David, Samuel and the prophets, [33]who through faith conquered kingdoms, administered justice, and gained what was promised; who shut the mouths of lions, [34]quenched the fury of the flames, and escaped the edge of the sword; whose weakness was turned to strength; and who became powerful in battle and routed foreign armies. [35]Women received back their dead, raised to life again. Others were tortured and refused to be released, so that they might gain a better resurrection. [36]Some faced jeers and flogging, while still others were chained and put in prison. [37]They were stoned[e]; they were sawed in two; they were put to death by the sword. They went about in sheepskins and goatskins, destitute, persecuted and mistreated— [38]the world was not worthy of them. They wandered in deserts and mountains, and in caves and holes in the ground.

[39]These were all commended for their faith, yet none of them received what had been promised. [40]God had planned something better for us so that only together with us would they be made perfect.

---

[a]18 Greek seed   [b]18 Gen. 21:12   [c]29 That is, Sea of Reeds   [d]31 Or unbelieving   [e]37 Some early manuscripts stoned; they were put to the test;

God Disciplines His Sons

12 Therefore, since we are surrounded by such a great cloud of witnesses, let us throw off everything that hinders and the sin that so easily entangles, and let us run with perseverance the race marked out for us. [2]Let us fix our eyes on Jesus, the author and perfecter of our faith, who for the joy set before him endured the cross, scorning its shame, and sat down at the right hand of the throne of God. [3]Consider him who endured such opposition from sinful men, so that you will not grow weary and lose heart.

[4]In your struggle against sin, you have not yet resisted to the point of shedding your blood. [5]And you have forgotten that word of encouragement that addresses you as sons:

> "My son, do not make light of the Lord's discipline,
>   and do not lose heart when he rebukes you,
> [6]because the Lord disciplines those he loves,
>   and he punishes everyone he accepts as a son."[a]

[7]Endure hardship as discipline; God is treating you as sons. For what son is not disciplined by his father? [8]If you are not disciplined (and everyone undergoes discipline), then you are illegitimate children and not true sons. [9]Moreover, we have all had human fathers who disciplined us and we respected them for it. How much more should we submit to the Father of our spirits and live! [10]Our fathers disciplined us for a little while as they thought best; but God disciplines us for our good, that we may share in his holiness. [11]No discipline seems pleasant at the time, but painful. Later on, however, it produces a harvest of righteousness and peace for those who have been trained by it.

[12]Therefore, strengthen your feeble arms and weak knees. [13]"Make level paths for your feet,"[b] so that the lame may not be disabled, but rather healed.

Warning Against Refusing God

[14]Make every effort to live in peace with all men and to be holy; without holiness no one will see the Lord. [15]See to it that no one misses the grace of God and that no bitter root grows up to cause trouble and defile many. [16]See that no one is sexually immoral, or is godless like Esau, who for a single meal sold his inheritance rights as the oldest son. [17]Afterward, as you know, when he wanted to inherit this blessing, he was rejected. He could bring about no change of mind, though he sought the blessing with tears.

[18]You have not come to a mountain that can be touched and that is burning with fire; to darkness, gloom and storm; [19]to a trumpet blast or to such a voice speaking words that those who heard it begged that no further word be spoken to them, [20]because they could not bear what was commanded: "If even an animal touches the mountain, it must be stoned."[c]

a6 Prov. 3:11,12   b13 Prov. 4:26   c20 Exodus 19:12,13

²¹The sight was so terrifying that Moses said, "I am trembling with fear."*ᵃ*

²²But you have come to Mount Zion, to the heavenly Jerusalem, the city of the living God. You have come to thousands upon thousands of angels in joyful assembly, ²³to the church of the firstborn, whose names are written in heaven. You have come to God, the judge of all men, to the spirits of righteous men made perfect, ²⁴to Jesus the mediator of a new covenant, and to the sprinkled blood that speaks a better word than the blood of Abel.

²⁵See to it that you do not refuse him who speaks. If they did not escape when they refused him who warned them on earth, how much less will we, if we turn away from him who warns us from heaven? ²⁶At that time his voice shook the earth, but now he has promised, "Once more I will shake not only the earth but also the heavens."*ᵇ* ²⁷The words "once more" indicate the removing of what can be shaken—that is, created things—so that what cannot be shaken may remain.

²⁸Therefore, since we are receiving a kingdom that cannot be shaken, let us be thankful, and so worship God acceptably with reverence and awe, ²⁹for our "God is a consuming fire."*ᶜ*

Concluding Exhortations

13 Keep on loving each other as brothers. ²Do not forget to entertain strangers, for by so doing some people have entertained angels without knowing it. ³Remember those in prison as if you were their fellow prisoners, and those who are mistreated as if you yourselves were suffering.

⁴Marriage should be honored by all, and the marriage bed kept pure, for God will judge the adulterer and all the sexually immoral. ⁵Keep your lives free from the love of money and be content with what you have, because God has said,

"Never will I leave you;
never will I forsake you."*ᵈ*

⁶So we say with confidence,

"The Lord is my helper; I will not be afraid.
What can man do to me?"*ᵉ*

⁷Remember your leaders, who spoke the word of God to you. Consider the outcome of their way of life and imitate their faith. ⁸Jesus Christ is the same yesterday and today and forever.

⁹Do not be carried away by all kinds of strange teachings. It is good for our hearts to be strengthened by grace, not by ceremonial foods, which are of no value to those who eat them. ¹⁰We have an altar from which those who minister at the tabernacle have no right to eat.

¹¹The high priest carries the blood of animals into the Most Holy Place as a sin offering, but the bodies are burned outside the camp. ¹²And so Jesus also suffered outside the city gate to make the people holy through his own

*ᵃ*21 Deut. 9:19   *ᵇ*26 Haggai 2:6   *ᶜ*29 Deut. 4:24   *ᵈ*5 Deut. 31:6   *ᵉ*6 Psalm 118:6,7 blood. [13]Let us, then, go to him outside the camp, bearing the disgrace he bore. [14]For here we do not have an enduring city, but we are looking for the city that is to come.

[15]Through Jesus, therefore, let us continually offer to God a sacrifice of praise—the fruit of lips that confess his name. [16]And do not forget to do good and to share with others, for with such sacrifices God is pleased.

[17]Obey your leaders and submit to their authority. They keep watch over you as men who must give an account. Obey them so that their work will be a joy, not a burden, for that would be of no advantage to you.

[18]Pray for us. We are sure that we have a clear conscience and desire to live honorably in every way. [19]I particularly urge you to pray so that I may be restored to you soon.

[20]May the God of peace, who through the blood of the eternal covenant brought back from the dead our Lord Jesus, that great Shepherd of the sheep, [21]equip you with everything good for doing his will, and may he work in us what is pleasing to him, through Jesus Christ, to whom be glory for ever and ever. Amen.

[22]Brothers, I urge you to bear with my word of exhortation, for I have written you only a short letter.

[23]I want you to know that our brother Timothy has been released. If he arrives soon, I will come with him to see you.

[24]Greet all your leaders and all God's people. Those from Italy send you their greetings.

[25]Grace be with you all.

James

INTRODUCTION

The Letter of James is an exhortation to practice virtue, to have concern for the poor, and especially to manifest one's faith through good deeds (2:14ff). It seems to have been written in answer to a misunderstanding about Paul's teaching about justification by faith. Paul emphasized that we are saved through the cross and resurrection of Jesus Christ whom we accept in faith, and not by doing the works of the law. But an antinomian spirit crept in at Corinth and elsewhere, whereby an insistence on faith, not works, was used as an excuse for non-virtuous behavior. This of course was contrary to the teaching of Paul, for whom faith "expressing itself in love" (Gal 5:6), produces "work" (1 Thes 1:3), and prompts "acts" (2 Thes 1:11). True faith must certainly inform the way we live; salvation is not automatic (cf. 1 Cor 9:27; 10:12; 1 Thes 3:5; 2 Cor 5:10; Rom 2:6). James points this out: "Show me your faith without deeds, and I will show you my faith by what I do" (2:18).

Authorship and date of this letter are disputed. "James, a servant of God and of the Lord Jesus Christ" (1:1) has been traditionally identified with "James, the brother of the Lord" who was very active in the Jerusalem church and who was martyred there in 62 A.D. (Mk 6:3; Gal 1:19; Acts 15:13; Josephus, *Antiquities,* XX, 200), but the letter is not mentioned in the earliest list of inspired books accepted by the church in Rome about 170 A.D. (the Muratorian fragment), nor by such third century Christian writers as Tertullian and Cyprian of Carthage. First notice of the letter is found in Origen (3rd c.) who stated that it was not generally acknowledged as part of Sacred Scripture; Eusebius (4th c.) placed it among the disputed books. Yet in the fourth and fifth centuries it was accepted as inspired by the great doctors of the Church. Today it is part of the canon of inspired books. Such a tortuous history might be more easily explained if the author were not the famous "brother of the Lord" but a later Christian clarifying the meaning of "faith" which seems to have lost its dynamic character and which could be predicated even of demons (2:19). It may well have been written toward the end of the first century.

James emphasizes the importance of Christ's second

coming at the parousia for judgment and final salvation (2:5, 13–14; 3:1; 4:12; 5:1–11). He urges the Christians to persevere in their life of faith and to be patient "because the Lord's coming is near" (5:8); they are to live in peace with one another and are warned that "the Judge is standing at the door" (5:9). This is why James is so insistent on the need for demonstrating one's faith by good deeds.

Respect and care for the poor are stressed (2:1–17; 5:1–6). An attitude of humility is commended (3:13; 4:10, 13–16); a taming of the tongue is urged (3:1–12); and the non-judgment of others is encouraged (4:11–12).

Special attention is given to prayer. Those who submit themselves to God's will have every reason to believe that their prayers will be answered (4:1–10). Those who are ill are to call the elders of the Church to pray over them and to anoint them with oil in the name of the Lord; they will be healed in body and soul. (5:13–18).

JOSEPH F. WIMMER, O.S.A.

Points for Reflection

1. How authentic is my faith? Do I live it in humble submission to God, in trustful prayer, in active service to the poor? Will I persevere in times of temptation and trial?
2. Do I judge others? Is my speech hurtful to others?
3. Am I a peacemaker? Do I promote mercy and understanding? Am I willing to waive my "rights" especially in relation to the needy?

1 James, a servant of God and of the Lord Jesus Christ,

To the twelve tribes scattered among the nations:

Greetings.

Trials and Temptations

²Consider it pure joy, my brothers, whenever you face trials of many kinds, ³because you know that the testing of your faith develops perseverance. ⁴Perseverance must finish its work so that you may be mature and complete, not lacking anything. ⁵If any of you lacks wisdom, he should ask God, who gives generously to all without finding fault, and it will be given to him. ⁶But when he asks, he must believe and not doubt, because he who doubts is like a wave of the sea, blown and tossed by the wind. ⁷That man should not think he will receive anything from the Lord; ⁸he is a double-minded man, unstable in all he does.

⁹The brother in humble circumstances ought to take pride in his high position. ¹⁰But the one who is rich should take pride in his low position, because he will pass away like a wild flower. ¹¹For the sun rises with scorching heat and withers the plant; its blossom falls and its beauty is destroyed. In the same way, the rich man will fade away even while he goes about his business.

¹²Blessed is the man who perseveres under trial, because when he has stood the test, he will receive the crown of life that God has promised to those who love him.

¹³When tempted, no one should say, "God is tempting me." For God cannot be tempted by evil, nor does he tempt anyone; ¹⁴but each one is tempted when, by his own evil desire, he is dragged away and enticed. ¹⁵Then, after desire has conceived, it gives birth to sin; and sin, when it is full-grown, gives birth to death.

¹⁶Don't be deceived, my dear brothers. ¹⁷Every good and perfect gift is from above, coming down from the Father of the heavenly lights, who does not change like shifting shadows. ¹⁸He chose to give us birth through the word of truth, that we might be a kind of firstfruits of all he created.

Listening and Doing

¹⁹My dear brothers, take note of this: Everyone should be quick to listen, slow to speak and slow to become angry, ²⁰for man's anger does not bring about the righteous life that God desires. ²¹Therefore, get rid of all moral filth and the evil that is so prevalent and humbly accept the word planted in you, which can save you.

²²Do not merely listen to the word, and so deceive yourselves. Do what it says. ²³Anyone who listens to the word but does not do what it says is like a man who looks at his face in a mirror ²⁴and, after looking at himself, goes away and immediately forgets what he looks like. ²⁵But the man who looks intently into the perfect law that gives freedom, and continues to do

this, not forgetting what he has heard, but doing it—he will be blessed in what he does.

²⁶If anyone considers himself religious and yet does not keep a tight rein on his tongue, he deceives himself and his religion is worthless. ²⁷Religion that God our Father accepts as pure and faultless is this: to look after orphans and widows in their distress and to keep oneself from being polluted by the world.

Favoritism Forbidden

2 My brothers, as believers in our glorious Lord Jesus Christ, don't show favoritism. ²Suppose a man comes into your meeting wearing a gold ring and fine clothes, and a poor man in shabby clothes also comes in. ³If you show special attention to the man wearing fine clothes and say, "Here's a good seat for you," but say to the poor man, "You stand there" or "Sit on the floor by my feet," ⁴have you not discriminated among yourselves and become judges with evil thoughts?

⁵Listen, my dear brothers: Has not God chosen those who are poor in the eyes of the world to be rich in faith and to inherit the kingdom he promised those who love him? ⁶But you have insulted the poor. Is it not the rich who are exploiting you? Are they not the ones who are dragging you into court? ⁷Are they not the ones who are slandering the noble name of him to whom you belong?

⁸If you really keep the royal law found in Scripture, "Love your neighbor as yourself,"ᵃ you are doing right. ⁹But if you show favoritism, you sin and are convicted by the law as lawbreakers. ¹⁰For whoever keeps the whole law and yet stumbles at just one point is guilty of breaking all of it. ¹¹For he who said, "Do not commit adultery,"ᵇ also said, "Do not murder."ᶜ If you do not commit adultery but do commit murder, you have become a lawbreaker.

¹²Speak and act as those who are going to be judged by the law that gives freedom, ¹³because judgment without mercy will be shown to anyone who has not been merciful. Mercy triumphs over judgment!

Faith and Deeds

¹⁴What good is it, my brothers, if a man claims to have faith but has no deeds? Can such faith save him? ¹⁵Suppose a brother or sister is without clothes and daily food. ¹⁶If one of you says to him, "Go, I wish you well; keep warm and well fed," but does nothing about his physical needs, what good is it? ¹⁷In the same way, faith by itself, if it is not accompanied by action, is dead.

¹⁸But someone will say, "You have faith; I have deeds."

Show me your faith without deeds, and I will show you my faith by what I do. ¹⁹You believe that there is one God. Good! Even the demons believe that—and shudder. ²⁰You foolish man, do you want evidence that faith without deeds is

ᵃ8 Lev. 19:18   ᵇ11 Exodus 20:14; Deut. 5:18   ᶜ11 Exodus 20:13; Deut. 5:17

useless*a*? [21]Was not our ancestor Abraham considered righteous for what he did when he offered his son Isaac on the altar? [22]You see that his faith and his actions were working together, and his faith was made complete by what he did. [23]And the scripture was fulfilled that says, "Abraham believed God, and it was credited to him as righteousness,"*b* and he was called God's friend. [24]You see that a person is justified by what he does and not by faith alone.

[25]In the same way, was not even Rahab the prostitute considered righteous for what she did when she gave lodging to the spies and sent them off in a different direction? [26]As the body without the spirit is dead, so faith without deeds is dead.

Taming the Tongue

3 Not many of you should presume to be teachers, my brothers, because you know that we who teach will be judged more strictly. [2]We all stumble in many ways. If anyone is never at fault in what he says, he is a perfect man, able to keep his whole body in check.

[3]When we put bits into the mouths of horses to make them obey us, we can turn the whole animal. [4]Or take ships as an example. Although they are so large and are driven by strong winds, they are steered by a very small rudder wherever the pilot wants to go. [5]Likewise the tongue is a small part of the body, but it makes great boasts. Consider what a great forest is set on fire by a small spark. [6]The tongue also is a fire, a world of evil among the parts of the body. It corrupts the whole person, sets the whole course of his life on fire, and is itself set on fire by hell.

[7]All kinds of animals, birds, reptiles and creatures of the sea are being tamed and have been tamed by man, [8]but no man can tame the tongue. It is a restless evil, full of deadly poison.

[9]With the tongue we praise our Lord and Father, and with it we curse men, who have been made in God's likeness. [10]Out of the same mouth come praise and cursing. My brothers, this should not be. [11]Can both fresh water and salt*c* water flow from the same spring? [12]My brothers, can a fig tree bear olives, or a grapevine bear figs? Neither can a salt spring produce fresh water.

Two Kinds of Wisdom

[13]Who is wise and understanding among you? Let him show it by his good life, by deeds done in the humility that comes from wisdom. [14]But if you harbor bitter envy and selfish ambition in your hearts, do not boast about it or deny the truth. [15]Such "wisdom" does not come down from heaven but is earthly, unspiritual, of the devil. [16]For where you have envy and selfish ambition, there you find disorder and every evil practice.

[17]But the wisdom that comes from heaven is first of all pure; then peace-loving, considerate, submissive, full of mercy and good fruit, impartial and sincere. [18]Peacemakers who sow in peace raise a harvest of righteousness.

*a*20 Some early manuscripts *dead*   *b*23 Gen. 15:6   *c*11 Greek *bitter* (see also verse 14)

Submit Yourselves to God

4 What causes fights and quarrels among you? Don't they come from your desires that battle within you? [2]You want something but don't get it. You kill and covet, but you cannot have what you want. You quarrel and fight. You do not have, because you do not ask God. [3]When you ask, you do not receive, because you ask with wrong motives, that you may spend what you get on your pleasures.

[4]You adulterous people, don't you know that friendship with the world is hatred toward God? Anyone who chooses to be a friend of the world becomes an enemy of God. [5]Or do you think Scripture says without reason that the spirit he caused to live in us envies intensely?[a] [6]But he gives us more grace. That is why Scripture says:

> "God opposes the proud
>   but gives grace to the humble."[b]

[7]Submit yourselves, then, to God. Resist the devil, and he will flee from you. [8]Come near to God and he will come near to you. Wash your hands, you sinners, and purify your hearts, you double-minded. [9]Grieve, mourn and wail. Change your laughter to mourning and your joy to gloom. [10]Humble yourselves before the Lord, and he will lift you up.

[11]Brothers, do not slander one another. Anyone who speaks against his brother or judges him speaks against the law and judges it. When you judge the law, you are not keeping it, but sitting in judgment on it. [12]There is only one Lawgiver and Judge, the one who is able to save and destroy. But you— who are you to judge your neighbor?

Boasting About Tomorrow

[13]Now listen, you who say, "Today or tomorrow we will go to this or that city, spend a year there, carry on business and make money." [14]Why, you do not even know what will happen tomorrow. What is your life? You are a mist that appears for a little while and then vanishes. [15]Instead, you ought to say, "If it is the Lord's will, we will live and do this or that." [16]As it is, you boast and brag. All such boasting is evil. [17]Anyone, then, who knows the good he ought to do and doesn't do it, sins.

Warning to Rich Oppressors

5 Now listen, you rich people, weep and wail because of the misery that is coming upon you. [2]Your wealth has rotted, and moths have eaten your clothes. [3]Your gold and silver are corroded. Their corrosion will testify against you and eat your flesh like fire. You have hoarded wealth in the last days. [4]Look! The wages you failed to pay the workmen who mowed your fields are crying out against you. The cries of the harvesters have reached the ears of the Lord Almighty. [5]You have lived on earth in luxury and self-

---

[a]5 Or that God jealously longs for the spirit that he made to live in us; or that the Spirit he caused to live in us longs jealously   [b]6 Prov. 3:34

indulgence. You have fattened yourselves in the day of slaughter.ᵃ ⁶You have condemned and murdered innocent men, who were not opposing you.

Patience in Suffering

⁷Be patient, then, brothers, until the Lord's coming. See how the farmer waits for the land to yield its valuable crop and how patient he is for the autumn and spring rains. ⁸You too, be patient and stand firm, because the Lord's coming is near. ⁹Don't grumble against each other, brothers, or you will be judged. The Judge is standing at the door!

¹⁰Brothers, as an example of patience in the face of suffering, take the prophets who spoke in the name of the Lord. ¹¹As you know, we consider blessed those who have persevered. You have heard of Job's perseverance and have seen what the Lord finally brought about. The Lord is full of compassion and mercy.

¹²Above all, my brothers, do not swear—not by heaven or by earth or by anything else. Let your "Yes" be yes, and your "No," no, or you will be condemned.

The Prayer of Faith

¹³Is any one of you in trouble? He should pray. Is anyone happy? Let him sing songs of praise. ¹⁴Is any one of you sick? He should call the elders of the church to pray over him and anoint him with oil in the name of the Lord. ¹⁵And the prayer offered in faith will make the sick person well; the Lord will raise him up. If he has sinned, he will be forgiven. ¹⁶Therefore confess your sins to each other and pray for each other so that you may be healed. The prayer of a righteous man is powerful and effective.

¹⁷Elijah was a man just like us. He prayed earnestly that it would not rain, and it did not rain on the land for three and a half years. ¹⁸Again he prayed, and the heavens gave rain, and the earth produced its crops.

¹⁹My brothers, if one of you should wander from the truth and someone should bring him back, ²⁰remember this: Whoever turns a sinner from the error of his way will save him from death and cover over a multitude of sins.

ᵃ5 Or *yourselves as in a day of feasting*

1 Peter

INTRODUCTION

After the Gospels, nothing would be more precious to Christians than authentic letters from Peter, the prince of the apostles. Yet the two New Testament letters bearing his name are very likely "pseudonymous," that is, written by others in his name and drawing upon his authority, but after his death.

First Peter is chiefly concerned with difficulties the community experiences from "outside." The specified recipients (1:1) live in rural areas of Asia Minor (modern-day Turkey) but are "aliens and strangers" (1:17; 2:11), resident aliens. As converts from both Jewish and Gentile quarters they are now considered by their fellow citizens as even greater threats to established order and well-being. The author addresses a wide spectrum of social classes and positions: leaders, families, slaves.

Because of similarities to Romans and 1 Clement, this first letter is believed to have been written from Rome. Its neutral attitude toward Rome suggests it was written long after the famous fire Nero blamed on Christians (65–67 A.D.) but before Domitian's hostilities (93–96 A.D.). Calling Rome "Babylon" (5:13) occurs only in literature composed after the fall of Jerusalem in 70 A.D. and thus 1 Peter very likely derives from the Petrine circle faithful to his theological heritage and social vision late in the first century, perhaps about 90 A.D.

Earlier scholarship overemphasized the exhortations to martyrdom and baptismal motifs in the letter. Present scholarly opinion views the letter as highlighting traditional morality (household duties), concern for the public reputation of the Church in its pagan milieu, and extensive Christian oral tradition.

JOHN J. PILCH

Points for Reflection

1. What advice does 1 Peter give to the "foreigners and strangers" in Asia Minor for remaining faithful to their beliefs in a suspicious and hostile environment? Is this citizenship style practical for believers today?

2. Recount the history and list the characteristics of "Church" in this letter: how God founded it, its structure and dignity, its call to holiness, its relationship to pagan society, etc.
3. Reflect on the author's advice to slaves (2:18–25), husbands and wives (3:1–7), Church leaders (5:1–5). How is it appropriate for the original recipients of the letter? What lessons do you draw for modern believers? What principles do you follow in adapting the patterns of our ancestors in the faith to contemporary life?
4. "Living the faith" is a perennial concern for believers. What concrete advice does 1 Peter offer in this regard? What is said about suffering? How does this relate to the way you "live your faith" today?

1 Peter, an apostle of Jesus Christ,

To God's elect, strangers in the world, scattered throughout Pontus, Galatia, Cappadocia, Asia and Bithynia, [2]who have been chosen according to the foreknowledge of God the Father, through the sanctifying work of the Spirit, for obedience to Jesus Christ and sprinkling by his blood:

Grace and peace be yours in abundance.

Praise to God for a Living Hope

[3]Praise be to the God and Father of our Lord Jesus Christ! In his great mercy he has given us new birth into a living hope through the resurrection of Jesus Christ from the dead, [4]and into an inheritance that can never perish, spoil or fade—kept in heaven for you, [5]who through faith are shielded by God's power until the coming of the salvation that is ready to be revealed in the last time. [6]In this you greatly rejoice, though now for a little while you may have had to suffer grief in all kinds of trials. [7]These have come so that your faith—of greater worth than gold, which perishes even though refined by fire—may be proved genuine and may result in praise, glory and honor when Jesus Christ is revealed. [8]Though you have not seen him, you love him; and even though you do not see him now, you believe in him and are filled with an inexpressible and glorious joy, [9]for you are receiving the goal of your faith, the salvation of your souls.

[10]Concerning this salvation, the prophets, who spoke of the grace that was to come to you, searched intently and with the greatest care, [11]trying to find out the time and circumstances to which the Spirit of Christ in them was pointing when he predicted the sufferings of Christ and the glories that would follow. [12]It was revealed to them that they were not serving themselves but you, when they spoke of the things that have now been told you by those who have preached the gospel to you by the Holy Spirit sent from heaven. Even angels long to look into these things.

Be Holy

[13]Therefore, prepare your minds for action; be self-controlled; set your hope fully on the grace to be given you when Jesus Christ is revealed. [14]As obedient children, do not conform to the evil desires you had when you lived in ignorance. [15]But just as he who called you is holy, so be holy in all you do; [16]for it is written: "Be holy, because I am holy."[a]

[17]Since you call on a Father who judges each man's work impartially, live your lives as strangers here in reverent fear. [18]For you know that it was not with perishable things such as silver or gold that you were redeemed from the empty way of life handed down to you from your forefathers, [19]but with the precious blood of Christ, a lamb without blemish or defect. [20]He was chosen before the creation of the world, but was revealed in these last times for your sake. [21]Through him you believe in God, who raised him from the dead and glorified him, and so your faith and hope are in God.

[a]16 Lev. 11:44,45; 19:2; 20:7

²²Now that you have purified yourselves by obeying the truth so that you have sincere love for your brothers, love one another deeply, from the heart. *ª* ²³For you have been born again, not of perishable seed, but of imperishable, through the living and enduring word of God. ²⁴For,

> "All men are like grass,
>   and all their glory is like the flowers of the field;
>   the grass withers and the flowers fall,
>   ²⁵   but the word of the Lord stands forever." *ᵇ*

And this is the word that was preached to you.

2 Therefore, rid yourselves of all malice and all deceit, hypocrisy, envy, and slander of every kind. ²Like newborn babies, crave pure spiritual milk, so that by it you may grow up in your salvation, ³now that you have tasted that the Lord is good.

The Living Stone and a Chosen People

⁴As you come to him, the living Stone—rejected by men but chosen by God and precious to him— ⁵you also, like living stones, are being built into a spiritual house to be a holy priesthood, offering spiritual sacrifices acceptable to God through Jesus Christ. ⁶For in Scripture it says:

> "See, I lay a stone in Zion,
>   a chosen and precious cornerstone,
>   and the one who trusts in him
>   will never be put to shame." *ᶜ*

⁷Now to you who believe, this stone is precious. But to those who do not believe,

> "The stone the builders rejected
>   has become the capstone, *ᵈ" ᵉ*

⁸and,

> "A stone that causes men to stumble
>   and a rock that makes them fall." *ᶠ*

They stumble because they disobey the message—which is also what they were destined for.

⁹But you are a chosen people, a royal priesthood, a holy nation, a people belonging to God, that you may declare the praises of him who called you out of darkness into his wonderful light. ¹⁰Once you were not a people, but now you are the people of God; once you had not received mercy, but now you have received mercy.

¹¹Dear friends, I urge you, as aliens and strangers in the world, to abstain from sinful desires, which war against your soul. ¹²Live such good

---

ª22 Some early manuscripts from a pure heart   ᵇ25 Isaiah 40:6-8   ᶜ6 Isaiah 28:16   ᵈ7 Or cornerstone   ᵉ7 Psalm 118:22   ᶠ8 Isaiah 8:14 lives among the pagans that, though they accuse you of doing wrong, they may see your good deeds and glorify God on the day he visits us.

Submission to Rulers and Masters

¹³Submit yourselves for the Lord's sake to every authority instituted among men: whether to the king, as the supreme authority, ¹⁴or to governors, who are sent by him to punish those who do wrong and to commend those who do right. ¹⁵For it is God's will that by doing good you should silence the ignorant talk of foolish men. ¹⁶Live as free men, but do not use your freedom as a cover-up for evil; live as servants of God. ¹⁷Show proper respect to everyone: Love the brotherhood of believers, fear God, honor the king.

¹⁸Slaves, submit yourselves to your masters with all respect, not only to those who are good and considerate, but also to those who are harsh. ¹⁹For it is commendable if a man bears up under the pain of unjust suffering because he is conscious of God. ²⁰But how is it to your credit if you receive a beating for doing wrong and endure it? But if you suffer for doing good and you endure it, this is commendable before God. ²¹To this you were called, because Christ suffered for you, leaving you an example, that you should follow in his steps.

²²"He committed no sin,
  and no deceit was found in his mouth."ᵃ

²³When they hurled their insults at him, he did not retaliate; when he suffered, he made no threats. Instead, he entrusted himself to him who judges justly. ²⁴He himself bore our sins in his body on the tree, so that we might die to sins and live for righteousness; by his wounds you have been healed. ²⁵For you were like sheep going astray, but now you have returned to the Shepherd and Overseer of your souls.

Wives and Husbands

3 Wives, in the same way be submissive to your husbands so that, if any of them do not believe the word, they may be won over without words by the behavior of their wives, ²when they see the purity and reverence of your lives. ³Your beauty should not come from outward adornment, such as braided hair and the wearing of gold jewelry and fine clothes. ⁴Instead, it should be that of your inner self, the unfading beauty of a gentle and quiet spirit, which is of great worth in God's sight. ⁵For this is the way the holy women of the past who put their hope in God used to make themselves beautiful. They were submissive to their own husbands, ⁶like Sarah, who obeyed Abraham and called him her master. You are her daughters if you do what is right and do not give way to fear.

⁷Husbands, in the same way be considerate as you live with your wives, and treat them with respect as the weaker partner and as heirs with you of the gracious gift of life, so that nothing will hinder your prayers.

ᵃ22 Isaiah 53:9

Suffering for Doing Good

⁸Finally, all of you, live in harmony with one another; be sympathetic, love as brothers, be compassionate and humble. ⁹Do not repay evil with evil or insult with insult, but with blessing, because to this you were called so that you may inherit a blessing. ¹⁰For,

> "Whoever would love life
>   and see good days
> must keep his tongue from evil
>   and his lips from deceitful speech.
> ¹¹He must turn from evil and do good;
>   he must seek peace and pursue it.
> ¹²For the eyes of the Lord are on the righteous
>   and his ears are attentive to their prayer,
> but the face of the Lord is against those who do evil."ᵃ

¹³Who is going to harm you if you are eager to do good? ¹⁴But even if you should suffer for what is right, you are blessed. "Do not fear what they fearᵇ; do not be frightened."ᶜ ¹⁵But in your hearts set apart Christ as Lord. Always be prepared to give an answer to everyone who asks you to give the reason for the hope that you have. But do this with gentleness and respect, ¹⁶keeping a clear conscience, so that those who speak maliciously against your good behavior in Christ may be ashamed of their slander. ¹⁷It is better, if it is God's will, to suffer for doing good than for doing evil. ¹⁸For Christ died for sins once for all, the righteous for the unrighteous, to bring you to God. He was put to death in the body but made alive by the Spirit, ¹⁹through whomᵈ also he went and preached to the spirits in prison ²⁰who disobeyed long ago when God waited patiently in the days of Noah while the ark was being built. In it only a few people, eight in all, were saved through water, ²¹and this water symbolizes baptism that now saves you also—not the removal of dirt from the body but the pledgeᵉ of a good conscience toward God. It saves you by the resurrection of Jesus Christ, ²²who has gone into heaven and is at God's right hand—with angels, authorities and powers in submission to him.

Living for God

4 Therefore, since Christ suffered in his body, arm yourselves also with the same attitude, because he who has suffered in his body is done with sin. ²As a result, he does not live the rest of his earthly life for evil human desires, but rather for the will of God. ³For you have spent enough time in the past doing what pagans choose to do—living in debauchery, lust, drunkenness, orgies, carousing and detestable idolatry. ⁴They think it strange that you do not plunge with them into the same flood of dissipation, and they heap abuse on you. ⁵But they will have to give account to him who

---

ᵃ12 Psalm 34:12-16   ᵇ14 Or *not fear their threats*   ᶜ14 Isaiah 8:12   ᵈ18,19 Or *alive in the spirit,*
¹⁹*through which*   ᵉ21 Or *response*

is ready to judge the living and the dead. [6]For this is the reason the gospel was preached even to those who are now dead, so that they might be judged according to men in regard to the body, but live according to God in regard to the spirit.

[7]The end of all things is near. Therefore be clear minded and self-controlled so that you can pray. [8]Above all, love each other deeply, because love covers over a multitude of sins. [9]Offer hospitality to one another without grumbling. [10]Each one should use whatever gift he has received to serve others, faithfully administering God's grace in its various forms. [11]If anyone speaks, he should do it as one speaking the very words of God. If anyone serves, he should do it with the strength God provides, so that in all things God may be praised through Jesus Christ. To him be the glory and the power for ever and ever. Amen.

Suffering for Being a Christian

[12]Dear friends, do not be surprised at the painful trial you are suffering, as though something strange were happening to you. [13]But rejoice that you participate in the sufferings of Christ, so that you may be overjoyed when his glory is revealed. [14]If you are insulted because of the name of Christ, you are blessed, for the Spirit of glory and of God rests on you. [15]If you suffer, it should not be as a murderer or thief or any other kind of criminal, or even as a meddler. [16]However, if you suffer as a Christian, do not be ashamed, but praise God that you bear that name. [17]For it is time for judgment to begin with the family of God; and if it begins with us, what will the outcome be for those who do not obey the gospel of God? [18]And,

> "If it is hard for the righteous to be saved,
>   what will become of the ungodly and the sinner?"[a]

[19]So then, those who suffer according to God's will should commit themselves to their faithful Creator and continue to do good.

To Elders and Young Men

5 To the elders among you, I appeal as a fellow elder, a witness of Christ's sufferings and one who also will share in the glory to be revealed: [2]Be shepherds of God's flock that is under your care, serving as overseers—not because you must, but because you are willing, as God wants you to be; not greedy for money, but eager to serve; [3]not lording it over those entrusted to you, but being examples to the flock. [4]And when the Chief Shepherd appears, you will receive the crown of glory that will never fade away.

[5]Young men, in the same way be submissive to those who are older. All of you, clothe yourselves with humility toward one another, because,

> "God opposes the proud
>   but gives grace to the humble."[b]

[a]18 Prov. 11:31   [b]5 Prov. 3:34

⁶Humble yourselves, therefore, under God's mighty hand, that he may lift you up in due time. ⁷Cast all your anxiety on him because he cares for you.

⁸Be self-controlled and alert. Your enemy the devil prowls around like a roaring lion looking for someone to devour. ⁹Resist him, standing firm in the faith, because you know that your brothers throughout the world are undergoing the same kind of sufferings.

¹⁰And the God of all grace, who called you to his eternal glory in Christ, after you have suffered a little while, will himself restore you and make you strong, firm and steadfast. ¹¹To him be the power for ever and ever. Amen.

Final Greetings

¹²With the help of Silas,ᵃ whom I regard as a faithful brother, I have written to you briefly, encouraging you and testifying that this is the true grace of God. Stand fast in it.

¹³She who is in Babylon, chosen together with you, sends you her greetings, and so does my son Mark. ¹⁴Greet one another with a kiss of love.

Peace to all of you who are in Christ.

ᵃ12 Greek *Silvanus*, a variant of *Silas*

2 Peter

INTRODUCTION

This writing is more like a last will and testament (1:12–15) than a letter, and its contents more similar to Jude than 1 Peter. The hint at a "collection" of Paul's letters (3:16) suggests an origin dating 100 A.D. or later and clearly points to an author other than Peter who died around 67 A.D. The letter is probably the "latest" document in the New Testament and exhibits well the second-century style of drawing upon the best of Jewish-Christian as well as pagan culture.

False teachers are attacking God's promises, his power, and his eternal plan for reward and punishment, resulting in division and dissent in the community. The author writes in Peter's name to convince present believers to remain true to their heritage, that "old time religion," while rebuking their skeptical "friends."

JOHN J. PILCH

Points for Reflection

1. The central idea of 2 Peter is the Christian doctrine of God. Pause to describe your personal beliefs about God, then compare them with those of the opponents mentioned in the letter as well as those of the author.
2. The author challenges the incomplete understanding of the second coming of the Lord by the false teachers (2:1–5). What is the correct understanding (3:1 –13)? How does this fit into your daily faith and life?

1 Simon Peter, a servant and apostle of Jesus Christ,

To those who through the righteousness of our God and Savior Jesus Christ have received a faith as precious as ours:

²Grace and peace be yours in abundance through the knowledge of God and of Jesus our Lord.

Making One's Calling and Election Sure

³His divine power has given us everything we need for life and godliness through our knowledge of him who called us by his own glory and goodness. ⁴Through these he has given us his very great and precious promises, so that through them you may participate in the divine nature and escape the corruption in the world caused by evil desires.

⁵For this very reason, make every effort to add to your faith goodness; and to goodness, knowledge; ⁶and to knowledge, self-control; and to self-control, perseverance; and to perseverance, godliness; ⁷and to godliness, brotherly kindness; and to brotherly kindness, love. ⁸For if you possess these qualities in increasing measure, they will keep you from being ineffective and unproductive in your knowledge of our Lord Jesus Christ. ⁹But if anyone does not have them, he is nearsighted and blind, and has forgotten that he has been cleansed from his past sins.

¹⁰Therefore, my brothers, be all the more eager to make your calling and election sure. For if you do these things, you will never fall, ¹¹and you will receive a rich welcome into the eternal kingdom of our Lord and Savior Jesus Christ.

Prophecy of Scripture

¹²So I will always remind you of these things, even though you know them and are firmly established in the truth you now have. ¹³I think it is right to refresh your memory as long as I live in the tent of this body, ¹⁴because I know that I will soon put it aside, as our Lord Jesus Christ has made clear to me. ¹⁵And I will make every effort to see that after my departure you will always be able to remember these things.

¹⁶We did not follow cleverly invented stories when we told you about the power and coming of our Lord Jesus Christ, but we were eyewitnesses of his majesty. ¹⁷For he received honor and glory from God the Father when the voice came to him from the Majestic Glory, saying, "This is my Son, whom I love; with him I am well pleased." ᵃ ¹⁸We ourselves heard this voice that came from heaven when we were with him on the sacred mountain.

¹⁹And we have the word of the prophets made more certain, and you will do well to pay attention to it, as to a light shining in a dark place, until the day dawns and the morning star rises in your hearts. ²⁰Above all, you must understand that no prophecy of Scripture came about by the prophet's own interpretation. ²¹For prophecy never had its origin in the will of man, but men spoke from God as they were carried along by the Holy Spirit.

ᵃ17 Matt. 17:5; Mark 9:7; Luke 9:35

False Teachers and Their Destruction

2 But there were also false prophets among the people, just as there will be false teachers among you. They will secretly introduce destructive heresies, even denying the sovereign Lord who bought them—bringing swift destruction on themselves. [2]Many will follow their shameful ways and will bring the way of truth into disrepute. [3]In their greed these teachers will exploit you with stories they have made up. Their condemnation has long been hanging over them, and their destruction has not been sleeping.

[4]For if God did not spare angels when they sinned, but sent them to hell,[a] putting them into gloomy dungeons[b] to be held for judgment; [5]if he did not spare the ancient world when he brought the flood on its ungodly people, but protected Noah, a preacher of righteousness, and seven others; [6]if he condemned the cities of Sodom and Gomorrah by burning them to ashes, and made them an example of what is going to happen to the ungodly; [7]and if he rescued Lot, a righteous man, who was distressed by the filthy lives of lawless men [8](for that righteous man, living among them day after day, was tormented in his righteous soul by the lawless deeds he saw and heard)— [9]if this is so, then the Lord knows how to rescue godly men from trials and to hold the unrighteous for the day of judgment, while continuing their punishment.[c] [10]This is especially true of those who follow the corrupt desire of the sinful nature[d] and despise authority.

Bold and arrogant, these men are not afraid to slander celestial beings; [11]yet even angels, although they are stronger and more powerful, do not bring slanderous accusations against such beings in the presence of the Lord. [12]But these men blaspheme in matters they do not understand. They are like brute beasts, creatures of instinct, born only to be caught and destroyed, and like beasts they too will perish.

[13]They will be paid back with harm for the harm they have done. Their idea of pleasure is to carouse in broad daylight. They are blots and blemishes, reveling in their pleasures while they feast with you.[e] [14]With eyes full of adultery, they never stop sinning; they seduce the unstable; they are experts in greed—an accursed brood! [15]They have left the straight way and wandered off to follow the way of Balaam son of Beor, who loved the wages of wickedness. [16]But he was rebuked for his wrongdoing by a donkey —a beast without speech—who spoke with a man's voice and restrained the prophet's madness.

[17]These men are springs without water and mists driven by a storm. Blackest darkness is reserved for them. [18]For they mouth empty, boastful words and, by appealing to the lustful desires of sinful human nature, they entice people who are just escaping from those who live in error. [19]They promise them freedom, while they themselves are slaves of depravity—for a man is a slave to whatever has mastered him. [20]If they have escaped the corruption of the world by knowing our Lord and Savior Jesus Christ and

---

[a]4 Greek *Tartarus*   [b]4 Some manuscripts *into chains of darkness*   [c]9 Or *unrighteous for punishment until the day of judgment*   [d]10 Or *the flesh*   [e]13 Some manuscripts *in their love feasts*

are again entangled in it and overcome, they are worse off at the end than they were at the beginning. ²¹It would have been better for them not to have known the way of righteousness, than to have known it and then to turn their backs on the sacred command that was passed on to them. ²²Of them the proverbs are true: "A dog returns to its vomit,"ᵃ and, "A sow that is washed goes back to her wallowing in the mud."

The Day of the Lord

3 Dear friends, this is now my second letter to you. I have written both of them as reminders to stimulate you to wholesome thinking. ²I want you to recall the words spoken in the past by the holy prophets and the command given by our Lord and Savior through your apostles.

³First of all, you must understand that in the last days scoffers will come, scoffing and following their own evil desires. ⁴They will say, "Where is this 'coming' he promised? Ever since our fathers died, everything goes on as it has since the beginning of creation." ⁵But they deliberately forget that long ago by God's word the heavens existed and the earth was formed out of water and by water. ⁶By these waters also the world of that time was deluged and destroyed. ⁷By the same word the present heavens and earth are reserved for fire, being kept for the day of judgment and destruction of ungodly men.

⁸But do not forget this one thing, dear friends: With the Lord a day is like a thousand years, and a thousand years are like a day. ⁹The Lord is not slow in keeping his promise, as some understand slowness. He is patient with you, not wanting anyone to perish, but everyone to come to repentance.

¹⁰But the day of the Lord will come like a thief. The heavens will disappear with a roar; the elements will be destroyed by fire, and the earth and everything in it will be laid bare.ᵇ

¹¹Since everything will be destroyed in this way, what kind of people ought you to be? You ought to live holy and godly lives ¹²as you look forward to the day of God and speed its coming.ᶜ That day will bring about the destruction of the heavens by fire, and the elements will melt in the heat. ¹³But in keeping with his promise we are looking forward to a new heaven and a new earth, the home of righteousness.

¹⁴So then, dear friends, since you are looking forward to this, make every effort to be found spotless, blameless and at peace with him. ¹⁵Bear in mind that our Lord's patience means salvation, just as our dear brother Paul also wrote you with the wisdom that God gave him. ¹⁶He writes the same way in all his letters, speaking in them of these matters. His letters contain some things that are hard to understand, which ignorant and unstable people distort, as they do the other Scriptures, to their own destruction.

¹⁷Therefore, dear friends, since you already know this, be on your

---

ᵃ22 Prov. 26:11   ᵇ10 Some manuscripts *be burned up*   ᶜ12 Or *as you wait eagerly for the day of God to come* guard so that you may not be carried away by the error of lawless men and fall from your secure position. [18]But grow in the grace and knowledge of our Lord and Savior Jesus Christ. To him be glory both now and forever! Amen.

1 John

THE LETTERS OF JOHN: INTRODUCTION

Since the New Testament refers to these three letters as 1, 2, 3 John we would presume that they were written by the author of the fourth Gospel. Such has been the tradition in the earliest centuries but even among the early Church fathers, not all agreed that all three letters were written by the same individual.

Today, scholars readily admit, based on linguistic arguments that the person or persons who wrote these letters (not all agree that one person wrote all three) was not the author of the fourth Gospel. Though the letters do not share a common author with the fourth Gospel, New Testament scholars admit that these letters have a close affinity to the thought of the Gospel of John and thus, in all probability, were written within the community of the Gospel.

In attempting to reach some conclusion as to date, a prevailing opinion today places the origin of the three epistles around the same time because they deal with the same problems of the Johannine churches. They are usually dated after the composition of the Gospel of John.

These letters show a shift in interest away from the external problems—the pressures from Jews and even Jewish Christians—and toward the internal problems since it seems that even the Christians themselves are not getting along. First John might even be considered as the first pastoral commentary on the Gospel of John directed to believers within the Johannine churches in order to help them make practical applications of the teachings found in the Gospel of John.

Because the author writes to a specific group of Christians he only alludes to problems or views he is opposing, leaving the modern reader with many unanswered questions. First John even contains somewhat independent sections which give us some hints as to the type of ethical exhortation that characterized the preaching of the Johannine community. Although called a letter, 1 John is not a letter at all but rather an instructional tract which may have been intended to circulate among several communities.

The author alternates between ethical concerns and doctrinal concerns. Believing, confessing Jesus, doing righteousness as a sign of being "born from God," love as the foundation for faith and faith as the foundation for love—each theme appears and reappears with slight variations and word associations. Some might be tempted to see the Christological themes as central, but rather it seems that the problems of the community are not caused by doctrinal disagreement but are instead on the level of praxis. The dominant theme is Christian fellowship, the unity that results from the faith commitment to the Lord and finds its completion in the mutual love of the brethren. The one who follows the teaching of the elder may have confidence concerning judgment and eternal life for that believer knows that the love of God shown in Jesus and made practical in the love of the brethren is the true foundation for the Christian community and the source of Christian sinlessness.

JOHN F. O'GRADY

Points for Reflection

1. The true believer is not deceived by the antichrists. What forces in my life take me away from God? How do I fight off these evils? What advice does this letter offer me in these situations?
2. Confidence in God is a characteristic of a true believer. Am I confident in God's love and care?
3. The love among brethren is a characteristic of a Christian community since God is love. Does my community express this characteristic?
4. A Christian community is also a praying community. Do I participate in communal worship? How does personal prayer better prepare me for praying during the liturgy?

The Word of Life

1 That which was from the beginning, which we have heard, which we
have seen with our eyes, which we have looked at and our hands have
touched—this we proclaim concerning the Word of life. ²The life appeared;
we have seen it and testify to it, and we proclaim to you the eternal life,
which was with the Father and has appeared to us. ³We proclaim to you
what we have seen and heard, so that you also may have fellowship with
us. And our fellowship is with the Father and with his Son, Jesus Christ.
⁴We write this to make our*ᵃ* joy complete.

Walking in the Light

⁵This is the message we have heard from him and declare to you: God
is light; in him there is no darkness at all. ⁶If we claim to have fellowship
with him yet walk in the darkness, we lie and do not live by the truth. ⁷But
if we walk in the light, as he is in the light, we have fellowship with one
another, and the blood of Jesus, his Son, purifies us from all*ᵇ* sin.

⁸If we claim to be without sin, we deceive ourselves and the truth is not
in us. ⁹If we confess our sins, he is faithful and just and will forgive us our
sins and purify us from all unrighteousness. ¹⁰If we claim we have not
sinned, we make him out to be a liar and his word has no place in our lives.

2 My dear children, I write this to you so that you will not sin. But if
anybody does sin, we have one who speaks to the Father in our defense
—Jesus Christ, the Righteous One. ²He is the atoning sacrifice for our sins,
and not only for ours but also for*ᶜ* the sins of the whole world.

³We know that we have come to know him if we obey his commands.
⁴The man who says, "I know him," but does not do what he commands is
a liar, and the truth is not in him. ⁵But if anyone obeys his word, God's love*ᵈ*
is truly made complete in him. This is how we know we are in him:
⁶Whoever claims to live in him must walk as Jesus did.

⁷Dear friends, I am not writing you a new command but an old one,
which you have had since the beginning. This old command is the message
you have heard. ⁸Yet I am writing you a new command; its truth is seen
in him and you, because the darkness is passing and the true light is already
shining.

⁹Anyone who claims to be in the light but hates his brother is still in
the darkness. ¹⁰Whoever loves his brother lives in the light, and there is
nothing in him*ᵉ* to make him stumble. ¹¹But whoever hates his brother is
in the darkness and walks around in the darkness; he does not know where
he is going, because the darkness has blinded him.

> ¹²I write to you, dear children,
>   because your sins have been forgiven on account of his
>   name.
> ¹³I write to you, fathers,

ᵃ4 Some manuscripts your   *ᵇ7 Or every*   *ᶜ2 Or He is the one who turns aside God's wrath, taking*
away our sins, and not only ours but also   *ᵈ5 Or word, love for God*   *ᵉ10 Or it*

because you have known him who is from the beginning.
I write to you, young men,
because you have overcome the evil one.
I write to you, dear children,
because you have known the Father.
[14]I write to you, fathers,
because you have known him who is from the beginning.
I write to you, young men,
because you are strong,
and the word of God lives in you,
and you have overcome the evil one.

Do Not Love the World

[15]Do not love the world or anything in the world. If anyone loves the world, the love of the Father is not in him. [16]For everything in the world— the cravings of sinful man, the lust of his eyes and the boasting of what he has and does—comes not from the Father but from the world. [17]The world and its desires pass away, but the man who does the will of God lives forever.

Warning Against Antichrists

[18]Dear children, this is the last hour; and as you have heard that the antichrist is coming, even now many antichrists have come. This is how we know it is the last hour. [19]They went out from us, but they did not really belong to us. For if they had belonged to us, they would have remained with us; but their going showed that none of them belonged to us.

[20]But you have an anointing from the Holy One, and all of you know the truth. [a] [21]I do not write to you because you do not know the truth, but because you do know it and because no lie comes from the truth. [22]Who is the liar? It is the man who denies that Jesus is the Christ. Such a man is the antichrist—he denies the Father and the Son. [23]No one who denies the Son has the Father; whoever acknowledges the Son has the Father also.

[24]See that what you have heard from the beginning remains in you. If it does, you also will remain in the Son and in the Father. [25]And this is what he promised us—even eternal life.

[26]I am writing these things to you about those who are trying to lead you astray. [27]As for you, the anointing you received from him remains in you, and you do not need anyone to teach you. But as his anointing teaches you about all things and as that anointing is real, not counterfeit—just as it has taught you, remain in him.

Children of God

[28]And now, dear children, continue in him, so that when he appears we may be confident and unashamed before him at his coming.

[a]20 Some manuscripts *and you know all things*

[29]If you know that he is righteous, you know that everyone who does what is right has been born of him.

3 How great is the love the Father has lavished on us, that we should be called children of God! And that is what we are! The reason the world does not know us is that it did not know him. [2]Dear friends, now we are children of God, and what we will be has not yet been made known. But we know that when he appears,[a] we shall be like him, for we shall see him as he is. [3]Everyone who has this hope in him purifies himself, just as he is pure.

[4]Everyone who sins breaks the law; in fact, sin is lawlessness. [5]But you know that he appeared so that he might take away our sins. And in him is no sin. [6]No one who lives in him keeps on sinning. No one who continues to sin has either seen him or known him.

[7]Dear children, do not let anyone lead you astray. He who does what is right is righteous, just as he is righteous. [8]He who does what is sinful is of the devil, because the devil has been sinning from the beginning. The reason the Son of God appeared was to destroy the devil's work. [9]No one who is born of God will continue to sin, because God's seed remains in him; he cannot go on sinning, because he has been born of God. [10]This is how we know who the children of God are and who the children of the devil are: Anyone who does not do what is right is not a child of God; nor is anyone who does not love his brother.

Love One Another

[11]This is the message you heard from the beginning: We should love one another. [12]Do not be like Cain, who belonged to the evil one and murdered his brother. And why did he murder him? Because his own actions were evil and his brother's were righteous. [13]Do not be surprised, my brothers, if the world hates you. [14]We know that we have passed from death to life, because we love our brothers. Anyone who does not love remains in death. [15]Anyone who hates his brother is a murderer, and you know that no murderer has eternal life in him.

[16]This is how we know what love is: Jesus Christ laid down his life for us. And we ought to lay down our lives for our brothers. [17]If anyone has material possessions and sees his brother in need but has no pity on him, how can the love of God be in him? [18]Dear children, let us not love with words or tongue but with actions and in truth. [19]This then is how we know that we belong to the truth, and how we set our hearts at rest in his presence [20]whenever our hearts condemn us. For God is greater than our hearts, and he knows everything.

[21]Dear friends, if our hearts do not condemn us, we have confidence before God [22]and receive from him anything we ask, because we obey his commands and do what pleases him. [23]And this is his command: to believe in the name of his Son, Jesus Christ, and to love one another as he commanded us. [24]Those who obey his commands live in him, and he in them.

---

[a]2 Or *when it is made known*

And this is how we know that he lives in us: We know it by the Spirit he gave us.

Test the Spirits

4 Dear friends, do not believe every spirit, but test the spirits to see whether they are from God, because many false prophets have gone out into the world. ²This is how you can recognize the Spirit of God: Every spirit that acknowledges that Jesus Christ has come in the flesh is from God, ³but every spirit that does not acknowledge Jesus is not from God. This is the spirit of the antichrist, which you have heard is coming and even now is already in the world.

⁴You, dear children, are from God and have overcome them, because the one who is in you is greater than the one who is in the world. ⁵They are from the world and therefore speak from the viewpoint of the world, and the world listens to them. ⁶We are from God, and whoever knows God listens to us; but whoever is not from God does not listen to us. This is how we recognize the Spirit*a* of truth and the spirit of falsehood.

God's Love and Ours

⁷Dear friends, let us love one another, for love comes from God. Everyone who loves has been born of God and knows God. ⁸Whoever does not love does not know God, because God is love. ⁹This is how God showed his love among us: He sent his one and only Son*b* into the world that we might live through him. ¹⁰This is love: not that we loved God, but that he loved us and sent his Son as an atoning sacrifice for*c* our sins. ¹¹Dear friends, since God so loved us, we also ought to love one another. ¹²No one has ever seen God; but if we love one another, God lives in us and his love is made complete in us.

¹³We know that we live in him and he in us, because he has given us of his Spirit. ¹⁴And we have seen and testify that the Father has sent his Son to be the Savior of the world. ¹⁵If anyone acknowledges that Jesus is the Son of God, God lives in him and he in God. ¹⁶And so we know and rely on the love God has for us.

God is love. Whoever lives in love lives in God, and God in him. ¹⁷In this way, love is made complete among us so that we will have confidence on the day of judgment, because in this world we are like him. ¹⁸There is no fear in love. But perfect love drives out fear, because fear has to do with punishment. The one who fears is not made perfect in love.

¹⁹We love because he first loved us. ²⁰If anyone says, "I love God," yet hates his brother, he is a liar. For anyone who does not love his brother, whom he has seen, cannot love God, whom he has not seen. ²¹And he has given us this command: Whoever loves God must also love his brother.

*a*6 Or *spirit*   *b*9 Or *his only begotten Son*   *c*10 Or *as the one who would turn aside his wrath, taking away*

Faith in the Son of God

5 Everyone who believes that Jesus is the Christ is born of God, and everyone who loves the father loves his child as well. ²This is how we know that we love the children of God: by loving God and carrying out his commands. ³This is love for God: to obey his commands. And his commands are not burdensome, ⁴for everyone born of God overcomes the world. This is the victory that has overcome the world, even our faith. ⁵Who is it that overcomes the world? Only he who believes that Jesus is the Son of God.

⁶This is the one who came by water and blood—Jesus Christ. He did not come by water only, but by water and blood. And it is the Spirit who testifies, because the Spirit is the truth. ⁷For there are three that testify: ⁸the*a* Spirit, the water and the blood; and the three are in agreement. ⁹We accept man's testimony, but God's testimony is greater because it is the testimony of God, which he has given about his Son. ¹⁰Anyone who believes in the Son of God has this testimony in his heart. Anyone who does not believe God has made him out to be a liar, because he has not believed the testimony God has given about his Son. ¹¹And this is the testimony: God has given us eternal life, and this life is in his Son. ¹²He who has the Son has life; he who does not have the Son of God does not have life.

Concluding Remarks

¹³I write these things to you who believe in the name of the Son of God so that you may know that you have eternal life. ¹⁴This is the confidence we have in approaching God: that if we ask anything according to his will, he hears us. ¹⁵And if we know that he hears us—whatever we ask—we know that we have what we asked of him.

¹⁶If anyone sees his brother commit a sin that does not lead to death, he should pray and God will give him life. I refer to those whose sin does not lead to death. There is a sin that leads to death. I am not saying that he should pray about that. ¹⁷All wrongdoing is sin, and there is sin that does not lead to death.

¹⁸We know that anyone born of God does not continue to sin; the one who was born of God keeps him safe, and the evil one cannot harm him. ¹⁹We know that we are children of God, and that the whole world is under the control of the evil one. ²⁰We know also that the Son of God has come and has given us understanding, so that we may know him who is true. And we are in him who is true—even in his Son Jesus Christ. He is the true God and eternal life.

²¹Dear children, keep yourselves from idols.

a7,8 Late manuscripts of the Vulgate testify in heaven: the Father, the Word and the Holy Spirit, and these three are one. 8And there are three that testify on earth: the (not found in any Greek manuscript before the sixteenth century)

2 John

INTRODUCTION

Second John has the classical format of a Greek letter: opening, greeting with well wishes, the body of the letter which contains the purpose of the letter, and the closing.

The author simply refers to himself as the "elder" which may or may not indicate an office in the Johannine community. Nor do we know if the letter is addressed to an individual or a community. Some see this letter as a cover letter encouraging the readers or listeners to pay attention to the instructions that are found in 3 John.

This letter along with 3 John shows us that the Johannine community was, in fact, several groups or churches spread over a region. These communities were linked by the traveling missionaries and their common Johannine tradition.

Since the letter is so brief, an outline based on the classical format will help the reader in understanding the letter:

1. opening and greeting (1–4) which includes a benediction and thanksgiving;
2. body (4–11) which warns of false teachers;
3. closing (12–13).

The true believer walks in love and avoids the deceivers and false teachers.

JOHN F. O'GRADY

Points for Reflection

1. This letter conveys the following themes: the true believer always remains with the community and false teachers are devious and try to entrap. How do the modern-day cults deceive and sway people, mostly the youth, into their organizations? What can I do to keep from being deceived? How can I help others?
2. "Love one another" (2 Jn:5) echoes the words of Jesus during his farewell discourse in Jn 15:17, "Love each other." How do I show my love to the brethren? To the Lord?
3. Salvation demands unity with the tradition of Jesus as expressed in the Johannine community. How is this expressed in the letters of John?

¹The elder,

To the chosen lady and her children, whom I love in the truth—and not I only, but also all who know the truth— ²because of the truth, which lives in us and will be with us forever:

³Grace, mercy and peace from God the Father and from Jesus Christ, the Father's Son, will be with us in truth and love.

⁴It has given me great joy to find some of your children walking in the truth, just as the Father commanded us. ⁵And now, dear lady, I am not writing you a new command but one we have had from the beginning. I ask that we love one another. ⁶And this is love: that we walk in obedience to his commands. As you have heard from the beginning, his command is that you walk in love.

⁷Many deceivers, who do not acknowledge Jesus Christ as coming in the flesh, have gone out into the world. Any such person is the deceiver and the antichrist. ⁸Watch out that you do not lose what you have worked for, but that you may be rewarded fully. ⁹Anyone who runs ahead and does not continue in the teaching of Christ does not have God; whoever continues in the teaching has both the Father and the Son. ¹⁰If anyone comes to you and does not bring this teaching, do not take him into your house or welcome him. ¹¹Anyone who welcomes him shares in his wicked work.

¹²I have much to write to you, but I do not want to use paper and ink. Instead, I hope to visit you and talk with you face to face, so that our joy may be complete.

¹³The children of your chosen sister send their greetings.

3 John

INTRODUCTION

Like 2 John, this also follows the classic division of a letter in the Graeco-Roman period, but unlike 2 John the problem here described is a lack of hospitality. Christians who traveled depended on local communities or house churches for hospitality and assistance as they brought news and letters from one community to another. The elder wishes to obtain hospitality from another group after they have been denied it by Diotrephes.

Whether the two communities are house churches of the same Johannine tradition or house churches of the Johannine approach and the more developed Church at the end of the first century remains unknown. Whatever happened, the lack of hospitality manifested a lack of true love of the brethren which was the hallmark of the Johannine community and the elder felt impelled to express his viewpoints.

Opening:	1	
Greeting:	2–4	health wish, thanksgiving
Body:	5–12	reputation for hospitality
		lack of hospitality
		request for hospitality
Closing:	13–15	

JOHN F. O'GRADY

Points for Reflection

1. Verse 8 of 3 Jn states, "We ought therefore to show hospitality." Hospitality characterizes the true Christian community. Have I, along with my parish, expressed this warmth and acceptance to outsiders and those who are in need?
2. Authority is to serve not to be served. How has our Lord Jesus Christ exemplified this statement? One example is found in Jn 13:12–17, with the washing of the disciples' feet.
3. One of the messages of this letter is peace and unity should exist even if opinions differ. How do I handle a difference of opinion? Do I, like Diotrephes (v. 9), insist on having my own way and refuse to even listen to others? In what ways can this be destructive to my family? To my parish?

¹The elder,

To my dear friend Gaius, whom I love in the truth.

²Dear friend, I pray that you may enjoy good health and that all may go well with you, even as your soul is getting along well. ³It gave me great joy to have some brothers come and tell about your faithfulness to the truth and how you continue to walk in the truth. ⁴I have no greater joy than to hear that my children are walking in the truth.

⁵Dear friend, you are faithful in what you are doing for the brothers, even though they are strangers to you. ⁶They have told the church about your love. You will do well to send them on their way in a manner worthy of God. ⁷It was for the sake of the Name that they went out, receiving no help from the pagans. ⁸We ought therefore to show hospitality to such men so that we may work together for the truth.

⁹I wrote to the church, but Diotrephes, who loves to be first, will have nothing to do with us. ¹⁰So if I come, I will call attention to what he is doing, gossiping maliciously about us. Not satisfied with that, he refuses to welcome the brothers. He also stops those who want to do so and puts them out of the church.

¹¹Dear friend, do not imitate what is evil but what is good. Anyone who does what is good is from God. Anyone who does what is evil has not seen God. ¹²Demetrius is well spoken of by everyone—and even by the truth itself. We also speak well of him, and you know that our testimony is true.

¹³I have much to write you, but I do not want to do so with pen and ink. ¹⁴I hope to see you soon, and we will talk face to face.

Peace to you. The friends here send their greetings. Greet the friends there by name.

Jude

INTRODUCTION

The Letter of Jude is a strong denunciation of false teachers who have entered the Christian community (v. 4), taken part in the Eucharistic love feasts as fellow Christians (v. 12), but whose lives are characterized by licentiousness (vv. 4, 7–8, 16, 18, 23). It is difficult to determine the precise teachings of these men, but they seem to be an early group of Christian libertine gnostics, similar in thought to those criticized in Revelation 2:14, 20 and in the Pastoral Letters, precursors of such later movements as described by Irenaeus (c. 180), Hippolytus (c. 200), and Epiphanius (c. 370). Gnostics believe in dualism, that matter—especially the human body—is evil, and that each person contains a divine spark which must be liberated from the flesh through secret knowledge. Hatred of the body led some gnostics towards asceticism, but others felt that since the flesh was worthless, acts performed in the flesh were unimportant, morally indifferent, and could be indulged in freely. The purpose of this letter was to counteract such pernicious doctrine.

The author is named "Jude, a servant of Jesus Christ and a brother of James" (v. 1). One thinks immediately of Jude or Judas, a relative of Jesus who is mentioned along with James (Mk 6:3; Mt 13:55). That would make him a contemporary of the apostles, but there are several indications in the text which point rather to the sub-apostolic age: reference to the apostles in the past tense as having predicted the present evils of the final age (vv. 17–19); definition of the faith in terms of a fixed deposit of truths to be accepted and defended (v. 3); and finally, the situation which occasioned the letter, the beginnings of Christian gnosticism. The author wrote in excellent Greek, a further indication of being removed from the Aramaic-speaking family of Jesus. He was most probably a Hellenistic Christian who lived toward the end of the first century. He manifests a profound knowledge of Jewish apocalyptic, alludes to the Assumption of Moses (v. 9) and quotes from the Apocalypse of Enoch (vv. 14–15).

While severely criticizing those who "change the grace of our God into a license for immorality" and who "deny Jesus Christ our only Sovereign and Lord" (v. 4), the

JUDE

Letter of Jude emphasizes some important aspects of the Christian faith. Christians are "called," "loved by God the Father," "kept by Jesus Christ" (v. 1); the priority of divine initiative in our salvation is duly expressed. Christians are to accept Jesus Christ as their "only Sovereign and Lord" (v. 4) and they are to persevere in their faith (vv. 4–6). All will be judged (v. 15); those who sin like the false teachers will "suffer the punishment of eternal fire" (v. 7); times of trial have been foretold, so they are relativized and should not disturb the faithful too greatly (vv. 17–19). Christians can grow in faith through prayer in the Holy Spirit; they are to remain in God's love, trusting in "the mercy of our Lord Jesus Christ to bring [them] to eternal life" (v. 21), in the power of God the Savior "who is able to keep [them] from falling and to present [them] before his glorious presence without fault and with great joy" (v. 24).

JOSEPH F. WIMMER, O.S.A.

Points for Reflection

1. How strong is my Christian faith in the presence of those whose lives and actions are a call to licentiousness? Do I oppose them with all the resources at my command? Am I concerned about others, as was Jude?
2. Do I realize that I will be judged some day by the Lord who is "coming with thousands upon thousands of his holy ones"?
3. Am I willing to pray to the Holy Spirit, to remain in God's love, and to trust in "the mercy of our Lord Jesus Christ to bring [me] to eternal life"?

¹Jude, a servant of Jesus Christ and a brother of James,

To those who have been called, who are loved by God the Father and kept by*a* Jesus Christ:

²Mercy, peace and love be yours in abundance.

The Sin and Doom of Godless Men

³Dear friends, although I was very eager to write to you about the salvation we share, I felt I had to write and urge you to contend for the faith that was once for all entrusted to the saints. ⁴For certain men whose condemnation was written about*b* long ago have secretly slipped in among you. They are godless men, who change the grace of our God into a license for immorality and deny Jesus Christ our only Sovereign and Lord.

⁵Though you already know all this, I want to remind you that the Lord*c* delivered his people out of Egypt, but later destroyed those who did not believe. ⁶And the angels who did not keep their positions of authority but abandoned their own home—these he has kept in darkness, bound with everlasting chains for judgment on the great Day. ⁷In a similar way, Sodom and Gomorrah and the surrounding towns gave themselves up to sexual immorality and perversion. They serve as an example of those who suffer the punishment of eternal fire.

⁸In the very same way, these dreamers pollute their own bodies, reject authority and slander celestial beings. ⁹But even the archangel Michael, when he was disputing with the devil about the body of Moses, did not dare to bring a slanderous accusation against him, but said, "The Lord rebuke you!" ¹⁰Yet these men speak abusively against whatever they do not understand; and what things they do understand by instinct, like unreasoning animals—these are the very things that destroy them.

¹¹Woe to them! They have taken the way of Cain; they have rushed for profit into Balaam's error; they have been destroyed in Korah's rebellion.

¹²These men are blemishes at your love feasts, eating with you without the slightest qualm—shepherds who feed only themselves. They are clouds without rain, blown along by the wind; autumn trees, without fruit and uprooted—twice dead. ¹³They are wild waves of the sea, foaming up their shame; wandering stars, for whom blackest darkness has been reserved forever.

¹⁴Enoch, the seventh from Adam, prophesied about these men: "See, the Lord is coming with thousands upon thousands of his holy ones ¹⁵to judge everyone, and to convict all the ungodly of all the ungodly acts they have done in the ungodly way, and of all the harsh words ungodly sinners have spoken against him." ¹⁶These men are grumblers and faultfinders; they follow their own evil desires; they boast about themselves and flatter others for their own advantage.

*a*1 Or *for; or in*   *b*4 Or *men who were marked out for condemnation*   *c*5 Some early manuscripts *Jesus*

A Call to Persevere

¹⁷But, dear friends, remember what the apostles of our Lord Jesus Christ foretold. ¹⁸They said to you, "In the last times there will be scoffers who will follow their own ungodly desires." ¹⁹These are the men who divide you, who follow mere natural instincts and do not have the Spirit.

²⁰But you, dear friends, build yourselves up in your most holy faith and pray in the Holy Spirit. ²¹Keep yourselves in God's love as you wait for the mercy of our Lord Jesus Christ to bring you to eternal life.

²²Be merciful to those who doubt; ²³snatch others from the fire and save them; to others show mercy, mixed with fear—hating even the clothing stained by corrupted flesh.

Doxology

²⁴To him who is able to keep you from falling and to present you before his glorious presence without fault and with great joy— ²⁵to the only God our Savior be glory, majesty, power and authority, through Jesus Christ our Lord, before all ages, now and forevermore! Amen.

Revelation

INTRODUCTION

The author of Revelation identifies himself as John (1:1) exiled on Patmos island (1:9). He is not the same John who wrote the Gospel but comes, as it were, out of the same mold. To console and instruct his community suffering persecution and martyrdom, he writes an "apocalypse." Like all "apocalypses," so too is Revelation a form of writing in which an otherworldly being discloses information to a human being about salvation and a better (supernatural) world. Though cryptic and puzzling to us, the symbolic language was evident and obvious to our ancestors in the faith. Modern believers should resist the urge to find a literalistic meaning for every detail (e.g., the number of the beast).

Scholars further agree that Revelation was probably completed late in the first century at a time of imperial persecution, perhaps that of Roman Emperor Diocletian between 81 and 96 A.D.

The enormous popularity of the book then and now is due to the hope and security it engenders in helpless humans. In the symbolic visions world history unfolds according to a plan which God has measured out. Ultimate victory is assured for good believers. It will be achieved by superhuman beings.

The author is partial to the number seven. There are seven letters, seals, trumpets, bowls, unnumbered visions, and beatitudes ("Blessed is" statements). The sevens tend to overlap and make an interlocking whole of the entire book.

Prologue 1:1–8
Scroll I 4:1—15:4
   7 seals - 1/4 earth (4:1—8:5)
   7 trumpets - 1/3 earth (8:2—11:19)
   7 unnumbered visions (12:1—15:4)
Scroll II 15:1—22:5
   7 bowls - all the earth
      (15:1—16:20)
   Babylon Interlude (17:1—19:10)
   7 unnumbered visions
      (19:11—21:8)
   Jerusalem Interlude (21:9—22:5)
Epilogue 22:6–21

The dominant themes of Revelation are persecution, suffering, martyrdom. Jesus is the faithful witness (martyr, 1:5) and model for the believer. He is the central figure king (1:4) and warrior (19:11–16) victoriously triumphant over death.

Believers are urged to be faithful and patient, for ultimate victory is assured. The only human options in the book are denying Christ, or dying for him. All are repaid according to their deeds (14:13; 16:6).

JOHN J. PILCH

Points for Reflection

1. The letters to the churches (Rev 2–3) describe internal (e.g., laxity) and external (e.g., persecution) threats to believers. Can you identify and validate similar challenges for modern believers?

2. How does Revelation's overwhelmingly critical attitude toward imperial power ("Babylon the Great," "the prostitute") help or hinder you in developing an appropriate religious aspect to your political beliefs?

3. Sometimes described as resistance literature for a time of crisis, Revelation advises a passive resistance to the point of death (martyrdom, see 13:9; 6:10). Does this advice guide and console, or discourage and depress you? Explain.

Prologue

1 The revelation of Jesus Christ, which God gave him to show his servants what must soon take place. He made it known by sending his angel to his servant John, ²who testifies to everything he saw—that is, the word of God and the testimony of Jesus Christ. ³Blessed is the one who reads the words of this prophecy, and blessed are those who hear it and take to heart what is written in it, because the time is near.

Greetings and Doxology

⁴John,

To the seven churches in the province of Asia:

Grace and peace to you from him who is, and who was, and who is to come, and from the seven spirits*ᵃ* before his throne, ⁵and from Jesus Christ, who is the faithful witness, the firstborn from the dead, and the ruler of the kings of the earth.

To him who loves us and has freed us from our sins by his blood, ⁶and has made us to be a kingdom and priests to serve his God and Father—to him be glory and power for ever and ever! Amen.

⁷Look, he is coming with the clouds,
  and every eye will see him,
  even those who pierced him;
  and all the peoples of the earth will mourn because of
    him.
So shall it be! Amen.

⁸"I am the Alpha and the Omega," says the Lord God, "who is, and who was, and who is to come, the Almighty."

One Like a Son of Man

⁹I, John, your brother and companion in the suffering and kingdom and patient endurance that are ours in Jesus, was on the island of Patmos because of the word of God and the testimony of Jesus. ¹⁰On the Lord's Day I was in the Spirit, and I heard behind me a loud voice like a trumpet, ¹¹which said: "Write on a scroll what you see and send it to the seven churches: to Ephesus, Smyrna, Pergamum, Thyatira, Sardis, Philadelphia and Laodicea."

¹²I turned around to see the voice that was speaking to me. And when I turned I saw seven golden lampstands, ¹³and among the lampstands was someone "like a son of man,"*ᵇ* dressed in a robe reaching down to his feet and with a golden sash around his chest. ¹⁴His head and hair were white like wool, as white as snow, and his eyes were like blazing fire. ¹⁵His feet were like bronze glowing in a furnace, and his voice was like the sound of

ᵃ4 Or the sevenfold Spirit   *ᵇ13 Daniel 7:13*

rushing waters. [16]In his right hand he held seven stars, and out of his mouth came a sharp double-edged sword. His face was like the sun shining in all its brilliance.

[17]When I saw him, I fell at his feet as though dead. Then he placed his right hand on me and said: "Do not be afraid. I am the First and the Last. [18]I am the Living One; I was dead, and behold I am alive for ever and ever! And I hold the keys of death and Hades.

[19]"Write, therefore, what you have seen, what is now and what will take place later. [20]The mystery of the seven stars that you saw in my right hand and of the seven golden lampstands is this: The seven stars are the angels[a] of the seven churches, and the seven lampstands are the seven churches.

To the Church in Ephesus

2 "To the angel[b] of the church in Ephesus write:

These are the words of him who holds the seven stars in his right hand and walks among the seven golden lampstands: [2]I know your deeds, your hard work and your perseverance. I know that you cannot tolerate wicked men, that you have tested those who claim to be apostles but are not, and have found them false. [3]You have persevered and have endured hardships for my name, and have not grown weary.

[4]Yet I hold this against you: You have forsaken your first love. [5]Remember the height from which you have fallen! Repent and do the things you did at first. If you do not repent, I will come to you and remove your lampstand from its place. [6]But you have this in your favor: You hate the practices of the Nicolaitans, which I also hate.

[7]He who has an ear, let him hear what the Spirit says to the churches. To him who overcomes, I will give the right to eat from the tree of life, which is in the paradise of God.

To the Church in Smyrna

[8]"To the angel of the church in Smyrna write:

These are the words of him who is the First and the Last, who died and came to life again. [9]I know your afflictions and your poverty—yet you are rich! I know the slander of those who say they are Jews and are not, but are a synagogue of Satan. [10]Do not be afraid of what you are about to suffer. I tell you, the devil will put some of you in prison to test you, and you will suffer persecution for ten days. Be faithful, even to the point of death, and I will give you the crown of life.

[11]He who has an ear, let him hear what the Spirit says to the churches. He who overcomes will not be hurt at all by the second death.

[a]20 Or messengers   [b]1 Or messenger; also in verses 8, 12 and 18

To the Church in Pergamum

¹²"To the angel of the church in Pergamum write:

These are the words of him who has the sharp, double-edged sword. ¹³I know where you live—where Satan has his throne. Yet you remain true to my name. You did not renounce your faith in me, even in the days of Antipas, my faithful witness, who was put to death in your city—where Satan lives.

¹⁴Nevertheless, I have a few things against you: You have people there who hold to the teaching of Balaam, who taught Balak to entice the Israelites to sin by eating food sacrificed to idols and by committing sexual immorality. ¹⁵Likewise you also have those who hold to the teaching of the Nicolaitans. ¹⁶Repent therefore! Otherwise, I will soon come to you and will fight against them with the sword of my mouth.

¹⁷He who has an ear, let him hear what the Spirit says to the churches. To him who overcomes, I will give some of the hidden manna. I will also give him a white stone with a new name written on it, known only to him who receives it.

To the Church in Thyatira

¹⁸"To the angel of the church in Thyatira write:

These are the words of the Son of God, whose eyes are like blazing fire and whose feet are like burnished bronze. ¹⁹I know your deeds, your love and faith, your service and perseverance, and that you are now doing more than you did at first.

²⁰Nevertheless, I have this against you: You tolerate that woman Jezebel, who calls herself a prophetess. By her teaching she misleads my servants into sexual immorality and the eating of food sacrificed to idols. ²¹I have given her time to repent of her immorality, but she is unwilling. ²²So I will cast her on a bed of suffering, and I will make those who commit adultery with her suffer intensely, unless they repent of her ways. ²³I will strike her children dead. Then all the churches will know that I am he who searches hearts and minds, and I will repay each of you according to your deeds. ²⁴Now I say to the rest of you in Thyatira, to you who do not hold to her teaching and have not learned Satan's so-called deep secrets (I will not impose any other burden on you): ²⁵Only hold on to what you have until I come.

²⁶To him who overcomes and does my will to the end, I will give authority over the nations—

²⁷'He will rule them with an iron scepter;
he will dash them to pieces like pottery'ᵃ—

just as I have received authority from my Father. ²⁸I will also give him

ᵃ27 Psalm 2:9

the morning star. ²⁹He who has an ear, let him hear what the Spirit says to the churches.

To the Church in Sardis

3 "To the angel*ᵃ* of the church in Sardis write:

These are the words of him who holds the seven spirits*ᵇ* of God and the seven stars. I know your deeds; you have a reputation of being alive, but you are dead. ²Wake up! Strengthen what remains and is about to die, for I have not found your deeds complete in the sight of my God. ³Remember, therefore, what you have received and heard; obey it, and repent. But if you do not wake up, I will come like a thief, and you will not know at what time I will come to you.

⁴Yet you have a few people in Sardis who have not soiled their clothes. They will walk with me, dressed in white, for they are worthy. ⁵He who overcomes will, like them, be dressed in white. I will never blot out his name from the book of life, but will acknowledge his name before my Father and his angels. ⁶He who has an ear, let him hear what the Spirit says to the churches.

To the Church in Philadelphia

⁷"To the angel of the church in Philadelphia write:

These are the words of him who is holy and true, who holds the key of David. What he opens no one can shut, and what he shuts no one can open. ⁸I know your deeds. See, I have placed before you an open door that no one can shut. I know that you have little strength, yet you have kept my word and have not denied my name. ⁹I will make those who are of the synagogue of Satan, who claim to be Jews though they are not, but are liars—I will make them come and fall down at your feet and acknowledge that I have loved you. ¹⁰Since you have kept my command to endure patiently, I will also keep you from the hour of trial that is going to come upon the whole world to test those who live on the earth.

¹¹I am coming soon. Hold on to what you have, so that no one will take your crown. ¹²Him who overcomes I will make a pillar in the temple of my God. Never again will he leave it. I will write on him the name of my God and the name of the city of my God, the new Jerusalem, which is coming down out of heaven from my God; and I will also write on him my new name. ¹³He who has an ear, let him hear what the Spirit says to the churches.

To the Church in Laodicea

¹⁴"To the angel of the church in Laodicea write:

These are the words of the Amen, the faithful and true witness,

ᵃ1 Or *messenger*; also in verses 7 and 14   *ᵇ1* Or *the sevenfold Spirit* the ruler of God's creation. [15]I know your deeds, that you are neither cold nor hot. I wish you were either one or the other! [16]So, because you are lukewarm—neither hot nor cold—I am about to spit you out of my mouth. [17]You say, 'I am rich; I have acquired wealth and do not need a thing.' But you do not realize that you are wretched, pitiful, poor, blind and naked. [18]I counsel you to buy from me gold refined in the fire, so you can become rich; and white clothes to wear, so you can cover your shameful nakedness; and salve to put on your eyes, so you can see.

[19]Those whom I love I rebuke and discipline. So be earnest, and repent. [20]Here I am! I stand at the door and knock. If anyone hears my voice and opens the door, I will come in and eat with him, and he with me.

[21]To him who overcomes, I will give the right to sit with me on my throne, just as I overcame and sat down with my Father on his throne. [22]He who has an ear, let him hear what the Spirit says to the churches."

The Throne in Heaven

4 After this I looked, and there before me was a door standing open in heaven. And the voice I had first heard speaking to me like a trumpet said, "Come up here, and I will show you what must take place after this." [2]At once I was in the Spirit, and there before me was a throne in heaven with someone sitting on it. [3]And the one who sat there had the appearance of jasper and carnelian. A rainbow, resembling an emerald, encircled the throne. [4]Surrounding the throne were twenty-four other thrones, and seated on them were twenty-four elders. They were dressed in white and had crowns of gold on their heads. [5]From the throne came flashes of lightning, rumblings and peals of thunder. Before the throne, seven lamps were blazing. These are the seven spirits[a] of God. [6]Also before the throne there was what looked like a sea of glass, clear as crystal.

In the center, around the throne, were four living creatures, and they were covered with eyes, in front and in back. [7]The first living creature was like a lion, the second was like an ox, the third had a face like a man, the fourth was like a flying eagle. [8]Each of the four living creatures had six wings and was covered with eyes all around, even under his wings. Day and night they never stop saying:

"Holy, holy, holy
is the Lord God Almighty,
who was, and is, and is to come."

[9]Whenever the living creatures give glory, honor and thanks to him who sits on the throne and who lives for ever and ever, [10]the twenty-four elders

[a]5 Or *the sevenfold Spirit*

fall down before him who sits on the throne, and worship him who lives for ever and ever. They lay their crowns before the throne and say:

> [11]"You are worthy, our Lord and God,
>   to receive glory and honor and power,
>   for you created all things,
>   and by your will they were created
>   and have their being."

The Scroll and the Lamb

5 Then I saw in the right hand of him who sat on the throne a scroll with writing on both sides and sealed with seven seals. [2]And I saw a mighty angel proclaiming in a loud voice, "Who is worthy to break the seals and open the scroll?" [3]But no one in heaven or on earth or under the earth could open the scroll or even look inside it. [4]I wept and wept because no one was found who was worthy to open the scroll or look inside. [5]Then one of the elders said to me, "Do not weep! See, the Lion of the tribe of Judah, the Root of David, has triumphed. He is able to open the scroll and its seven seals."

[6]Then I saw a Lamb, looking as if it had been slain, standing in the center of the throne, encircled by the four living creatures and the elders. He had seven horns and seven eyes, which are the seven spirits[a] of God sent out into all the earth. [7]He came and took the scroll from the right hand of him who sat on the throne. [8]And when he had taken it, the four living creatures and the twenty-four elders fell down before the Lamb. Each one had a harp and they were holding golden bowls full of incense, which are the prayers of the saints. [9]And they sang a new song:

> "You are worthy to take the scroll
>   and to open its seals,
>   because you were slain,
>   and with your blood you purchased men for God
>   from every tribe and language and people and nation.
> [10]You have made them to be a kingdom and priests to serve
>   our God,
>   and they will reign on the earth."

[11]Then I looked and heard the voice of many angels, numbering thousands upon thousands, and ten thousand times ten thousand. They encircled the throne and the living creatures and the elders. [12]In a loud voice they sang:

> "Worthy is the Lamb, who was slain,
>   to receive power and wealth and wisdom and strength
>   and honor and glory and praise!"

---

[a]6 Or *the sevenfold Spirit*

¹³Then I heard every creature in heaven and on earth and under the earth and on the sea, and all that is in them, singing:

"To him who sits on the throne and to the Lamb
be praise and honor and glory and power,
for ever and ever!"

¹⁴The four living creatures said, "Amen," and the elders fell down and worshiped.

The Seals

6 I watched as the Lamb opened the first of the seven seals. Then I heard one of the four living creatures say in a voice like thunder, "Come!" ²I looked, and there before me was a white horse! Its rider held a bow, and he was given a crown, and he rode out as a conqueror bent on conquest.

³When the Lamb opened the second seal, I heard the second living creature say, "Come!" ⁴Then another horse came out, a fiery red one. Its rider was given power to take peace from the earth and to make men slay each other. To him was given a large sword.

⁵When the Lamb opened the third seal, I heard the third living creature say, "Come!" I looked, and there before me was a black horse! Its rider was holding a pair of scales in his hand. ⁶Then I heard what sounded like a voice among the four living creatures, saying, "A quart*a* of wheat for a day's wages,*b* and three quarts of barley for a day's wages,*b* and do not damage the oil and the wine!"

⁷When the Lamb opened the fourth seal, I heard the voice of the fourth living creature say, "Come!" ⁸I looked, and there before me was a pale horse! Its rider was named Death, and Hades was following close behind him. They were given power over a fourth of the earth to kill by sword, famine and plague, and by the wild beasts of the earth.

⁹When he opened the fifth seal, I saw under the altar the souls of those who had been slain because of the word of God and the testimony they had maintained. ¹⁰They called out in a loud voice, "How long, Sovereign Lord, holy and true, until you judge the inhabitants of the earth and avenge our blood?" ¹¹Then each of them was given a white robe, and they were told to wait a little longer, until the number of their fellow servants and brothers who were to be killed as they had been was completed.

¹²I watched as he opened the sixth seal. There was a great earthquake. The sun turned black like sackcloth made of goat hair, the whole moon turned blood red, ¹³and the stars in the sky fell to earth, as late figs drop from a fig tree when shaken by a strong wind. ¹⁴The sky receded like a scroll, rolling up, and every mountain and island was removed from its place.

¹⁵Then the kings of the earth, the princes, the generals, the rich, the mighty, and every slave and every free man hid in caves and among the rocks of the mountains. ¹⁶They called to the mountains and the rocks, "Fall on us and hide us from the face of him who sits on the throne and from

---

*a*6 Greek *a choinix* (probably about a liter)   *b*6 Greek *a denarius*

433

the wrath of the Lamb! [17]For the great day of their wrath has come, and who can stand?"

144,000 Sealed

7 After this I saw four angels standing at the four corners of the earth, holding back the four winds of the earth to prevent any wind from blowing on the land or on the sea or on any tree. [2]Then I saw another angel coming up from the east, having the seal of the living God. He called out in a loud voice to the four angels who had been given power to harm the land and the sea: [3]"Do not harm the land or the sea or the trees until we put a seal on the foreheads of the servants of our God." [4]Then I heard the number of those who were sealed: 144,000 from all the tribes of Israel.

[5]From the tribe of Judah 12,000 were sealed,
from the tribe of Reuben 12,000,
from the tribe of Gad 12,000,
[6]from the tribe of Asher 12,000,
from the tribe of Naphtali 12,000,
from the tribe of Manasseh 12,000,
[7]from the tribe of Simeon 12,000,
from the tribe of Levi 12,000,
from the tribe of Issachar 12,000,
[8]from the tribe of Zebulun 12,000,
from the tribe of Joseph 12,000,
from the tribe of Benjamin 12,000.

The Great Multitude in White Robes

[9]After this I looked and there before me was a great multitude that no one could count, from every nation, tribe, people and language, standing before the throne and in front of the Lamb. They were wearing white robes and were holding palm branches in their hands. [10]And they cried out in a loud voice:

"Salvation belongs to our God,
who sits on the throne,
and to the Lamb."

[11]All the angels were standing around the throne and around the elders and the four living creatures. They fell down on their faces before the throne and worshiped God, [12]saying:

"Amen!
Praise and glory
and wisdom and thanks and honor
and power and strength
be to our God for ever and ever.
Amen!"

¹³Then one of the elders asked me, "These in white robes—who are they, and where did they come from?"

¹⁴I answered, "Sir, you know."

And he said, "These are they who have come out of the great tribulation; they have washed their robes and made them white in the blood of the Lamb. ¹⁵Therefore,

"they are before the throne of God
    and serve him day and night in his temple;
and he who sits on the throne will spread his tent over
        them.
¹⁶Never again will they hunger;
    never again will they thirst.
The sun will not beat upon them,
    nor any scorching heat.
¹⁷For the Lamb at the center of the throne will be their
        shepherd;
    he will lead them to springs of living water.
And God will wipe away every tear from their eyes."

The Seventh Seal and the Golden Censer

8 When he opened the seventh seal, there was silence in heaven for about half an hour.

²And I saw the seven angels who stand before God, and to them were given seven trumpets.

³Another angel, who had a golden censer, came and stood at the altar. He was given much incense to offer, with the prayers of all the saints, on the golden altar before the throne. ⁴The smoke of the incense, together with the prayers of the saints, went up before God from the angel's hand. ⁵Then the angel took the censer, filled it with fire from the altar, and hurled it on the earth; and there came peals of thunder, rumblings, flashes of lightning and an earthquake.

The Trumpets

⁶Then the seven angels who had the seven trumpets prepared to sound them.

⁷The first angel sounded his trumpet, and there came hail and fire mixed with blood, and it was hurled down upon the earth. A third of the earth was burned up, a third of the trees were burned up, and all the green grass was burned up.

⁸The second angel sounded his trumpet, and something like a huge mountain, all ablaze, was thrown into the sea. A third of the sea turned into blood, ⁹a third of the living creatures in the sea died, and a third of the ships were destroyed.

¹⁰The third angel sounded his trumpet, and a great star, blazing like a torch, fell from the sky on a third of the rivers and on the springs of water—

¹¹the name of the star is Wormwood.ᵃ A third of the waters turned bitter, and many people died from the waters that had become bitter.

¹²The fourth angel sounded his trumpet, and a third of the sun was struck, a third of the moon, and a third of the stars, so that a third of them turned dark. A third of the day was without light, and also a third of the night.

¹³As I watched, I heard an eagle that was flying in midair call out in a loud voice: "Woe! Woe! Woe to the inhabitants of the earth, because of the trumpet blasts about to be sounded by the other three angels!"

9 The fifth angel sounded his trumpet, and I saw a star that had fallen from the sky to the earth. The star was given the key to the shaft of the Abyss. ²When he opened the Abyss, smoke rose from it like the smoke from a gigantic furnace. The sun and sky were darkened by the smoke from the Abyss. ³And out of the smoke locusts came down upon the earth and were given power like that of scorpions of the earth. ⁴They were told not to harm the grass of the earth or any plant or tree, but only those people who did not have the seal of God on their foreheads. ⁵They were not given power to kill them, but only to torture them for five months. And the agony they suffered was like that of the sting of a scorpion when it strikes a man. ⁶During those days men will seek death, but will not find it; they will long to die, but death will elude them.

⁷The locusts looked like horses prepared for battle. On their heads they wore something like crowns of gold, and their faces resembled human faces. ⁸Their hair was like women's hair, and their teeth were like lions' teeth. ⁹They had breastplates like breastplates of iron, and the sound of their wings was like the thundering of many horses and chariots rushing into battle. ¹⁰They had tails and stings like scorpions, and in their tails they had power to torment people for five months. ¹¹They had as king over them the angel of the Abyss, whose name in Hebrew is Abaddon, and in Greek, Apollyon.ᵇ

¹²The first woe is past; two other woes are yet to come.

¹³The sixth angel sounded his trumpet, and I heard a voice coming from the hornsᶜ of the golden altar that is before God. ¹⁴It said to the sixth angel who had the trumpet, "Release the four angels who are bound at the great river Euphrates." ¹⁵And the four angels who had been kept ready for this very hour and day and month and year were released to kill a third of mankind. ¹⁶The number of the mounted troops was two hundred million. I heard their number.

¹⁷The horses and riders I saw in my vision looked like this: Their breastplates were fiery red, dark blue, and yellow as sulfur. The heads of the horses resembled the heads of lions, and out of their mouths came fire, smoke and sulfur. ¹⁸A third of mankind was killed by the three plagues of fire, smoke and sulfur that came out of their mouths. ¹⁹The power of the horses was in their mouths and in their tails; for their tails were like snakes, having heads with which they inflict injury.

ᵃ11 That is, Bitterness   ᵇ11 *Abaddon* and *Apollyon* mean *Destroyer*.   ᶜ13 That is, projections

²⁰The rest of mankind that were not killed by these plagues still did not repent of the work of their hands; they did not stop worshiping demons, and idols of gold, silver, bronze, stone and wood—idols that cannot see or hear or walk. ²¹Nor did they repent of their murders, their magic arts, their sexual immorality or their thefts.

The Angel and the Little Scroll

10 Then I saw another mighty angel coming down from heaven. He was robed in a cloud, with a rainbow above his head; his face was like the sun, and his legs were like fiery pillars. ²He was holding a little scroll, which lay open in his hand. He planted his right foot on the sea and his left foot on the land, ³and he gave a loud shout like the roar of a lion. When he shouted, the voices of the seven thunders spoke. ⁴And when the seven thunders spoke, I was about to write; but I heard a voice from heaven say, "Seal up what the seven thunders have said and do not write it down."

⁵Then the angel I had seen standing on the sea and on the land raised his right hand to heaven. ⁶And he swore by him who lives for ever and ever, who created the heavens and all that is in them, the earth and all that is in it, and the sea and all that is in it, and said, "There will be no more delay! ⁷But in the days when the seventh angel is about to sound his trumpet, the mystery of God will be accomplished, just as he announced to his servants the prophets."

⁸Then the voice that I had heard from heaven spoke to me once more: "Go, take the scroll that lies open in the hand of the angel who is standing on the sea and on the land."

⁹So I went to the angel and asked him to give me the little scroll. He said to me, "Take it and eat it. It will turn your stomach sour, but in your mouth it will be as sweet as honey." ¹⁰I took the little scroll from the angel's hand and ate it. It tasted as sweet as honey in my mouth, but when I had eaten it, my stomach turned sour. ¹¹Then I was told, "You must prophesy again about many peoples, nations, languages and kings."

The Two Witnesses

11 I was given a reed like a measuring rod and was told, "Go and measure the temple of God and the altar, and count the worshipers there. ²But exclude the outer court; do not measure it, because it has been given to the Gentiles. They will trample on the holy city for 42 months. ³And I will give power to my two witnesses, and they will prophesy for 1,260 days, clothed in sackcloth." ⁴These are the two olive trees and the two lampstands that stand before the Lord of the earth. ⁵If anyone tries to harm them, fire comes from their mouths and devours their enemies. This is how anyone who wants to harm them must die. ⁶These men have power to shut up the sky so that it will not rain during the time they are prophesying; and they have power to turn the waters into blood and to strike the earth with every kind of plague as often as they want.

⁷Now when they have finished their testimony, the beast that comes

up from the Abyss will attack them, and overpower and kill them. [8]Their bodies will lie in the street of the great city, which is figuratively called Sodom and Egypt, where also their Lord was crucified. [9]For three and a half days men from every people, tribe, language and nation will gaze on their bodies and refuse them burial. [10]The inhabitants of the earth will gloat over them and will celebrate by sending each other gifts, because these two prophets had tormented those who live on the earth.

[11]But after the three and a half days a breath of life from God entered them, and they stood on their feet, and terror struck those who saw them. [12]Then they heard a loud voice from heaven saying to them, "Come up here." And they went up to heaven in a cloud, while their enemies looked on.

[13]At that very hour there was a severe earthquake and a tenth of the city collapsed. Seven thousand people were killed in the earthquake, and the survivors were terrified and gave glory to the God of heaven.

[14]The second woe has passed; the third woe is coming soon.

The Seventh Trumpet

[15]The seventh angel sounded his trumpet, and there were loud voices in heaven, which said:

> "The kingdom of the world has become the kingdom of our
>   Lord and of his Christ,
>   and he will reign for ever and ever."

[16]And the twenty-four elders, who were seated on their thrones before God, fell on their faces and worshiped God, [17]saying:

> "We give thanks to you, Lord God Almighty,
>   the One who is and who was,
>   because you have taken your great power
>   and have begun to reign.
> [18]The nations were angry;
>   and your wrath has come.
>   The time has come for judging the dead,
>   and for rewarding your servants the prophets
>   and your saints and those who reverence your name,
>   both small and great—
>   and for destroying those who destroy the earth."

[19]Then God's temple in heaven was opened, and within his temple was seen the ark of his covenant. And there came flashes of lightning, rumblings, peals of thunder, an earthquake and a great hailstorm.

The Woman and the Dragon

12 A great and wondrous sign appeared in heaven: a woman clothed with the sun, with the moon under her feet and a crown of twelve stars on her head. [2]She was pregnant and cried out in pain as she was about

to give birth. ³Then another sign appeared in heaven: an enormous red dragon with seven heads and ten horns and seven crowns on his heads. ⁴His tail swept a third of the stars out of the sky and flung them to the earth. The dragon stood in front of the woman who was about to give birth, so that he might devour her child the moment it was born. ⁵She gave birth to a son, a male child, who will rule all the nations with an iron scepter. And her child was snatched up to God and to his throne. ⁶The woman fled into the desert to a place prepared for her by God, where she might be taken care of for 1,260 days.

⁷And there was war in heaven. Michael and his angels fought against the dragon, and the dragon and his angels fought back. ⁸But he was not strong enough, and they lost their place in heaven. ⁹The great dragon was hurled down—that ancient serpent called the devil, or Satan, who leads the whole world astray. He was hurled to the earth, and his angels with him. ¹⁰Then I heard a loud voice in heaven say:

> "Now have come the salvation and the power and the
>   kingdom of our God,
> and the authority of his Christ.
> For the accuser of our brothers,
>   who accuses them before our God day and night,
>   has been hurled down.
> ¹¹They overcame him
>   by the blood of the Lamb
>   and by the word of their testimony;
> they did not love their lives so much
>   as to shrink from death.
> ¹²Therefore rejoice, you heavens
>   and you who dwell in them!
> But woe to the earth and the sea,
>   because the devil has gone down to you!
> He is filled with fury,
>   because he knows that his time is short."

¹³When the dragon saw that he had been hurled to the earth, he pursued the woman who had given birth to the male child. ¹⁴The woman was given the two wings of a great eagle, so that she might fly to the place prepared for her in the desert, where she would be taken care of for a time, times and half a time, out of the serpent's reach. ¹⁵Then from his mouth the serpent spewed water like a river, to overtake the woman and sweep her away with the torrent. ¹⁶But the earth helped the woman by opening its mouth and swallowing the river that the dragon had spewed out of his mouth. ¹⁷Then the dragon was enraged at the woman and went off to make war against the rest of her offspring—those who obey God's command-

13 ments and hold to the testimony of Jesus. ¹And the dragon*a* stood on the shore of the sea.

a1 Some late manuscripts And I

The Beast out of the Sea

And I saw a beast coming out of the sea. He had ten horns and seven heads, with ten crowns on his horns, and on each head a blasphemous name. [2]The beast I saw resembled a leopard, but had feet like those of a bear and a mouth like that of a lion. The dragon gave the beast his power and his throne and great authority. [3]One of the heads of the beast seemed to have had a fatal wound, but the fatal wound had been healed. The whole world was astonished and followed the beast. [4]Men worshiped the dragon because he had given authority to the beast, and they also worshiped the beast and asked, "Who is like the beast? Who can make war against him?"

[5]The beast was given a mouth to utter proud words and blasphemies and to exercise his authority for forty-two months. [6]He opened his mouth to blaspheme God, and to slander his name and his dwelling place and those who live in heaven. [7]He was given power to make war against the saints and to conquer them. And he was given authority over every tribe, people, language and nation. [8]All inhabitants of the earth will worship the beast—all whose names have not been written in the book of life belonging to the Lamb that was slain from the creation of the world.[a]

[9]He who has an ear, let him hear.

> [10]If anyone is to go into captivity,
> into captivity he will go.
> If anyone is to be killed[b] with the sword,
> with the sword he will be killed.

This calls for patient endurance and faithfulness on the part of the saints.

The Beast out of the Earth

[11]Then I saw another beast, coming out of the earth. He had two horns like a lamb, but he spoke like a dragon. [12]He exercised all the authority of the first beast on his behalf, and made the earth and its inhabitants worship the first beast, whose fatal wound had been healed. [13]And he performed great and miraculous signs, even causing fire to come down from heaven to earth in full view of men. [14]Because of the signs he was given power to do on behalf of the first beast, he deceived the inhabitants of the earth. He ordered them to set up an image in honor of the beast who was wounded by the sword and yet lived. [15]He was given power to give breath to the image of the first beast, so that it could speak and cause all who refused to worship the image to be killed. [16]He also forced everyone, small and great, rich and poor, free and slave, to receive a mark on his right hand or on his forehead, [17]so that no one could buy or sell unless he had the mark, which is the name of the beast or the number of his name.

[18]This calls for wisdom. If anyone has insight, let him calculate the number of the beast, for it is man's number. His number is 666.

[a]8 Or *written from the creation of the world in the book of life belonging to the Lamb that was slain*
[b]10 Some manuscripts *anyone kills*

The Lamb and the 144,000

14 Then I looked, and there before me was the Lamb, standing on Mount Zion, and with him 144,000 who had his name and his Father's name written on their foreheads. [2]And I heard a sound from heaven like the roar of rushing waters and like a loud peal of thunder. The sound I heard was like that of harpists playing their harps. [3]And they sang a new song before the throne and before the four living creatures and the elders. No one could learn the song except the 144,000 who had been redeemed from the earth. [4]These are those who did not defile themselves with women, for they kept themselves pure. They follow the Lamb wherever he goes. They were purchased from among men and offered as firstfruits to God and the Lamb. [5]No lie was found in their mouths; they are blameless.

The Three Angels

[6]Then I saw another angel flying in midair, and he had the eternal gospel to proclaim to those who live on the earth—to every nation, tribe, language and people. [7]He said in a loud voice, "Fear God and give him glory, because the hour of his judgment has come. Worship him who made the heavens, the earth, the sea and the springs of water."

[8]A second angel followed and said, "Fallen! Fallen is Babylon the Great, which made all the nations drink the maddening wine of her adulteries."

[9]A third angel followed them and said in a loud voice: "If anyone worships the beast and his image and receives his mark on the forehead or on the hand, [10]he, too, will drink of the wine of God's fury, which has been poured full strength into the cup of his wrath. He will be tormented with burning sulfur in the presence of the holy angels and of the Lamb. [11]And the smoke of their torment rises for ever and ever. There is no rest day or night for those who worship the beast and his image, or for anyone who receives the mark of his name." [12]This calls for patient endurance on the part of the saints who obey God's commandments and remain faithful to Jesus.

[13]Then I heard a voice from heaven say, "Write: Blessed are the dead who die in the Lord from now on."

"Yes," says the Spirit, "they will rest from their labor, for their deeds will follow them."

The Harvest of the Earth

[14]I looked, and there before me was a white cloud, and seated on the cloud was one "like a son of man"[a] with a crown of gold on his head and a sharp sickle in his hand. [15]Then another angel came out of the temple and called in a loud voice to him who was sitting on the cloud, "Take your sickle and reap, because the time to reap has come, for the harvest of the earth is ripe." [16]So he who was seated on the cloud swung his sickle over the earth, and the earth was harvested.

[17]Another angel came out of the temple in heaven, and he too had a

[a]14 Daniel 7:13

sharp sickle. [18]Still another angel, who had charge of the fire, came from the altar and called in a loud voice to him who had the sharp sickle, "Take your sharp sickle and gather the clusters of grapes from the earth's vine, because its grapes are ripe." [19]The angel swung his sickle on the earth, gathered its grapes and threw them into the great winepress of God's wrath. [20]They were trampled in the winepress outside the city, and blood flowed out of the press, rising as high as the horses' bridles for a distance of 1,600 stadia.[a]

Seven Angels With Seven Plagues

15 I saw in heaven another great and marvelous sign: seven angels with the seven last plagues—last, because with them God's wrath is completed. [2]And I saw what looked like a sea of glass mixed with fire and, standing beside the sea, those who had been victorious over the beast and his image and over the number of his name. They held harps given them by God [3]and sang the song of Moses the servant of God and the song of the Lamb:

> "Great and marvelous are your deeds,
>   Lord God Almighty.
> Just and true are your ways,
>   King of the ages.
> [4]Who will not fear you, O Lord,
>   and bring glory to your name?
> For you alone are holy.
> All nations will come
>   and worship before you,
> for your righteous acts have been revealed."

[5]After this I looked and in heaven the temple, that is, the tabernacle of the Testimony, was opened. [6]Out of the temple came the seven angels with the seven plagues. They were dressed in clean, shining linen and wore golden sashes around their chests. [7]Then one of the four living creatures gave to the seven angels seven golden bowls filled with the wrath of God, who lives for ever and ever. [8]And the temple was filled with smoke from the glory of God and from his power, and no one could enter the temple until the seven plagues of the seven angels were completed.

The Seven Bowls of God's Wrath

16 Then I heard a loud voice from the temple saying to the seven angels, "Go, pour out the seven bowls of God's wrath on the earth."
[2]The first angel went and poured out his bowl on the land, and ugly and painful sores broke out on the people who had the mark of the beast and worshiped his image.
[3]The second angel poured out his bowl on the sea, and it turned into blood like that of a dead man, and every living thing in the sea died.
[4]The third angel poured out his bowl on the rivers and springs of water,

[a]20 That is, about 180 miles (about 300 kilometers)

and they became blood. ⁵Then I heard the angel in charge of the waters say:

> "You are just in these judgments,
>   you who are and who were, the Holy One,
>   because you have so judged;
> ⁶for they have shed the blood of your saints and prophets,
>   and you have given them blood to drink as they deserve."

⁷And I heard the altar respond:

> "Yes, Lord God Almighty,
>   true and just are your judgments."

⁸The fourth angel poured out his bowl on the sun, and the sun was given power to scorch people with fire. ⁹They were seared by the intense heat and they cursed the name of God, who had control over these plagues, but they refused to repent and glorify him.

¹⁰The fifth angel poured out his bowl on the throne of the beast, and his kingdom was plunged into darkness. Men gnawed their tongues in agony ¹¹and cursed the God of heaven because of their pains and their sores, but they refused to repent of what they had done.

¹²The sixth angel poured out his bowl on the great river Euphrates, and its water was dried up to prepare the way for the kings from the East. ¹³Then I saw three evilᵃ spirits that looked like frogs; they came out of the mouth of the dragon, out of the mouth of the beast and out of the mouth of the false prophet. ¹⁴They are spirits of demons performing miraculous signs, and they go out to the kings of the whole world, to gather them for the battle on the great day of God Almighty.

¹⁵"Behold, I come like a thief! Blessed is he who stays awake and keeps his clothes with him, so that he may not go naked and be shamefully exposed."

¹⁶Then they gathered the kings together to the place that in Hebrew is called Armageddon.

¹⁷The seventh angel poured out his bowl into the air, and out of the temple came a loud voice from the throne, saying, "It is done!" ¹⁸Then there came flashes of lightning, rumblings, peals of thunder and a severe earthquake. No earthquake like it has ever occurred since man has been on earth, so tremendous was the quake. ¹⁹The great city split into three parts, and the cities of the nations collapsed. God remembered Babylon the Great and gave her the cup filled with the wine of the fury of his wrath. ²⁰Every island fled away and the mountains could not be found. ²¹From the sky huge hailstones of about a hundred pounds each fell upon men. And they cursed God on account of the plague of hail, because the plague was so terrible.

The Woman on the Beast

17 One of the seven angels who had the seven bowls came and said to me, "Come, I will show you the punishment of the great prostitute,

ᵃ13 Greek *unclean*

who sits on many waters. ²With her the kings of the earth committed adultery and the inhabitants of the earth were intoxicated with the wine of her adulteries."

³Then the angel carried me away in the Spirit into a desert. There I saw a woman sitting on a scarlet beast that was covered with blasphemous names and had seven heads and ten horns. ⁴The woman was dressed in purple and scarlet, and was glittering with gold, precious stones and pearls. She held a golden cup in her hand, filled with abominable things and the filth of her adulteries. ⁵This title was written on her forehead:

MYSTERY

BABYLON THE GREAT

THE MOTHER OF PROSTITUTES

AND OF THE ABOMINATIONS OF THE EARTH.

⁶I saw that the woman was drunk with the blood of the saints, the blood of those who bore testimony to Jesus.

When I saw her, I was greatly astonished. ⁷Then the angel said to me: "Why are you astonished? I will explain to you the mystery of the woman and of the beast she rides, which has the seven heads and ten horns. ⁸The beast, which you saw, once was, now is not, and will come up out of the Abyss and go to his destruction. The inhabitants of the earth whose names have not been written in the book of life from the creation of the world will be astonished when they see the beast, because he once was, now is not, and yet will come.

⁹"This calls for a mind with wisdom. The seven heads are seven hills on which the woman sits. ¹⁰They are also seven kings. Five have fallen, one is, the other has not yet come; but when he does come, he must remain for a little while. ¹¹The beast who once was, and now is not, is an eighth king. He belongs to the seven and is going to his destruction.

¹²"The ten horns you saw are ten kings who have not yet received a kingdom, but who for one hour will receive authority as kings along with the beast. ¹³They have one purpose and will give their power and authority to the beast. ¹⁴They will make war against the Lamb, but the Lamb will overcome them because he is Lord of lords and King of kings—and with him will be his called, chosen and faithful followers."

¹⁵Then the angel said to me, "The waters you saw, where the prostitute sits, are peoples, multitudes, nations and languages. ¹⁶The beast and the ten horns you saw will hate the prostitute. They will bring her to ruin and leave her naked; they will eat her flesh and burn her with fire. ¹⁷For God has put it into their hearts to accomplish his purpose by agreeing to give the beast their power to rule, until God's words are fulfilled. ¹⁸The woman you saw is the great city that rules over the kings of the earth."

The Fall of Babylon

18 After this I saw another angel coming down from heaven. He had great authority, and the earth was illuminated by his splendor. ²With a mighty voice he shouted:

"Fallen! Fallen is Babylon the Great!
　　She has become a home for demons
　and a haunt for every evil*ᵃ* spirit,
　　a haunt for every unclean and detestable bird.
³For all the nations have drunk
　　the maddening wine of her adulteries.
The kings of the earth committed adultery with her,
　　and the merchants of the earth grew rich from her
　　　excessive luxuries."

⁴Then I heard another voice from heaven say:

"Come out of her, my people,
　　so that you will not share in her sins,
　　so that you will not receive any of her plagues;
⁵for her sins are piled up to heaven,
　　and God has remembered her crimes.
⁶Give back to her as she has given;
　　pay her back double for what she has done.
　　Mix her a double portion from her own cup.
⁷Give her as much torture and grief
　　as the glory and luxury she gave herself.
In her heart she boasts,
　　'I sit as queen; I am not a widow,
　　and I will never mourn.'
⁸Therefore in one day her plagues will overtake her:
　　death, mourning and famine.
She will be consumed by fire,
　　for mighty is the Lord God who judges her.

⁹"When the kings of the earth who committed adultery with her and shared her luxury see the smoke of her burning, they will weep and mourn over her. ¹⁰Terrified at her torment, they will stand far off and cry:

" 'Woe! Woe, O great city,
　　O Babylon, city of power!
　　In one hour your doom has come!'

¹¹"The merchants of the earth will weep and mourn over her because no one buys their cargoes any more— ¹²cargoes of gold, silver, precious stones and pearls; fine linen, purple, silk and scarlet cloth; every sort of citron wood, and articles of every kind made of ivory, costly wood, bronze,

ᵃ2 Greek unclean

iron and marble; ¹³cargoes of cinnamon and spice, of incense, myrrh and
frankincense, of wine and olive oil, of fine flour and wheat; cattle and sheep;
horses and carriages; and bodies and souls of men.

¹⁴"They will say, 'The fruit you longed for is gone from you. All your
riches and splendor have vanished, never to be recovered.' ¹⁵The merchants
who sold these things and gained their wealth from her will stand far off,
terrified at her torment. They will weep and mourn ¹⁶and cry out:

> " 'Woe! Woe, O great city,
>   dressed in fine linen, purple and scarlet,
>   and glittering with gold, precious stones and pearls!
> ¹⁷In one hour such great wealth has been brought to ruin!'

"Every sea captain, and all who travel by ship, the sailors, and all who
earn their living from the sea, will stand far off. ¹⁸When they see the smoke
of her burning, they will exclaim, 'Was there ever a city like this great city?'
¹⁹They will throw dust on their heads, and with weeping and mourning cry
out:

> " 'Woe! Woe, O great city,
>   where all who had ships on the sea
>   became rich through her wealth!
> In one hour she has been brought to ruin!
> ²⁰Rejoice over her, O heaven!
>   Rejoice, saints and apostles and prophets!
> God has judged her for the way she treated you.' "

²¹Then a mighty angel picked up a boulder the size of a large millstone
and threw it into the sea, and said:

> "With such violence
>   the great city of Babylon will be thrown down,
>   never to be found again.
> ²²The music of harpists and musicians, flute players and
>   trumpeters,
>   will never be heard in you again.
> No workman of any trade
>   will ever be found in you again.
> The sound of a millstone
>   will never be heard in you again.
> ²³The light of a lamp
>   will never shine in you again.
> The voice of bridegroom and bride
>   will never be heard in you again.
> Your merchants were the world's great men.
>   By your magic spell all the nations were led astray.
> ²⁴In her was found the blood of prophets and of the saints,
>   and of all who have been killed on the earth."

Hallelujah!

19 After this I heard what sounded like the roar of a great multitude in heaven shouting:

> "Hallelujah!
> Salvation and glory and power belong to our God,
> ² for true and just are his judgments.
> He has condemned the great prostitute
>   who corrupted the earth by her adulteries.
> He has avenged on her the blood of his servants."

³And again they shouted:

> "Hallelujah!
> The smoke from her goes up for ever and ever."

⁴The twenty-four elders and the four living creatures fell down and worshiped God, who was seated on the throne. And they cried:

> "Amen, Hallelujah!"

⁵Then a voice came from the throne, saying:

> "Praise our God,
>   all you his servants,
> you who fear him,
>   both small and great!"

⁶Then I heard what sounded like a great multitude, like the roar of rushing waters and like loud peals of thunder, shouting:

> "Hallelujah!
>   For our Lord God Almighty reigns.
> ⁷Let us rejoice and be glad
>   and give him glory!
> For the wedding of the Lamb has come,
>   and his bride has made herself ready.
> ⁸Fine linen, bright and clean,
>   was given her to wear."

(Fine linen stands for the righteous acts of the saints.)

⁹Then the angel said to me, "Write: 'Blessed are those who are invited to the wedding supper of the Lamb!' " And he added, "These are the true words of God."

¹⁰At this I fell at his feet to worship him. But he said to me, "Do not do it! I am a fellow servant with you and with your brothers who hold to the testimony of Jesus. Worship God! For the testimony of Jesus is the spirit of prophecy."

The Rider on the White Horse

[11]I saw heaven standing open and there before me was a white horse, whose rider is called Faithful and True. With justice he judges and makes war. [12]His eyes are like blazing fire, and on his head are many crowns. He has a name written on him that no one knows but he himself. [13]He is dressed in a robe dipped in blood, and his name is the Word of God. [14]The armies of heaven were following him, riding on white horses and dressed in fine linen, white and clean. [15]Out of his mouth comes a sharp sword with which to strike down the nations. "He will rule them with an iron scepter."[a] He treads the winepress of the fury of the wrath of God Almighty. [16]On his robe and on his thigh he has this name written:

KING OF KINGS AND LORD OF LORDS.

[17]And I saw an angel standing in the sun, who cried in a loud voice to all the birds flying in midair, "Come, gather together for the great supper of God, [18]so that you may eat the flesh of kings, generals, and mighty men, of horses and their riders, and the flesh of all people, free and slave, small and great."

[19]Then I saw the beast and the kings of the earth and their armies gathered together to make war against the rider on the horse and his army. [20]But the beast was captured, and with him the false prophet who had performed the miraculous signs on his behalf. With these signs he had deluded those who had received the mark of the beast and worshiped his image. The two of them were thrown alive into the fiery lake of burning sulfur. [21]The rest of them were killed with the sword that came out of the mouth of the rider on the horse, and all the birds gorged themselves on their flesh.

The Thousand Years

20 And I saw an angel coming down out of heaven, having the key to the Abyss and holding in his hand a great chain. [2]He seized the dragon, that ancient serpent, who is the devil, or Satan, and bound him for a thousand years. [3]He threw him into the Abyss, and locked and sealed it over him, to keep him from deceiving the nations anymore until the thousand years were ended. After that, he must be set free for a short time.

[4]I saw thrones on which were seated those who had been given authority to judge. And I saw the souls of those who had been beheaded because of their testimony for Jesus and because of the word of God. They had not worshiped the beast or his image and had not received his mark on their foreheads or their hands. They came to life and reigned with Christ a thousand years. [5](The rest of the dead did not come to life until the thousand years were ended.) This is the first resurrection. [6]Blessed and holy are those who have part in the first resurrection. The second death has no

[a]15 Psalm 2:9

power over them, but they will be priests of God and of Christ and will reign with him for a thousand years.

Satan's Doom

⁷When the thousand years are over, Satan will be released from his prison ⁸and will go out to deceive the nations in the four corners of the earth—Gog and Magog—to gather them for battle. In number they are like the sand on the seashore. ⁹They marched across the breadth of the earth and surrounded the camp of God's people, the city he loves. But fire came down from heaven and devoured them. ¹⁰And the devil, who deceived them, was thrown into the lake of burning sulfur, where the beast and the false prophet had been thrown. They will be tormented day and night for ever and ever.

The Dead Are Judged

¹¹Then I saw a great white throne and him who was seated on it. Earth and sky fled from his presence, and there was no place for them. ¹²And I saw the dead, great and small, standing before the throne, and books were opened. Another book was opened, which is the book of life. The dead were judged according to what they had done as recorded in the books. ¹³The sea gave up the dead that were in it, and death and Hades gave up the dead that were in them, and each person was judged according to what he had done. ¹⁴Then death and Hades were thrown into the lake of fire. The lake of fire is the second death. ¹⁵If anyone's name was not found written in the book of life, he was thrown into the lake of fire.

The New Jerusalem

21 Then I saw a new heaven and a new earth, for the first heaven and the first earth had passed away, and there was no longer any sea. ²I saw the Holy City, the new Jerusalem, coming down out of heaven from God, prepared as a bride beautifully dressed for her husband. ³And I heard a loud voice from the throne saying, "Now the dwelling of God is with men, and he will live with them. They will be his people, and God himself will be with them and be their God. ⁴He will wipe every tear from their eyes. There will be no more death or mourning or crying or pain, for the old order of things has passed away."

⁵He who was seated on the throne said, "I am making everything new!" Then he said, "Write this down, for these words are trustworthy and true."

⁶He said to me: "It is done. I am the Alpha and the Omega, the Beginning and the End. To him who is thirsty I will give to drink without cost from the spring of the water of life. ⁷He who overcomes will inherit all this, and I will be his God and he will be my son. ⁸But the cowardly, the unbelieving, the vile, the murderers, the sexually immoral, those who practice magic arts, the idolaters and all liars—their place will be in the fiery lake of burning sulfur. This is the second death."

⁹One of the seven angels who had the seven bowls full of the seven last plagues came and said to me, "Come, I will show you the bride, the wife of the Lamb." ¹⁰And he carried me away in the Spirit to a mountain great and high, and showed me the Holy City, Jerusalem, coming down out of heaven from God. ¹¹It shone with the glory of God, and its brilliance was like that of a very precious jewel, like a jasper, clear as crystal. ¹²It had a great, high wall with twelve gates, and with twelve angels at the gates. On the gates were written the names of the twelve tribes of Israel. ¹³There were three gates on the east, three on the north, three on the south and three on the west. ¹⁴The wall of the city had twelve foundations, and on them were the names of the twelve apostles of the Lamb.

¹⁵The angel who talked with me had a measuring rod of gold to measure the city, its gates and its walls. ¹⁶The city was laid out like a square, as long as it was wide. He measured the city with the rod and found it to be 12,000 stadia[a] in length, and as wide and high as it is long. ¹⁷He measured its wall and it was 144 cubits[b] thick,[c] by man's measurement, which the angel was using. ¹⁸The wall was made of jasper, and the city of pure gold, as pure as glass. ¹⁹The foundations of the city walls were decorated with every kind of precious stone. The first foundation was jasper, the second sapphire, the third chalcedony, the fourth emerald, ²⁰the fifth sardonyx, the sixth carnelian, the seventh chrysolite, the eighth beryl, the ninth topaz, the tenth chrysoprase, the eleventh jacinth, and the twelfth amethyst.[d] ²¹The twelve gates were twelve pearls, each gate made of a single pearl. The great street of the city was of pure gold, like transparent glass.

²²I did not see a temple in the city, because the Lord God Almighty and the Lamb are its temple. ²³The city does not need the sun or the moon to shine on it, for the glory of God gives it light, and the Lamb is its lamp. ²⁴The nations will walk by its light, and the kings of the earth will bring their splendor into it. ²⁵On no day will its gates ever be shut, for there will be no night there. ²⁶The glory and honor of the nations will be brought into it. ²⁷Nothing impure will ever enter it, nor will anyone who does what is shameful or deceitful, but only those whose names are written in the Lamb's book of life.

The River of Life

22 Then the angel showed me the river of the water of life, as clear as crystal, flowing from the throne of God and of the Lamb ²down the middle of the great street of the city. On each side of the river stood the tree of life, bearing twelve crops of fruit, yielding its fruit every month. And the leaves of the tree are for the healing of the nations. ³No longer will there be any curse. The throne of God and of the Lamb will be in the city, and his servants will serve him. ⁴They will see his face, and his name will be on their foreheads. ⁵There will be no more night. They will not need the

---

[a]16 That is, about 1,400 miles (about 2,200 kilometers)   [b]17 That is, about 200 feet (about 65 meters)   [c]17 Or *high*   [d]20 The precise identification of some of these precious stones is uncertain.

light of a lamp or the light of the sun, for the Lord God will give them light. And they will reign for ever and ever.

⁶The angel said to me, "These words are trustworthy and true. The Lord, the God of the spirits of the prophets, sent his angel to show his servants the things that must soon take place."

Jesus Is Coming

⁷"Behold, I am coming soon! Blessed is he who keeps the words of the prophecy in this book."

⁸I, John, am the one who heard and saw these things. And when I had heard and seen them, I fell down to worship at the feet of the angel who had been showing them to me. ⁹But he said to me, "Do not do it! I am a fellow servant with you and with your brothers the prophets and of all who keep the words of this book. Worship God!"

¹⁰Then he told me, "Do not seal up the words of the prophecy of this book, because the time is near. ¹¹Let him who does wrong continue to do wrong; let him who is vile continue to be vile; let him who does right continue to do right; and let him who is holy continue to be holy."

¹²"Behold, I am coming soon! My reward is with me, and I will give to everyone according to what he has done. ¹³I am the Alpha and the Omega, the First and the Last, the Beginning and the End.

¹⁴"Blessed are those who wash their robes, that they may have the right to the tree of life and may go through the gates into the city. ¹⁵Outside are the dogs, those who practice magic arts, the sexually immoral, the murderers, the idolaters and everyone who loves and practices falsehood.

¹⁶"I, Jesus, have sent my angel to give you^a this testimony for the churches. I am the Root and the Offspring of David, and the bright Morning Star."

¹⁷The Spirit and the bride say, "Come!" And let him who hears say, "Come!" Whoever is thirsty, let him come; and whoever wishes, let him take the free gift of the water of life.

¹⁸I warn everyone who hears the words of the prophecy of this book: If anyone adds anything to them, God will add to him the plagues described in this book. ¹⁹And if anyone takes words away from this book of prophecy, God will take away from him his share in the tree of life and in the holy city, which are described in this book.

²⁰He who testifies to these things says, "Yes, I am coming soon." Amen. Come, Lord Jesus.

²¹The grace of the Lord Jesus be with God's people. Amen.

---

*16 The Greek is plural.